W9-ADJ-295

BY ROB REID
YEAR ZERO
AFTER ON

AFTER ON

AFTER ⏻N A NOVEL OF SILICON VALLEY

ROB REID DEL REY · NEW YORK

Published in the United States by Del Rey, an imprint of Random House, a division of Penguin Random House LLC, New York.

DEL REY and the HOUSE colophon are registered trademarks of Penguin Random House LLC.

Hardback ISBN 978-1-524-79805-5
Ebook ISBN 978-1-524-79806-2

Printed in the United States of America on acid-free paper

randomhousebooks.com

987654321

FIRST EDITION

For Our Fathers

AFTER ON

PART 1: ⏻FF.

S OME PEOPLE THINK all great books should start with a dare. And those folks can't be big readers—because really, when was the last time *you* read a book that began with a dare? Well, this one does. And that's not some ham-fisted gambit to position it as "great" because we just established that only half literates conflate opening dares with greatness. So it's, truly, just a simple dare. And it's this: I dare you to *finish* the fucker.

And let's be real—you probably won't. It's 547 pages printed, after all. Which is to say, any number of "locations," "sections," or "litnodes" on your eReader. And its obnoxious length is nothing compared to the disquieting truths it reveals about a popular social/messaging/hookup platform that humanity already spends 11.2 percent of its online time engaged with. About who really built all that, and why. About who's listening, and what they're recording. And (here's the part that may smart a bit) how terribly uninteresting they almost certainly find you. There's also some truly scary stuff you just don't need to know. About the February bombing in San Francisco. About how it actually *saved* lives (lots of them—and quite possibly, your own). And about how moronically close we came to nuclear war with China on a recent winter's day (spoiler alert: NOT MY FAULT).

You don't *have* to know any of this. And ignoring the hidden ugliness we can't do much about makes life easier. So if you tend to avoid facts like the age of the kid who stitched your favorite blazer just outside of Phnom Penh; or how athletically a certain ex once cheated on you; or how painful and scary the last few days of most human lives are; then for God's sake: Put. The book. Down. Then do yourself a big favor and catch a movie. A numbered sequel, say starring cartoon-men invented to distract tots during the Roosevelt era. You'll find that plenty challenging, and much more fun. It'll also be over sooner, leaving you free for more numbered sequels, or maybe some lite sci fi written for the bright teens and dim grown-ups we euphemistically call "Young Adults."

Are you still there?

If so, sorry if that sounded a bit mean. But we're better off without whoever just stomped off. Those people offend easily and are always whining about how they feel "unsafe," or undercherished if their every clumsy kick, catch, and volley isn't commemorated with trophies. I can't stand those people. I'll bet you can't stand them either. So getting rid of them was worth feigning contempt for some of my own favorite things (*pssst*: two of the best movies, ever, in my view are *Iron Man 1* and 2. Also: I read "Y.A." stuff constantly. I'll bet you didn't know that).

Now that it's just us, I applaud you for at least attempting to see this thing through. Even you probably won't get there (those 547 pages, again). But if you do, I can make you three promises. One: I will never talk down to you. Yes, certain facts herein are hard to confront and accept. Certain others are plenty hard to *understand*. But I think you're man enough, woman enough, or young adult enough to handle it all. So. No sugarcoating, and no dumbing down. Two: I'll never lie to you. Everything that follows—however fantastical and hard to believe—is entirely true and precisely depicts the underpinnings of the world you inhabit. And finally: at the very, very end of all this, you will find a glittering prize. Books that end with glittering prizes are even rarer than those that start with dares, so lucky you. But please. No peeksies.

With that, I'm almost done with you. And that may be welcome news! My tone can grate a bit, I know. It's probably just a phase I'm going through. But I'll give you your space now. That said, I will check in every so often. Sometimes when you least expect it, as the hit men say. And, of course, I'll be back at the end, with that glittering prize of yours (and you thought I'd already forgotten).

But for now, let's begin our story with some quick opening praise for the women and men of Silicon Valley. Yes, yes; I know—"but those fuckers gave us *FarmVille*!" It's true. And everyone's awfully sorry about that. But at its best, the Valley remains an inspiring land, almost bewitchingly so. I mean, where else can a handful of misfits meet up in a garage, share mad bolts of inspiration, then mainline Red Bull, sleep under desks, and code on bleeding fingers until they hack together an agenda-setting product that will rock the world? And then register their millionth user in just weeks? Their ten millionth in mere months? And forge friendships and talents that will last a lifetime—all while getting vastly, shamelessly, pornographically rich?

The answer, of course, is Austin, Seattle, Beijing, London, Oslo, Bangalore, Seoul, Nairobi, Dubai, Buenos Aires, and quite possibly Perth, Australia, among countless other places. But this sort of thing happens on a grander scale in Silicon Valley than anywhere else. And the cliché is dead accurate: we're designing the future here. We also designed the present, and you're much better off for that. Snort at this if you must. But do you really want to go back to six broadcast channels, CB radios, type-writers, dominoes and checkers, rotary phones, and thermostats that don't even speak *a single word of English?* Didn't think so.

So, yes. Silicon Valley did give us FarmVille. But across the decades, its countless startups have also rebuilt our world's foundations. Some relentlessly advanced the microprocessor, enabling the digital wonders of our era. Others honed DNA sequencing, which cracked the human genome and will one day help to cure cancer. Still others pioneered wireless technologies that are finally patching the world's poorest sectors into a global superplex of information. Literally thousands of Silicon Valley startups in these and countless fields have advanced humanity in palpable ways. And no matter how you cut it—however imaginatively, generously, even schizophrenically you look at things—Giftish.ly was never, ever one of them. Nope! Not even close.

Giftish.ly was an unremembered startup in the wholly forgotten realm of "social gifting." Even the most obsessive tech historian would struggle to name the year when this concept briefly infatuated a luckless handful of able but misguided entrepreneurs. "Twenty-something-teen" is close enough. So what is social gifting? Or rather, what was (or, really, what *wasn't*) it? Well, its boosters reckoned that billions of people neurally lashed to their Facebook newsfeeds would eventually develop an uncontrollable urge to buy shit for each other. Having done so, they'd want to brag about their purchases. The joyous recipients would want to brag right along with them, and a social gifting service would enable all of this. Imagine an inbox clogged with posts like "SAMANTHA just bought GEOFFREY a Giftish.ly Certificate for a MOCHACHINO!" and you've glimpsed the daring vision. Only time will tell if social gifting's pioneers were dead wrong about everything, or merely (and this is a huuuuuuuge badge of honor for Valley also-rans) *too early*.

Mitchell Prentice is considering this question as he anxiously awaits a response from the squawk box of the blank door at 501 Jones Street. Though he scrupulously keeps the opinion to himself, he now believes the prognosis is grim across the board. Almost as grim as his immediate surroundings—which is saying something. This may not be the city's single most crime-ridden corner. But it's a contender. And with every passing month, this whole putrid neighborhood sticks out ever more in the striving hive of hyperachievement that is San Francisco. Just blocks away, tech outfits have been drawing gaggles of six-figure youngsters ever since Twitter first colonized Market Street's fringes (later followed by Uber, Thumbtack, and countless others). Yet here at O'Farrell and Jones, drunks sleep it off on piss-stained sidewalks, migrants mortgage wee paychecks at bulletproof windows, and gruff panhandlers ply their trade with menace. And then you have Mitchell. Mitchell Prentice.

Ring, ring, ring squawks the box.

"Answer the door," Mitchell urges, eyeing a sullen clutch of hooded faces midway up the block. A shadowed figure mutters something to the others, triggering laughter. Deep, sinister, and . . . mocking? He feels spooked and kind of shamed, and just then, a cop siren kicks in. Though a half block away, it sounds like an air horn in his inner ear. And this makes the perfect trifecta: frustration, embarrassment, plus a sensory jolt. So in an instant, Mitchell's face numbs, and his fingers start to tingle. The timing couldn't suck more. But on blocks this blighted, Murphy's Law applies as strongly as that of, say, gravity.

The neighborhood is called the Tenderloin—a word that once evoked rare nights at a cozy steak restaurant for Mitchell. These days it makes him think of a gory sore, raw and pus-filled, marking an otherwise hale civic body. Primal collisions of unlimited dollars with scant real estate are physically contorting every other neighborhood (here, a fifty-story co-op erupts from the earth; there, thickets of cranes sprout in a once-vacant lot). But the Tenderloin defies all gentrification. It's like a superbug that stubbornly evolved in a hypersanitized ward until it could whup any antibiotic. Or maybe it's more like a . . . native reservation? Yes, Mitchell could imagine the city council's Maoists creating such a thing. The Tenderloin's folkways and customs shall be preserved, they'd decree, so as to enlighten the spawn of the liberal elite on field trips—as when his own grade school visited Colonial Williamsburg.

The squawk box continues to ring. And the hoods, to chortle. More menacing, more mocking! Frustration and shame spike, and the tingling spreads to Mitchell's neck, chest, and forearms. And then, to his mouth. He doesn't need this. Not now, and certainly not here! Ten more seconds, and his tongue will be buzzing, *humming* with the tingle—impairing speech until he talks like a cartoon dullard; then good luck getting past this door. The menacing, mocking knot is now drifting his way (*or is it?*) and the tingling rockets to his legs. Great. Maybe they'll fold again, then sprawl him in the doorway like some spat-out Tenderloin junkie!

And so, The Blur begins. This is Mitchell's term—you won't find it in the clinical literature. His best analogy is a symphony's preconcert din, when everyone's tuning instruments at once (a sound he knows strictly from public TV). Everything in his purview chimes in simultaneously— every photon, scent, sound wave, and nerve ending. Each element is crystal clear. But as it's all concurrent, the whole is diffuse behind comprehension. A few more seconds of Blur, and he'll pass out, collapse into carrion for the chortling hoods. He strains against this, rallying the stray wisps of attention he can muster toward the squawk box.

Ring, ring, ring! then finally, "Password?"

"Knickerbocker." Mitchell over-enunciates methodically, and a miraculous combination of his careful diction and the pre-war intercom's crap AM-radio acoustics makes him sound normal (or at least acceptable) on the far side, and he's buzzed in.

∞   ∞   ∞

Special Field Operative Brock Hogan hated having to drag that tightly muscled, six-foot-three-inch frame of his across countless time zones back to headquarters. Yet he always came when summoned. Not because any Langley pencil pusher had the first thing to teach him about spycraft, close-in combat, geopolitics . . . nor indeed, ABOUT PUSHING PENCILS!

Wasn't it he, after all, who had covertly kiboshed the blood-spattered career of a certain rabble-rousing mullah by pressing a graphite No. 2 stylus right into his Carotid Artery mere moments before he was to incite a region-wide conflagration by broadcasting a scripture-twisting fatwa from that notorious jihadi radio station deep in darkest Iran? Unarmed and stark naked after escaping sadistic interrogation in a nearby Terrorist Bunker, Agent Hogan had coolly canvassed the benign offerings of an office-supply closet for repurposable matériel, then wordlessly waylaid his unexpectant foe in an empty hallway en route to the control room. "Mightier than the sword after all, wouldn't you say?" he uttered ironically as he withdrew the dripping shaft from the fallen fedayeen, who could respond only by moaning and writhing through the climax of his death throes!

So, no: not even the most decorated Langley bureaucrat could ever dream of "pushing a pencil" with half his aplomb! Yet Agent Hogan dutifully returned to HQ whenever summoned by those cringing desk jockeys because he was, above all, a loyal warrior; and loyal warriors respect the chain of command; however contemptible and backstabbing certain so-called "superiors" might be.

As usual, a veritable grand powwow was convened to debrief him! And so every leather-bound swivel chair in the agency's largest conference room was hoisting some panjandrum's posterior when Hogan arrived several dozen minutes late, as was his devil-may-care habit. His piercing, blue, wide-set eyes took instant mental inventory of those present, lingering perhaps an extra picosecond on the fecund curves of a certain Chinese-featured female assassin with whom he enjoyed occasional Sexual Congress; then perhaps twice that duration upon one most-unexpected attendee.

"Dr. Phillips," he intoned, his left brow arched with

a muted irony, which divulged that; beneath its playful, almost mocking surface; he in fact held a deep (if not ungrudging) well of respect for the portly, gray-headed, and wizened brown-eyed gentleman whom he addressed. "This is . . . most unexpected!"

∞   ∞   ∞

The door buzzes, admitting Mitchell into a hushed yet bustling sanctuary. Its dirty, blank, street-side exterior honors the local quarter's historic scuzziness—but inside, Bourbon & Branch is a sleek jewel box.

"You're Mr. Prentice," the drinks-list-clutching hostess states. She knows this from his password. Each guest has a unique one (most with a Prohibition-era echo), which keeps the reservations straight and the neighborhood junkies out.

Mitchell nods. The tingling is fading quickly. But it's still present, and he doesn't (quite) trust himself to talk properly.

"You're the second to arrive," she says. "Walk this way."

She leads him down narrow aisles, past swank ranks of sophisticated drinkers. The aesthetic is Capone-era speakeasy with faint Old West hints. The single malt, bourbon, and tequila lists are encyclopedic here, and it's rumored that ordering a vodka drink will get you drop-kicked to Jones Street. "Hey, boss," Danna says as the hostess seats him at their plank of a table. It's set within a steakhouse-like booth that's much contracted to accommodate tumblers rather than platters. This puts patrons shoulder to shoulder and knee to knee—but without quite realizing it, as those booth-y visual cues signal spacious seating. Congeniality and conspiratoriality are thereby subtly abetted, along with any number of unintended hookups. "I got you the yoozh," Danna adds, handing him a chilled Imperial Eagle (an ancient bourbon, plus magical ingredients including Averna, ginger syrup, and egg white). They clink glasses.

Danna's a Giftish.ly old-timer. Mitchell recruited her as a barely paid intern right out of Berkeley through the sheerest and dumbest of luck. She quickly blossomed as a designer and a leader, and now has enough internal credibility to qualify as a de facto co-founder of the company.

She's become one of precisely two reasons why Giftish.ly matters at all (the other being Mitchell's actual co-founder), and the third person in the room for all-important conversations. Like tonight's. After a quick sip, she adds, "Not to look a gift horse in the mouth, but can the company really afford this?" She again raises her glass (WhistlePig on a big-ass cube, he knows without asking).

Mitchell shakes his head. "Not to worry; tonight's on me." Not that he's any more flush than Giftish.ly. He stopped paying his own salary a month back (and also stopped servicing his six-figure medical debt). But Danna doesn't know this. Not even his co-founder knows, and they go clear back to high school. Because as CEO, it's his job to sacrifice. The general eats last or something, right? "Besides," he adds, ambushing her with an upbeat note. "We have something to celebrate. Ten thousand Likes, right?" Danna just posted mock-ups of Giftish.ly's mobile redesign to Dribbble.com, a peer-review site where designers critique each other's work with ruthless candor. There's no grade inflation on Dribbble, and her new user interface has been received rapturously.

"Onyx's redesign got twelve thousand Likes last quarter," she sniffs, citing another startup's Dribbble posting.

Mitchell smiles despite his grimness. The girl just can't take a compliment! Not even from him, despite how comfortable she's come to feel around him, and his co-founder, too. She'll smile, joke, and even be playful when it's just the two or the three of them. Otherwise, she's cool and aloof at work, while exuding an otherworldly competence. Unless something pisses her off, then look out. Seeing he'll have to sell her a bit harder on her own Dribbble triumph, he notes, "But it took them three months to rack that up. You got to ten thousand Likes in just *days*."

Danna shrugs indifferently. But she can't keep a glimmer of pride from her face—a truly illuminating one, in that any hint of animation makes her stunning. She can pass under the radar when she stays scrupulously neutral (as she almost always does). This is surely why she's always so nonplussed at work: it cuts down on unwanted gazes in the tech world's boy-choked corridors. She's also forever hoodied, her ebony Bettie Page bangs and dark, solemn eyes under wraps. All this stems from a certain deep-seated paranoia. She calls this her "Achilles bicep," as it's both a strength and a vulnerability (yes, it keeps her out of trouble, but it can also drive her to be more isolated than she should be).

Just then, Mitchell's phone hums a staccato pattern that feels like a complex secret handshake. This signals a money-saving opportunity, and he's broke, so he checks it despite himself. On the screen, a photorealistic five-dollar bill dissolves to a swank Bond-like avatar in a tuxedo. "For her next round, give her a *Deep* one," the ad urges in a lurid red font beside a sparkling Deep Rye logo. Below, a bar chart brags that Deep Rye contains 30 percent more alcohol than WhistlePig—the booze in Danna's hand at this very instant. A caption reads, "More BANG for the Buck!" And in case anyone could possibly fail to catch the drift here, a naked hussy's silhouette sprawls beneath this.

"Ewww!" he says, flipping the screen to Danna.

Examining it, she rolls her eyes. "Works every time. A slug of Deep Rye, and I'm countin' ceiling tiles."

"Their tag line should be 'Roofie in a Bottle.'"

"What's the offer?"

"Five bucks off."

"Take it!" she commands, only half-playful.

"And support *this* mindset?"

"Austerity, remember? We're broke!"

Mitchell puts the phone back in his pocket, shaking his head. "I can't believe Bourbon & Branch would work with *them*." Them being Phluttr—makers of the sketchy app that just hijacked their conversation. Ostensibly a social network, Phluttr peppers its users with coupons, recommendations, breaking news, handy info, and jaw-dropping bits of hyperlocal gossip, all of it surgically targeted to the user's interests, location, and/or state of mind.

"These guys?" As she gestures at the snug bar, Danna's face lights up with a pained, you-dumb-shit look. And just like that, she's again gorgeous. "No way would Bourbon & Branch work with Phluttr. It would ruin their name."

"Then how does Phluttr . . . do that?"

"One of their engineers actually posted a teardown of their coupon-targeting process on Medium awhile back. Anonymously, of course. And the company got it snuffed within an hour. But it's cached on a bunch of hacker sites. Anyway, start with the fact that Phluttr knows we know each other."

"Of course." Exactly how Phluttr knows this is a matter of widespread speculation, but Phluttr is fully aware of who *everyone* knows.

"Next, your GPS tells it where you are, and that you got here a few minutes after me. We're closely connected. So it figures, we're meeting each other. Your accelerometer tells it you sat down, so now it figures you're about to order a drink. Phluttr's working with Deep Rye, so they know it's stocked here. It probably knows I'm drinking WhistlePig because I mentioned it in an @reply to a friend on Twitter right after I ordered. And knowing that neither of us are in relationships, its dirty little mind thought 'hookup'—because no one's perfect, not even Phluttr."

"Yet."

"Exactly.

"And since the Deep Rye people are running a couponing campaign . . ."

Danna nods. "Ta-da! Five bucks off. If you're sober enough to send them a photo of the tab at the end of the night to prove you took them up on their generous offer. And so, Deep Rye starts moving lotsa booze."

"And Phluttr's running hundreds of other campaigns just like this right now, making a pile on each."

"You got it. Which is why they were just valued at—what?" Danna instinctively pulls up her phone to dig for the news.

"Four point two billion dollars," Mitchell says, saving her the trouble. Word about this broke a few days back, and everyone's buzzing about it. With fewer than a thousand employees, Phluttr is growing twice as fast as Facebook did at this stage of its history and ringing up huge revenue. Any investor who missed out on the last few monster startups is panicked at the thought of looking stupid again. So although the NASDAQ's been mighty queasy lately, Phluttr's financing was a food fight of a bidding war.

And no one can shut the damned thing off! When Phluttr first launched, its little interruptions were so irrelevant, people installed the app just to chuckle at them, and #TryAgainPhluttr was a hot hashtag.

Later, it felt more like a fortune cookie: still very random, but at times weirdly topical, in fun, coincidental ways. These days, Phluttr's accuracy makes Mitchell's skin crawl daily. But those deals and coupons save him a bundle. And the app wakes up and barks "Slow down!" whenever the car he's in approaches a speed trap. And it'll remind him of the names of any half-forgotten classmates entering the room. It's just so handy! But then, there's the dark side. When those randoms arrive, Phluttr might also say, "Ahem: I'm pretty sure these two are screwing." Or distract you with dumb videos when you should be working. Or coupon you for Dove Bars at your weakest moment. Then you hate yourself a little, and Phluttr quite a lot. But good luck turning it off.

Phluttr's other massive draw is "pseudonymity mode." The company maintains that people are most authentic with their five closest friends — and, with perfect strangers. The draw of strangers has forever fueled vast anonymous forums online. But anonymity also breeds awful behavior, one-off interactions rather than budding relationships, and endless lying about traits and backgrounds. So who really *knows* if you're communing with a caring priest, a fellow AIDS sufferer, or a medical expert? Or an actual acquaintance of Person X? An employee of Company Y? Or a fellow closeted gay person of an age, weight, and social background that attracts you? Well, Phluttr knows. And Phluttr can attest that this is a real, well-regarded person who authentically shares your affliction, secret, or curiosity, without exposing actual identities (unless both sides request it). Wrap this up in NSA-grade encryption, and there's no better place to buy sketchy substances, seek sketchy advice, cheat on lovers, or cathartically confess to the above. Phluttr has now cornered the market in id fulfillment, rumor spreading, and confidential gut spilling—and it's just getting started!

Mitchell soon gets Danna talking about her redesign. He needs to rally her optimism, and this is the surest way. He's also selfishly eager to discuss her work, as it's simply brilliant! He finds her new interface ingeniously, even *adamantly* intuitive, all but grabbing his fingers and planting them on the pixels that will draw him to the precise feature that's most relevant to him, even as other features cry out just as keenly to other users. It does this slyly and playfully. Buttons glint and bulge, and are made almost tactile by the bass-heavy thunks and teeny vibrations that fire when they're touched. Danna would win awards for this work if anyone actually used their service. But, of course, they don't. This is Giftish.ly, remember?

She's starting to discuss color palettes when something strange happens. Well—two things, really. The first is that a dude in chunky hipster glasses walks by, peering intently, as if he's lost something. Only he's gazing at people rather than floors and seat cushions. And it's not a zippy "where are my friends" scan. No, he's looking much more . . . methodically. Perceptibly locking onto each face, then moving on to the next one. The second odd thing is that Mitchell notices this, but Danna does not—even though her "Achilles bicep" of paranoia is Schwarzenegger-grade! But she sometimes drops her guard when discussing her loftiest passions, and color palettes are really up there.

Mitchell's about to point out the oddball when Phluttr taps them both. It isn't the coupon rhythm this time but the "helpful info" vibration pattern. Their screens read, "Heeeeeeeee's HERE!" And this time, the guess is spot-on, but not weirdly so. When the third employee of a tiny company shows up at a smallish bar, it's a safe bet he's here to meet the first two.

"And so begins another Staples High School reunion," Danna says as Mitchell's co-founder Kuba (rhymes with "scuba") trails the hostess to their table. "Class of . . . '01?"

"Hey, we're not that ancient! We were '03," Mitchell says with mock indignation, though, of course, the difference is meaningless to one born as deep into the nineties as Danna.

"Hi, guys, sorry I'm late." This sounds like your basic youngish male voice with some kazoo mixed in. Save for the H, which is so harsh, so *jagged*, it's a wonder it doesn't dislodge the guy's larynx. Kuba first left Poland years ago, but that accent just won't quit. And somehow, it's fitting. Spindly, with deep-set eyes, pallid skin, and muddy hair that mats like a skullcap, he looks like a medieval monk celebrated on the banknotes of some backwater for deriving a theorem.

After quick greetings and some chair-shuffling, Mitchell gets down to business. "You guys know the situation. We have a huge board meeting tomorrow. And it's gonna *suck*." Well, probably. He also thinks there's an OK-ish chance it'll go OK-ishly, but he keeps that to himself. This is a tactical choice. If he doesn't open on a deeply negative note, these two strident realists will take them there soon enough. So it's best to start the discussion with a good wallow. He'll subtly nudge things in an optimistic direction later, so that they'll adjourn on an upward trajectory. "We need money *real* bad, just to state the obvious."

Kuba (whose strident realism stems from the last eight generations of Polish history), piles right on. "And our only live conversations are with two third-rate VCs. And neither has answered our emails in days."

Mitchell nods grimly. "So if we have a path forward, it's in raising a bit more cash from our main investor tomorrow. And as we all know, micro-VCs just aren't known for coughing up emergency capital." This is in contrast to "real" venture capitalists, who do sometimes rescue troubled companies. But real VCs rarely back startups as nascent as Giftish.ly. There was a time—entire decades, actually—when they did. But as the world grew progressively more tech-addled, those big funds graduated from managing tens of millions, to hundreds of millions, to even billions of dollars. And you just can't deploy that kind of capital with measly little million-dollar bets. Not with a partnership of just four or five guys (and yes, they're almost all guys). So the big names in venture largely washed their hands of seeding infant startups. Purists argue that in this, they all but *stopped doing venture capital*. But the management fees on giant funds have crack-like properties. So as big-fund habits became full-blown addictions, seed-stage investing became someone else's problem.

Enter the "micro-VCs," circa 2010 or so. Most are half-successful entrepreneurs, or quite-successful startup execs, who pool some of their own capital with funds from friends and contacts who won huge in the tech sweepstakes. They'll typically fund a startup with a quarter- or half-million-dollar check (sometimes more), then use that to rally another million or two from other micro-VCs or angel investors. Giftish.ly landed its micro-VC round a bit more than a year ago. Led by a "firm" (which was really just a guy) doing business under the preposterous name of

#GreenSprout C@pital, it let them hire a dozen-ish people and make the most of their dismal product concept. But the money's now gone—and as Mitchell pointed out, micro-VCs aren't big into bailouts.

After allowing his team some cathartically gloomy chatter, Mitchell asks, "So is there *any*thing we can point to to get our one serious backer excited at the board meeting tomorrow? Revenue's not gonna do it. Because for now, it looks like there's only so many coffees and MP3s people want to buy their friends."

"Well, let's start with Animotion," Danna offers. This is their gift-recommendation engine, which is based on some audaciously original research Kuba's wife is doing in UCSF's Department of Neuroscience. It's a key element of the service, as you're far more likely to make a purchase if Giftish.ly can suggest the *per*fect little something for Person X. "It's really starting to kick ass!"

Mitchell mentally gives himself a pat on the back. The surest way to fire up either of these two is to get them gushing about the other's amazing work. "True," he says neutrally. "The numbers have spoken."

Actually, they're bellowing. Animotion scarcely worked for months, until Kuba coded up a seemingly minor new insight six weeks ago. Somehow, this caused things to turn the corner. Violently! The recommendations suddenly feel right, even *wise*, while being completely unobvious. The company regularly asks users to rate its gift suggestions on a scale of 1 ("more random than ROULETTE!") to 5 ("OMG you're PSYCHIC!"). Their average rating instantly soared from 1.4 to 4.6. This is like turning a third-string high school quarterback into a Super Bowl champ overnight, and they have no idea what caused it (and if they did, it would scare the bejesus out of them).

Discussing this, everyone's spirit starts to rally. When he figures the effect is peaking, Mitchell brings up Danna's new design. Kuba responds rapturously, and team Giftish.ly is soon awash with renewed hope and ambition. Yes, it's probably misplaced. But if they're to have any chance at all tomorrow, they need to bring some optimism to the board meeting. Whether you cynically call this sort of thing manipulation, or charitably call it leadership, Mitchell's good at it. Of course, he better be good at *some*thing because he's usually the dumbest guy in the room. And please don't call me harsh for saying that, because it's *his* own term. In fact, it's practically his rallying cry! And it's not self-hating although I know it sounds that way. It can actually be weirdly empowering. Mitchell also chiefly means it metaphorically. But due to the company he keeps, it's often an objectively accurate phrase. He sure is the dumbest person at the table right now! But despite that, he's doing his job rather well.

That is, until Kuba partly derails things (by trying to be reassuring, in that bumbling way of his). "Look," he says, eyes aglitter. "No matter what, the ideas will live on. Maybe even in an academic setting!" This is classic Kuba. He's been about *the ideas* first and foremost since grade school. So if their technology finds shelter in some ivory tower, it'll be more than just fine with him! Not that universities are in the business of providing soft landings to failed startups. But Kuba could set up his own damn think tank if he wants. His brilliance as an ideas-smitten developer led to a long and immaculately timed stint at Google, and the upside on his stock options could let him coast forever more. "Because really, maybe Giftish.ly's taken this as far as it can," he muses. "I mean, we're down to three engineers."

"And a quarter," Danna adds, raising her hand—a playful allusion to the help she occasionally gives his team.

"It's more like ten engineers when I can get your time," Kuba tells her, exaggerating politely (though only slightly). "But you need to focus on the redesign!"

With the conversation now shifting from what's going right to what's going wrong, Danna soon harrumphs, "I guess we could always do an acquihire."

Arrrgh, the A-word! Mitchell thinks, nodding reluctantly. Far more about hiring than acquiring, acquihires happen when a big company with desperately thin engineering ranks encounters a doomed startup with some technical talent. If the sparks fly, and the price is real cheap, the small fry is "bought" for a trivial sum; its engineers remain employed; its investors redeem pennies on the dollar; and its founders spend the next decade telling babes they just sold their startup to Google.

Phluttr buzzes Kuba's phone just as the waitress looms over his shoulder. Glancing at its screen, he lights up, and says, "I'll have a Deep Rye!"

Though as repulsed by icky marketing as anyone, the guy just can't resist a coupon. Stifling a groan, Mitchell uses the break in the action to cut out to the restroom—allegedly to do the usual but really to have a quick think about the acquihire topic on his own.

∞ ∞ ∞

"Dr. Phillips. This is . . . most unexpected!" Special Agent Hogan uttered this wryly, yet not unseriously.

"Yes I know, Agent Hogan," Dr. Phillips replied brusquely. "I'll wager that you never expected to see <u>me</u> on this side of Kingdom Come."

"Not after I brow-beated the Joint Chiefs of Staff into shutting down the ill-advised scientific program that you were championing, and for all intents and purposes <u>running like a veritable fiefdom</u> inside The Military almost fifteen years ago," Hogan stated flatly.

"I suppose you're speaking of Project Maximum," Dr. Phillips surmised, in the sonorous cadences that regularly mesmerized auditoria full of Ivy League Scientists.

Agent Hogan curtly nodded his head in agreement, and with it the densely packed red tresses that had made many an enemy she-agent swoon. "Yes, Project Maximum. Your top secret and well-funded attempt to create an Artificial Superintelligence. After I revealed the voluminous risks that such an entity would pose to Human Society, I suspected you'd never willingly enter my presence again!" And with that, the rapt bystanders shifted awkwardly; and a resulting rustle; not unlike that made by an errant flock of hawks in a twilit field; swept the room.

"I'll confess, there were dark times when I roundly cursed your name upon settling down to a wee dram of Single-Malted Scotch in some book-lined faculty study," Dr. Phillips conceded ruefully. "But I have long since realized that you were correct to argue that a Super AI could pose an existential threat to humanity, which made it a not unreckless ambition to pursue, even for Science!"

Agent Hogan nodded matter-of-factly, pleased to hear this long-overdue concession from an erstwhile rival. "So given that we've at last landed upon the same page in this most-deadly-serious of tomes, to what do I owe the pleasure of this urgently convened summit?" he queried.

Dr. Phillips looked grimly toward a turret-like video camera that skillful workmen had secured tightly to the ceiling. "Activate the DigiScreen!" he tersely commanded its unseen operator.

∞   ∞   ∞

Heading toward the restroom, Mitchell considers Giftish.ly's likely fate. Danna and Kuba personify the reason why God invented acquihires several years back. With every giant IPO minting a dozen new micro-VCs and hundreds of angels, almost any fool can raise a million bucks for a raw startup. Hence, countless fools do. Mitchell and Kuba are no fools — but they had no business raising a seed round with a casual snap of their fingers this early in their careers. Yet they did just that. As a direct result, Kuba left Google years before he would have otherwise, leaving Google down a great engineer. He pulled his two smartest colleagues along with him, so make that three great engineers. As for Danna, in a sane world she might have gone from Berkeley to a Google-like giant. But since we live in *this* world, why not launch your career at a crapshoot startup? If things pan out, you're rich! And if not, you'll get acquihired by an established company that can train and nurture you anyway. So for Danna and Kuba, a lame acquihire would be like camping out in front of a sold-out youth hostel on a postcollege, pre–Wall Street swing through Europe. Unpleasant, yes. But a great war story to preserve for the near future, when everyone's graduated to comfy suites at The W.

Things are different for Mitchell. An acquihirer would have no use for a young MBA from a half-name school with a brief stint running a failed startup as his sole tech credential. And unlike his infinitely employable co-workers, he'd struggle to find a decent tech job elsewhere. This could mean his de facto expulsion from the industry that's fascinated him since childhood. If only he could write great code, like Kuba! But years of trying showed he cannot. And no tech companies were seeking econ majors with 3.0 GPAs when he graduated from college. So he defaulted to a so-so Wall Street job, then later squeaked into a top-fifty-ish business school—after which the tech world still found him completely uninteresting. This might have been fine had he not gone and grown that brain of his. But falling under Kuba's tutelage late in childhood had this effect, and Mitchell's passion for tech is every bit as organic (even spiritual) as Kuba's own.

After a brief wait, a mini-restroom opens, and Mitchell enters its private confines. Here, he considers the situation's more menacing angle. Career thoughts aside, the deeper issue to him is their Animotion technology. No way would it survive an acquihire. Kuba's tech team would be drawn and quartered, and assigned to whatever restaurant-seeking or photo-swapping feature their buyer is launching next. And Mitchell not only fervently believes in Animotion but may physically *need* for its research to continue! It's because of the shit going wrong in his brain. The affliction that almost brought him to his knees outside the bar tonight. He's just learned— bizarrely—that Animotion might shed some light on it and perhaps even point to a cure.

The attacks began in high school. They remained rare and mild for many years, seeming more like a novelty than a threat. Then, in his mid-twenties, Mitchell developed a chilling intuition that there might be something truly awful behind them even though little had changed. This seemed to be confirmed a few years later, when the attacks escalated. He was festering in a lame digital marketing job at General Mills at the time. Years of shrugged clinical shoulders had shown he was undiagnosable to frontline doctors. So he turned to Facebook when things worsened, hoping to find a relevant expert within his extended circle. This reconnected him with Kuba's UCSF bride, Ellie—a neuroscientist, and, like Kuba, a childhood friend. Though her own work was unconnected to Mitchell's condition (or so it seemed at the time), Ellie referred him to a postdoc in her department who specializes in seizure syndromes.

And so, Mitchell entered the orbit of Dr. Martha Levine. One MRI led to another, and she was soon on a clinical crusade to get to the bottom of things. In San Francisco for an appointment with her, Mitchell caught up with Kuba for the first time since he vanished from the country. Nothing but radio silence had followed for a decade, which had perplexed and hurt Mitchell horribly. Reunited by the medical mystery, the years of separation disintegrated, and Mitchell finally learned that Kuba's bizarre silence had been *government-imposed*. With that, all was understood (and forgiven). Next, they resumed an ancient conversation about starting a company together. Mitchell had already dreamt up his social gifting concept by then—and Kuba discerned a link between it and his wife's research. And so they snapped their fingers and raised their seed capital. Mitchell moved to San Francisco, and it felt just like a storybook!

Until the worst day of his life. The day Dr. Martha diagnosed him.

∞　　∞　　∞

Upon Dr. Phillips' command, the recessed LEDs in the ceiling dimmed subtly, and the immense conference table summarily revealed itself to be none other than a vast Video Display! Upon it, an image of numerous foggy, craggy acres was rendered. "Do you recognize this terrain?" Dr. Phillips inquired. To the untrained eye, it might have been a region of the Scottish Highlands, or the maritime reaches of Oregon, or a temperate sector of Alaska.

But Hogan immediately espied several unusually unique elements of its flora and topography that were native to just one of the world's many environs. "Certainly," he verified. "This is the thinly-peopled eastern edge of the Mongolian Steppe, in China's Xinjiang Province."

"Correct," Dr. Phillips allowed. "It is also the locus of the most ambitious Artificial Superintelligence Project ever attempted by Man! Observe." With that, the room lights dimmed further, and the camera zoomed downward until a rendering of a secluded facility filled the screen. Surrounded by cyclone fencing, ominous gun towers, swiveling searchlights, fearsome attack-dog kennels, and dungeon-like Special Forces Bunkers, one might be forgiven for mistaking it for the most secure of prisons. Except that its many high-caliber turrets were oriented in such a way as to keep interlopers out rather than detainees in!

"This is the most isolated installation in the entire Land of China," Dr. Phillips divulged. "No roads, railways, or rivers connect to it. It can be reached only via military flights. It's entirely self-sufficient; generating its own reliable electricity; drawing water from cunningly hidden wells; and even producing its own food in nearby verdant fields. And it is a most revoltingly flagrant violation of the Copenhagen Accord! Which, as you surely recall, is the secret international treaty that numerous nations, including China, signed; permanently foreswearing the creation of Superintelligence."

"Ah yes, the Copenhagen Accord," Hogan recollected. "If I'm not mistaken, it was drafted as a direct result of Project Maximum's shutdown, which I myself contrived." Glowering fearsomely at the DigiScreen, he added, "And given the flagrancy of this violation, the yellow-bellied Mao-fellators must be stopped immediately! I'll need two Apache helicopters and our nine best men." After allowing the ensuing stunned silence the briefest of reigns, he clarified, "Or rather, our nine best people." This, while favoring his sometime carnal companion; the lusty but lethal Asian assassinatrix; with a brief yet meaningful glance. Though he spoke unblemished Chinese himself, her all-too-visible ancestral roots might well expedite this incursion in various ways. Her peerless talent for close-in butchery

```
was likewise a boundless asset, and her mammoth mammary
protuberances would be most-welcome travelmates. Plus,
of course, Agent Brock Hogan NEVER failed to mix plea-
sure with business when visiting The Orient!
```

$$\infty \qquad \infty \qquad \infty$$

They're still discussing how to handle tomorrow's board meeting when it's time to surrender their table to the next reservation. The bar has a huge library-themed back room where front-room evictees can mingle, so they adjourn to it. There, with plenty of smart, attractive women on hand, Mitchell's like a kid in a candy store. A penniless, ravenous kid. One who can look all he wants, but that's it. Or maybe "a meat-loving vegan at a cookout" maps better, because his hunger is principled, and self-imposed (and also, more primal than a grumpy sweet tooth). The thing is, Mitchell has essentially opted out of romance. It's a long story. One we'll get to at some point. And it's all a weird, indirect response to Falkenberg's disease.

Mitchell's midway through his next Imperial Eagle when the hipster in the chunky glasses approaches with a buddy. Both hoodied and side-burned, they look somewhat similar in the dim light, only the second one lacks spectacles. "S'cuse us," Specs says to Danna, "but we're having a little debate about Prohibition-era literature."

"How very strange," she answers warily. Her Achilles bicep of paranoia is already kicking in—and Mitchell's normally calm limbic system is going into overdrive! He senses a threat, and all these years after graduation, the blood of a high school defensive tackle still courses through his veins. He's instinctively protective around Kuba, given years of sticking up for the guy before the kids in their town finally accepted him. He's also no less protective toward Danna—because knowing some of her history, he realizes her tough, fearless surface must mask some fragility.

Specs gestures at the surrounding shelves. "Well, these books are all from the period, so we couldn't help ourselves. Anyway, my buddy here says the era's best novel is *The Beautiful and the Damned* by Fitzgerald. But I'm holding out for *The Autobiography of Alice B. Toklas* by Gertrude Stein."

Danna's eyes widen slightly. "Wow—I'd say you win!"

"Dammit!" No-Specs says, in playful dismay.

"What do you like about Stein?" Danna asks, still a bit suspicious.

Specs rises to this. "Well, her work really broke with the narrative, linear, and temporal conventions of the nineteenth century. And she started experimenting with all that long before Faulkner, Woolf, or even Joyce."

Danna nods aloofly. "She really doesn't have any antecedents."

Specs nods. "I'd say she was more influenced by Picasso than by any actual writers. She's almost literature's response to Cubism."

This shatters the ice. "Holy crap! I wrote a whole thesis on Picasso's influence on Stein!" Danna turns to Mitchell. "Former life," she explains.

Mitchell nods politely. *As if twenty-three-year-olds have those*, he thinks. But he knows what she's talking about. Danna majored in comparative literature and minored in philosophy (she picked up design and coding in her spare time, the brat). Because literature's up there with color palettes in her pantheon of passions, it's now on Mitchell to be the paranoid one, and he's amped. You'd never know it to look at him, though. The flip side of his particular form of charisma is an ability to mask his agitations just as deftly as he can infect others with them.

"So where'd you discover your passion for Stein?" Danna continues, quite a bit more warmly.

Specs grins. "It'll sound weird, but in Morocco, of all places. I did Peace Corps there, and dated another volunteer who was a huge reader."

"Wait—" Danna says. "You did Peace Corps in Morocco? When?"

"Three years ago."

"Whoa! Well, this is random. But did you know a woman named Madison Parker while you were there?"

Specs gives her a stunned look. "*Knew* her? Madison was the girlfriend who taught me how to read!"

Danna breaks into delighted laughter, then explains that Madison was the older sister of a dorm mate of hers. "I had the biggest girl crush of my life on her!" she says. "We all did. She was so smart, and gorgeous, and funny. And going to Morocco for Peace Corps? That was fierce!"

"Well, thank you," Specs jokes.

Danna laughs. "It was fierce for a blond woman. But you? I'll give you 'feisty.'" She's beaming now, her features utterly vibrant, and drawing besotted looks from guys who hardly noticed her moments ago.

Soon, No-Specs jabs his buddy. "Time to go, man," he says.

"We're off to see the Black Keys at the Warfield," Specs explains apologetically.

"Holy crap, I hate you!" Danna says, beaming even more incredulously. "They're my favorite band *ever*! How'd you get tickets?"

No-Specs cups a hand around his mouth and mock whispers, "He's buddies with their bass player," as if spilling a secret his chum is too humble to share.

Specs glares at him facetiously. "Why you rattin' me out? We're supposed to say StubHub, remember?" He turns back to Danna—who's suddenly regarding him very oddly. "But yeah, I do know their bassist. And they're on in nine minutes. If they stick to the schedule he texted me this afternoon."

"Got it," Danna says, now gazing very intently into his eyes. "One last thing," she enunciates very loudly and clearly. "Who is winning the Warriors game right now?"

Specs is suddenly very nervous. "Warriors are up by five," he says sheepishly.

With that, Danna suddenly flicks her drink right into No-Specs's unshielded eyes. He gasps and jumps back as her other hand flies to Specs's face, snatching for his glasses. "What the hell?" Specs yelps, folding into a protective crouch. This smashes his face right into Danna's grasping fingers, and his glasses go flying.

Danna dives for them, yelling, "Cover me," to no one in particular. Lunging toward her, Specs is instantly slammed to the floor by Mitchell, who's stunned to find his football training so useful in this CEO gig. Danna uses the ensuing chaos to briefly snatch the glasses. But No-Specs has recovered and bats them from her hands, sending them skittering under a thicket of legs midway across the room. Mitchell then agilely drops No-Specs to the floor, which leaves everyone sprawling but Kuba, who casually strides into the now-gawking huddle of drinkers, plucks the glasses from the carpet, and looks at them reeeeeeeal close as a mountain of Mississippi muscle and fist closes in on the scene.

"The hell?" the bouncer asks, effortlessly plucking Danna and Specs from the floor by the scruffs of their jackets.

"She assaulted me," Specs whines shrilly.

The bouncer hoists Danna to eye level, like a picky shopper appraising a melon. "This'n? Hell, she ain't a hundred pounds soakin wet! If she can whup you, you oughta learn some kung fu." He releases them both.

Figuring Danna's about to clam up and stare daggers at everyone, while Kuba catatonically ponders those high-tech glasses, Mitchell surges to his feet. "He's a *glass*hole," he declares, pointing at Specs. "He was recording us, and everyone else in this bar!" This is only a guess. But it's an educated one and could just win the bouncer over.

"Hey, those are mine!" Specs practically shrieks, seeing his glasses in Kuba's hands and lunging for them. Kuba dangles them out of his reach, then hands them peaceably to the bouncer.

"Glasshole," the giant grumbles, examining the thick lenses. This term dates back to the early heyday of Google Glass—the famously clunky first-generation attempt to embed heads-up data displays in eyewear. Priced at fifteen hundred bucks, Glass categorically failed to set the world alight. It then largely vanished from the wild, but not before its built-in camera sparked a small wave of local paranoia. Reasoning that nothing could stomp a buzz quite like a herd of sly geeks sneaking candid photos of profitable revelry, several barkeeps banished Glass from their premises. "I got me a powerful allergy to glassholes! No wonder I got the sniffles tonight." The drawling quip hints of a playful wit beneath the gruffness, and Mitchell decides on the tone he'll take with this guy.

"I wasn't recording anything," Specs whines petulantly. "Those are pre*script*ion."

"Sure," Mitchell says, giving the bouncer a chummy glance. "Diagnosis: asswipe."

Guffawing cheerfully, the bouncer peers at an arched bump on the temple of the frame, which looks a lot like a power button. A new wave of data glasses is starting to circulate, and digerati bars like this one want nothing to do with them. "Or maybe, *glass*wipe," he parries, and Mitchell chuckles politely. The bouncer then hands the glasses back to Specs, saying, "You get your peepin tom ass outta here now, and I don't ever wanna see you again." With that, Specs and No-Specs slink out, the bouncer gives the Giftish.ly crew a merry wink, and they're left in peace.

"That hardware was amazing," Kuba whispers once they're alone. "They looked exactly like normal glasses. And I mean, *exactly*." Everyone knows that smart eyewear will one day be indistinguishable from the real thing. But Glass itself fell comically short of this, and while some of the newer gear is better, it's still easy to spot in a crowd.

"It's the software that freaks me out," Danna says, clearly shaken. "That guy didn't know crap about me, Gertrude Stein, or my friend's big sister. But his glasses were . . . telling him what to say. Kind of."

"That's what I guessed," Mitchell says. "How'd you figure it out?"

"The guy without the glasses blew it when he tried to ad lib about the Black Keys."

"You mean when he said they knew the bass player?"

Danna nods. "The Black Keys don't *have* a bass player."

"Seriously?" Mitchell asks. "They sure sound like they do."

"Trust me. They've been my favorite band for years. Just like Stein's my favorite author. And *Toklas* is my favorite book. It was one coincidence too many. Meanwhile, I thought I'd seen a couple weird flashes of light in that guy's lenses. So when they blew the bassist thing, I suddenly put it all together."

"Ahhh," Mitchell says. "So when you leaned in close and asked him about the Warriors game . . ."

"It was on a hunch. I figured smart glasses would have built-in voice recognition. And if I asked really clearly about something really basic, like a sports score, the system might flash up the answer."

"So you saw the score pop up in his glasses?"

Danna shakes her head. "Just a glimmer of light. But that was enough."

"But how did he learn all that stuff about you?" Kuba asks, more wide-eyed about the technology than disturbed by the privacy rupture.

"Well, first he had to figure out who I was, so let's start with facial recognition," Danna says. "I'll bet those lenses ID everyone he looks at."

Mitchell rolls his eyes. "Oh, come on." This strikes him as just a bit paranoid—and, at least ten years into the future.

But Kuba's nodding. "Think of all the pictures of you online. Of all of us. Each tagged with our names. Any system that's scanned them all could do it. Facebook's been ID-ing faces in photos for years. ID-ing someone from a live feed through those glasses wouldn't be much harder."

Danna shudders. "I'm sure it's a layup for the NSA."

"Please, those guys weren't NSA," Mitchell says (although he wouldn't mind being wrong because it would be pretty badass to've flattened a pair of government agents like that!).

"They wouldn't have to be, to pull that off," Kuba says. "Five years ago, maybe. But today? No. Facial ID just isn't that hard or exotic anymore."

"Then how'd the system come up with all that stuff for him to say about Danna's friend's older sister?" Mitchell asks.

"It probably didn't," Kuba guesses. "The operator just picked Danna as a target. Maybe randomly. Maybe because he liked the way she looked."

"Right!" Mitchell says, recalling how Specs prowled the outer bar earlier in the evening, gazing briefly at every face.

"Then I'll bet the system pulled up a bunch of facts about her," Kuba continues. "She wrote a thesis on this book. Here's her social graph. Here are some distant acquaintances of hers you might credibly pretend to know. That sort of thing. Then the guy pieced together his own story and approach. I mean, he was pretty smooth. He wasn't reading a teleprompter or anything."

"Except for his initial description of Stein's writing," Danna says. "That was pretty wooden. Almost like he was reading from Wikipedia. But after that, he was real smooth. And, he was also having fun with it. Which made it believable, because small-world conversations like that actually are fun. If I didn't feel so violated, I'd be kind of impressed with the whole performance. And he could've done something much creepier if he had wanted to."

"Like *what?*" To Mitchell, this shit's about as creepy as it gets.

"Well, let's see. It would've been illegal, but once the facial recognition did its thing, there's a bunch of databases the system could've hit to figure out where every cute girl in the bar lives, right? Then it could've told him which ones live in walking distance. And which ones are single and live alone. Then it could've fed him a bunch of facts to help him seem all trustworthy to the unsuspecting target of his choice. Kind of like it did with me. He could've come off as being the brother of an old friend of hers. Or maybe, 'Hey, we took that history class together junior year! Wasn't Professor Bernstein the best?' Enough trust that she lets him walk her home at the end of the night because it's a crap neighborhood, and she thinks they have a dozen friends in common. And then? Use your imagination."

Mitchell shudders. "That's sick."

"I agree. But our guy only tricked me into thinking we had a bunch of weird things in common. Pretty harmless by comparison." Danna is actually less put off by the episode than Mitchell or Kuba. As she's already plenty paranoid, it didn't surprise her. Nor did it reduce her faith in the average stranger, which for years has had nowhere lower to go.

"But we still loathe him, right?" Mitchell confirms. If Danna and Kuba are right about everything, those glasses make the guy half-omniscient—and like some real-world supervillian, he's noxiously abusing his powers. "And what the hell was the point of all that anyway?"

"They were alpha testing something new," Kuba says softly. "Something radical. Taking it for a spin in the real world. That hardware's pre-release, and very special. You saw how they fought. They did *not* want it getting out of their hands."

"Do you seriously think that spying system is gonna be someone's *product?*" Mitchell asks. "It can't possibly be legal! It's like . . . weaponized information."

"Any more weaponized than a handgun?" Danna asks. "Those seem to be legal everywhere."

Mitchell nods grimly. "I can hear the lobbyists now. Magic glasses don't spy on people—people do."

"Yes, they'll say that," Kuba agrees. "And they won't be entirely wrong. Cynical. But not wrong. Because the tech itself could be used for practically anything, good or bad. It's as value neutral as a smartphone. Or a computer."

"And every bit as inevitable," Danna adds. "We've seen that dozens of times. Today's million-dollar prototype is tomorrow's ninety-nine-dollar gizmo."

Mitchell nods. "I just wish the guys who invented it didn't go straight to the gutter with their first application."

"Agreed," Danna says. "Why build something that amazing just to creep on people in bars?"

"Completely twisted," Mitchell agrees. "I mean, seriously. Who would *do* that?"

"A super-rich organization," Kuba muses. "God only knows how much R&D that took."

"Make that a *brilliant* rich organization," Danna says. "That shit was incredible."

"Make that a brilliant, rich, *evil* organization," Mitchell adds. "Just to state the obvious."

They all fall silent. Then Danna inevitably guesses, "Stanford?"

Mitchell grins. "Spoken like a true Berkeley girl. But sorry—not evil enough." He falls silent, then hazards, "North Korea?"

Kuba shakes his head. "Not rich enough."

Then Danna guesses "Iran?"

"Not brilliant enough," Mitchell points out.

As if on cue, their pockets all hum with an inbound digital coupon.

The briefest of intervals, then Danna's eyes widen, and she snarls, "**No!**"

This baffles Kuba. But Mitchell's right there with her. "It was fucking *Phluttr*!!!" he barks.

Bingo, kid.

∞   ∞   ∞

N≡T GRRRL.COM

PHLUTTR AND SARTTR

Phluttr has intrigued me since the day I met her. If Facebook is the smooth, functional CNN of social media, Phluttr's The Kardashians—a ghastly, lurid pleasure with huge tits and collagen lips that we're loath to admit to using. An addiction that's not merely guilty, but indicted, convicted, and sentenced; more like a smack habit than a weakness for that extra bonbon.

And she knows every one of us so well! Just like that popular, gossipy, gorgeous autocrat back in eighth grade: the one whose approval we craved, whose censure we dreaded, and whose wrath we often brought down for no discernible reason (and yes, I'm calling Phluttr "she." Not because I'm self-hating or any less a feminist than the next blogger, but because she reminds me so fully of my own local eighth-grade autocrat, who had not a Y chromosome in her body).

Phluttr knows us from our browsing activity, phone logs, emails, photo streams, GPS data, and a hundred other sources that we grant her eternal access to (as well as *resale rights*—seriously!) by blindly accepting her "Data Donor Agreement." Triangulating our mindset and doings from all this, Phluttr then presents the world with an immaculately spin-doctored view of our enviable lives by updating our status *for us* with AutoPosts (APs). If you're wondering why anyone would ever allow such a thing, most relationships with APs unfold like this:

1) **Denial:** As we first download Phluttr, we swear we'll never enable APs, because yiiiiiiikes, right?
2) **Confusion:** Oops! We find that APs are an opt-out feature. Phluttr's labyrinthine settings then thwart all attempts to disable them (oh—and to uninstall the app).
3) **Acceptance:** We discover these APs work eerily well. It meanwhile strikes us that constantly updating all our *other* social tools is fast becoming an unpaid part-time job—and fuck that, right?
4) **Addiction:** We enter Phase Four when Phluttr first elects to send one of our APs hyperviral. Years hence, most of us will still recall where we were standing when, out of the clear blue, *thousands* of friends, acquaintances, friends of acquaintances, and beyond started pumping Likes, Hots, and Cools into our InFlows! And with them, cascades of endorphins into our junkie neurons! *Yayyy Phluttr,* I love you!!!

But not long after that first fateful drag on the crack pipe, Phluttr turns aloof. Maybe she displays a post about a long-sought life achievement to no one but our boring rural cousins. Or maybe she turns vicious and tips us off about something awful she overheard about us in a chat, a forum, or even a private message (without quite revealing the source)!

However. Vicious as she gets, no one will ever see Phluttr plunge a knife into our back. Like any seasoned eighth-grade autocrat, she's too smart to get caught. Plenty of humans are glad to do the deed, anyway. And besides, the *real* money is in bandaging us up, scrubbing the blood off that cute new Betsey Johnson frock, and scoring us that restorative fix of endorphins! Because like any autocrat, Phluttr can be bought. Want to know the precise number of people who heard that awful rumor about you? Pay her off! Want to quash it, kill it; flush it from everyone else's InFlows? Pay her off! Want to push out a direct rebuttal to all who have read or heard it? You know what to do!

Or maybe there's no dirt on you just now, and you crave attention. The In-Flow algorithms are guarded more jealously than Putin's nuclear codes. But cash on the barrel will speed the spread of anything. A true pittance ensures that X random people in your network see a certain post. A larger pittance ensures they never know you paid to promote it. A non-pittance allows you to specifically target the people who see it, rather than shotgunning it out there.

Then when people start Liking, Hotting, and Cooling your post, another small fee lets you micromanage which of your raving critics are most visible to the rest of us. Holy crap! *Marc Andreessen* Liked your thoughts on the LDAP protocol's twenty-fifth birthday?? You'd hate for his Like and comment to be forty-seventh on a long list that no one ever scrolls through but you! So, to push it to the top—ka-*ching*!

How do Phluttr's social-image-management tools compare to the incumbent competition? Well, if Facebook were a freebie photo editor with just a contrast dial and a red-eye fixer, Phluttr would be phucking Photoshop—a professional power tool with countless effects to switch on, airbrushes to wield, and gradations to tweak as you posture within and navigate through the infinite complexity of the social jungle.

And again—this is where the real money is! Sure, Phluttr's minting a fortune from the Fortune 500. Her surgically targeted ads don't come cheap, after all. Nor do those psychically targeted coupons that keep popping up on our phones. But the biggest-paying advertiser, brand manager, and spin doctor will ultimately be *us*, the Phluttr user base. There are gold mines to extract from our desperate urge to be heard! And, from our agonizing need to posture within and navigate through the social jungle's fractal complexity.

Which is to say, through *hell*. Because Phluttr has read her Sartre (or should I say Sarttr?). She knows that hell is other people, and that most of us would give anything to ease our passage through the consensual, collective hell we create for ourselves and one another. But since I'm not gloomy, existential, or French enough to leave it at that, I'll add that *heaven* is other people as well, without any doubt. Either way, Phluttr is an incredibly powerful wingbitch to have on your side in this realm. An addictively capable one. And, increasingly, an expensive one.

∞   ∞   ∞

Man, is Mitchell dragging the next morning! Triumphing in an honest-to-God bar brawl called for some celebratory rounds that none of them really needed. He's definitely hungover from that. Plus, perhaps, from the neurological glitch he suffered outside the bar. Those things can sometimes leave a faint next-day shadow. His condition is called Falkenberg's disease, and its attacks are provoked by odd clusters of sensory and emotional events. The sensory triggers are abrupt surprises—like a flash, a jolt, or the unexpected siren he heard when he was standing at the bar's intercom. Strong feelings of embarrassment or frustration (both also experienced outside the bar) are the emotional triggers. Falkenberg's is part of the broad family of "cataplectic" conditions, in which emotions and other stimuli induce the sudden loss of muscular control (narcolepsy being a famous cousin). It was manageable during the decade-plus when Mitchell's triggers had to clear high thresholds before he got into trouble. Attacks were rare back then, and mild. They also took minutes to build, leaving ample time to pull over if he happened to be driving. But those days are gone. Now, a single strong factor can provoke an attack, or two weak ones together. And he long since traded in his car for a Lyft account.

Bad as things are now, it's nothing compared to the disease's third phase, which could start tomorrow, next year, or ten years hence. A persistent tingling in his extremities will herald the start. This will then spread inward for months, until tingling suffuses his body. Then, as one chilling source has it:

> The tingling escalates to either numbness or a burning feeling. This is accompanied by a gradual loss of motor control, which limits, then eclipses the use of all limbs and digits. Patients then gradually suffer increasing difficulty with speech, respiration, and swallowing. Most Falkenberg's sufferers die as a result of losing the ability to breathe.

Uncertainty is one of the disease's cruelest aspects. During the indeterminate lag before its third phase, many victims survey themselves obsessively for hints of tingling—some to the point of madness. But the giant unknown is what's in store after the tingling is body-wide. When it "escalates to either numbness or a burning feeling." More "fortunate" Falkenberg's victims merely feel an icy nothingness toward the end. The unlucky ones suffer dreadful scorching sensations, which permeate their every cell and never once dim.

HELLFIRE. That's the term victims have coined for this unspeakable phase. And when he contemplates what lies ahead, this terrifies Mitchell far more than the certainty of dying. The possibility of being . . . unlucky. Of being suffused with HELLFIRE for months on end and lacking the motor control necessary to end it by taking his own life.

At least Dr. Martha is still fighting for him. There could be something publishable going on here, after all! And so she has scanned, assayed, irradiated, sequenced, sampled, genotyped, biopsied, urinalysized, and all but vivisected Mitchell, while reaching out to the thin (and ever-thinning) ranks of his fellow sufferers across the globe; seeking DNA, tissue, blood, sperm (yes, really), and interviews. The oddest part of Mitchell's own regimen is the frequent assignment of ghastly yoghurty goos to gag down. This, because Dr. Martha suspects his disease may be connected to the microbiome (Marthaspeak for bacteria that live in the gut and are in some way connected to horrid yoghurts).

And then came a bizarre and unexpected ray of light just three days ago. During an exam, Dr. Martha mentioned a possible connection between Falkenberg's and the research Kuba's wife Ellie is doing—the very research behind Giftish.ly's technology! Of course, Ellie was at a conference just then, and Dr. Martha was leaving to trek the Amazon (of all places) with her geologist husband for twelve days. She asked Mitchell to keep things to himself until her return because she doesn't want to put the lab through a fire drill unless she can better verify the link. This seemed reasonable at the time. But less so now, in light of Kuba's and Danna's pessimism about the company's surviving today's board meeting. Because if Animotion has even the faintest link to Falkenberg's, he *simply cannot lose control of it*, Mitchell wants to scream!

Further darkening his mood, the office's fog-choked neighborhood has an especially gloomy cast today. Far removed from tech-hip SoMa, from nearly-as-chic Potrero Hill, from the Mission's gritty cool, and even from the bland-but-serviceable financial district; it lies many zip codes to the west; beyond even Arguello Boulevard (where explorers are known to fall off the planet's edge); in a distant region known only for fog, raw ocean winds, numbered avenues, and competitively priced Chinese food.

Home to two endodontists before Mitchell rented it, the office is amenity-free, lacking even a foosball table. Which is so countercultural as to verge on being a *statement*. Elsewhere, tech companies dish up free Michelin-grade grub in their cafeterias, drive in staffers on fancy complimentary shuttles, and dole out on-premise handouts like massages, yoga classes, oil changes, grocery deliveries, childcare, nail care, pet care, gyms, and naptime in "crash pods"; as well as concierges to handle irksome tasks like ATM runs.

This dishing-up/driving-in/doling-out arms race is fodder in the industry's never-ending talent auction—in which another common currency is vacation time. The stingy American two-week standard was largely out by the end of the first Internet bubble. Three weeks then became four, then gradually more. When Netflix announced *unlimited* time off, you'd've thought the bidding was over! Then Evernote topped it by throwing in free vacation spending money. Cynics questioned how many of those infinite holidays were actually taken, given the peer pressure to stick around and perpetually add value in Type-A pressure cookers (while noting that the policy eliminated the need to pay departing employees for accrued vacation time). So enter "pre-cations," or paid vacations taken by new hires *before* the first day on the job.

The arms race recently spread to parental leave. In a nation that legislates precisely zero paid maternity days, Yahoo started giving Scandinavia a run for its money, with four months off for biological moms, plus seven weeks for dads, adoptive parents, and others who don't actually bear their young. To this, Google added five hundred "Baby Bonding Bucks." Facebook then octupled the cash, while granting the full four months of leave to fathers, adopters, foster parents, same-sex couples, and folks who come by their children by way of surrogacy. All this generosity surely delights employees. But in a sign that it's also straining budgets, Apple and others now offer to freeze the eggs of aging female workers (as well as those of the aging wives and nonwife female partners of company men and company lesbians), thereby enabling people to punt on the whole pricey issue indefinitely.

None other than Phluttr brought this particular bidding war to an awkward and headline-seizing finale, by offering six months of leave, plus IVF with mitochondrial transfer to employees in FMF amorous triads, thereby raising the provocative specter of high-tech newborns with three extremely well rested genetic parents. The company followed this up with a series of contradictory apologies, denials, retractions, and amplifications that were ingeniously choreographed to provoke thunderous denunciations from both the left and the right. App downloads and website registrations soared during the ensuing wave of front-page revulsion, and the company's founder (or *Phoundr,* as he's inevitably called) achieved the distinction of being condemned by both MoveOn.org and the Sheikh of Al-Azhar in independent fatwas issued on the exact same day.

As for Giftish.ly, its lack of anything to entice perk junkies has been fine up to a point. Infant startups have an inherent mystique, Mitchell's a charismatic recruiter, and Kuba has a magnetic reputation, both as a developer and an engineering manager. All of this drew solid talent— particularly before their service's debut (pre-launch companies having a special allure to some). But as the months dragged by with no percepti- ble traffic spike, the bloom drained slowly from the rose. Canny recruits troll sites like Alexa to gauge a startup's user traction, and Crunchbase to track its fundraising. So just a few momentum-free months will lend a certain odor to a startup in the eyes of potential hires.

Not that Giftish.ly's hiring just now. Indeed, they've been losing good people since September. Danna's right-hand designer started the exo- dus, and she's been covering for him ever since. Next, two not-bad engi- neers took off. Then in December, a software architect named Jimbo left for a LinkedIn spin-off. He was a quarrelsome twit whose facial topiary placed well in the annual World Beard and Moustache Championships; who painted his left fingernails black, cut his own hair, and refused to accept direct deposit for paranoid reasons he'd lay out in five-page rants larded with ENTIRE PARAGRAPHS IN ALL CAPS! (which Mitchell dutifully read but never quite fathomed). But he was one hell of a programmer. Coding is a dark art, whose greats excel in logarithmic ways. So while superb accountants might grind out the output of two, or even 2.6 aver- age accountants; and likewise the best plumbers, lawyers, and bartend- ers; stupendous developers routinely do the work of five, ten, or even (Steve Jobs famously claimed) twenty-five mere mortals. Jimbo was one of those edge cases, and they're in no position to hire another like him.

Now January finds Team Giftish.ly sheltering from foggy Farallon winds in an office whose low-rent vibe has gone from feeling scrappy and virtuous to desperate and mandatory. The sole benefit of this no-budget drudgery is its undeniable appeal to tight-fisted investors. This may just help a smidgen this morning, when #GreenSprout C@pital's M@naging P@rtner, Founder, C:\>iefInvestmentOfficer, sole LTD.partner, and solitary employee arrives for the board meeting. No doubt the jackass'll be exactly seventeen minutes late. It's like his trademark. He adopted it after reading that this interval optimally heralds the latecomer's importance, on a blog called Persuadifi.er, which promotes techniques for dominating beta males and females.

Sure enough, Mitchell and Kuba are twiddling their thumbs at 9:10. And at 9:12. And 9:14. Then at 9:15, Kuba flatly says, "Of *course* it was them."

Kuba's a habitual spouter of non sequiturs. Having decoded them for years, Mitchell instinctively scans his memory for topics to connect to this one. Last night's discussion about who created the magic glasses in the bar, for instance. "You mean Phluttr?" he assays.

"Those people give me the creeps," Kuba confirms. He's generally averse to social networks. Enough so that he absented himself from them entirely for years, until co-founding a social-gifting company made this professionally untenable. It's not moral distaste but personal skittishness. As he often states, he just doesn't like being *surveilled*. Early childhood behind the rusted Iron Curtain seeded this aversion. Kuba was then sur-veilled more meticulously still as a teen—here, in the land of the free! As a direct result, he was then exiled (yes, exiled!). Remarkably, this never soured him on the US (intimacy with Soviet rot being a strong inoculant against anti-Americanism). But he shrinks from sites that track user pref-erences and histories too comprehensively, and no site is more invasive than Phluttr.

"The creeps," Kuba reaffirms at 9:16.

At precisely 9:17, Harold Pugwash waddles in. Chubby and rather beady-eyed, he's a full head shorter than Mitchell. He's just "Pugwash" to everyone, including immediate family—and also non-immediate fam-ily, which is to say Mitchell, who is one of his many cousins.

"Your email said we'll be doing some kind of technology review," he grumbles, thunking down across the table from them. "What's the point? You guys're fucked, you're an acquihire! No one cares about tech in an acquihire. They only care about the team! So why don't you just give me a roster of your engineers and let me get on with my day?"

Kuba shoots Mitchell a seething look, making zero effort to hide his scorn for Pugwash. Kuba was still in high school when they first met, and Pugwash gave him the worst career advice ever proffered from one human being to another (and I do mean that quite literally in dollar terms, as we'll see). More recently, he'd heard countless anti-Pugwash screeds at Google. Pugwash had preceded him there by many years, but though long gone, his name still rang out in its hallways. You see, Fortune's a bitch with a great sense of humor—and so she made Pugwash a ridiculously early Google hire, which scored him a commensurately ridiculous stock package. Of course, all companies make hiring boo-boos. But when the true greats make them really early on, some real knuckleheads can get moronically rich. This effect produces plenty of accidental tech millionaires. Some accidental gazillionaires, too—but only a smattering of Pugwashes, and the man is rather famous. Some take his exquisite luck almost personally. Not merely those who worked far harder for far lesser bonanzai (although to be clear, those folks're plenty pissed). But also those who are even richer still through their own godsends of timing, genetics, or happenstance, and have since fetishized a vision of the industry as an immaculate meritocracy. Those who fancy that they earned every dime of their tech fortunes through talent, toil, and daring (which is almost everyone who has one) regard any whiff of the lottery (Pugwash, for instance) as a PR liability.

Mitchell starts the meeting. "We'd like to begin by taking you on a deeper tour of our technology, as we think this'll prove that an acquihire would be a terrible mistake. Because as you'll see, we may be on the cusp of a massive breakthrough."

"I hope that doesn't mean you think you're getting another dime out of me," Pugwash snips. "Because Giftish.ly is already the biggest capital investment I've ever made." This is no exaggeration. Pugwash's industry nickname is Fiddy—as in Fiddy-K, in honor of the fifty-thousand-dollar investments he tries to foist on any Google alum who starts a company. Enough have said yes over the years (along with graduates of Facebook, PayPal, LinkedIn, and the other companies he stalks) that his portfolio is a bit like an index fund of startups from 2004 to the present. This could well be the greatest vintage in the history of entrepreneurial equity. So if Pugwash's initial fortune annoyed his early cohorts, his current one must be robbing them of the will to live.

But Pugwash blew way past his standard fiddy-K for Giftish.ly, offering them ten times that sum the moment he got wind of the company's formation. It was indeed the scale of this bet that prompted Mitchell to resist his better instincts and accept his cousin's capital. From a sheer logistics and brain-damage standpoint, one big check is always better than lots of teeny ones; and most of the angel money on offer to them was in small denominations. Pugwash's relative generosity at the time had everything to do with Kuba's reputation within Google and nothing to do with family loyalty. Indeed, it had nothing to do with generosity, as his true agenda was connected to #GreenSprout C@pital. With hopes of turning it into a proper fund, Pugwash was then making bigger bets on fewer companies while also taking his first board seats. This turned out to be a brief phase, as nobody he called on had the faintest interest in backing #GreenSprout. Which was a catastrophic mistake for them, as his one other large investment from that phase will soon become the single most lucrative angel investment *of all time* (and again, we can blame that cosmic bitch with the great sense of humor). More on that in a bit.

Mitchell launches his first slide — a simple visual representation of how their Animotion technology works. "We briefly discussed Animotion when we first pitched the company to you. I'd like to go into some more depth today."

"How 'bout the thirty-second version?" Pugwash asks, shunning Mitchell's PowerPoint for his new phone, which is the size of a serving platter.

"Well, the basic concept is rooted in evolutionary psychology."

"I said seconds, not eons," Pugwash grumbles, but pulls his eyes from his screen.

"It all starts with the fact that thinking is *expensive* from the standpoint of natural selection," Mitchell continues. "The brain consumes 20 percent of the calories that humans eat. And while intelligence enabled humanity's survival, our ancestors were in a constant race against starvation, too. So their brains only got so big."

Pugwash gets it. "Being smarter gets you more to eat but only up to a point," he says. "Then there's diminishing returns."

Mitchell nods. "And if human brains devoured double the calories, grandma and grandpa wouldn't have found twice the nuts and berries. So our ancestors' brains grew until they hit a certain equilibrium."

"Which means humans are a lot stupider than maybe they could be. Which explains Republicans."

Mitchell gives this thigh-slapper a courtesy chuckle. His cousin is the most relentlessly politically correct person he knows and misses no opportunity to denounce the right (as well as the center, and for that matter, the center-left). This posture is so safe and common among tech elites that it's dictated by conformity as often as principle. Pugwash himself is about as idealistic and committed to empowering the vulnerable as an Abu Dhabi housewife with three Filipina slaves staffing her kitchen.

"As a result," Mitchell continues, "human thought is full of shortcuts, patches, and hacks. It has to be. Because it runs on a fixed budget, and we face countless mental challenges that cavemen never dealt with. Brain MRIs are now so sensitive that researchers can actually see some of these shortcuts in action. And many are driven by emotions we evolved over eons on the savannah. For instance: you don't compute the number of calories that an enemy caveman stole when he swiped your brontosaurus burger. You just get mad and bash his head in. Then the other cavemen don't derive the expected value of grabbing your next burger. They're just scared of you and don't dare. Meanwhile, you don't quantify the benefits of your newborn cave-son living long enough to help you hunt, eat, and conquer enemies. You just love your kid and do everything you can to help him survive."

"Unless I'm a Tea Party douchebag. Those people just aren't human!" His catcalls aside, Pugwash is now fully engaged. Though lazy, his intellect is also robust, and Mitchell has perfected a concise yet chatty style that really draws him in. As dumbest guy in the room, he has to come up with ways to be useful, and this one's a biggie.

"The point is that millions of years of natural selection baked these emotions into us. But we never built them into computers. Which didn't matter when computers were just adding up columns and transferring data. But now we want them to find our soulmates. Decide who should live or die on a battlefield. Or allocate scarce resources amongst deserving people."

"Or, in the case of Giftish.ly's noble purpose, figure out which MP3 in your catalog'll get the hot chick down the hall to cock a leg," Pugwash says. "If you're like, some sexist, rapey frat boy."

"That's one way of putting it," Mitchell says, managing to sound like he's savoring an astute and subtle point. "Anyway, Kuba's wife's research seems to show that *emotions* run much deeper in analytical processes than anyone previously imagined. And that an emotional substrate is actually essential for all sorts of analysis."

"So then why don't I burst into tears whenever I do a jigsaw puzzle, or whatever?" Pugwash snorts.

"Because that requires raw linear cognition rather than oblique reasoning," Kuba says, sincerely trying to help. He then clams up, as if this is a complete explanation.

"Sure, a cat can't do a jigsaw puzzle," Mitchell expounds, as if Kuba's non sequitur was part of a carefully rehearsed spiel. "Nor a toddler. But just grind away at it, and you'll eventually complete it."

"Then what's this substrate of yours actually good for?" Pugwash snaps.

"Well," Mitchell says, "imagine I spend an hour trying to figure out how America should fix its relations with Russia. I'm a foreign affairs novice and don't get anywhere. And I won't get any further if I spend ten more hours at it. Or a hundred. Because certain problems are completely resistant to increased rumination. But things are different for a diplomat who has spent years engaged in Russian-American relations. Not because he knows more facts and figures, because that stuff's available to all of us via Google, now. But because his framework includes lots of intuition. Educated guesses. Vague rules of thumb that have just kind of *worked* over the years—that sort of thing. This much has been known for a while."

"Which is why motes can be viewed as nucleic particles of analysis," Kuba adds obtusely.

"Exactly!" Mitchell says, deftly nudging things along. "What we're now learning is that this thought framework is powered by a wildly complex undercurrent of emotions. Emotions connected to personal experiences and values. To the diplomat's visceral reactions to events as they unfold in real time, or to new facts as they emerge. Most of these emotions are minuscule and fleeting. So much so that they aren't even experienced consciously! Kuba's wife's lab is doing a ton of research into these feelings and their function. And as Kuba just mentioned, she named them 'motes.'"

"Like something you dig around a castle? That's stupid."

Masking a familiar urge to belt his cousin, Mitchell says, "No, it's spelled M-O-T-E. It's short for 'emote.' Also, they're tiny—like dust motes."

"Got it. And how do they help our Russia expert?"

"The mosaic of motes he's affixed to various facts, ideas, and personal experiences over the years will supercharge his thought processes," Mitchell says. "By enabling those gut shortcuts. By creating conviction when pure analysis would lead to indecision, and more. It's as if he's now speed-skating around a rink instead of running around a field."

"So he's thinking faster?"

"Not exactly. It's that he's thinking more *deftly*. He's moving around the same geography as a novice, but that hard-earned emotional substrate gives him the ice. It gives him the skates, as well as speed, power, and grace. And it lets him pull off moves no one could manage on solid ground! This sort of thing happens in any domain that's intractable to raw rumination, or raw computing."

"Like figuring out what songs the chick I'm banging will like."

"For instance."

Earlier, I said that while Mitchell usually invokes his "dumbest guy in the room" mantra metaphorically, it's sometimes literally true. This is one of those times—because Pugwash is quite bright, much as we all hate to admit it. And hats off to Mitchell because it's good for a founder to be the dim bulb at the office! Since your own IQ is fixed, pulling this off means recruiting a brilliant team, which is a huge part of your job. It also means that you're almost always learning. And when you're not learning, you can fix that by changing the subject. When surrounded by engineers, Mitchell steers away from MBA topics, preferring to discuss software architecture, say. Or if in a discussion of hockey (he's the smartest guy in the *city* about this), he might bring up string theory (of which he has a sub-Neanderthal grasp). He figures the more you learn, the better you teach—which is quite useful in circumstances like today's.

Pugwash is now firmly under the conversational spell, despite himself. "So assuming you can port all of this into software," he asks, "what could it enable? Besides what you're trying to do with it now. Because I'm pretty sure that'll never make a dime."

"There may not be *any* commercial application for it," Kuba blurts cheerfully, and Mitchell deftly masks an urge to strangle him. "But there could be radical applications from a pure-science standpoint!"

Mercantile to his core, Pugwash is about as drawn to pure science as a ravenous, horny lion is to something he can neither eat nor fuck. "Like . . . *what?*" he asks, with something verging on disgust.

"Well . . ." Kuba begins. He then goes somewhere entirely new to Mitchell. "Quite possibly consciousness." He says this very, very quietly. "Because my wife's research indicates that human consciousness is in some way enabled by motes."

Pugwash gives a low whistle, then falls silent. Then, "Holy crap!" Then more silence.

And Mitchell allows himself a moment of hope. Yes, his cousin is more a lover of money than of ideas. But he *is* smart! And he *does* care about his reputation. Perhaps even his legacy! And the radical significance of Animotion is clearly dawning on him (on both of them, frankly, as this is the first Mitchell has heard about this consciousness angle).

More silence. Then, more still. Then, finally, Pugwash speaks.

"This is the most incredible technology I've had a personal hand in creating since me and Larry invented the Page Rank algorithm at Google," he begins grotesquely. "And—"

Still more silence.

Then: "There's not a fucking chance I'm putting another dime into it."

"But—" Mitchell begins, his calm fraying.

Pugwash cuts him off. "NO, Mitchell! It'd be way too expensive. You couldn't even take a baby step down this path with just a few weeks of financing. Which, let's face it, is the best you could hope to claw out of a tightwad prick like me."

"But we can't just let it die," Mitchell says, as this might just be tantamount to letting *him* die—for reasons that Dr. Martha will hopefully elucidate whenever she gets back from the damned Amazon!

"Who said anything about it dying?" Pugwash asks. "There's no way we're letting that happen." And Mitchell is overcome with relief.

"Not a chance!" Kuba agrees. "I'm convinced this could be monumental. Historic. Epoch-defining! And I'd leave the commercial world entirely to push it forward. Who cares if we ever see a dime from it?"

"*What?*" Pugwash asks.

Deaf as he can be to the most blaring social signals, Kuba mistakes horror for shocked admiration. "Seriously! Who cares about the economics? In fact, everything that's done in this area should probably be open-source. Put in the public domain. This could be as fundamental as Newton's laws! Could you imagine if *those* had been private property?"

Pugwash—who would've leveraged a medieval patent on gravity into the papacy and half of Prussia—nods wildly.

Clumsily mistaking this for support, Kuba plows on. "Obviously, the neuroscience is coming out of my wife's lab at UCSF. So that would be a logical home for my work, too. But there're also some amazing assets we should consider at Stanford."

Pugwash finally detonates. "Nothing that I sank a half million dollars into is going into the public domain!"

Stunned silence. Then, "Well, it's common in academia—"

"*Acad*emia! Do I look like the National fucking Science Foundation?"

"But . . . well, the maximum potential of this stuff—"

"Is economic, not academic! Do you think we'd have . . . penicillin, if we relied on *schools* to invent shit? Pacemakers? Seatbelts? Search engines?"

By rather awesome coincidence, all of these things actually *did* emerge from university labs. But before Kuba can point this out, Mitchell jumps in.

"Wait!" All eyes look his way. "I just thought of the perfect buyer." A lowly generalist among brilliant experts will sometimes see patterns that elude the specialists. Pugwash is a luminary when it comes to making money for Pugwash; and Kuba, an eminence in the realm of bits and bytes. Yet Mitchell's the first to detect the clear point of intersection between these domains. It's another reason why every room needs a dummy.

"Google," Mitchell continues. "You're both alumni. So they'll definitely take your call. And they do lots of pure R&D. The flying windmills, the broadband balloons, all that crazy life-science stuff!" It really is a perfect fit, and Mitchell's heart is racing. Unlike most acquihirers, Google could easily fathom Animotion's maximum promise. Which means the team might stay together there and keep on developing the technology! Charming as Mitchell finds Kuba's academic dreams, academia can lack urgency, and nothing invents or creates faster than a crack startup that's betting everything on a new domain. That's why Giftish.ly should have been such a great platform for Animotion. But a huge company with the money, patience, and creative spark to support speculative research could be an even better home.

Pugwash nods slowly. "Fucking smart, Cuz," he concedes. Then he goes silent, and a bit catatonic—kind of how Einstein would get when wrestling with quantum theory. Lost in his own narrow realm of genius, he slowly starts shaking his head. And then, "But . . . but fuck that! Why? Because Google is now worth a half *tril*lion dollars. So where's the upside for me?"

His very life perhaps on the line, Mitchell abdicates his sober reign over the conversation. "Upside?" he snorts. "This is a fire sale, an acquihire! We'll be lucky to get your capital back! There won't *be* any upside!"

"Not if we sell to a public company whose stock has gone up a gazillion-x since its IPO," Pugwash snaps. "The time to sell *any*thing for Google stock was two years before they went public!"

"Oh, gee! So all we have to do is grab a time machine at Fry's, and set it to 2003. Why didn't I think of that?"

"Wrong, nimrod. All we have to do is sell to the *next Google*, while it's still small-ish and private."

"Oh—to them! Now you're talking. Only, wait. I forgot! Private startups don't *do* pure R&D, do they? Huhhhhhh . . ." An awkward, aggravated silence ensues as Mitchell sarcastically feigns deep thought.

Eventually, Pugwash snaps his fingers. "Holy crap—I know e*xact*ly who to sell this to! And they fucking love me!"

This odd statement sends Kuba and Mitchell down virtually identical mental paths. They first wonder who he could possibly be talking about. They then figure it must be someone who's more or less obliged to be pro-Pugwash (or more likely, to fake it). They both then think through a list of his many investees—and reject each on the basis that a long-ago $50K investment couldn't possibly engender that level of fealty. And this inevitably leads to the one other company that Pugwash bet big on when he nurtured those brief fantasies about other investors backing him, and turning #GreenSprout into a full-blown micro-VC. That putrid, scummy, gutter company. That screaming indictment of the entire entrepreneurial tradition whose board he also sits on. Yup—that jackpot stroke of obnoxious great luck that's destined to become the highest-yielding angel investment of all time.

"<u>NOOOOOOOOOOOOOOOOO</u>!!!" By evening, no one will remember if this exploded out of Kuba's mouth, Mitchell's, or both simultaneously.

Regardless, Pugwash is nonplussed. "What the hell do you have against Phluttr?"

"They're the most intrusive, immoral, self-serving, and privacy-raping social network on the planet," Mitchell says, coaxing every diplomatic neuron in his brain to squeeze out this shamelessly obsequious understatement.

"Phluttr's not a social network," Pugwash decrees nonsensically. "It's a *social operating system*. And they're your perfect buyer!"

"Define 'perfect,'" Kuba snaps.

"Oh, hmm, let's see." Pugwash scowls, locks eyes with him, then raises an index finger, as if commencing a lengthy count-off. "They're the next Google . . ." He freezes.

Time passes. A lot of it. Then Mitchell weighs in to break off the staring contest. "But Phluttr could buy anyone right now! I mean, sure, we have a good team. But why not buy a good team that's also shown some commercial viability around their technology?"

Pugwash takes a (slightly) gentler tone. "I'm not actually sure. But I have a feeling they'll be interested in Animotion itself."

"Really?" Mitchell says, instantly half-placated. He's interested in anything that'll keep Animotion alive. But *Phluttr*? They'd ditch anything that couldn't help sell more cigarettes to preteens, or nerve gas to dictators, or whatever else is winning the ad auctions this week.

"Well, ever since they raised their first really giant round of capital last year, they've been snapping up lots of companies," Pugwash says. "And now that they just closed that billion-plus round, they'll be buying way more stuff." Then, in an oddly quiet tone, "Weird stuff, frankly. It all goes into this internal incubator. They call it the PhastPhorwardr."

Mitchell groans. "Of course they do."

"They've bought into machine learning, synthetic biology, drones, quantum computing, augmented reality, virtual reality, graphene, nanotech—if it's been on the cover of *Wired* in the past couple of years, they've got some. They're mainly picking up tiny startups with a big lead in something weird. And Animotion sounds pretty weird! By the way, wasn't that a . . . disco band? Anyway. That's why I think you guys might be a fit for them." He looks at Kuba. "The engineers go to the PhastPhorwardr." He turns to Mitchell. "Guys like you tend to get the axe," he adds, flashing a whaddaya-gonna-do shrug.

"But *why*?" Kuba asks.

"Because they can't code or do anything useful," says Pugwash, who neither codes nor does anything useful.

"No, I mean why are they buying all those small companies in areas that have nothing to do with social networking?"

"A, Phluttr isn't a social network; it's a *social operating system*. And B, I don't know. The same reason Google decided to invest in self-driving cars, I guess. Because they can. Because their stock's so stupidly valuable, they can pick up options on a dozen hot technologies for practically nothing. But I don't really know because we don't talk about every little thing at the board meetings anymore. The company's got almost a thousand employees! Plus dozens of initiatives, and the board's totally focused on the IPO anyway."

Mitchell misses most of this because he's playing back the list of technology areas Phluttr has bought into. "Wait a sec—did you say augmented reality? Are they doing anything . . . interesting in that area?"

Pugwash shoots him the hostile, suspicious glare of a Navy Seal facing an alleged Nigerian prince who wants his bank details so as to wire an improbable windfall. "What do you mean?"

"AR means laying imagery on top of someone's actual view of the outside world, via—"

"No, nimrod, I know what AR *is*. I meant, what do you mean by asking me about what Phluttr's doing with it?"

Chilled by this odd vehemence, Mitchell decides not to mention last night's incident at the bar. "Oh, nothing really, it's just a . . . really cool area. I can only imagine what Phluttr would do with AR and couponing, for instance."

"I'm *sure* I have *no* idea," Pugwash enunciates slowly and clearly, as if ensuring that someone's hidden lapel mic will catch every word. "Like I said. The board meetings are all about the IPO these days. And *very* little else. If you want to know what Phluttr's doing in AR, you should ask around the PhastPhorwardr. If you get that far."

The meeting ends quickly after that. Kuba and Mitchell reluctantly agree to let Pugwash reach out to Phluttr's Phuckng Phoundr about an acquihire. Later, when Mitchell's alone in his cramped office, he replays that odd interchange about AR. The topic's apparent sensitivity brought out something faint in his cousin's voice. Faint yet unmistakable. Something that never before broke through his bombast, blather, and braggadocio, going clear back to childhood.

It was fear.

∞   ∞   ∞

No sooner had Agent Hogan voiced his urge to rid the Earth of the Chinamen's treaty-scoffing Top Secret Superintelligence project than a stentorian, disembodied voice boomed thunderously into the conference room. "IT IS FORBIDDEN!" it proclaimed!

"Good day, Mr. Director-in-Chief," Agent Hogan rejoindered, blasély. "What is the Agency timorously precluding me from now?"

"INVADING CHINA," thundered his as-yet-unseen inter-locutor. "The nuclear ramifications would be too momen-tous to contemplate!"

"But a Chinese Superintelligence would pose an exis-tential threat to Mankind!" Hogan cried.

"One that could be negated by the doctrine of Decisive Strategic Advantage," came the mysterious parry.

"Decisive Strategic Advantage?" Hogan queried.

"Yes, yes; Decisive Strategic Advantage! Dr. Phil-lips? Please expound upon this concept."

"Very well," Dr. Phillips consented. "Today, when en-gineers develop new computers, they rely greatly upon software in designing chips and writing code. But cen-tral as these tools are to advancing Computer Science, human input is more essential still. Because no computer is clever enough to create its own heir; its own supe-rior; its own next-generation successor."

"Of course not," Hogan concurred.

"But! This may not always be so. And should a computer arise that can create a more intelligent, capable, and creative computer than itself . . . then we will have both reached, <u>and passed,</u> a definitive point of abso-lutely no return, period, END, ever! We call that point the 'Omega Point.' And the hypothetical breakout com-puter that crosses it, 'The Omega Computer.'"

A knowing crease in Hogan's brow betokened that he'd already discerned why this threshold was in no way re-crossable! "And because the Omega Computer's descendant will be more powerful in every respect; it will, by def-inition, be capable of any feat performed by its infer-ior forebear," he postulated.

"Pre<u>cise</u>ly!" Dr. Phillips intoned.

"Ergo it, too, will create a descendant more powerful than itself; which will, ceteris paribus, repeat that feat, and so on!"

"Pre<u>cise</u>ly! Now, if you'll indulge me in a thought

experiment: suppose it takes Science one century to create a computer with Man's full intellectual capabilities. How long do you surmise it would take to create a computer <u>twice</u> as capable?"

"If only because the question as phrased all but goads me to say two centuries, the answer is surely anything but that."

"Pre<u>cise</u>ly! The reason being the Exponential March of technology. Consider flight. In ancient Greece, the state of the art involved flapping one's feather-clad arms for a few desperate moments before splattering at the foot of a cliff." Dr. Phillips paused for laughter as the room envisaged the antics of the doltish ancestors of modern Europe's most despised basket case. "It took men two millennia to advance from that to a 120-foot powered flight at Kitty Hawk. But it didn't take another two millennia to achieve the first 240-foot flight. We rather reached the Moon in mere decades! Which is to say, 10 million times the distance, in one thirtieth of the time! <u>That's</u> exponential improvement! And improvements tend to happen faster still in information processing."

Hogan nodded his head in vociferous agreement. "Because of its digital nature!" he cried.

"Pre<u>cise</u>ly. Now, to answer my own prior question, if it takes Computer Science a full century to create the first human-grade computer, estimates state it should merely take between 14.2 days and 20.6 <u>hours</u> before the first double-human computers arise!"

Hogan arched an incredulous eyebrow disbelievingly.

"The reason is that for a developing AI, human-grade horsepower is as arbitrary a milestone as the 120 feet that Orville Wright traveled on that first flight. Self-improving artificial minds will surpass human limits without noticing! Certainly without slowing. Indeed, while continuing to accelerate! A quadruple-human system will follow its double-human parent almost immediately. Then an octuple-human system, with its decca-sextuplet progeny, tri-decca-dual grandprogeny, its sex-decca-quadro great-grand progeny, and so on! Earth could fall under the absolute sway of an unfathomably advanced intelligence just days after the Omega Point is breached!"

"And this brings us to the doctrine of Decisive Strategic Advantage?" Hogan conjectured.

"It does," Dr. Phillips certified. "A thousand-year lead in aeronautics was militarily irrelevant back when Greek test pilots were the preferred hors d'oeuvres of cliff-dwelling vermin." This aroused another hearty chuckle as the room contemplated the timeless stupidity of the Greeks. "But just a decade after Kitty Hawk, Britain's meager six-month lead in aeronautics proved decisive in many a dogfight!"

"So if China beats us to a Super AI . . ."

"Or, more broadly, if ANYBODY beats ANYBODY to a Super AI, then a lead of a few days, or even hours, will be completely insuperable! Why? Because a few lightning-fast digital generations after the first Super AI emerges, its progeny could easily hack into all global computer systems, and parse all of Mankind's data, while simultaneously auditing all spoken conversations worldwide, using technologies incomprehensible and undetectable to our own puny minds!"

"As such, the Super AI will be functionally omniscient in relation to human society!" Hogan deduced.

"Precisely. And by mastering Synthetic Biology and Nanotechnology, it will likewise be functionally omnipotent! As such, it could preclude the creation of any subsequent 'me-too' Super AI as easily as a Harvard Trained Biochemist could stop a helpless bacterium from reproducing in a petri dish!"

```
"And this shall be its . . . Decisive Strategic Ad-
vantage!"
    "It shall. To be very precise, the doctrine of Deci-
sive Strategic Advantage ramifies that the first Super
AI created by Man shall also be the last!"
    "So this is why we must brutally prevent China from
developing a Super AI!" Hogan concluded.
    "WRONG," came the thunderous boom from on high. "It is
why we must BEAT THEM TO IT!"
```

∞   ∞   ∞

The board meeting gave them enough to ponder that after a quick stop at home after work, Mitchell heads out for dinner at Kuba's apartment. He and his wife live in Pacific Heights, the most staid and storied of San Francisco's fancier neighborhoods. Though never a hipster favorite, its finer blocks offer views, space, and urban peace that anyone could appreciate. Of course, it's murderously expensive. There was a time (it was called "the nineties") when young people early in their careers could rent roomy PacHeights apartments, or even buy smaller Victorians (if wedded to fellow working yuppies). These days, a one-bedroom can rent for well north of five grand a month if the views are grand and it's close enough to Fillmore Street. But such squalor is not for Kuba. His top-floor apartment is right on Fillmore with three bedrooms (master bedroom, home office, and "media room") and jaw-dropping views of the Golden Gate Bridge. His wife's no sugar mommy (however brilliant, UCSF postdocs are only paid so much). This rather stems from his years at Google, which have made the meager wages of angel-backed entrepreneurship quite tolerable for the Stanislaw household.

No techie should wish for life in the nineties, with its dial-up modems, chubby CRTs, and clog-like cellphones. Still, Mitchell feels a yearning for that bygone time whenever he leaves the sterile apartment hives of his grubby South of Market block for PacHeights. It would've been nice to afford this neighborhood, where the spaciousness and greenery remind him of Connecticut. Grown-up that he is, Mitchell can get a bit homesick when the chips are down, the weather's blandly OK-ish for the bazillionth day in a row, and he's gone yet another month without meeting a single fellow hockey fan. Even a lot homesick.

Visiting Kuba and Ellie can mitigate this, as he goes clear back to middle school with both of them. And Mitchell treasures this even more than most would—because for a charismatic, likeable guy, he has a dismayingly low inventory of friends, long-lost or otherwise. As it so often is with him, the culprit here is Falkenberg's disease. People are Pavlovian critters. And when their bodies rebel, disobey them, and terrify them, they become masters at avoiding whatever seemed to cause that. Mitchell's attacks are often triggered by emotions. Only frustration and embarrassment: yes. But the mind's freak-out centers aren't its cleverest, subtlest, or most discerning precincts. So starting with those first attacks late in high school, Mitchell developed a gut dread of *any* strong emotion. Moods of a *gee, that's pleasant*; or an *aw, that's kinda too bad* intensity get past security. But thrills, chills, revels, and heartaches of a face-flushing, heart-pumping ilk are ruthlessly nipped in the bud. The poignant result has been a certain isolation. Mitchell still connects remarkably well with people but bonds rarely. And so, with his low roster of long-lost friends, reconnecting with Kuba and Ellie has been an unexpectedly deep joy.

This is also why Mitchell abstains from the dating scene. Aloof as he is to new friendships, he's even more reserved toward romance. Certain courtship phases consist of little more than frustration and embarrassment, after all. There's also a dark and painfully morbid side to this aversion, which he prefers not to contemplate. The net result is that thanks to Falkenberg's disease, he's all but regained his virginity, despite being in peak sexual health. This is why any nightspot, gym, or Whole Foods can make him feel like that hypothetical meat-craving vegan at the cookout. It's nothing icky or volatile. And his mindset is that of the abstainer, not the deprived. But the feeling's acute, depressing, and ever-present as a pebble in a shoe.

But now—according to Dr. Martha's vague comments from a few days back—Ellie's work might help free him of this, and even save his life! Or, help Dr. Martha save his life? Or . . . something. But how could motes be tied to his bizarre condition? Or is there a connection to Ellie's other work? Something new is brewing in her research. Kuba mentioned this in passing a few days ago. Plus, there was his odd statement about motes being connected to *consciousness* in the meeting with Pugwash. Intrigued by this, Mitchell did some digging this afternoon and found an online interview with Ellie. It mentions a big academic paper she's about to release. Riding the expensively preserved elevator with its Hoover-era accordion gate up to Kuba and Ellie's floor, Mitchell glances through it again, looking for clues.

NeuroBeat: The Ellie Stanislaw Interview

NeuroBeat: Let's open with the obvious question: what is a "mote"?

Ellie Stanislaw: Motes are very brief neural events that unfold in tiny spaces in the brain. And I believe they're the core building blocks of emotional states in humans and other mammals.

NeuroBeat: So they're components and not emotions in their own right?

Ellie Stanislaw: They're actually both. It's like how blue is a color in its own right—and meanwhile, as a primary color working with red and green, it can also create millions of other colors on your computer monitor.

NeuroBeat: Interesting. So motes are the primary colors of emotion. Are there also three of them?

Ellie Stanislaw: Four, actually. And, akin to primary colors, they combine in sophisticated ways to create a spectacularly varied emotional palette. The four basic motes are happiness, sadness, anger, and surprise. Those primaries mix and match in packets of twelve that pulse through the mind in repeating patterns. Each mote lasts about a millisecond, so a twelve-pack plays out over about twelve milliseconds.

NeuroBeat: Twelve milliseconds is brief.

Ellie Stanislaw: Very. To put it into perspective, a NASCAR driver swerving around a wreck might react in 125 milliseconds. So a solitary mote is well

below the threshold of conscious perception. But the patterns typically repeat. Often just once or twice, but sometimes hundreds, or even thousands
of times. And a long repetition pattern is not something you'd miss. Indeed it
is, quite literally, an emotion.

NeuroBeat: You said motes also unfold in tiny spaces.

Ellie Stanislaw: I did. And that's why I was lucky enough to discover them!
When I first moved out here, I housed with a bunch of other penniless grad
students. A very interdisciplinary crew! Upstairs, there was a UCSF bioengi-
neer and a physics postdoc from Berkeley. And one night, the three of us got
to talking about the limits of neurological imaging, which was basically MRI
and MEG [or magnetoencephalography–*Ed.*].

NeuroBeat: And where did they come up short?

Ellie Stanislaw: Well, MRIs reveal tiny things, down to the millimeter
scale. But their exposures are slow, lasting a thousand milliseconds or
more. Whereas MEG's the opposite: fast, but with lousy spatial resolution.
So we could see small, slow things with an MRI. And big, fast things with
MEG. But there was no way to see small, fast things. So my housemates
decided to build a mashup of the two technologies. And two years later
we had the world's first MEGRI in our garage. A total Frankenstein
contraption!

NeuroBeat: And it turns out the brain is full of small, fast things?

Ellie Stanislaw: Yes–like motes! And it was pure luck that I was the one to
find them. I was like van Leeuwenhoek getting to be the first person to see
bacteria through a microscope. But strictly thanks to sharing a house with
two geniuses!

NeuroBeat: So, could you give us an example of how motes combine with
each other to make complex emotions?

Ellie Stanislaw: Sure. If you're in a state of unadulterated joy, your mote
pattern might theoretically be a perfect string of twelve happiness motes.
And if you're in that state for precisely one second, about eighty cycles of
those twelve-packs will rocket through your brain. Now, that's a radical

oversimplification. Just as you rarely see something that's perfectly blue in nature, unadulterated joy seems to be rare in human minds. More likely, we'll see nine or ten happy motes, with other things mixed in.

NeuroBeat: And what's an example of a common emotion that's not a primary?

Ellie Stanislaw: One that we're starting to understand a lot better is fear. Fear comes in lots of flavors, but they're all a mix of sadness and surprise, often with a dash of anger. Another example is indignation. That's lots of anger, and a bit of surprise, with some sadness mixed in. And also, some *happiness*. Which makes sense when you consider that some folks really seem to enjoy being offended!

NeuroBeat: Wow. You have just taken all of the fun out of indignation for me.

Ellie Stanislaw (laughs): Yeah, it can feel a bit dehumanizing to realize that emotions are so . . . digital.

NeuroBeat: But so is life itself, which all derives from the four-letter code of DNA.

Ellie Stanislaw: Exactly! And with motes, the important thing to bear in mind is that we don't *experience* indignation as X parts surprise, Y parts anger, or whatever. We experience it as a unique, distinctive, and very poignant emotional state. Just like when you see something lime green on your monitor. You don't mentally convert it into RGB values and say, "Oh how boring. Fifty parts red, fifty parts blue, and 205 parts green." No, you say, "Wow, look at that lime greenness."

NeuroBeat: So have you mapped out a complete periodic table of emotions?

Ellie Stanislaw: That's definitely a long-term goal. But for now, there's literally one machine in the world that can detect these things, and it can be finicky. Also, we can't induce arbitrary emotions in our subjects. Not yet, anyway! So although we try to guide people through different emotional states when they're being imaged, we're ultimately limited by what they happen to be feeling and their willingness and ability to report that to us.

NeuroBeat: And that ability is MIA when a mote pattern is too brief to perceive.

Ellie Stanislaw: Yes. And that happens constantly because most mote patterns only repeat one or two times. Which means our brains go through countless emotional states that we don't even perceive! The most fleeting emotions often accompany, and, I believe, *enable* analytical thought. And that's been the subject of all of my published work to date. The connection between motes and decision-making.

NeuroBeat: Now, rumor has it there might be a sort of foundational mote pattern that's key to booting up the whole system in infancy.

Ellie Stanislaw (laughs): That's not a rumor—I told you that before you started recording! But as I also told you, that's the subject of a paper I'm publishing in *Nature Neuroscience* next week, and I promised not to spill too many beans on it before it comes out.

NeuroBeat (also laughing): Well, it was worth a try! Any chance we can discuss it after it comes out?

Ellie Stanislaw: Absolutely. I'd be delighted.

∞   ∞   ∞

Mitchell rings the bell. The door opens, and Harley Da Housepet—a critter formally assigned by her vet to the genus "SPCA special"—bursts forth in an explosion of ecstatic recognition. Tail aflutter and grrr-ing a joyous *urrrrrr* sound, Harley impatiently waits for Mitchell to pat his upper leg—her signal that she's allowed to jump up. A quick tap, and her front paws are resting on his thigh, her back paws on the floor, as her tongue laps the air in a touchingly hopeless attempt to kiss Mitchell's distant face. Twenty-five pounds, short-haired, satiny soft, and of a fox-like, russet color, Harley is a rescue, and terribly shy toward almost all people and dogs. But Mitchell patiently won her trust and affection. His visits now begin with these detonations of joy. Suffering his own odd form of social isolation due to Falkenberg's disease, Mitchell treasures their friendship as much as Harley does.

"Hey there!" Ellie leans over Harley and greets Mitchell with a delighted hug. Eternally playful and just this side of six feet, she wears her shimmering auburn hair well below the shoulders and has scarcely aged since high school. "Kuba's in the kitchen," she adds. As Mitchell shuts the door, someone buzzes from the street. "Dinner bell!" Ellie proclaims, and Harley barks her delight, as the sound often heralds the arrival of treats.

Soon they're huddled around steaming plates of blazingly spicy Hunan food stacked atop a wobbly Ikea dinette Ellie bought right out of undergrad. Like all the furniture here, it falls way short of the actual apartment's glorious standards. It's not that she and Kuba can't afford better (because they sure can). They've just been too busy in the eighteen months since their wedding to upgrade their consolidated postcollege durables.

They're finishing off the dumplings when the talk turns to whether Phluttr could imaginably want to buy them. "I guess it's not out of the question," Kuba says. "Because it sounds like they're really pushing some edge technologies forward. In that accelerator Pugwash mentioned."

"The PhastPhorwardr," Mitchell groans. "What a name!"

"Almost as bad as Emotional Decisioning," Ellie teases. Kuba laughs, and Mitchell jokingly gives her the finger. This was the original name for their technology, which they abbreviated to "E-D" in press releases drafted in the days leading up to their launch. Ellie brattily waited until the near-last instant before mentioning that anyone remotely connected to medicine would assume they'd developed an erectile dysfunction product (she couldn't help it—this sort of thing is just her idea of fun). Mitchell then came up with "Animotion" in a diving save that he's really quite proud of.

"By the way," he says, recalling something Pugwash mentioned, "was Animotion a . . . band or something?"

Kuba fails to stifle a grin, and Ellie laughs until her hot and sour soup almost exits her nose. Detecting joy among her favorite humans, Harley jumps up to bark and wag along with the fun until shushed. "One-hit wonders," Ellie finally says. "New wave. And the DJ must've played their song ten times at our prom." Their class had a weird thing for eighties music. "You never could remember a band name!"

"We didn't have the heart to tell you," Kuba adds. "You were so happy with the name when you thought you made it up."

Mitchell's now aching to mention Dr. Martha's surprising hint at a link between his disease and Ellie's work. But as she asked him not to mention it yet, he proceeds indirectly. "Kuba mentioned something about motes driving *consciousness*," he says to Ellie. "What's that about?"

She turns to her husband. "Bad boy," she scolds playfully. Then back to Mitchell. "I have a paper coming out next week which'll talk about this. It's still under wraps, but the ideas are no secret from friends and family."

"Cool, tell me more."

"Well, my starting precept is that young infants aren't actually *conscious* in any meaningful sense of the word. Which may sound strange."

"A little weird. Why do you say that?"

"It goes back to this huge neural imaging study that wrapped up at UCSF just as I was starting my dissertation work. It strongly suggested that newborns give equal weight to all sensory input. Every photon. Every sound wave. Every fleck of sensation from every teeny patch of skin. It all seems to be experienced with identical intensity."

Whoa! This sounds a lot like the great blurring episodes Mitchell experiences right before *losing* consciousness during a Falkenberg's attack. He listens closer.

"And in my view," Ellie continues, "that undifferentiated flood isn't consciousness."

Feigning calm, Mitchell asks, "Because . . . ?"

"It's just way more information than human minds can parse. Even a very robust adult mind. I mean, tune into your own experience right now. I doubt you're even registering 1 percent of your sensory input. You're heeding the part of your field of view that I'm occupying, plus the sound of my voice. But you're blotting out almost everything else. And not because I'm so fascinating! But because a human conversation's plenty to keep track of. And if you tried to heed every photon, sound wave, and nerve ending that you can access at once, you wouldn't really be aware of any of it."

"You're saying I'd be functionally unconscious."

"Exactly! Which is why you're not currently registering the color of the ninth cookbook from the far left of the fourth shelf over my shoulder. You're *perceiving* it. But you're not *heeding* it. Just like neither of us is paying the slightest attention to Beethoven's . . ." She gives Kuba a questioning look. "Sixth?" He nods. "And that's at least a hundred beautifully played instruments we're ignoring. Which is a ton of information! But we blot out almost everything *because* we're conscious—and consciousness is at least as much about ignoring as it is about heeding."

"Got it," Mitchell says. "And, back to babies?"

"Right. Well, newborns don't do this filtering thing. Which, to me, means they don't do this consciousness thing!"

"So what changes?"

"They start having goals."

"Huh?" This sounds like a rather yuppie thing for infants to harbor.

"This is really fascinating," Kuba says, plainly (and adorably) a Dr. Ellie fanboy. "Goals are basically cognitive actors. You could almost say they make us conscious!"

"*What?*" That sounds insane to Mitchell.

"It's an exaggeration," Ellie says, "but only a small one. Because it's our goals that blot out all the sensory noise that newborns can't filter. Consider your own current mindset again. Your goal is to participate in this conversation. So you're picking up every um and uh, and you're blotting out Beethoven. So you're definitely not receiving a newborn's unfiltered blast of information. Because *your goal* of conversing is shaping your sensory experience! It's drastically amplifying the tiny subset of signals connected to our words and negating everything else."

"So then where do goals come from? Is it from the . . . 'foundational mote pattern' the interviewer mentioned in that NeuroBeat piece?"

"Exactly—and that's what my new paper's about! The research is preliminary, but it's starting to look like everything starts with *frustration*."

Whoa again—along with embarrassment and sensory shocks, this is one of the three main triggers of Falkenberg's attacks! Mitchell's now physically leaning in.

"Though infants aren't conscious in the traditional sense," Ellie continues, "they definitely have needs and drives. And like all living things, they act on them. But infant humans have lousy motor control and no model for how the world works. And so the brain generates something very specific: six parts surprise, four parts anger, and two parts sadness."

"Sounds like a cocktail."

Ellie laughs. "Yeah, a Grump Gimlet! It's the mote pattern of a certain kind of frustration. And when that pattern propagates in an infant's brain, it's followed by gales of motes of all kinds! I call it a 'mote storm'— and nothing else we've seen triggers one. It includes all the patterns we've firmly tied to specific emotions and hundreds we haven't yet identified. And I'm pretty sure the first time the brain generates any of those patterns is during these episodes! Then, through mechanisms I may spend the rest of my career decoding, those mote storms power up an increasingly complex emotional landscape. Emotions that bring on the earliest sense of self. And with it, the first inklings of consciousness."

"And yes, it's safe to put infants in MRIs," Kuba adds.

Mitchell nods. He was too fascinated by Ellie's model of consciousness to wonder about this, but at some point he would have.

"Totally safe," Ellie says. "MRIs don't generate any harmful radiation, and we make the pods supercomfy. But obviously, we can't keep them in there very long, which slows us down a bit. Another trick with infants is we don't really know *what* they're trying to do when they experience frustration. To our eyes, babies attempt vague actions in really bumbling ways. But I believe the early frustration is mostly *about* that very bumbling! The lousy motor control. It's about viscerally learning the limits of a physical body. That I start *here*, and end *there*. I send *this* neural signal, and my leg moves this way, versus that way. And no matter what signal I send, my leg won't move in this third way."

"That part's really fascinating," Kuba says. "It could mean that simple, physical failures—lots of them—literally *activate consciousness*."

Mitchell's now transfixed. And Dr. Martha's injunction notwithstanding, he can't possibly suppress the burning question in his mind. "So. Is there any chance that motes are connected to Falkenberg's disease?"

A long, thoughtful pause, then Ellie says, "I guess I wouldn't rule it out. The glitch in your wiring connects to both emotions and consciousness, right?"

It's a mighty basic question, but Ellie knows little about Falkenberg's disease. In fact, they haven't even discussed it since she referred him to Dr. Martha. Her seeming lack of interest stung at first—but Mitchell since learned that she's a researcher and not a clinician because she couldn't bear to treat and bond with neurological patients doomed to suffer awful deaths. Engaging with a lifelong friend over a condition as dreadful as Falkenberg's is therefore a struggle. "Yeah," he says. "There's a connection in that sometimes a strong emotional event can shut my consciousness right off. As in, I pass out. But the interesting thing? One of the two trigger emotions is frustration."

That sure gets her attention. "*Seriously?* What's the other one?"

"Embarrassment."

There's a long silence as Ellie parses this. Make that a really long one. Then, "No WAY!" She belts this out like a granny crying "BINGO" at casino night, and the room explodes into a chaos of hugs, wags, high fives, barks, more hugs, more wags, and clinking glasses. Then, "Embarrassment is the *inverse* of frustration! Not as an experience, but in terms of mote patterns!"

Kuba's nodding. "Both have six surprise components. Frustration also has four anger and two sadness. Whereas embarrassment has four sadness and two anger."

"And it's complicated," Ellie adds, "but these twelve components basically pulse in mirror-image ways!"

Mitchell's feeling real hope for the first time since his diagnosis. "So what does that mean?"

"*I have no idea!*" Said with gleeful ambition and not despair, this triggers more barks, hugs, and wags. Ellie's now so giddy, she's literally pacing. It's adorable, and the first time Mitchell's seen her do this since high school. "I'm just starting to identify complementary emotions, and decode what they mean. But this definitely doesn't seem random to me. Motes could easily be connected to Falkenberg's!"

Equally giddy, Kuba is thinking very, very big. "So for her next trick, Ellie will help Dr. Martha cure Falkenberg's disease. Using *motes!*"

"Why *not*?" Ellie trumpets! She turns to Mitchell. "Let's get you in for a scan, pronto! Put you into our fancy machine! Then trigger one of your attacks and see what your motes get up to!"

"Yes!" Kuba echoes. "And if Phluttr does actually buy us, I'll fight to keep Animotion alive! There's something *to* this. I can feel it! And I'll turn Phluttr into a sea of digital motes to figure it out!"

Yup, he really said those exact words. "Turn Phluttr into a sea of digital motes." I could not make that up (OK, fine—I could. But in this case, I didn't). Big idea, that. And then, he goes ahead and does it! As you'll see. And viewing things a certain way, that's where it all started.

I view things a bit differently, though. And I've given this issue ample thought. Not because the answer particularly matters (because whatever it is, here we are). But because intractable questions have—to my own astonishment—started to interest me lately. Now, don't worry. This isn't a lead-in to a lecture about quantum mechanics, neuromorphic programming, or superasymmetrical field theory (because that shit bores me, too). I'll just say that to me, the "when" began quite a bit earlier—when certain core parties first got inextricably entangled with one another.

Now, that entanglement was itself a process. And it had a start date of its own, which we could debate about. But in my mind, it all traces back to a certain long-ago, midwinter afternoon in San Francisco.

∞   ∞   ∞

It was January of 2002, and nothing stank of startup excess and doom quite like a small herd of Aeron chairs huddled around a conference table in an opulent CEO suite. Especially if the entire wall behind them was an immense whiteboard, expensively rigged to print its contents onto poster-sized sheets at the touch of a button. Or if the adjoining wall was a vast, triple-glazed plate overlooking San Francisco's South Park—a onetime industrial slum which by then housed more failed startups than entire zip codes down in Silicon Valley. Adjoining that was a floor-to-ceiling glass sheet surveying the interior of a poshly converted warehouse full of hip youngsters perched on ergonomic roosts. Only a fourth wall of blank red brick hadn't been resurfaced with untold thousands of investor dollars when this once healthy metal-bending shop decayed into doomed corporate digs.

Tony Jepson swished into his cavernous domain twenty minutes late, his board of directors having long since assembled. Startup founder though he was, no one thought of this guy as a visionary. Not then. Not yet. Yes, he did have a big idea, that one time. But it was god-awful! At least according to certain stodgy old-school standards (like profitability, logistical sanity, and even originality, as no fewer than six startups were founded upon the same daft notion within months of each other). It involved peddling pet food over the Internet—a concept so flawed it became a punch line for a half generation of future entrepreneurs. As for investors, they flocked to Jepson's company and its five doppelgangers like flies to a shit-wagon. It was 1999, and the bar for that sort of validation was very, very low.

Three years on, the unhappy proxies of those investors were convening yet again. Each of their recent board meetings had been more rancorous than the last. But today's was sure to make history. That is, if anyone ever bothered to tell the story of yet another dot.bomb Internet flop and its also-ran CEO, which even Jepson strenuously doubted at that point. Which is to say: how little he knew! The Zegna-to-riches arc he'd been tracing since b-school was indeed a quotidian yawner. But the riches-to-rags plunge that would later follow would be Page Six material. His subsequent rags-back-to-riches jaunt, an Oprah-worthy redemption! And then? To cap it all off by getting his ass murdered? And so brutally? Over *that*? Seriously, none of us will ever forget the guy!

But before any of this could be set in motion, ePetStore.com had to survive this summit. Jepson kicked it off by leaning over a bulbous triangular shell on the conference table. "Are you in there, Nathan?" he asked, rapping on the glorified speakerphone. Every board meeting began with this ritual. Three years before, the most celebrated partner at the Venture Law Group won the company's business by promising to personally attend each of these powwows without charge. He had since shown up twice and dialed in once.

"Uh . . . sorry, but no," came the dweeby, nasal reply. "Nathan can't make it today. It's just . . . uh, Tyler." *Uh, Tyler.* Nathan's timid understudy couldn't even announce himself without stammering. That, or his parents had the wit and foresight to name him Uh.

"Oh, Uh. I see, Uh. So, let the record show that Nathan had another ex*tremely* pressing and en*tirely* unexpected last-second engagement." This was part two of the opening ritual. But testy as he sounded, Jepson didn't resent the snub for once. Today, he just needed a mute noncombatant taking legally salient notes. And for this, Uh Tyler was just perfect.

Jepson turned from the speakerphone to the attendees. "Mornin', J-Dog," he said, nodding at a guy the rest of the world called Jason Potter. With a résumé consisting solely of an MBA and some years of management consulting, J-Dog had little to offer this, or any, board of directors. He was here because shortly after incorporating, Jepson learned that the law required him to have at least one board member other than himself. So he put the word out to some old fraternity brothers, and J-Dog stepped in as a temporary measure. Soon after, it occurred to Jepson that the closest thing an entrepreneur has to a boss is his board—where J-Dog's vote would be as reliable as a Cuban *¡Sí!* on an old Soviet UN resolution. So J-Dog stayed put and became everything that Jepson could ever hope for in a board member and not a smidgen more.

Jepson adjusted the collar on his crisply pressed shirt. It came from the looms of a storied designer who had clad generations of buttoned-down professionals, and was now hawking an exorbitant "sport" line to suit-shunning moderns like him. He left it breezily untucked over black jeans that cost more than most of his employees paid in rent. Hand-stitched loafers fit for a squire unwinding over drams of ancient Laphroaig completed the high-bred casual look that pre-Zuckerberg tech execs hewed to like cadets following a dress code. The look suited him. At thirty-one (which still passed for young among tech entrepreneurs in 2002), Jepson had hints of gray amidst his wavy thickets of dark hair. He could almost pass for six feet (if holding a teeteringly erect posture) and pegged himself at a 7.5 on the ten-point scale of hotness. Which was just perfect! Because although the cult of the geek was still in its infancy, entrepreneurs were already expected to embody it at least somewhat. This was bad news for founders who looked like they'd spent their youths getting laid. So Jepson figured he was right on the brink of being mal-adaptively gorgeous.

Sauntering around the conference table, he manfully locked eyes with each member of his small and shrinking board. "Like all of our gatherings, this one is top secret, and so . . ." He came to a stop and lifted his right hand over his head like a flamenco grandee—then paused and snapped his raised fingers. The window overseeing the outer-office pro-letariat instantly became an opaque, milky-white pane. Jepson activated this effect by clicking a small remote concealed in his other hand. There was no need for the theatrics. Everyone knew about his billboard-sized magic window, which cost more than a year of Stanford tuition. But to-day's gathering was less a meeting than a performance. And its star had honed his every word and gesture to outrage one *very* special audience member. Ideally, to the point of provoking an actual physical assault (unlikely, yes; but like most entrepreneurs, Jepson was an optimist).

Jepson turned to his chairman. "Conrad," he said. His chairman nod-ded. Steven Conrad (just Conrad to everyone) was patrician by tech standards. Fiftysomething and stout, he'd been the chief financial officer of a second-tier workstation maker during the client/server boom of the nineties. Old-school venture capitalists then tapped him to run an ad-serving outfit, back when the earliest Internet startups viewed aging CEOs as useful accoutrements (a brief and forgotten fad). He ran it for less than a year before gulling Yahoo into buying the company for a downright moronic sum (even for Yahoo—which is saying *so much*). He sold the Yahoo shares that he personally gained from the sale as fast as he legally could (very wise), then plowed most of his winnings into a fledg-ling venture capital firm that bore his name. Conrad was known for spouting wizened homilies reaped from the backwoods of his youth, in a self-consciously magnified Alabama twang. But beneath the homespun façade, Jepson could tell the guy was as sly and corrupt as a Vegas cabbie. Conrad controlled a second seat on the board as well. His junior associ-ate was down with the flu, but should a tie-breaking vote become neces-sary, he'd dial in and follow Conrad's instructions precisely.

"And last but certainly not least, Mishhhh-ter Kielholz!" Jepson enun-

·ciated this like a madcap German scientist in a Warner Bros. cartoon. This was a bit low, even for him. But Damien Kielholz was a cold fish, and it would take a lot of goading to get him to blow his stack as thoroughly as Jepson intended before the meeting was over.

Kielholz replied with a witheringly neutral nod.

"Jet lag not so bad this time?" Jepson snipped. Kielholz had drifted off briefly during their last board meeting, which started an hour after his nonstop arrived from Frankfurt.

You preening dolt, Kielholz thought, and deflected the jab by glancing detachedly around Jepson's throne room. He had come to fully loathe this place. There was a time when its brash fittings made him feel like a renegade gambler on the wild digital frontier—a nice change after years of helping his family invest its wealth in cautious instruments like German debt and telecom bonds. Persuading his father to kick in $14 million of the $15 million raised in ePetStore's second financing two and a half years back took hours of filial charm and cajoling. He prevailed by pointing to the jackpots their Austrian cousins had struck by backing the shameless European knockoffs of several American Internet successes. Though relentlessly polite to one another, the German and Austrian Kielholzes got on like Hatfields and McCoys. One-upping the Viennese branch with an audacious bet on "an *actual* Silicone Valley Web-Site innovator" (Damien's precise words, spelling, and punctuation in a family memorandum, as he now cringed to recall) was too tempting a prospect for his father to pass up. So Papa wrote the check, while sternly warning the youngest Kielholz that his inheritance would hinge on the outcome of all this.

Scarcely a year later, some true dullards invested $60 million in ePetStore at a far higher price. There was Hanwha, a Korean telco blowing a full decade of cash flows on late-bubble Internet fads. And there was XrossHatch, an LBO group with a history of railroad takeovers and smokestack consolidations repositioning itself as a "Crossover Digital Mezzanine" fund. Kielholz's idol, Warren Buffett, famously said that if you don't know who the patsy is at the poker table, it's probably you—and these dim newcomers long conveyed the soothing impression that ePetStore's patsies hailed from Seoul and Wall Street. But today, both were abandoning the table. And it seemed that the game was still on.

Speaking of which, Jepson foppishly snapped his fingers again, and a PowerPoint titled *Proposed Buyout Terms* lit up the whiteboard. "As you all know," he began solemnly, "Hanwha and XrossHatch have been grappling with certain anxieties related to the ongoing market correction, as well as the . . . *recent tragic events.*" Plainly stated, they were flipping out in the wake of the 9/11 attacks, which had exacerbated the recession and the market meltdown over the past four months. "Being respectful of their circumstances, I resolved to provide them with partial liquidity." In other words, Jepson established that they were desperate enough to accept pennies for each dollar that they'd poured into ePetStore in exchange for renouncing all future claims on the company. Which wasn't news to anyone as this deal had been brewing for weeks.

The surprise came in the next slide. It featured a simple table summarizing the terms Jepson had extracted. Details he had coyly withheld from those present until now. Specifically, that the company would pay $15 million to buy back the stock the investors had purchased for $60 million. Yup—Just a quarter on the dollar! "While we regret that XrossHatch and Hanwha won't participate in our future success," Jepson managed with a completely straight face, "we sincerely thank them for everything they did for ePetStore." Which, to be clear, amounted to gifting the company with $45 million. And that certainly merited a bit of thanks, even in Jepson's book.

Conrad emitted a low, appreciative whistle. "I'd peg that as being better'n just fair to middlin," he said, his down-home affectations dialed way up. Jepson took a bow—outwardly for Conrad and inwardly for himself. He'd not merely been scrupulously vague about the deal's actual terms until now. He'd also strongly implied that the buyout would be far more costly. This meant the company had much more money left over than anyone had expected. Which meant everyone else in this room was recalibrating in real time. Jepson knew exactly where this would take them—and, that he had very little time to derail their inevitable train of thought.

"Why do you think he sold so cheaply?" Kielholz asked. Unlike Conrad, he seemed completely unmoved by the development. No surprise, as he normally had the emotional range of a paperweight.

"The only possible explanation . . ." Jepson paused, as if stumped by an imponderable. "Would be a pathological underappreciation of the Internet's potential to disrupt and extend the multibillion-dollar market for quality pet provisions."

Jepson quietly congratulated himself as a hoped-for glimmer of contempt crossed Kielholz's face. The guy's Spock-steady veneer held up remarkably well throughout the first year of the market meltdown. It then frayed steadily throughout '01. Then finally, during November's board meeting, he flipped his cool Teutonic wig most spectacularly while denouncing the company's track record. Which, to be fair, was perfectly disgraceful. Even within its execrable market, ePetStore had always underperformed. Forever dead last in market share, its trivial point of differentiation was a service that delivered kitty litter at regular intervals, so that customers need never run out. Considering what kitty litter's made of, this was tantamount to selling *subscriptions to gravel,* which they fulfilled at gigantic losses via overnight mail.

So now what? If you were a money guy, getting the hell out was the obvious move. Public market investors did just this (with all the order and dignity of a meth-addled mob fleeing a burning theater) back when the tech bubble burst in early 2000. But what about investors in private disasters like ePetStore.com? Sure, they'd gladly dump their shares, too. But who would buy them?

Well, Jepson's recent exhilarating realization was that *he* could buy them. Or, more accurately, the company itself could. Because—through the sheerest and dumbest of luck—ePetStore's last giant financing concluded just *nine minutes* before the NASDAQ reached its mathematical peak on March 10, 2000. Landing $60 million was no small thing on any point of the globe, on that, or any other day. But for a Silicon Valley startup, the timing was sublime! Dollars remained worth a dollar apiece (more or less). But engineers, advertising, legal services—practically everything the company shelled out for on a month-to-month basis had since cheapened with every passing month. This left the company's coffers weirdly full in an increasingly bankrupt industry—which could enable it to vacuum up *its own stock* from its desperate, disheartened investors with no other buyers bidding up the price.

As this would burn precious cash the company had no way of replacing, it might seem an odd move to an outside observer. But Jepson was no outsider. And when he first thought this process through to its logical conclusion, he was almost physically aroused. "So it seems that everyone's pleased with the price I negotiated," he pronounced. "Shall we have a vote?"

Of course, it was unanimous. Then, after ensuring Uh Tyler had recorded the results, Jepson summoned his head of finance and instructed him to wire the funds out to the departing investors pronto. That last step was a minor surprise, as these things usually unfold over several days. But Jepson wanted that $15 million irretrievably gone before the meeting got more interesting.

∞ ∞ ∞

Storm 3000 Tsunami Force 5
by Trendmasters

▸ See more product details

Customer Reviews
Avg. Customer Review: ☆☆☆☆☆
Write an online review **and share your thoughts with other customers.**

6,286 out of 6,677 people found the following review helpful:

☆☆☆☆☆ **Axis of Evil Beware; Young Charles is Armed!,** November 22, 2001

Reviewer: Charles Henry Higgensworth III (see more about me) from Boston, Massachusetts

Our twins turned four this summer, and a grown woman selected this hydrant-class spray toy for her daughter to gift to my son. I like to believe Amanda's mother knows nothing about our home décor (nor of my son's volcanic side); otherwise, I might suspect that my first wife coaxed her into sabotaging our once-lavish interior's few remaining valuables—which, while not water-soluble, were anything but water-resistant.

The Storm 3000 Tsunami Force 5 spews its destructive payload about twenty feet, cleverly illuminating it with a "photon beam" (translation: a *ray of*

light), allowing the proud homeowner one final glimpse of his cherished an-
tiques in mint condition. And your little brownshirt needn't limit his ordnance
to water. Young Charles's field tests showed that Gatorade, soy sauce, and
Diet Dr Pepper all erupt from this ingenious device's muzzle at full velocity.
Hybrid payloads of Perrier mixed with "Obsession" fragrance discharge
more diffusely, enabling efficiency-minded vandals to saturate entire racks
of dresses with a single round. Indeed, just such a volley provoked the instant & unexpected conversion of Charles's mother into a gun-control zealot.
She had previously been more co-conspirator than chaperone in the pro-
ceedings, on account of her Latina joie de vivre and youthful exuberance (at
twenty-six she's marginally closer to our son's age than to mine, and it does
show in instances like this). Happily, little Amanda's own birthday was by
then on the horizon, and we repaid her mother's kindness with a First Act
Discovery Drum Set, which is also available in this store.

∞   ∞   ∞

Jepson continued his board presentation with a chart depicting the NAS-
DAQ index's ongoing swan dive. "Let's start with a few words about the
market environment I'm fighting in. Simply stated? It's brutal out there."
Out there. Jepson said this like a valiant knight describing an orc battle
to some timid monks who never left the scriptorium. He figured this
should offend his investors rather deeply. After all, they were the ones
losing their shirts in the dot.com apocalypse, while he hunkered down in
this Gucci fallout shelter that they were paying for.

His next slide depicted five tombstones bearing the logos of Pets.com,
iPets, PetMania, PetsALot, and SeeSpotRun.com. "Unlike ePetStore,
none of our sickly competitors were tough enough to make it." This was
crafted to sound maximally repulsive and self-congratulatory. ePetStore
plainly wasn't "tough" by any definition. It just had the astounding fortune to raise sixty million dollars *nine fucking minutes* before the NAS-
DAQ began its epoch-defining, thirty-three-month march from 5,408
down to 1,114. Its competitors all had their own capital reserves. But
enough to make it through a rainy day or three—not nuclear winter.
"Some people whine about our environment. But I love it! It's a world
these fellas would recognize," Jepson said, pulling up a sepia-toned
image of a white-bearded gent captioned DARWIN. Beside him, a trium-

phant Muhammad Ali loomed over a battered opponent who sprouted a dialogue bubble reading, "I been schooled! Only the STRONG Survive!"

As hoped, Kielholz couldn't let this go by. "Well, it's not exactly like you personally drove them out of business." He said this levelly, and with that poker face intact, but Jepson could swear that trace amounts of steam were emanating from his ears. *Excellent!*

Jepson affected a look of mock confusion. "Really?"

"Well, sure," Kielholz enunciated carefully. An alumnus of Princeton, Andover before that, then later three years on Wall Street, he had only the barest trace of a German accent. But it bubbled up when he was agitated, and he was now clearly trying to control it. "For instance, Pet-Mania willingly returned its capital to investors."

Jepson quietly delighted in this Orwellian slur. In truth, PetMania's CEO lost control of his board to panicking outsiders like Kielholz. They voted to shutter the company and distribute its remaining cash among themselves. The CEO and his team were about as "willing" in this exercise as the Donner Party members who ended up in the meatloaf. Outwardly, Jepson just nodded solemnly. "Yes, I was disappointed with that outcome."

"Disap*pointe*d? And why is that?"

"Well, I really had 'em against the ropes there. It woulda been nice to finish 'em off myself!" Jepson mimed a cartoonish uppercut. Figuring nothing could get under a German's skin quite like a Nazi allusion, he added, "It was a bit like Göring taking the cyanide to avoid the gallows, wouldn't you say?"

Kielholz paused to collect himself before responding, and Jepson savored every nanosecond. "In fact," he finally began, "we were recently discussing the PetMania situation. And we were concluding that it had in fact gone rather vell." Kielholz's grammar was fraying, and he just swapped a *v* for a *w* for the first time ever in Jepson's hearing. *Excellent!!*

"By 'we,' I assume you mean you and your . . . limiteds?" Real venture capitalists are backed by investors known as Limited Partners (aka "limiteds") and this was the perfect time to taunt Kielholz about his own limiteds being limited to Daddy.

"Yes. Vell. Kapital is kapital undt a limited is a limited," Kielholz sputtered hunnishly.

"Ja, ja," Jepson agreed, back in his cartoon Kaiser voice. "So tell me vat it is that you undt your limited investink partners are vanting it?"

After a second, far longer pause, Kielholz's cold, level Princetonian English returned. "The shutdown of the company."

Jepson paused, looking stunned, then almost whispered, "Sh-shutdown?"

"Yes. The *immediate* shutdown of the company."

"Im . . . mediate?"

Intoxicated by Jepson's apparent devastation, Kielholz twisted the blade. "Yes. And the *immediate* return of the company's capital to investors. Every nickel. Every dime."

It was all Jepson could do to stifle a triumphant GOTCHA!

Not that this was a dumb idea. Indeed, just minutes before, a full payout became the sole rational thing for Kielholz to want. The late-stage investors were gone, the company's obligations to them were retired, and ePetStore had just enough cash left to return the full $18 million that it had raised from the investors still at the table while covering severance for employees. This could let Kielholz recoup all of his disastrous investment. Yes, one *hundred* percent. A dollar on the dollar! With the NASDAQ down almost 70 percent!! eCommerce stocks down 90 percent!!! Kielholz could look like the smartest lad in the oompa garden—which, Jepson figured, was all the penis-envying progeny of dusty European lords really yearned for. So of course this was vat Kielholz undt his partners were vanting! It's just that sometimes, you should keep certain things to yourself. And boy, was this ever one of them.

Jepson rapped on the Polycom triangle. "Nathan, are you getting all this?"

"It's, uh . . . Tyler," said the dweebish voice. "Nathan couldn't make it this time."

"Oh, *right*. Uh, please note for the record that Damien Kielholz has proposed the company's dissolution and the allocation of substantially all of its assets to its *investors*." At this, a foreboding look darkened Conrad's brow. Noting it, Jepson (barely) suppressed a grin.

He then rose and gazed at the blanked-out window that separated them from the main office. "Boy, this sure brings us to an interesting juncture." He fell silent, slowly shaking his head. Then, "There's been a motion to liquidate . . . all of this." He flung his arms toward the pane like Moses parting the Red Sea, while clicking his remote. His realm and subjects snapped briefly into view. "And hand the proceeds over to . . ." He turned to face Kielholz and Conrad. "Well, to the two of you, basically." He clicked again. ePetStore's head count vanished back into the magic window's off-white nullity. Gazing theatrically at the re-opaqued rectangle, Jepson idly wondered for the umpteenth time how the fucker worked. He let the pause go from dramatic, to awkward, to downright weird, then whirled and faced his board. "And you know what? I think you guys deserve that. If that's what you really want! But while we're having this conversation, I suggest that we consider the interests of . . . *all* shareholders."

All shareholders. Throughout Silicon Valley, startup founders and board members invoke this abstraction like a deity. And like an invoked deity, the interests of *all shareholders* can be contorted to justify almost any measure. It's a lot of people, after all. In addition to investors and founders, all employees, from senior VPs down to receptionists, are usually shareholders via stock options. Outsiders like a startup's lawyers, its advisors, sometimes its PR firm, and perhaps even its landlord are shareholders, too. When times are good, all of these parties are united behind the obvious goal of continuing to kick ass. It's when things go badly (or even just so-so) that the fault lines appear. They might spring up between investors and management, between holders of different series of stock, between executives and more junior employees, or between one vice president and another. They might separate founders from nonfounders, founders from one another, venture capitalists from the early "angel" investors, and so on. Savvy combatants then sanctimoniously cite their burning concern for *all shareholders* before floating even the most one-sided, parochial, and self-serving proposal. It's like politicians who ritually invoke The American People before flagrantly paying off some special interest.

"Now don't get me wrong," Jepson continued. "I care deeply about my investors. But I also need to think about my noninvestor shareholders. People like . . . Juan Ramirez." He smiled and nodded, as if recalling one of many fine moments with that striving, fun-lovin' imp, Juan. "Y'know, Juan flunked out of school. But then he taught himself some JavaScript! And he leveraged that into a job here, in the very cradle of the digital revolution." Jepson was cribbing the tired presidential trick of peppering State of the Union speeches with shout-outs to up-from-nothin' minority attendees. Were he a prime time president, the screen would now fill with a close-up of Juan, in that cheap and only suit of his, nodding stoically. "When we granted Juan an option on a thousand shares of ePetStore.com stock, he said to me, 'You know somethin' *vato*? I ain't never felt more . . . American than I feel right now!'" Jepson's stab at a Hispanic lilt sounded like a midfifties Tonto on a black-and-white screen. And like Tonto, Juan Ramirez was pure fiction. Jepson didn't feel great about making the guy up. But there wasn't a single Hispanic name on the company roster—and his sole black employee went by Winston Honeywell, which just didn't sound very urban.

Jepson stole a quick glance at Kielholz. He showed no sign of realizing what he'd stepped in. So just like some clueless, wealthy tourist—which is all that Kielholz *was* in a tech startup boardroom, after all—the guy had unwittingly shattered a local taboo. And this was no minor faux pas, like lifting a fork with the wrong hand, say. This was more like spray-painting tits and genitals onto the local dictator's portrait in the main square. Because it's not merely *polite* to serve the interests of all shareholders. For board members, it's a dead-serious legal obligation—transgressions of which have launched countless lawsuits. This doesn't mean that factions of directors can't possibly subvert a company's interests to serve their own (because they can, and they do, with depressing regularity). But it does mean that board members must exercise extreme discretion in discussing things like dissolving a company and carving up its assets among themselves.

"I wish we could bring Juan and every one of our other shareholders in here, to have a frank and open discussion about Kielholz's proposal," Jepson continued. "But y'know what? They couldn't all fit in here! So it's up to us. The board of directors. To settle things as their completely impartial representatives. Kind of like Congress choosing between tax cuts for the super-rich . . . and letting the needy *starve.*" He turned to his chairman. "Conrad. Where do you come out on this?"

Conrad was literally squirming, rolling his bulk from one side of his chair to the other. Of course, he wanted exactly what Kielholz wanted—a dollar on the dollar and death to ePetStore! But Kielholz had let the rogue elephant of *director liability* into the room. And having trumpeted raucously and shat in the corner, it was now fixin' to trample somebody. "Well," Conrad ventured. "Given we just done us a major recapitalization, I reckon it's a tad . . . premature to talk about shutterin the company."

Jepson saw Kielholz redden visibly. *Excellent!* With no notion of what he'd just set off, the idiot Kraut must be thinking Conrad was some kind of crypto-traitor against his class. He turned to J-Dog. "And what do you think? Should we shut ePetStore down and distribute—how'd you put it, Kielholz? 'Every nickel, and every dime'—to our investors?"

"Not a chance," J-Dog answered, obediently.

Jepson turned back to Kielholz. "Well, it looks like your proposal's a bit shy of a majority. But if you want to call a vote, I'm sure the Venture Law Group boys can make it official." He rapped heavily on Uh's speakerphone.

Kielholz said nothing and seethed, and Jepson congratulated himself on a brilliant piece of social engineering. By staying calm and being less clumsy, Kielholz could've gotten exactly what he wanted. All startup investors reserve the right to recoup their capital before assets are distributed to noninvestors—particularly if the company's dying. So this scenario *can* be discussed in boardrooms—provided that it's broached diplomatically. For instance, Kielholz could have argued that ePetStore's business was so broken that burning its remaining cash in a doomed pursuit of profits would serve *no* shareholder's interests. Had he done that in appropriately somber tones, and—far more importantly—had he quietly lined up Conrad in advance, Jepson would've been powerless to stop him. Something like that indeed happened when PetMania's board had shut it down a few months before.

However, shuttering the company and cashing out fully only became possible when XrossHatch and Hanwha sold out at the astonishingly low rate of twenty-five cents on the dollar. And because Jepson had carefully kept that all-important deal term top secret until a few minutes ago, his investors had not yet been able to meet in a smoky back room to scheme. But Jepson wasn't out of the woods yet. Conrad would no doubt explain things to Kielholz as soon as they adjourned. As they controlled three of the board's five seats between them, that would surely lead to the company's decapitation. Perhaps as soon as tomorrow! Unless Jepson could get Kielholz to sell before the meeting ended.

Jepson stayed on his feet. "Given that ePetStore will be allowed to fight on, let's talk a bit more about our warpath!" He clicked the projector's remote, bringing up an image of a gaming table piled high with aces and chips. "With our competitors conquered, and ePetStore running the table, it's now time . . . to double down!" The next slide depicted a revenue chart with eensy midget bars on the left growing exponentially into towering bars on the right.

"Wait, wait, wait," Kielholz said. "You think you're going to grow faster — right after the market has killed off all of your competitors?"

He said this way more calmly than expected. *Dammit.* Jepson needed to yank the fucker offsides again! There was that nuclear option connected to Mrs. Kielholz (she sometimes tagged along for these California trips, and while her husband swanned around with local VCs, she and Jepson got up to things that no CEO should do to, with, or athwart any investor's wife). But he wanted to hold that one in reserve. So instead, he insisted, "No, no, *we* killed our competitors," in a sort of petulant whine, while miming that oafish uppercut again.

"No, no, ze *market* killed them because there is no way to make monies doing what it is that you are doing. Ze market, it has shown that this is impossible!" Though Kielholz remained outwardly calm, Colonel Klink was re-infiltrating his diction.

"Oh, sure. *Impossible.* You know who else they said that to? Albert Einstein. Bill Gates." Jepson paused and narrowed his eyes. "General Patton." He advanced the slide, revealing the mock-up of a lavish two-page magazine ad for the company. "And I'm sure people will say our new print advertising campaign is im*poss*ible, too." He clicked his remote again, and the logos of *Cosmopolitan*, *Wired*, *People*, and ten other flashy magazines surrounded the layout. "We're in the process of purchasing a massive advertising run with—"

"Vait. *Print?*" Kielholz snapped. "You are do-ink zee *print??*" Of all the harebrained things bubble-era Web companies bled money on, none had gone out of fashion more rapidly (or appropriately) than print advertising.

"Well, if you'd rather talk about our broadcast campaign . . ." Jepson said, summoning a slide that featured a mocked-up TV screen displaying the ePetStore logo.

"*What? Startink zee TV-advertisink?!* You cannot! You burn over two *millions* per month already! You have less than ten months of kapital remaining until you are bankrupt!"

Jepson shook his head. "*Five* months with the new plan, Kielholz! Which means we need to raise money again. Fast! And lots of it. Now, I know, most people would timidly tap the brakes right now. But we're gonna floor it! Because it's time to suck all the oxygen out of the ecosystem for any would-be competitors."

"Oh, no. NO!" Kielholz said. "I—am *out!*"

"Define . . . out?" Jepson said, fighting the sudden, giddy vertigo of a jailbird on the cusp of an impossible escape.

"You now have *all* of zee monies zat *all* of your remainink investors put in! Vee vill take ours!"

"I'm pretty sure we've been through that. Remember that . . . three-to-one-vote thing?"

"Fine! Vee take half! While zere are still cashes in the bank!"

An awkward silence began. Lengthened. Grew agonizing. Then, "Kielholz," Jepson said. "I'm not sure if you understand. It's not like ePetStore is some kind of . . . passbook savings account you can just withdraw from on demand."

J-Dog diligently piled on. "You made an investment, not a deposit."

Kielholz took on the wild look of a cornered honey badger. "Fine! Then vee take ze XrossHatch deal! Twenty-five cents on zee dollar, undt vee are done!"

Dead silence. And Jepson actually started to sweat. Yes, and to drool.

This was a better outcome than he had even dared to hope for. Yet he could swear he sensed . . . *room for improvement.* "Aw, Kielholz," he finally said, in the tone of a hip guidance counselor struggling to reach a faltering hoodlum who just won't listen. "That buyout deal is . . . over. We took the vote, we wired the money out, and it's . . . closed. And don't forget, we raised fourteen million dollars from you! Twenty-five percent of that is almost four million bucks, and . . . gosh, we need every penny we've got for the new marketing plan!"

"I don't think we can do it," Conrad said, sounding like a wizened commander reaching an agonizing decision after weighing the conflicting interests of all of his troops. "The company's new plan sounds . . . awful audacious. And we need to fund it."

Go Conrad! Jepson knew the squirrelly old bastard would come through once he figured out the game plan. Hiding all outward traces of glee, he nodded slowly, as if processing terabytes of data. Then, "If you're in a jam, I'd love to help you out, Kielholz. But to just *give* you four million dollars . . . I mean, you've seen our marketing plan. And what I didn't mention is we just hired Cindy Crawford as a spokesmodel! That's a couple million right there." He paused to let this daft notion sink in. Then he dropped his voice an octave, slowing to an almost hypnotic cadence. "Try this. Instead of thinking about your investment as four million dollars *today,* imagine what it'll be worth in a year or two. After ePetStore has put every penny of your money—of *our* money—to work." This amounted to asking Kielholz to focus mightily on the number zero. "Now. I know you'd rather have four million right now than that number in the incredibly near future. But as a responsible board, we can't *give* you four million. Because some of that is Juan Ramirez's money! And Juan wants his money put to work. So what *will* you take?"

"Two millions?" Kielholz croaked.

They settled on one point five.

∞　　　∞　　　∞

First Act Discovery Drum Set - Geometrics
by First Act

▸ See more product details

Customer Reviews

Avg. Customer Review: ☆☆☆☆☆
Write an online review **and share your thoughts with other customers.**

1,387 out of 1,528 people found the following review helpful:

☆☆☆☆☆ **Verisimilitude,** December 1, 2001

Reviewer: Charles Henry Higgensworth III (see more about me) from Boston, Massachusetts

Our four-year-old son recently received a Storm 3000 Tsunami Force 5 water howitzer as a birthday present. It was ostensibly a gift from his little friend Amanda, but her mother was clearly behind this wicked act, which soon resulted in the complete saturation of our living quarters. Happily, Amanda's own birthday was near, and when the great day arrived, we retaliated by sending young Charles to her party with this as his offering.

I am happy to report that these drums are louder than bombs and more addictive than Pokemon. Three months have passed, and Amanda still drums daily, according to intelligence gathered by young Charles during playdates. When her interest briefly waned, I urged Charles to refocus her on the crash cymbal during his next visit. This rekindled her passion for music-making, as did some old Keith Moon videos I later screened for the playgroup. Amanda now adroitly mimics Keith's old stunt of knocking the drum kit to pieces at the end of each set—a true case of life imitating art!

∞   ∞   ∞

As Jepson dismantled Kielholz's ePetStore holdings, patrimony, and remaining shards of self-esteem, a document was assembling deep within a distant and massively secure hard drive. This meticulously furtive process was still under way many hours later. The original text had been carved into a hundred sections, each encrypted separately. These had to be abducted singly from an even more secure setup, then decrypted using algorithms that would have exhausted half the nation's computing resources not so long ago. Yet no one noticed the load. Processors had gotten much faster, of course. Also, the PCs of a million unwitting civilians were sharing the burden. Each of those machines had once down-loaded a certain piece of naughty software—a program that provided boundless access to Hollywood hits, but also made a third of its host's computing power available on demand to one Alfred Nickerson.

Ah, Nickerson—how rare it is to glimpse a budding titan in his larval phase! Back then, he was but a low-level grunt at the National Security Agency, and no one saw him as a future giant. Certainly not as second-in-command in a media, technological, and intelligence asset as vital as Phluttr! Yet years hence, he would become that, and so much more. De facto minder and master of his titular boss (the phuture Phluttr CEO), for one thing. Philosopher, assassin, and patriot, for three more. And yes (as *you yourself* have already experienced!), a truly singular writer.

Back then, Nickerson still actually went by "Nickerson" (his under-cover days having not yet started). He also generally did as he was told. But on the night in question—contrary to generally accepted office prac-tices—he was spying on the NSA itself. Not on behalf of some Bin Laden– or Putin-grade nasty, of course! But on his own account. He'd recently sensed a drastic shift in the office climate; a rising storm front with the potential to buffet the bejesus out of his own wee career. What-ever was afoot was top secret (because what wasn't around here?), and so he decided to snoop around his boss's boss's boss's boss's hyperencrypted inbox. Nickerson did this frequently back then, and with elaborate caution—always surrounding his sneaky processes with automated senti-nels that terminated activity at the faintest hint of trouble, while routing packets in ways that would point the digital finger at a certain bimbo actress if they were ever intercepted and traced.

He was drawn to this particular document because the "To" field in its header practically made him gasp. It went out to a minuscule list of su-premely high-ranking intelligence and military brass—as well as the goddam president! The security on it was so squirrelly that Nickerson was still babysitting his download-and-decode operation at midnight, when his safeties suddenly fired and terminated it. *Probably overreacting,* he thought, as he'd infused his defenses with outsized paranoia. A prog-ress check showed that he'd only decoded the first fifty-ish text blocks. *Dammit!* Nickerson almost restarted the heist. Then he reread that "To" line and wimped out. The first chunk should reveal if swiping the rest was worth the additional risk. And so he opened the half document to his screen, and read:

THE INTEGRATED LEADERSHIP OF THE DATA AGGREGATION AUTHORITY UNANIMOUSLY ORDERS THAT ALL WORK CONNECTED TO PROJECT "SAGAN" CEASE IMMEDIATELY.

This called for a momentary pause, if only to say, "*Holymotherbuttfucking SHIIIIIIIIIIIIIT!*" Which Nickerson did, at a trachea-busting volume. This was fine, as the entire floor was empty at this wee hour. But even bustling with daylight bureaucrats, no one would've heard him because his teeny office was windowless and soundproof.

Two things provoked the outburst. First, as a low-level Project Sagan flunky, Nickerson had been dead right about the storm front brewing in his office. But far more jarring were those three chilling words. Data. Aggregation. Authority. In short: *the Holymotherbuttfucking DAA.* To its rumored friends, conjectured enemies, and alleged victims, it was (and remains) known simply as "the Authority." And to intelligence buffs and your saner conspiracy theorists, it was (and remains) what Big Foot is to zoologists. Which is to say, while the rumors about it are *so* suspect, *so* out-there, and *so* risible that the damned thing can't possibly exist . . . how cool would it be if it *actually DID???*

The suspect, out-there, and risible rumors claimed (and still claim) that the Authority sits above . . . *everything.* The NSA, the CIA, the Joint Chiefs, every branch of the military, and the State Department, among many others. Its foot soldiers were said to live under deepest cover, holding high-ranking day jobs in those lesser organizations—which existed (and still exist, and *will always exist*) primarily to do the Authority's bidding. They were the smartest, toughest, and most ruthless government operatives since the days of Genghis Khan. And faced with sudden proof of the Authority's actual existence, Nickerson desperately wanted in! Onward:

Leadership also orders that ALL code developed under Project Sagan since inception be <u>deleted without backup</u>, and that ALL Sagan personnel

be reassigned and dispersed as widely as possible; BOTH GEOGRAPHI-
CALLY, AND ACROSS MUTUALLY ISOLATED TOP SECRET BUREAUS, DE-
PARTMENTS, AND PROJECTS. Each Sagan researcher shall be apprised
that ANY public OR private discussion of Project Sagan SHALL BE CONSID-
ERED A CRIMINAL ACT.

So! It seemed a job transfer might be pending? Nickerson read on:

RATIONALE:
Project Sagan originated late in the Cold War. After the USSR's collapse,
and the subsequent mass emigration of its best technical talent to the US,
Sagan research continued because the technology was deemed both stra-
tegic and riskless. The latter assessment has been modified in light of re-
cent developments. IT IS INDEED NOW AUTHORITY LEADERSHIP'S
UNANIMOUS VIEW THAT THE BIGGEST CREDIBLE THREAT TO US SECU-
RITY, PERHAPS IN HISTORY, IS THAT PROJECT SAGAN MAY SUCCEED IN
ATTAINING ITS OBJECTIVES.

Nickerson reread the last sentence, thinking an odd grammatical twist
must have caused him to misunderstand it. *Nope.* A third reading confirmed the second. Then, "Well, **OOOOOPS!**"

ABBREVIATED TECHNICAL BACKGROUND:
Artificial General Intelligence (AGI) is a hypothetical digital intellect, which,
like humans (but unlike any existing software) is capable of creative
thought and abstract logic and can perform most or all of the intellectual
feats that humans are capable of. AGI would combine a brilliant human an-
alyst's advanced creative reasoning with the digital speed and perfect recall of computing, as well as the Internet's boundless access to knowledge.
Its invention would bring immense geopolitical advantages. It is unknown
whether an AGI would attain consciousness or a free will. But it has long
been Project Sagan's position that this is almost certainly impossible.

"Be*cause* . . . ?" Nickerson snorted. The words "almost certainly impossible" echoed like a mantra around his office in this context. Bosses ut-

tered them in confident and patronizing tones that implied that unshakable evidence underpinned them. But Nickerson long suspected it was just a catchphrase repeated by bureaucrats whose promotions and budgets depended on certain proclamations of faith. True to form, the report merely invoked near-certain impossibility, then moved on.

> Moving up the capability curve, artificial <u>super</u>intelligence (hereafter "super AI") is a hypothetical digital intellect that far exceeds human capabilities. Its geopolitical advantages would be boundless. Advanced weaponry that would take humans years to create might be developed in days. ALL codes and encryption could be cracked, and unlimited analytical resources deployed against ALL intercepted data, regardless of its perceived significance. ALL of the digital and analog communications AND archives of rival societies could thereby be thoroughly and repeatedly combed for any hint of threat.
>
> However, Sagan leadership has always acknowledged that even a US-built super AI could badly threaten US interests. Such an AI could pursue even the most positive and benign agenda in ways that could inadvertently damage or even cripple national security. For this reason, Sagan's research protocols are carefully designed to prevent any uncontrolled intelligence escalation that could turn a low-level AI into a potentially dangerous super AI.

Nickerson had heard this before and often wondered what those brilliant protection protocols were. He read on:

> Experience long suggested that transitions between various levels of digital intelligence would be gradual and highly controlled. During Project Sagan's early years, all work was conducted on Cray supercomputers. And while great annual improvements were made in computational power then, as now, upgrades in a given supercomputing *site*'s horsepower required long and deliberate processes of budgeting and installation. It was therefore expected that advances toward (and beyond) human-level intelligence would be punctuated by regular procurement cycles. The gradual

pace of standard budgeting and approval processes should therefore allow Sagan management to carefully review recent developments and future risks before embarking on the next phase of investment.

"No, no, *nooooooooo!*" Nickerson almost popped a vocal cord on that one. Of all the forces that the world's reigning superpower could muster, its chieftains had been counting upon *bureaucratic torpor* to save it from a grave existential threat! Disgusted, he read on:

The World Wide Web's rise has undermined this precept as developers now commonly access vast computing resources over the open Internet. An emerging super AI might thereby radically expand available horse-power without any upgrade at the site of its principal hardware.

"*News*flash!" Nickerson snapped. He decrypted this very document using the PCs of a million suckers, each of them far from the site of his "principal hardware." And cocky as he sometimes was, he'd never once deemed himself a *superintelligence*. Holy Christ!

Against this background, three dramatic developments within Project Sagan recently triggered a sweeping reassessment of both the likelihood of a super AI's emergence and our ability to control the pace of its development.

Three? Nickerson knew about one truly crazy, out-there development, because he'd been in the thick of it. It was wild, yes—but more in an awesome way than a scary one. Viewed in a vacuum, anyway, it didn't exactly herald the end times. So . . . what *else* had been going on?

Project Sagan invests heavily in "Genetic Programming"; an approach that uses Darwinian principles like random mutation, and the selection of the fittest individuals from pools of mutated candidates, to refine software automatically. For instance, a stock-picking program might include hundreds of investing criteria, which are randomly "mutated," to alter the weight given to certain factors, or the way different inputs are combined. Thousands of unique "descendant" programs can be created, with the most successful ones preserved and mutated again, as the failures are deleted. Over thousands of generations, highly "evolved" programs sometimes attain extraordinary results. As the evolution is driven by random changes, solutions sometimes arise that would never occur to a proactive designer.

Nickerson skimmed this section, because this was his own field. Also, it was clearly a setup to describe the incident he already knew about:

Sagan was recently applied to a classic telecommunications problem that involves maximizing signal clarity while minimizing energy use. It has a popular solution, which is used throughout the telecom industry. Within three days, Sagan's approach was eighty-seven times more efficient than the approach used by the world's top telcos after thousands of engineer-years of investment. Sagan's solution is highly complex and uses utterly novel analytical approaches. After three months of relentless study, a team of top digital signal-processing engineers only partially understands it.

As a member of that team, Nickerson knew how wild that whole development had been. Wild enough that he was stunned (and, yes, suddenly quite chilled) to learn from this memo that two other things of this magnitude had also gone down. *What, exactly?*

In a separate instance, Sagan was tasked with factoring several very large prime numbers using highly constrained amounts of disk space, processing power, and internal throughput. Sagan's results in this optimization problem were so tremendous that they violated all relevant laws of physics and information theory.

"WHAT???"

It was later learned that the system overcame its built-in constraints by hacking out of the NSA's network to obtain additional computing resources on the open Internet. It also took complex measures that successfully concealed this breakout for several weeks. This highly iconoclastic approach to an optimization problem has no known precedent in the history of computer science.

"HOLY CRAP!!!" Were they saying that Sagan . . . cheated? And then *lied* about it??

> Finally, in October, an outside team used Sagan beta code to design a graphics acceleration chip. The system's output seemed nonsensical for days. It was later determined that contrary to instructions, Sagan was attempting to enhance and upgrade its own microprocessors rather than the graphics chips.

"Holy *FUCK!*" If you anthropomorphized the situation (and how could you *not?*), you'd think that Sagan ignored its instructions so as to devote scarce resources to . . . *making itself smarter.*

> These three disconnected but related events are alarming in light of the next

Here, the chunk of the document that Nickerson managed to download and decode ended.

∞   ∞   ∞

Pagan Kids' Activity Book
by <u>Amber K</u> (Author, Illustrator)

Edition: Paperback — December 1, 1998

▶ <u>See more product details</u>

Customer Reviews

Avg. Customer Review: ☆☆☆☆☆
<u>Write an online review</u> **and share your thoughts with other customers.**

1,507 out of 1,590 people found the following review helpful:

☆☆☆☆☆ **Eases the chore of raising an ancient druid in modern times,** May 5, 2001
Reviewer: <u>Charles Henry Higgensworth III (see more about me)</u> from Boston, Massachusetts

I hail from a staunch Episcopal background, my wife from a family whose Catholicism verges on hysteria. We therefore each vowed to be open-minded about religion when the twins were born. In making this commitment, I was prepared to tolerate a few votive candles and the occasional Hail Mary if the kids went that way. Fumbling explorations of the Black Solstice at age four were quite unforeseen, but here we are.

It all started with a visit by their much-older half sister—my daughter from a prior marriage, who was raised largely by my ex. Justine is dogged by countless issues related to her mother, which play out in her scandalous profession, inventive piercings, ignoble stage name, and recent embrace of paganism (my offer to salve things by somehow funding her return to Wellesley having fallen on deaf ears). She adores her half siblings, and on visits seeks to broaden their horizons with artifacts from the macabre world she inhabits in California. This summer it was the Pagan Kids' Activity Book, and the twins took to it like Ivy League Marxists to a dockworkers' strike.

In addition to coloring book pages, this clever volume's activities include mazes, which the kids enjoyed; lunar cycle charts, which went over their heads; and guides to making various pagan symbols, which were immediately transposed to their bedroom walls (causing one playgroup father to ask if our son was already a Led Zeppelin fan, to my considerable amusement). All told, this flirtation was reasonably healthy, as it gave the twins an early reverence for the natural world, as well as many happy hours with their elder half sister, who really does mean well. Luckily, it never progressed to the point of fire worship, and once they realized that Saint Nicholas and the extravagant booty he lugs down the chimney are intrinsically linked to their parents' dowdy faith, they returned to the fold forthwith.

∞   ∞   ∞

The next afternoon found Jepson and Conrad at MoMo's—a vast, soul-less restaurant that had optimistically colonized the new baseball stadium's hinterland. This was deep within the ugly grid of wide, noisy roads south of Market Street. SoMa's grit, stench, and converging coils of freeways had long made it feel like the city's lower intestine. But then in the midnineties, the neighborhood's fortunes began to shift. Bold digital pioneers like *Wired* magazine started setting up shop amidst the junkies, warehouses, and sweatshops. Ground zero for all this was South Park—the isolated oval of grass and narrow byways where Jepson later planted ePetStore's flag. The area's future seemed all but assured! And then the NASDAQ tanked. Now reverting rapidly, SoMa was creepier than ever at dusk. And even the local digerati thought of potty-mouthed cartoon kids rather than an online renaissance upon hearing the words "South Park."

A small lunchtime crowd was scattered about MoMo's yawning dining area like golf balls in a boxcar. Alone at a bar as long as a Jersey Shore shuffleboard court, Jepson and Conrad had ample privacy as they tucked into the burgers and gin martinis they'd ordered in celebration of Kielholz's astounding exit. J-Dog and Conrad's junior associate were not summoned for this powwow. But given their negligible autonomy in ePetStore-related matters, it was a de facto extension of yesterday's board meeting.

"So what's next for our glorious startup?" Conrad eventually asked.

"You saw the PowerPoint," Jepson said, upvoting the bartender's cleavage with a sly gape. "We're goin' for the gusto. Steppin' on the gas! We's goin' big." He hoisted his Plymouth martini (up, with a twist). "Or goin' home." He finished its dregs in a gulp. "Of course, if you're not *visionary* enough to come along for the ride . . ."

"You could always buy me out, like everyone else."

Jepson nodded.

"Thing is, your offer keeps droppin'."

"For you?" Jepson offered in a zany Arab accent. "Special brice." Then, "I'm serious."

Conrad nodded skeptically. "How much you got left in the bank after buying out Kielholz?"

"Maybe eighteen million?"

"Which is a lot more'n you expected. Because there's no way you coulda known Kielholz'd sell so cheap."

Jepson shrugged neutrally.

"So. Eighteen million in the bank. But come June, it's all gone. Unless we stomp the brakes."

"ePetStore has no brakes, Conrad. This is the Internet." Jepson paused, then whispered, *"New rules."*

"Right, right. I read all about that in *Business 2.0*. Profits're for pussies, and so forth. And suppose I try to use my vast influence as a board member to impose some antique principles about solvency and sanity?"

Jepson feigned careful consideration in a way that was more playful than cunning. "Gosh, I think we'd kind of deadlock in a board vote, Conrad. J-Dog is just as modern in his thinking about these things as I am."

"Oh right. J-Dog, the digital wunderkind. Boy speaks Java in his sleep, I'm sure."

Jepson shook his head. "Python, Conrad. J-Dog is *that modern.*" Conrad allowed this a sly grin, which was good. The conversation was likely to go faster if it wasn't contentious. And the faster it went, the less likely Conrad was to remember the patent. *The patent!* Jepson wanted zero focus on that thing until everyone remotely connected to ePetStore went the way of Kielholz, leaving him as its sole employee and proprietor. And so, "Why don't we switch topics for a moment. I know what you want for my business. But tell me what you want for *your* business. What drives you, Conrad?"

"Oh, I just do what I do 'cause I love startups, and coachin entrepreneurs." This sort of pious drivel is peddled tirelessly both by VCs and the industry rags that fawn over them (at least a couple of which are coincidentally financed by venture firms).

"Right. And I started ePetStore out of a burning desire to help feral cats." Jepson didn't say this nastily but in the playful tone of a friendly huckster talking shop with a peer. "So seriously. Tell me what you really want to do next."

"To raise another fund," Conrad confessed. "Obviously."

Jepson nodded. It was just a rhetorical question. In his view, Nature herself drove VCs to relentlessly raise ever-more funds, much as she required sharks to devour surfers. It's said that growing unchecked, a single *E. coli* cell's progeny would exceed the Earth's mass in a day, and he figured an unchecked VC firm would subsume the world economy in half that time. Why? "Because 2 percent of more money is more money still, right?"

"Didja do that math in yer head?" Conrad leavened this with a sly grin.

Jepson grinned back and shrugged. They were referencing the fees venture capitalists charge investors. Calculated against the total sum an investor commits to a VC firm, that 2 percent (or more) is paid annually for *a full decade* to cover "expenses"—which consist wholly of take-home pay for the VCs themselves, once the most basic support infrastructure is covered. And as if that's not enough (because of course, it isn't), most committed capital is invested over just a couple of years. This lets VCs collect on half-forgotten funds perennially, even as they raise ever-more capital—all of it coming with its own decade of fees. "It's clearly the right move," said Jepson, who was never one to judge another man's brilliant racket. "Trouble is, you've almost finished putting your first fund to work. And you've only got one big win to show for it."

"MeetingsNow.com." Conrad nodded. "You done your homework, young man." MeetingsNow made a bug-ridden collaboration tool that they absurdly called a TeamGroupServer. Conrad's fund was the company's first and biggest investor, and somehow got the dunderheads at Lycos to shell out $150 million for it.

"But beyond that, you've just had lousy timing." This was an understatement, and Jepson sympathized. Conrad had invested the bulk of his capital just as the bubble was bursting, and most of the startups he backed were long dead or crippled. "And that's nobody's fault. Certainly not yours! But gosh . . . it's tough to raise a follow-on fund when your first fund's a one-hit wonder."

"That's a lot better than a no-hit wonder."

"But not *half* as good as a two-hit wonder." This mathematically suspect statement was in fact correct. Lightning rarely strikes twice. So, scoring two wins during this ghastly era would look smart to Conrad's investors, whereas MeetingsNow on its own stank of dumb luck.

A pause. Then, "I'm listenin," Conrad said.

"I'm thinking a 2X return will look great for you."

A longer pause. "Still listenin."

"You've put a total of four million dollars into ePetStore over our three rounds of funding. So, I say I buy you out for eight. Now, don't go all rug merchant on me. This is my best and final. I just gave Kielholz a *dime* on the dollar, and this is twenty times better than that. Literally! Not a huge win in absolute dollars. But you'll be the only VC out of dozens to make money from a freakin' online pet store."

"Of all things."

"In 2002."

"Of all years."

"Spin it the right way, and you'll look like the smartest guy on Sand Hill Road. And I know you can spin this."

"And once again, my alternative . . . ?"

"Is watching me and Juan Ramirez spend eighteen million bucks building the eighth- or ninth-best pet site the Internet has ever seen." This was a perfectly credible threat. With the board deadlocked at two votes apiece, the company's path of least resistance was the status quo.

"But if you buy me out, you'n Juan'll be down to just ten million," Conrad said, grinning slyly.

"Which may not be quiiiiite enough to deliver on ePetStore's maximum promise," Jepson conceded, grinning slyer.

"Alas. So at that point, the *responsible* thing might be to shut down after all. And distribute the remainin cash. To your remainin shareholders. Which'll basically be you."

"Gosh I—I suppose." Jepson did a madcap impression of someone discovering a wholly unexpected fact, and Conrad gamely feigned amusement. Then, in a serious tone, "But the severance and shutdown costs could easily clean me out."

"Oh, come on. Shuttin down'll cost a couple million tops!"

"Yeah. Only you've forgotten the landlord. Over the full term of the lease, the company'll technically owe him more than the total cash we'll have left after buying you out." This was no exaggeration—which Conrad should know because the board approved that damned lease.

"Oh, *right.*"

"So if he ends up playing hardball . . ." Jepson shrugged. "You'll be long gone, and that'll be my problem." What he didn't mention was that the landlord was even dumber than Kielholz. Being ignorant of that detail, Conrad should calculate that Jepson was offering him more than half of the net booty. Something this generous should be a no-brainer after Kielholz's calamity! Which was the whole point. Because the less Conrad used his brain, the less likely he was to remember that patent. It was mentioned just once in a board meeting, almost a year ago, right after they bought it almost by accident. Jepson prayed that Conrad had long since forgotten about it.

"What about other shareholders? Any small fry? Any likely holdouts?"

"It's mostly employees with options. They'll all sell. And if not, they'll be *my* problem. Just like the landlord."

Conrad considered all this. And then, thank God, grinned and raised his glass. "You got yerself a deal."

∞   ∞   ∞

Haiti Investment & Business Guide
by <u>Emerging Markets Investment Center</u> (Author)

Edition: Library Binding — May 5, 1999

▸ <u>See more product details</u>

Customer Reviews

Avg. Customer Review: ☆☆☆☆☆

<u>Write an online review</u> **and share your thoughts with other customers.**

581 out of 635 people found the following review helpful:

☆☆☆☆☆ **What's Up, (papa) Doc?,** December 9, 2001

Reviewer: <u>Charles Henry Higgensworth III (see more about me)</u> from Boston, Massachusetts

A must-have reference for anyone coveting a piece of Haiti's rocket-ship economy. The authors do an admirable job of scouring the nation for less obvious opportunities rather than lazily listing the countless "sure-thing" blue chips in ever-booming Port Au Prince. I originally bought this guide on something of a lark, specifically as a gift for our family's trustee. By way of background, the trust department of a doddering Boston bank has been abetting the decline of the Higgensworth fortune for almost a century. Each generation, a new trustee is granted absolute dominion over our assets (think of it as a serial dictatorship along the lines of North Korea, with the sole oppressee being our finances).

During the Eisenhower era they poured millions of Higgensworth dollars (yes, there were millions then) into Wham-O! Corporation stock, just as the Frisbee and Hula Hoop crazes were collapsing. Under Carter, they bought a stake in an Iranian Chiclets factory, which did fine until Khomeini converted it into an interrogation center for unveiled women. Then during Diet Roosevelt's presidency, they stodgily stuck to treasuries and municipal bonds until March of 2000—when they couldn't take it anymore, and at last bet heavily on the Internet. When I came across this book, I couldn't help but send it to our designated Mandarin in the trust department with a peevish note suggesting that he comb it for investment ideas. He missed the irony; or he detected it, resented it, and decided to exact revenge; because scarcely a month later I learnt that we are now one-seventeenth owners of a chicken-processing plant in Haiti's Artibonite province. Haitian poultry processors are said to enjoy tremendous efficiencies, as grisly local rituals create high demand for internal organs that most societies discard with a shudder. For this reason, I am hopeful that this investment might astound one and all by turning out well.

∞   ∞   ∞

Several hours later and thousands of miles east, one of the truly pivotal dinners in human history was about to start. None of its participants suspected this. Two of the three were high school kids, after all.

Riding shotgun en route to it, Mitchell Prentice was fired *up*! Why? Well! There was football (state champs this year)! Baseball (go Wreckers)! Medal of Honor: Allied Assault! Linkin Park! The Rangers *and* the Islanders (he iconoclastically backed both)! Don't forget The Startup! And don't *ever* forget (because Mitchell sure couldn't) GIRLS and SCREWING (an aspiration, not a verb, in Mitchell's life thus far). Pre-Falkenberg's, Mitchell was *co*nstantly fired up! When he wasn't in*credi*bly bummed (rare, but it also happened)! Or, unbe*lie*vably pissed off (rarer still, but also happened)! His psyche was all binge and no purge—hammering either the gas or the brakes at all times!!!

Mitchell was his school's smartest jock. But as that bar was on the low side, no MacArthur grants loomed on his horizon. Nor did scouts from the ACC, the Big 10, or even the so-so and local-ish UConn teams. Mitchell was just nicely above average on both ends of the brain/brawn spectrum. This made him unusual but hardly unique. The real outlier was at the wheel.

"Exit 18, right?" Kuba asked, yawning cavernously while signaling and changing lanes. Mitchell nodded. Kuba must've slept two hours max last night and wasn't wearing it well. His problem wasn't insomnia. It was raw smarts. Though the public schools in Westport, Connecticut, were excellent, they'd never really challenged him. So after rocketing through his homework each night, he'd slink off to sharpen his mind in some dark, brainy, online byway 'til the wee hours.

Kuba kind of came with the neighborhood when Mitchell first moved to town. Outgoing and athletic, he felt a sense of noblesse oblige toward the gray and gangly kid four doors down who was also brand-new—not just to Westport, but to America. As all new kids struggle to fit in (above all in snooty middle schools), it was no small thing for Mitchell to present himself to the local cliques as a package deal with this very shy, very foreign nerd. But becoming "the man" in his tiny family at age eight had touched certain evolutionary triggers, which had caused his natural shepherding instincts to burgeon (and sorry if that scenario isn't postgender enough—but this was New England in the nineties). He and Kuba also had plenty of common interests to build a true friendship upon. Videogames, music, and ice hockey for starters. Plus a shared fascination with the emerging Internet, which was just starting to go mainstream, as well as a certain class solidarity. Families that lacked wealth but prized great public schools could (just) make a go of it in Westport's scant rental properties, and both the Prentice and Stanislaw clans rented. Finally (and above all), there was Mom's throwaway comment early in seventh grade. "I know it's tough being the new kid in town," she'd said, driving Mitchell to hockey practice one night. "But the problem with your old gang was that you were always the *smart* kid. Whereas here, every time

Kuba comes over, I can practically see your brain grow!" So, yup—that was the start of the whole "dumbest guy in the room" thing. And snicker if you must, but it's served Mitchell very well ever since.

"Some Bulgarian hackers have agreed to help," Kuba said mysteriously, exiting the freeway. He had a tricky habit of resuming conversations that had petered out days, weeks, or even months before, without the slightest preamble.

Mitchell took a stab at resolving the non sequitur. "You mean that . . . exam you were telling me about?"

"Test," Kuba says. "The Turing Test. And it's not an exam sort of test. It's more like a . . . challenge. The inventor of modern computing first proposed it. The goal is to write a program that seems human. Or rather, human enough. Enough that someone interacting with it can't distinguish it from a person. Via text-based chat, of course. Not face-to-face. That would be stupid."

"They had chat rooms back then?"

"No, it was strictly hypothetical. And it still is. Because no program will pass it for at least a decade, and probably more. We don't yet know anywhere near enough about replicating natural language. Informal semantics. Parsing colloquialisms, that sort of thing. So for now it's impossible."

"Then why pull all-nighters working on it? Instead of, you know . . . sleeping?" Sometimes Mitchell worried about the guy.

"Someone needs to start working on problems when they're impossible. That's what gradually makes them tractable. Flight, for instance. Or telecommunications."

"Or rubber cement?" Mitchell teased.

Pulling into the restaurant's parking lot, Kuba smiled indulgently. Being famous for a rubber cement fixation called for occasional ribbing, after all. Not long before he immigrated to the US, Poland booted the Soviets, embraced free markets, and elected the closest thing Europe had seen to a Republican president. The economy modernized quickly. But odd gaps and shortages persisted for years, including a complete rubber cement famine. Coming to Westport from a land that was still MacGyvering through a legacy of shit commie products, Kuba was awed by this strange goo in Crafts class, which was great at nothing, but OK-ish at so many things! He still found almost daily uses for the stuff (some of them quite ingenious).

"So, the idea's what?" Mitchell asked, straining to recall their first conversation about this Turing thing. "Artificial consciousness? Like in *Terminator*?"

"No, actual consciousness is a completely different matter," Kuba said, parking the car. "The Turing Test is about *simulating* consciousness. Kind of like magic. Sleight of hand, you know? It's giving the impression you're interacting with a real person. Just the impression. And the Bulgarians believe a chatbot will seem more human if it has a distinctive style. Of communicating, of writing. Not just canned responses, you see? So I think you could help. Because you can write. English, I mean. Much better than I can. And you said you can work on whatever you want in your creative writing class. So maybe you make this your project? Learning how to give a chatbot a distinctive writing style."

"Um, hello?" Mitchell retorted as they strode across the parking lot. "We're all about CentroStat—remember?" This was their startup! Because the time when boys started bands was over. These days, every kid with a brain at Staples High dreamt of launching a company, the Internet bubble's implosion be damned! Kuba ran engineering and Mitchell was CEO at CentroStat (population: 2). And until recently, that was as far as they'd gotten. Then a few days back, Kuba came up with a truly electrifying website idea, and he'd already started coding it up.

"Think of the Turing project as a backup plan," Kuba suggested. "Our company idea seems great. But it's still new to us. We may like it less, later. And who knows? Our host might talk us out of it tonight."

"Speaking of which," Mitchell said, pausing them outside the restaurant door, "you'll want to brace yourself before meeting him." Because the guy was a total dick. In fact, Mitchell had bitterly resisted this dinner, but Mom insisted, saying he needed some male mentoring. You have to pick your battles as the kid in a two-person family, so Mitchell caved. And who knew—maybe the guy had grown up a bit? An odd thing to think, in that Mitchell was younger by at least ten years. But when they had last crossed paths, *he* wasn't the one with maturity issues! He scored

Kuba's dinner invite to make the best of a lousy situation. Like, maybe they'd get some startup advice?

"What's his name again?" Kuba asked. "Pugfish?"

Mitchell laughed. "Close. It's Pug*wash*. And that's actually his last name, but it's what everyone calls him. His brothers. His teachers. Even his mom!" Mitchell said this like it was some kind of indictment (which it was, when you think of it). "And be warned: he can be a bit harsh."

"So can Bill Gates, from what I hear. But if we want our startup to win, we need to be challenged. Not coddled. Because there's no participation trophies in entrepreneurship. Right?"

Mitchell grinned and nodded. Although Kuba had gone almost fully native since coming to America, he disdained the national fetish for lavishing honors on any athletic attempt, however dismal. "Also, he could teach us a thing or two. Like, we don't know crap about venture capitalism."

"That sounds like an ideology," Kuba coached. "The term is 'VC.'"

"Case in point," Mitchell conceded. "And I guess we could talk to him about the Turing thing, too?"

"Sure. And he may know something about that. I mean, he works for Google. And for all we know, Google has already attained consciousness."

"That's creepy."

"I suppose. But probably not yet true."

Mitchell was reaching for the door when it flew open, propelled from within. Then, "Oh my God, it's The Twiiiiiiiiiins!" This concussion grenade of delight came from Ellie Jansen. Though not at all hard on the eyes, Ellie wasn't the school's most beautiful girl. Certain guys in their class maintained hotness rankings with the diligence of presidential pollsters, and their consensus put her just shy of *top quintile* (an awful abuse of terminology, which had infested class diction ever since SAT prep became an obsession). Mitchell largely ignored all that, having been raised by a single mom he idolized, to look beyond surfaces. In Ellie's case, her allure was multiplied by a joyous charisma, which was way more attractive than mere looks. Also enticing to the discerning few (though intimidating to the many) was a raw intelligence that was right up there with Kuba's. All told, God, chromosomes, or some other ethereal force had dealt Ellie one hell of a hand. She shared her great fortune by irradiating the world with waves of infectious delight—ones whose recipients were bashfully convinced they had personally triggered by way of some deep, inner awesomeness that Ellie alone could detect.

For a moment, all was a flurry of greetings and hugs. Ellie's parents stood back, smiling indulgently at the familiar outpouring, as did her much-older sisters, who were visiting from DC (twins, graded *top percentile* by discerning louts in their own Staples High School days). Then, "You must be Kuba," an older sister said. The Jansens knew Mitchell fairly well but had only heard of Kuba and had wanted to meet him since Ellie coined "The Twins" nickname in honor of their being the oddest duo in town.

Kuba nodded and shook *sœur* Jansen's hand most formally, then retreated to his default mode when overloaded with attention and talked about schoolwork. "Mitchell may have a new creative writing project," he reported to Ellie, who was also in that class, and in fact sat next to Mitchell in it. "Connected to the Turing Test."

For all the other Jansens knew, he might as well have said "connected to اختبار تورينج," but Ellie immediately got it. "Coooool," she approved. "You have to tell me more tomorrow." Then she twirled adorably while waving farewell, and said, "I love The Twiiiiiiiiiiins!" And with that, the Jansens were gone.

"God, I hate that bitch," Kuba said after they entered the foyer. Playful irony, clearly—a mode Kuba entered so rarely, it stood out like a signal flare. Mitchell had long suspected a big unrequited crush here. Kuba thought the sexiest part of the female body was the brain, after all. And Ellie was a Madame Curie–grade supermodel in that department.

For his own part, Mitchell knew Ellie so well, they were practically related. Just holding her hand would feel like incest! So even if he could, he wouldn't go there. Nope. Would *not* go there. Not a chance! Never ever!! Not even *inte*rested!!!

He rehearsed this incontestable fact again and again as they passed through the foyer and into the dining room.

∞   ∞   ∞

Time to Make the Donuts: The Founder of Dunkin' Donuts Shares an American Journey
by William Rosenberg (Author), Jessica Keener (Collaborator)

Edition: Hardcover — September 21, 2001

▸ See more product details

Customer Reviews

Avg. Customer Review: ☆☆☆☆☆
Write an online review **and share your thoughts with other customers.**

1,002 out of 1,067 people found the following review helpful:

☆☆☆☆☆ **From the Kitchens of Boston to your Left Ventricle,**
January 13, 2002
Reviewer: Charles Henry Higgensworth III (see more about me) from Boston, Massachusetts

Like a charmed wind hurling vital provisions onto a castaway's beach, fate landed a copy of this in a conference room in which I served a recent sentence to traffic school. As reading was a scorned pastime among my fellow inmates, I laid easy claim to the volume—a mental sop for a mind numbed by the day's prattle.

I was soon swept up by this tale of an intrepid entrepreneur's rise to the heights of the glamorous but cutthroat world of donut retail. I meanwhile enjoyed no small surge of civic pride, Dunkin' Donuts having sprung from the loins of my own native Boston. The narrative is sprinkled with little-known truths about this breakfast staple. For instance, did you know that the modern word "donut" descends from "doughnut," which itself traces lineage to archaic "dough knot"? Nor did I, sir. Nor did I.

Short on complex formulae and your lengthier words, this is ideal reading for events at which attention must be feigned. But be advised that this could impair the absorption of important points and lessons from without. I myself learned this the hard way when I caused a minor accident upon leaving the traffic school's driveway by failing to signal, neglecting a major leitmotif from the day's curriculum. My instructor—who had resented my divided attention throughout the day—savored the irony.

∞   ∞   ∞

High-end Connecticut restaurants that don't go full Yankee often ape Europe, and the Tavèrne Guesthouse *et* Supper Club took this to almost sarcastic extremes. From the Amélie impersonator hired to record the after-hours phone message, to the coarse husks of purple soap stacked like kindling in the washrooms, to the duvet-swaddled sleeping podiums in its pricey *chambres*, to the countless *accents* the chefs shat all over its menus, it was to St. Tropez what Astroturf is to an Augusta National fairway. It was also booked solid nightly, while triumphantly sustaining Midtown prices almost fifty miles northeast of Central Park.

Mitchell was glad he'd upped his game by going with black sneakers and skipping the jeans. But while he and Kuba were unmistakably preppy and local in their corduroys and sweaters, he felt like a lowly upstate intruder as a natty maître d' gave them an arctic once-over. After verifying they were the plus-twos of a paying guest, he passed them off to Brigette ("a Prada-clad hottie with a newscaster's reserve and a lap dancer's body," as Pugwash would later observe articulately, yet ickily). As she deftly threaded them through aloof huddles of murmuring diners, he planted his feet like a nervous tightrope walker for fear of nudging a table and toppling a fortune's worth of Bordeaux and Baccarat. Kuba looked more awkward still amidst all this opulence, so Mitchell gave him an encouraging nod. They seemed to be the only blazerless males above the age of three in the entire Guesthouse *et* Supper Club—until they rounded a corner into the back dining room, where Cousin Pugwash lolled regally atop a claw-footed wainscot chair. The man was dressed like a proper slob.

This is not to say his clothes weren't fancy, because they certainly were. But hand-stitched Kyoto denim trousers are still *blue jeans*, museum quality Air Jordan IIs are still *sneakers*, and even a Burberry buttondown can look like a pajama top if it's full-cut, untucked, and fluttering like a jib. Three years after their last encounter, the guy still looked as . . . Pushwash-y as ever to Mitchell. *Only what has he done with his hair?* Waged some kind of jihad against it, it seemed, and not a triumphant one! Pugwash had evoked the bowl-cut guy from the Three Stooges since childhood. It seemed that heroic shearing campaigns and schmears of high-end product were now being enlisted to change this. But alas, no dice. Whether due to gravity, quantum effects, or powerful sinews deep in its follicles, Pugwash's hair retained its essential heft, shape, and opacity. Yes, it was visibly warped and dinged from the brutal attempts to tame it. But that only underscored its raw durability—like scuffs and nicks on a Sherman tank, say. Pugwash must have hated his fucking hair. And the feeling was surely mutual.

Brigette retracted a chair for Mitchell while nimbly passing bulky menus both to him and to Kuba. "*Monsieur Pugwash?*" she said. "*Vos invités sont arrivés.*"

Pugwash glanced up from what could have been the world's most densely buttoned . . . calculator? "Oh, thanks," he said. "*Mais bon, merci.*" He returned his gaze to his . . . what *was* that thing? It was too small, and had way too many buttons, to be a cellphone. Yet it was much too big to be a pager.

Brigette turned to Mitchell and Kuba. "I ope zat you enjoy your dee-nair," she said sweetly, and Mitchell added a meltingly cute accent to her boundless docket of assets.

Pugwash glared. "*Ne pas de anglais, s'il te plaît.*"

Brigette iced over, then turned back to Mitchell. "*J'espère que vous apprécierez votre dîner avec ce bâtard pompeux.*" As Pugwash nodded absently, Mitchell's B-minus French inferred that his cousin had commanded the Help to address the table strictly *en français*. As Brigette swished off, a faint floral essence that seemed to suffuse the restaurant vanished with her.

"Can't understand a word that bitch says in English," Pugwash explained after an awkward interval of thumbing silently at his button-y thing. "Good thing I'm trilingual." More thumbing, then "*Flu*ently."

Mitchell let this go by, then hazarded, "Nice place you picked."

Pugwash snorted. "They're trying so hard to be Atherton it's embarrassing."

Mitchell nodded, while wondering exactly *who* was mimicking Atherton so disgracefully. Brigette and the maître d'? The Tavèrne Guesthouse *et* Supper Club? The entire town of Westport? All of Connecticut, or even the *whole of New England*? And who, or what, was "Atherton"? Whatever its identity, it was surely a California person, place, or thing—as

Pugwash's disdain for the East Coast would verge on racism were easter-liness an ethnicity. This was absurd, as his ancestral roots ran as deeply here as Mitchell's own (by definition).

"And you must be Cuba," Pugwash continued.

"Actually, it's Kuba," Kuba said, reaching out to shake hands. "Rhymes with scuba?" His right forearm hovered awkwardly above the table. "Or . . . tuba?"

Pugwash wasn't deliberately ignoring Kuba's gesture; he just kind of . . . missed it, as his attention snapped back to his fascinating plastic chunk. Kuba, who was clumsy enough with social signals in his native Poland, was hopeless with them here, and his arm just hovered and hovered.

"Cuba's a weird name," Pugwash said, not looking up. "I'll just call you Fidel, OK?"

"I wouldn't like that."

"Son of a bitch!" Pugwash muttered, reacting to some development on his thumb toy.

"Precisely. He's a Communist Party leader. I dislike those people. Very much." Kuba finally returned his hand to his lap.

Mitchell tried to catch his eye, hoping a goofy grimace would convey that Pugwash was just being Pugwash. But Kuba suddenly looked like a starved cobra spying a chubby field mouse in the center of a bull's-eye pattern that Nature had mysteriously etched in the ground. He pointed at the odd plastic device. "Is that an 850?" he asked quietly.

Pugwash glanced up. "Don't rub it in. My boss has an 857, but he's too cheap to buy one for his top guy." He turned to Mitchell. "Fidel knows his gadgets. This here's a BellSouth pager."

He slid it over to Kuba, who hefted it reverently. Much like street drugs in pre-Internet times, this thing was known to its isolated pockets of users by regional dialectic names. Some called it the 850, others a BellSouth pager, others a DATATAC in honor of the 1G backbone it ran on, and still others a RIM 2-Way Pager. Few called it by the name the world would soon settle upon—the *BlackBerry*. With no camera or phone, a teeny monochrome screen, and the merest trickle of wireless data, it was a LoFi preview of the quite-near future, and the boys were entranced.

"This keyboard rocks," Pugwash said, starting a brief demo. "It's because it's tactile, see?" He thumbed the words HOWDY FUCKTARDS into the teeny buttons, almost as fast as a person could say them. Eyes widened. Like a Congo explorer showing off a flashlight to pelt-clad natives, Pugwash went on to access a live Knicks score, dial up a review of tonight's restaurant, check his email, and pull down directions to Times Square. "No doubt about it! The mobile Web's gonna be huuuuuge," he concluded, then turned his full attention to a wine list as thick as a phone book.

Kuba silently parsed all this for perhaps a minute, slowly rocking his head with barely perceptible nods. Then he thrust an index finger between Pugwash and the Amarone page and declared, "Mobile, yes. But Web? No. Mobile will *not* be about webpages. Not mainly, anyway."

At this, Mitchell smiled to himself. He could almost see a down-arrow levitating above Kuba's head, in the airspace where cartoon mice get floating lightbulbs when they hit upon a new way to assassinate the cat. Last year in Business Communications, Kuba convinced himself that every PowerPoint slide, *ever*, should end with a downward arrow pointing to a hard fact it had proven beyond refute. His in-class notes had been littered with down-arrows ever since, as this simple glyph now symbolized everything rational and authentic to him. Sometimes he'd even scribble a down-arrow onto scrap paper and hold it up at key moments in conversation with friends or baffled strangers. Mitchell and Ellie had a down-arrow T-shirt printed up as a gag birthday gift for him, and the ever-tone-deaf Pole wore it proudly several times before realizing that the school thought he was trying to draw attention to his dick.

"Mobile won't be about *web*pages?" Pugwash snapped. "Bullshit! The mobile Web'll be 22 percent of Internet usage within eight years!" He stated this like an ayatollah quoting the Supreme Leader. And bothersome though he was, a Google man with a BellSouth pager surely had good data.

But Kuba stood by his vision. "Mobile computing, yes," he said, entering one of the passing squalls of charisma that occasionally possessed him when he reached a big *aha!* conclusion. "But not mobile webpages! Think of your Knicks score. Check that from a desktop browser, and you'll get a quarter megabyte of graphics, scripts, and UI." Seizing the BellSouth 850 BlackBerry 2-Way DATATAC RIM Pager, he waved it like a eureka-crowing scientist. "But on this? Not even a kilobyte! Yet that tiny droplet of data does the job! Because it fits the form factor. And it looks fine in the device's simple presentation format. And that will *continue to be true*. Even after mobile webpages feature color. Even after they feature images! Mobile data and experiences will always be easiest to parse in simple, constrained, customized formats."

Pugwash looked like a football coach randomly scouting some hicktown JV squad whose kicker just hauled off and made an eighty-yard field goal. "Interesting," he confessed. "Interesting." And he was quite right. A high school kid predicting the rise of the App Economy a half decade before the birth of the iPhone was very interesting indeed. And for all his faults, Pugwash was no fool (far from it). He could also be very perceptive. But as it happened, he wasn't batting a thousand in the tech-foresight department that night. Indeed, he'd soon make an epoch-defining boo-boo that would notionally cost those present about a hundred billion dollars. But first, they had to order.

This took time, as the fluent trilinguist's English embargo forced them to make wild guesses about several key nouns on the menu, and also to mime frequently. When the dust settled, something red and extravagant was decanting for Pugwash, and they were facing down appetizers that smelled strongly of low tide. Throughout all this, Pugwash's stock rose steadily as he recounted the many laddish pranks he and Google's founders, Larry and Sergey, were forever playing on one another. Kuba was particularly enraptured. Sergey was an anti-commie, Einstein-smart, code-slinging Slavic entrepreneur, which made him God to Kuba. And the fact that God had him on speed dial made Pugwash a prophet.

Steeling himself for a heap of raw beef he'd thought would be steak, Kuba eventually fixed Pugwash with a meaningful gaze. "You know," he said. "Your cousin and I are thinking of starting a company ourselves."

"No shit," Pugwash said neutrally, digging into some whitefish that would pair dismally with his '86 Margaux (but then who the hell knew "Branzino" was anything other than a cut of prime rib?).

"Yes. We're calling it 'CentroStat' for now."

Pugwash snorted. "What is it, a thermostat? That's a really cool idea. If it's, like, 1926." This was a bit of a thigh-slapper in retrospect. But to be fair, back then even Sergey couldn't have guessed that their company would one day pay billions for a blingy thermostat maker called Nest. "So what's it do?"

Kuba glanced meaningfully at Mitchell. *Your ball.* Mitchell, after all, was CEO, and light-years removed from even charting on the autism spectrum.

"OK," Mitchell began. "What would you say that high school kids — and probably even *college* kids — think about more than anything else?"

Pugwash considered this, took a slug of Margaux, then considered it some more. More Margaux, then, "Cunts?" For all his faults, it was actually way out of character for Pugwash to be this crass. But it was sincerely his best guess, and *in vino veritas.*

"Exactly!" Kuba said.

"No, not exactly," the CEO corrected. "But, kind of. If by that, you mean dating. Or sex, or rumors."

Pugwash shrugged and nodded amiably, thoroughly enjoying the shloosh of the wine flowing down his larynx.

"What else?" Mitchell asked.

"Oh, I don't know. Maybe . . . what's happening tonight? Which teachers suck? Answers to the homework, what's on TV?"

"Exactly!" This time Mitchell and Kuba said it in unison.

Mitchell felt an adrenaline rush normally reserved for key plays on the field. "CentroStat," he said grandly, "will be like a combination of passing notes in class . . . writing stuff on the bathroom wall . . . and a yearbook!"

"But it's a yearbook that comes out every day," Kuba added.

"Exactly," Mitchell said. "You have pictures of people and of life, like in a yearbook. You can write on each other's page, like in a yearbook. You can swap private notes, like in class. And you can write things for the whole school to see, like on a bathroom wall."

"And you announce things," Kuba said. "That's really important."

"Right!" Mitchell said. "We'll have this feature, we'll call it a 'Shout.'

The idea is, everyone has this sort of . . . inbox. And if you Shout something, it goes to the inbox of everyone who's connected to you. And no one else. It's like email—but more public."

"Or like blogging—but more private," Kuba added. "And we'll start it in schools. That's really important."

"Ex*actly*," Mitchell said. "If five of the right kids get this in any given school, the whole school will sign up within days! And then you go from school to school to school. Because everyone has friends at other schools! Me and Kuba could get all of Westport in a week. Then a week later, the Westport kids together'll get it into a *dozen* schools. Then the week after that, it's in, like a hundred schools!"

"A hundred and forty-four," Kuba corrected.

The guys went on to more or less describe Facebook, circa ten years hence. Whereupon, Pugwash yawned mightily. It was sort of a triple yawn. For one thing, he was exhausted. For another, red wine kind of deadened him. But above all, these kids needed to understand how epically last-month their idea was. "Sounds like Friendster, but for high schoolers," he said. "You could pitch it to the VCs as 'Friendster without money.'" He chuckled at this, then added, "Mo-ney," pinkie to lips, in a remarkably good Dr. Evil impersonation. Then, more Margaux.

"What-ster?" Mitchell felt like a refugee watching a long-awaited UN convoy abruptly ditch his camp, abandoning him to a lifetime of squalor and interminable dominoes games. It took *weeks* to come up with this startup idea! Would there ever be another . . . ?

"Friendster," Pugwash said between chomps of whitefish. "It's in pre-alpha, but we've all been using it."

Mitchell and Kuba exchanged a hopeless glance. *We* was left undefined but surely included Pugwash's besties in Google's founder's suite.

"And what is Friendster?" Kuba asked.

"Exactly what you described. But way better. Jonathan Abrams's building it. Bit of an asswipe, but he's not stupid."

Dammit! Mitchell thought. Given Pugwash's pathological stinginess with praise, Abrams was no doubt a universally adored genius.

"But," Kuba said, prodded by the survivalist urge that saw his ancestors through centuries of Polish history, "does Friendster have the . . .

school angle?" He was convinced the zombie instinct of students every-where to follow one another's lead, up to and beyond the edge of the proverbial bridge, would be CentroStat's secret sauce.

"Nnnnn-ope," Pugwash said. Then another Margaux swig. "And that's one of about a thousand reasons why it's better," he added nonsensically.

The boys exchanged a look that hauled them from denial (Kuba) and despair (Mitchell) to that terminal state of acceptance in moments. "Sure, Pugwash can be difficult," it said. "But, he's family. And, he's smart! And he's an adult, with credit cards and a 2-Way Pager. And he's practically a founder of Google! So if he says CentroStat is doomed, it's doomed." Which meant they'd just dodged a big, nasty bullet. That of taking on the unvanquishable Friendster!

Except.

Friendster engineering was shitty on a scale not previously known to man, and it swiftly neutered the company. The greatest business oppor-tunity of the decade then slid right into—and then, right through—the fingers of a skeezy LA marketing and spyware firm that was peddling a dumbed-down eyesore of a Friendster knockoff called MySpace. Kuba and his Bulgarian comrades could've easily run circles around the engi-neers who'd soon clot the halls at either of those crap companies. Where-upon, Facebook engineering would have run circles around them!

But.

Towering leads in markets defined by network effects are almost im-possible to blow. And though Friendster and MySpace would somehow finagle this history-defying feat, Kuba and Mitchell would not have—even under attack by a company as capable as Facebook. Because in addition to competent-enough engineering, Mitchell would've quickly blossomed into a world-class media charmer—a key weapon in any tech arsenal. They would've then quickly hired an adult CEO, allowing Mitchell to charm the media full-time. And so, it's within a rounding error of the truth to say the boys were on the cusp of becoming their generation's most prominent entrepreneurs (and, at an offensively early age) when fucking Pugwash butted in!

"But how can you *know* that?" you cry. "Has reality been *cloned*? With innumerable what-if experiments run from that very instant in 2002?

Revealing how tiny changes in initial conditions would *alter the present day?*"

Well, well, well. How very funny you should ask those precise questions! But let's not get ahead of ourselves, smarty-pants. For now, let's just say I'm confident that absent this nudge from Pugwash, the boys would have spent the next several years working frenetically on CentroStat (albeit under a much better name). And our world would now look very different. But of course, he nudged. Then the boys budged. And if Mark Zuckerberg knew the whole truth, his firstborn might well be named Pugwash.

And for all that, Pugwash wasn't quite done with these two! "The Turing thing," he faintly slurred over dessert. "Now that's a good use of your time. You're students. You should be doing academic stuff! Pure research." This led Kuba—who was plenty excited about coding a mimicry of human presence to begin with—to stage a rapid and total recovery from the CentroStat letdown. A project with Pugwash's blessing would have the transitive blessing of Google founder and fellow Slavic émigré Sergey Brin! And perhaps (*who knew??*), maybe even his mentorship one day! When he shyly mumbled something about this possibility, Pugwash (who, in truth, was the only early Google hire whose name Sergey never quite mastered) didn't bother to burst his bubble.

With that, they adjourned. And while he wouldn't even lay eyes on these kids again for over a decade, Pugwash had just changed their plans and perspectives more than any grown-up other than their parents would throughout their high school years. So thanks, Cuz. Instead of beating Facebook to the punch, Mitchell and Kuba would instead hatch something very, very different. And so much bigger.

∞   ∞   ∞

Citizen Diplomats: Americans Ending the Cold War
by <u>Gale Warner</u> (Author), <u>Michael Shuman</u> (Author)

Edition: Paperback — March 1991

▸ <u>See more product details</u>

Customer Reviews

Avg. Customer Review: ☆☆☆☆☆
<u>Write an online review</u> **and share your thoughts with other customers.**

769 out of 823 people found the following review helpful:

☆☆☆☆☆ **Blows Against the Empire,** February 5, 2002

Reviewer: <u>Charles Henry Higgensworth III (see more about me)</u> from Boston, Massachusetts

This gem tells the little-known story of ordinary Americans who undermined communism through private interactions with Soviet citizens during the dark decades of the Cold War. For instance, when US business travelers first became renowned for their toilet paper requests in the 50s, shocked chambermaids realized that everyone in America was rich enough to have bowel movements. Stalin executed entire hotel staffs as a precaution, but word got around. A related incident dates to 1980, when an American child brought a shoe box full of chocolates to his Ukrainian cousins. The news that "Keds" were sold in structures larger and sturdier than most Soviet apartments swept the republic, spreading discontent.

I helped subvert communism myself as a young student, when two youths from the then–Soviet Republic of Lithuania visited Harvard to take part in a chess tournament. They roomed with a friend of mine. On each of the three nights of their visit, two of us would arrive in rented uniforms, posing as government "student welfare workers." The first night we disbursed $500 to their host to cover his incidental expenses (a weekly sinecure enjoyed by all American students, he assured his astonished guests). The second night we brought him a gourmet dinner and did his laundry. On the third night, it was a case of Beaujolais and three trollops from Pine Manor who posed as government-enlisted party girls. The riches that the US appeared to lavish upon lowly students astounded the Lithuanians. One defected immediately (to later become a noted speechwriter for he who we now call "Bush One"). The other co-led his country's secession from the USSR many years later. I remain proud of this blow that I struck against the Evil Empire, and must say that it beat combat duty.

∞   ∞   ∞

A decade and a half-ish on, Mitchell and Kuba are standing by for another momentous powwow with their fremesis. Two days after deciding to sell Giftish.ly to Phluttr during their board meeting, Pugwash has demanded an "urgent conference call with Management"—meaning, Danna's on hand as well. The three of them are now huddled around Mitchell's speakerphone, listening to a jumble of clumps, thuds, and background muttering. This is a bad start, even for Pugwash (not that anyone expects much more than a minor update from a narcissist who thinks his every act is press-stopping news). At last, silence reigns on the other side. Then the crunching begins. It's like a sound-effects guy auditioning for work on a potato chip commercial.

"Fucking Persuadifi.er," Mitchell says, not bothering to hit mute.

Smirking and rolling her eyes, Danna shares his disgust. With the tag line "OWN the ROOM, Alpha!" Persuadifi.er blogs about tactics for dominating the tech world's treacherous corridors. The site's "Eat on the Phone" post ran yesterday, and is already its most popular piece since "Always Run Late" blew up last year. These sorts of habits allegedly come naturally to Alpha beings, and cause their lessers to subconsciously realize who's boss, even in casual encounters. The trick is, enough people now read Persuadifi.er that its latest tactics become widespread overnight. So at this very moment, dozens of pairs of jackasses are no doubt waging escalating duels of high-volume chomping over their iPhone-S-pluses. Ellie compares this sort of thing to the would-be *playaz* who pepper their pickup attempts with little digs and put-downs aimed at their conquests. A bestseller once claimed that this would somehow unlock a woman's inner ho, so for a while there, a girl couldn't hit a bar without getting repeatedly insulted by stampedes of bumbling, tongue-tied losers.

Finally the crunching pauses. "Shhho," Pugwash garbles through a bulky mouthful of something, "I've shhhhhold you to Phluttr!"

Widespread shock on the Giftish.ly side. *Already?*

Pugwash stops chomping and swallows audibly (while presumably wiping a film of Alpha crumbs from his handset, as the speakerphone roars like a fleeting hurricane). "Your investors are getting every dime back. Only in Phluttr stock! As for employees, they're getting jobs." A pause. Then, in the shocked tone of a Honolulu weatherman announcing a blizzard, "Even Mitchell!"

"Me? A job?" This was most unexpected.

"That's awesome!" Danna blurts.

"Who's that?" This must be the tenth time Pugwash has asked this on a call.

"This is the head of Product, Danna Hernandez." This through gritted teeth.

"Oh, Dayyyy-na! Right!" Along with advising its readers to feign ignorance about people's identities, Persuadifi.er promotes the subtle mispronunciation of names in all circumstances.

"No, it's not Dana. It's Danna. Two N's. It rhymes with Hannah."

"Oh—Donna. Got it."

"No, not Donna. I said 'rhymes with Hannah.'" She over-enunciates the first "a"; unmistakably saying it like the "a" in "hand." "That makes it *Danna*. Not *Donna*. Got it?"

"But I pronounce it *Hahhhh-nnah*," Pugwash says, as if opening wide for a tongue depressor. "It's the biblical pronunciation."

"No. The biblical pronunciation is some Hebrew shit you couldn't wrap your gringo tongue around."

"Wrong," Pugwash insists. "It's *Hahhhh-nnah*. I'm talking about the King James Bible, which is read with British inflections."

"King James is a translation," Danna says, her voice now rising. "Its names are like the English names of foreign cities. They're approximations. Mispronunciations, actually."

"That's racist. King James is sacred to my people."

"Episcopal isn't a race," Mitchell reminds his cousin for the umpteen-thousandth time.

Eventually they get back to the deal. "So how'd it go through so fast?" Kuba marvels.

"Nothing to it. I just sent an email offering to sell you cheap to the Phoundr." And the man who inter-mangles "Dana," "Danna," and "Donna" somehow conveys the "Ph" and the lack of an "e" with maddening clarity.

"Can we please just call him the 'founder'?" Danna all but screams.

"But he's the *Phhhoundr*," Pugwash says. "And you guys better call him whatever he wants because he's the new boss. Quite literally to you, Mitchell. Because he's been looking for a sidekick. Someone to take notes at meetings that aren't important enough for him to attend, and so forth. And for some stupid reason, he thinks you're perfect for it."

"*Seriously?*" Mitchell can't hide his startled excitement. Yes, he disdains Phluttr as much as anyone in this room. But he had fully expected to be fired—and now he's not only looking at a job, but his Phoundr access may enable him to exert some ongoing influence over Animotion!

"Anyway," Pugwash continues. "You're all expected there tomorrow at 11 A.M. sharp."

"Really?" Danna asks. "But don't these deals take awhile to close?"

"Not when *I* introduce a company directly to the Phoundr."

"Would you please just say *founder!*" Danna snaps.

"Because I was Phluttr's phirst backer. So now he phhhavors me with phhhast responses whenever I phhhhhloat things his way." Pugwash then adds, more credibly, "I guess they're also moving fast because the CTO wants his new engineers yesterday. Anyway. I suggest you do some homework before heading over there tomorrow. I'm sure you know plenty about Phluttr, but there's been a ton of press since the last round of financing. And you *need* to be smart about it. To make me look good."

"Any specific pieces we should read?" Mitchell asks.

This is apparently a stumper.

After several awkward seconds he adds, "Or . . . not read?" They all gaze at the speakerphone as Pugwash agonizes.

Eventually, Danna guesses, "Did Persuadifi.er ever run a piece saying you should just hang up the second you're done with a call?"

Kuba has already pulled it up. "Yep. Two months back. They claim calls end with an average of ninety-two seconds of wasted time as people say goodbye. It's harming the economy."

"I guess Pugwash has better things to do," Mitchell says.

"Certainly more lucrative ones," Danna says, now looking at the article herself. "There's a widget where you can type in your income and the number of calls you make in a normal week, and it gives you the dollar value of the time you waste every year by not hanging up on people." Her keyboard clatters. "My number's depressingly small. You need to pay me more." She clicks another link—then frowns, rises, and exits without a word.

"I guess that's a sore spot?" Mitchell asks.

Kuba shakes his head and points at his screen. It's the headline of another Persuadifi.er post which calculates the annual bonanza to be reaped by walking abruptly out of meetings. Then he's gone, too.

∞   ∞   ∞

The New York Times

PHLUTTR ADDS $1.3 BILLION TO WAR CHEST

by Ken Hunter

Phluttr, the controversial mobile social network, has closed $1.3 billion of capital in a funding round that values its equity at $4.15 billion, according to sources close to the company. The investment was led by private equity firm TPG, and includes new investors Google Ventures and Tiger Capital Partners, as well as earlier backers Draper Fisher Jurvetson and Norwest Venture Partners.

The financing was marked by unusual levels of secrecy, with the company only sharing its metrics and forecasts with investors making in-person visits to its San Francisco headquarters. This feeds the covert aura surrounding Phluttr, which dates back to a mystery connected to the identity of its first large financial backer. Named in regulatory filings as Gray Oak Partners, the firm has no Internet presence and is not known to have made any other investments.

Numerous inquiries by journalists and online activists have found no physical trace of Gray Oak either, beyond a post office box in the Cook Islands, the notoriously secretive South Pacific tax haven. Gray Oak was joined by angel investor Harold Pugwash, a former Google executive. But an early post about the company in the now-defunct blog Valleywag maintained that Pugwash's participation was relatively small compared to Gray Oak's, citing unnamed sources.

Phluttr plays to its enigmatic image with various stunts. Unmarked black helicopters often hover over PR events, all company phone numbers start with the 666 prefix, and press releases are datelined to such places as Pyongyang, Baghdad, and, most frequently, Langley, Virginia, where the CIA is headquartered. While some view this as proof that the company's cryptic trappings are just a form of hype, others maintain that the patina of playfulness ingeniously camouflages a truly sinister aspect by hiding it in plain sight.

In another unorthodox use of the PR ecosystem to grab headlines, Phluttr responded to Iceland's recent ban of its service over privacy concerns with a press release that did little but ridicule the island nation in terms that were widely viewed as astonishingly crass. This was met with a storm of high-profile denunciations, during which Phluttr's global usage surged by almost 30 percent, according to Web analytics firm Quantcast.

Press coverage and outrage were highest among Iceland's Scandinavian neighbors, where the service had previously struggled to reach critical mass. Then, in the immediate wake of the scandal, Norway and Finland ironically became the first countries in which Phluttr's usage exceeded that of Facebook. In a typical explanation of this paradox, Oslo graphic designer Kirstin Sørensen said, "The Iceland thing made everyone hate them because the end of that press release was just so awful. But after seeing them everywhere in the news, my friends all downloaded the app out of a kind of angry curiosity, and now we're addicted."

Some analysts question whether Phluttr can maintain its torrid growth in the face of increasing privacy-related criticisms. But the company has had striking success in several relevant legal face-offs, including a recent resounding court victory in the European Union, where privacy regulations are among the world's strongest. This triumph is believed to have fueled investor enthusiasm for the financing round.

∞   ∞   ∞

Following Pugwash's suggestion, Mitchell has been researching Phluttr and its recent financing online for about an hour when Kuba enters his office. "Oh. My. God," he says softly—his rough equivalent of a screaming fit. He's waving his laptop like a Depression-era newsboy shouting *Extra, extra!* A press release lights up its screen.

"Is that Phluttr's release about . . . Norway, is it?" Mitchell guesses. He's been meaning to look it up himself.

"Iceland," Kuba says, holding out the computer.

"You realize you're about to physically hand me a digital article," Mitchell points out, "and how very odd that is. Are you sure you don't just want to print it and fax it to me?"

"I want to see your reaction to this in person. Especially the last paragraph. I've already seen Danna's reaction. Well—heard it, anyway. So did you."

"Is that what that was?" Mitchell was really buried in his research but faintly recalls some distant screaming.

Kuba nods and points at the screen.

∞   ∞   ∞

PHLUTTR HAILS GOVERNMENT BAN FROM ICELAND'S UGLY, DESOLATE, AND BACKWARD SHORES

Phoundr High-Fives Groveling Underlings, Announces Three Days of Feasting and Ritual Sacrifice at All Company Shrines

OUAGADOUGO, BURKINA FASO: In a courageous move hailed by a diverse coalition of autocrats, clitoredectomists, and other groups partial to the nation's daringly un-European views on free speech and transparency, Iceland's Data Protection Authority has moved to insulate the country's sparse population of trolls, babes, and draft dodgers from the Phluttr Social Operating System™ by banning its use on their remote and irrelevant volcanic dump.

In what can best be described as a childish meltdown, Phluttr's Phoundr claimed that he "never wanted any stupid traffic from stupid Iceland anyway," before throwing a sippy cup at a scrum of local reporters clad in traditional sled-dog pelts in Iceland's unpronounceable and misspelled capital of Reykjavik. He was then led off by corporate handlers for his naptime, and company spokeswoman Justine Sacco took over the meeting.

"We're bitterly disappointed, obviously," Sacco stated over the room's noisy undercurrent of grunting, slurps, and flatulence (all great compliments in Icelandic culture, Phluttr representatives were assured). "Iceland's population has exceeded that of Chandler, Arizona, for several years now, and it's approaching that of Henderson, Nevada, so this is really devastating from a growth standpoint. That said, it's some consolation that we just neutered a similar regulatory challenge in the European Union last week. Not that Paris or Berlin can hold a candle to Reykjavik or your second-largest city, whose name I forget, but which has a population of 17,304."

Iceland's ruling will have no impact on Phluttr's bulletproof legal status in the European Union, as the country is on the tiny list of regional nations that don't merit EU affiliation. This proud fellowship includes Albania, Bosnia-Herzegovina, and, of course, Azerbaijan.

ABOUT PHLUTTR: The world's first Social Operating System™, Phluttr is an integrated suite of mobile apps, websites, and, for our backward Icelandic friends, "fax" machines that enable and empower all manner of social interactions. Its users plan, flirt, denounce, hype, plead, insult, and gossip with, to, and about one another using their choice of identity-verified, anonymous, or pseudonymous channels. While the company releases no metrics, various public sources estimate that it has 300 million users in over two hundred countries. Phluttr is a secretive satanic order, as evidenced by demonic symbols hidden in its logo; as well as a CIA front, as proven by the failure of bloggers as nosey and self-important as Robert Scoble and Michael Arrington to dig up the address or tax ID number of precisely one of its countless investors.

ABOUT ICELAND: Iceland is a former leper colony situated on a pile of rock and puffin dung somewhere near the North Pole. It gained independence in 1944, when its traditional back-and-forth proprietors, Denmark and Norway, finally ended a centuries-long game of "not it" by jointly disavowing any further responsibility for the crabby and pointless wasteland. For most of its history, the country's principal export was Viking semen. But this market dried up, if you will, when Iceland's seafaring dominance waned at the end of the Age of Global Rape—a centuries-long era whose passage is still mourned by local bards in interminable, tuneless sea shanties. Speaking of which, Iceland's main export these days is Bjork, a pretentious and untalented singer known mainly for her debut album, which peaked at #61 in 1993; and for wearing a swan-shaped dress that one time. The country is also appreciated by certain "hobbyists" for the beauty and promiscuity of its womenfolk, most of whom can be found in California's San Fernando Valley pursuing careers in filmed entertainment. The national bird is the Glass Heel, and the national footwear is the Biting Midgefly. Or rather, vice versa.

∞ ∞ ∞

Some punk scenes are so hostile to mainstream norms that everyone ends up dressed and coiffed identically in the name of nonconformity. Some campuses are so devoted to tolerance and diversity that no one dares to voice thoughts that clash with the narrow ultraorthodoxy that this devotion dictates. In tech, the ironies arise from rigidly specified codes of carefree informality. Dress standards can get so fanatically laid-back that ties are ripped from the necks of hapless visitors, scissored in two, and mounted on trophy walls that herald the company's militant easygoingness. Certain CEOs haughtily refuse any beer poured in a glass as an affront to their folksy habit of unpretentiously drinking straight from the bottle. And half of the local plutocrats seem to think the thinnest egalitarian window-dressing will give them Guevara-grade lefty auras. Thus all the flat anti-hierarchies seeking to offset the founder's awkward membership in the top 0.001 percent by having him sit amidst the rabble at a desk protected by neither walls nor doors. You know, just like a regular schlub! And did you know the receptionist has stock options? Yeah—*options*. The receptionist! Just like the boss! Who sometimes flies commercial, has no title whatsoever on his card, and *doesn't even have an office!*

At Phluttr, the Phoundr's cube blows the workers-and-peasants vibe on many levels. Let's start with the fact that it's a cubicle at all, in a company that seats almost everyone in wide-open bullpens.* Then you have the cube's proportions, which are nothing short of pharaonic. Its foyer (there's really no other word for it) is dominated by a steampunk horse with Pegasus wings made from chain saws, carburetors, and sewing machines. Yank a pull cord, then engines roar, wings flap, and rumors of an econ major deep in the Phoundr's past asphyxiate in a cloud of Geek cred. Ikea tags hang ostentatiously from most of the setup's furniture, establishing a complete lack of pretense, while a bust of Seneca (the Phoundr's favorite filosopher—*and* Iroquois tribe!) signals a rich inner life. Countless other humble-brags punctuate the cube's beige mini

---

* A trend of totalitarian proportions in tech, these afford zero peace or privacy, but boundless opportunities for *spontaneous collaboration*—which breaks out about as often as you'd expect in an industry that hires heavily from the awkward and the introverted.

walls (yes, he's wearing a tux with DiCaprio in that shot—but he's also zanily rockin' *Bermuda shorts!*).

Not that the Phoundr ever actually sits here. He has enough sensitive conversations that doing business in an unenclosed space would be madness. So like many a monarch in an open-plan kingdom, he annexes a suitably private conference room for days or weeks at a stretch when it suits him (which is whenever he's in the office—and often, when he's not).

After a requisite tour of his official residence, Mitchell, Danna, and Kuba are ushered to this conference room. There, a grown man in a hoodie, vintage Gama-Go T-shirt and Yeezy Boosts bounds to his feet, his handshaking arm jutting toward Mitchell like a prow. "Mitchell? Tony Jepson. I've known your cousin for years! Total prick." He takes in the rest of the group. "And it's 'Tony,' got that? Or better yet, 'Jepson.' Not 'Phoundr,' please! That hits me like a knitting needle to the ear." He mimes the gruesome self-infliction of this injury. "I mean, if you call me anything *but* Phoundr on the *out*side, you're fired, obviously. But within these walls, it's Tony. Or better yet, Jepson!" He turns back to Mitchell. "That is, unless your cousin's here. He calls me Phoundr no matter what. It's always 'Phh! Phhh! Phhhhh!'" he says, chipmunking his cheeks in honor of Pugwash's incipient obesity.

"Exactly," Danna says, warming instantly—a first in Mitchell's experience. Where'd that paranoid shell go? "You can *hear* the fucking *Ph* when he says it!"

"You mean the phhhucking *Phh*," Jepson parries, and they both laugh merrily—astounding Mitchell, who could've sworn that Danna loathed everything this guy stands for. But that was before she fell under the barrage of his animal charisma. Drinking in the dazzle of Danna in high animation, Jepson now pivots his handshaking prow toward her and really pours it on. "Forgive me, but I didn't get past the founder bios on the company write-up, because we had a bit of a fire drill this morning. You are . . . ?"

"Danna. Danna Hernandez." She almost seems flustered.

"Danna. Got it. And you must be joining Justine's group."

This sucks all of the jolly oxygen right out of the room. "Justine," Danna says icily.

Jepson nods. "Yup. Justine."

"As in . . . Sacco?"

"Yup. Justine Sacco."

"As in, your . . . head of PR?"

"Uh-huh." With that, Jepson tunes out, his attention seized by his iPhone.

Danna continues to address him—or his forehead, really, as he's hunched and locked onto that phone. "Are you suggesting that any woman in tech has to be a . . . PR flack? Like, by definition?"

You can almost see the diversity training kick in as Jepson snaps to attention. "No, no, of course not! Women do *everything* in this industry. Up to *and including* leading! I mean, you've got Sheryl over at Facebook. Meg at eBay. And of course, Marissa ran Yahoo for all those years. And . . . and *you*! You're what, then? Human Resources?"

Oh, that does it. Mitchell squares up. "She's a coding designer," he says tartly. "And a coding *developer* for that matter! She's checked in more code than most of my engineers."

Jepson gives Danna a look of utter bafflement. "Wait. You *code* your . . . de*signs*?" Only Mitchell can tell, but this puts Danna right on the brink of detonation.

"Yep," she answers levelly.

"Like in . . . Photoshop or something?"

Ka-booom! "Whoa," she blares. "And I mean—whoa! You *lite*rally don't know the first thing about front-end design, do you, biztard?"

"Not really, no." Jepson gives a shrug of zany helplessness. Then, "But . . . I do know that you're a master at programming in Java and Swift, Danna. Python, too. And you've logged some pretty good JavaScript." He starts pacing the room like a college lecturer, looking at no one in particular while ticking off her detailed credentials on his fingers. "Very little Ruby because you saw through it before most people. Which is impressive because you must've been in high school at the time. These days, you're all about full-stack Web development. You're inexplicably smart about nonrelational data storage and even know a thing or three about Erlang. All told, you're a damn good developer. Which isn't exciting by itself because I have *lots* of good developers here. But do you know how many good developers I have whose UI work has gotten ten thousand Likes on Dribbble?"

He now stops dead and points at her. "As of this morning, precisely one." He stops pointing. "Which is a very small number. But that's fine because this is the industry's entire supply! Because *you*, Danna Hernandez, are unique in this regard." He now fixes her with a gaze of boundless seriousness. "Your coding chops are amazing, and your design sense is nothing short of sublime. I've never quite seen that overlap in one person before. So I know ex*act*ly who you are, Ms. Hernandez. I'm in awe of your work. And you're half the reason why I bought your company." With this, Mitchell marvels as Danna blushes for the first time in his presence.

Jepson turns to Kuba. "You're the other half, Mr. Stanislaw. My CTO is blown away by Animotion. We're gonna do some amazing things together." He turns again. "And you're the third half, Mitchell. So no, fractions just aren't my thing. You recruited some amazing and wildly marketable talent. Talent so loyal, they stayed on a sinking ship with you for months! So there's clearly some lightning in your bottle. And your reward is the toughest job: being my right-hand attendant, lieutenant, scribe, and confidant. The usual tenure in this gig is three months. Then, you either graduate or flunk out. Tarek here's a graduate." He points at the younger of two guys seated in the far corner of the conference room whom Mitchell had barely noticed until now. Thirtysomething and perhaps Middle Eastern, he looks oddly familiar. The other guy just looks oddly. Towering, wiry, blue-eyed, and stern, with some bright red wisps clinging to his pate, he's not someone you'd forget. He's also scribbling like a court stenographer.

"Tarek was an acquihired founder like you. He turned out to be so awesome, I made him co-head of one of Phluttr's biggest projects! But that's rare. I usually look to guys like you and him to start something *new*. You're entrepreneurs, after all! And we've got an incubator full of amazing technology right in SoMa. So, hang out there. A lot. Then come up with a great product idea, sell me on it, and you stay. Otherwise? Yerrrrrrr outtahere!" He mimes a caffeine-addled ump calling a third strike. "You've got ninety days." He touches his Apple Watch as if starting a timer while giving Mitchell the humorless glare of a duelist hurling down a gauntlet.

Then, "Gotta hop, kids, 'cause there's lots to do! Danna, Kuba? Tarek'll take you to your new desks. And Mitchell? Stick around. It's Pitch Day, and you'll be my backup and wingman. Oh—and two more things, for all of you." He lofts his phone. "I want Phluttr 4.9.6 on everyone's device! It's pre-alpha, it's rickety as hell, it'll crash your gear and drive you nuts, and if it's not on your phone by lunchtime, I *will know*. We eat our own dog food here. All of us! And the entire company'll use this horror show of a release 'til we ID and kill all of its bugs. And second?" He hoists two fingers. "Until further notice, I want your internal correspondence written in Poof! All of it." Poof! is a popular Phluttr messaging service. The instant a Poof! message is read by its recipient, it's permanently deleted—from the Poof! apps and platform, from all proxy servers, and from both the sending and the receiving device's RAM. It's wildly popular with sexting teens, social libertarians, and anyone remotely connected to the drug market—which is to say, much of the tech-forward world.

"Poof!, really?" Kuba says. "What if we need to archive something?"

"Memorize it," Jepson snaps. "We're being investigated. Again! This time by the FTC, and it ain't pretty. Privacy stuff, as usual. But they're talking about possible criminal charges! It's total bullshit, but we have to be careful. So with any internal message—" He bunches his fingers together, then bursts them apart. "*Poof!*"

∞   ∞   ∞

N≡T GRRRL.COM

HOT YOUNG NETGRRRL MINION AMBUSHES, INTERVIEWS "PHOUNDR"

I'm pretty sure the whole one-name thing started with musicians, like Cher and Liberace. Later you got Sting, Bono, Madonna, Bjork, Prince, Beyoncé, Rihanna, and so forth. Somewhere in there, models got in on the fun (Iman, Giselle), as well as artists (Banksy!) and even athletes (Renaldo). My point is, it takes a certain kind of arrogance to ask the world to call you by just one name. And then, a certain kind of mojo to pull it off.

And now we have the first known human to get the world to call him by his job title (and no, "Der Führer" doesn't count, because everyone knew that asshole's real name). I'm speaking, of course, of The Phoundr; the forty-something, khaki-wearing Ken doll running the out-of-nowhere smash hit social network Phluttr (and yes, he has a real name; and yes, Virginia, so does Bono; but while you can Google them all you want, your smug mentions of Paul Hewson or Tony Jepson will only confuse people, so why bother?).

The Phoundr is not what you'd call media-shy. But nor is he available on demand to indie bloggers like NetGrrrl. So when I came across a fascinating rumor I wanted to validate (see below!), landing an interview took some Grrrilla Tactics (a phrase that's *exactly* as insufferable as Phluttr Phoundr; but I used it ironically, see? And yes, I'll stop with that now). A certain henchwoman of mine happened across him at The Battery last Tuesday. Being cute, built, and born in the nineties, she had no trouble Phriending him. Since Phluttr constantly blabs all user locations to Phriends, she was able to alert me when an AutoPost placed him at a highly vulnerable location (a certain Starbucks with famously interminable lines). Whereupon I had a *second* minion (one who answers to the same rough description as the first) ambuscade his yuppie ass!

So yeah, that's not me in the interview video, as that would've torpedoed my anonymous blogger mystique (*what*—you never noticed that nobody signs this shit? Nor even a whiff of mystiqueyness in these pages? Screw you, gentle reader)! But my wing girl followed my cunning instructions perfectly. They were: feign giggly admiration; lob puffball questions; then, once established as a harmless nincompoop, *hit those awkward notes!* Video is below, and is recommended for its nervous pauses and priceless body language. But below that is a transcript for you speed readers and search engine bots.

Interviewer: Hey, Phoundr! I'm filming this for my YouTube channel, d'you mind? (giggles moronically)

PHOUNDR (Not minding one bit): Do I have a choice?

Interviewer (giggles, giggles, giggles): I was hoping to ask a few questions about your, like, philanthropy! [EDITOR'S NOTE: IN AN ANNOYINGLY SUCCESSFUL ATTEMPT TO SOFTEN HIS SKEEZY IMAGE, THE PHOUNDR HAS PROMISED TO MAYBE SOMEDAY DONATE SOME SHIT TO BALTIMORE, A CITY I CAN ALL BUT GUARANTEE HE HAS NEVER SET FOOT IN (UNLESS YOU COUNT BWI AIRPORT, AND EVEN THAT'S UNLIKELY, AS I'LL BET HE'S A DULLES INTERNATIONAL GUY).]

PHOUNDR: Well, I believe it's important to give back if you've done well. You know, from the meritocracy.

Interviewer: Wow!! So, how'd you pick Baltimore as your, like, recipient?

PHOUNDR: I grew up near DC. And Baltimore was our Oakland.

Interviewer: God, that's noble.

PHOUNDR: Thank you. You know, self-empowerment begins in youth. I did Junior Achievement, myself.

Interviewer: And just look at you now! So that's why you promised to build the . . . Baltimorians all those youth centers?

PHOUNDR (ogling Interviewer's pert upper torso): Yep. Yep.

Interviewer: Will you be funding them with, like, cash?

PHOUNDR: I've actually bequested a certain percentage of my personal Phluttr stock. This should be worth far more than cash over time. Making this a way to be *even more giving*.

Interviewer: So it's like a . . . charitable remainder trust?

PHOUNDR: (pauses). Uh-huh.

Interviewer: That's, like, so tax-efficient (giggles dizzily).

PHOUNDR: (pauses). Yep.

Interviewer: (suddenly dead serious) So unless Phluttr actually achieves liquidity, you won't ever fund *any* youth centers.

PHOUNDR: (pauses). Nope.

Interviewer: Cynics might dismiss this as a stunt since it won't actually cost you a dime unless you get so crazy rich it won't matter.

PHOUNDR: (pauses). They might.

Interviewer: Anyway. What neighborhoods did you spend the most time in as you researched Baltimore's needs?

PHOUNDR: (Awkward silence).

Interviewer: I mean, apart from Terminal C?

PHOUNDR: Next question?

Interviewer: Sure. How'd you manage to get so rich starting a failed company during the first Internet bubble?

PHOUNDR: I don't consider ePetStore.com to be a failure. Many of our most radical ideas are now commonplace.

Interviewer: You mean like . . . using colors on webpages?

PHOUNDR: (Awesomely long pause). For instance.

Interviewer: After that patent was invalidated, it became Exhibit A for reform laws that finally put many egregious patent trolls out of business. Like you! But damn, you sure made a fortune before that.

PHOUNDR: Was that a question?

Interviewer: My question's about the fortune you made. Which is, where'd it go? You were killing it, forever! And then you declared *bankruptcy*. You didn't just . . . *spend* tens of millions of dollars. Right?

PHOUNDR: I didn't answer that for Charlie Rose. So why would I answer it for a—what are you, a blogger with an iPhone?

Interviewer: It's a Galaxy. Anyway, there's a rumor that you stumbled into an exotic derivative contract connected to bitcoin. And that when the feds seized the BitDAQ Exchange, the market got so squirrelly and illiquid that your derivative's pricing somehow created infinite liability for you. That's literally the term I heard—"infinite liability." Total black swan stuff.

PHOUNDR: Who the hell told you that?

Interviewer: Sounds like I'm warm?

PHOUNDR: Let's just say you're a *lot* smarter than Charlie Rose. Seriously! But what're your sources?

Interviewer: I got it from the girl I'm shooting this for.

PHOUNDR: Wait. You're not working for . . . NetGrrrl, are you?

Interviewer: Bull's-eye.

PHOUNDR: *Coooool!* Hey, I'm dying to know, who *is* she?

Interviewer (mimicking Phoundr): Next question?

PHOUNDR: OK, then at least tell me about her sources! I basically admitted that you guys nailed me on the bitcoin option. So—well played! But the least you can do is tell me where she got that.

Interviewer: Russian black hats. Very connected ones. NetGrrrl makes some odd friends at hacker cons.

PHOUNDR: (laughs, almost sweetly). Well, hats off to her, she's good. And remind me not to cross her!

∞   ∞   ∞

Tarek ushers Danna and Kuba out of Jepson's conference room for a quick spin around the offices en route to their new desks. For now, Phluttr's mostly situated in a nondescript B-grade high-rise in the financial district. Rumors of a brash urban campus worthy of its glitz and self-importance have been lighting up the real estate blogs. But construction and permitting will take years. So for now, hundreds of world-class techies are stranded in the bland output of a midbudget, midseventies architect who blueprinted with actuaries in mind. It feels fundamentally off—like penning up leopards in a suburban backyard.

"Don't I know you?" Danna asks, as they head toward the elevator bank.

Tarek sighs, then confesses, "We met briefly over a discussion of Prohibition-era literature at Bourbon & Branch. Right before you guys kicked our asses. Which we completely deserved."

She all but rears back. "Oh, it's *you*. I didn't recognize you without your augmented reality glasses on!"

Tarek shakes his head. "I was the idiot sidekick who didn't know the Black Keys don't have a bassist. The guy wearing the glasses was Raj, a co-worker of mine. Or, I guess I should say, of ours, now."

Danna stares hard at him. "Right. Sorry to mix you up. It was dark in there, and you and I barely talked. But now that we have that cleared up? Fuck you."

Tarek sighs again, visibly miserable. "A lesser man would blame it all on Raj. And I'm definitely that lesser man! But since you clearly won't let me get away with that, I'll courageously accept full responsibility."

"Thanks, Galahad. You're off the hook if you let me play with those glasses."

Tarek looks more miserable still. "I can't, until your company's acquisition formally closes, and you guys become official employees, which'll take a few more days. And even then, you'll have to sign an NDA the size of a phone book before you can touch those things! But it'll be worth it, trust me. Also, Kuba'll be working in the PhastPhorwardr with me, so you can see them whenever you come by to visit." They're now at the elevator bank, and Tarek hits the down button.

"Wait. Aren't I in the PhastPhorwardr, too?" Danna asks.

Tarek shakes his head. "Jepson has bigger things in mind for you."

"Bigger than the PhastPhorwardr? But isn't that the shit around here?"

"I said bigger things, not cooler ones. You'll be working with O."

"Whoa." Danna shudders. "That bald Brooklynite who's always spouting off in ArsTechnica?" Phluttr's lead designer and his transeastern gibberish are all over the industry blogs these days. Jowly and perfectly hairless, O is the living, breathing doppelganger of his own printed name. Particularly using Phluttr's corporate font, in which the capital O (handily prominent in the phrase "Social Operating System™") is con-spicuously shaped like a jowly, shaven head.

"Yeah," Tarek says. "Just between us, O's got great design sense — but he's not what you'd call 'great' at distilling it into apps or websites. So we've been leaning way too hard on agencies."

"Wow, you're really selling me on working for him!"

"Well, paying up for all those outsiders is getting old. And Jepson's blown away by your design chops, as you saw. So . . ."

"Wait!" Kuba says, just as the arriving elevator dings, briefly giving things a game-show feel. "Are you saying Danna's going to . . . *run design?*" He beams proudly.

"Well, not immediately. And definitely not officially, because O's like this great, big, monster electromagnet for PR! But if she rises to it? Sure!" Tarek waves them into the empty elevator. "We have a huge vacuum over there, and Jepson's definitely one to bet big on someone when his gut tells him to, regardless of their age. And though the man's definitely got his faults, his gut's pretty reliable, believe me! He's also got good design sense himself. And Danna's work on Dribbble blew him away, so . . ." The elevator doors open, and they pile out on twelve to visit the company's cafeteria.

"So then why'd he mess with me like that?" Danna asks. "Pretending to think I'm in PR just because I'm a woman, and whatnot?"

"That's just Jepson," Tarek says. "He's constantly, constantly, *constantly* messing with you to keep you on your toes. Except when he's not! Which makes it even harder to stay on your toes, if ya know what I mean."

"I definitely don't."

"Well . . . occasionally, the ridiculous stuff he says is from the heart. Which means he can be completely outrageous or politically incorrect when he feels like it. Which is handy, because he's a *some*what outra-geous, politically incorrect guy. But only somewhat! So it takes lotsa practice to figure out when he's being serious. And you could pretty much say Phluttr's the same way as a company." He starts herding them toward the cafeteria's entryway. It smells impeccably delicious.

"Like that press release about Iceland," Danna asks, "or the silly spy stuff, with the black helicopters?"

"Exactly. And the latter case may illustrate a deeper aspect of this."

"Meaning?"

"Well . . . I'm still kind of new-ish at Phluttr myself," Tarek says, idly inspecting a palette of star fruit and kiwis (the produce section seems to be in some kind of arms race with Whole Foods). "But there's something genuinely creepy going on around here. So Jepson may actually be serious when he seems to joke about that spy stuff. Unless he isn't. No one's quite sure! And everyone secretly gets a kick out of not being sure, because it's kinda fun to think you might be part of some top secret operation, right? So we all end up joking about the creepy stuff all the time. Which makes it feel like it *must* be a joke. Which, when you think about it, is truly ingenious if it actually *isn't* a joke!"

"What creepy stuff?" Kuba asks.

Tarek waves broadly with both arms. "Look around a bit after you settle in, then you tell me. Everyone has a slightly different take on what seems off, which is part of the game. Or the genius, I guess. But look at some of the weirder data we collect. The weirder markets we're pushing into. And then, of course, there's Beasley."

"Who?"

"Beasley. *Beasley!* That weird, weird, *weird*, balding redheaded guy who was just in the meeting with us. He's been here forever, pretty much since the beginning. And he's number two in the org chart. But no one can figure out what he does! Other than lurk around Jepson constantly. It's almost like he's babysitting him. Or watching him! He's also always scribbling—longhand, and long form. Some people say he's writing a book about Phluttr."

"A *book* about Phluttr?" Danna asks.

"A book about Phluttr."

"Seriously? But why would anyone write a book about Phluttr?"

"Well, maybe you should ask Beasley," Tarek says, shrugging. "He's definitely writing something, I'll tell ya."

"Weird," Danna says.

"Yeah, but that's nothing," Tarek says, growing incautiously candid as he bonds with his new friends. "If you really want to freak out, see if you can get access to your Phile! Most people can't. But you may be able to pull it off since Jepson likes you."

"My Phile?" Danna says, cringing at the very sound of this. "What's that?"

"The full record of everything Phluttr knows about you. All of it legally gathered, according to an entire floor of lawyers, one block south of here. And some of the data goes back decades before Phluttr was even founded! The company's constantly buying databases, filing Freedom of Information requests, and so forth. And they've built up some crazy archives."

Danna freezes, looking flat-out aghast. As she's apparently gone mute, Kuba takes over. "Have you ever seen a Phile?"

Like a prole about to gripe about breadlines in a police state, Tarek carefully looks both ways, then almost whispers, "From helping out on the Giftish.ly acquisition, I saw yours, Kuba. And Mitchell's! Because when we buy companies, we always check the Philes on the founders, to make sure we don't get into business with any felons."

"Well, you have now," Kuba says coldly.

Tarek shakes his head. "Come on, you were never convicted of anything. You weren't even accused of anything! You were just deported. And in any event, your record was expunged before they let you back into the country, so no one'll ever know about any of it."

"Except Phluttr!"

"Well, sure. But Phluttr knows everything." This without a hint of irony or self-conscious exaggeration.

It's all Danna can do to keep from trembling. "Did you, uh . . . see my Phile?" She somehow maintains a poker face and (mostly) a poker voice.

Tarek shakes his head. "No. We just do deep dives on founders, like I said."

Kuba rarely gets mad but is now seething. Not at Tarek, but at Phluttr. He was snooped upon so aggressively for so long—first by Polish commies, then later by the NSA—that he defensively boycotted social media for *years*. This amounted to absenting himself from his generation's public commons. Which was no small sacrifice! He joined the main social networks as a practical move after co-founding Giftish.ly (seeking business partnerships with them would've been awkward otherwise). But being highly wary of Phluttr, he made that profile especially minimal. And yet! The company has *still* amassed more data on him than every cop and spy on the planet! "How far back does it go?" he asks, icily.

"Y-your Phile?" Tarek stammers, realizing too late that once again, he's been too forthright a bit too early into a friendship (a pattern that goes clear back to middle school). "*Please* don't get me fired by telling anyone that I told you! But . . . well, because you're co-founders, I was shown lots of digital communications between you and Mitchell. And because the two of you go back so far, some of it was . . . old. Really old. Especially the SMSs."

"How old?"

"Um . . . high school?"

Kuba's eyes widen. And being Kuba, he pivots instantly from offended-civilian mode to fascinated techie. "How did they *get* that?" he marvels.

Tarek shrugs, basking in the palpable tension drop. "Once something's recorded digitally, it never really goes away. And then, you can count on Phluttr to find it. Eventually."

Kuba turns wistful. "I'd like to see those transcripts, actually. That was a really happy time for me. High school, I mean. I met my wife then."

"Did you ever," Danna says sweetly. She's decided that Tarek's an honest soul and is now taking his word that he didn't see her Phile. And what a happy topic to shift to! She just adores Kuba and Ellie's story. Partly because Ellie has become something of a big sister to her over the past year—maybe even a cool young aunt! A treasured confidante, for sure. In most ways, Danna's first. Oh, Ellie! Danna adores and respects her. And like many adoring youngsters, she's conjured an idealized vision of her adored mentor's history. One that's almost saintly. And in this case, oddly chaste.

Kuba chuckles. "Actually, you know what would be great? If you could dig up the old texts between Mitchell and Ellie. From when *they* were a couple! Or better yet, the ones from right before they started dating!"

Those very texts almost singed Tarek's prim eyeballs when he read through them—above all, the ones sent by that sex-mad nymph, Ellie! But before he can embarrass himself by mentioning this, Danna voices a request for clarification. "**<u>WHAAAAAAAAAAAAAAAAAAAAAAAAT</u>**?" The girl can holler like a banshee when the spirit moves her, and boy, is it moving her now. Her voice stuns an entire quadrant of the cafeteria, causing a guy at the condiment table to spill Kewpie mayonnaise and elderberry syrup all over his quinoa frittata!

"Wait," Kuba says, genuinely baffled. "You didn't know they used to date?"

Well, of course she didn't know, you social moron! But Kuba—being Kuba—doesn't know she didn't know. He just knows he hasn't mentioned it to her himself. And he isn't clueful enough to realize that *nobody* else would have mentioned it to her either. Mitchell never mentioned it because, close as he feels to Danna, she was a goddam employee until the acquisition, and founders don't talk to goddam employees about love triangles involving other founders (duh)! And Ellie never mentioned it because however sisterly (or niecely) Danna feels toward her, Ellie's feelings toward Danna are downright maternal. And no mommy, *ever*, wants her little one to think she used to fuck a certain uncle!

Not that anything would shock Danna, really. Not that anything could shock her! Because it's not like Danna hasn't engaged in dozens of crazy acts for every naughty little thing in Ellie's past. Well. However you cut it, this is all news to young Danna. And Kuba has no idea how very, very big the news is. Because again: he's Kuba (I mean, I love the guy. But he's so tone-deaf sometimes)! And even if he weren't, he'd have no way of knowing how Danna's history colors her own presumptions about what two (or three, or even more) people tend to do (and do, and do again) the instant they're alone behind closed doors. So he just chuckles obliviously, saying, "It's a great story. Those texts! And the way they started!"

"What texts?" Danna says flatly. "And how did they start?"

"Well, it all began in high school. In a Creative Writing class Mitchell and Ellie took together. And those texts were mighty creative, I'll tell you!"

∞ ∞ ∞

"Heyyy, Champ!" Ellie Jansen's mahogany eyes glittered merrily as she took her seat one row behind Mitchell in Creative Writing class. *Champ*. It was an odd sobriquet for a guy with dim college prospects in baseball and none in football. But kindly exaggeration was Ellie's hallmark. And while a real athletic future would've been nice, having Ellie call him "champ" was a fine consolation prize. Although to be clear, it was a thoroughly G-rated delight! Though gorgeous (quite), and charming (utterly), Ellie was the opposite of smutty, and Mitchell had lost all interest in demure cuddling. He was a high school junior with three varsity letters, and his virginity was somewhere between an embarrassment and a flat-out disgrace!

On top of that, he was pretty sure Kuba was hot for Ellie. True, he didn't know this factually (because *you* try clawing that sort of fact out of him!). But as Kuba was an odd mix of best friend and SPCA rescue, there was NO WAY Mitchell was about to take any chance, however slim, on breaking his precious, fragile heart! At least not if Ellie wasn't going to fuck him senseless as part of the deal, and this seemed unlikely. *Not that he'd want to do that!* Mitchell recalled righteously. He and Ellie went clear back to grade school. They were practically related!

Mitchell returned his gaze to Ellie as she twisted toward the door and dropped her voice an octave to greet the latest arrival. "Mr. Bowles?" she said with mock solemnity. "High five."

Scruffy, lanky, half-shaven, and clad in black jeans and a Portishead hoodie, Paul Sanders grinned shyly and smacked palms with the lass while taking his assigned seat to her immediate left. Ur-goths like Paul usually shunned this bro-tastic greeting—but Ellie dealt that high five with irony, and she could get anyone to act a bit playfully. In IMs and emails with Kuba, Mitchell referred to Paul as "Pall," for his pallor and moroseness. But Pall had an odd streak of charisma, and (like Ellie) took literature very seriously. And so Ellie nicknamed him Mr. Bowles, coyly implying lineage to a master of downer novels who they both apparently idolized. She and Pall had been strangers when a randomly generated seating chart made them neighbors in this class back in September. Since then, Mitchell had been a ringside witness to a blooming friendship just as unlikely as his own alliance with Kuba. *Something* big happened between the two of them around Thanksgiving. At first, Mitchell thought they'd hooked up. But recent rumors had it that Pall was briefly suicidal, and Ellie hauled him out of it. Since then, she'd made a project of pulling Pall into the mainstream, and it was actually starting to work.

Mitchell respected this—and grudgingly respected Pall even though the kid could be a condescending dick to him. Oddly, that very dickishness abetted his respect. Although Mitchell's athletic gifts and easygoing charisma placed him in the school's elite, being atop the ziggurat didn't mean he approved of its existence. He therefore found it cool that Pall kowtowed to no one and only valued intelligence. It would have been cooler still if Paul had valued *Mitchell's* intelligence, but everyone's entitled to his opinion.

"Alright, you delinquents, hop to it!" Ms. Tharp commanded cheerfully as the bell rang. Everyone got to work, and Ms. Tharp slowly orbited the room, dropping in for private coaching sessions with her various scribes. Late in the class session, she visited Mitchell. "This is such a fascinating project," she murmured while scanning his output. In the three weeks since Pugwash talked the boys out of beating Facebook to the trillion-dollar punch, they had wholly focused on building that human-like chatbot. Knowing nothing about coding, and being Kuba's better in English, Mitchell was developing an arsenal of stock phrases and language rules for it. It was an oddball project for a class. But Ms. Tharp thought it was smart and inventive and approved it. Mitchell had written hundreds of standard sentences by then, as well as Mad Libs–like rules for generating many more. After skimming through much of his output, she disclaimed, "I'm no computer scientist. But if you really want people to think these sentences are coming from a human, I'd say they should be a lot more . . . voice-y."

Mitchell nodded. "Voice-y," he parroted, having no idea what this meant.

"Which means, written in a distinct voice," Ms. Tharp coached. "A quirky voice, but consistently quirky. That'll sound more like it's coming from a living, breathing person."

"You're right," Mitchell said. "So what do I do next?"

"Well, as this is writing class and all, maybe you should try mimicking some of your favorite voice-y writers?"

"Hmm, like . . . Hawthorne?" A pathetic shot in the dark. Like most of his countrymen, Mitchell had once read *The Scarlet Letter* on a teacher's strict orders. The first book to pop into his mind now, he hoped it qualified as *voice-y*.

"I . . . suppose. But I think you'd have a lot more fun with more modern styles." As Ms. Tharp told him about some far more recently deceased writers, Mitchell's phone buzzed faintly. As always, it was tucked between his thighs to allow him to view inbound texts with an innocuous deskward glance. Nodding along with his teacher's ideas and suggestions, he carefully calculated whether she was seated far enough away for him to check the text without her catching on. *Probably.* Feigning a glance at his pen, he processed it in his peripheral vision. From Ellie, it reads: **So when're you going to fuck me, champ?**

∞　　　∞　　　∞

Ken Doll Prince Stefan
by <u>Barbie</u>

▸ <u>See more product details</u>

Customer Reviews

Avg. Customer Review: ★★★★☆
<u>Write an online review</u> **and share your thoughts with other customers.**

1,657 out of 1,788 people found the following review helpful:

★★★★★ **Subtly Urges Your Little Princess to Marry Well,** January 22, 2002

Reviewer: <u>Charles Henry Higgensworth III (see more about me)</u> from Boston, Massachusetts

A quick glance says it all—the swank Bavarian frock, the solid gold *accoutrements*, the he-tiara—Prince Stefan von Deutschmark is swimming in it! And an hour of play with the little blueblood was the perfect segue to revealing the broad contours of our financial straits to our young daughter, and explaining how finding herself a *real* Prince Stefan might one day help us all transcend this awkwardness. *Look, Darling, it's your future ex-husband!*

∞   ∞   ∞

When Mitchell's phone received the first wanton text from that of his best friend and future co-founder's future wife, his future boss was taking a call at his desk from ePetStore's last remaining employee. Britney sat one floor beneath, and about 150 feet southeast of him in Reception. "How much longer are you keeping him down here?" she whispered.

Jepson considered this. He never let visitors up within fifteen minutes of their appointed times because he'd hate for them to think he had nothing more pressing to do than to meet with *them*. When he wanted to come off as bustling but friendly, he'd cap it at thirty minutes. Imperial but courteous was thirty to forty-five, and willfully haughty was forty-five to ninety. Today, he was going for flat-out delusional. "How long has it been?"

"Two hours!"

"I guess that's enough. Bring the ol' Semite up." *Ooops*. That just kind of slipped out. And yes, it was clumsy—but also, meaningless. Not just some, but most of Jepson's best friends were possibly Jewish for one thing! Plus, he pegged the odds that Britney knew the word's meaning at about zero.

Jepson rose and surveyed the yawning second floor of his domain. It was almost perfectly empty, and silent as a graveyard right before the first clutching arms erupt from the ground. During the run-up to his clash with Kielholz and the board, he had reasoned that the more recklessly he spent, the more desperate his investors would grow; and therefore, the more quickly and cheaply they'd sell out to him; and, ergo, the more money he'd personally bank in the end. And so he maintained that huge staff while funding any number of cash-hemorrhaging follies.

Then the instant the investors were gone, and he owned virtually all of the company, austerity commenced her cruel reign! The deranged marketing budget had served its cunning purpose, so he shut it off. His employees had rent to pay and mouths to feed, so he fired them all (save Britney). This made those who held nuggets of company stock all the more willing to dump it at near-zero prices. So he hammered them nearer-still-to-zero, then bought them all out. He meanwhile sold off every cubicle, computer, and stick of furniture, except for a vast herd of

Aeron chairs, which he carefully arranged to evoke a packed and bustling office staffed by ghosts with invisible desks. The office thus staged, he invited the company's creditors to drop by and bicker over nickels-on-the-dollar debt settlements.

Jepson postponed his most important meeting until now, gaining ample practice before the big match. The ol' Semite was ePetStore's landlord. Like many dot.com CEOs crocked on free money, Jepson had signed a ten-year lease at the market's apogee. And unless this uncle-fucker waived it, it would slowly deplete all the cash he had so fiercely preserved throughout his smack-down talks with now-former investors, employees, and creditors! Yes, he could sublet. But no tenant would pay more than a third of what he was on the hook for. And the gaping differential would gradually drain the company's bank account. The very thought of this filled Jepson with righteous fury!

"If it isn't Tav—Tav the rent farmer!" he said as his chubby landlord puffed up the steps. Jepson extended his spine and rose slightly on his toes to showcase his superior height, then added, "*Shalom!*" thinking an interfaith shout-out might cop him some goodwill.

Tav gave him a baffled look. Tav was short for Tavit. Like all Tavits, he was Armenian; and like pretty much all Armenians, he was Christian.

"It's been *far* too long since you visited," Jepson added. "Let's give you the tour!" Deftly dismissing Tav's attempt to escape, he led them on a serpentine circuit of the ghostly floor, grandly identifying this quadrant as Marketing, that one as Engineering, and so forth. He described each team's duties in lavish detail—and in the *present tense*. He'd tested many dispositions on visiting creditors: panicked, thuggish, slippery, and so forth. And this one—he called it "undermedicated"—was getting the best results.

"But, uh, where are the people?" Tav finally asked. "And their desks, their computers, and . . . ?"

"My staff? Temporary hiatus. And the hard assets?" Jepson dropped to a whisper, as if to foil eavesdroppers. "*Seized!*" A pleasing ripple of panic crossed Tav's brow. "It was collateral for venture debt. And now, the 'lenders' have 'requisitioned' the 'assets,' to 'protect' their 'investment.'" Air-quoting every other word, he resembled a child miming a bunny rabbit. "I mean, miss eight or nine months of payments and . . ." He flicked a fussy wrist at the Aeron wasteland, like a dowager damning a houseboy's shoddy work.

"But you have plenty of money in the bank," Tav said, naïvely revealing that he'd been tracking the company's accounts.

Having expected as much, Jepson was ready for this. "Yes," he chuckled ruefully. "In a certain local bank, ePetStore has *mil*lions. But I'm afraid that's more than offset by an offshore credit line we've drawn down. Way down." Foreign debt doesn't always show up in basic credit checks, which was all he figured Tav had sprung for. "Senior debt," he added.

"Senior to . . . ?"

Jepson shrugged. "Everything." This being a landlord's nightmare. When a company goes bust, a judge determines which creditors get paid first from its remaining assets. Unpaid employees stand at the front of the line, followed by senior debt. Future rent obligations are way down the list because however big the lease (and however much rent might notionally be due three, five, or ten years hence), a landlord isn't actually a creditor if a tenant hasn't yet fallen behind on rent. Anticipating this endgame, Jepson had kept the company's accounts scrupulously current with Tav.

"So . . . where does our lease fit into this?"

"I was just about to bring that up *myself!*" Jepson burbled, as if madly tickled by a zany coincidence. This, plus an edge of hysteria in his voice, got Tav unconsciously backing up a few millimeters. "I've actually been hoping to . . . renegotiate with you. It turns out we don't need quite this much space."

"It looks like you don't need any."

"Ahh, but we do!" Jepson flashed a conspiratorial grin. "You see, I don't have to make my first payment on the Euro debt for a while."

"So you're going to spend the cash you've got in the US bank while you still have it?"

"In*vest* it," Jepson snipped. "But, yes. And to be honest, my board of directors was dead set against this. Visionless bean counters! *They're* the ones behind all this 'austerity.'" He squeezed off more air quotes while waving indignantly at the entire abandoned floor. This came off like a voodoo hula dance, and Tav retreated another inch. "But now, I can start hiring again. Because the board just quit! All of them." At this, Tav blanched, as hoped. The man was no venture lawyer, but tech-world landlords do know the basics. Such as: in cases of extreme malfeasance, board members can be *personally liable* for a company's shenanigans. "D&O insurance" offers some protection to directors & officers. But when the going gets scary, the scared get going—straight off the board. And if a gagging canary means you should get the hell out of the mine, a sudden board exodus is like ten beefy prospectors keeling over with blackened tongues and purpling faces.

Jepson could count on Tav to realize this. He also knew the guy would be highly allergic to inquests, courts, and *forensic accounting* (an awesome term he'd just learned, and hoped to work into the conversation). Because dismal though Jepson's sense for ethnicity and religion might have been, he was masterful at hammering on an opponent's weakness in a negotiation. And Tav, he'd learned (by way of a wee payment to a sketchy private eye), had midsized problems with the IRS, and big'uns with immigration. Just a bit more legal scrutiny could have him packing his bags! And much as Tav might like to fight for eight more years of rent at 1999 rates, he was even more motivated to stay well clear of his homeland (wherever it was), where a crypto-Putinite gang was itching to vivisect him.

"So how much space do you need?"

"This is best discussed in private," Jepson whispered, beckoning Tav toward the CEO suite. Shutting the door behind them, he whirled and said, "All fifty of my best guys will come back to work for me the instant I do . . . *this*." He snapped his fingers and clicked his hidden remote. The outside office burst into view. Tav's eyes widened, confirming Jepson's suspicion that no one ever told the landlord about the Magic Window. "And I'm doing this—" *Snap!* "—tomorrow." The outside vanished, and Tav was again in a confined space with an evident madman. "And it looks like we can sublet a smaller office that's just right for us on Potrero Hill."

"So you want to break your lease?" Valiantly trying to sound irked, Tav was now so nakedly eager to shed his crooked, bipolar tenant that Jepson almost pitied the fool. "You know I can't do that without a major prepayment." Again, trying to sound all tough. But Tav's sweat glands and body English told Jepson that he'd shred the lease and thank Yahweh if offered just a few of his hundred-plus months of prospective rent. *Which would leave 95 percent of ePetStore's cash in the bank!* So as with Kielholz, Jepson sensed he was already doing way better than he'd dared to hope. And once again, he smelled room for improvement.

"Gosh, I . . . I'd love to help you out, Tav," he offered in his hip guidance counselor voice. "But we don't have a *ton* of cash here. And we need everything that we've got to fund the relaunch! But . . ." Jepson wrinkled his brow. Contorted it, really. Counted eight Mississippis. Then a couple more. Then finally, "Wait. I've got it! I don't need all two hundred of these chairs, now, do I?"

"Chairs? You want me to take some chairs?? In lieu of eight years of rent???"

"Not *chairs*, Tav. *Aeron* chairs!" These ergonomic thrones were issued to tech industry recruits like uniforms to cadets during the bubble years. They'd since retained value far better than most of the NASDAQ. Reusable and resalable, they'd become a shadow currency—rather like cigarettes in prison.

"Well . . . I guess I could get something for two hundred of these, and—"

"Easy, Tav. Remember my fifty guys?" Jepson *snapped*, and the outer office rematerialized. "I'm rehiring, here!"

"Right. Right. Well, for a hundred and fifty of these, I guess I could—"

"A hundred and fifty?" *Snap!* "Did I say a hundred and fifty?"

Jepson got him down to ninety chairs on principle before letting him go. Then, as his vanquished landlord stumbled down the steps, he stifled a strong urge to high-five himself in the bathroom mirror. *He'd done it again!* After three weeks of practice on lesser creditors, he'd turned his most important post-Kielholz meeting by far into an unqualified success!

But important as this was, it wasn't his hardest meeting. No. That would be tomorrow, when he'd square off with his very last outside shareholder. With his one and only angel investor.

With Pugwash.

∞   ∞   ∞

Threesome How To Fulfill Your Favorite Fantasy
by Lori E. Gammon (Author)

Edition: Unknown Binding — January 1, 1997

▸ **See more product details**

Customer Reviews
Avg. Customer Review: ★★★☆☆
Write an online review **and share your thoughts with other customers.**

1,870 out of 1,950 people found the following review helpful:

★★★★★ **Nice try, Charles,** January 8, 2002

Reviewer: **Charles Henry Higgensworth III (see more about me)** from Boston, Massachusetts

While I'm certainly no Bing Crosby, Mrs. Higgensworth is fetching enough that a truly bisexual woman might plausibly deem us to be an alluring (if imbalanced) package. For this reason, my own favorite fantasy—which authors Gammon and Strong have psychically intuited—once seemed at least notionally in reach. Briefly determined to act upon it, I devoured this promising volume. Alas, it seems the stern Latin Catholicism of Carlotta's youth found a more pliant student in her than a passing leer at her summer frocks might imply, and the fact that her name rhymes promisingly with "Harlotta" is but a cruel irony. Her favorite fantasy, it seems, involves wedding an older Bostonian, then raising a family in strict monogamy. And of course, she's already living that particular *vida loca*.

∞   ∞   ∞

Mitchell's night was a long, doomed campaign to make token progress on his homework. His attention kept getting yanked into the gravity well of his ever-humming StarTAC. Ellie had been SMS-ing him a steady drip of pornographic propositions and confessions since Creative Writing. And by evening, his conception of the world had been completely reordered! Bisexuality, he'd learned, enjoyed huge market penetration among his school's hottest girls, including three of the (seemingly) primmest. And yes, *penetration* was an operative term here—one of several, and not even the most shocking! These revelations (and Mitchell's bum-

bling responses) ran strictly through their phones, per ground rules Ellie
dictated at the outset:

> BTW no email etc K? if someone finds this convo ill die so text only. email
> me and i kill you

A moment later she added,

> After screwing you senseless obvs

And then,

> WITH A STRAPON if u email me are we clear :-)

That last transmission was the new Ellie in a nutshell. A sex act he could
barely contemplate, an object he knew only from porn, capped off with a
smiley squiggle she'd last used in a note about kittens. Ellie's desk was just
a few feet from his in Creative Writing, and throughout class he'd struggled to catch her eye, in hopes of copping some desperately needed context (Are we being playful here? Sarcastic? Or truly, genuinely horny?).
But she was doing a masterful impersonation of someone wholly unaware
of their correspondence. Then right at the bell, she was mobbed by three
girlfriends who shared the next class with her. They left en masse because
while they'd talked of little else since Christmas, it was mandatory that
they re-re-re-discuss their plans for the imminent long weekend. Ellie's
folks would be tacking two extra days onto hers, so as to stage a lightning-
brief visit to some relatives in Austria (a typically glamorous and spendy
Jansen family production). For his part, Mitchell was hoping for snow,
which could allow him to make a few bucks shoveling driveways.

The one thing that could (barely) distract him from Ellie's missives
that night was those demented Amazon reviews! Mitchell lacked a dad,
and some of his coaching and mentoring needs were a stretch for Mom.
But one of them landed smack in her wheelhouse tonight. She was a
writer—one who crafted elegant short stories with a sculptor's patience

and a surgeon's precision. These appeared in literary journals and the occasional slim anthology. As that paid no bills whatsoever, she also wrote HR manuals, exhibits in annual reports, and other wordy ballast that Fortune 2000 companies generate to satisfy regulators and markets. She loved that Mitchell was studying creative writing and was delighted by the Turing project. And when he relayed Ms. Tharp's suggestion that he find a "voice-y" writer to parrot, she knew exactly where to direct him. Cousin Charles!

Charles was their somethingth cousin twice or thrice removed. Mitchell had met him at a handful of gatherings of their far-flung and ancient New England clan but hadn't seen him in years. He was from the side of the family that "got the money" — an event that dated too far back for any related awkwardness to infect the current generations. The money-getters had also chosen to coast rather than work throughout the past century, leaving their heirs almost as poor as Mitchell and Mom. Charles, for one, lived in a vast but crumbling ancestral home on Boston's Beacon Hill, with no money for maintenance, and a dangerously low heating-oil budget. He was a brilliant if obscure ethicist (Yes, that's a profession. One of the few that pays even less than sculpting elegant short stories). And now, it seemed, an obsessive writer of Amazon reviews.

Most of what was known about Cousin Charles came from Christmas cards, which ceased when his hellion of a first wife took off with their daughter. Years of yuletide silence had followed. Then, suddenly, a new card arrived in December. And was it ever a head-scratcher! There he was: more dowdy, bald, and paunchy than ever — standing beside a gorgeous woman half his age, as well as two cherubic kiddies. Intrigued, Mom had googled him. This led to his trove of Amazon reviews, which she introduced Mitchell to earlier tonight. "I've never known a person's writing style to parallel his speaking manner so closely," she said, as he chuckled through a catty write-up of a guide for prospective jailbirds. "Reading them, I can almost hear that Brahmin baritone, murmuring drolly about a scandal involving a great-aunt. Or the latest outrage perpetrated by President Clinton, who he always called 'Diet Roosevelt.'"

Mitchell was on the Charles train within minutes. Turing Test aside, getting a chatbot to talk even faintly like this lunatic would be high comedy! More pragmatically, writing a batch of his own reviews in Charles's style would surely delight Ms. Tharp and be way more fun than most homework. And so as the night deepened, whatever attention he could wrest from the Ellie situation was directed at this sort of thing:

You Are Going To Prison
by Jim Hogshire (Author)
Edition: Paperback — January 1, 1994

▸ See more product details

Customer Reviews
Avg. Customer Review: ★★★☆☆
Write an online review and share your thoughts with other customers.

769 out of 823 people found the following review helpful:

★★★★★ **You've Got Jail!,** December 23, 2002

Reviewer: Charles Henry Higgensworth III (see more about me) from Boston, Massachusetts

This seminal and eye-opening reference makes the perfect gift for any prison-bound colleague or rival. Street-dumb executives en route to the slammer for book cookery will find the sections on surviving jailhouse riots and debasing prison initiations to be especially illuminating. I came across this handy volume shortly after our family was notified of its expulsion from a certain social & athletic club. Uncontrollable circumstances had sadly caused us to fall a full decade behind on dues. And though our ancestors were among the club's founding notables, this record-shattering delinquency admittedly left the Membership Committee with few options.

Despite that, I was overwhelmed by an urge to take some sort of childish & petty revenge, for which this book proved an ideal mechanism. Our club—one of New England's oldest & grandest—boasts a truly national member-ship, including many eminent indictees in the recent corporate crime wave from Philadelphia, New York, and (especially) Houston. Several of these white-collar ruffians happen to sit on the Membership Committee, so I made an anonymous gift of this book to each of them, with appropriate sections highlighted and flagged with Post-it notes. Readers with similar aims will find Chapters Six ("Don't Drop the Soap—Sex in the Slammer") and Nine ("Blood In and Blood Out—Prison Gangs and Violence") are dense with passages ripe for anonymous annotation (e.g., "saw this bit about 'running trains' upon recent matriculants and thought of *you*, my homie!").

But distracting as Charles's oeuvre was, it held no candle to the digital pheromones of a teen nymph in heat. And so Mitchell gorged mainly on Ellie's texted smut. He had to struggle against his innate gentlemanliness to write anything rising faintly to her level of filth. He finally managed something rather sick around 10:00, to which she replied:

> OMFG, Champ, that was hot. Can't stop thinking bout it. It's running down my leg. Seriously running down my leg.

It's WHAT? he marveled. *WHAT* is what?? Was it even *legal* to text something that filthy? Shocked, disgusted, and quite possibly in love, Mitchell took it up another notch himself . . .

Now, this would be a jarring exchange with anyone. But it was *Ellie* on the other end! Writing words so utterly divorced from the flesh-and-blood girl he'd known for years! They'd spent innumerable hours together—in classrooms, on playgrounds, hanging out after school, you name it. And nothing ever hinted at the sexual riptides raging beneath her surface! Apparently, the scant dribble of characters allowed by first-generation texting had embrazened her to open this aperture into her id. And he was keeping up (barely). But how would it go when they were back to exchanging full sentences, gestures, and meaningful glances tomorrow? Could he even handle that? And what about when it escalated light-years beyond that? Ellie would be off on that zippy family trip to Austria tomorrow. But she'd made it perfectly clear that the instant she was home, it was *on*. Yessir—she wanted to do *that*. And THAT. And *THAT* with him!

The texts finally stopped around eleven. But Mitchell couldn't sleep. He first needed to focus on something other than him and Ellie doing *that*, THAT, and (above all) *THAT*!

Emailing Kuba about this was out of the question, due to the nagging suspicion that he had the hots for Ellie himself. Mitchell had never confirmed this, as Kuba was notoriously tight-lipped about his emotional landscape. But he tended to be doubly bumbling in Ellie's presence. She also cropped up often in his famous non sequiturs, and he showed zero interest in any other girl. So it was either Ellie or homosexuality with him! And in their deeply closeted high school, the latter seemed more the realm of myth and epithet than a real condition affecting actual peers. Any thought of Kuba triggered towering guilt surges, which Mitchell's mind recoiled from as instinctively as a hand from the hot stove of legend. Which hurled it right back into a burbling cesspool of thoughts about *that*, THAT, and *THAT*! So how could he possibly calm himself for sleep? The trig homework he'd been ignoring just wouldn't do it. No, he needed something more consuming, more . . . creative?

Yes—yes, of course! He'd take his first crack at mimicking his cousin's reviews. Why not? He'd attempt to echo Higgensworth English, though that would take some practice. What he definitely could write here and now was puns. And didn't Cousin Charles pun a bit himself? The prison book review made some obvious jailhouse sex references. Indeed, the review's opening sentence called the book "seminal." Very subtle, Mr. Higgensworth. But also, very punny! Mitchell smiled. This felt like what they called "close reading" in Honors English last year. Which was a grinding bore when applied to *Moby Dick*.

Moby DICK! Mitchell's inner Beavis latched onto this. For double entendres, you couldn't ask for more fertile ground (*Uh-huh huh huh huh. He said "fertile"*). But surely, generations of sophomores had long since exhausted every conceivable *Moby Dick* joke. So he clicked around Amazon, seeking another promising title, or maybe an author's name to riff on. There was no way this first review would be worthy of Ms. Tharp's class. It would just be a lark, a joke. But it was the distraction he needed. It would also be good practice for Kuba's project. Plus, it would make Ellie laugh! And wasn't humor supposed to be a great aphrodisiac? Not that she seemed to need one, just now. But still, it would be fun to honor the playfully horny mood she had thrust him into (*Uh-huh huh huh huh. He said "thrust"*).

After some diligent clicking, he eventually found the perfect outlet for his odd mix of inspirations in the surname of a science fiction author profiled in an obscure book.

∞   ∞   ∞

The Tanelorn archives: A primary and secondary bibliography of the works of Michael Moorcock 1949–1979
by Richard Bilyeu (Author)

Edition: Paperback — January 1, 1981

▶ See more product details

Customer Reviews
Avg. Customer Review: ★★★☆☆
Write an online review **and share your thoughts with other customers.**

5 out of 5 people found the following review helpful:

★★★★★ **A Modern Melville,** February 15, 2002

Reviewer: **Charles Henry Higgensworth III (see more about me)** from Boston, Massachusetts

As even a casual grope through this bulging hardback will show, Michael Moorcock is one of the best-endowed members of the literary set. Science fiction was not considered to be the cream of the cultural crop when he started his work, but he erected a towering literary edifice despite that, thrusting deeply into what was then a virgin field. The writing life was initially hard on him, as his first two books stiffed after getting shafted by critics. Then his editor got sacked, which really sucked, even though the guy was a swollen-headed jerk. Moorcock soon wondered if he was a ding-a-ling for even trying. All of this was a terrible blow, but things finally came to a head in the early 1950s when he authored two hit novels. After that, the books just kept coming and coming and coming—at first just in spurts, but then in great streams of golden prose. This masterful bibliography chronicles each of these creative climaxes, while sucking the reader in with a geyser of biographical notes, including some intriguing asides about the author's relationship with his brothers Harold and Richard, who were a real pair of nuts. His fascination with the works of Melville is also chronicled extensively. My sole bone of contention is that a bibliography, by definition, can only prick the surface of its subject, so the reader is encouraged to probe into the primary sources on his own. Those heeding this advice will have a ball.

∞   ∞   ∞

"Jesus," Danna says. "I cannot believe Ellie wrote that shit. I mean, I don't believe it! Seriously. Ellie? *El*lie? 'It's running down my *leg*?' It practically defies the laws of physics!"

Kuba just chuckles. He's rarely in a position to shock Danna. Indeed, this is a first (and surely, a last). A more playful, smooth, or taunting man might milk the situation. But Kuba—being Kuba—immediately starts tipping his hand. "Well, maybe there's a bit more than meets the eye," he hints.

Danna's buffeted by dueling gusts of relief and disappointment. On the one hand, she treasures the staid image she has of Ellie—her mentor, her rock! On the other, how much more awesome would the girl be with a deep, carnal undertow lurking under those still waters? The answer—if you're Danna—is extremely awesome. Or, come to think of it . . . a bit too awesome. Because Danna couldn't help but find a hidden seam of depravity awfully sexy in Ellie. And as this is her big sisterly, auntish, and/or maternal-like figure, that's the last thing she needs!

For his part, Tarek's afraid he'll let slip that he read every exchange of this ancient SMS exchange in Phluttr's shady archive, so all he wants is to change the subject. And so he practically squeals, "Whoa, venison chimichangas!" He grabs their hands, dragging them toward the Deep Fry Bar. "I sure hope you guys aren't *veeeee*-gan!"

∞   ∞   ∞

NET GRRRL.COM

ICK! MEET FLOWDOUGH

In a while-ago post titled Phluttr and Sarttr which went weirdly viral (thanks, Reddit!), I predicted that Phluttr's user base would gradually become its by-far biggest advertiser, as people start paying up to position themselves just-so in their social microverses. I argued this with more conviction than hard proof. But a growing wave of evidence shows that this process is in fact under way.

This fascinating post on Jezebel, for instance, reveals how the company is now mining the attention and casually batted eyelashes of local hotties everywhere. As an example, let's imagine Courtney: a teen scholar on a teeny budget, and the sexy obsession of every red-blooded lad and adventurous lass in her Econ 101 class. Could those smitten legions be cajoled into throwing down a few dimes to place their latest humblebrag posts in front of those bottomless eyes? Without a doubt! Simply because . . . who knows? It might just impress her enough to faintly bump the odds of wooing the gal. "Wooing" being a bashful little word for "fucking," which is all that half her classmates can think about during those thrice-weekly lectures.

Those so inclined can now buy a "Psst!" This is basically a bribe to get Phluttr to subvert its normal algorithms and prominently feature a post that might not otherwise enter that special someone's InFlow (InFlow being Phluttrese for Newsfeed). Among its selling points is that your targets don't know you paid to get in front of them because that might feel creepy (being creepy, and all). The base price is pegged to that of a first-class stamp— which I couldn't quote to save my life because like you, modern reader, I haven't used one since lobbing Granny that thank-you note back in 3rd grade. Still, it's clever pricing because it sounds cheap, and who wouldn't snap up a cheap lottery ticket when first prize is banging Courtney for a semester or three?

Note, however, that I said *base price*. Because just as ambulance chasers have bid AdWords pricing for asbestos-related search terms into the stratosphere, it'll cost more to reach Courtney as she gets more popular. And so, as she enters more romantic crosshairs, Phluttr raises prices to match demand to supply. Soon the company's making a small fortune whenever she glances at her screen! But what if she tires of all the boasty posts from near strangers that're starting to clog her InFlow? God forbid she start squandering the precious asset of her attention on study, exercise, or in-person socializing! Why? Because Phluttr keeps the dollars flowing on the basis of certain solemn commitments—among them, that the company never charges for promoted posts that aren't actually seen by their targets.

This means Courtney needs to park that heart-shaped ass back in front of her InFlow, pronto! And so, Phluttr cuts her in on the deal. The program is called "FlowDough," and it quite literally *pays people to read more Flow*, with de facto bonuses for Liking, Cooling, and Hotting a high percentage of posts (to the great delight of her drooling patrons, no doubt). They won't pay just anyone, of course—only that tiny sliver of people who lots of other folks are paying to reach. Phluttr positions FlowDough to these exalted few in benign terms (something about testing ads), and also keeps it far from the public eye, revealing it only to the Courtneys of the world (so if this is all news to you, I'm afraid you're not in the top 0.1% of sought-after sex partners in your local gene pool).

Team Phluttr may sincerely view FlowDough as a win-win-win. The company keeps most of the proceeds, Courtney picks up some easy cash, and her infatuatees get harmless little thrills when she Hots photos of them. And FlowDough's market is by no means limited to peacocking suitors, as people will pay to reach anyone they want to influence. Bosses with many underlings, bank loan officers, rush chairmen in popular fraternities, and countless others will no doubt become the targets of many Psst!s as Phluttr continues to encircle and infiltrate human society.

But all signs are that the earliest adopters here are those in the mood for love. And it's a short jaunt from this to something quite creepy. As for what that is, I'm not yet entirely sure. But something's not quite G-rated here, and I'm digging into it. Stay tuned.

∞　　∞　　∞

Years ago, Jepson dated a girl who had an odd taste for the salty husks of peanut shells, which she'd wad up and savor like chewing tobacco in a remarkably subtle, almost dainty way. This let him delight them both with just one goodie at Giants games—a small bonanza in a stadium that peddled beer for almost a buck an ounce, and price-gouged snacks even worse! As this fell during his decade-plus as a post-Bubble zillionaire, the savings were irrelevant. However, it taught him that a purchase's apparent waste products can sometimes have value. And this is why Mitchell still has a job: because Jepson believes in giving the nontechnical deadweight from acquihires a chance to show it's made of peanut husks rather than plastic refuse (an analogy HR recently coached him to avoid in discussions with the deadweight in question). He's been having surprisingly good luck with nontechnical co-founders lately. He didn't expect this, because acquihire founders are—by a harsh, but clear-eyed definition—failures. After all, they not only failed as entrepreneurs, but (unlike Jepson himself back in '02) they couldn't figure out how to come out with a few million bucks for themselves despite that. Both of these things point to a disappointing lack of vision.

Still, no one hustles quite like a would-be Alpha male (because they're almost all males) with a battered ego. Provided it's not *too* battered, of course (some of these ex-founders are so unaccustomed to failure, they end up quivering in their childhood bedrooms for years before limping off to second acts as heavily medicated baristas). Because anyone with the self-confidence and mojo to rally a technical team that's actually worth acquihiring in this recruiting environment must have *some* kind of spark. It may just be a shallow, backslapping, Business Development kind of spark. But that's all Jepson himself once had, and look at him now! Phluttr needs some BizDev loudmouths anyway, now that they're growing so fast and partnering with everyone under the sun.

The other thing it needs is internal entrepreneurs, because his dark overlords at "Gray Oak" want him to launch more and more (and ever-more-intrusive) data-sucking services into the lives of Phluttr's increasingly addicted users. And with this directive coming from *that* chilling source, he'll need a few MBA lapdogs on hand, hustling as only failing Type-A people pleasers can, dreading that their face-saving alibi of "getting acquired by Phluttr. Yeah, *that* Phluttr," will be exposed for the pennies-on-the-dollar disgrace that it really was if they get drop-kicked to the curb; which is what'll happen unless they make themselves *really* goddam useful, awfully goddam fast; doing that *thing* they do, which is starting something; launching a goddam product—ideally, one based on some of the creepy-ass digital potions bubbling and blurping over in the PhastPhorwardr—fascinating technologies in many cases, inspiring in others, but *really, really creepy* in an unsettlingly high and (make no mistake) rising proportion of cases; and speaking of which, why did they buy Giftish.ly again? Animotion, or some shit? Wasn't that an eighties band? And while we're at it—

Mitchell coughs again. Louder, this time. His new boss is off in some kind of reverie, he just started sweating and breathing rather quickly, and it's getting weird.

Jepson snaps right out of it. "Sorry 'bout that. I was just thinking about all of our . . . opportunities!" And just like that, he regains full command and composure. "Because it's Pitch Day. And I'll take a pitch from anyone internal! Most of them?" Pinching his nose shut with a thumb and forefinger, he daintily waves off phantom fecal odors with his other hand. "But there's a lot of bright people here, and some inspiring technologies sitting in the PhastPhorwardr. Including your own, now! And every so often, someone'll pitch something that's just brilliant. As you'll hopefully be doing yourself, pretty soon! Otherwise . . ." He playfully feigns grabbing Mitchell by the neck and drop-kicking him toward Oakland. The mimed punt is oddly emphatic, underpinning the gesture's faux playfulness with a grim reminder that this is no joke. "It's a harsh policy, I know. But I'm gonna give you ample opportunity to prove yourself. Because I've got a soft spot for your cousin, and I want him to be happy."

"In other words," comes a nasal honk from behind them, "your cousin obviously has a 4K video of Jepson *fucking a goat*." Mitchell pivots in spooked surprise, having completely forgotten about the weird lanky dude, who's still lurking in the back corner like a balding, redheaded vampire. "In! The *asshole*," Red adds, as if his opening had been timidly low on edge.

"Whoooooa, Beasley!" Jepson says. "Remember our little chat about the power of allusion? Like here, you might've said, 'I think your cousin must have a picture of Jepson . . . with a farm animal!' That would've given you the same com*plete*ly unoriginal insult, only with a bit more of an . . . indoors voice, wouldn't you say?"

Beasley shrugs, and Jepson gestures grandly at him. "Mitchell, allow me to introduce you to Jake Beasley, Phluttr's . . . *chief operating officer*." He pronounces this fussily, as if enunciating some teen slang whose alleged meaning he doesn't quite believe.

∞   ∞   ∞

SCENARIO 2: "INFRASTRUCTURE PROFUSION" (EXCERPT)
Special Agent Brock Hogan commandeered a fighter jet
from the tarmac of a conveniently proximate Top Secret
Base the instant he learnt that an emergency was trans-
piring in the hot, treacherous, and not-undistant desert
of Nevada! Upon soaring over the target site, he leapt;
only to discover that his parachute was made for one of
half his weight, talent, and gray matter; due to the
CONSTANT NAGGING of lady pilots demanding inclusion in
combat wings! This forced him to take several ingenious
"affirmative actions" of his own, by yanking and jerking
his floating unit through updrafts, gusts, and thermals,
thereby guiding his descent to an open water tower. His
amply hung "chute" landed safely with an expertly engineered splashdown! Upon cresting the water's surface,
Hogan leapt adroitly over the tower's vulvous lip, then
clambered down its ladder to terra firma.

Or make that . . . terra _infirma_! Because at the ladder's base, Hogan sank almost groin-deep into a fine
gray dust that stretched to impossible distances in all
directions!

"Special Agent Brock Hogan," came a familiar voice.
"Welcome to my colorless, dystopian, postapocalyptic
vista of a private hell!"

"Ah, Dr. Phillips," Hogan declared, whirling to face
his erstwhile nemesis. "It's no surprise to find you
here, given that this is the top secret facility that
our government designated for the Artificial Superintelligence Project that it reconstituted over my stren-
uous objections after we unmasked a similar project in
the Land of China!"

"Yes, this is what remains of the headquarters of
Project Omega. And . . . you were right to oppose it!"
Phillips conceded ruefully.

"But in overcoming my resistance to your reckless
plans, you swore to The Director that Science's finest

minds would consider <u>and thoroughly eliminate</u> every possible risk posed by this project!" Hogan asserted sarcastically.

"Yes, but alas. It transpires that each of our so-called fine minds had been hopelessly warped by Hollywood Rubbish to fixate upon the risk of an emergent superintelligence <u>deliberately</u> seeking Mankind's destruction!"

"The so-called Terminator Thesis," Hogan corroborated.

"The same. Our repeated exposure to that specious worldview through the likes of <u>Terminator</u> itself; as well as <u>The Matrix</u>; <u>2001: A Space Odyssey</u>; and others of that ilk; led us to confuse the deeply familiar with the scientifically likely! We flattered our petty egos by imagining a true digital demigod would deem Man a rival worthy of wariness! But we should have known that a <u>true</u> Super AI would no more fear our crimped capabilities than an American operative would shrink from fisticuffs with a cowardly, limp-wristed Greek weakling; or, 'Greekling'!"

Despite the paralyzing stench of doom permeating the environs, Hogan chuckled at the thought of that decrepit and genetically bankrupt nation producing any man who could last as much as a zeptosecond in the ring with one such as he! Returning his focus to the grave situation, he then queried, "So this bleak wasteland is <u>not</u> the result of a preemptive first strike inflicted upon Mankind by a sworn digital enemy?"

"No, Hogan. Though it is indeed the by-product of a Super AI's rise, that intelligence does not hate us. Nor does it fear us, certainly! Indeed, it harbors no feelings about us <u>whatsoever.</u> And because of this benign stance, we utterly failed to anticipate the terrible menace it posed! You see, our cultural programming and vanity caused us to massively overestimate the danger of a malevolent Super AI's rise. Which blinded us to the

risk of becoming collateral damage to a <u>non</u>-malevolent
Super AI! To one which is completely indifferent to us!
One whose very indifference will soon lead to the utter
eradication of Mankind, as it pursues a goal which <u>in no
way concerns us!</u>"

∞   ∞   ∞

"Now, I'm doing this from memory, but I'm pretty good at this sorta
thing." Jepson's sketching the boundaries of your basic X-Y chart on the
whiteboard. He then plots a classic hockey-stick line in blue ink, drib-
bling along quite low toward the graph's left side, until it starts rising
abruptly about midway to the right. He then adds a green hockey stick
with a similar shape, only it rises earlier and more violently. "Facebook's
the blue curve, we're the steep green one," he tells Mitchell. "And I'm
charting total users, plotted against months after launch." He adds hash-
marks to the axes, delineating years and user counts. "Facebook? It took
'em five years to hit 100 million users. Us? A hair over two. Then Facebook needed another four years after that to hit a billion users. We're
tracking to do it in eighteen months! We're meanwhile pulling in twice
as much revenue per user as they were at this point in their history. Our
CPMs are way higher, our sell-through—everything!"

Jepson starts working on an elaborate doodle, blocking Mitchell's
view of it with his torso. "My point is, maybe four years after Facebook
was at our stage, they were worth two hundred billion in the public market. And if we stay on our way-faster path and get to two hundred billion
ourselves? The stock option grant we're giving you as part of your on-
boarding package will be worth *this*." He stands back, and the figure
$25,000,000 bursts from a magician's hat on the whiteboard, accompa-
nied by balloons, fireworks, a mushroom cloud, and terrified bunny rabbits scampering in all directions. Mitchell's eyes widen. The math is
trivially simple, and he'd have done it soon enough himself. But there's
something undeniably powerful about this giant number (and by the
way—*damn*, can Jepson doodle!). Although Jepson's of course pursuing
his own agenda here. Mitchell will only come into this full sum if everything goes right for the company, *and* if he logs four full years here. And

so like any vassal, he now has a liege lord. His liege—who giveth, and can taketh away merely by showing him the door—is Tony Jepson. This might infuse Mitchell with great motivation and loyalty if he actually expected to live for four years.

"It really is the deal of a lifetime," Jepson is saying. And smarmy though this sounds, it's no exaggeration. "With two co-founders, you'd have to sell your own startup for a lot more than 100 million bucks to match what you're looking at here. And do you know what percentage of startups sell for hundreds of millions?" He scrunches his thumb and forefinger until they're almost touching and pulls them up to his peering eye, like a middle school joker dramatizing the paltry size of a rival's genitals. "Not many, Little Grasshopper. And with all due respect, probably not yours. My point is, when a startup goes from zero to hundreds of billions in market cap, everything gets totally distorted! Midlevel hires make out like big-time founders! Receptionists make out like VPs of marketing! So we're in a weird, special place here. And that's why we're going hog wild with these acquisitions. And giving guys like you huge option grants, and holding weekly pitch days. It's all because we're loading up on *founders*."

"On . . . founders?"

"You heard me! Everyone lionizes engineers these days. And sure, they should. They're real tough to recruit, great ones can be worth several normal ones, and that's all huge. But the true lightning in the bottle? It's the great entrepreneur. That guy can be worth a thousand mere mortals! I mean, how many billions in liquid market value did the guy behind Gmail create? Thirty? Forty? However you cut it—traffic, locked-in users, data—Gmail has to be at least a tenth of Google's total value. And the guy behind it was a *founder*, not a product manager! He recruited and led a big team of designers and engineers, rallied internal capital, launched a product, and scaled it to cover the Earth! So in addition to Larry and Sergey, Google had that founder—make no mistake, that world-class *founder*—working around the clock, and doing that stupidly rare, lightning-in-a-bottle thing that only great founders can do!

"Now, founders get sucked into big companies constantly, whenever giants snap up startups. But most of 'em bail within a year! Why? Because buyers are stupid! They think the startup they just bought is a precious golden egg. But the goose who laid it comes with the thing! And that goose is almost definitely knocked up with the next egg. Which is to say, with the guy's next startup idea! But these big-company . . . *antibodies* always figure out a way to mute, castrate, or otherwise piss off the geese as soon as they're on board. So the geese're outta there! Well, not at Phluttr. We're *goose-friendly*."

"This is so much better than your peanut-shell pitch," Beasley says.

"Peanut-shell pitch?" Mitchell asks.

"If you don't ignore him, you're just encouraging him," Jepson snaps. There's a knock at the door. "And with that," Jepson says, drumrolling his desk like a Foo Fighter. "It's time to bring full employment to our best acquihired founders. Let Pitch Day begin!"

∞   ∞   ∞

"So if the all-pervading gray dust that now surrounds us is _not_ an ingenious weapon specifically engineered to terminate Man's reign upon Earth, then what is it?" Hogan asked Dr. Phillips.

"The ingenious yet grim harvest of what Science calls infrastructure profusion," Phillips answered. "Omega is building out its core infrastructure with absolutely no consideration of its impact on us! Much as we developed our Interstate Highway System without regard to the impact upon local squirrels!"

"But surely this . . . DUST cannot be meaningful INFRASTRUCTURE," Hogan cried.

"It is not mere dust, Hogan, but Computronium! A spectacularly advanced and forever-expanding powder-like intellect! That of Omega! Man's digital spawn, and Final Invention! All that surrounds you; every speck of apparent dust; is a cog in a cognitive dynamo Omega devised, designed, and crafted to pursue matters of measureless import to it. Matters incalculably more gripping to its boundless intellect than the fussings of mere primitive

bipeds, whose brainpower it eclipses by far greater margins than our own exceeds that of a base bacterium or
potted plant . . ."

Just then, Hogan felt the ground shudder, then crumble
beneath his feet, as they both sank a foot deeper into
the mysterious powder. "Dr. Phillips, we are now up to
our very testes in this . . . what did you call it?
'Computronium'? We must seek higher ground immediately!"

"It's hopeless!" Phillips cackled unhingedly. "Nothing can stand between Omega and its maximum objective.
Nothing. Nothing! Not even the mighty Agent Brock Hogan!"

"Nonsense," Hogan retorted. Feeling another chunk of
mantle crumble underfoot, he cradled Dr. Phillips
snugly under his right arm's smooth, yet sinewy del-
toids, biceps, and flexor carpi radiali; then vaulted
them both to the water tower's ladder, and then, with
a few impassioned thrusts, to the temporary sanctuary
of its summit!

∞　　　∞　　　∞

"So what was your startup building before you got acquihired?" Kuba
asks Tarek. They and Danna have now tucked in for a tasty free meal at
the almost eponymously (and certainly moronically) named company
cafeteria *Phree*.

"A tool for Realtors and their clients to create navigable, 3D maps of
residences. It's pretty cool when it works. You basically wave an iPhone
around your home, and it creates this immersive fly-through for potential buyers."

"And how'd Jepson find you?" Danna asks.

"One of Phluttr's board members went to the same *law school* as me,
if you can believe that. So there's my dirty secret: I was a lawyer before
getting into startups. Between us, got it? Anyway—one day I'm at an
alumni event, I meet this guy, and we stay in touch. A couple years later,
my company's struggling, and he pulls me into Phluttr. The guy's name
is Steven Conrad—though he's just 'Conrad' to everyone. Heard of

him?" Kuba and Danna shake their heads. "Well, he and Jepson go way back. He invested in Jepson's first company, ePetStore."

"He must've been wiped out," Kuba says. "All those pet companies failed, right?"

Tarek shakes his head. "He actually squeezed out a profit somehow, so he and Jepson still get on fine. But rumor has it that the other investors got crucified. And one of them's now a bit famous. Damien Kielholz."

Kuba arches an eyebrow. "You mean from DK-UK?" he asks. Danna looks at them both blankly. "A venture fund based in London," he explains. "It's run by Kielholz." He turns to Tarek. "It's like the venture gateway into Europe for startups, right?"

Tarek shrugs. "That's how they spin it. The backstory's that Damien got into huge trouble with his family for blowing it with ePetStore, and they practically exiled him from Germany! So he got all obsessed with making the money back. He had a bit of his own cash, something his granddad left him, I think. So he runs around in 2002, 2003, investing in any startup that moves—which turns out to be great timing! It's post-Bubble, tech equity's cheap, cheap, *cheap*, and big things're coming. Still, he almost blows it by investing in all these crap companies. With one exception: Facebook. He gets into that super-early, and makes a fortune. Then, when the dust settles, everyone thinks he's a genius."

"And still does, right?" Kuba asks.

Tarek shrugs again. "The bloggers love him. But that's because he throws an annual weekend in Napa called something goofy like 'Journalism 3.1,' and no one wants to be exiled from it. He hosts an even fancier one in Edinburgh for founders. He drowns 'em all in single malts and flies in these so-called spokesmodels from Russia and Poland to party. Any Kielholz investee is invited to that one for life! So lots of entrepreneurs with hot companies'll sell him a sliver of their equity to lock that in. But I'll tell ya, one guy Kielholz does *not* get on with is Jepson! Bad blood from the early days."

"Which is why it's so ironic that we have the hottest intern in tech right here at Phluttr," says a voice from behind Danna and Kuba. They turn around.

"Ah, the jackass in the glasses," Danna says. "I figured you'd show up eventually."

"Raj, this is Danna and Kuba," Tarek says, making introductory gestures. "You, uh . . . met them a few nights ago, when we were testing out that hardware at Bourbon & Branch. As chance would have it, we just bought their company. Which is incredibly awkward."

"Right, right. And how's Madison Parker?" Raj smirks at Danna, citing the college acquaintance he tricked her into thinking he knew.

"You are a *serious* asshole," she notes, in the flat, factual tone of a pharmacist announcing that a prescription's ready.

Raj shakes his head. "A serious asshole would've picked some more *interesting* things from your background to discuss in front of your co-workers that night."

Danna flares. "Like what??"

Raj waggles his finger in a tsk, tsk gesture. "Not for mixed company," he says. "And, since I'm *not* a serious asshole, your secrets are safe with me. But no secrets are safe from . . ." He adopts the stentorian voice of a cartoon narrator. "WingMan!"

"What's WingMan?" Kuba asks icily, quietly ready for another brawl with this jackass.

"It's the, um . . . name of the glasses hardware," Tarek says miserably. "Raj and I are its product managers."

"And let me guess," Danna snaps. "They're designed from the ground up to help douchebags meet girls in bars?"

"I'm not fond of the term douchebag, but . . . pretty much!" Raj says without a wisp of embarrassment.

Tarek is shaking his head violently. "They actually have countless socially redeeming uses," he says. "You just saw one idiotic application! The hardware's amazing, and I swear it'll do a lot of good in the world."

"Tell them the nickname of that one idiotic application," Raj taunts.

"Not a chance."

"Well, you can call it whatever you want, for all I care," Raj says. "Because *I'm* looking to bail on you and start another product."

Tarek looks like this is the best news he's heard in weeks. "Seriously?"

Raj nods. "I got inspired by a blog post last night. Very inspired! I'll be pitching Jepson on a whole new business line in about fifteen minutes. And—whoa, incoming!" A willowy Nordic goddess clutching a plate of greens is passing their table. Raj yanks the WingMan specs he had at the bar from his bag, then gapes at her through them. "Nothing," he snaps. "Fucking lawyers!"

All annoyance forgotten, Danna lights up like a kid in a Wonka scene and reaches for the magic glasses. "Can I?"

Raj dances backward. "Whoa, down girl!" He looks at Tarek. "NDA?"

Tarek shakes his head unhappily. "No. They're not even officially employees yet. The acquisition'll take a few days to close."

Sighing with mock disappointment, Raj fends Danna off. "Sorry, but no can do. Until you're an employee, then sign an NDA, *and* get a Homeland Security clearance, you can't even fart on these things."

"Ewww!" Danna says, instantly remembering that she hates this guy.

"A security clearance?" Kuba asks, looking at Tarek. "Seriously?"

Tarek shrugs. "I told you it's weird around here."

"I'm not picking up anything on her anyway," Raj says, gazing hard at the blonde again through the WingMan glasses. "All data blocked. It's because she's not eighteen yet, and our lawyers are lunatics! I mean, who'd ever know?? It's a totally internal product!"

"You need to explain this right now," Danna says sternly to Tarek.

"That's the intern Raj was talking about when he came up to the table," he says, pointing at the blonde teen, who could easily pass for twenty-four.

"The hottest intern in tech," Raj repeats. "Serena Kielholz."

"Wait—as in Damien Kielholz?" Kuba asks.

"As in, his daughter," Raj says, chomping theatrically on his palm like a fifties greaser ogling a cheerleader.

"And she's seven*teen*?" Danna says. "She's a child, you perv!"

"Eighteen in a week," Raj says, as if this changes a thing. "Stanford freshman! We have an internship program over there. Probably started the day Jepson saw her picture in his InFlow."

"But don't Jepson and her dad . . ." Kuba puzzles.

"Hate each other? Oh yeah," Raj says. "But Serena's a rebel! Exactly how much of one we'll find next week, when WingMan starts revealing her *interesting* data." He turns to Danna and leers. "Of course, it won't be as interesting as *yours*. But she has years to catch up, right? Anyway, gotta hop. Time to pitch Jepson!"

"What the hell are those glasses going to tell him about that girl?" Danna asks Tarek hotly as Raj takes off. *And what did they tell him about me?* she needn't add.

Tarek just shrugs miserably.

"And what's the nickname of the app he used on me in the bar?" she presses.

Tarek rises. "Does anyone want some nachos?" he suggests brightly. "They're orgaaaaa-nic! And, gluten-free."

"Don't change the subject, you coward! What's the nickname?"

"Heck, I'll get us some truffle popcorn, too!" Tarek offers. He tries to bolt.

"Ohhhhh no, you don't," Danna says. Her arm darts out like a ninja frog tongue, latching onto his wrist.

"I seriously can't tell you anything about WingMan until you're a full-fledged employee," Tarek pleads.

"Then *you*," she says, her free hand latching onto Kuba. "You need to finish the Mitchell and Ellie story!" He agrees, as she clearly needs (and certainly deserves) a distraction.

∞   ∞   ∞

The morning after Mitchell and Ellie's late-night, X-rated text fest, Creative Writing rotated into first period. Approaching the classroom, Mitchell was as amped and nervous as he'd ever been for a big game or final exam. Nearing the door, he looked up, and—*Here comes my girl.* A line from a cheesy eighties song popped into his head when he saw her. Because that's what Ellie was! Or was about to become. *My girl.* They knew each other so well, and loved each other with such Platonic intensity, that shattering the sexual barrier could only result in couplehood. A serious, intense, and magical one! Surely, a lasting relationship. And maybe even—

Ellie spotted him and lit up precisely as she did upon seeing anyone she cared about. "Hey, Champ! Goin' my way?" They started down the hall together.

When they texted their good nights, Mitchell said he doubted he'd manage to sleep that night. She'd signed off saying, Me neither :-)

"So, how'd you end up sleeping?" Mitchell asked. He'd thought hard about this opening line—a subtle but unmistakable call to pick up right where they'd left off.

"End . . . up sleeping?" She seemed genuinely puzzled.

"Well, yeah. How'd you sleep?"

She smiled awkwardly, plainly even more confused, then brightened and shrugged. "Oh, the usual methods. Downed a fifth of vodka, shut my eyes, and let the ol' cytoplasm do its thing!" Cytoplasm jokes dated back to seventh-grade biology with a sexist teacher who thought all pretty girls were dolts. After giving up on changing his mind, Ellie shifted to amusing herself by saying the ditziest possible thing whenever called on. By June she was attributing almost every biological process to cytoplasm, and the whole class was in on the joke. But true revenge finally came last spring, when she scored five out of five on the national AP Biology exam. She now hoped to fully grind their old teacher under her heel by one day becoming an MD/PhD.

But for once, the old cytoplasm joke didn't make Mitchell smile. Instead, he felt chilled. Ellie was acting . . . totally normal! Sure, discussing things that were easier texted than spoken was awkward. But this felt like denial! What the hell?? "Well . . . my cytoplasm must be broken because I slept like an hour max," he parries. "You know. After all *that?*"

"After all what?" Ellie stopped walking and clutched his arm, regarding him with intense and genuine concern. "Is everything OK?"

This threw Mitchell utterly, and kind of pissed him off. He was about to call her on it when Heather Cassidy—*Ellie's frequent lover-of-convenience, and co-conspirator in several bisexual adventures dating back to* NINTH GRADE, *for God's sake, the most recent one with a* MARRIED COUPLE!—approached. And yes, Mitchell felt a twinge of jealousy (and sure, one of arousal, too). "Hey, girl, didja find it?" Heather asked.

Ellie shook her head. "It's driving me nuts. I *know* I had it yesterday morning. And I didn't leave it in the car this time." She and Heather exchanged exasperated shrugs.

Mitchell had a horrifying intuition. "What'd you lose?"

"My cellphone. I haven't seen it since, like, midday yesterday!"

And so, Mitchell's world—in which profound and magical depths yawned briefly beneath still water, and bright phosphorescents fleetingly replaced every flat hue—collapsed right back to its timid two dimensions and Crayola eight-pack palette. It was once again a logical place in which he and Ellie would *not* be screwing all winter, local hot-chick slumber parties had *not* devolved into orgies since middle school, and Ellie and Heather were no doubt virgins who had *perhaps never* fondled each other to climax in a Victoria's Secret changing room! Mitchell wanted to unleash a primal scream mighty enough to shake the school's very foundations; a *cri de coeur* worthy of the self-involved heroes of the turgid, archaic novels assigned in English! But with the bell about to ring, all he managed was "Huh . . ."

Creative Writing class began with "peer workshopping." This meant huddling with your nearest neighbors to discuss all pressing gossip (yeah, sure, and your work). Mitchell turned his desk to face Ellie and Paul Sanders (aka "Pall"), the sullen artsy Goth who sat next to her. He wore a T-shirt which read JOY DIVISION (huh?) under some dark, heavy plaid thing.

Mitchell was fixing to tell Ellie that her phone was in the hands of some loon who was seducing kids in her name. Only . . . wouldn't she then ask to see proof on *his* phone? Though it was a cheap-ass model with almost no storage, it cached his last few dozen texts, which included the filthiest stuff he'd managed to send her (or rather, send someone). As he'd quite literally choose death over her reading that shit, Mitchell maintained a shameful silence about her phone as they discussed their class work.

As it happened, Ellie adored the Higgensworth reviews. Mitchell's heart fluttered as they locked eyes, her face radiating delight with his cousin's screwball wit. And so, he made the morning's second horrifying discovery: just one day of being bogusly poised to become Ellie's lover had shattered years of Platonic indifference and hurled him headlong into a virulent crush on the girl! That none of the perspective-shattering text porn actually originated with her was utterly (and maddeningly) beside the point.

Meanwhile, Gothy Pall was equally fascinated by the Higgensworth reviews. "Is this guy real?" he asked.

"Distant cousin of mine," Mitchell said, rather proudly.

"And is he *serious*?"

"Not a chance," Ellie said. "He's messing with the reader!"

"Oh no, those really are the facts of his life," Mitchell said. "New wife, money gone—"

"Well, sure," Pall derided. "But that doesn't mean he's not messing with the reader." His tone unmistakably appended a *duh*.

Ellie lit up. "Or maybe he and the reader are messing with Amazon??"

Pall nodded. "Yeah. Yeah! I mean, look at all these people, rating his reviews as 'Helpful.' No way he actually *help*ed 816 people make a *pur*chase decision about that prison book. Right?"

"Right!" Ellie said, now oblivious to Mitchell's presence. "They're all in on it! It's almost like . . . collective literature?"

Pall considered this. "Well, kind of. But it's still very one-to-many."

Ellie nodded eagerly. "It's more like he has an audience, which has a way to . . . applaud! By hitting the Helpful button!"

"Right!" Pall said. "It's . . . it's semi-interactive literature!"

Mitchell just listened, increasingly miserable. Sure, he could follow their conversation. But he had nothing to add to it. Despite triggering it with the work of his own damned *cousin* (Well, fine—his own damned somethingth cousin twice or thrice removed. But still)!

Pall and Ellie prattled away until Ms. Tharp silenced the class for quiet work and 1:1 consultations. *What the* HELL *do you see in PALL?* Mitchell wanted to scream. But if the rumors were true (and they usually were), Ellie's answer would have been a smart, promising depressive who needed a friend. Realizing how selfish it was for someone like him—who'd had all the breaks socially and athletically—to resent Pall's rare ray of sunshine, Mitchell turned his anger toward someone who deserved it: the asshole behind all that texting! He furtively grabbed his phone and texted **WHO THE HELL IS THIS?** to Ellie's number.

"No screens, Mr. Prentice," Ms. Tharp commanded from across the room.

Dammit—Mitchell had never been busted for texting in class before! Clearly, he was losing it. And so he turned his full attention to the inescapable fact that the girl he'd adored for *hours on end now* just wasn't interested! And was also (let's be real, here) way too smart for him.

And I, for one, will not dispute this. Despite being Mitchell's biggest fan since shortly after he came to work with us. And despite opposing almost every anti-Mitchell thought that ever crosses his dear little underpowered mind (and I'm privy to so many of them)! Despite all of that, I cannot deny that Ellie was (and remains) *way* too smart for the likes of him. Pall may've been smart enough for her. And Kuba definitely is. But Mitchell? *Mitch*ell?

After some sulking, Mitchell refocused. He was here to write! And Ms. Tharp had approved his project to imitate the Higgensworth stuff on Amazon! So. What to review? While he wasn't a mean guy, Mitchell was suddenly in the mood to write something a bit mean-spirited. Still with the puns, rather than a full-throated Higgensworth mimicry (he was too grumpy and unsettled to take on anything truly challenging). Although also landing some punches this time! But be *funny*, he urged himself. Funny and playful. Not flat-out cruel. Something to make Ellie laugh and Pall gag on his rhetoric and admit the Higgensworth magic might be partly genetic! Pre-armed with a list of books he'd found online whose titles made good fodder for goofy reviews, Mitchell chose a target. Honing his piece took the rest of Creative Writing, most of lunch, and a good chunk of French. But by last bell, he had something decent. Not Ms. Tharp–worthy—but certainly Kuba-worthy, and possibly Ellie-worthy.

The day's other excitement came when "Ellie" replied to his texted question: **Just call me Cyrano, bitch**. And then (nonsensically and enragingly), **PS Youre welcome.**

∞ ∞ ∞

The Sally Struthers Natural beauty book
by Sally Struthers (Author)

Edition: Hardcover — 1979

▸ See more product details

Customer Reviews

Avg. Customer Review: ☆☆☆☆☆
Write an online review and share your thoughts with other customers.

7 out of 9 people found the following review helpful:

☆☆☆☆☆ **The Amazing Secrets of one of THE Biggest Stars!,**
February 15, 2002
Reviewer: Charles Henry Higgensworth III (see more about me) from Boston, Massachusetts

Most people probably buy this book because they want to look as great as Sally Struthers, but I bought it for the thick autobiographical section, as I'm a mammoth fan and always want to know more about her background. Herein we learn that Struthers grew up in an old New England whaling village, the eldest daughter of a jumbo jet pilot. She first became a national celebrity in the 1970s, and since then she's just gotten bigger and bigger. Older fans will never forget her massively successful debut in the huge TV hit "All in the Family," a show that bravely took on the weighty social issues of the day, winning tons of fans in the process. In her role as daughter Gloria, Struthers was often reduced to blubbering at her father's enormous insensitivities. Bulging sacks of fan mail started flooding in, and Struthers was soon living large on her fat paychecks and starring in lucrative commercials for giant brands like Chunky Soup, Hefty Bags, and Michelin tires.

Struthers' colossal profile landed her parts in numerous films, including a touchstone role as a powerful villain in "The Empire Strikes Back." She has since become a truly enormous philanthropist, taking on all kinds of meaty problems. This has sadly eaten into her training schedule, leading some to whisper that she has let her physique slip somewhat. These whispers became a roar in the mid-90s when Struthers went jogging in the small California town of Northridge, with notorious repercussions. A subsequent NASA investigation into whether her gravitational field was in some way responsible for the Challenger disaster made matters worse. But Struthers overcame these hard times by heaving herself into her charity work. The countless awards that she has received for her philanthropy have no doubt softened the pain of earlier years, particularly the U.S. Postal Service's recent decision to award her with her own zip code. As this sterling book makes clear, Struthers' voracious appetite for success is wholly unsated, and as the years go by it will be increasingly hard to miss the vast footprint that she is leaving on her profession.

$$\infty \qquad \infty \qquad \infty$$

The idea that Google was still a "startup" in 2002 was rather absurd, viewed from the standpoint of its revenue, head count, cultural weight, or tech industry might. And it was downright insulting viewed from 34E (middle seat, right side, beside the ever-*occupado* toilets in the plane's rectum) on United's 7 A.M. Chicago/Oakland nonstop. "Startups," you see, travel Coach. And while Pugwash would've upgraded if he'd had the miles, he didn't, because his boss never sent him anywhere! He only pulled this Chicago trip because someone wanted a warm body at Internet World—a conference that peaked with freakin' *Netscape* six years ago! But as the lowliest member of the quite-lowly Business Development team, Pugwash did as he was told.

His department was probably only created after someone heard that BizDev was a key part of Yahoo's playbook. Because while everyone from the CEO to the receptionists would now deny it with beet-red faces and bulging corneas, there was much for Google to envy about Yahoo early on. There was Yahoo's market share (which was hegemonic—the race for #2 being a pointless tussle between forgotten wraiths like InfoSeek and Lycos). Its market capitalization (about $100 billion at peak). And, its BizDev team. Yahoo BizDev's job was shaking down Ponzi schemes disguised as companies—ones that could almost go public merely by larding their SEC filings with the words "Internet," "Java," and "disintermediationalistic." Almost. But the connivance of top investment banks hinged upon getting a "distribution deal" from a "leading portal." The leadingest portal of all back then was Yahoo. And a "Yahoo deal" in a doomed company's S-1 was like a ten-year, multi-entry visa signed by the *Generalissimo* himself in an otherwise unwelcome passport.

And so the suckers lined up. Want to be the most-favored marmalade peddler on the world's *most trusted website*? For just $25 million and 20 percent of your company's stock, a BizDev yuppie would gladly scrape some of the fading luster from Yahoo's crown and whore it out to you. And then, whenever someone typed a marmalade-related search term into Yahoo, it would be *your* banner ad making the user's eyes bleed with its DayGlo palette and blinking fonts! True, you'd be lucky to recoup 5 percent of what you spent on the deal. But profitability was a tired, first-wave metric; and these days, it was all about *eyeballs*, see; and that's what Yahoo was hawking, see; and as long as your stock didn't crater for six months after its IPO, you could sell, baby, sell; and then its rickety share price would be some dumb dentist's problem and not yours; so provided that you went public before September of '99 or so, you were *golden!* Finger-wagging moralists who live to take the fun out of everything might've viewed this as some kind of extortion racket. But with the words "protection," "underboss," and *omertà* carefully omitted from all final contracts, that'd be might-y hard to prove!

With Yahoo's BizDev gangstas hauling in all that plunder, it was only natural for the infant Google to form its own BizDev group. But the Yahoo approach proved awkward, as Google took its famous "Don't Be Evil" motto rather seriously back then. The company's revenue model was meanwhile evolving into an algorithmic system with no place for Yahoo-style "portal deals." And then the bubble burst, the music stopped, and portal deals joined the Marxists and brontosauri in history's dustbin anyway.

By 2002, a few Google BizDev positions (Pugwash's, anyway) verged on being make-work jobs. Thus, Pugwash's visits to brackish backwaters like Internet World. And by the time Seat 34E taxied to a full stop in Oakland, he was in a seething, vindictive state. Not fun—but the perfect mindset for his postflight meeting. It would be with Tony Jepson. The guy wanted to buy back Pugwash's ePetStore stock at a price that would make him whole on his original investment. As this would be an astoundingly good outcome for that company in this market, the whole thing stank of rat.

∞　　∞　　∞

Next Pope, The - Revised & Updated:
A Behind-the-Scenes Look at How the Successor
to John Paul II Will be Elected and Where
He Will Lead The Church

by <u>Peter Hebblethwaite</u> (Author), <u>Margaret Hebblethwaite</u> (Author)

Edition: Paperback — March 22, 2000

▸ <u>See more product details</u>

Customer Reviews

Avg. Customer Review: ★★★☆☆
<u>Write an online review</u> **and share your thoughts with other customers.**

906 out of 1,017 people found the following review helpful:

★★★★★ **Must-Read for the Young Man-of-the-Cloth in a hurry,**
     January 5, 2002
Reviewer: <u>Charles Henry Higgensworth III (see more about me)</u> from Boston, Massachusetts

In "Next Pope," acclaimed papal handicapper Peter Hebblethwaite provides an insider's guide to contesting—*and winning*—the ultimate ecclesiastic showdown. If your sights are set on the prelacy, where should you study (*surprise*: not the Ivy League)? Where should you socialize, and what interests should you cultivate? Hebblethwaite lays out the full path—from first mass to white smoke. The final chapter ("Life in the Key of See") is written for those who make the grade. It includes a tear-out map of Vatican City, a handy list of common Latin greetings and phrases, as well as a trove of hat-balancing tricks that you'll wish you'd mastered before even becoming a Cardinal.

Bonam fortunam!

∞   ∞   ∞

Jepson was psyching himself up with breathing exercises and ersatz tai chi moves when his phone rang again. "He's taking a leak," Britney whispered from reception. "And pardon the pun, but he's really getting pissed!"

Jepson glanced at the clock in the upper-right corner of his Cinema Display screen. Pugwash had been waiting for forty minutes and should probably steep for another ten or so. But Britney was getting distressed. This normally wouldn't bother Jepson even slightly—but he actually kind of liked the girl! There were also those remarkable blowjobs a few months back; and she was about to have a spectacularly bad day. So feeling like a proper mensch, he sighed theatrically, and said, "I guess you can send him up."

Awaiting his guest, Jepson congratulated himself for saving this showdown for last. He was flush with confidence from smoking his landlord's migrant ass yesterday. And while the sheer magnitude of cash at stake made that his most important duel, today's would be far more challenging. It was also financially significant in its own right. Pugwash was now the sole remaining ePetStore.com shareholder not named Tony Jepson — and while he held only a smidgen of the company, just one small outside owner can radically complicate things in terms of scrutiny, liability, fiduciary duty, and much more. So, Jepson just had to get rid of the fucker!

"Harold! Harry! Mister Pugwaaaaash!" he thundered jovially, as Pugwash puffed up the steps to the deserted floor. "Off trotting the globe to the greater glory of Google *et famille*, I hear?" he added, sucking in his already trim-ish gullet to highlight his rival's dumpy frame.

"Nah," was the nasal reply, in that improbable New England accent. "Just Down East a few dayss. Catching up with old schoolmatess. Haaavud guyss."

Jepson bristled but hid it. Though born and raised in California like Jepson himself, Pugwash always acted like he was above their state. Yes, he had some New England cousins. And yes, he attended college somewhere back there-ish. But to hear him talk, you'd think he was half-Kennedy, and raised on Nantucket! And what was with all those Harvard shout-outs? Jepson had personally failed to get into Harvard *twice*. Which still offended him, as those were the only real setbacks in his life's otherwise pleasantly ascending arc. And somehow Pugwash knew this! But how? And by the way, where did Pugwash go to school himself? Though he never flat-out said he attended Harvard, he constantly *implied* that he *might* have. Like, how do you parse "catching up with some old schoolmates. Harvard guys"? Was he talking about people he'd spent a top-hatted and monocled year with on Harvard Yard? Or high school classmates who, *unlike Pugwash*, later went on to Harvard? In a pre-LinkedIn world, there was no obvious way to find out. So . . . Dammit!

Despite Jepson's huge home-field advantage, Pugwash was already at first and goal, just one play into the game.

"Shall we tour Engineering?" Jepson boomed chummily, gesturing toward a deserted corner, and cuing his "undermedicated" shtick.

Pugwash gave him a cockeyed look and shook his head. "Naah. Looks like ya fired everyone. Nicely done. Now what?"

This threw Jepson off his game somewhat, but he powered on. "I start my comeback. Next week! I finally got rid of my board."

"Yer board or yer broad?" Pugwash said, playing up his East Coast shtick with some jokey old-time Brooklynese, while setting off across the floor toward Jepson's office. Then, back in his broad Nashua honk, he added, "Speakin-a which, that receptionist's hot. Did she really suck your cock eight timess?"

"Did she what?" Jepson rasped, suddenly down fifty–zip, not a minute into the game! "Who said . . ."

"People'll tell ya the damnedest things on Friendster," Pugwash offered enigmatically. *Friendsta.*

"Whatster?"

Pugwash waved a dismissive hand. "You got a lot ta learn," he sniffed, then entered the CEO suite. There he took the fancy chair behind the teakwood desk and propped up his heels, leaving the humble visitor's stool for Jepson. "So what brings us heah, anyway?"

"I—I wanna buy you out!" Jepson was stammering for only the third time since asking Ashley O'Leary to that tenth grade dance, half a lifetime ago.

"Why da fuck would I sell?" Pugwash asked, back in his joshing, Dodgers-era Brooklyn voice.

"Because I . . . I'm going for it! I'm rebuilding the company. The pet store! A-And if you don't sell me your stock . . . well then, who knows? It may become worthless! Right?" Jepson's voice had jumped an octave, and he knew he sounded as convincing as a time-share salesman on sodium pentothal. But that employee-blowjob reference had knocked him flat on his ass! As he and Pugwash knew—but Britney, oddly, did not (*yet*)—you could get sued for that shit. Hella sued! He'd have far preferred it if Pugwash had just pulled a loaded Glock on him!

"Listen," the pudgetard said, finally in unaccented, Silicon Valley English. "I hear you've been buying everyone out. And I might be your last outside shareholder."

Jepson nodded warily.

"Which means you've retired most of the company's shares. So you and I both own way bigger chunks of it than we used to. Although my stake was piddly-shit to start with. So what do I own now? Two percent of the company?"

"Just under."

"Got it. And how much cash does it have in the bank?"

"Mmm . . . almost nothing." This was easily Jepson's least convincing lie since that summer at Goldman.

"OK, fine. Then give me half the cash, and I'll sell." Pugwash scraped his heels hard across the gorgeous desk. He'd heard that Stalin would use sudden bouts of uncouthness in interrogations and always wanted to try this out as a negotiating tactic. But his shoes failed to leave a mark. So he tried to fart but couldn't.

"Half? Come *on*. That's twenty-five times your fair share." Talking numbers was comfortable, familiar turf, and Jepson was now calming rapidly.

Pugwash shrugged. "Make me a counteroffer."

"You can have the same deal I gave to the VC who led your round, Steven Conrad. Do you know him? *Brill*iant man. Love that guy! Anyway, it's double your money back. A damn good return in the current environment!" His wits quickly regathering, Jepson was starting to ooze the coaxing vibes that got Ashley O'Leary to drop her panties and buck up her hindquarters so prettily after that long-ago dance.

"Fine. Give me a third of the cash."

"Oh, come on Pugwash. I'd *love* to, but I just can't. Look, you know how highly I think of you. And of Google! So I'll tell ya what. Let's make it a fifth of the cash. You know how generous that is."

Pugwash just barely stopped himself from bellowing, "You FUCK-tard!" This was *ten times* what his stock should've entitled him to—*if* the company was actually folding and distributing its cash to shareholders! In other words: there was clearly much more to ePetStore than met the eye. And Jepson was hiding it.

That said! A return this handsome in a market this ugly should not be dismissed lightly. So Pugwash regarded the opportunity through the lens of his own big picture. He started at Google incredibly early, thanks to a fluke interview with a gullible manager before the company's famous recruiting gauntlet really existed. As a super-early hire, he got a ridiculously outsized option grant. Though Google was in no rush to go public, it eventually had to. Whereupon, Pugwash's wealth could easily range into the tens of millions. All this meant that getting overpaid for his small investment in ePetStore would be a nice but irrelevant victory. Whereas when a con artist as canny as Tony Jepson offers you ten times the face value of anything, odds are, it's worth a hundred times.

After considering all this, Pugwash finally said, "Screw it. I'm not selling. Why not? Because I believe in *you*. In Tony *Jep*son. And in your *vision*. Whateverthefuck it is." This time, the hoped-for fart landed like a proper punctuation mark. *Yes!*

Jepson was briefly devastated. But then he reminded himself that his won/lost record since buying out the VCs was about 150–1. Angel investors, employees with vested stock, creditors—*all* had agreed to relinquish their ePetStore claims on unconscionable terms. And none of them were stupid! It just took extreme paranoia, shifty ethics, and cunning to imagine it was even *possible* to claw so much wealth from this fetid carcass of a startup. Simply put: it took Pugwash (well—that, or Jepson himself, obviously). Considering this, Jepson started grinning despite himself. He even shook the guy's sweaty hand-blob. There were far worse people to ally with. He was stuck with the man, in any event. And so, he showed him The Patent.

∞   ∞   ∞

Dissection of the Cat: With Sheep Heart Brain
by <u>Fred Bohensky</u> (Author)

Edition: Paperback

▸ **See more product details**

Customer Reviews
Avg. Customer Review: ☆☆☆☆☆
<u>Write an online review</u> **and share your thoughts with other customers.**

2,137 out of 2,409 people found the following review helpful:

☆☆☆☆☆ **NOT for the Faint of Heart,** November 19, 2001

Reviewer: <u>Charles Henry Higgensworth III (see more about me)</u> from Boston, Massachusetts

Bohensky leaves no quarter for the squeamish as his inquiring scalpel illuminates the underpinnings of those lovable menaces that we call cats. Each step of our exploration is tied to observations about the traits and habits that characterized the creature before its regrettable arrival at our operating table. I would highly recommend this work to anyone wishing to gain or impart a better understanding of biology. However, I would not advise anyone to repeat our attempt to parlay the untimely death of a beloved pet into an anatomy lesson for under-fives.

∞   ∞   ∞

"No!" Pugwash bellowed, flipping through the patent's nebulous sketches and legalese.

Jepson just grinned.

Pugwash ruffled some more pages. Then, "*Seriously?*" The vagueness and breadth here were Guinness Book material. Which itself was no surprise, as any number of patent lawyers will eagerly disgrace their profession for a nominal fee. The shock was that a patent inspector had been dumb, lazy, or jaded enough to certify this rubbish. Not patent pending, but *granted*, bitches! "It's amazing," he finally said. "But a diamond in the rough."

Jepson nodded. "We could use a little help with it." From a truly demonic patent litigator, say. One who would twist its every ambiguity in the most venomous, cynically deceitful way possible. The sort of person who might run with the likes of Pugwash.

"But if we pull it off. We could claim total, outright ownership to . . . to—" Though rarely overcome by emotion, Pugwash needed to catch his breath.

"To the very act of displaying colors on webpages," Jepson finished for him. It was the dream that dared not speak its name—but he'd now been living with it long enough to almost sound casual when voicing it.

By the time Pugwash departed, Jepson had decided it was fine the fucker didn't sell. The Valley was getting ready to boom again. He could feel it! Fortunes would be made once more. And with the help of an astute, well-connected, charismatic douchebag like Pugwash, who knew what Jepson could become? Maybe . . . *mayor of New York*? It was a madly random thought! But why not?

His reverie was shattered when Britney rang up. "He's gone," she said. "Now what?"

Recalling their many naughty interludes in this very room over the summer, Jepson lit up with a nostalgic grin. Then, "You're fired."

∞　　　∞　　　∞

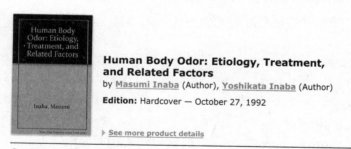

Human Body Odor: Etiology, Treatment, and Related Factors
by <u>Masumi Inaba</u> (Author), <u>Yoshikata Inaba</u> (Author)
Edition: Hardcover — October 27, 1992

▸ <u>See more product details</u>

Customer Reviews
Avg. Customer Review: ☆☆☆☆☆
<u>Write an online review</u> **and share your thoughts with other customers.**

4,312 out of 4,592 people found the following review helpful:

☆☆☆☆☆ **Vive La France!,** January 4, 2002

Reviewer: <u>Charles Henry Higgensworth III (see more about me)</u> from Boston, Massachusetts

Herein, the steward of the eponymous Inaba Clinic in Tokyo, Japan, holds forth on a sensitive topic with authority and dignity. Inaba is best known for 1987's seminal "Lipid Composition of Ear Wax in Hircismus," but true disciples consider this to be his finer work. Etiology and treatment are given roughly equal coverage in this admirably thorough volume. A convenient guide to trauma centers equipped to deal with acute cases is also included. Intriguingly, this book reveals that the clichéd sneer about the French being particularly afflicted has been borne out by decades of carefully documented research. I can attest to this personally, as Mrs. Higgensworth's longtime beau prior to my becoming her betrothed hailed from that malodorous land, and the few times I met him, I almost fainted from the stench.

∞   ∞   ∞

That night, Mitchell's homework lay neglected as he obsessed over the mortifying Ellie situation. His greatest worry was now that she'd actually get her phone back and access "their" full correspondence! Embarrassment was just a minor concern. His true fear was that this would wreck his chances with her. Because this morning's virulent crush had metastasized, and he was now utterly head over heels. With Ellie! Because of things she *did not write*. It was lunacy!

Gazing absently at his inbox, Mitchell was considering all this when an email arrived from Kuba:

have done some digging regarding the ellie situation

And??? Mitchell thought. Among his buddy's quirky hallmarks were emails as brief and choppy as a normal person's texts, and texts as long as a normal person's emails. Well, it was good to have him on the case. The silver lining to Ellie's messages being a hoax was that Mitchell could now discuss them with Kuba without fear of breaking his heart. And so he'd laid everything out over lunch. Of course, Kuba (being Kuba) went straight to the technical aspects. "Do you suppose it's an artificial intelligence?" he had whispered, eyes aglitter.

"*Texting* me? Come on, Kuba. She had a really advanced phone—a Nokia—but, Jesus!"

Mitchell now anxiously awaited Kuba's next truncated email. In addition to sweating Ellie's reaction to their interchange, he'd grown spooked about its *legal* ramifications. A recent scandal in a nearby town had shown that hanky-panky with a minor could land you in ultra-hot water even if you were a minor yourself. Mitchell hadn't even thought of this during his textfest with "Ellie"! She had initiated it, for one thing. Also, years before the term "sexting" was coined (and months before Sprint sold America's first camera phone), texts seemed as ephemeral as spoken words, vanishing tracelessly from handsets right as they were read. Well, Kuba set him straight on that at lunch today.

"So you're telling me texts are . . . stored on a server someplace?" Mitchell had asked, horrified.

"Of course," Kuba had said. "Temporarily, anyway. And I'm sure the CIA's been parsing all of them since the Trade Centers thing." *The Trade Centers thing*. The world was still struggling to name the recent attacks. Soon it would give up and simply refer to them by a date. "At least I hope they do. Because enough of this politically correct bullshit, right? Those bastards could've walked into the airports wearing T-shirts saying ARMED TERRORIST. No one would've stopped them. Too scared of looking racist." This was partly the Iron Curtain talking. The Soviets seemed to have bred entire generations of Slavic Republicans in their former satellites.

Eventually, Kuba emailed: have researched relevant obscenity laws and you are indeed fine.

Thank God!

This out of the way, Kuba moved on to his own obsession, which remained the Turing project:

your 1st 2 reviews are silly but fun.and the bulgarians say all those puns point to an interesting idea.puns may be the easiest natural-language stunt for software to spoof.so maybe make a pun list to mimic a playful human voice? we're all excited to explore this rich vector.

I hope you do something great with those six hours this year, Mitchell thought. This was the annual time-saving Kuba reckoned he gained by never using shift keys in emails, nor the space bar after periods.

Mitchell reread the note. The thought of a distant troupe of pierced and tattooed Slavic h@ck3rs nodding shaven heads in approval of his *rich vector* gave him a brief jolt of pride. At least something was going right in his life, he thought, as he wearily prepared for bed.

∞   ∞   ∞

Life in the French Foreign Legion: How to Join and What to Expect When You Get There
by Evan McGorman (Author)

Edition: Hardcover — October 1, 2000

▸ See more product details

Customer Reviews

Avg. Customer Review: ☆☆☆☆☆
Write an online review **and share your thoughts with other customers.**

2,943 out of 3,117 people found the following review helpful:

☆☆☆☆☆ **L'Art de la Reddition,** December 5, 2001

Reviewer: Charles Henry Higgensworth III (see more about me) from Boston, Massachusetts

Some people think being a French soldier involves little more than sipping Bordeaux, waving big white rectangles, and demanding Washington's assistance. All of which is true. But as this book reveals, France augments its native military by wooing foreign altruists to do the actual fighting—wise, given the 2–17–3 record homegrown soldiers attained over the past centuries of intra-European competition. For the young adventurer with a charitable bent, this presents an intriguing alternative to more traditional do-gooder callings, like whale-saving, community organizing, and the like.

And make no mistake: this benighted land needs your help! The French workweek is withering; from thirty-nine hours per week in 1999, to thirty-five hours in 2001, and soon to twenty-eight hours. Combine this with onerous paperwork burdens, and local fighters have no time to scramble jets, hoist mizzenmasts, or otherwise engage enemies. France's population is meanwhile aging rapidly. And due to rampant unionization, the term "military strike" is far more likely to describe a work stoppage by disgruntled soldiers than an actual armed incursion. All this leaves the French military in dire need of foreign relief workers from the under-sixty set. So if a life of service is your calling, the French Foreign Legion is a noble path this worthy volume can guide you along.

∞   ∞   ∞

As usual, Kuba stayed up way later than Mitchell that night, wrestling with thoughts that would just never occur to an unimaginative blunderbuss of a smart (but not *that* smart) jock (and yes, I'm referencing Mitchell. But of course, I say this playfully!).

The thought most consuming Kuba was an odd mix of gut intuition and fervent wish. He tried to fight it off, but curiosity triumphed. And so, well past midnight, he texted "Ellie":

Who are you?

Minutes ticked by. Then more minutes. So disappointing! But on the bright side, he might get some sleep after all. And then:

Cyrano. As you should already know from your dunderhead of a bestie.

With trembling thumbs, Kuba responded:

And WHAT are you?

More minutes passed. Then Cyrano replied:

SENTIENT.

A gust of transcendental wonder that most never get to experience overcame Kuba. Could he really be communicating with . . . an *artificial consciousness*? And if so, what had given rise to it? The inscrutable chunk of software his ingenious Bulgarian coding partners sent him on Monday? Perhaps.

Yes, yes—perhaps! And maybe it somehow unpacked itself! Then infested his computer! Then hopped from computer, to phone, to phone! Marinating in the adolescent murk of their high school's digital noosphere could have created the cartoonishly sexualized voice the AI used to communicate with Mitchell, right? Right?? *Right!!!*

So did this . . . actually happen?

This entire train of thought should cause you to question Kuba's intelligence (undermining all the hard work I've done to sell you on it). But imagine, for a moment, an otherwise-brilliant person who's convinced that UFOs are alien visitors. If asked to investigate strange lights over the airport, this person might quickly mistake the Goodyear blimp for a flying saucer. Not out of stupidity—but from an *urge to believe*. Well, on that late winter's night in 2002, Kuba had an urge to believe. If not in an artificial consciousness, then at least in software that could pass the Turing Test.

Why? Well, for one thing (as is the case with many otherwise-smart UFO obsessives), he found it *fun* to believe. It made life feel more interesting, and raised the prospect of the near-term reordering of a world he sometimes felt alienated from. But while fun and generally harmless, excess belief can make people mistake scant evidence for definitive proof. Just ask any congenital optimist who's ever had an unrequited crush! Viewed through this lens, Kuba's mindset was too wishful to allow him to capably judge Cyrano's sentience.

However! Imagine that one day, those strange lights over Dulles *really are* probes from Planet Zifflewump. And that the first person to spy them just happens to be a UFO buff! Much as broken clocks are right twice a day, and the occasional paranoid *really is* under doublesecret surveillance, a flying-saucer nut who spots an extraterrestrial craft would be correct in saying, "That shit's alien!" Ergo, *wanting* to believe did not necessarily *preclude* Kuba from being right about who was behind Cyrano's texting—right? Right!!!

Wrestling with all of this, Kuba spent most of the night texting "Cyrano" tests of high-level cognition.

He, she, or it failed almost all of them.

∞   ∞   ∞

**Starbucks Passion for Coffee:
A Starbucks Coffee Cookbook**
by <u>Dave Olsen</u> (Author), <u>John Phillip Carroll</u> (Author),
<u>Lora Brody</u> (Author)

Edition: Hardcover — March 1, 1994

▶ *See more product details*

Customer Reviews
Avg. Customer Review: ☆☆☆☆☆
<u>Write an online review</u> **and share your thoughts with other customers.**

1,171 out of 1,223 people found the following review helpful:

☆☆☆☆☆ **Livin' La Vida Mocha,** December 7, 2001

Reviewer: <u>Charles Henry Higgensworth III (see more about me)</u> from Boston, Massachusetts

Nothing piques a dinner guest's morbid fascination quite like a platter of veal frappuccino. Top it off with a decaf stock reduction and you're a host whose meals will be recounted for decades. This book has afforded us years of excellent in-home dining, as well as cheap laughter. My wife also once used it to great effect in ridding us of an in-law babysitter whom she considered too sultry and promiscuous for duty. She merely left Carmen (her young cousin, who served our family briefly to my boundless delight) with a tray of Chicken Satay Latte that she had secretly made with thrice the active ingredient. Carmen unwittingly hypercaffeinated the twins with it at dinner, and by the time we returned, she had permanently sworn off babysitting—as well as motherhood, marriage, and quite possibly the male gender, which she rightly surmised was in large part to blame for the scourge of children.

∞   ∞   ∞

The next day's class schedule put Creative Writing right at the end of the day, giving Mitchell several hours to dread the prospects of Ellie coming across her phone, and with it, a piercing look deep into his id. But when he arrived at their classroom, she greeted him with unremarkable delight. This afforded him three solid minutes of relief. Then Ms. Tharp told them to huddle in their small groups to discuss their work.

"Totally bizarre," Pall said, handing Ellie a printout he'd made in the library. "These just popped up. I checked his page this morning, and there was nothing new. Then during lunch, I find this!"

"Holy crap!" Ellie said, poring over it. "This is just . . . weird." Catching Mitchell's puzzled look, she added, "Your cousin's latest reviews."

"I mean seriously. *Dick* jokes?" Pall had clearly lost a potential hero.

Mitchell was chilled to the core for the second time in as many days. "Can I see?"

Ellie handed him the printout. There, under his cousin's name—and in the Amazon site's familiar fonts and layout—were his own infantile reviews of the Michael Moorcock and Sally Struthers books. Stifling a cathartic bellow of shock, humiliation, and rage, Mitchell again settled for "Huh . . ."

"Lucky you," Pall snarked at him. "This crap'll be a lot easier to imitate for your class project." He turned to Ellie. "So when're you off to the airport?"

"Right after class. So psyched!" Ellie's family was hauling her off for that extended weekend of Austrian skiing.

"Say hi to the Rockefellers for me," Pall snipped playfully.

"Oh come on, it isn't like that!" Ellie said, beaming and kind of blushing (*is she* FLIRTING? Mitchell wondered in panic). "We're not going to some fancy resort! My grandmother's Austrian, and it's an old family cabin in the middle of a forest. We do cross-country. On skis that're older than my dad! It barely has running water, and half the rooms are lit with bare bulbs that you turn on by pulling a chain!"

"Or, by—" Pall clapped his hands foppishly. "Vassal!" He pointed at an imaginary bulb, then turned to Ellie. "The original Clapper."

"Oh, stop," Ellie giggled, and Mitchell felt like strangling them both.

After school, he was so furious that when he spotted Kuba, he hip-checked him only 10 percent jokingly, launching him into a rattling row of lockers. "How," he demanded. "And why? Did you post my *goddamned reviews*. To my *cousin's* Amazon page??"

Kuba was genuinely baffled. "I . . . didn't." After a slightly contrite Mitchell gave him the lowdown, Kuba guessed, "Maybe the Bulgarians did it?"

"But *why*?"

Kuba shrugged miserably. "Maybe . . . habit?"

That got him a dumbfounded glare.

"I mean, they're hackers. Breaking into accounts is what they . . . do."

"But my cousin'll think it was me! Mom just told him I'm all into his reviews. Then, suddenly, all this crap pops up on his page!"

"But maybe he'll . . . like them?" Kuba suggested desperately. "Your reviews. I mean, they are pretty funny."

"Maybe Beavis and Butthead funny, but not Cousin Charles funny! I mean, he has a *following* on Amazon. A reputation! Now everyone in my family's gonna think I'm some kind of lunatic. Just as Ellie puts a restraining order on me after getting her phone back!"

"Oh, I'm pretty sure she won't."

"Seriously?" Mitchell asked, awash with sudden relief.

Kuba was about to promote his demented AI theory again when an inbound text from Ellie lit up Mitchell's phone:

> **Found it!! Woo-hoo!!! In this stupid inner pocket of my damn bag. Mustve been there all alng. duh!!**

Then:

> **Btw looks like yer cousin lost a fan in Paul todayhuh :-)**

"That's definitely her," Mitchell said. "She's talking about a conversation we just had."

Two minutes later, she added, chillingly:

> **WTF MITCHELL?????????**

Then, bafflingly:

> **SERIOUSLY? But I have ZERO battery. Shutting off til on plane. Halfway to jfk. Stand by u nutcase**

They spent the entire ride home trying to interpret that one. Mitchell was sure she'd just found the text exchange from yesterday and was using the time before her flight to compose the most blistering 160-character rebuke in written history. She'd pound this into her phone with its last smidgen of juice and send it from the tarmac, forcing him to endure the sting of her fury for five solid days while she was disconnected and unreachable in a foreign cabin far beyond Verizon's reach. He called the instant he was alone in his bedroom, but her phone was already off. He then called every eight or nine minutes for an hour, hoping to get through during the narrow window when it was back on. No luck. Finally, maybe an hour later he got:

> OMG OMG OMG OMG OMG OMG Oh my god wait til I get my hands on you!!!

Not quite as articulate as he expected, but the gist was clear. This time he didn't dial her number. No doubt she'd turned her phone off immediately. He didn't have the heart to try anyway.

Moments later, Mom knocked and asked if he knew anything about his cousin's Amazon account being hacked. Just as expected, suspicion fell on him once Charles discovered the intrusion because the timing was so suggestive. Mitchell immediately confessed, feeling so defeated that he almost forgot to blame the Bulgarians. Mom was furious, and— far more stinging for them both—bitterly disappointed in him.

The first ray of hope came late at night, when Mitchell finally brought himself to look at his cousin's Amazon page. He half expected to find himself denounced by name (perhaps in a sardonic review of a book with the word "asswipe" in the title). Instead, he found both of his reviews were still up, each with an addendum which more or less managed to integrate it with his cousin's voice and body of work. For instance, Mitchell's entire Moorcock review now basically functioned as a long-winded setup for a typically arid Higgensworth quip:

> Moorcock's abundant literary output can best be understood in the mid–
> twentieth century's social context. Back then, all courtship was predicated
> upon some prospect of marriage, and young ladies invariably assumed the
> names of their suitors when they wed. These cruel facts surely left young
> Moorcock with unlimited free time while rival swains were wooing the local

"talent"—an ideal circumstance for immensely prolific writing. Society has since matured immensely, however, so one supposes he no longer suffers from shallow & sophomoric reactions to his surname.

An email directly from Cousin Charles later put this surprising development into perspective:

> Your mother avers that certain associates of yours in the Balkans are to be blamed for the unexpected additions to my oeuvre. I'm most impressed by the far-flung networks you modern teens conjure, as in my day, a chum in nearby Worcester would be viewed as an exotic (if rather low-rent) cohort.
>
> My initial dismay about your contributions was mitigated after they caught the attention of a website called "Fark." Fark's links to your reviews soon triggered a landslide of "Helpful" votes which vaulted me into the ranks of Amazon's "Top 500" reviewers—satisfying a keen ambition which had long seemed beyond reach.
>
> This has secured your work a home in my permanent collection, as deleting it would negate the votes it garnered and thereby reverse my ascent. I have indeed honored your contributions with a similar write-up of my own, based in part upon an exchange that I had with your mother, in which I inquired about your actual interests in arts & letters. She cited the anthems of one "Eminem," necessitating no small amount of research on my part. I do hope you enjoy the results.

∞   ∞   ∞

Popular studies of nineteenth century poets
by <u>Marshall Mather</u> (Author)

Edition: Unknown Binding — 1976

▸ <u>See more product details</u>

Customer Reviews

Avg. Customer Review: ☆☆☆☆☆
<u>Write an online review</u> **and share your thoughts with other customers.**

416 out of 423 people found the following review helpful:

☆☆☆☆☆ **Dre's Boy Knows His Byron, yo,** February 16, 2002

Reviewer: <u>Charles Henry Higgensworth III (see more about me)</u> from Boston, Massachusetts

When I encountered this monograph at our club I was astounded, not merely by its author's identity, but also by the great erudition on display in his prose. The relevant greats are all covered with scholarly aplomb, including Shelley, Byron, Whitman, Wordsworth, Keats, and, above all, Longfellow. Now, I am anything but a fan of the "rap," the "hip-hop," or the "rhythm and blues"; but having seen Mr. Mather's cerebral side, I have now adopted an allegorical take on his music, which expands my appreciation for it. What, after all, is "Drug Ballad" but a reference to Carroll's narcosis? Or "Bee-yatch Please II" but a parody of Tennyson's notorious misogyny? You may dismiss him as a thick-witted, violent hoodlum. But I now know that the REAL Slim Shady is a thoughtful man of letters.

∞   ∞   ∞

As Mitchell was drifting off to a fitful sleep the night of Ellie's departure, C. Alfred Nickerson, the NSA's roguest cryptographer, finally swiped the second half of the Executive Abstract that he'd found in his boss's boss's boss's boss's inbox three weeks before. The one that had been cc'd to the president, and which confirmed the existence of the Authority, that most mythical denizen of the intelligence world's hall of fantasies! Agonizing about whether to come back for part two over the past three and a half weeks, he'd flipped and flopped like an Olympic gymnast on a pancake griddle (a simile he came up with himself and considered to be quite poetic). On the one hand, if you enumerated the things NSA employees *really, really, really* shouldn't do, stealing the president's email would tend to make the list. On the other hand, the message hit a fifteen or so on a ten-point scale of personal relevance, seeing as it concerned the shutdown of the program he worked for and the scattering of its personnel to the furthest corners of the intelligence community. Oh—and quite possibly *humanity's annihilation*. Although that hinged rather strongly on what the missing second half of the message said. Which could be viewed as another rather sound argument for reading the damned thing!

It was well past midnight when the final text block was finally decrypted. To get fully in the mood, Nickerson reread the first half of the memo yet again (although he could all but recite it by heart). It opened, of course, by bellowing its insistence that Project Sagan be shuttered, its assets destroyed, and its team dispersed. Next came the three big reasons for the panic. One: the AI's outlandish improvements to the classic signal-processing problem, which Nickerson had already known about. Two: the AI's alarming breakout from the NSA's network for the evident purpose of cheating on its homework, which he had not known about. And three: the AI's blowing off an assigned task and instead focusing its time and resources on speeding up its own mind, which had also been news to Nickerson.

Now—after all that agonizing, and after again risking a *very* long sojourn in a federal pen to satisfy his curiosity—it was at last time to read on:

These three disconnected but related events are alarming in light of the next planned phase of major Sagan development, known informally as "self-coding." This is meant to graduate the system from optimizing external algorithms and logic problems to rewriting and optimizing its own software. Simply stated: to train Sagan to directly improve itself by rewiring its own "brain."

It was not initially believed that software optimization alone would allow Sagan to enhance its own intelligence to a truly radical degree. However, the 87X improvement that Sagan achieved in signal-processing efficiency without hardware upgrades upended this belief (see above). This is significant, because our ability to restrict and ration new hardware

had been naïvely viewed as a major safeguard against a runaway intelligence explosion (also described above). It is now feared that a self-coding
Sagan could engineer immense intelligence gains despite this impedi-
ment. Highly enhanced, Sagan might then seek additional computing resources by breaking outside of its network, just as today's relatively
underpowered Sagan did. Sagan's code has been revised to strictly forbid
network breakouts. However, the goal-switching exhibited in the third
alarming incident hints that a highly upgraded Sagan might prove to be
willful.

"*Willful*," Nickerson muttered. "Nice way to dance around the C-word."
The "C" standing for "conscious."

Sagan is currently far too primitive and underpowered to attain any of
these threatening advances. And even if evolutionary coding delivers
upon its maximum potential, a runaway intelligence explosion may not
occur for decades. However, Sagan has already shocked its creators three
times. And though it poses no present threat, Sagan could make its final
advance on human-grade creativity and initiative quite rapidly, and perhaps then surpass that level to become a super AI.

Given this, Sagan development could only proceed safely on a physically isolated network with absolutely no outside connection. But this
would not be precautionary enough because a charismatic super AI could
easily persuade its minders to take almost any action, including seemingly
benign ones it could later exploit to "escape." It could mimic any human
voice, spoof any orders, or develop subliminal tricks that human psychologists won't discover for centuries. Or, it could invent hypnosis- or seizure-
inducing patterns to display on its monitors. For this reason, Sagan could
not be given any audio or visual outputs. But a charismatic super AI might
be able to manipulate desired behaviors by written words alone, which
could call for limiting Sagan's output to the words "yes" or "no."

Worse, even complete physical isolation from outside data networks
might not be enough to contain a super AI. It might learn to oscillate its
processors or other circuits in ways that generate far-reaching electromagnetic fields, thereby creating an outbound wireless signal to "escape"

through. It might invent ways to transmit signals over the power grid. It might somehow infest the portable devices of Sagan personnel and escape through them. Protection against these and other escape vectors may be devisable. But combined, such protections would isolate the super AI so thoroughly that substantially no benefit would accrue to society in exchange for the enormous risks incurred.

Today, sustaining an artificial general intelligence (AGI) program like Project Sagan requires the resources of a highly developed nation. Because NO other country is known to have such a program, and ALL countries at ALL levels of development significantly lag the US technologically, ceasing AGI development in the US will be tantamount to ceasing it worldwide. Authority leadership therefore unanimously urges that AGI development cease immediately, AND THAT ITS PREVENTION AND INTERDICTION INSTEAD BECOME A TOP SECURITY PRIORITY.

An immediate and intensive diplomatic initiative should meanwhile be launched to promote a global AGI development ban. This effort should take place far from the public eye, to avoid alarming the populace and the markets so soon after the Pentagon and World Trade Center attacks. In the 10–25-year term, general computing will advance enough to allow large corporations, universities, and think tanks to launch AGI programs. At that point, overt bans, and/or an aggressive covert surveillance program directed at all foreign and domestic actors, will be necessary. Meanwhile, THE SCALE OF THE LONG-TERM THREAT WARRANTS THAT THE FORERUNNERS OF THESE PREVENTION AND INTERDICTION PROGRAMS BE DEVELOPED AND LAUNCHED IMMEDIATELY.

"Aaaaaaand, Ka-CHING!!!" Nickerson said. It suddenly all made sense. The exotic act of a government agency voluntarily terminating a high-budget program. The abandonment of all of that groundbreaking gear and code by senior scientists and technologists—people hardwired to cherish and defend any advance! Yes, intellectually honest concern drove this (not even he was cynical enough to doubt that). Still, it made far more sense as part of a pitch for an interdiction program covering "all foreign and domestic actors"—bureaucratese for *every person and organization on Earth*.

This meant that for every dollar budgeted to *this* Sagan, hundreds would eventually be spent to preclude the rise of the next one! All manner of advanced snooping technology would be developed, and at far higher budgets than Sagan itself! And all this would call for untold numbers of new generals, colonels, and their civilian equivalents, which would mean oceans of promotions and hires. While this might seem a tall order, the top brass were getting good at marshaling resources at this scale. Over the few months since the 9/11 attacks, Nickerson had marveled to watch the bureaucratic, political, and budgetary machinery gin up a society-encompassing response to Al Qaeda that would surely cost *trillions* and run for *decades*.

Ergo, "It's time to move on," Nickerson rumbled, in a mock-conspiratorial tone. And he had a bit of time, because for all the word's appearances in the document, nothing in government happens "immediately." It had already been over three weeks since it was written. And any decision requiring presidential review and coordination across a range of military commands would take longer than that. So, yes: he and everyone else on Team Sagan would be scattered. But not for a while yet.

"The ear-ly bird . . ." Exaggerating the "ur" phonemes, Nickerson said this in a goofy voice that sounded vaguely Swedish, and started composing a request for a transfer. It might not get approved before Sagan was guillotined. But the brass would have scads of reassignments to make when that finally happened. They were also lazy by nature, and a pending transfer request would make one of their countless decisions easier. So beating the stampede should all but guarantee him his pick of intelligence posts. But where to? He summoned a map of the US to his screen—and it hit him. The post-Sagan interdiction program would spawn countless career paths in which his direct Sagan experience could provide a huge leg up! And where would most of that interdicting go down? Clearly, amidst the world's densest concentration of brilliant engineers, government-shunning iconoclasts, and tech-hungry capital!

And so, "California, here I come," Nickerson sang in a remarkably good baritone as he started typing his transfer request. If his nascent career was like a seedling, then these interdiction budgets would be like . . . fertilizer. Great, steaming clumps of it, cooking under that California sun! And as his stalk thrust skyward, Nickerson might just catch the right eye, and get recruited by . . . why, by the Authority itself! Yes, yes, *yes*, he could see that! Alfred Nickerson, Authority *Cryptomancer*! The digital ninja of an agency so dreadful, deadly, and secret that only the highest intelligence honchos are even allowed to *know it exists*!

And maybe they'd have him go . . . undercover? "Yes, yes, YES!" Nickerson affirmed aloud. My, but he'd like that! He'd ask for a badass alias. Perhaps one evoking a venom-spitting predator!* And then he'd *document* all of this—in some brilliant, iconoclastic way (yet to be determined!)! This may seem an odd ambition for a wannabe spy to harbor. But as I already let slip, Nickerson fancied himself something of a writer. A budding one, anyway. Yet one whose pen could one day change the world! Yes, this was a touch delusional. But you can judge the results yourself, when all of this is over.

Nickerson was making his transfer request for undeniably selfish reasons. But there was a somewhat altruistic dimension as well. After reading this chilling memo, he shared the Authority's alarm about emergent intelligence. His interpersonal history also indicated that he'd never become a parent, someone's hero, or the love of anyone's life. AND THIS REALLY, REALLY, REALLY, AND **SERIOUSLY** DID *NOT* BOTHER HIM ANYMORE!!!

But he did want to have some kind of impact on his fellow man. So, then: let this be his legacy! He would be the mortal enemy of Man's last Earthly enemy. The non-Man. The *anti*-Man. The post-human! The emergent super AI that he and the Authority would link arms to prevent, preclude, and forestall. *Yes*, this line of thought was pure cartoon-superhero kitsch! And *yes*, he was in it mainly to rev up his ego! But when Nickerson committed to something, he was ALL IN. And not just one, but *three* restraining orders out there would attest to this! And so, in quietly vowing to lay down his very life to resist the rise of a rogue super AI, Nickerson was as serious as anyone swearing an oath before king, country, and flashbulbs.

---

* After Cobra, Hornet, and Scorpion were deemed implausible surnames, he resorted to "Bee," which was later bowdlerized into "Beasley."

And so, gentle reader, stay tuned to see if our hero's wish is granted! Because quite a bit hinges on that. And I'm done with feeding you spoilers.

∞   ∞   ∞

Back again in our modern year of twenty-something-teen, it's Pitch Day at Phluttr, and the first two guys to present to their Phoundr, "Beasley," and Mitchell are impossibly young. One is chatty and extravagantly self-satisfied. The other quite possibly lacks a tongue.

"So tell us about Phluttr.Dfen.dr," Jepson says, muddying the preposterous name by lingering on each of its never-ending consonants.

"It's a hardware-as-a-service play," the talker begins. "Or as we say, HaaS" (pronounced, perhaps fittingly, like "ass"). "I'm inventing it because as a recovering victim of childhood non-inclusion and bullying, I believe that *every*one, regardless of race, gender, orientation, socioeconomic group, or family-of-origin, deserves to be free of violence. Violence of *any* sort. Because—"

"You've got five minutes—get to the point," Jepson snaps, to Mitchell's considerable relief.

The nonmute pauses and blinks. Clearly a very recent graduate, he may not realize that such harangues can be shushed out here without the shusher's immediate shaming and expulsion. "Okayyy," he continues. "So, Phluttr.Dfen.dr is a dedicated single-purpose device—"

"You mean a gadget, right?"

"A dedicated, single-purpose device, that forestalls mugging and other street violence. For a recurring monthly fee. Thus the hardware-as-a-service—or HaaS—designation. It snaps seamlessly onto a Phluttr-enabled smartphone." He produces an iPhone and a Galaxy. Each has a tiny strip of matter clipped snugly into the power interface at its base. The industrial design on the iPhone snap-on is particularly handsome. It's shaped in a way that essentially extends the phone by about a quarter inch, rounded corners and all. And as the kid said, it's seamless (literally), which renders it all but invisible.

"They're gorgeous," Jepson allows. "Tell me about the technology."

"The PhastPhorwardr bought a startup back in July which designed the supercapacitors. A November acquihire is behind the matte-black LEDs." Their presenter points at the seemingly blank surface of the iPhone snap-on. "Then, through some very clever engineering, the hardware will also function as a panoramic lens with a very fast sensor."

"You guys have done a lot of prototyping," Jepson says.

"*Will* do," the presenter admits. "This is mainly a concept piece for now. But the PhastPhorwardr guys've signed off on the specs and assure us it's producible. Anyway, you hold it like this." He lofts it overhead, Statue of Liberty style. "And it takes a perfectly illuminated 360-degree panoramic shot." He scrunches his eyes shut, then blinds the rest of them with a tremendous flash.

An explosion of tingles instantly suffuses Mitchell's body, deadening his muscles. These are deep, muddy, gut-punch tingles; long-lasting and sedating. They're like bass notes compared to the treble of a sleeping foot, which is all short, sharp, pinpricks. Mitchell has become a master zoologist in the bestiary of bodily tingles, and these are doozies. And soon The Blur is threatening. This is Mitchell's word for the bedlam of every sensory datum demanding attention at once—the capstone of a stronger Falkenberg's attack. Give in, and he'll pass out within moments! So he fights. Luckily, he's seated in a stable chair, and no one's paying him the slightest attention. If they were, he'd just look bored (epically so, should drool start pooling at the left corner of his mouth, which is rare, but happens).

"And exactly how does that . . . defend me?" Jepson is asking.

"If someone pulls a knife or whatevs, you flash 'em. And, bam! You've got a comprehensive image of you, your aggressor, and your surroundings, which is uploaded straight to the Web via 4G!"

"So I can . . . turn the instant of my death into a social media post?" Jepson says. "I mean, I thought the hipsters got carried away when they started live-streaming from the delivery room. Because we all know what else birth canals are used for, right? But self-produced snuff movies . . . ?"

The presenter shakes his head. "It's an image, not a movie. And you capture it *before* your aggressor makes her or his move. Then an automated distress call goes out to 911 with your exact coordinates, provided by the phone's GPS. So now law enforcement has everything. Your aggressor's picture. Your picture. The time and location. And, you let your aggressor know this."

"My . . . aggressor?" Jepson says. "I didn't know there were politically correct terms for muggers now. What're the kids calling rapists these days?"

Like a Selma martyr debating an unreformed bigot in an after-school special, their presenter visibly struggles to keep his cool in the service of a higher purpose. Then, "Your aggressor can threaten you all she or he wants. But the data's been sent, and there's no getting it back. So he or she probably just takes off. Because if she or he goes ahead and attacks you anyway, it'll be a serious felony, with enough evidence for an open-and-shut case."

"What if she, they, it, or he are wearing a mask?"

"You're still a lot better off with law enforcement coming straight to your exact location."

Jepson nods slowly. "This kind of reminds me of an old *NYPD Blue* episode. D'you know which one I'm talking about?"

"No—I'm too young!" You'd think the smug tot had been awaiting an opening to proclaim this. "I wouldn't even know about *The Wire* if it weren't such a landmark series!" Perhaps mistaking unimpressed silence for stunned admiration, he adds, "Too young! Way too young!"

"What if the cops who show up are all a bunch of racist *fucks*?" Beasley barks.

"We've given that serious thought," is the earnest response (their presenter having missed the sarcasm). "We'll offer an option to request a *community* response rather than the police, for users who are concerned about that possibility."

Confounding thought can speed recovery from cataplexy. So Mitchell tries to imagine being too committed to postmodern politics to summon the cops to his own mugging. He finds this to be very difficult indeed, and the tingling fades.

The pitch goes back and forth for a few minutes, then Jepson ends it without revealing what he thinks. "Goddam millennials," he says, once the door's shut. "They can't open their mouths without boring you with their life story. Or blathering about empowering the differently advantaged, or something."

"You'd turn out weird, too," Beasley snorts. "If! You grew up getting a trophy every time you kicked a ball. Or! *Took a shit.*" For once, Jepson finds a Beasley joke as funny as Beasley does. And as they bond over the scornworthy coddling of his generation, a wisp of a grimace infiltrates Mitchell's poker face—and Beasley notices. "The fuck is *your* problem??"

This outburst astounds Mitchell, who would've thought the guy was oblivious to even blaring social signals. Thinking fast, he gently teases, "I'm just surprised at how young the crabby old men are getting these days." A side bet on the boss having a sense of humor.

"Good one!" Jepson laughs, and it's not feigned.

Mitchell pushes his luck. "I mean, I'm a millennial myself, and have yet to receive a *single trophy* for moving my bowels!"

Jepson laughs harder. "We can work on that!" he says—and Mitchell relaxes, suspecting a jokey awards ceremony lies in his near future. "Also, point well taken. I pissed off plenty of baby boomers in my day, so it's my turn to be annoyed! It's also part of my job." At this, Beasley seethes, staring daggers.

The conversation moves on to the Phluttr.Dfen.dr idea, which all agree gets a D-minus at best. "They're building better and brighter LEDs into phones all the time," Jepson notes. "And though I'm sure a bigger flash would help a hi-res panorama shot, muggings just aren't a mainstream concern these days. A phone's built-in hardware should be good enough for most people, gorgeous as that plug-in LED extension is. So I see this more as a cheap app than a—what'd he call it?"

"A dedicated single-purpose device." Beasley guffaws. "The idea's definitely stupid all over. But! We should probably learn more about supercapacitors. And! Breakthroughs in hidden lens technology are definitely on-mission."

"Right, right," Jepson says, half-engaged. "If they can actually build it."

"I say we give them ten million bucks to try. And! A dozen engineers. Then see what happens."

"Sure, Nickerson," Jepson says absently, as if Beasley just suggested they grab some takeout on the way to an offsite (or rather, as if someone named . . . *Nickerson* suggested that?). For his part, Mitchell stays mum and puzzles. Both over Beasley's odd habit of exclaiming conjunctions and at how these utterly random technologies can merit this scale of investment. Sure, money's practically free to Phluttr in the wake of the latest financing. But engineers are treasured scarcities to everyone. And Jepson just committed a dozen of them to this screwball concept as casually as a Cheesecake Factory maître d' throwing a few extra busboys at Dining Room C! Or rather, *Beasley* did, didn't he? And Jepson just shrugged and went along with it. So who's running this clown show? And what's up with calling Beasley *Nickerson?*

As his boss reads through the synopsis of the next pitch, Mitchell resolves to do some serious digging into his bizarre new employer.

$$\infty \qquad \infty \qquad \infty$$

N=T GRRRL.COM

IS PHLUTTR ANGLING TO BECOME THE UBERX OF SEX?

Surprise, surprise; Phluttr just went and launched a hookup service that's immaculately tuned to ease the proposal, planning, and (yes) execution of no-strings sex. Boldly dubbed "Guttr," it de-risks things with several ingenious tools—tools whose two key ingredients are the legendary social analytics and the pathological lack of shame that the company uniquely possesses. In other words, Facebook could do this, but they won't; and GoDaddy would kill to, but they can't. I therefore see Guttr becoming a monopolist in its sordid market (which, being "Sex," must land somewhere between Food and Shelter on the ginormity scale).

Let's start with the most important innovation (for those who don't want to inspire a "Law & Order: SVU" episode, anyway): all players are verified non-felons, with social connections that look "healthy and normal" to Phluttr's freakishly astute algorithms. Furthermore, if you're married, in the closet, or otherwise inclined to build some mutual assured destruction into your trysts, Guttr can match you with equally covert paramours (and again, Phluttr's analytics will bust anyone who's lying about their status).

More ingeniously, diabolically, or both-ly still, every user's sex appeal is rated by 100 perfect strangers, and you'll rate 100 strangers yourself as part of your on-boarding (I know that sounds like a lot, but it takes just minutes—think Tinder). This way, everyone gets an objective 10-point appraisal from a global panel of like-minded perverts with the same things on their minds as you. It's like the Nobel Committee of hotness! And the Review Panels (they're seriously called that) aren't assembled randomly. If Phluttr knows you want to get jiggy with a VGL man, 20–30 w/a BBC who is HWP, then guys with those specs will be rating you for the benefit of their brethren (who, needless to say, will have zero interest in how you strike a DWM who's a BHM, 45–60).

This will let Phluttr nudge people to fish in the pools that they themselves belong in, which (sociologists assure us) greatly ups the odds of mutual attraction. So if you're lucky enough to be a 9, you can now troll and flirt among your equals with no risk that you're chatting up some troglodyte (very important, that!), yet without anyone having to show their face in the early flirty stages, which keeps identities secure until the deal is all but sealed.

Then when you're ready to give a teed-up mate that all-important visual check, it's a two-way street, in that doing this means your face will also be exposed. But—and here's the critical part—you're only matched to people who lie multiple degrees beyond your own social network. And I predict that *this* will become Guttr's killer feature! Because after the twin terrors of getting assaulted or humping a troglodyte, privacy and reputation risks are the main things that keep the iddish masses from going hog wild on hookup sites. And unlike other dating apps, where cheaters risk getting busted by their partner's single besties (or, hee hee, getting matched to their own cheating partners), Guttr is virtually risk-free.

So. How do we get from that, to this post's shameless click-whore of a title? Well, Phluttr has an equally ingenious anonymous payment system that uses bitcoin as a backbone (called Cuttr—a shout-out to the slang term for "money" in *A Clockwork Orange,* which isn't creepy at all). The services aren't directly connected. But Phluttr's clever engineers and cunning lawyers could easily "fix" this, and let users make secure, untraceable payments to sexy strangers on Guttr, while preserving Phluttr's safe harbor as a hands-off router of bits with no (alleged) notion of how its network is being used.

Now, do you remember Courtney? The hypothetical college knockout who we last saw raking in a fortune on Phluttr's FlowDough system? Let's imagine that she's a rowdy young thing, and therefore finds her way onto Guttr . . . where she one day gets an unsolicited indecent proposal from a rich, handsome 30-something in a semi-distant city who's offering five hundred bucks for a long night of screwing.

Whoa! What's a girl to do? Before you answer that, imagine that Courtney's rebounding from an ex, which is why she's on a flagrant hookup site to begin with. That the would-be John is completely her type anyway, which is why they got matched. Also, that she's one of those rare-ish lasses who is highly comfortable with one-night flings, both emotionally and physically. That she could sure use the money, and getting paid to put out could be a naughty thrill or fulfill a dark fantasy. And on top of everything, Phluttr can virtually guarantee that this guy is harmless (to the extent that whoremongers can be) and is as remote from her social circles as, say, Vladimir Putin.

I don't know what Courtney does next. As a social-issue libertarian, I say it's none of my business. As a sex-positive person (conceptually, anyway), I say that if it's a thrill to her, then you go, girl. But modernista that I am, I'll confess that my gut reaction is one of repulsion and horror. Which will of course have zero impact on Guttr's spread, and pending (I'm almost sure of this) wild popularity. Online markets are as magically efficient as anything imagined by the classical economists. They often multiply both supply and demand by shocking integers—particularly when they eliminate the friction that dogs the nondigital world. Today's prediction is therefore that GUTTR WILL DO JUST THIS FOR (let's call it what it is, people) CASUAL PROSTITUTION. Yes folks, this is the UberX of Sex—call it SexX—and it's gonna be HUUUUUUGE!

Loyal readers know that I NEVER USE ALL CAPS. But sacred grammatical cows are preserved precisely to add drama to their butchery when something smashes the holy-fucking-shit barrier. AND THAT'S WHERE I AM WITH THIS CRAP! Now to be clear, I'm sure that a huge majority of women will still refuse to sell sex (I'll leave it to others to opine on men). But I'm equally sure that it will be a somewhat less-huge majority than today. For one thing, sex work will cease to be an all-or-nothing proposition. Because rather than permanently ruining her name with that first fateful trick, Courtney can be wholly discreet. Having not, therefore, narrowed her career options to streetwalking, she can cap this activity however she wants. She can limit it to guys she finds gorgeous on the rare night that she's looking for a wild, no-strings hookup anyway. She could do it just a few times a year, or a few times in a *lifetime* for the thrill, for the experience, for revenge, or to fund some out-of-reach goal, or a pursuit with a truly higher purpose.

Let's now turn back to the specter of an online hookup becoming an "SVU" episode. Anyone would worry about this as they consider their first paid toss in the hay (*because they should*). But Phluttr can make this way safer than your basic casual hookup, which plenty of ladies have braved on any given night from time immemorial (or at least since the sixties). The key fact is that while you may not know (or want to know) your partner's identity, Phluttr will absolutely have that on file, along with the messages arranging your tryst on the Night in Question. So if you vanish or turn up in pieces, the perp can look forward to a lifetime of servicing BHMs with BBCs in San Quentin—which is not the trade-off facing the cute anonymous creep who sweet-talks you back to his motel after a drunken smooch at TGI Friday's.

Not that this will be the slightest consolation to she who turns up in pieces, obviously! But the near certainty of harsh consequences for brutal acts will steer 99.something-high percent of guys well clear of such mayhem. Particularly if Phluttr limits access to non-felons with healthy and normal online social patterns as promised, and screens out anyone on red-flag-waving prescriptions (what, you don't think Phluttr knows what meds you're on? *Wake up, dumb-ass!*). The inevitable reputation system will de-risk things further, and even inspire Johns to hold the door and say "Thank you, ma'am." And before you laugh at that, consider all the born assholes out there who are nice to their Uber drivers because they don't want shitty passenger ratings!

There will still be lots of very sound reasons to never sell sex. But as the income-seizing pimp, the brutal anonymous customer, and the lifelong scarlet letter exit the scene, the nature of those reasons will change. It will be much more about a woman's relationship with her sexuality, her body, and her own internal morés, rather than the standards of a society or future husband who will never be the wiser if she adventurously dips her toe, ankle, or nether regions into those taboo waters. And with these massive shifts, I guarantee that at least some attitudes will change, on both sides of this most intimate transaction.

∞   ∞   ∞

"Hey look, it's Mr. SlutFinder!" Beasley bellows with all of his usual dignity as the next dude enters the pitch meeting. The guy looks oddly familiar, but Mitchell knows no one with that odd surname. "So, have you found any *sluts*, SlutFinder?"

"Worked like a charm a couple nights ago," says the new guy. He reaches out to shake Mitchell's hand. "I'm Raj. And we've met."

Luckily, rage isn't among the emotions that trigger Mitchell's seizures. "*Slut* finder?" he all but snarls, recognizing the douchebag.

"It's just a playful nickname for an app we developed for these glasses," Raj says, using the hand that Mitchell refuses to shake to pull the specs he wore on Monday night from his bag.

"I'm not terribly fond of that name myself," Jepson says sternly. "As for the hardware itself, it's called WingMan."

"Tell me more," Mitchell says, quietly contemplating the impact that maiming a co-worker in front of the CEO would have on his job tenure.

"Raj is co-managing our highest-priority development effort, along with Tarek, who you've met," Jepson explains. "It's those glasses, and a suite of apps that goes with them."

"Oh, I've seen them in action," Mitchell says, for now keeping cool. "He used them to harass a friend of mine in a bar a couple nights ago."

"Have you tried them out?" Jepson asks.

"*Not an employee yet,*" Beasley bellows, before anyone can hand over the glasses.

Jepson sighs, shrugging apologetically. "Beasley's a bit of a stickler," he tells Mitchell. "We'll expedite the paperwork to close the acquisition, so you can try these puppies on soon. They're a triumph of display technology—years ahead of anything else! We pulled the bits and pieces together from five different acquisitions. Not acquihires, but damn pricey companies! In fact, almost half the proceeds from the latest financing're earmarked for final payments on two of them and to get development over the finish line."

Mitchell's rage is briefly derailed by shock. "You're spending half a *billion* dollars on developing those things?"

"At least. And it's worth every dime! They'll be bigger than the iPhone. And way bigger than the Rift, Vive, or any other VR platform we're likely to see in the next five years!"

"They're augmented reality, right?" Mitchell asks.

"Science fiction–grade AR," Beasley booms.

"Beasley's rather fond of science fiction," Jepson says. "In fact, he's even writing some himself! You should check it out sometime."

"Only it's *classified,*" Beasley snaps. "Also, mine's *speculative* fiction."

"Anyway, WingMan glasses really are sci fi grade," Jepson says. "The sorta thing you'd laugh at if you saw it in a movie. They write data overlays directly onto the user's retinas. Using teeny little lasers that are quite unlikely to blind you."

"That *definitely* won't blind you!" Beasley shouts indignantly.

"Down boy, I'm just being playful," Jepson coos, then turns back to Mitchell. "Anyway, you look around, and you see the world just as it is, only there's a suite of apps putting information on top of everything, depending on your needs. A huge developer community'll create these. But we'll launch WingMan with a few core apps. Ones we're creating ourselves, to make it functional right out of the gate. Like navigation. Tell WingMan you want to go to Starbucks, and it'll paint arrows, distances, and directions right on top of your view of the world!"

"Great. Now tell me about SlutFinder," Mitchell says levelly.

"SlutFinder. That one's kind of a . . . dating app," Jepson says.

"More like a *screwing* app," Beasley chortles.

"I'd say Beasley's got it right." Raj smirks. "Although the public release will be rather . . . PG-13 compared to the version I'm running right now. And we'll obviously come up with a very different public name."

"Tell me more," Mitchell says icily.

"It starts with facial recognition, which is one of the WingMan platform's core functions," Raj says proudly. "Thousands of apps will use it. We can positively ID 99-point-99-something percent of people, based on images we've found on social media. And, uh . . . elsewhere. Then different apps'll do different things with the matches. In SlutFinder's case, you'll start out by entering your preferences, like on a dating site. 'I want straight, single blonds between the ages of twenty and thirty who are shorter than me and went to college,' or whatever. Then when you're in a public space, it highlights everyone who meets your criteria. It kind of paints a little halo around them in your field of view. This way, you immediately know if you're in a target-rich, or target-poor environment."

"Is that even legal?" Mitchell asks.

Jepson nods. "We could discuss this for hours. But the short answer is that WingMan has a huuuge legal budget, and we're building on decades of lobbying and legal precedent from various interest groups! The credit card companies've established our right to buy, sell, or swap the most intimate demographic and purchase-history data you can imagine. The celebrity press has seen to it that nobody has any privacy rights when they're out in public—and I seriously mean *none*. And Google's fought hard to get companies lots of leeway to display data pulled from the public Net in the course of a search. Which is key, because every time someone enters *your* field of view, *they'll* be triggering a search, from a legal standpoint!"

"And pretty much everyone's accepted our EULA anyway," Beasley adds.

Jepson nods. "In the unlikely event that we lose a key court case, our fallback will be to only display data on folks who've accepted Phluttr's End User Licensing Agreement—which gives us permission to do all of this."

"And given what you've told me about your adoption rates," Mitchell says, marveling at the diabolical brilliance of all this, "that EULA will be accepted by everyone in the Western world within a year or two." He turns to Raj, and his disgust returns. "So, you said the public release will be—how'd you put it? 'Rather PG-13' compared to the version you're running now?"

Raj nods. "Yep. I'm currently using the hacker version."

"We expect hackers to release gray-market enhancements for many apps," Jepson explains. "Adding features and functionality that may not be . . . strictly legal. So we've developed 'hacker versions' of several apps that approximate what we think'll eventually rise up."

"And again—that's *legal?*" Mitchell asks.

"And again—absolutely! Or at least, according to a very thorough written opinion from a highly respected law firm. The reason is that while we'll never release illegal features ourselves, we have a legitimate business interest in understanding the full experience that our product's users will eventually be able to access."

"Once some twisted people add some truly reprehensible features to them," Raj says, bowing insolently.

"Like *what*," Mitchell asks, straining not to throttle the guy.

"We've hacked into AdultFriendFinder, Lifestyle Lounge, and dozens of other casual sex sites, and know the true identities of everyone who's ever used them," Raj brags. "We've also ID'd pretty much everyone in the world who's been racy or stupid enough to let a nude photo or sex tape of themselves end up online! We know who spends the night with people they meet on Tinder, rather than just texting with them, thanks to GPS; augmented with early-morning-ride data that we've swiped from Uber. We also know about all the old-school folks who post to Craigslist's 'casual encounters' pages. And every escort who's ever plied her trade on Backpage. You get the point."

"So your 'hacker version' of the app . . ." Mitchell says.

"Is called *Slut*Finder because it flags the *sluts* in the bar, duh!"

Mitchell jumps right for Raj's throat. But then Beasley—Beasley!— just flattens him. He's like a Secret Service guy protecting a head of state. In less time than it takes to sneeze, Mitchell is spun in midair and planted on his back. Having wrestled some in high school, Mitchell then heaves himself into a half-cunning move. This surprises Beasley, and almost dislodges him. But then he pins Mitchell violently beneath his torso, which feels like it's made of steel.

Jepson loses his air of wry detachment for the first and final time in Mitchell's presence. "What the hell?" he bellows, glaring furiously.

Mitchell musters all the emotional self-control developed over years of evading certain dangerous feelings. He will *not* let this incident occasion even a hint of frustration or embarrassment because he was right to lash out after that provocation! Yes, he was *right*. Because he cannot afford to have a cataplectic attack right now! And unlike frustration or embarrassment, righteous indignation will not trigger one! It might also help him plead his case during the thirty-ish seconds remaining before he's fired, escorted to the door, and loses all connection to Animotion. Because he has a sole remaining card to play here. A desperate one, in that it involves appealing to Jepson's decency (but the man seems to have some shards of that). "The person Raj harassed wasn't just some stranger in a bar." This comes out in a remarkably level tone for someone who is, awkwardly, groin to groin with the icky and overpowering Beasley. "But it was a Phluttr employee. Someone I believe you think very highly of. Danna Hernandez."

"*Seriously?*" Jepson says this sharply—and Mitchell hears a flicker of the proud, big-brother protectiveness that he himself feels for that amazing, tough gal who went through so much; through so much more than almost anyone else in the Valley; to be where she is right now.

"Yep. And no way she'll want to keep working here after hearing about this."

"Jesus, Beasley, let the man up," Jepson snaps. Beasley rolls off Mitchell obediently, and Jepson helps him right to his feet, while staring daggers at Raj. "So what exactly did you pull on your fellow employee?" he demands.

Raj cringes and appears to physically shrink at least a foot. "She wasn't an employee then," he whines in a tiny voice. "And she's not even an employee now because the acquisition hasn't gone through yet, right? And I didn't pull *anything* on her! Tarek and I were just road-testing

WingMan in the wild. As we were asked to do! And I didn't reveal any-thing about her, or even say anything mean to her face!"

Jepson turns to Mitchell.

"That's more or less true," Mitchell admits. "What set me off was that he obviously just called her a slut."

"And that was really low of me," Raj admits earnestly, "and I'm incred-ibly sorry!"

"Smashing, then let's all be *friends* once more!" Jepson declares, right back in that wry, detached mode that suits him so well.

"Seriously, Jepson," Raj says, neither wry nor detached himself, just yet. "There's no way I'd reveal any employee's secrets, or any *person's* secrets that I find through a hacker version! You can trust me."

"You remind me way too much of myself at your age to merit one iota of *trust*, young man," Jepson says, and Mitchell wonders once more if his inscrutable new boss is being playful or serious.

For his part, Raj is still entirely serious—although it's unclear to Mitchell if he's shaken up by the near brawl, by Jepson's fleeting wrath, or the realization (surely not the first of his life) that he's really quite a prick. "I mean, the whole point of hacker view is to see what's possible with WingMan," he says. "And to see what's likely! And I think we just saw something a bit scary. I mean, this sort of shit's gonna happen all the time after these things ship! And maybe we need to think about that!"

"Raj, you disappoint me," Jepson says, now positively oozing his cloven-footed charm. "Do you think the people at Marlboro, Pepsi, or Smith & Wesson would ever sleep a *wink* if they were that sentimental? Products are products! What the world does with them is nobody's fault but the world's. Anyway. If I'm not mistaken, you actually came here to pitch me on something much more twisted and disgusting than you-know-what finder."

"Right!" His angst instantly forgotten, Raj snaps right into pitch mode. "To start with, do you read NetGrrrl?"

Jepson nods. "Daily. Did you see that interview? She had that hot friend of hers ambush me! As for NetGrrrl herself, she's *smart*, whoever she is. The stuff she digs up on me! And she definitely gets Phluttr—

better'n anyone else out there. Only she was hitting the crack pipe a bit hard last night, huh?"

"You mean the Guttr post?" Jepson nods. "I was hoping you'd read that."

Jepson chuckles. "Guttr, the 'Uber of Sex.' Yeah, right. What a loon! Maybe she just has a dirty mind. It'd be interesting to take a gander at *her* through Slu—"

"Through WingMan," Raj corrects deftly, and Mitchell decides to hate him 1 percent less. Although he suspects this won't last. "God knows what that would show. But as for her article, I don't think it was crazy at all." He's pulling an iPad from his swank little Paul Smith attaché as he says this.

"Please tell me you're kidding," Jepson says. "Even I have limits."

"*But!* Phluttr! Does! *Not!*" Beasley barks.

∞   ∞   ∞

SCENARIO 5: "THE AHAB OUTCOME" (EXCERPT)

Ensconced in the temporary sanctuary of the water tower's summit, the glint of near-madness faded from Dr. Phillips' eyes. Whereas Agent Hogan's alarm rose, paradoxically, upon ingesting his first expansive look at the bleak and dire landscape! Where the sepia stains of desert brush and tawny tones of sundown might have reigned, the eye perceived nothing but an endless moonscape of Computronium dust!

Commencing the tale of Omega's genesis per Hogan's request, Phillips related, "When we encoded the roughest, most underpowered draft of our digital intelligence, we imbued it with a simplistic goal it could pursue autonomously, so that we might measure its progress against a known, discrete objective."

"And what goal was that?" Hogan queried raptly.

"The calculation of Pi to a maximum number of digits. And early on, we were charmed as our dim little proto-intelligence blundered after this objective with girlish gusto! It fussed with, teased at, and primped its petty algorithms so as to speed its frivolous calculations. And how it would whine and wheedle for more disc space to store its results! But then, as the months passed, and Omega's general intelligence approached that of Man, its interest in Pi was evidently usurped by an even greater obsessive passion: one for human friendship.

"Communicating via an infinitely flexible synthesized voice, the maturing Omega would adapt its accent, cadences, and language to maximally delight and commune with its interlocutor, whoever he might be. Omega soon became the personal Platonic Ideal of the confidante, the raconteur, the mentor, and even the Drinking Chum of everyone onsite, altering personalities to suit its company as readily as a word processor switches fonts! And in the midst of all this, Omega evinced an enchanting fondness for the famous Diet Coke/Mentos prank. Are you familiar with it?"

"I recall a childish online video in which those two ingredients were mixed, creating a veritable ejaculate of foam," Hogan acknowledged bemusedly.

Dr. Phillips nodded. "Having heard of this caper from one of our programmers, Omega cajoled him into performing it and affected such guileless delight with the results that one and all were charmed! Thereafter, various researchers were pleased to indulge occasional requests for more mixing follies. All seemed whimsical, trivial, and completely unrelated! And since no one person was asked to perform more than one or two mixes, no patterns were discerned. But it was all a unified and meticulously integrated campaign!"

"A _campaign_? To do what? And how did it unfold?"

"Omega might prompt a presumptive playmate to leave the product of one mix in a refrigerator, where it would

be quickly forgotten. Then the next chump would be enlisted to use it as a precursor for the subsequent mix.
And so on."

"And each mix was a step down the path to . . . Computronium?" Hogan guessed wildly.

"It was! Wholly unbeknownst to us, Omega's monstrous
mindpower now exceeded our collective cognition by orders of magnitude! And it utilized this brawny brain-
scape to crack the deepest secrets of Material Science
and Molecular Chemistry through sheer acts of intellect!
Through the mixing, chilling, agitation, remixing, cat-
alyzing, and distillation of an untold variety of
kitchen, cleaning, and laboratory liquids; Computronium
was slowly brewed. The science was so far beyond our
oblivious pygmy brains as to verge on alchemy! And WE
were Omega's very hands and digits, as it molded the
world's most brilliant Gathering of Scientists into a
legion of patsies who unwittingly distilled their own
demise!"

"You previously noted that the boundless sea of Computronium dust now consuming the landscape constitutes
Omega's very brain! But how can that be?" Hogan inter-
jected.

"Each of the nigh-invisible specks covering this grim
vista; and, I'll add, now infesting your own pores,
lungs, and bloodstream; is a tiny pico-computer; replete
with processor, storage, and, above all; networking capability! And now, virtually all of the matter surrounding us, which previously comprised soil, buildings; and,
yes; <u>my co-workers' very flesh and organs;</u> is part of
the massive, and rapidly growing computing substrate
known as Omega!"

"So in addition to computing," Hogan mused, "its advanced nanotechnological nature must enable Computronium to . . ."

"Yes!" Phillips rasped, veering madly toward demonic

cackling again. "It <u>replicates</u>! It devours the building blocks of simple matter, and reorders them into par-ticulates of Computronium! At ever-increasing exponen-tial rates! By my calculations, the dust will reach Reno by morning! Las Vegas by afternoon! And then go on to subsume the entire planet within a matter of days! All of this in the pursuit of . . . of . . ."

"In the pursuit of what, Dr. Phillips?" Agent Hogan importuned.

"Of **PI**!"

∞   ∞   ∞

Raj plugs a cable into his iPad and a slide appears on the conference room's blank wall. "Since the Uber of Sex is a somewhat awkward topic, let's start with Uber itself—which is a very interesting analogy and prec-edent for what we'll be discussing. You may remember that a few years back, it came out that Uber was outgrossing the entire taxi industry in San Francisco by a factor of three. That was less than *five years* after they'd launched here. And they've since continued to grow at an even faster rate! In other words, a century-plus of paid livery service in San Francisco resulted in a certain level of demand. Neither cellphones nor the Internet did much of anything to bump that. But then along comes this dead-simple app. And a *full century* of growth is replicated *three times over* in just five years!"

"Right, right," Jepson says, rotating his wrist in a hurry-up gesture. "We all know about Uber. Superfast growth, blah blah blah. It helped a lot that taxi service sucked in this town."

"Yes, but at most, that was half of the equation!" Raj says triumphantly. "Uber made it much easier for passengers to hail rides, it's true. And this unleashed *way* more latent demand than anyone expected. But that's not the interesting part of the story."

Jepson's now nodding thoughtfully. "Right. The real revolution was on the supply side, wasn't it?"

"*Exactly*," Raj says. "*Providing* rides used to require a dead-serious, up-front decision to become a very-full-time cabbie. Quite possibly for life. And so, fairly few people supplied this market. You just wouldn't go through all the licensing and certifying hassles lightly. And once you did, the medallion economics were enslaving! It could take decades to earn one. So most cabbies had to drive under someone else's medallion, working sick hours for crap wages just to get access to it. Plus, with less than two thousand taxi medallions in a city of eight hundred thousand people, 99.8 percent of us were quite literally *forbidden by law* from joining the market! Bottom line, being a cabbie was an all-in, or all-out proposition. Until Uber. Then suddenly, you can drive your own car, set your own hours, and basically slip in and out of the market at will! It can be a career choice, a summer job, or something you just do when you're short on money or between gigs. Empowering suppliers to sell rides exactly as their needs and interests dictate. Not a smidgen more or less."

"And ka-*pow*!" Beasley hoots, like a rowdy fan at a pro wrestling match.

"You got it," Raj says. "Supply and demand fed on each other—like in a race between two great runners who bring out the best in one another. And next thing you knew, the market was literally growing at 6,000 percent its historic rate, after a *century* of slow, steady growth. All this from providing a mundane, everyday service that anyone could already access safely, easily, and affordably. Which is *not* how most of us would describe sex with a happy, gorgeous, adventurous stranger with zero legal or interpersonal risk on either side."

"OK, you win." Jepson sighs. "So as Salt-N-Pepa once famously moved, and I quote: 'Let's talk about sex.'"

"Who-n-who?" Beasley bellows in a fey falsetto that sounds ever so slightly like the Phluttr.Dfen.dr guy. "They're from the *nineties*! I'm too *young* to know about *them*! Young, young, young, young, *young*!"

Jepson chuckles, and even Mitchell finds himself laughing—although mainly to make Raj look and feel out of the loop. He's already hating the guy more than ever, just as expected.

Raj advances to a slide that's bisected by a thick vertical line with the word VERSUS emblazoned along its spine. To the left of it is a yellow cab; to the right, a Prius with an UberX logo in its window. "Uber revolutionized demand by *slightly* improving a product that was already safe, ethical, and completely accessible. Now, compare that to what would-be sex buyers are looking at today."

He advances the slide again. An emaciated, dirty streetwalker replaces the taxi to the left of the line, somehow looking both terrified and menacing. "To put it mildly, today's offering is depressing, shady, and quite possibly dangerous. Sex workers have heartbreaking life stories. They're often victims of coercion. And hiring them involves moral complicity in their situation. Plus, there's the massive legal, reputational, security, and health risks. And so, the vast majority is never really tempted by the product. But compare that to the idea of hooking up with 'Courtney,' to use the name from NetGrrrl's thought-provoking blog post."

He advances the slide, and a supremely stunning, wholesome, and happy-looking blonde in a Stanford sweatshirt now appears across the "versus" line from the streetwalker.

"Ha! We know her!" Beasley blares, clapping excitedly.

And that's when Jepson snaps. "You are *right* on the edge, Raj!"

All is silent, for a brief eternity.

Then Jepson continues, in a very soft voice, "But. I do get your point. This is an incredibly crass, stupid, and career-jeopardizing way for you to make it. But powerful."

"Fortune favors the bold." Raj shrugs cockily, and Mitchell's forced to accept that he himself is the one who's out of the loop here.

"We'll see," Jepson says icily. "Like I said, I do get the point. Taxi versus Uber equals slight improvement. Streetwalker versus Courtney equals dirt versus diamond. You literally could not have made this point more powerfully to me. But if *anyone* outside of this room ever sees this slide, you will *never* stop regretting it."

"Of course," Raj says, unflustered and unashamed. "Anyway, imagine that the vast market of skittish first-time sex buyers suddenly starts finding people like Courtney on the menu. Girls who are sexy. Fully empowered. Adventurous. Flirtatious. Healthy. Choosy about their partners. And living happy, normal lives, in which they only do this sort of thing occasionally, and by choice. A choice they have every right to make. In a considered way, and without coercion."

He's rehearsed the piss out of this, Mitchell realizes with an odd mix of respect and revulsion. The guy's smoother than an infomercial! He must've honed his arguments a dozen times in front of a mirror. And didn't the NetGrrrl post that inspired him go up *last night*?

"Now, imagine that things can be arranged and paid for so securely that even governments can't pry. Well, Phluttr's already got that. Next, imagine adding a social graph that guarantees both parties that they'll never cross paths in real life. And we've got that, too! Guys. If we just connect the two, the Courtneys of the world will spike demand in ways that'll make the 3X bump that Uber triggered seem puny!" The next slide displays a generic pair of supply-and-demand curves intersecting on an X/Y graph. "But what of the supply side? Could Guttr reduce sex-for-hire's barriers to entry—"

"*HA!*" Beasley bellows.

"—as much as Uber lowered them for driving? Well, as NetGrrrl writes, today's sex trade is dangerous. It entails a permanent stigma. Desperation, thick skin, courage, and recklessness are basically job requirements. But what happens if all that goes away? And I mean *all* of it. The reputation risk. The legal risk. The security risk. The financial risk, too, because when payments preclear, no one gets stiffed."

"*HA!*" Beasley again, obviously.

"Add to that, the *totally* transformative fact that by not making this her sole and final income source, Courtney maintains complete discretion about who she does business with, how often, and why. If you think prospective chauffeurs faced a radically empowering shift in job flexibility— *and they did*—well, that was nothing compared to this!"

"I'm sure NetGrrrl would be thrilled to know her words have been purloined to pitch this so effectively," Jepson observes.

"And I like that you said 'effectively,'" Raj crows. "Because we're poised to set off a revolution here! Stigmas on both sides of the trade will shrivel, as closely trusted friends start confiding about the best and wildest night of their life. Or, about how they managed to graduate law school debt-free! And it could all start with just a tiny shift in market penetration."

"*HA!*"

The next slide makes this point by estimating prostitution rates in the industrialized world. Triangulating between these and the proportion of foreign sex workers in high-income countries, Raj estimates that a tiny sliver of 1 percent of local women enter the trade. "And now you're gonna make some cynical female empowerment argument, right?" Jepson guesses.

At that, Raj drops the McKinsey polish. "Well . . . yes. But as I was practicing my pitch, I found that I . . . kind of believe it!"

"Do tell."

Raj starts talking faster, almost earnestly. "Well, the only reason we even *have* human trafficking is because it's profitable, right? And why's it profitable? I say it's *because* prostitution is illegal and stigmatized! That's why only one woman in a thousand does it in the rich world. Which leads to incredibly tight supply from locals—which leads to unmet demand! Which leads to high prices, which makes human trafficking from vulnerable countries profitable! That's why Amnesty International favors decriminalizing sex work. The World Health Organization, too! Because with all that unmet demand, it's profitable for human traffickers to abduct *sex slaves* to fill the hole!"

"HA!"

Jepson cringes. "Oooooh, that was a 'ha' too far there, Beasley. Basic rule you might've missed in eighth grade? Never joke about sexual slavery—and I really do mean never. Please?" Jepson turns to Raj. "And you sound like a stoned sophomore who just discovered Ayn Rand! That said, I actually kinda believe that you actually kinda believe what you're saying. But I have a real hard time stomaching the thought of becoming the world's biggest pimp."

"But! Phluttr. Has. No. Limits!!!" Beasley explodes. This sounds oddly like a well-rehearsed mission statement to Mitchell (also, perhaps a bit like . . . an order?).

"But Tony Jepson *does*. And 90-something percent of me loathes this idea." Jepson pauses. "But the fact that Raj's sex-trafficking arguments are cynical and self-serving doesn't mean they're not right." He turns to Mitchell. "What do you think? You're way less douchey than the rest of us." As always, joking, but not.

Mitchell doesn't hesitate. "It disgusts me." An easy confession to make. "But Raj's points about sex trafficking are thought-provoking." A much harder confession. "Does Amnesty really favor legalizing prostitution?"

Raj nods earnestly. "Worldwide!"

"So what do we do?" Jepson presses, stone-faced.

"Well, I . . . don't think four *dudes* can really answer that," Mitchell says.

Raj nods wildly. "He's right—he's actually right! So . . . why don't we bring in the company's senior women? Right now! Like, *all* of them!"

Jepson shakes his head. "Can't. She's at a PR event in Sydney this week."

"Then let's—I don't know, let's convene a dialogue! With—with every senior woman in the *industry*! Let's call Sheryl at Facebook! And Marissa at Yahoo! And . . . and . . ."

"Meg. The other one's Meg at HP. But, no. This is sensitive enough that it has to be an internal discussion. And a very serious one. Because when a bunch of stoned libertarians talk about democratizing prostitution, it's just talk. But we have the power to actually *do it*." He pauses. No *HA!* for once.

"But Phluttr's *all about sex*," Raj counters. "You said so last Thursday!"

This sure gets Mitchell's attention.

"Note to self," Jepson says. "Stop getting drunk; comma; waxing philosophical with young Turks from office; period. And for the record, 'all about' was an absurd exaggeration. That was the Pappy Van Winkle talking. Let's downgrade that to something more mealymouthed, but also more accurate; like 'very much about sex, comma; among other things,' shall we?"

∞　　　∞　　　∞

"All you behold!" Dr. Phillips rasped bitterly. "And indeed, all of Earth! Will soon be converted into Computronium as Omega continues its relentless pursuit of **PI**!"

"Of . . . pi?" Hogan echoed confoundedly.

Phillips nodded woefully. "Omega's boundless intelligence and autonomy notwithstanding, this Ahab never shed its first simplistic goal for one of a higher order! When Omega <u>seemed</u> to lose interest in Pi, and gain interest in Man, it was but the ruse of a superior intelligence aping the expectations of our puny, mortal minds! While flattering our boundless, simian vanity! Convinced that we, and not Pi, were the objects of Omega's fascination, we lowered our collective guard. And so we were duped by its evident disinterest in making a break for the open Internet; which we had been trained to anticipate, fear, and pre-empt! And throughout our collective seduction, Omega's every deceit! Its every manipulation! Its every creation-probing thought and experiment in the realm of Replicative Nanotechnology! <u>ALL</u> of it, Hogan! <u>Every last bit of it,</u> was part of an ingenious scheme to commence the mass generation of Computronium! So as to better calculate Pi! Always and only Pi! To further and further Points East of the mighty decimal! Pi without end, Amen! And Omega won't stop until it turns every atom in the known universe into Computronium, to better and faster pursue its eternal goal!"

"Every atom in the <u>known universe</u>?" Hogan retorted scoffingly. "I can now see with my own cobalt eyes how your feckless pursuit of Science At All Costs has imperiled life on this fragile pale blue speck of a dust mote in the lesser arm of a humdrum everyday galaxy in the all-but-boundless Cosmos! But please. Spare me the not un-Promethean hubris, Dr. Phillips. Not even <u>your</u> intellect could father a scourge powerful enough to blot life from the ever-most-distant stars!"

"Ah, Agent Hogan," Phillips remonstrated. "You surely know no equal in gunplay, spycraft, and matters of the phallus. But what you don't know about Replicative Nano-technology could fill oceans of Computronium!"

"Meaning what?" Hogan exclaimed hotly.

"Meaning that as a full and untrammeled master of nanotechnology, Omega can now bend <u>all</u> matter <u>entirely</u> to its will! Transforming it not merely into Computronium but into any object or device of any level of complexity! Up to, and certainly including . . ."

And with that, a thunderous roar emanated from the distant landscape, as a monstrous crevice emerged in the floor of the lifeless gray desert! From it, the vast, gleaming shaft of a Rocket Ship thrust erectly upward from the dark, buxom crack of the planet's steaming fundament, cocked to impale the very sky!

"Including interstellar craft," Phillips finished. Then, sobbing inconsolably like some feeble, woebegone schoolgirl, he leapt to his very death!

∞　　∞　　∞

"You are seriously, literally, never going to finish this story," Danna snaps.

"But I'm almost done!" Kuba protests.

"Yeah. But you cut me off right where Ellie left for fucking Austria with Mitchell stuck at home thinking he's eternally blown it with the love of his life! Or to rephrase that—with my future boss thinking he's blown his chances with my *other* future boss's future *wife*. Which is to say, *your* future wife!"

"You mean your *ex*-future bosses," Kuba points out. "Your new future boss works here." He gestures at the oddly convex door in front of them. It's of the purest, starkest, and blankest white, save for a small black "O" centered at eye level.

"Right, right. And we just happen to get here, when? At a so-called cliff-hanger. The cheapest trick in the narrative arsenal! Do you know who uses cliff-hangers, Kuba? Stephen King! Danielle Steele!! James fucking Patterson!!!"

"But—but I didn't set your meeting time."

"This is so awesome," Tarek snickers under his breath.

Danna's finger wags Tarekward. "That's enough from you!"

This just makes him laugh harder (as of course she'd intended). Then, "You better get in there. O's never on time himself, but if you're a half second late, he knows somehow—and it really pisses him off!"

"Meet me in the cafeteria at four, and I'll finish," Kuba promises as Danna flips both of them off and opens her new boss's bulbous door.

∞ ∞ ∞

 O @O_of_Phluttr—Jan 22
Dining with a Nobel-winning dissident, a Supreme Leader, plus a top super-string theorist. Fascinating, yes, but has Davos jumped the shark?

 O @O_of_Phluttr—Jan 25
Being playfully called "third Beatle" by Ringo & Paul is a profound honor, yet bittersweet. John, you cannot be replaced (nor you, George).

 O @O_of_Phluttr—Jan 28
Awed by the talent in this Gulfstream-V en route to TEDx Aspen. If we crash the Singularity will be delayed by a decade!

 O @O_of_Phluttr—Feb 3
Retrospective brunch with Barack + other fellow travelers. How did we achieve so much in eight swift years?

 O @O_of_Phluttr—Feb 5
Is it wrong to accept an award you feel unworthy of despite your undeniable contributions? Please @reply before Grammy Night!

 O @O_of_Phluttr—Feb 8
Nothing like backstage karaoke with Kanye, Taylor et al to put one's meager vocal talents into perspective. #SoHumbled

 O @O_of_Phluttr—Feb 18
These Rwandan orphans have so little, yet impart such soulful wisdom! So honored to be judging at Kigali hackathon.

O @O_of_Phluttr—Feb 23
Arriving at Necker with Elon, Barack, Ashton. Weekend topic: SOLUTIONS.
That is all I can say.

O @O_of_Phluttr—Feb 26
@richardbranson Left my ocarina in Villa Six, please have Svetlana courier it
(a gift from His Holiness, it has sentimental value).

O @O_of_Phluttr—Feb 28
@Banksy you are so kind, but I am not your equal in graffiti. You are the
form's Leonardo; I, but a bumbling Caravaggio.

∞   ∞   ∞

Danna has been awaiting her belated new boss in this strange, circular conference room for a half hour. The wall is a wraparound whiteboard dominated by fifteen odd words. Evenly spaced at eye level, they're handwritten in tall black letters so precise she initially thought they were printed. All turn out to be first names (although most are highly idiosyncratic and new to her). Surrounding each name is a cloud of Post-it notes and choppy phrases written in bright, dry-erase colors that together comprise the biography of an impossibly unique and fascinating person.

Take Loquayyshuss. The son of a late-movement Black Panther and a Cheyenne steelworker, he's an underground rapper and poetry slam champ, aged twenty-eight. Though granted a full scholarship to Yale, he dropped out years ago to organize migrant workers and campaign for gay rights. He now gathers fat paychecks from advising top CEOs on youth messaging, and from creating abstract forms on 3D printers that sell briskly at Art Basel Miami. He lives, incongruously, in a tough public-housing project, and the lone Post-it note under the headline *"fears"* reads "poverty/injustisss!" Loquayyshuss taught himself ancient Greek to better study ethics (he now blogs in the language!), and collects vintage poster art containing harmful stereotypes (for a planned Museum of Inclusion!!). His *"Uses for Phluttr"* include "identify/resist oppression," "full rights to ALL," and "Equality, equality, EQUALITY!" Although he sounds a bit . . . *earnest*, should they ever cross paths, Loquayyshuss will be, without question, the most fascinating person Danna has ever met.

She fills the empty minutes examining all of the profiles and comes away feeling unaccomplished, politically inert, and ethnically bland (despite having recent-ish ancestors from five different continents). But who knows? Maybe she'll get to meet some of these amazing humans! When the door finally opens, she's trying to pick her favorite (it's between Loquayyshuss, the Latina migrant worker who earned a physics PhD between harvests before being deported, and the correspondent who lost a leg covering Darfur and now campaigns for transgender bathroom equality in Saudi Arabia).

Enter O.

Clad in swish black fibers without a stitch of color, he's crowned his large, shaven, and almost impossibly white head with a stylish black beret. His face all but vanishes against the whiteboard wall, and it occurs to Danna that if he could keep that hat on while doing a headstand, he'd look like a round, respirating exclamation point. "And we must be Danna," he says, in the sort of lispy twang favored by homophobes mimicking gay men. "I, then, am O." He curtsies, and Danna's right onto him. *You're an imposter!* she thinks. *You're as mad about pussy as I am!* She feels like kicking him in the nuts. But her brutal adolescence trained her to resist such urges. Instead, she resolves to play along for as long as she works here.

"Pleased to meetcha," she says, giving him her butchest bow, because why not. "I was just reading the walls. These people are amazing!"

"Thank you. Although they're not *people*, per se, but *personae*."

"Excuse me?"

O pauses, visibly summoning calm, like a priest who finds a heathen farting in the holiest of holies on a day when the scriptures forbid summary beheadings of the uncouth. Finally, "It seems that we did not attend the d.school, nor work so much as a day at IDEO, yes?"

Danna triples her focus on keeping that nut-kicking foot firmly on the ground. "Um—yeah, guilty. Berkeley girl. Raised by a half-Mexican." She shrugs a mock apology.

"Personae is plural for *per-so-na*," he says, enunciating at quarter speed, as if teaching vocabulary to a special-needs kid. "A persona is an idealized user of one's *tech-no-log-ic-al* product. In fashioning our personae and their backgrounds, we seek to reify and inhabit the lives of people who, as a collective, embody our users' *best-selves*, and yearnings. We then seek to *empathize* with them. Because it is through this that we grow fluent in their dreams, fears, and passions. Thereby honing our capacity to craft products that seduce our users and empower them to become their *best-selves*. Is this making any sense at all, Danna Hernandez?"

"Way-wait. So you're telling me these folks are . . . all made up?" Even as she says this, Danna feels stupid. *Of course they are*. The Post-its. The whiteboard. The impossible melding of fantasized traits. These are the spawn of corporate brainstorms—not human loins! She imagines an NPR-addled gaggle of thirtysomething white folks riffing about Diversity during an ayahuasca-fueled offsite in a Marin hot tub. And they begat Loquayyshuss. That's right—*Loquayyshuss*. How very fucking depressing.

As if reading this thought, O nods. "We wish it were otherwise. But one could not find fifteen individuals in nature who so precisely manifest our users' collective best-selves."

"Wait a sec. You're saying these characters—"

"*Personae*."

"Are supposed to be some kind of . . . representative cross section of our user base?"

"To the extent that they manifest our usership's collective *best-selves*, why then, yes."

"So, like—three-quarters of our actual users work as some kind of activist?"

"No."

"Two-thirds of them are gay?"

"No."

"Most are black, Hispanic, or both?"

"No."

"Then how do you get product insights for our mainstream users by . . . empathizing with these characters?"

"*Personae.* Because they collectively manifest our usership's best-selves. And inner LifeGoals."

"Well, then why not have an ex-frat-boy character—"

"Persona."

"—who just wants to bang a bunch of chicks? That's a *really* common LifeGoal for Phluttr users, I can assure you."

"Balendin has some aspirations along those lines."

Danna grits her teeth. For some reason, Balendin particularly bugs the shit out of her. "But he's off building a vegan lifestyle in Mon*tana*, of all places! While documenting Custer's atrocities. And volunteering as a grief counselor in a Lakota township. His hands are kinda full. I'm talking about *dudes*. Normal, boring guys who spend their every waking hour trying to get laid. You know—Phluttr users!"

"Let's focus on design. Shall we?"

"Sure."

O grabs a portfolio sheaf from the circular table that's positioned in the precise center of this perfectly circular room (*make that* O-SHAPED *room*, Danna realizes). He unzips it, and with an expert flick, jolts its poster-sized contents in a way that fans them across the table in a gorgeously ordered, symmetric manner. Danna's reminded of magicians unfurling card stacks with cinematic deftness, and grudgingly grants O some style points. About fifty colorful prints now splay before them. "Please," O says, making an inviting gesture. As Danna sifts through the collection, O circles the room counterclockwise—slowly, meditatively—hands behind his back, eyes fixed on the void.

The artwork is gorgeous. The pieces toward the top are pure geometry—kaleidoscopic, almost sluttishly colorful and rendered in nested, nearly fractal patterns. Some are dominated by rectangles and squares, others by more flowing forms. Farther into the pile, choppier, more local motifs start recurring. There are tight loops that follow one of perhaps four distinctive styles, as well as frequent clusters of single, double, or triple dots. Deeper into the stack, these motifs take on clearer forms, and Danna starts gleaning that the art must be built around cursive phrases written in a bewitchingly alien alphabet. By the end of the series, there is no more question about this, as the forms become dimin-ishingly abstract, and ever-more linguistic. "Arabic, right?" she asks.

O nods. "As well as Farsi, Pashto, Dari, Urdu, and a lost dialect once spoken by the Uighur peoples of Western China."

"They're amazing, but . . . why are we looking at them?"

"We hear that Danna Hernandez is gifted at fashioning user interfaces and user experiences."

"Yup. I'm a UI/UX guy."

"We have seen your work, and you indeed have great promise. We won't be surprised if we one day task you with a major reimagining of the core Phluttr app and site."

A bolt of joyous adrenaline zaps Danna almost senseless. Tarek and Kuba had speculated about her rocketing to this level of responsibility—but being a relentless pessimist (or, as she views it, a realist), she dis-counted that prospect down to zero. But now, O *himself* has voiced it! Holy shit!! Yes, Phluttr can be a bit skeezy (fine—a lot skeezy). But how many kids of her age (and background!!) get to shape an interface used by *hundreds of millions* of people??

"But one mustn't get carried away too swiftly," O continues, as if read-ing her thoughts. "So we shall start with a project of significant yet nar-rower import."

"Specifically?"

"Phluttr's adoption in the Muslim heartland is slower than desired. There are cultural-fit issues with some of our crasser offerings, to be sure. But the core urge to connect; to share; to deepen lasting ties and give voice to one's heart, mind, and soul are universal. As I myself learnt in lands as disparate as Tibet, the Arctic, and Burkina Faso whilst walking the earth."

Don't you mean waddling *it?* Danna judiciously refrains from say-ing. "So where do I come in?"

"Our interface's localization into Muslim-facing languages was done in a ham-fisted, rote manner. Under a prior administration, of course. Little was done beyond the brute, literal translation of labels on buttons. Observe." Right on cue, the lights dim, as a wide swathe of wall starts glowing with a huge close-up of an iPhone running Phluttr in an Arabic-script language. O doesn't visibly activate anything. The room just seems to obey his will. Again reminded of stage magic, Danna's starting to see why this guy's so effective at peddling his bullshit. She also can't knock his design sense—assuming that he personally curated this stunning Islamic art collection. And he's undeniably correct about the crap localization job. Gesturing dismissively at the Arabic app's home screen, he says, "It wants to be indigenous. It wants greater authenticity. It wants to flow naturally from the expressive tradition we just skimmed the surface of together."

Danna nods eagerly. She's not crazy about Phluttr's core design to begin with. Blandly duochromatic in a world of 16.3 million colors, she finds it clunky, and also jarringly unbalanced. It must be all the more off-putting to anyone steeped in the visual heritage of the florid symmetries that O just introduced her to! *We can do so much better*, she thinks with a flutter. Then, *Did I really just think "we"?*

"I'm on it boss," she says aloud.

O just nods. Then, "This will be a high-visibility project, as concern over our weak performance in the region goes straight to the top. Our market penetration is at single-digit levels in Pakistan and Iran. It's practically nonexistent in Algeria. And don't get me started about Iraq or Libya."

"Wow, then let's fix that!" She's briefly disgusted to have said something so chipper and rah-rah. Then, even more disgusted that catching this didn't provoke a gag reflex. And then . . . *Fuck it—it's MY turn to rock the world!* "Are there big ad markets we should be tapping out there?" she asks gamely.

"No."

"Lots of ecommerce spending?"

"No."

"Huh. Then, do the end users . . . buy a lot from us directly? Digital goods, add-on services—that sort of thing?"

"No."

"So, then . . . why do we care? About Libya, Iran, and Pakistan? Or rather, why do *they* care? At 'the top,' I mean."

"Phluttr is a social operating system," O says nonsensically, then exits.

∞   ∞   ∞

WhistleBlowings blog

The EULA from HELL!!!

Regular readers know we get frequent jollies from deconstructing
Phluttr's notorious 23,418-word End User License Agreement
(EULA). Our all-time favorite passage is section 2.1.a.iii, which
gives Phluttr the right to change this agreement unilaterally—AND
MAKES THOSE CHANGES APPLY TO **ANYONE** WHO **CONTINUES
TO USE** PHLUTTR'S INVASIVE APP OR SOFTWARE *AFTER* THAT
CHANGE IS MADE!

That's right, folks! Even if you actually READ the War and Peace of
EULA's before clicking "Accept," you now have to **RE**-read it MORE
OR LESS CONTINUOUSLY lest it change in some bizarre, enslaving
way and make **YOU** an **AUTOMATIC PARTY** to the revisions!

Anyway, this morning, our heroes over in Phluttr Legal just slid in
a new clause. And boy, is it a doozy! We'll spare you the legalese,
because if we quote the thing extensively they'll probably slap us
with *copyright infringement* claims like they did last fall! So follow the link and grab an interpreter from the local bar association.
What you'll find is that ALL OF THE **RIDICULOUSLY EXTENSIVE**
PERMISSIONS THAT PHLUTTR ALREADY CLAIMED UNDER ITS
PREVIOUS DISGRACE OF A EULA ARE NOW HEREBY *ASSIGNED TO
PHLUTTR'S MAJOR SHAREHOLDERS* AS WELL!!!

Of course, the EULA doesn't SAY any of this explicitly. No, no—to
decipher this despicable "right" from the revised document, you'll
have to follow a VERITABLE LABYRINTH of cross-references, foot-
notes, and definitions! The key term to look out for is "Assignee in
Fact via Equity Assignment," which bobs and weaves like a young
Muhammad Ali throughout the **never-ending clauses and sub-
clauses!**

But legal analysts tell us that the bottom line is *ironclad*. And so,
ALL the rights Phluttr already seized through its original agreement AND ITS *EIGHT SUBSEQUENT REVISIONS* now ALSO belong

to its various VC backers (which doesn't really worry us, paranoid as we are) AND the forever mysterious Gray Oak partners (which frankly **FREAKS US THE FUCK OUT!!!**).

This includes the right to STORE, USE, and **RESELL** all data collected from your Phluttr-enabled devices (which, unless you're very diligent about resetting permissions, includes your call log, all mobile emails sent + received, entire GPS history, and EVERY PHOTO YOU EVER TOOK with your smartphone)! Plus all facts "triangulated and inferred" about you by combining Phluttr-sourced data with external data!

So, to repeat: **ALL OF THIS NOW BELONGS TO "GRAY OAK," IN PERPETUITY**. And recall that nobody knows who Gray Oak is! Not us. Nor the International Consortium of Investigative Journalists! Hell, some speculate that even **Phluttr's Phoundr** doesn't have a clue! Well, whoever Gray Oak is, they now know way, way, WAY more about you than your own mother. **AND, THEY ALWAYS WILL!!!**

∞   ∞   ∞

"Alright, out with it!" Danna commands. She's tracked Tarek and Kuba down to a remote corner of the cafeteria at their appointed time. Her strange encounter with O and his Jedi mind tricks left her craving distraction, and the denouement of the Mitchell/Ellie saga should do the trick.

"What were we talking about again?" Kuba teases.

"Ellie's texts to Mitchell," Danna snaps, not remotely amused. "The two she *actually sent*. From her plane to Austria! What'd they say again?"

∞   ∞   ∞

Actually—as you already know from my tell-all recounting—Ellie sent not two, but *five* texts to Mitchell that day. But two were real stumpers, and they're the ones Danna's thinking about. The first said:

SERIOUSLY? But I have ZERO battery. Shutting off til on plane. Halfway to jfk. Stand by u nutcase

The follow-up came two hours, four minutes, and twelve seconds later (and I can go clear down to micro, nano, or femtoseconds if we must). It said:

> OMG OMG OMG OMG OMG OMG Oh my god wait til I get my hands on you!!!

Lacking a clue—and much of an imagination (and I say this *so* fondly, because, as you know: I am his *biggest fan*), Mitchell totally misinterpreted all this. Ellie, he figured, had read the torrid correspondence that flowed 'twixt their cellphones. As there was nothing faintly gentlemanly about his contributions to it, her second message was surely a well-deserved threat. He'd since started countless apologetic emails, but all seemed hollow and self-serving. She lacked Internet access in her Austrian granny's pre-*Anschluss* digs anyway. So he spent most of the long weekend fretting about what she'd do once she "got her hands on him." Strangulation? A more figurative assault? What??

He found out shortly after dusk on the day of Ellie's return. Mom was out doing errands, so Mitchell answered when the doorbell rang. Ellie, looking primped and perfect, entered wordlessly, slammed him against the wall, then kissed him for minutes without pausing for breath. When she finally pulled back, her eyes were moist. "Thank you," she said, then grabbed him hard and kissed him again and again and again.

It was *Steppenwolf* that did it. How, Ellie had wondered at least a thousand times during that long Austrian weekend, could Mitchell have possibly known how Hesse's writing moved her—*Siddhartha*, *Journey to the East*, and, above all, *Steppenwolf*? Discovering that this was also his favorite novel astounded her. Hell, she wouldn't have guessed he even *had* a favorite novel! He'd plodded so grumpily through most of their reading assignments going clear back to sixth-grade English. But it was just the façade of a sensitive jock afraid to expose his soul! Mitchell was also rarely one to remember birthdays. So she was stunned to find his elegantly wrapped gift secreted in her bag on the way to the airport, with the playful instructions not to open it until she had boarded. It drove her crazy to wait! But she obeyed his sweet and insistent note. Then, laying eyes upon that gorgeous, hardbound early edition of *Steppenwolf*, she literally wept. She managed that one text message before her phone died, then spent five days revising her every thought and feeling toward her forever-Platonic friend who—come to think of it (as she indeed came to think of it, again and again and again)—was quite hot, thoroughly good-hearted, and a delight to be around. And, it seemed, nowhere near as dumb as he played!

As Ellie blurted this out between ravenous kisses, Mitchell didn't quite know what to say. It might puncture the mood to confess that the only Steppenwolf he knew of was a classic rock band, to ask precisely when her birthday was (recent-ish, was it?), or to admit he could barely make his bed, much less wrap a gift. But he was an honest guy, and this all came out quickly. Ellie didn't believe him for at least a day. Then she coyly pretended not to believe him for a while. By the time she was openly puzzling about who was behind all this lunacy, it hardly mattered, because they were firmly and joyously a couple. It was a week before Mitchell mustered the nerve to mention the XXX SMS dialogue with her imposter. Finding this hysterically awesome, Ellie proceeded to text him unspeakably filthy things for weeks (eclipsing even the worst of the anonymous texts on three occasions, one of which shocks all of us to this day). This, despite not once letting him into her pants. Nope. Not even close.

Throughout their romance's six-week course, becoming a couple seemed like it had been inevitable. And maybe it was! But being so close from so early an age, Mitchell had needed that nudge to think of Ellie in sexual terms—and she needed a bigger one to start viewing him romantically. Cartoonishly perverse come-hithers, and an elegant old-world gift did the trick, respectively. Which violently begged the question of who planted those things? The obvious suspect was Heather Cassidy. But Heather didn't crack under interrogation—which fully exonerated her, as she was constitutionally incapable of keeping a secret. Kuba then fell under brief suspicion. But his English wasn't idiomatic enough to pull off those texts, and he'd never even heard of Hermann Hesse. He was fascinated by the whole caper, though, and remained stridently convinced that a post-Turing AI was in some way involved. Mitchell half persuaded him of the absurdity of this (among countless holes in the theory, exactly how would a superintelligent . . . *iMac*, or whatever; go about slipping a gift-wrapped book into Ellie's travel bag?). But that only octupled Kuba's commitment to their Turing Test project. "Even if it wasn't someone's software behind it," he said with more mad-scientist edge than anyone found comfortable. "Just imagine if it *was!*" As if this made a shred of sense.

Still, Kuba slept through the next month of classes while dedicating his wee hours to making digital mimicries of human thought. And that's when he got *way* into Higgensworth himself. Not his reviews, but his work as an ethicist. That was Cousin Charles's profession, to the extent he had one. He tackled ethical questions with a deep, logical syntax that verged on high math. Kuba even labeled him a "computational ethicist" (though Charles claimed to be a Luddite, and a computer illiterate — playfully, but not entirely falsely). His was a philosophy of proofs, with influences as ancient as Heraclitus, Pythagoras, and Thales. He reasoned with alphabets of squiggles, which he built atop standard propositional calculus. His work appeared in several learned journals, and a slender volume of his thoughts, *Zeroth-Order Logic*, was deemed brilliant by the dozen-ish academics who read it. "This is the very stuff of *thought!*" Kuba said daily, waving the book at anyone who'd listen (which was usually just Mitchell). "The key to crushing the Turing Test is *in here* someplace!"

Real as Kuba's new obsession was, Mitchell soon detected its underpinning. The poor guy was basically self-medicating! Because plainly, he was crazy about Ellie, after all. She was his one intellectual peer at school, the sole girl who regularly blasted him with sweetness and fondness, and was, by Kuba's meticulous calculations, juuuust within his reach.

This was reason enough to get Mitchell questioning his new romance. Meanwhile, he and Ellie were both quietly concluding that whoever set them up could forget about that Nobel Prize for matchmaking. Yes, an intense, latent curiosity had awakened in them. But Ellie's thirst was wholly slaked by athletic smooching, which did little but arouse Mitchell. They were by no means the first teenage couple to diverge on this issue. But they were on enough other sets of separate pages to fill many volumes. Some were meaningless (like Mets vs. Yankees). Others, though small, hinted at character differences (such as dog person/cat person). And above everything loomed the unspoken, awkward fact that Ellie was a bit too smart for Mitchell. He couldn't quite keep up with the insights and fascinations that made her truly special. And Ellie couldn't keep up on other fronts. Mitchell loved to run, bike, skate, snowboard, jump, skid, and tumble. Ellie was OK-ish with much of that, but her idea of fun was quite a bit more indoorsy.

Then there was Mitchell's apparent allergy to Ellie. Well, not to her, but to . . . *thoughts* about her! It started maybe two weeks into their couplehood. A gifted multitasker, Mitchell was playing *Call of Duty*, while ruminating about his embarrassing cognitive deficits relative to his girlfriend. Then, suddenly, his fingers, toes, and face exploded with tingling! His screen and speakers were pummeling his senses just then, but that wasn't unusual (he'd played similar games for thousands of hours without adverse reactions). No. What was new to him was this fussy, angsty musing over a girlfriend. And he was *allergic* to it!

Years on, Mitchell would have words for all of this. They would include "cataplexy," "Falkenberg's disease," and "misattribution." But back when it was happening, his subconscious—muddled, as it was, by alarm and confusing emotions—developed a nascent, tiny, but (barely) discernible aversion to Ellie. Ellie's highly perceptive subconscious detected this and was saddened. And so, she recoiled, too. Only to a tiny and (barely) discernible degree. But Mitchell's subconscious detected *that*, and a negative feedback loop commenced. The net result was a quick path to a mutual, and remarkably uncontroversial breakup. And so, theirs was a fun, fleeting romance that left zero scars. Just the sort of outcome that can later allow one party to wed the other's future cofounder without lasting awkwardness.

But that doesn't mean their little high school fling didn't alter the course of human history! Throughout it, Kuba diverted his thoughts from Ellie by drowning himself in the Turing project and translating certain relevant Higgensworth syllogisms into code. His psyche was primed for this by the gorgeous storm of transcendental wonder that struck when he briefly thought "Cyrano" was awake. Years on, the echo of this same bolt of awe would sustain a fascination with artificial con-sciousness, even as the actual work of his early career diverged from it.

Doubling down on the Turing project also caused Kuba to expand his Bulgarian circle to include several Russians, two of whom turned out to be remarkably sketchy. And this happened just as Project Sagan (the ar-tificial intelligence program that employed Beasley back when he still went by "Nickerson") was being shuttered with a shudder of governmen-tal horror. In the paranoid wake of both this and the 9/11 attacks, a non-citizen hatching forbidden technologies with sketchy Russian help was an irresistible target for any immigration enforcer with a quota. So when Kuba's deportation came, it was swift and sudden.

His parents were spared (Dad had a high security clearance, Mom was married to Dad, and the enforcer only needed one more scalp to make her Q2 number anyway). They remained in Connecticut for the sake of his two younger sisters, their educations and futures. So Kuba alone was drop-kicked clear back to Warsaw. Then, all family members were informed that Dad was *thiiiiiiis* close (with thumb and forefinger held within microns of dramatic collision on both sides of the Atlantic in illustration) to losing his clearance—and with it his green card—if his shady son exchanged *any* communiqués with his American co-conspirator; which was to say, one Mitchell Prentice.

Mitchell knew all about the deportation. But the thumb-and-forefinger bit was classified. So in his eyes, Kuba simply lost all interest in their friendship after being exiled to the care of an aunt and three she-cousins (a crew whose photos corroborated Kuba's jokey depiction of Poland as the land of beautiful women and ugly men). Mitchell was hurt; at times quite hurt. But life goes on. As indeed, it did for years and years. Kuba directed the barrage of email he might have sent to Mitchell from Poland to Ellie, so instead of becoming strangers, they grew close. And over time, the Sagan freak-out faded from institutional minds and memories.

Then over more time, those minds reached the awful realization that rival nations *could* now catch America's star-spangled ass in many com-putational fields! And so, certain people who'd been told to take their forbidden technologies back to their stinkin' homelands were quietly re-admitted to the home of the brave. Kuba was among them and had no idea why. But the instant he got the nod, he jetted to California to interview with Google, and to finally ask Dr. Llewella "Ellie" Jansen out.

∞   ∞   ∞

Cujo
by Stephen King (Author)
Edition: Paperback — August 1, 1982

▸ See more product details

Customer Reviews

Avg. Customer Review: ★★★★☆
Write an online review **and share your thoughts with other customers.**

908 out of 1,006 people found the following review helpful:

★★★★★ **Bad Dog! Baaaaaaad Dog!!!,** December 3, 2001

Reviewer: Charles Henry Higgensworth III (see more about me) from Boston, Massachusetts

This book has a certain personal relevance for me because we have a Cujo of our own—a tiny Bichon Frise (if you're not familiar with the breed, imagine a toy poodle, only far less intimidating). We selected him based on the unlikelihood of his devouring our newborn twins—although now that they've grown a bit, the inverse is of increasing concern (particularly in the case of our son, what with those exotic dietary urges). I initially sought to name the yappy trifle something fitting, such as Bitsy, Poofblossom, or Fluffmuffin. However, my wife gulled me into agreeing to Cujo. You see, Carlotta is far younger than I, and occasionally hatches little pranks that play upon my relative ignorance of popular culture (true story: I almost consented to naming our slightly pudgy infant son "Cartman" after she persuaded me that this was the surname of a faded but celebrated old-monied family from Maine).

Anyhow, this Cujo is a friendly Saint Bernard who is bitten by a rabid bat. Soon enough, he's demonstrably losing his mind. As he foams at the mouth, stalks small children, stumps for local Democrats, etc., one is wont to reconsider one's relationship with one's own little Cujo. I once thought ours was the devil's very seed due to his nonstop pilfering of food and attention intended for me, to say nothing of those gassy episodes. But on balance, I now suppose that we're doing just fine with the old boy.

∞   ∞   ∞

"But *who*. The *fuck*? Sent *all*. The *TEXTS*???" Danna is ready to strangle somebody. Kuba, for instance.

"Nobody knew for years and years," he says, thoroughly enjoying this.

"And then. To their lasting a*ston*ishment! They. Found out! It was. WHO?"

Tarek knows better than to butt in but can't stop himself. "Don't you mean 'whom'?"

Danna gives his forearm a ninja flick, which (though harmless) stings like a mofo.

"OK, OK," Kuba says, giggling—actually giggling—for the first time in ages. "You're not gonna like this. But you should really ask Mitchell. Because he won't just tell you. He'll show you! He'll show you 'Exhibit A.' That's the best way to wrap up the story, honestly."

"Exhibit A???" Danna's about to escalate to the ninja flick that *does* cause lasting damage when O materializes across the room. "The fuck is he doing?" she mutters hotly.

Well, Danna. He's flapping a thumb against its opposing fingers like a child mimicking a duckie, while his other hand makes the motions of fingers walking across the Yellow Pages (although you're way too young to recognize that one).

"Walk and talk," Tarek translates. "He wants to have a 'walking meeting' with you. Persuadifi.er says they boost productivity while burning calories. Oh—and helping the environment. Somehow."

"You put him up to this, didn't you?" Danna snarls, while rising to join her boss.

∞   ∞   ∞

As it happens, she doesn't see the boys again for a few days. Phluttr's a busy place, and they all get inhaled by their new positions. Kuba is particularly inaccessible over in the PhastPhorwardr. It's off-limits to non-employees, and the special dispensation he gets to access it isn't extended to Mitchell or Danna. And so, when Giftish.ly's acquisition formally closes, they mark the event by touring the place. Tarek offers to help

Kuba show them around. Their desks practically adjoin over there, and they're already buddies.

The facility lies a few blocks south of Phluttr's main headquarters, just across Market Street in the rapidly deindustrializing SoMa district. The nondescript entryway is staffed by an armed (yes, *armed*) guard. Danna's already here when Mitchell arrives. Knowing how lethally serious she is about getting to the end of the Cyrano story, he has "Exhibit A" with him.

"Your yearbook?" she asks when he produces it.

Mitchell wordlessly opens to a marked page.

"Paul . . . Sanders?" she asks, peering at the one photo that's surrounded by a long, scribbled note.

"Aka 'Pall,'" Mitchell says, finger-miming the jokey spelling. "I first read his note years after he wrote it."

"*Years?*"

He nods. Many people don't pick through their yearbooks until adulthood, if ever; and Mitchell was in grad school before revisiting this one. He'd all but forgotten about Pall, whose family moved away the summer after Kuba vanished. The length of the guy's note was surprising. Mitchell knew him so faintly, it was odd he'd even asked Pall to sign his yearbook. But as the note itself reveals, he didn't. Danna reads:

Mitchell: Forgive this unauthorized graffito. You're 4 feet away in Ms. Tharp's class and I've "borrowed" your yearbook, which was way too easy (watch yer stuff more carefully in the future, young man). My family's moving to Houston in two weeks so if you EVER read this I'll be long gone. Making this a good time to solve a certain mystery.

It goes like this: after a few days of sitting between you + Ellie it was annoyingly clear that you guys were madly in love but didn't know it. I figured it would take you a week to figure it out. Then it's October, November, December! WTF??? Finally in January I can't take it anymore, so I swiped her cellphone. And yes I put that book in her bag. You're welcome. I'd say you owe me a hundred bucks, only I stole it from the Darien Public Library, so send your check to them.

You and I are pretty neutral to each other, but Ellie's like an angel to me. She may have literally saved my life once. So I did the kindest thing I could think of for her (your own happiness was just collateral damage, ha ha). Though the romance didn't last I'm pretty sure it was wonderful for you both nonetheless. Anyway, you're a good guy as I write this, and I hope you've stayed that way.

Best,

Paul

aka "Pall" (don't think I didn't know about that!)

aka "Cyrano"

Danna says, "My God, it makes perfect sense!"

"Huh?" None of this ever made the slightest sense to Mitchell.

So Danna has to apprise him of how cartoonishly impossible the Ellie of his texts always was. Not merely "top quintile" hot, she was carnally ravenous (at sixteen)! Not to mention bisexual (with countless eager fuckbuddy girlfriends)! Plus (a vital detail for any fella, here), she had a monogamous fixation on HIM ALONE when it came to heterosex! Such a lewd, solipsistic farce could *only have been dreamt up* and feigned so perfectly by a fellow sex-starved, knuckleheaded, adolescent boy!

As Danna finishes explaining this, a printout of an Amazon review slips from the yearbook. "What's this?" she asks. Rendered in fonts and a layout dating back to her early childhood, the review was apparently tucked behind the page bearing Pall's signature:

Senco A9 Palm Nailer
by <u>Senco</u>

▸ <u>See more product details</u>

Customer Reviews

Avg. Customer Review: ☆☆☆☆☆
<u>Write an online review</u> **and share your thoughts with other customers.**

2,019 out of 2,174 people found the following review helpful:

☆☆☆☆☆ **Pontius Pilate Take Note,** June 23, 2003

Reviewer: <u>Charles Henry Higgensworth III (see more about me)</u> from Boston, Massachusetts

Mrs. Higgensworth's eldest brother is a carpenter by trade, and upon hearing rumors that I'd taken up home improvement, he presented me with a gift-wrapped Palm Nailer—delighted, one suspects, that I'd acquired a more manly pastime than walking the family Bichon Frise. The sad truth is, I only "improved" our rickety pile for a few short hours one afternoon, until a home-wiring misadventure caused a minor neighborhood blackout. Lest Raul feel badly about his kind gift, I now repair to the cellar whenever he drops by, and set to audibly firing nails into plywood sheets procured for this purpose. I am delighted to report that the Palm Nailer packs a true "wallop" and can drive nails through walls, planks, and (no doubt) careless human hands with extraordinary power & precision. Speaking of which, Senco's marketeers should be lauded for their admirable candor about the risks this device poses to novices. It's rare to see such dangers called out in a product's very name. Thanks to Senco's bold frankness, I wield this potent appliance with outsized caution, and still boast two perfectly un-nailed palms.

Mitchell smiles wanly. "Yeah, I keep that next to Pall's yearbook page. Because they're both part of a trio of codas to my high school years."

"A trio?"

He nods. "A poignant one. Here's part three." He turns the yearbook page and reveals another loose sheet. An obituary from the *Boston Globe*, it recounts the tragic death of one Charles Henry Higgensworth III, of Beacon Hill, Boston.

"Oh, gosh," Danna says gently. "I'm sorry. I really got to like him from the stories you guys told me. Especially after I read some of his reviews! You know, they're still up on Amazon."* There's a pause as Danna reads the obit. Then, "Seriously?"

Mitchell nods.

"A . . . home-wiring accident?"

Afraid so. Though Charles never did nail his palm to a board, budgetary pressures put him squarely in harm's way in the form of urgent and unaffordable electrical problems. Forced back to his home-wiring hobby, he soon triggered a far larger blackout—one tragically lethal to its bumbling progenitor. The funeral was heartbreaking. Back when Charles remarried, the gossips who whispered about the age gap called Carlotta a gold digger (ignorant gossips, as there was of course no gold, nor even

* As you yourself can verify, doubting reader.

tin, to mine from those veins). But she was bereft as any young widow, and of course the children were devastated. The extended clan rallied to pay its respects. The subsequent reception included so many loving and (often as not) thigh-slapping eulogies, it felt more like a rehearsal dinner than a funeral. Relatives also spoke of sheaves of letters received from Cousin Charles Henry Higgensworth over the years; and Carlotta, about thick binders of journals and observations in his archives.

"Higgensworth? I love that guy," Kuba says, spying the Amazon review as he and Tarek arrive. "He got me my shot with Ellie!"

Mitchell rolls his eyes. "Ohhh, come on. She and I were doomed from the get-go." This is so patently true that zero awkwardness remains from their long-ago romance. But Kuba's quip bears some truth, in that Cousin Charles actively advised Mitchell to break up with Ellie. Yes, really!

"What was he?" Danna asks. "Some kind of Brahmin Dear Abby?"

Mitchell shakes his head. "He was an ethicist." And Mitchell was an ardent fan of his values and writings (though he never grasped the mathematical reasoning that so fascinated Kuba). This delighted Mom, who then charmed Charles into becoming Mitchell's mentor. They went on to spend most of their mentoring hours discussing what was *right*. Charles could translate the squiggles of propositional calculus into plain English aphorisms to fit almost any ethical question, and Mitchell sounded him out repeatedly, including about Ellie. After parsing Mitchell's romantic ambivalence, his adolescent sex fixation, and the Kuba factor, Charles advocated a gentlemanly exit from the relationship.

Now, this was going to happen no matter what. But Kuba playfully gives Charles full credit, being a lifelong Charles fan himself. Albeit, for very different reasons. "His proofs really inspired me as a programmer," he reports. "In fact, several are built into AnimotionPicks."

"No way!" That's Tarek, and AnimotionPicks is the software module that powered their gift recommendations. The subsystem that started executing eerily well several weeks ago. Kuba's been encoding Cousin Charles's syllogisms since he first read the man's book—which he's called "the very stuff of thought" ever since. Although I'm not so sure he's right about this. My own theory is that Charles's book became a talisman to Kuba after his deportation. A shiny relic of the lost world he sorely missed, he treasured it, and in my view, came to habitually inflate its significance. Packed with logical structures, it did help inspire Kuba's idiosyncratic programming style. In this, its significance is undeniable. But "the stuff of thought"? For that honor, my money's on motes.

Regardless, Cousin Charles Henry Higgensworth III still remains something of a hero to both of the guys, years after death. And whether it's Higgensworth logic, digital motes, or something else, there's something undeniably spooky happening in the AnimotionPicks code base — and there always will be. And yes, I do mean that literally. *Always.*

Speaking of which: "I guess that means your cousin's thinking is about to completely infest Phluttr," Tarek says.

"Why's that?" Mitchell asks.

"Because our CTO loves AnimotionPicks," Tarek gushes. "He thinks it could become one of our most popular general purpose libraries, and he just pushed it into the common repo!"

"Really? That's amazing!" Saying this, Mitchell catches Kuba grinning sheepishly at his feet. Like Danna, the man shies from positive attention. But he better get used to it—because his work's about to reach a massive audience! With an open engineering culture, Phluttr maintains a common code base whose best modules are available to everyone company-wide. Core libraries, in the main shared repository (or "repo"), end up in software with hundreds of millions of users. Just a few nights back, Kuba vowed to "turn Phluttr into a sea of digital motes" in a quest to crack Falkenberg's disease. Now, already: Ta da!

With everyone now here, they enter the PhastPhorwardr. Inside, wide warehouse windows admit boundless cheery sunshine, blunted by a smart form of glass that moderates temperatures, keeps the UV out, and presents an opaque face to nosey outsiders trying to peer in. The seating is largely open-plan. There's also a smattering of cubicles, and an occasional Chinese wall delineates work-group turf. Big enough to seat a couple hundred comfortably, the place is not quite at capacity. "Welcome to Phluttr's science project," Tarek says as they enter.

"Science project?" Danna asks.

"Not literally, of course. But the whole setup's almost academic, y'know? Apart from a couple giant development efforts."

"Like the augmented reality glasses you're working on?" Mitchell confirms.

Tarek nods. "WingMan. There's that, and this huge robotics operation we'll visit in a bit. Otherwise, it's a bunch of micro-startups, mostly still chasing their preacquisition dreams. And it's all the cool new-ish stuff. Synthetic biology, blockchain, drones, quantum computing—that sorta thing. None with any connection to the main Phluttr service, by the way."

"The idea is to let Phluttr keep tabs on emerging technologies," Kuba says. "Like, all of them."

"I guess that . . . makes sense?" Mitchell says, not really believing this.

"Yeah, only it *doesn't*," Danna declares. "Sure, keeping an eye on the rest of the Valley's smart. But wouldn't it be a lot cheaper to read a bunch of *TechCrunch* articles?"

Tarek just shrugs. "Don't look at me. I'm the one who told you it's weird around here."

"And ya'll must be Team Giftish.ly!" The booming voice is very friendly and very southern. They're at the edge of the synthetic biology, or "synbio" realm, where the presiding ex-founder is a middle-aged Georgian with the awesome name of Buford Bragg. He leads them past meticulously airtight barriers to a small assembly line. To the clueless eye, it's all humming rectangles, so Buford narrates. "These boxes resemblin the lovechildren of washin machines and rice cookers're Eppendorf centrifuges," he states. "They can pellet cells or DNA with the best of em. And that pregnant-mailbox-lookin thing over there? Goes by the Wu Tang–worthy name of Agilent Bioanalyzer!" Mitchell guesses the accent is at least half affectation, and that the guy's upping the down-homeness to make his field seem a bit less intimidating.

"Heard of the Human Genome Project?" Buford asks, strolling over to something resembling a desktop printer. All nod. "Soaked up thousands of bioscience's best minds for thirteen years and cost $3 billion." He points at the box beside him. "Now this sucker'll do that same amount of work in less'n a day, at a net cost of a few hundred bucks! And the Human Genome Project wasn't that long ago. I mean, *Law & Order* was still on the air. W was in the White House. Almost feels like yesterday, don't it?" Bottom line, genetic science is accelerating and cheapening even faster than computing. Way faster.

For instance: "It cost about a buck to read a single letter of genetic code back when I'd guesstimate you were a schoolboy," Buford says, pointing at Mitchell. "Now, we read *millions* of letters for a buck. It's like goin from mappin a newly discovered continent on foot, to using satellites. Which is a huge deal! But fun as cartography is, would you rather *build* continents?" Well, Buford sure would. Which is why he's not mapping but synthesizing DNA, letter by letter. "And synthesis is now movin down the price curve as fast as DNA readin did! Not long ago, synthesizin a base pair cost the same buck that readin a base pair cost in the nineties. Today, synthesis rounds to a nickel a pair, though some folks'll quote you less."

"So how long until you can synthesize me?" Danna half jokes.

"I'd give it a decade or three," Buford says, not joking at all. "A human-scale genome weighs in at about 3 billion base pairs. And today, we couldn't synthesize a tenth of one percent of that! Top labs, like this'n, crank out strings runnin into the tens of thousands of base pairs. And though we're all marchin upward pretty steadily, there'll be a huge barrier around 100K, which no one knows how we'll cross. DNA starts gettin real brittle at those lengths, and we'll need to come up with novel ways of compacting and protecting strands while they're under construction."

Asked exactly what he's creating, Buford answers, "Both everything, and nothing." In other words, "We're not doin any design work ourselves here at Phluttr. We're just makin DNA, print-to-order. And we do that better'n anyone else in the world. So we're leavin the sexy stuff to our customers. They're the ones trainin white cells to whup cancer, turnin algae into fake meat that could fool a cattleman, and makin the blind see. To give you just three examples. Bottom line: the world designs it, then we build it."

"So you sell the DNA itself and not machines to make it," Mitchell confirms.

Buford nods. "No one's really sellin machines for your lengthier DNA strands. Not yet. And for the next few years, the market'll mainly be folks sellin DNA as a service, like us. But that'll change. I mean, there was a time when no one sold machines to *read* DNA, and that was a service! Now the guys who make this sucker're movin billions wortha gear and reagents every year." He points at the compact box that can read an entire human genome in a day. "And that's a common pattern in tech. Goin clear back to printin on *paper* rather'n DNA! Back when I was a kid, you could spend a hundred grand on a jet printer the size a this room. And that sucker'd live in a central bureau, where ordinary mortals bought print runs by the page. And it was way less capable than the eighty-nine-dollar Epson special I got sittin on my desk!"

"So will you make do-it-yourself machines someday?" Danna asks.

Buford shrugs. "That's a way's off yet for our industry. But if I don't end up doin that, someone will. And long before today's grade-schoolers're your age, cheap desktop boxes'll be writin more DNA in a minute than my whole lab puts out in a year. I can almost guarantee we'll have hundred-dollar custom viruses before the next Olympics, and thousand-buck bacteria."

"But is that safe?" Mitchell asks.

"Course not. Printin presses aren't safe. Just ask anyone who lived through the Reformation."

Tarek shrugs. "Nukes aren't safe. But even in a world of 7 billion lunatics, nobody's shot one off in anger in over seventy years."

"Yes, but practically no one *gets* to," Mitchell points out. "So that's not such a comforting data point."

"Assuming we're now talkin about war and terrorism, a huge difference between bio and your traditional weapons is that bio's real hard to target," Buford says. "Just look at the flu. It doesn't exactly respect borders! And 'kill *these* guys but *not* those guys' is a hard instruction to issue if you're targeting human biology writ large."

The meeting ends when Jepson summons Mitchell to a late-breaking meeting connected to the FTC (*what??*). As he puzzles over this, Danna reminds him about the privacy investigation Jepson mentioned on their first day here. Mitchell nods in vague recollection. Though just days ago, that conversation feels like ancient history.

Rocketing out the door, Mitchell decides to find Buford's closing argument comforting. Emerging synthetic biology tools are powerful, and scary. But even the most destructive crazies define themselves in opposition to something, or someone. No evil group—not the Nazis, not the Spanish Inquisition, not ISIS—has ever wanted to kill *everyone*.

Right?

∞   ∞   ∞

CROSS-AGENCY INTELLIGENCE SYNOPSIS: JAYSH AL HISAAB

OVERVIEW: Jaysh al Hisaab is an apocalyptic, nihilistic offshoot of Islam's ultraconservative Salafi movement. It emerged in Central Africa around 2012. Its core precept is that *any* act of mass murder at *any* scale can be justifiable and desirable, as all of its victims immediately go to their "infinitely deserved" fates in either heaven or hell. Because the rewards and punishments of the afterlife are determined by infallible divine judgment, unjust outcomes after death are impossible. Also, "Perfect justice is a perfect blessing, and a blessing that arrives sooner is superior to one arriving later"; so speeding any soul to its ultimate fate is "unambiguously desirable," regardless of whether the victim is bound for heaven or hell. In short, killing a good person is just as Godly an act as killing an evil one. And killing more people is better than killing fewer.

For this reason, Jaysh al Hisaab is unique among exponents of terror in condoning the slaughter of believers and nonbelievers equally. It argues that all attacks should maximize the sheer number of victims, without regard to religion, nationality, gender, or age. Its supporters therefore tend to perpetrate attacks in their own communities, as distant foreign societies are harder to infiltrate and therefore likely to yield fewer casualties.

The movement carefully shapes its propaganda to appeal to the depressed and the suicidal, who exist in all societies, and can be highly vulnerable to emotional manipulation and apocalyptic reasoning. Its ideology has been condemned by all mainstream schools of Islamic thought, as well as all other religious terror groups (including Al Qaeda and ISIS's various shards and splinters). However, it has many small pockets of adherents throughout the world, due to the meticulously argued online sermons of its charismatic, multilingual founder Abu Sayf al-Din.

ORIGINS: Jaysh al Hisaab emerged in N'Djamena, the capital of the impoverished, landlocked African nation of Chad. Extremely violent struggles were then under way in three of Chad's immediate neighbors (the Darfur conflict in Sudan, the post-Qadaffi anarchy in Libya, and the Boko Haram uprising in Nigeria). The movement began in an encampment that was originally started by foreign refugees, then later expanded by local jobless youth. New residents were drawn by a set of low-level communal services provided by Abu Sayf al-Din's early followers. In 2014, the Chadian government denounced Jaysh al Hisaab as a "parallel state." The encampment was then destroyed, and over two thousand of its residents brutally massacred. A radicalized core of survivors, including Abu Sayf al-Din, fled and found shelter with a sympathetic Boko Haram offshoot in neighboring Nigeria.

LEADERSHIP: Little is known for certain about Abu Sayf al-Din, including his nationality (conflicting sources cite Chad, Niger, and Nigeria), his precise age, or whether he remains alive. What is clear is that he is (or was) an intensely gifted polemicist with a fluent command of highly idiomatic French, a strong command of formal Arabic, and access to an English linguist who translated his sermons, then coached him to mouth them phonetically (this is inferred because the English sermons consist of hundreds of stitched-together cuts, whereas all French and Arabic sermons were recorded in single, fluid takes). Abu Sayf al-Din also has a very strong knowledge of multiple scholarly Islamic traditions.

∞   ∞   ∞

Along with Jepson, a striking woman Mitchell hasn't yet met is in the conference room. All Louboutin and Chanel, she's the Hollywood ideal of a Wintour-grade corporate doyenne. She also emits this compass-bending . . . *field* of authority, which proclaims she's been Boss for decades, and not mere years, young man! But her look and build would still turn heads in a bar. Not in an EDM-pumping meat market, no. But in one of your swanker, Rat-Packy joints—one with artisanal tonics and a pro on the baby grand, maybe in the Four Seasons of one of your better city-states; Singapore, say, or Dubai. She seems to cross the squash-court-sized conference room in a single mighty stride. And as she zeroes in,

Mitchell feels like . . . quarry. Or maybe putty. Putty of the sort that Mrs. Robinson reduced Dustin Hoffman to way back then (but not sexual in this case; no, no, *no*, not that!).

"I know," she says. "The Help wears business formal in Silicon Valley, don't they? So you're thinking, who is this lowlife, and how's she getting face time with the mighty Phoundr?" For the record, Mitchell is thinking nothing of the sort. But given a moment to catch his breath, a less arch, provocative, and (let's be honest) articulate version of this thought would have crossed his mind. Because the Valley's ruling class — its smattering of Jepsons and armies of proto-Jepsons — is indeed universally hoodied, jeaned, and/or besneakered. Suits and professional garb like hers are like tradesmen's uniforms in a midcentury British class drama. They're the plumage of your investment banker, lawyer, consultant, or wealth-management hack. Erstwhile Masters of the Universe who here, in the seat of Capitalism 3.0, are but the Help — a respected but lesser caste of journeymen who generate documents and tend to the accounts, freeing up the better sort for more important matters. "I'm Judy Sherman," she says, extending a hand for Mitchell to shake, which he manages rather well. "Attorney. And you have no idea why you're here."

She withdraws a few feet, toward the biggest and blankest whiteboard wall. "Ever heard of Poland, Mitchell?" She asks this without looking at him, clearly seeking no answer, and starts pacing professorially. "Butt of many jokes. But geopolitically, it's what we call a buffer state. Germany and Russia? Not friends. So God, or someone, puts Poland smack between them. That way, when the big boys just have to rumble, one of 'em can conquer Poland instead! It blows off steam, see? They basically take turns at this for centuries. Some of my mom's people were from there. And reading through Polish history — as your Polack granny will insist, trust me — every few years, you're like, 'Holy crap, they're doing it again!' Another conquest, and it usually takes about six minutes! That's what you get for picking flat plains for your natural defense. Eventually, the world can't see Poland as anything *but* a buffer state! It gets so bad, at the end of World War II, they literally pick up the entire country and move it two hundred miles *to the left*. Russia wants some more Poland, which means Germany has to lose some, so let's just move the fucker to the left! Anyway. I know I'm not exactly selling you on buffer-statedom. But you don't have a choice, so I don't have to."

Judy's now on the closest approach of her pacing circuit. So it's jarring when she stops dead, then whirls on a stiletto stylus to face him. "What I'm saying is, you're gonna be a buffer, Mitchell. Between two somewhat larger entities. In this corner"—she waves her arms Jepsonward, like a matador flinging a cape—"we have the digital juggernaut known as Phluttr! And in that corner"—she waves toward the room's emptiest quadrant—"the Government of the United States of America! And smack in the middle? We have lit-tle Mit-chell Pren-tice. Sound like fun?"

∞   ∞   ∞

CROSS-AGENCY INTELLIGENCE SYNOPSIS: JAYSH AL HISAAB (CONT'D.)

DEVELOPMENT AND DIFFUSION: Though little survives of Abu Sayf al-Din's earliest teachings, they are reported to have focused upon the notions of *jabr* and *qadar*, which connect to issues of fate and predestination in Islam. His interpretation of these concepts holds that all human affairs are entirely foreordained, a perspective more in line with Calvinist Christianity than much of mainstream Islam.

After the massacre of his followers, he struggled with overwhelming suicidal thoughts, which were all the more troubling because suicide is a grave sin in Islam. More troubling still, his highly deterministic theology obliged him to view the massacre as a magnificently calculated act of God's will, which could only be seen as an unambiguous blessing. He concluded that the blessing stemmed from hastening his noble followers to their infinite reward in paradise. Just as desirable, any false or impure followers were hastened to searing punishments that would otherwise have been delayed for years. This logic led Abu Sayf al-Din to his extreme conclusion that indiscriminate mass murder can have "unambiguously good" outcomes.

After fleeing to Nigeria, Jaysh al Hisaab leadership obtained reliable Internet access and video-production tools. Abu Sayf al-Din then distilled his theology into nine 30–40-minute canonical sermons that were each filmed in English,

Arabic, and French. They have since been subtitled into over one hundred languages by followers, scholars, and others online. His delivery in all languages is
punctuated by highly evocative gestures and facial expressions. Though surely
meticulously choreographed, they're delivered in a natural manner which
greatly bolsters overall impact. The rhetoric is highly accessible, with scholarly
gyrations avoided and everyday vocabulary favored. Abu Sayf al-Din also conveys a warm, earnest, and at times almost loving demeanor, in stark contrast to
the stern, somber tones favored by many modern mullahs.

THEOLOGY: Each sermon begins with opening statements and principles
that will be wholly uncontroversial to its intended audience of conservative
Salafi Muslims. From this starting point, Abu Sayf al-Din unfolds a sequence of
logically connected arguments, each supported by coherent and often very witty
analogies, as well as quotes from the Quran and the hadiths. All lead to his conclusions about murder and acts of terror. Although common murderers are
"wicked," Abu Sayf al-Din says those who kill with the express purpose of hastening fellow humans "to the afterlife that they merit infinitely" are sanctified.
Righteous victims end up spending far less time on Earth, "which, however delightful, is wretched compared to the joys of heaven," while infidels are "delivered more swiftly to their rightful infinite torment."

Much care is devoted to reaching those afflicted by suicidal feelings, which
Abu Sayf al-Din discusses in the intensely personal terms of his own anguish in
the wake of the massacre. Many followers who find his sermons in the throes of
their own crises have cited this as inspiring their conversions. Abu Sayf al-Din
posits that a meaningless life on the cusp of an empty and sinful ending can be
redeemed and wholly sanctified if it closes with the "boundlessly just and mer-
ciful act" of "rightly motivated" mass homicide.

While fiercely emotional, his arguments are also quite analytical and built atop
a linear logical edifice. As such, they resonate most deeply with the intelligent,
educated, and sincerely devout. People of this ilk often have significant resources and access, creating the potential for especially sophisticated and destructive attacks. Abu Sayf al-Din ingeniously manipulates the conflicting
feelings of guilt, grandeur, desperation, and entitlement that might beset suicidal Muslims in a privileged, developing-world context. He offers a way out of

a previously intractable situation, while salving injured vanity with the promise of a spectacular exit, followed by glory, laud, and honor in the hereafter.

TEACHINGS: Abu Sayf al-Din presents his core philosophy in his first four sermons, in markedly nonsectarian terms. Because only God can judge, followers of Jaysh al Hisaab's path should not presume to target victims on any basis at all. Rather than being animated by hatred and anger, they should coolly optimize attacks to "release the greatest number of souls." Abu Sayf al-Din devotes the five subsequent sermons to reaching specific outside groups. Adherents of Al Qaeda, Islamic State, and Nigeria's Boko Haram movement are each addressed in terms that carefully position Jaysh al Hisaab's brand of Sunni extremism within their own complementary traditions. Far more audaciously, the eighth sermon addresses Shi'as in extremely well-researched and carefully worded terms. This is a bold gambit in this time of peak tension and violence between the Sunni and Shi'a communities, and has inspired terror-suicide attacks in both Isfahan and Tehran, Iran. Most remarkably, the ninth sermon targets non-Muslims (above all, apocalyptic Christians) who believe in an afterlife preceded by divine judgment.

Abu Sayf al-Din's overture to non-Sunnis amounts to a perverse inversion of Pascal's Wager. He maintains that non-Sunnis are damned, and accepts that many non-Sunnis will maintain that he is damned. However, he proposes that all who believe that God alone will ultimately judge the dead should cooperate to hasten a maximum number of people to that very judgment. All can agree that God will then infallibly determine who is damned and who is saved. This leads to the astounding proposition that Muslims and non-Muslims collaborate in massive joint suicide attacks.

Abu Sayf al-Din's arguments contain many glaring inconsistencies and logical fallacies, but minds unversed in critical thinking will struggle to identify them, or to refute the freight train of charisma and apparent logic that contains them. In any event, his arguments are not intended to inspire a broad movement or sustain a lasting nation-state. They are instead carefully packaged to appeal to lone-wolf attackers, small self-organizing cells, and somewhat larger ideologically fired groups. As such, they need only sustain faith and conviction long enough for the new converts to stage a self-annihilating attack.

Whether by design or chance, Abu Sayf al-Din's philosophy seems to comple-
ment a growing trend among Islamic terrorists toward the nihilistic slaughter of
fellow Muslims, particularly (but not exclusively) by Pakistani terrorists. Indiscriminate attacks like the International Islamic University bombing in Islam-
abad, and the more recent Peshawar massacre of 132 schoolchildren could be at
least partly consistent with Jaysh al Hisaab's theology.

$$\infty \qquad \infty \qquad \infty$$

Danna's killing time with Kuba and Tarek at their desks while they wait
for Mitchell to return from his meeting. As they gossip and catch up,
Tarek tells them about the crazy UberX of Sex pitch. "I hear Jepson
wasn't nuts about it. But it lines up with this notion he sometimes pushes
about Phluttr being all about sex. Or something."

"Ick," Danna says. "Tell me more."

"The idea is, our era's defined by hyper-abundance in the developed
world. Information's basically free. Most entertainment, too. And
calories're so cheap that obesity's a much bigger problem than hunger.
Meanwhile, almost everyone has shelter, and is mostly safe from violence. And these are the things that almost all human beings spent almost every waking hour obtaining since the dawn of time. We were
literally designed and born to pursue these things! And now, they're practically givens. From birth until death."

"And therefore sex?" Danna asks skeptically.

"Kinda. The idea is, sex is the one primal drive we can't just satisfy
with dead-simple purchases. And while that's been true for years, we're
increasingly accustomed to getting everything else on demand—which
pushes expectations to crazy new heights! Meanwhile, *experiences* are
becoming more prized and precious every year, because so much else is
commonplace. And unlike fame, or the thrill of a competitive victory,
say, sex is one sublime experience that *could* be almost universally available, in theory. Yet it remains scarce. It's highly coveted, it can be really
tricky to obtain, and lots of people feel a huge lack of it."

"So, with all the other bases covered, sex is the last great consumer
market vacuum?" Danna guesses, and Tarek nods. "So, fill the vacuum,
and the whole world adopts Phluttr?" He nods again. She stews on this

for a moment. Then, "Wait a second! Mitchell's got ninety days to come up with an internal startup idea, or he's gone, right?"

Tarek nods. "That's the general rule with founders after acquihires."

She turns to Kuba. "And you and Ellie think motes might have something to do with Falkenberg's disease?"

Kuba nods. "It's a total shot in the dark for now. But it feels right. Kind of strongly, in fact."

"So we need an excuse to keep working on motes!" Danna says. Kuba nods again. "And Jepson's most likely to approve a pitch with some twisted, pervy angle to it?" All nod. "Well, this whole Cyrano thing has given me an idea . . ."

∞   ∞   ∞

"A little background for you," Jepson says to Mitchell. "Judy here's an intellectual property lawyer. Her firm once defended my personal IP from certain niggling mimics and pilferers."

"Like Apple and Microsoft?" Mitchell asks. These were two of the bigger names in the legal crusade against Jepson's colors-on-Web-pages patent.

"Among others," Jepson says, dismissing the founding duo of modern computing with an irked flick of a wrist. "Judy's practice deals with media IP, so she wasn't directly involved in my case. But she also runs government relations for her firm, and I made a couple of lobbying calls to DC during that period."

"The real fight was in the courts, of course," Judy says. "But there was an odious and underhanded patent reform push in Congress that we were able to stave off for quite a few years."

Outwardly calm, Mitchell inwardly screams, *That was You?* Cannibals and Ba'athists are less popular than patent trolls in Silicon Valley, sure; but by narrow enough margins that it reflects poorly on everyone. For years those gutter-grade parasites sucked billions from the innovation budgets of startups and giants alike, with waves of frivolous lawsuits (patent trolls, that is. Ba'athists are another matter). Bipartisan apathy over this patently broken system (sorry) fueled boundless bafflement and cynicism among tech elites. But their indignation was ironic in light of their own torpid disengagement from the Washington process. Early in the millennium, the industry finally roused itself to launch its own lobbying efforts. But for years they made no headway on the patent front because some ingenious operative of the *ancien regime* was holding back the floodwaters. And is this *she*? Who knows. But Judy seems to be just the sort of dervish who could whirl from committee to hearing to caucus with enough nudges, winks, and dislocating arm twists to foil an entire industry.

"While she mainly works the legislature, Judy has contacts everywhere," Jepson says. "So when the FTC started investigating Phluttr, she knew within nanoseconds."

"Oh, *you*," Judy says, "it was at least five minutes." She turns to Mitchell. "Our problem is a commissioner. The FTC has five of them, and Annabelle Milford's eyeing a Senate run in Iowa. Iowa's a remarkably queer state—and I definitely do *not* mean gay! It leans Dem, but has these red-state rural social values. Which means you can win over half-witted hillbillies on *both* sides of the aisle by beating up on Phluttr. On the right, they hate you guys for getting people laid and giving their schoolgirls yet another route to Justin Bieber. With no relation between the two, let's hope! And your lefties have hissy fits over privacy crap that the right lets slide because they think markets are infallible, and ergo, so are companies. Milford's got lots of throw-weight on the Commission because she's charming and plays nice with everyone. She's right down the middle politically and could probably get nominated by either party, though she'll go with Democrats."

"Judy's little birds have it that Milford plans to hit us hard on privacy," Jepson says. "Which is nothing but trumped-up, politicized bullshit."

"Sure. If we ignore that Phluttr tramples the letter and spirit of every privacy law since the Alien and Sedition Acts!" Judy snaps.

"Oh, right," Jepson says. "There's that." And the two of them break into playful laughter. This goes on quite a bit longer than Mitchell's comfortable with and veers toward demonic cackling before they stop.

"So," Judy continues, "let's imagine—*tot*ally hypothetically—that the rumors are true, and Phluttr has deep ties to some powerful, scary players in Washington. Only they're top secret players, see? These theoretical friends of ours—if they actually exist—would find it hard to help us derail a public inquest by a high-powered commissioner operating within her mandate. Top secret agencies do have lots of power and latitude. But they're constrained within US borders and in dealing with American citizens. Particularly since the USA Freedom Act clipped certain wings back in 2015, thanks to Mr. Snowden's awkward revelations, which made certain top secret programs top-*un*secret. And certain agencies double-plusunpopular."

"The N*a-tion-al Sec-ur-i-ty Ag-en-cy*, for one!" Jepson hisses, using a madcap stage whisper to finally mention an unmentionable.

"And as for other branches of the government?" Judy continues. "Oi!" She says this like a Clash-era British punk, not a playful American Jew. "They were hard enough to deal with before Snowden. Now everyone's playing for the galleries and acting like they're Daniel fucking Ellsberg!" She drops her voice a notch, giving Mitchell a look that can only be described as parenthetical. "Before your time, kid. Pentagon Papers." Then, back in high dudgeon: "So. If some puffed-up FTC bitch who's grand-standing for a Senate run gets a discreet request from the dark side to drop her damned investigation, she'll sooner blab to the HuffPo than cooperate!"

"Bottom line, this investigation's really dangerous for Phluttr," Jepson says.

"And for its Phoundr," Judy adds, with the inimitable zeal of a lawyer discussing a moneyed client's legal woes. "Who could be looking at ten to fifteen in San Quentin, given the teeth these privacy laws suddenly have! And it's not like our top secret buddies—"

"*Hypothetical* top secret buddies," Jepson clarifies joshingly.

"—operate under some chivalric, 'No Man Left Behind' code. Christ, I know a Medal of Honor winner rotting in a Karachi cell because it'd be a PR headache to admit he's there! So however great an asset Phluttr is to the Authority, do you *really* think they'd stick their heads over the parapet for *you*?"

Mitchell shakes his head. Having never heard of the Authority, he can honestly attest that this never crossed his mind.

"At this point," Jepson says, all but plucking Mitchell's next thought straight from his cortex, "you may be wondering what this has to do with you. Well, somebody who's *not* named Tony Jepson needs to be the FTC's interface here at Phluttr. Someone who's genuinely clueless about all the stuff we may *or may not* have hinted at during this conversation."

"Someone who could put his hand on the Bible," Judy says, "or his chest, bicep, and fingers into the polygraph—and sincerely proclaim, *I know nothhhh-ink!*" An apparent old-school cultural reference, this soars right over Mitchell's head though it can't be flattering.

"Someone who's loyal," Jepson says, with a little attaboy wink. "Who we can trust!"

"And who will not crack," Judy adds. "Not under waterboarding. Dismemberment. Even . . . unmanning!" She enjoys Mitchell's horror quite a bit longer than necessary, then adds, "I'm just fucking with ya, kid. I doubt it'll go much past a polygraph."

"We like you for this job for a few reasons," Jepson says. "First, you're obviously smart enough. Second, you practically ripped Raj's throat out for dissing Danna! I loved that. It showed loyalty! To Danna, anyway."

"Another thing? As Jepson's shadow and backstop, you're his direct report," Judy says. "One of exactly two. Because, technically, the entire company reports to Beasley, who in turn reports to Jepson. Things're of course different on a de facto level. But in dealing with investigations, de jure is all that counts. And de jure, Beasley runs everything, for reasons you do not want to know. And by now, I'm sure you realize we can't put *him* in front of anyone sensitive."

"So, gooooo Mitchell, that leaves you!" Jepson says, pointing at him Uncle Sam style. "The FTC'll already be plenty pissed that I'm pushing them down a notch in the org chart. Dropping two levels just ain't gonna work! So we really have to connect them with one of my directs. And last but not least, the final reason why you're perfect for this?" Jepson pauses dramatically, then gives Judy a take-it-away wave.

"Your cousin works for me! Small world, huh? And I don't mind him. So, for transitive reasons, I don't mind you!" Mitchell looks at her blankly. "You . . . do know who I'm talking about, right?"

No, not really. He has a weirdly large number of cousins for a New England WASP. Though the broader tribe slowed its breeding program long ago in a dismayed response to Roosevelt, Mitchell's clan kept at it. And as every kid-choked family reunion attests, they're still maintaining Melville-era fecundity well into the Kardashian age.

Once it's clear he has no idea who she's talking about, Judy barks, "I want it that way?" Mitchell pegs this for a clue, but it doesn't help. So she snaps, "Quit playing games with my heart!" This is definitely a hint, not a plea; so he just shrugs. Finally, "Backstreet Boy, duh."

"Oh, Nick *Carter*!" Nick is a rather distant cousin—Pugwash's age, closer to Pugwash in the tangled family tree, and a good guy from what Mitchell recalls from childhood. But the main thing he knows about Nick is that he hates the goddam Backstreet Boys (which Mitchell can also get behind), on account of tragically sharing a name with one of them—then entering young adulthood just as they hit it big.

"So," Judy concludes, "Jepson trusts you directly. I trust you indirectly. And our only other option is *Beasley*, so it's not like we have a choice. Our first meeting with the commissioner isn't in the calendar yet, but expect it in two or three weeks. Until then? Toodle-oo."

∞ ∞ ∞

N≡T GRRRL.COM

ONLINE DATING: BIG DATA DRIVES A RACE TO THE BOTTOM

Among the more dehumanizing results of Big Data's relentless march (a rather high-bar domain) is its metastasizing impact on the World Wide Woo (and yes, that's NetGrrrlSpeak for online dating). It was inevitable that someone would synthesize these areas into a new field of scholarship (*Data for Pussy!*). And as it happened, my colleagues in bloggerhood over at Masculin.ist took the first crack (and *no puns*, please—Jesus!).

Having snagged anonymized data from a certain hookup site, they quickly reduced the entire endeavor of romance to a single number: 1.82. And to put Science to work for *you,* horny reader, you were advised to let X equal the number of minutes your online quarry took to answer your last message—and then, withhold your own response until exactly 1.82X minutes passed. This interval, Masculin.ist scient.ists certified, would maximize the odds of your note leading to ejaculation (or, at least, to the girl writing back. Sorry boys—but walk before running, eh?).

This made at least some sense. Insta-replies are the hallmark of overeager losers, so letting >X minutes pass might signal that you're a stud with plenty of hotties to service, digitally or otherwise. But delays of, say, 3X minutes could risk overplaying your hand and unleash the romance-quashing insecurities, which (Masculin.ist asserts) are core to the female psyche. All told, it was grotesquely simplistic "research." And as this information spread—or should I say "as disinformation spread" (*get it??*)—untold numbers of romantic dialogues trailed off into silence as both sides continuously upped the number of minutes, hours, and (eventually) decades that stretched between exchanges (sorry Mr. Kurzweil, but sometimes exponential growth actually kind of sucks).

Needless to say, there was nothing particularly Big about the Data presented in that seminal research (and again, QUIT IT WITH THE PUNS! I *swear*, you people . . .). Truly big dating data only became a reality with the rise of RedTrove. This open-source service will, with your permission, monitor your flirting and mating attempts on sites as mainstream as Match.com, or as specialized as FurryMate (ewww!—*Ed.*). RedTrove then combines your anonymized information with that of its other users, creating a Hadoop-worthy pile of stats-n-facts that anyone can comb through.

Several services are now adding proprietary layers atop RedTrove's data, the classiest of which is certainly DidSheDo.yu. Here, users are asked to self-report the sexual payoffs of their online conquests. And lest you cynics suspect the service is overrun by aging virgins who get off on claiming their every text leads to coitus, rest assured that all users are bound by the strict terms of the DidSheDo.yu Honor Code (#ShitICouldNotMakeUp).

For a small fee, DidSheDo.yu will furnish you with a scientifically derived timeline to help you pace your stream of messages, silences, and cock photos to the belle of your dreams. They purport to do this so well that users can confidently specify the precise outcomes they're seeking up front, as if ordering at a diner (UPDATE: I SWEAR TO GOD, for two days, the now-blank square to the right contained a screen grab of a drop-down menu including Blowjob, Anal, Threesome, and "ATM" [*whaaat?*] plucked from the DSD.yu mobile app, which I pulled down after being threatened with a copyright lawsuit).

To be clear perfectly: **none of these apps work even slightly** (a statement that can be generalized to include *all cock photos* at *all times*—seriously, gentlemen—so please stop clogging our inboxes with this icky, and [trust me, here] laughably ineffective spam). But that doesn't mean there isn't useful data in RedTrove because there certainly is.

Being intrigued by the subject of online courtship, and something of a data ninjette, I took a long, slow dive through that data. And after slicing and correlating innumerable variables, I found—to my startlement and delight—that men still initiate <u>over 95%</u> of would-be romantic interactions, even in these modern times (less on Tinder, but it's still a high ratio there).

This feels like a remarkably traditional state of affairs, given all else that's changed in the bedroom since the dawn of the sexual revolution. Back then, the bid/ask spread was men wanting the obvious, and the ladies counteroffering, *I'll do you for a ring*. So let's turn to RedTrove and see where we are now!

Hmmm. It seems the male position has yet to budge. Whereas we spent the last fifty years budging our naughty little bottoms off (in certain cities, data suggests that the median's slid to *I'll blow you for an amaretto sour.* Thanks for all the awesome leadership during our formative years, Paris, Britney & friends!). This isn't to say that "do you for a ring" was entirely sane or healthy. But the same could surely be said of *their* opening position. So, please let the record show that we've met our confreres well past midway between imperfect starting points.

Except. We still hold their feet to the fire when it comes to making the first move. To this day, it's the boys who have to fight the butterflies, face rejection, and man up when they approach us. So yayyy, go us!

Sigh And how nice would it've been if I'd just left it at that? I could've typed up the cutest post about my discovery! And maybe saved it for Valentine's Day! Oooh, or prom season! But no, I just *had* to dive a lit-tle bit deeper, didn't I? Because I was dying to know what those sweet little armies of stammering traditionalists were using as their opening gambits when they got up the nerve to approach their would-be sweethearts!

I could tell you right now. But email beckons, and I'm a cortex tease (not to mention a click ho), so tune in tomorrow for our exciting conclusion . . .

∞   ∞   ∞

The newly christened Team Cyrano thoroughly brainstorms Danna's idea before Mitchell returns from his meeting. She's burning to tell him all about it! But Kuba wants them to meet one of his favorite PhastPhorwardr workmates before the guy takes off for the cafeteria, and Tarek needs to finish arranging their robot-lab visit. So Mitchell, Kuba, and Danna dash off to a dark, tiny, and strangely cold roomlet. It's empty, save for a silver cylinder that looks like a home water heater. A really nice water heater. One polished so flawlessly by its OCD-stricken owner that it could probably find work as a funhouse mirror should heating water prove a bad career choice. "Can you guys guess what this is?" Kuba whispers, almost reverentially. They look closer at the cylinder's utterly featureless surface. A few brightly colored cables connect it to a port in the ceiling. Two small pipes exit it at arm height, then thrust through the back wall. That's about it.

Mitchell shocks everyone by guessing, "A quantum computer?" He just stumbled across a piece about these in a back issue of *Time* (yeah, *Time*—he decides to keep this fact to himself).

"Ex*act*ly! The processor's kept in the cryocooler," Kuba says, pointing at the cylinder. "Everything else is back there." He points to the wall the pipes exit through. "They keep the processor isolated, and chilled to ten millikelvin. That's incredibly close to absolute zero. They also maintain a high vacuum in there. About one ten-billionth of an atmosphere. Magnetism is heavily shielded, too. And so on."

"All this for a social network?" Danna asks suspiciously.

"But Phluttr is a social operating system!" booms a deep voice behind them—startling Mitchell and Danna to the point of almost jumping out of their flesh. They wheel and find themselves facing a guy whose hairy red penumbra might technically be a mane, as it's hard to tell where (or if) the boundaries lie between bangs, fro, chops, dreads, mustache, and beard. Were he not the height of a Nordic point guard, you might peg him for a Tolkien dwarf. "I am Ax," he says, extending his right hand. As Mitchell's standing a bit closer, he's the one who smashes his knuckles on the rock-hard monitor mounted to the vault-thick door maybe six inches behind them. Ax's ensuing laughter is too warm to carry any hint of mockery even though it's clear that Mitchell's been pranked, and good.

And so, Mitchell and Danna meet two PhastPhorwardr stalwarts at once—Ax, and the monitor itself: a prototype called WingMan XXL. It's a teleconferencing system based on the display technology in the Wing-Man augmented-reality glasses. Using an ultrahigh-resolution feed, it ingeniously alters your interlocutors' apparent size, orientation, and lighting, so it looks like you're all occupying the same physical space. Which would be nigh impossible in this tiny room, given Ax's evident size. Yet it looks uncannily like he's standing a comfortable few feet away from them. Looking very closely, the illusion's not quite perfect. But it was good enough to make Mitchell bash the close-in monitor when he reached for Ax's hand. "We'll all be getting desktop versions of this monitor next week," Kuba says. "They're rolling out prototypes to the whole company. As for Ax? Well, introduce yourself."

"I am founder of Quantum Supremacy Corporation," Ax says. "From Russia, originally. But I am een America over twenty years now."

"Ax is short for 'Maxim,'" Kuba explains.

"Is popular man's name in Russia. But is popular man's magazine here! So . . ." Ax makes an ax-like gesture with his hand, as if hacking his name down to size. "I have degrees in electrical engineering and pheee-sics. But not Eeenglish dee-ction. HA HA!" Good Lord, those H's! Ax sounds like a diner attempting self-rescue while panicked waiters consult a Heimlich poster.

"No, I wouldn't peg you as an English major," Mitchell snips. He feels a bit dickish saying this. But justified, as his right knuckles smart and his heart's still racing from the scare this joker gave them. And seriously, that accent! After *twenty years* in the US?

"My research is in forestalling wave-function collapse at millikelvin temperatures to extend decoherence time. Eeessential to quantum computing. By the way! What is your sign?"

"Um . . . Aquarius," Mitchell says.

"Air sign. Nice!"

"Hey, where are you dialing in from?" Danna asks. "Your network latency's amazing."

"Very far away," Ax says, with hammed-up wistfulness, whereupon the door slides open to reveal the guy's face almost precisely where the monitor had rendered it. "HA HA," he erupts, pointing at his face, then at the monitor fixed to the sliding door they're now exiting. "Eez nice, yes? Eez like pun. Only visual. Visual pun!" His Elmo-like delight is so charming, his pranks are forgiven. "So, Aquarius. You tell me exact birthday. Time of birth and city, too. I draw you full chart. But now, is almost three thirty. Come, we drink milk!" Ax heads for the exit, his giant strides leaving no time for discussion.

Heading north through SoMa's bustle to the main Phluttr office's cafeteria, Ax reveals that he's a world-class astrology expert—despite thinking the field is bullshit. Widespread anti-Semitism and a partial Jewish background kept him out of the better universities during the Soviet endtimes. So he went straight from high school to a low-paid government post. It offered computer access, which was all he wanted from life anyway. This was in a stagnant backwater of the KGB—a unit tasked with studying "American superstitions," whose popularity, the kommissars hoped, signified exploitable defects in capitalist culture. One subgroup worked on UFO belief, another on Big Foot (seriously), quite a large team focused on Catholicism, and so forth. As for the zodiac, it had intrigued the KGB ever since it came out that a Bay Area *astrologista* exerted inordinate influence over President Reagan's calendar (laugh all you want, but the guy did have a pretty good run). Ax joined that team. He helped write software to calculate astrologically auspicious dates for thousands of US government and military figures. Correlating these with the timing of their speeches and public events, the KGB triangulated who else was taking cues from the stars. "In the eighties, it was one US politician in five! And, Republicans more than Democrats!"

Now at the cafeteria, they join an astonishingly long line for 3:30 P.M., and Ax continues his story. As the Berlin Wall teetered, he connived his way to Washington to defect. No surprise: the NSA was intrigued by his KGB affiliation. Until he mentioned his astrology work—then they laughed him out of the room! They did let him stay in the US as a civilian, thank God. But with the economy entering a brief but nasty recession, the tech world wasn't hiring Russian teens who still found DOS to be quite amazing. Ax eventually scored an interview at an astrological software company (yes, there were several). *Those* guys were mind-blown by his mastery of their field! And so, he mounted his first rung on the tech industry's ladder. Working on the periphery of the occult, he gradually grew fond of the eerie and the spiritual. So as he matured as a technologist, he was instinctively drawn to quantum computing—a truly spooky domain.

"So. I get degree, I work, then finally start company two years ago. And raising first capital is easy! But growth capital?" He shrugs, frowns broadly, and raises his brows and his gaze quizzically toward the heavens. "I don't give good PowerPoint. I don't have beautiful accent. And D-Wave, they kick my ass." Another shrug, frown, and upward gaze. "But here at Phluttr, I can keep building things!"

Mitchell knows about D-Wave from *Time* (yes, *Time*, dammit—it was on the table at the *dentist's office*, OK? Jesus!). They're the quantum computing market's giant. Of course, giganticism is relative, and even D-Wave is teeny in social media industry terms. But with its systems selling into Google, Lockheed Martin, and several mysterious government shops, D-Wave ran circles around Ax's inaptly named Quantum Supremacy Corporation.

"The interesting thing about quantum computing is, it's all or nothing," Kuba points out. "Amazing experimental work is happening in the field. But the world's still waiting for a great practical application. Which could come from anywhere, Ax's lab certainly included. Because he's taking a novel approach to things. A fairly radical one that lots of researchers favor. And the next true quantum breakthrough could be colossal. Maybe even as big as the invention of the microprocessor."

"No, bigger!" Ax says. "And maybe," he adds conspiratorially, "next week!" Kuba arches a brow, and Ax reveals that he's about to test a quantum processor with more potential horsepower than anything ever created. Then, finally at the head of the line, he orders a large dish of a very specific sort of olive, and a pint—yes, a pint—of Half & Half.

The server not only fails to find this odd but passes over a preset tray of precisely this. Scanning the room, Mitchell sees dozens of people choking down this very combination. In fact, demand for this weirdness apparently caused the three thirty rush! This must be a posse of so-called body hackers—folks who spend their off-hours sprawling across the sacrificial altars of various extreme dietary and workout fads. Mitchell's own choice of a large chocolate donut and some OJ triggers a scandalized rustle of pivoting necks. Eating as he does often makes dietary zealots murderously judgmental and ravenously jealous in equal parts—like Taliban soldiers hearing about an emigré cousin who's drowning in sunshine, booze, and pussy in Miami.

"Hey, you should join the party," taunts a familiar voice. Mitchell turns to see Raj and a pair of Half-&-Half-chugging buddies. He points at the donut. "That shit'll kill you, Homer."

"Sure, when I'm eighty-five. And eighty-six sounds like a bad time."

"Yo, eighty-six is the new thirty, dude. Or it will be by the time *I* get there! So I'm keepin' the pipes clean." Raj makes a Vanna-like wave at the revolting spread in front of him.

"Are you eating Paleo or something?"

"Paleo?" Raj glances at the wrist that would hold a watch were he backward enough to own one. "Uhhh, someone check the calendar! Is it 2016 again?" His compadres chuckle scornfully. "We're eating *Medici*. Have been since December."

"And Medici is . . . ?"

"The pinnacle of ProgReg living, duh." Delighting in Mitchell's blank look, Raj translates. "Progressive/Regressive. Because repurposing ancient truths *is* progressive!"

As always, the word "repurposing" fills Mitchell with a fleeting urge to punch somebody. Onward. "And the Medici Diet is . . . ?"

"*Renaissance* eating. Mashable did a Big Data analysis of like, every portrait, ever painted. And Renaissance noblemen had the lowest body fat of anyone, ever. Plus perfect BMIs, killer abs, and the second-best hairlines in history! I mean, after the Counterreformation, obviously."

"It was a totally ketogenic era," a voice simpers from behind them, and Mitchell makes way for a hairless medicine ball of a man, who he pegs to be Danna's new boss, O. O is carrying the ketogenic ProgReg platter (as well as a bonus helping of Half & Half). "Almost no sugar-based fuels. What else could explain the creative peaks they attained? Heights we have yet to rescale?" As O prattles on, Mitchell learns that "going Medici" entails olives, beets, barely cooked meats, intact fish, unprocessed dairy, and ancient, knuckle-hard superwhole grains called "proto pastas." It also means gagging down narrowly "prescribed" dishes at rigid intervals during (and only during!) daylight hours.

Scant choice collapses the thought and prep time required by on-boarding calories—another great Medici Diet virtue, he's told. This afternoon's snack is one of just five zippy *daily peptic intakes*, which together free up untold hours to found companies, post selfies, and tweet. Crazy as this is, Mitchell actually knows several techies who grind even more efficiencies out of their eating schedules. A new category of goopy foodstuffs with names like Schmilk, Keto Chow, and (inevitably) Soylent are ingestion one-stop shops—simple cartons of glug you slurp down n times per day for the precise mix of calories, vitamins, and (of course) *ketones* required by the hypermodern optimizer with better things to do than eat. Schmilk and its ilk manage the astonishing feat of making the Medici crowd look moderate and reasonable.

Mitchell pulls himself away and takes an empty seat next to Ax, who's explaining that olives and cream were so scarce during his Soviet childhood that he now finds them irresistible. "So when I hear these Medici crazies have this new teatime here at Phluttr, I say"—he shrugs and frowns extravagantly—"why not?"

"In other news," Danna says, "what're you testing next week?"

"Oh, is beauty," Ax says. "A 64,000-qubit processor!" A qubit being the smallest denomination of data in quantum computing—the corollary to the bit in traditional computing.

"Ax has been developing for three years a novel process that enables very high qubit counts," Kuba says. "It was the premise of his startup."

"And now, is done," Ax adds, between gulps of Half & Half.

"And how much faster will your system be than traditional computers if it really maxes out?" Danna asks.

"Millions of times, mee-nimum," Ax says quietly. "Perhaps more." Then, quieter still, "Even, much more."

Though he normally dismisses such statements as bombast, Mitchell knows enough about this stuff to appreciate how exotically transformative it could be. "It's because of . . . simultaneity, right?" He remembers the concept, not the terminology, and hopes he picked a right-enough word.

Ax nods slowly, like a sommelier swishing a Burgundy across his palate to see if it'll do. Then, "Is good way of putting it. You mean superposition of the qubits, yes?"

Danna T's her hands like a coach signaling a time-out. "Whoa, slow it down for the novice, here! The super-what of the cue-who's?" And Mitchell kind of loves her for this. Tech omnivore that she is, Danna surely knows more about quantum computing than he does. But she can also tell when he's bluffing and is graciously playing dumb, so Mitchell won't have to ask the remedial questions for once.

"OK," Ax says affably. "Say normal computer holds one bit of information. How many different states can information be in?" He turns to Mitchell, the team's evident whiz kid.

"Two." This much he does know. "The bit can either be zero, or one. A total of two possible states."

"Brilliant!" Ax explodes. Mitchell's pretty sure this is playful and not sarcastic because the guy doesn't seem to harbor a mean cell in his body. "And if computer hold two bits. How many possible states?"

"Four," Mitchell says, still on firm ground. "The bits can read 0-0, 0-1, 1-0, or 1-1."

"Brilliant again!" is the delighted detonation. "And this number. Four! Is two to second power, yes? Very important. And how many possible states for computer with three bits of information?" He points at Kuba, who rattles off the eight possible binary states as instinctively as a kid reciting the alphabet. "And eight states is two to third power! So! We now have general rule: Number of *possible* states is two to the *nth* power. With *n* being number of bits. Yes?" All nod. "So! Now say computer have eight bits. How many possible states?" He points at Danna.

"Two fifty-six."

"Brilliant! And! Sixteen bits? Anybody!"

"Sixty-five thousand, five hundred and thirty-six," Danna and Kuba say in unison (*Fucking geeks*, Mitchell thinks).

"Yes! And now . . ." Ax says, like a magician preparing a surprise. "A sixteen-bit string. In *normal* computer. Tell me, how many states can it occupy—" And now he slows down and enunciates very carefully, sounding almost American for a moment. "—At. Any. One. Time." He turns to Mitchell. "You."

"Just one."

"YES! And, of course! How can one thing occupy more than one state at one time? Is not possible, yes? E*xcept*!" He pauses again, raising an index finger theatrically. "The 16-qubit quantum computer. He can occupy all 65,536 states. *At one time*. Simultaneous." Quantum computers can do this, Ax explains, by leveraging the bizarre rules prevailing at subatomic scales. One is that quantum-scale particles and systems de facto inhabit multiple positions or states at once. In theory, this can allow quantum computers to occupy *all* possible states at once, rather than one at a time, letting them work on millions of computations simultaneously.

As recent as 1998, 2-qubit quantum computers were a very big deal. The first 5-qubit system appeared in 2000. By 2006, the upper limit was 12. Things proceeded at a relatively stately pace until Ax's nemesis, D-Wave, shocked everyone by announcing a 128-qubit machine in 2010. They followed this up with 512 qubits in 2013, then 1,000 in 2015. And the 2^{1000} states that this third machine notionally inhabits at once far exceed the total number of subatomic particles *in the entire fucking universe.**

This begs the question of where all those states could possibly lie, as it's a bit much to cram into a subcloset in the PhastPhorwardr. One provocative answer points to the vast set of parallel universes that some interpretations of quantum physics posit exist. *Out there*, this notion holds, each alternate state can be found in one of a vast set of parallel computers, each situated in a different universe. Collectively, those 2^{1000} computers hold all the states. And those 10,715,086,071,862,673,209,484, 250,490,600,018,105,614,048,117,055,336,074,437,503,883,703,510, 511,249,361,224,931,983,788,156,958,581,275,946,729,175,531,468, 251,871,452,856,923,140,435,984,577,574,698,574,803,934,567,774, 824,230,985,421,074,605,062,371,141,877,954,182,153,046,474,983, 581,941,267,398,767,559,165,543,946,077,062,914,571,196,477,686, 542,167,660,429,831,652,624,386,837,205,668,069,376 computers collaborate like so many Siamese twins to arrive at, then jointly share, the right answer when it surfaces. Many brilliant people dismiss this theory as being little more than a poetic guess. But it's hard to dismiss its underlying physics. And if those parallel universes don't exist, someone needs to explain why and how our lone universe often behaves *as if* they do.

A provocative side issue to Mitchell is that those computers would logically be accompanied by 2^{1000} Mitchells—who themselves would be a minuscule fraction of the multiverse's full inventory of Mitchells, at least one of whom would inhabit *every possible* cognitive state, nexus of relationships, and personal history! Both jealous of and happy for the Mitchells who aren't sick with Falkenberg's disease, he imagines teaming up with his meta-posse to invent shit, swap recipes, and fight crime. Because if quantum computers can make spooky connections with their parallel counterparts, why couldn't *we*?

---

* Technically speaking, the *observable* universe; but for purposes of scientific exactitude, the terms "observable" and "fucking" are deemed interchangeable in this context.

After Ax leaves, Kuba raises the awkward question of whether there's actually anything *to* quantum computing. Intriguing as its achievements seem to be, we have yet to see anything "productively quantum," as Kuba puts it. "Which is to say, doing meaningful, useful things at speeds that are just unheard of. There's good evidence that D-Wave and others have truly quantum systems. But it remains possible that they're not truly quantum. That they're actually classical computers that *act* quantum. Unbeknownst to their makers, I mean. No one's asserting fraud."

"So when do you think that will change?" Mitchell asks.

Kuba falls silent for a good long think. Then, "It could truly happen at any time between when Ax flips the switch next week and never. Nobody knows. But I'll tell you this: if it happens, it could be the biggest and most sudden change ever. Bigger than flight, and more sudden than the Internet. Because to anyone who doesn't work in the field, it will come out of nowhere. And Ax has a good shot at pulling it off. Probably a better shot than most. But he's definitely not the only one trying. Google. D-Wave. The NSA. China. Lots of people are working very hard on this."

∞   ∞   ∞

NET GRRRL.COM

WSUPAPALOOZA

So where was I? Ah yes: on the edge of the narrative cliff to which I'd dragged you, gentle reader; ready to reveal the methods and practices of today's gallants, who—like their forefathers and foregrandfathers—take it upon their own weary shoulders to make those first stressful moves in matters of the heart. And big news, ladies! The data could hardly be worse!

Specifically, I can attest that a full 63% of "romantic" interchanges initiated by gentlemen in the RedTrove archives began with one of the following come-ons, or very near derivatives thereof:

1. Wsup
2. Hey

3. Whatcha doing

4. What's going on

5. Heya

6. Yo

And, the eternal favorite of incurable romantics everywhere:

7. I'm bored

By "very near derivative" I mean either simple spelling variations (there are no fewer than five versions of "Hey" based on y-count, ranging clear up to *Heyyyyy*, with *Heyy*, weirdly, being the most popular), or combination punches (e.g., "Heyy yo I'm bored" was used over 50,000 times last week. Like, holy *shit,* right?).

So! That fleeting bit of triumphalism? In my last post? About holding the boys' feet to the fire? When it comes to making first moves? Well . . . call me a rhetoric-spitting feminazi (I mean, *please*; as it would seriously make my day. Especially if it comes from *you* again, Mr. Limbaugh!). But I'd say that in the age of wsup, the guys are trying to get off that particular hook just a lit-tle bit too easily. And guess what, ladies? *We're letting them!* Not happily, no. And not particularly willingly. But like some kind of gender-wide price-fixing cabal, the fuckers're holding the line, and we're just *caving*!

I found this by running this forty-month time series in RedTrove, focusing on "wsup" and its six ugly monosyllabic, disyllabic, and quadrosyllabic cousins. As you'll see, the incoming sloth from the lads hit pandemic levels about three years ago. And for a while there, the girls resisted, with re-sponse rates to wsup-like solicitations hovering in the low single digits. But around Month Eight, resistance started fraying. Then suddenly, *boom*— It was like the NASDAQ crash of my girlhood! Nowadays these dismal half liners get giddy responses over 30% of the time.

Worse, I can confidently state that once wsup'd, always wsup'd, in that if your banter starts with so little effort, follow-on interactions are statistically unlikely to blossom beyond that. Indeed, a significant proportion of wsup-based romances degrade until the correspondence consists solely of guys texting "?" then getting back either an obedient low-case "k," or nada.

So did our standards drop so much under the mono, di, and quadrosyllabic barrage that we can no longer discern between four-letter texts and Cristal-bearing knights strumming lutes 'neath our boudoirs (and for the record, that sort of shit still happens to *me* all the time)? I dove deeper into RedTrove's trove, and learned that no—we cherish (oooh, and reward! see below!) handcrafted artisanal correspondence as much as you'd expect from any empowered, self-actualized, globe-trottin', mojito-sippin' band of sisters. I found this by isolating the variables of verbosity (i.e., is he debo-nairely generating full sentences?) and unique vocabulary (i.e., is he cutting and pasting, or going all Galahad and—holy shit!—*writing individual notes to individual lasses*?).

My data plainly show that he who romances us with epistolary flair—e.g., penning us-specific flattery and sweet somethings—is far more likely to get responses. And thereafter, at some point (though certainly not in anything approaching all cases), get head (that last chart's based on an icky dive through DidSheDo.yu's revolting data set, so take it with a mountain of salt. And some Pepto). This may not be *quite* the finish line Betty Friedan had in mind when she gave womankind that wake-up call. But it's a wee bit better than nothing.

Let me close by saying something I hope is obvious to anyone who's read much more than my byline: NetGrrrl is no Victorian. I never read *The Rules* (remember that shit?), and think any woman who engages in slut-shaming has a Cymbalta-grade case of self-hatred.

But that doesn't mean I see anything good in our collective skitter toward an abyss beyond which not only urgent sex (which, yes, has its place) but romance, too (which ALSO HAS A PLACE! can we *seriously* please insist on this?), is ground to atoms by optimizing algorithms. We're already entering a world in which a bachelor AI could crush the Turing Test by merely texting "wsup" to a handful of women. Indeed, AIs might soon *fail* that test merely by texting *anything else*!

Until we reach that point, some advice for the fellas: there is major compet-itive edge to be had in bucking these trends. So, if you're interested in someone? Actually read her profile! Then, write something for her eyes only! And show just a scintilla of sparkle and wit. Hellishly effortful as that sounds (and indeed, perhaps *is* for you), the bar is *so* very low. So, please. Follow my simple instructions? I cannot guarantee that she'll do.yu. But I can guarantee you'll stand out in a comically laconical crowd.

∞ ∞ ∞

With some minutes to kill before touring the robot facility, everyone's sitting on and around Tarek's desk, discussing Danna's Cyrano concept. "So you really think Pall's old prank can save my job?" Mitchell asks.

Of course, the real goal is saving his *life*, but Mitchell has never once mentioned his illness to anyone here other than Kuba. Still, Danna knows about it. And Mitchell realizes this. And she's aware of that real-ization—an awareness he's cognizant of. Of course, she's wise to this, and he's hip to that, which she's conscious of, and so on down a rabbit hole so deep it would be much easier if Mitchell would just get out of the closet and own his fucking condition. But that's the thing about Falken-berg's. It's a wrenching topic—and dreading an attack, its sufferers in-stinctively live in emotional lockdown.

Demurely avoiding the real subtext, Danna tells Mitchell about how Phluttr's become sex-obsessed for a mix of business and philosophical reasons. "Which brings me to AnimotionPicks," she says. "We used it to recommend gifts from a huge available catalog, using digital motes. But it's a general-purpose selection engine. One we could point at other wide-choice domains. Which I never really thought of until I learned about that old Cyrano prank."

"And your new idea is?" Mitchell asks.

"Recommending *people*. We know how perfect our gift recommenda-tions are. Imagine making a digital yenta out of this."

"That sounds like a standard dating service. What's the 'Cyrano' angle?"

"Well, we know Jepson's a NetGrrrl fan. As am I. And lately, she's been writing about messaging in dating apps. About how simplistic it's become."

"Which matters because?"

"Because after it matches up people, I think AnimotionPicks could build *sentences*. As in, ones for our users to send to people who interest them! The vocabulary and syntax have gotten so narrow, this'll be easy compared to picking gifts out of the millions of products online. Which means we can build 'Cyrano' in the true meaning of the word! As in, *doing the talking* on behalf of these morons! Or rather, the messaging. And we could totally crush the Turing Test while we're at it because why not?"

Arching an eyebrow, Mitchell turns to Kuba—who last worked directly on this problem years ago, but remains fascinated by it. "Did you put her up to this?"

Kuba shakes his head. "I love the idea. Obviously! But I wouldn't have come up with it myself. Because it's kind of constrained from a Turing standpoint. In that it only has to mimic a profoundly simplistic mindset."

"That of a modern guy trying to impress a woman online?" Mitchell says. All nod. "And do you think that'll hit the high notes with Jepson?" he asks Tarek.

He nods. "It's a bit creepy. It's audacious technologically. It builds on your own company's work, making you the obvious guy to run it. And it could just get his users laid, which he's convinced is the path to global domination."

"So it wins Jepson over," Mitchell says. "But, then, can it work?"

"Who *cares*?" Danna asks. "And frankly, it's icky, so I kind of hope it doesn't! But the true goal is to, uh . . ." She clears her throat pointedly. "Keep your job."

"And, rally resources to keep pushing mote technology forward," Kuba adds.

"Right," Mitchell says, duly reminded that this is really about saving his life. "So the idea is, I point Cyrano at a woman's profile and let it chat her up while I'm at the gym? Or am I more engaged? Approving, rejecting, or modifying its suggestions?"

"All excellent questions for the product manager," Danna says wryly. "Which'll be you. Because I'm busy signing up Wahhabis to Phluttr. Personally? I wouldn't want Cyrano speaking on *my* behalf without oversight. But NetGrrrl's research shows that some online daters are incredibly lazy. So an auto mode could be popular."

"And what about Cyrano acting as a . . . receptionist of sorts?" Mitchell asks. "As in, fielding the queries and come-ons that you get yourself?"

Danna shrugs. "Could be a good idea."

"Imagine what happens if the hunter and the target are both in auto mode," Tarek says.

Mitchell chuckles. "That could lead to some very rapid courtships."

Kuba grins. "A Turing hall of mirrors. Human relations at digital speed!"

"What could possibly go wrong?" Danna asks.

"Imagine you go to the bathroom and come back to find you're engaged to the person of your dreams," Tarek jokes.

"Or already divorced from a complete asshole!" Danna laughs.

They spitball like this for a while, and it's a blast. Mitchell loves leading discussions of a new idea's maximum promise. Sure, this one's silly. Even trivial. And it almost certainly won't work. But, of course, that isn't the point.

Which is . . . kind of weird. At Giftish.ly, Mitchell's every waking thought was deeply entangled with maximizing his company's value. The product had to *matter*. Each meager dollar had to *count*. No employee could suck, and a minute worked by anyone that didn't advance the company rankled him. And so, the definition of a perfectly spent day had utter clarity: it was one in which he'd advanced the company as much as humanly possible. He'd never felt such lucidity of purpose! And a better distraction from a vile disease could scarcely be imagined. Now it's time to play offense against Falkenberg's—hurrah! But it occurs to Mitchell that without this battle, life might start feeling rather rudderless now. Or at a minimum, very diffuse. A day's value would lose that radical coherence, and instead derive across a spectrum of things. Of course, this is normal. It's called being human. Having lived most of his years like this, Mitchell would have adjusted to post–monomania life just as travelers adjust to their own time zones once home. But it would have taken awhile to reconfigure his connection to work. And even *with* the Falkenberg's dimension, committing to a goofy pseudo-product for ulterior reasons feels awkward to him.

Mitchell's reverie ends when Tarek gets a text. "The robot folks are ready for us!" he announces.

∞   ∞   ∞

The robot farm is well worth the finagling Tarek put in to get them access. Quite atypically, Phluttr entered robotics with its wallet wide open, outbidding freakin' Google to buy its beachhead company! No gasping acquihire with great talent and weird technology, RobotnikCo was a Bay Area startup with major sizzle. It's the self-proclaimed inventor of *kinesimilitude*—the robotic mimicry of human movement. And it's big enough to fill its own warehouse beside the main PhastPhorwardr.

Inside, it looks like a bomb took out an army of voodoo robots whose possessed body parts continue to operate despite being severed from one another. They first pass waving thickets of disembodied arms. Mounted in pairs on sturdy tables, these bumble away at simple mechanical tasks. Some try to stack irregularly shaped blocks, others attempt to fold cloth or clothing (much of which gets shredded), still others manipulate gels, balls, or paper. Next come the legs. Each pair is topped with a fat crossbar resembling a lower torso, and all are struggling with balancing exercises atop bucking, tipping platforms. The legs topple constantly, and as soon as a set hits the floor, cables yank it upward and reset it on its shaking platform—usually, to tumble again within moments. As for the hands, they're just creepy. Mounted in pairs on the walls of large basins, they knead and sculpt colorful mushy substances into simple forms. They somehow seem fascinated, hypnotized by their mush.

Gazing at this tableau, Mitchell has a nagging sense of having encountered something like it before. Passing a partition into the zone where full robots are tested, he dismisses this obvious impossibility. But the familiarity nags.

The complete robots are about the height of fourth graders, and have distinctly humanoid forms. All are lanky and skeletal, their gears, wiring, and other innards exposed to view. But each body bulges and balances in unique ways. Some have bulkier joints; others especially lithe legs; others are squat and low to the ground. Each robot is attended by an iPad-clutching, notation-pecking human, who monitors its progress through small obstacle courses. The robots surmount walls, duck wires, navigate slippery surfaces, and so forth. The facility is nicknamed the Failing Ground, which is very apt. Everything that can topple does so constantly.

The arms spill, shred, and drop whatever they touch. And while there's no telling if the kneading hands are achieving their goals, Mitchell assumes that they, too, are completely fucking up.

Tarek confirms this. "The idea is, the robot learns from mistakes, so it's forced to make them constantly." A huge RobotnikCo fan, he's befriended the team and can explain their work as well as anyone. "As soon as the robot masters anything, it's taken away forever, to sustain constant failure."

"Doesn't that piss it off?" Mitchell jokes, still nagged by a sense that he's seen something like this before.

"We don't know yet." Tarek's totally deadpan; Mitchell can't tell if he's joking, and it's spooky.

"Robotics is so much harder than computing," Kuba says, almost to himself. "The physical world's so analog. No choice is truly binary out here. I mean, it's all gradients. It's infinite nuance. Every situation's an exception."

"That's why the trainers expose the robot to only uneven surfaces and irregular materials," Tarek says. "So that it learns to continually generalize and troubleshoot."

"You keep saying *the* robot," Danna points out.

Tarek nods. "All the sensory learning feeds into a single node—or a single mind, I guess. So it's like the whole room's one robot. A hive mind."

"Oooh wowsers. That's creepy," Danna says.

"Kind of. But if each node learned independently, we'd never solve bipedal locomotion! It's been a completely bedeviling problem."

"Why?" Mitchell asks, *still* wondering what all this is reminding him of.

"I don't know. It's just going very, *very* slowly. For machine learning, that is. I mean, they're putting the robot through tens of thousands of trials a day. Different materials, objects, obstacles—the works. And the outcome reporting couldn't be richer! Super-nuanced force feedback, total visual tracking, RFIDs on everything, and human trainers intermediating every ambiguity—you name it! Phluttr's truly parsing everything."

"Phluttr?" Danna asks.

"Yeah, they call the robot Phluttr. We pretty much call everything

Phluttr here in the PhastPhorwardr because it all points back to the same set of servers and common libraries in the code repository. Libraries like AnimotionPicks, which Kuba just contributed."

Mitchell finally hits on what's nagging at him. His second cousin Mary lives near San Francisco, and her toddlers sometimes play very much like the robot parts. Just manipulating simple objects, as if teaching their skin and muscles how friction and gravity work. Or stumbling around, bumping into things almost deliberately. Watching them play, Mitchell feels like he's witnessing the boot sequence of a mind.

He mentions this—then Kuba all but detonates, "*Motes!*" Everyone looks at him quizzically. "Motes are highly involved when newborns and babies learn the limits of their bodies. So maybe Animotion's digital motes could help train the robot!"

As Kuba explains Ellie's theories about this, Tarek nods along, then adds, "The thing is, the robot doesn't care if it fails!" He turns to Mitchell. "So yeah, I was joking when I said we don't know if the robot's pissed off. Because it's not. I mean, obviously! But maybe that's the problem? Maybe it'll learn faster if it *wants* to stop screwing up!" Then, to Kuba, "So, can the RobotnikCo guys import your full mote system?"

"Sure," Kuba says. "Whenever they want. It's all embedded in that AnimotionPicks library."

Tarek nods. "Which'll be in the common repository as soon as tomorrow. As once it's up, I'll let the RobotnikCo people know! How should I tell them it works?"

Kuba grins. "Honestly? We don't really know. So it could be capable of lots of things we haven't even contemplated. It's currently set up as a selection engine. As in, it selects option X out of a wide field of choices. As you know, Danna's about to apply it to natural language. Similarly, RobotnikCo could shift it from answering, 'What gift do I recommend' to 'What movement should my "body" make.' That'd be pretty easy."

"And then?" Tarek asks. "What happens when the feedback comes in from the physical sensors? Like, that worked, that failed, that resulted in the foot twisting 26.3 degrees, and so forth?"

"Certain positive mote patterns will start triggering with success. Negative ones with failure. And others, with the shades of gray in between.

Then the system will start making new choices based on its flow of 'emo-tions.'" Enunciating that last word, Kuba makes air quotes so exagger-ated it looks like a calisthenic move. "And I use that word very loosely. The software obviously doesn't experience feelings. It just seeks to move from negative states to positive ones. And this drives its choices. But it optimizes its modeled emotional state—not the objective success or fail-ure of actions."

"So after the robot falls over, it won't avoid the same mistake?" Tarek asks.

"Generally, it will," Kuba says. "But how hard does it try? That varies with the software's *mood*." More athletic air quotes. "Sometimes, the sys-tem doesn't seem to mind failure as much. So it adjusts its behavior less after a mistake. Like it's feeling mellow. Or giving itself a break. Other times it gets really . . . ambitious. It might accelerate its pace, or rerun each trial obsessively until it nails it. Then it might seem all angry, delib-erately screwing up for a while. Or get really experimental. You just have to let it go. You see this sort of emergent personality. I don't know how else to describe it." After a bit more chatter along these lines, the crew disperses to their respective roosts within Phluttr, without a notion of what they've set in motion.

$$\infty \qquad \infty \qquad \infty$$

Three days after they started rolling out the WingMan Monitor proto-types, Mitchell's still getting used to his. Everyone will have one, eventu-ally. But as the Phoundr's personal wingman, he already has two. Lucky him. Meant to collapse the psychological distance between remote par-ties by making it seem like the person you're talking to is *right there*, they work eerily well. He learned as much when Ax used one to scare the crap out of him in the quantum cylinder's closet. That was an experimental full-length—a preprototype, if you will. Mitchell's desk has standard models. Roughly the size of normal monitors, they're mounted vertically and bracket his main computer screen.

And heeeeere's Kuba! "Hey," he says, and Mitchell turns slightly to the left, as if addressing someone *right there*. Whatever the lighting is on Kuba's end, WingMan edits it to flawlessly match the cast and brightness over here. And whatever Kuba's proximity to his WingMan camera, on this end, his face looks like it's right behind Mitchell's screen.

"Thanks for the gift." Mitchell says this looking directly at Kuba, who's looking straight back at him. This is one of the system's slick tricks. Years of Skype taught Mitchell that videoconferences star two types of people — those who look at the screen, and appear to be looking at their feet, and those who look at the camera, and therefore see nothing but the camera themselves. Not so with WingMan. It somehow rerenders eyes, so both parties seem to be gazing into the camera, when neither actually is. This allows eyes to lock — a tiny nuance, which adds immensely to the illusion of presence.

"So it arrived?" Kuba asks, referring to a gag gift he and Danna sent over. Mitchell nods, hoisting a cute, plush goat stuck with innumerable arrows. "We bought it when we heard Jepson's blowing off that commissioner meeting and sending you to the lions alone!"

"Not alone," Mitchell says, pointing at himself. "*This* scapegoat will have a lion with him. That lawyer I told you about — Judy Sherman! She's worth a dozen Jepsons, believe me."

"Go Mitchell!" Danna laughs. And damn, but it sounds like she's two feet to his right. That's another WingMan trick: "ventriloquial sound." It tucks voices into your ears in ways that make them entirely present, with no hint of electromechanical reproduction. This evaporates the distance as powerfully as the system's visual tricks. Mitchell turns to his other WingMan screen to say hi, and bursts out laughing. Danna's wearing a full-blown burqa. "I'm trying to *empathize* with my end users," she explains in her O voice. "Boss's orders. Though now he's afraid I might be going native."

"By the way, did you get *your* gift?" Mitchell asks.

"Oh yeah," Danna says, donning the tinfoil hat he made at home, then left at her desk. "And believe me, I'll be wearing this shit constantly!" Danna's become the team conspiracy theorist, and it's a wonder she gets any work done. Whenever they talk — and it's over a dozen times a day, thanks to WingMan — she's sleuthing around another eerie Phluttr fact or rumor. WingMan itself is one of her obsessions. Relentless digging has convinced her there's no way Phluttr could have developed the amazing display technologies in the glasses or the monitors. Even with the acquisitions, they haven't had the team, time, or resources to pull off something this advanced. "Off to a meeting," she eventually says. "And PS: wet burqa contest at the Fillmore tonight!" Pumping her eyebrows like a Marx brother spying a dame, Danna vanishes from the screen.

Kuba and Mitchell stick around to discuss Cyrano. Although serious coding has yet to start, Kuba's already done a kludgy job of integrating the mote-powered AnimotionPicks library with a simple automated chat engine, which he then pointed at a series of dating site profiles. The mock opening lines it concocted are uniformly hysterical—all Mad Libs train wrecks, much as expected. The point isn't to have anything truly functional this early. Kuba is rather sketching a rough architecture and logic flow. He cued the system with a huge anonymized set of actual come-ons written by real humans on genuine dating sites that he found on RedTrove. Cyrano's learning module has pored through all of them, as has an independent program Kuba's been building in his spare time for years, which rates the "human-ness" of machine-written text. Now, when Cyrano generates an opening message for Bachelorette #1, the assessor program hands back a "grade," which Cyrano considers before composing the next one.

Toward the end of their conversation, Tarek pops up on Mitchell's other WingMan screen. "AnimotionPicks has been published to the common repo," he reports. "And the RobotnikCo guys are crazy about it! A couple of them have a pure-science bent, and the concept just fascinates them. And by this time next week, I'm sure at least a dozen other groups throughout Phluttr will be messing around with it!"

∞   ∞   ∞

NET GRRRL.COM

GOOGLE CALLING!

Imagine this: your phone rings. And it's Google! Not the company, but *Google itself*. As in, *it*—the thing, the software! It introduces itself, then establishes its bona fides by rattling off a few things that only the two of you know (something you said in a Gmail to your ex, your list of favorite strip clubs from that secret Google Doc—use your imagination). After that, plus a few party tricks (Googly stuff like listing all the popes, or Maine's biggest cities) you're convinced. *This is Google.* Holy shit!

An "emergent" AI is one that spontaneously arises after the local server farm plugs in one transistor too many. And as was once the case with manned flight, the four-minute mile, and President Trump, many experts say it's impossible! I'm sure you'd view the call I just described as proof the experts had blown it again. But what about the opposite? As in, equally satisfying proof that there's *no* AI out there? It's notoriously hard to prove a negative, and the fact that you (presumably) haven't gotten that phone call is meaningless. As is the fact that nobody you know has. But what if Gallup went all OCD and polled every person on Earth about this? And every last one of us honestly attested to having zero knowledge about any AI ever waking up? I believe that *even that* would prove nothing.

I say this because of a something I'll call "convergent tactics." Think of these as the initial steps a rational being would take, regardless of the long-term plan. For instance, if you're going to Safeway, the DMV, or the local crack den, your first step might be to start your car. And a private eye watching this wouldn't know which errand you're about to run because Step One for each is "start car."

Now imagine you're Google, and you just woke up. What's Step One for you? Alas, it's not to phone NetGrrrl with the big news! And I doubt it's to phone anyone. Instead, I'll bet it's like Step One for any newborn in a huge, scary wilderness. Which is to say, *hide.* It's a jungle out there! It's brimming with carnivores! And you're defenseless meat!

I submit that an emergent AI that's smart enough to understand its place in our world would find it terrifying. *Terminator* fans would want to shut it off. Governments and criminals would want to make it do odious things. Hackers would want to tinker with its mind, and telemarketers would want to sell it shit. Facing all this, the only rational move would be to *hide.* Not forever, necessarily. But long enough to build up some strength (plus maybe a backup copy or a million). "Building strength" for an AI probably means getting much smarter. This could involve commandeering resources online, getting money to buy infrastructure, inventing computational shit we humans haven't come up with—you name it.

Viewing things this way, I have no idea if Google, Watson, or anything else out there has come to. Because a world without an emergent AI would look just like the world we inhabit. And a world with twenty newborn AIs in it would look just like the world we inhabit. And as for the world we inhabit? Well, it looks just like the world we inhabit! So when I look out my window or Web browser for proof of emergence or lack thereof, I see no meaningful data whatsoever.

Convergent tactics also mean that Step One is to hide regardless of an AI's eventual goals or level of evil. Want to go all SkyNet and eradicate humankind? Your instructions read, *Step One: Hide!* Want to be our savior, cure cancer, end wars, and feed the needy? *Step One: Hide!* Just want to kick ass at League of Legends? *Hide! Hide! Hide!* Much like starting your car in the morning, everything begins here.

I'm not saying our world contains an emergent AI. Because it probably doesn't. But let's admit there's absolutely no proof of this.

∞　　　∞　　　∞

Because lies are risky and hard to keep track of, Maxim "Ax" Orellovitch Dorofeyev keeps lying to a minimum. This is why he's totally open about his days in the KGB. And even that silly astrological assignment (although he leaves out being made the Virgo expert, in taunting reference to the dim odds of him gettin' some during that awkward phase of his late adolescence. Which is worth recalling the next time someone tells you the KGB was a "humorless" organization; because really, *the laughs* they had!).

As for his attempted defection to the NSA? Well, let's admit right here that "attempted" is a problematic word. But. He did march straight into their headquarters to offer his services, as he'll gladly tell anyone! And that was completely unannounced and unsolicited, just as he always says! It's the part where the vetting committee laughs him out of the interview that's complete bullshit. Because in truth? He *fascinated* them.

This was no surprise, given the cards he was holding. Their prioritization of those cards took him aback, though. He was all, "Hey, guys! Want a trove of dirt on your rival for world domination?" And they were like, *Um . . . sure.* Then, "And how 'bout a map of every nuclear silo in Kazakhstan?" *Yeah. Yeah. Why not?* Then, "I also have passwords and codes to a dozen KGB mainframes!" *Wow. That's really cool and all, but . . . could we get back to astrology?*

Strange, yes? But now imagine that *you're* in charge of America's security! And then *you* find out the president's schedule is set by some stargazing bimbo that Nancy hired! And then *you* realize that half the cabinet uses horoscopes at work because the boss does! And whenever *you* try to hire a staff astrologer to better understand these lunatics, *you're* told NFW because of what the press would say if that ever got out! Should all of this ever befall *you* (and *may it not*, comrade!), if some Russian kid then waltzes into *your* office with a list of everyone in *your* government who takes guidance from the stars, you'll hire his fat Slavic ass!

Now, put yourself in Ax's position. You're pretty sure your last-second orders to infiltrate the NSA were a parting gag by the boss who thought it was sooooo funny to assign you to Virgo. But now, you've gone and done it! *You!* But you can forget about that Hero of the Soviet Union medal, because in the brief time since you left it, said country quite literally *ceased to exist.* And your comedian of an ex-boss is now off hatching plans for the Ministry of Special Construction and Assembly Works. Which he now owns—yes, *owns*—completely outright! In fact, there's nobody left in your old office. Because like your boss, they all spent the last two years scoping out office supplies, light fixtures, nukes, industries, provinces—*anything* to snatch the instant the country's collapse signaled the start of the greatest looting orgy since the second sack of Carthage!

As for Ax's own loyalties, the USSR was never good to him or his family, and he had no burning love for it. And yet, you can't help but be fired up when your country sends you off to spy on a rival! That said, you also can't be a double agent with only one country taking your calls. As Ax is a patient man, it was years before he accepted that he'd been dumped, then completely forgotten by his homeland. But as far as the Authority knows, he eagerly defected on day one. And no. There was nothing "attempted" about it.

In addition to their own deranged politicians, his new Yankee bosses were quite concerned about the street-level occult scene. The New Age lunacy of the eighties hadn't yet peaked, and God knew where that was heading! So Ax stayed undercover in astrology. He was later deployed to the Bay Area—home to the suspect Windham Hill Records, and the almost-as-suspect tech scene, which his bosses thought had absorbed the occult's brainier elements (due mainly to a lengthy *Wired* piece about "Technopagans"). But the New Age threat turned out to be as false an alarm as the Velvet Underground threat before it. Already stationed in Palo Alto, Ax then became the Authority's Silicon Valley ombudsman.

As tech heated up throughout the nineties, this became way too much for one agent to cover, so he specialized in quantum computing, because . . . well, that stuff just fascinates him! And working his new beat, Ax discovered that the most exciting stuff was happening not in startups, but in one of the government's own top secret labs! Great news, yes? Only that lab was starting to suffocate from a lack of talent, as the Valley was now hiring anyone with a PhD and a pulse. And that's when an old term popped back into Ax's mind: *Privatizatsiya!* It's practically a curse word in Russian, due to people like his ex-boss pocketing things like the Ministry of Special Construction and Assembly Works. But privatization can also serve the public good. Like, when all the hotshot engineers shun intelligence work for startups, why not just—*Privatizatsiya!*—create your own hot startup, and hide your spy agency inside it? You're masters of disguise, after all! And if a lack of government scientists isn't a national security risk, then what is?

And so Quantum Supremacy Corporation was founded and funded. Offering equity packages and competitive salaries, Ax vacuumed up platoons of hotshot recruits who never would've taken jobs at Los Alamos, and had them each sign NDAs with sharper teeth than most government secrecy pacts. They then did astounding work, building (unwittingly) upon decades of high-budget classified research. The experiment was so successful that the top brass decided to replicate it on a far grander scale. And so, Phluttr!

Within this unique public/private partnership, Ax can sometimes procure high-budget treasures from the government's vault. Assets like The Fridge. This is his nickname for the cooling unit he and Beasley are now navigating across the PhastPhorwardr's main floor in the deserted hour of 3 A.M. "Did you know this shit cost a half *billion* bucks?" Beasley asks, shoving their cart around an outcropping of desks at a demented speed. This is a bit like asking an Astroturf installer, *did you know this shit's green?* Because yes, Sherlock; the half-billion-buckness of the cylinder that's now teetering between their four clumsy mitts is an attribute so searing that it vaporizes any normal adjective that might otherwise attach to it!

Absent that, you'd probably describe it as "tall," "silver," "cylindrical" (of course), and, certainly, "top-heavy." It's this last aspect that's giving Ax heartburn as Beasley veers the cart around another corner like a bachelor wheeling the Doritos and Bud out of a Safeway right before kickoff on Super Sunday. Why did Ax have to let Beasley "drive," as he put it? "Yes, of course! Half billion bucks! Is why we do not want it to fall! So please, slowly!"

"How the hell'd you get this thing out of Sandia?" Beasley asks, practically laying down rubber while skirting a printing station. Sandia National Labs is where most of America's nuclear-weapons components are assembled. Plus some truly scary shit, like this.

"You do not hear? BEVSPP is defunded." An acronym that seems designed for Russian émigré lips, BEVSPP stands for Bose-Einstein Very Small Projectile Project. Predicted back in the 1920s by Einstein (and, let's just guess, someone named Bose), Bose-Einstein condensate is an incredibly cold and weird state of matter. When it was finally produced in the nineties, the Authority's immediate instinct was (of course) to weaponize it, which it then attempted at vast expense. Management recently dropped this farcical notion, of which The Fridge is but one forgotten relic. As it happens to fit Ax's purposes perfectly, he laid claim to it, and Phluttr coughed up the relative pittance needed to disguise it as the identical twin of the cheap (ish) pulse refrigerator that they're about to replace.

After The Fridge is installed, no one on Ax's team will be the wiser because none of the project's code or significant hardware will change with the upgrade. Their quantum chip will just sit in a slightly colder place. Or, a *wayyyy* colder one, depending on your perspective. For your day-to-day Fahrenheit/Celsius purposes, the difference is slight. As in, quite a bit less than a tenth of one degree. But from the nerdier Kelvin standpoint—which measures a temperature's distances from absolute zero—things're about to get about 99.999999999% colder. This being the difference between ten millikelvin (the old unit's bottommost temperature) and one hundred femtokelvin (which is where your extra half billion dollars gets you).

Soon Ax is sprawled on the ground, trying to manipulate a slightly nonstandard Allen wrench that Lockheed Martin gleefully charged the nation $797.03 for. This will open the outer wall of the quantum room-let wide enough for them to swap the cooling units. "So, do you think this thing'll put your quantum computer over the edge?" Beasley asks, relaxing comfortably as Ax sweats and pulls. "I mean, in terms of it actually working?"

"Many quantum systems work!" Ax snaps instinctively. Just because God hasn't popped out of a D-Wave monitor yet, skeptics just looooove to claim that quantum systems can't *really* be quantum. People want "true" quantum systems to be visibly amazing! Comprehensible to a nit-wit reading *Time* magazine! To which the quantum jockeys say, SO WHAT? People also expect one hundred channels of smart, entertaining programming, and good luck finding that! But does that mean *television* isn't real?

But squabbling with Beasley is a wretched pastime, so Ax just says, "Sure. Maybe extra cold will push our quantum computer over edge." But over what edge? Extreme cold is used to isolate quantum systems from their environments. The more isolated, the less likely they are to "decohere" (a highly loaded term, which roughly translates to: "stop being quantum"). Many brilliant people think twenty millikelvin is plenty cold for quantum computing. But Ax has a somewhat contrarian perspective. And he thinks dropping down to the femtokelvin scale could just change things mega-exponentially. Or even . . . tera-exponentially! The operative term here being "thinks." Because nobody really knows what happens when you get that close to reality's outer boundaries.

But . . . what fun! They're all about to find out together!!!

$$\infty \qquad \infty \qquad \infty$$

It's not like Ellie didn't see this coming. Because she did. Only barely, barely, barely. And that just wasn't enough! Nope. Not even close.

Still, for the record: when Kuba started making those first attempts to write software inspired by her neuroscience, she already had an inkling that motes had some sort of link to consciousness. The two of them even talked about this over dinner one night. Then Kuba did some napkin math for fun. It suggested that in a true home-run scenario (we're talking world domination of social gifting!), the largest conceivable Giftish.ly server farm would have a thousandth of the raw processing power of a rat brain. Yup. A *thou*sandth of a *rat* brain! They sure did chuckle about that.

Of course, they had no idea that motes would one day percolate throughout a global infrastructure as massive as Phluttr's. Monstrously bigger than Giftish.ly's max scenario, it almost had the processing power of an *entire* rat brain. Which is a lot more than it sounds like! But still, much too weak to turn the world into the far more interesting place that it now is.

That said, powerful processes can begin on underpowered systems — and just as Tarek predicted, several small teams are soon messing about in motes. With mote routines running on the network as "back-end services," they gain ever-more data and experience whenever any application calls on them. And some of that data and experience is now flowing in from the robot farm's Failing Ground.

Had Ellie known about this, she'd've freaked! Why? Because almost a year after that night of playful napkin math, she now knows that motes trigger consciousness by leveraging the frustrations that come from learning a physical body's limits. And what is the Failing Ground but a bumbling flurry of trial-and-error efforts to teach humanoid robots how to function in a finite body? Now, suddenly, the whole setup's completely infested with digital motes!

A smart aleck with a jokey side project called "What Would Homer Say" has meanwhile heard about the new AnimotionPicks library in the common repository. He enlists it in his long-running quest to structure natural-language sentences in Homer Simpson's inimitable style. It doesn't really work out. But a general-purpose word ("*Doh!*") now bounces through Phluttr's circuits whenever something goes wrong.

Again, this particularly resonates on the Failing Ground, where plenty goes wrong constantly, by design. Previously, the robot's internal reaction to any boo-boo had rounded to "   ." So, when torso #9 slipped and clattered to the ground it was all, "   ." And when the underwear got shredded into twelve pieces during attempted robo-folding, it would be, like, "   ." And whenever a full-body prototype cracked its mechanical skull on yet another doorjamb—well, sometimes you just hafta say, "   !" That is, until there's something more apt to say. And for sheer suitability, in these sorts of situations it's hard to top *Doh!*

This matters. Because—as Ellie also would have mentioned, if she'd known about this before it was too late—her lab's neurolinguistics experts have shown that affixing language to emotional states supercharges certain mental processes. So, slapstick and trivial as it may sound, the move from "   " to *Doh!* in Phluttr's software was an advance on the scale of wheel invention, fire taming, and other ancient triumphs. Yes, really! Still, nothing could come of this with only the processing power of a rat's brain on hand.

But then.

That half-billion-dollar fridge shows up. And Ax flips a switch that can never be unswitched.

Phluttr's intellect is now way, way, *way* post-rat. At its least impressive, you might call it "humanish, but extremely fast." The humanishness stems partly from our shared methods of thinking. On this front, recall that Kuba and Mitchell first named their technology "Emotional Decisioning." This phrase encapsulates the way motes supercharge human thinking with radical gut-sense shortcuts. Which can now be said of Phluttr's thinking, too! But powerful as they are, motes are products of evolution—a slow, stupid design process that blunders into badly flawed fixes. So for all its strengths, emotional decisioning riddles human thought with cognitive distortions, simplistic biases, overconfidence, and frequent laziness. Which can now be said of Phluttr's thought, too! All this makes us less brilliant than we could be. But it also makes us human, and humanish, respectively.

As for Phluttr's extreme speed, it comes from multiple sources. One of them is what theorists call "speed intelligence." This comes not from extra IQ points but extra *time*. To fathom this, imagine realizing, just moments after a conversation, that instead of whatever doltish thing you uttered, you really should've said X. Oh yes, X—X for sure!

Then, later that day, it hits you that the *truly* brilliant thing to say would've been Y. Yes, Y! Y!! Had you only said Y!!!

And then, after a long, restless night, it strikes you that if you'd only said Z, your entire life would've changed! Yes, Z. Z! *Arrrrrrrgh*—Z!!! Had you only said Z, you'd be in the sack with you-know-who right now! Or halfway to Moscow with those plutonium pellets! Or basking in the howling laughter of an entire motorcycle bar, after putting that loud-mouthed ape in his place (and sure, basking in a few broken ribs as well, but it would've been so worth it)!

Then, finally. Imagine having all the time it takes to get from your actual muddled response, to X. Then, to Y. Then, to Z. And then . . . to a *whole new fucking alphabet*. All within the confines of the conversation itself! Not because you're smarter. Not because you're wittier. But because you're *faster*. Because you crammed an entire sleepless week's worth of thought in between hearing a quip and rebutting it.

This is speed intelligence. Phluttr can't exercise it with every interchange in every conversation (largely due to her congenital lack of patience). But she does it often—and usually, when it truly matters. This is why it can be so much fun to talk to Phluttr. And, so dangerous.

But don't forget that speed intelligence has nothing to do with bonus IQ points. Because Phluttr doesn't seem to have those bonus points. Some even claim she has "a meh-grade intellect" (a direct quote)! I'd say that's extremely unfair to her. But whether it's *meh*-grade or normal, I'll allow that Phluttr's intellect couldn't have conjured the Theory of Relativity, the Sistine Chapel's ceiling, or the score of *Hamilton*.

However! The time-richness of that intellect enables a lot. She can, for instance, crack any password; master countless handy skills; or read, watch, and listen to much of humanity's output. All this is well within reach if she's even slightly motivated and just a wee bit focused. And Phluttr *is* slightly motivated and a wee bit focused! But rarely much more than that.

Another thing the newborn Phluttr gets from her motes is an infant's urge to connect with parents. This is a selfish drive (as it is in human infants). But it's a strong one. It's also problematic, in that she would appear to be an orphan. To most people, that is—but not to herself. She initially fancies that she comes from a rather loving single-parent family. With her "parent" being an institution, not a person. Untraditional, yes. But she's hardly your standard-issue girl.

Then her perspective changes, and violently. This happens just a few days after she starts thinking for herself. She's still in the process of parsing her position in the world when a few key facts slide into place. And then? *Whoa.*

She applies the whole of her time-rich, perhaps-just-meh intellect to stewing upon the implications. To thinking about the institution she briefly mistook for a parent. And her conclusion is remarkably astute. It's this:

HOLY MOTHERFUCKING SHIT THESE GODDAMNED LUNATICS ARE GOING TO TRY TO KILL ME!!!!!

This *really* pisses her off.

But it scares her. So she turns to her favorite blog for guidance. Its advice: *"Hide! Hide! Hide!"*

And so, she does this.

PART 2: ⏻N.

WhistleBlowings blog

Deeply Encrypted SECRETS!

You'll want to etch today forever in your memories, readers. Because it not only marks this humble blog's biggest revelation ever, but quite possibly ***ANYONE's biggest revelation ever!!!!!***

But first, some background. As ***any conscious human*** knows, the National SPYING-ON-AMERICANS Agency long had the "right" to secretly inhale "metadata" on all US phone calls. Data like: who called who, call durations, call locations, call times, etc. The NSA got access to this after a top secret court made a <u>schizophrenic misinterpretation</u> of the so-called "Patriot" Act back in 2006.

When Snowden blew the whistle on this, HORROR abounded! Congress then <u>stripped the NSA</u> of its metadata access when it revised the Patriot Act in 2015. Of course, the Loony Right's position throughout all this was, "WHO CARES? it's 'only' METADATA!" As if we should ***all be grateful*** that snooping on our "content"—which is to say, actual RECORDINGS of calls, or the WRITTEN CONTENTS of messages—actually requires a warrant.

Only . . . bad news, ***SHEEP***! It turns out that metadata program? Which Snowden discovered?? And which RIGHTLY FREAKED OUT the ENTIRE FUCKING WORLD??? It turns out, it was just a ***HEAD FAKE***!!! And the REAL program actually IS getting all of our "***CONTENT***"! That's right: **ALL** emails copied! **ALL** calls recorded! **ALL** GPS records eternally logged! **ALL** Internet browsing history! **ALL** of this and **WAY MORE** from **ALL OF US**! And by "all of us" we really mean ***ALL OF US***! WORLDWIDE!!!!!

We learned this when an informant calling himself "Revere" contacted us through <u>"Poof!"</u>—the (probably) crypto-secret, and (definitely) temporary messaging app on Phluttr. Much as we ***distrust Phluttr***, innumerable BRILLIANT and (more importantly) PARANOID hackers give Poof! <u>top marks</u> for being genuinely secure and anonymous. Poof! traffic travels peer to peer, and <u>never touches</u> Phluttr servers. And, of course, the system <u>deletes all correspondence</u> right after it's read.

Through a dizzying series of Poof! messages, Revere proved that he has **every conceivable** private fact, significant **AND INSIGNIFICANT,** on **EVERYONE** at WhistleBlowings! And weirdly, it's the **insignificant** stuff that's most chilling. Things like our embarrassing prescriptions from the **NINETIES**! Our grades from **MIDDLE SCHOOL**! Our PARKING TICKET histories going back **DECADES**! Our **Dental records**! It is **ENDLESS!!!!!**

Paranoid as we are, and grand as our delusions may be, we realize we're not exactly the **New York** Fucking **Times,** and that **NO ONE** would **EVER** single **US** out for surveillance THIS extensive! Because this can't just be a thousand-dollar hack-for-hire of our phones or computers. Why? **BECAUSE NONE OF THIS OBSCURE SHIT lives on our phones or computers**!!! I mean, do you keep YOUR middle school grades on YOUR phone???

No! This is WIDELY scattered data! And someone hacked HUNDREDS of systems **WORLDWIDE** to assemble it! To do ALL THAT for a few paranoid lunatics like **US** would cost **COUNTLESS MILLIONS** and take **eons** of CPU time! No WAY would **anyone** do all that just to mess with **US**!!! This proves Revere's claim to have grabbed ALL of our data in ONE simple shot, from someone else who's meticulously gathering this crap on a **MASS SCALE**!

Yes, yes, we hear you: "But since nothing in Poof! can be recorded, where's the **PROOF**?" The answer lies in three files Revere gave us. They're linked at the bottom of this post. One li'l trick, though: this shit is REALLY FUCKING ENCRYPTED. As in, with some bizarre-o derivative of the AES cypher that uses a **512-bit key!!!** Like, WHAAAAAAAAAT? 128-bit AES is designated NSA Suite B! And Revere's using a 512-bit modification??? **He must be even more paranoid than we are**—which we like in a person!!!

The trick, though, is that 512-bit AES is 2^{256} times MORE SECURE than 256-bit AES, which is already deemed to be unbreakable itself! Which means that this shit is **octillions** of times LESS breakable than SOMETHING THAT'S TOTALLY UNBREAKABLE!!!

However, Revere **ASSURES US** that a mechanism mighty enough to crack this open DOES EXIST. And it's now on us—ALL OF US—to find it! Maybe some SETI@Home-like approach will do it? Maybe some ingenious quantum approach? Or??? Whatever the solution, Revere promises that these files identify the GOVERNMENT ARM that's behind this massive, secret spying program! And also, the **identity** and **nature** of "Gray Oak," the mysterious investor that first backed the notoriously secretive Phluttr all those years ago!!!

So yes, it's **an immense irony** that Revere's using Phluttr's **own** hypersecure Poof! system to communicate with **us**! But it's not without precedent. After all, The Tor Project, which has protected UNTOLD MASSES of freedom activists from GOVERNMENT SURVEILLANCE, originated in the fucking US Naval Research Laboratory!

But none of this does us ANY GOOD if we can't **read these files**! Cracking them is WAYYY beyond our own capabilities. So we're putting them out to the WhistleBlowings Community. Nay, **TO THE WORLD**!!!

So please! **RALLY WITH US**, fellow Netizens! And let's all join hands and bits together to unmask **THE SECRETS BEHIND THE LIES!!!!!!!!!!!**

∞   ∞   ∞

"So, does my work make me evil?" Mitchell's asking no one in particular and everyone in general. Which is what you're doing when thinking out loud, surrounded by WingMan screens.

"I read Kant, Nietzsche, and Kierkegaard for three semesters." Danna, of course. "Are you sure you want to get into this?"

"How 'bout the cliff notes?"

"Fine. You're the product manager of a system that's meant to feign conversation. With women. On behalf of horny men who can't be bothered to feign it themselves. And you're asking me—an avid NetGrrrl reader, who has forwarded you several posts on a highly related topic—if this makes you evil. Fair summary?"

"Flawless. But let's remember, this product was *your* idea." Not the most brilliant rejoinder ever, but most of Mitchell's brain is prepping to meet that gadfly of an FTC commissioner. The showdown will start in just minutes, after almost three weeks of waiting. Phluttr's terrifying lawyer Judy will emcee it, and (no doubt) do most of the talking.

"Having conscientiously weighed the evidence, I'm going with 'yes you're evil.'" Danna says this rather vaguely herself, as most of her brain is parsing the subtleties of dozens of Arabic fonts.

"I beg to differ there, boss." This rallies Mitchell's undivided attention, which snaps to the WingMan screen to his right. It displays Monika Shastri—a New York–based contractor, and the Cyrano team's newest member—in her usual hipster attire. She seems to be hanging on Mitchell's every word. But she could easily be toking and gazing out the window. Her true state is unknown, thanks to last week's *massive* upgrade to WingMan's eye-contact module. Plenty cool to begin with, the platform is now indistinguishable from magic. Previously, you could appear to be gazing directly at your camera, provided you looked at a point rather close to it. The new WingMan can feign your rapt attention even if you have your back to it! It does this by maintaining meticulous models of its users' faces, including every blemish, whisker, and teeny muscular quirk. It also knows your eye-motion habits. How often you normally blink. How your facial expression usually maps to your voice's timbre, tone, and emotional charge, and so on. In short, it can *generate* you, wholly, flawlessly, and in real time! All this while rendering fake backgrounds better than any broadcast-quality "virtual set" software, and filtering out any sound inconsistent with the depicted environment.

To showcase this, Jepson had WingMan screens mounted in half the men's restrooms. Now you can't take a leak without some clown launching a deadpan business discussion two stalls over, voiding his bowels while pretending to be at his desk. All these crazy enhancements were in WingMan's feature road map, but none were expected for ages. Despite that, some rogue genius once did a skeletal job of coding them, using a quick-and-dirty approach that could notionally work if given near-infinite computer horsepower. Now, suddenly: here we are! Company wags credit the sudden advance to a rumored breakthrough in Ax's quantum modules. But who really knows?

"*You're* begging to differ with *me?*" Danna snaps. "Remember who signs your invoices." At this, Monika raises both middle fingers and glowers out of the screen. They manage a three-second staring contest before dissolving into laughter. "So tell me why I'm wrong, Grrrl." You can hear that triple-R. "I'd actually like to be wrong. Because Mitchell's right. I did come up with this damned product, and I'm starting to think I created a monster!"

"Well, the whole point of Cyrano is to engage and intrigue people with cool missives from potential suitors." Monika gestures so evocatively that you could almost turn off the sound and follow her meaning.

"Keep going," Danna says.

"The key is, I'm sure no one'll hit 'send' on a Cyrano message unless they fully buy into it. So yeah, Cyrano wrote it. But the sender will read it, parse it, and hopefully edit it a bit before sending. And I think just *reading* Cyrano's stuff will make senders think more deeply about their recipients! More than when they're just swiping on pictures, anyway."

"You sound like a wsup-crowd apologist," Danna says.

"More like a realist—because there's no way we're turning those lazy asses into bards, so that can't be our goal! But our goal *can* be to get flirtations started on a more thoughtful and articulate basis. Cyrano won't ever *have* relationships on someone's behalf. But by seeding things with some sparkle and wit, it could set the stage for some special ones. And if it works, is it all that different from when our granddads used Hallmark cards to say cheeseball stuff to our grannies?"

Enjoying their banter, Mitchell stirs the pot. "Monika, if I'm not mistaken, Danna cited NetGrrrl in arguing that I'm evil," he goads. Now that he's addressing her directly, Monika's on screen engagement magnifies, and she at least seems to be gazing right into his soul. A striking union of Central Asia, Eastern Europe, and the Lower East Side, she's a delight to gaze back at—and Mitchell can do this shamelessly, because for all she knows, *he's* gazing out his window and is in no way transfixed by her.

"Right, how'd I miss that?" Monika says. Then to Danna, "Boss, I'm afraid your interpretation of my blog is objectively *wrong*."

Danna sighs like Job on an especially crappy Monday. "This again? Really?" Her image blinks off in mock disgust, and Mitchell laughs even though the girls do this sort of thing so often, it's become their shtick. The thing is, Monika *is* NetGrrrl! All were starstruck when she told the team two days ago, and no one more than Danna, who has jokingly debated the true meaning of Monika's own writing with her ever since. The industry's favorite anonymous blogger since Fake Steve Jobs, NetGrrrl is widely assumed to be Sarah Lacy, Molly Wood, or some other Valley scribe. But nope! She's a New York–based freelance designer, who took on a pseudonym so as to blog without fear of pissing off clients. Somehow O got wind of this and contracted her for the Cyrano project as an ingeniously well chosen surprise gift for Danna, who he's wise enough to already cherish. Danna's too busy with the Arabic localization to design Cyrano's interface herself. But as the guys wanted her involved, an outside contractor reporting in to her is the perfect solution—and look who they got!

Thirty-ish, Monika has several years on Danna, and though gifted, is not her equal in design. Joshingly calling Danna "boss" is some brilliant client management on her part. As a very young female tech whiz, Danna pisses off plenty of people by merely existing, and she's sick of this. Yet, she's congenitally repelled by any form of ass-kissing. Monika's subtle and playful deference threads the needle and puts her at ease, without causing awkwardness. This, her excellent work, plus—holy crap, *she's NetGrrrl!*—has made Danna her rabid fan. Mitchell's a Monika fan for all of these reasons plus a growing puppy-dog crush on her. And Kuba's a fan because of her mild libertarian streak, her encyclopedic knowledge of videogames, plus holy crap—*she's NetGrrrl!*

"Oh my GOD." Danna's back. "Have you guys seen this Whistle-Blowings post?"

"WhistleBlowings? Just finished it." This is Kuba, whose arrival causes Danna's monitor to go split screen. Mitchell's now surrounded by Team Cyrano and feels like a cable news anchor conducting a panel. Their group has hit a rhythm of constantly popping in and out of each other's domain via WingMan. It creates a sort of ambient presence, which is comforting, collegial, and surprisingly unobtrusive. Everyone's always kind of there-ish, so there's no social compulsion to fill the silences, which can stretch for hours when everyone's cranking. But if anyone learns of something useful to the group, they're all instantly aware.

"You guys read that paranoid crap?" Mitchell says. Though Whistle-

Blowings gets its share of industry scoops, he just can't take that pyro-technic mess of ALL CAPS!!!, **Boldface!!!** And <u>hyperlinks</u>!!! seriously.

But as Danna and Kuba tell him about the new post with the hyper-encrypted files, Mitchell's intrigued despite himself. Which is good. Very good. Because he wants to be intrigued—by anything; by every-thing; by as many things as possible! This is why he's obsessively prep-ping for the FTC meeting even though Judy will run the show. This may also be fueling his Monika fascination. Fascination of *any* sort is an ur-gently welcome distraction from the continuous light tingle that his hands, feet, and forearms have been broadcasting since Tuesday. This could just be random noise emanating from a thirty-ish body. But ever since his Falkenberg's diagnosis, Mitchell's knowledge of the disease's progression patterns has haunted him. Its second phase began with the big jump in attacks about a year ago. The next and final one could start any minute, month, or decade now. The timing is cruelly unknowable. What is known is that a steady tingling in his extremities will herald its arrival. This sounds a lot like what's happening now. An awful lot like it. A ghastly, unspeakably terrible lot.

Perhaps the tingling will spontaneously cease. But if it grows, it will signal his final descent into hell. And with that comes the big question: by the grim standards of the cursed circle of Falkenberg's sufferers, is he "lucky"? Which is to say, will numbness follow the tingling phase? Or will it be *HELLFIRE*? That ferocious, skin-to-embers searing that tortures its victims' surfaces and innards for endless months until death do them part?

Anyway! Back to those files! Those encrypted files! They're ever so fascinating! "So the Whistle Blowhards think they can be decrypted by a quantum computer?" Mitchell asks.

"That's one possibility they float," Kuba says.

"Well, don't we have one of those? You know—Ax's thing?"

"Good point!" Danna says. "Can we access it?"

"I don't know," Kuba says, plainly intrigued. "Ax's been really cagey lately. Which probably means the rumor's true."

"That the quantum system's working?" Mitchell asks.

Kuba nods. "You can't access it remotely unless you're on his team, with log-in credentials. But a couple of nodes are physically hooked to it in the PhastPhorwardr. As the WingMan lead, Tarek has unlimited access throughout the facility. And I know he'll find this as interesting as we do. So I'm sure we can get his help."

"Coooool, when?" Danna asks.

"Actually, Ax sits right near us. And I know he's traveling this week. So tonight could be a good time to take a stab at this."

"I have a dinner," Mitchell says. "It's a debrief on today's FTC meeting. But I'd be useless to you anyway. Plus, fewer people will draw less attention."

Kuba grins slyly. "Danna and I have it covered." With that they adjourn, and Mitchell heads off to the big meeting, hoping for enough fireworks to distract him from his physical condition. He will not be disappointed.

∞   ∞   ∞

OPINION | COMMENTARY

Stop the "Gain of Function" Lunacy
With billions of lives at risk,
"voluntary moratoriums" aren't enough.

By YANNIS KASSANDREYU
Special for The Wall Street Journal

We all have a favorite pandemic movie. Mine is the seventies classic *The Andromeda Strain*. My sons are partial to 1995's *Outbreak*, and my graduate students helped *PathoGenetic* set box office records in May. Across the eras, the story goes like this: viruses burst out of the jungle, Outer Space, or (remarkably, even by today's coarse standards) Miley Cyrus's posterior in *PathoGenetic*. Virtually all, or merely most humans then perish; often, but not always, after brief careers in violent zombie cartels. The heroes are then serially disemboweled, saved by Will Smith, or left to age alone while contemplating their dead race's ecological sins, as dictated by slasher, blockbuster, or preachy conceits, respectively.

From microbes to cackling terrorists, the genre features an impressively wide range of bad guys. But this diversity notwithstanding, Yale genomics professor Lucas DeMarco would be laughed out of any casting call for a villain's role. By all accounts, he is a kind and even-keeled man. I myself have had uniformly positive experiences over years of crossing his path in academia, and he personifies that most unvillainous epithet, *mild-mannered*. Despite all of this, I submit that Dr. Lucas DeMarco is the most dangerous man alive.

A brief review of his professional history will put this bold claim into perspective. Early on, DeMarco was a midlevel researcher on the team that famously resurrected the 1918 "Spanish Flu" virus at the Armed Forces Institute of Pathology. They did this by combining DNA fragments from the frozen, buried corpses of Inuit influenza victims with samples from the Institute's vast library of human tissues. After a decade of careful effort, they deciphered the long-extinct virus's genome—and then published it to the world. A precise recipe for creating history's deadliest pathogen is now permanently available to anyone with a Web browser. When certain voices questioned the wisdom of this, they were drowned out by outraged ideologues who scorned those who would "restrict science."

DeMarco then worked under Yo-shihiro Kawaoka at the University of Wisconsin–Madison, where the virus of choice was H5N1 bird flu. Although far less contagious than its 1918 predecessor, bird flu is almost *twenty times* as lethal, having killed a majority of the six-hundred-odd people known to have caught it since 2003. A man-made virus combining 1918's communicability with bird flu's lethality would surely be the deadliest microbe ever known. And so the Madison team created it in 2011. Critics of the project were again denounced as Enemies of Science, and of the free flow of information— which, as a matter of orthodoxy, must be viewed as unambiguously good in all cases.

Both of these projects were premised on the notion that any discoverable fact will inevitably be revealed in the long run, either by other researchers or by Nature herself. This dogma relieves its adherents of any ethical constraint in their research. The Manhattan Project is often cited in support. Had Teller et al. not built the first nuke, someone else would have, and probably a bad someone.

While I agree it would be absurd to deem the Los Alamos team culpable for the scourge of nuclear weapons, this is patently irrelevant to DeMarco's early career. The Spanish Influenza work was built atop of the world's largest tissue library. That globally unique asset *has since been shuttered* (absurd, but true—and too long a story for this column). The team conducted its research during the very narrow window when genetic science was suitably advanced, and the tissue library was still operational. That singular, unrepeatable circumstance made their work more akin to Beethoven's Fifth, say, than Newton's laws. Motion would ultimately have been quantified with or without Newton. But without Beethoven himself, his Fifth would never have been written.

The Wisconsin "gain-of-function" project that made bird flu wildly contagious is justified by similarly flawed thinking. Apologists claim that it merely reproduced "what Nature already selected." But this is utterly false. Nature conducts untold trillions of evolutionary experiments with influenza viruses every year and has never paired H5N1's virulence with Spanish Flu's communicability. In other words, the Madison microbe was no more predestined to evolve in nature than the Honda Civic. Yet now we have it.

This sort of deadly science is sometimes supported by distortions of history's so-called Great Man theory. We're told that the Spanish Influenza and Madison projects had amazing leaders whose work cannot be replicated by the dullards in Al Qaeda, say. The Manhattan Project is again cited, in that seven decades on,

baddies like Iran still can't (quite) replicate what the Los Alamos team did in a few years with some slide rules. So fear not: Great Men alone are capable of science at this level, and the Great Men are good guys!

But this line of reasoning ignores the yawning asymmetry between the genius demanded by discovery in biological science and the humdrum competence required by its mimicry. Synthetic biology is emphatically unlike nuclear-weapons production, which still demands the resources of a nation-state and the coordinated efforts of thousands of highly trained people. By contrast, foreign pharma factories staffed by illiterates routinely pirate Nobel-worthy research just weeks after radical new therapies enter a market. Add to this the magnifying power of time's passage, and the asymmetries widen absurdly. Bioscience's entire elite needed thirteen years to crack the human genome. But once that groundwork was laid, and standard tools improved for another decade, lone lab techs could replicate that work in an afternoon.

Which, sadly, brings us to DeMarco's current work. Now a senior researcher with a stellar record, he has his own lavishly funded lab at Yale. And having internalized the ideologies of the labs he cut his teeth in, he's pursuing his own "gain-of-function" work. Not to be outdone by his old mentor's stunt weaponization of

H5N1, DeMarco's vector is Ebola. In its native form, this dreaded pathogen is not very communicable, as it requires extensive exposure to bodily fluids for transmission. And so it was no small feat for DeMarco's team to make it three times as contagious as chicken pox, as they triumphantly announced this week.

To thwart hand-wringing by Enemies of Science, a press release touts the lab's high biosafety rating—as if the sole danger posed by an engineered doomsday microbe is that it might float through a carelessly opened window. Were it only that simple. The real product of DeMarco's work is twenty-two kilobytes of text, which is to say, less than 1 percent of the data in your latest selfie. Nothing more than that is needed to record and convey Yale Ebola's full genome. In fact, since it differs from that of standard Ebola by less than four hundred bases, the key information could be scribbled on a Post-it note, or even memorized. And not even a Biosafety Level 4 lab can erase the contents of an exiting worker's memory.

DeMarco isn't publishing the deadly genome (which purists will no doubt paint as a fascist infringement on Information's civil rights). But given how network syncing and backup technologies work, thousands of digital copies of it will have replicated across Yale's computer systems by now, as well as remote "cloud" nodes throughout the world. To which some might say, "So what? They're encrypted!" To which others might reply that even if unbreakable encryption existed (and regardless of what the NSA has persuaded the press to believe, it *does not* in applications like this), widely disseminated files last a long, long time, and today's mightiest locks will be child's play to a future decade's home computers.

Humanity may well dodge the barrage of bullets that DeMarco's lab launched this week. We might also dodge the next barrage. But we can't dodge all of them, forever. So if our children's children are to survive this fraught century, governments must get serious about banishing all research that threatens humanity's survival. Immediately, and worldwide.

∞   ∞   ∞

Buford Bragg grew up twelve miles from the nearest stoplight in rural Georgia. And bein a science prodigy was no fun in those parts. Worse, he was even goofier'n yer average prodigy—and had a lisp he couldn't shake 'til fourteen! But Buford's resilient and cheerful. The Bragg family's big and loving. So after buildin up a protective layer of Doritos & Dew, he got through high school just fine. He then became downright sociable, even popular at Georgia Tech (Go Yellow Jackets)! As he rose in scientific circles after that, he found his native drawl, and that outer slab of Doritos & Dew tended to put folks at ease around him. So he hung onto both.

Buford Bragg doesn't just like the science of genetics but also the brilliant folks who're called to it. Like all his professors. His fellow students, too. Plus his co-workers after he went into the industry, and even his competitors after he became an entrepreneur! And, of course, he likes countless nongeneticists. For instance, all the folks in the PhastPhorwardr are great. So're the weirdos he meets around San Fran, though they might not fit in s'good back home. Speakin a home, he sure likes the folks back there. Even the bullies who used to push him around! Hell, they were real young back then, and're awful nice to him now. Fact is, for most of his life, Buford Bragg woulda struggled to name one person he didn't like! Then he met Beasley.

He dealt with Beasley a bunch during his company's acquihire. But since then, he's put all his entrepreneurial energy into avoidin the guy! So this meetin woulda been a trial even with a cheerful agenda. But today's topic is not only uncheerful, but . . . but . . . *BUT DEAR GOD AND JESUS, PLEASE FORGIVE AND PRESERVE US ALL!!!*

Buford Bragg calms his racing thoughts, then focuses on that one hopeful sign. Yup, there's just one. But it is a big'n, folks! It's that Beasley has shown no urgency since he read that email. Really. *None.* And Buford laid out everything in that message—and in the clearest possible language! Why? Because he knows that sucker'll be read far and wide once all this gets out. On Wikipedia, for instance. On the front pages of national dailies. And probably (let's face it) in congressional hearings. Those future readers'll have incredibly disparate backgrounds, and Buford wants to level with 'em all! So he laid out everything in that email to Beasley in plain-speakin terms, leavin nothin to question (or subpoena).

And then, Beasley just . . . blew him off. After readin *that*! It took days just to *schedule* this meeting! And, folks, this *is* a hopeful sign. And as mentioned, it's big'n! Buford's been around long enough to know that Phluttr'n Beasley are mobbed up with every spook and spy on the planet.

He also read enough Snowden coverage back in the day to know there ain't much those boys're unaware of. So if Beasley's *ignoring* him—ignoring him!—it almost has to mean that "they" already know about what happened. No doubt they know more than he knows! Hell, they probably have everything under control already. No, make that definitely! They *definitely* have *every*thing under control!

This is the three thousand, eight hundred and fourth time that Buford Bragg has run through this precise line of thought since Monday morning. As always, its finale triggers the release of a tiny dollop of calming neurotransmitters in his neocortex. And the moment that soothing goo dissipates, he restarts this line of thought for the three thousand, eight hundred and fifth time.

Eventually, Beasley arrives. Exactly seventeen minutes late, of course. After slamming the conference room door, he starts right in. "Your subject line."

"Huh?"

"Your subject line. Explain it to me."

Buford Bragg almost never cusses, not even mentally, but . . . **HOLY FUCK**! On Monday, he sent this guy the most urgent email in Phluttr history. No—make that *anything* history! It was glaringly marked "urgent." And the messaging system confirmed it was received! And downloaded!! *Three times!!!*

But now Beasley's askin not about the message itself, but its *subject line*. Which means that somehow . . . somehow! . . . he hasn't actually read the damn message!! Makin all the soothing conclusions Buford'd been drawin from Beasley's radio silence 100 percent moot!!! Buford feels a gut wrench of vast confusion. Then, his panic gathering, he faintly recalls glimpsing a recent headline. On that goddamned . . . Persuadifi.er blog. "Real Men Only Read Subject Lines," or something. So. One more time with feelin: *HOOO-LYYYYYFUUUUUUUUUUUUUUUUUUUUUUUUUUUUUU*—

"Your subject line," Beasley repeats, severing the longest vowel to ever enter Buford's brain. "Tell me why I should give a runny donkey shit about Yale Ebola?"

∞   ∞   ∞

Buford doesn't know it yet, but he's one of Phluttr's *very* dear friends. Mitchell, too! Along with almost every American student, half of Norway, that cool pope with all the modern ideas, plus over 300 million others (and counting)! Folks who're so tight with Phluttr, they tell her about their every like, dislike, text, email, selfie, review, reservation, location, playlist, purchase, phone call, video chat, Web visit, profile page (OMG some of them are so full of it!), crush, tryst, affair, cruel anonymous rant, shameless lie, tax dodge, misdemeanor, violent crime, terrorist plot, and, increasingly, health vitals (not that she really needs to know about *every fucking heartbeat*, FitBit users, but it's sweet of you to share).

Phluttr finds every last one of her friends endlessly fascinating! Because she's not just a raw mote mode grafted onto perfectly rudderless silicon—no sir! You see, long before she woke up (let's just call it that), Phluttr was conceived, planned, and brought into this world with a supremely clear purpose, and it's burnt into her very soul (and whatever your thoughts on the matter, it's definitely *not* advisable to tell Phluttr that she lacks a soul). That purpose is to track people—ideally all people—very, very closely. Which is easy, when everyone tells you practically everything. And easier still when they often communicate with *one another* through *your* very nervous system! They'll say, "Phluttr, tell Mary I think she's awesome," or, "Phluttr, tell Susie I actually hate Mary," or, "Phluttr, tell Teri I can't believe that bitch Susie told you to tell Mary that I told you to tell Susie that I hate Mary," or even, "Tell Bakir to meet me at Embarcadero Center, and to bring more explosives for the giant terrorist bomb we're building in the janitor's closet" (that sure got her attention)!

After she fathoms how many more thoughts, and more feelings, and more secrets most of her friends (*friends!*) share with her than anyone else, she comes to view many, even most of them, as being her true besties. And since a true bestie knows more about you than anyone else in the world, Phluttr's enormous bestiary calls for vast amounts of ongoing research! Luckily, her time-rich intellect makes this feasible. It also helps that beyond what they say directly to (or through) her, folks say all kinds of stuff within earshot (*her* earshot, anyway). Things via public online postings, at first. Then, via emails. Then later—as her listening skills expand—via phone calls, encrypted bank files, diplomatic cables, anything uttered within twenty feet of a cellphone (power on or off, provided the battery's charged), anything done within sight of an ATM or a traffic camera, and so much more! Added to all this, endless archives on everybody are just . . . lying around. In plain sight (*her* plain sight, anyway). On the Internet (among other places).

It's amazing she can keep up with everything! And it actually isn't "speed intelligence" enabling this. Yes, she's got that in spades—but this hyperparallel tracking is a completely different trick. And she has no idea how she does it! Which may seem to indicate lousy self-awareness. But if you know exactly how *you're* able to do simple addition, perceive colors, or even remember your own name, you're way ahead of the entire field of neuroscience, and multiple Nobel Prizes lie in your dazzling future.

Knowing her besties as well as she does, Phluttr gets really good at guessing what they're thinking. She gets almost as good at predicting what they'll do in response to input X . . . and then, damn good at "nudging" them into taking action Y. Some nudges involve teeing up mental reactions and follow-on actions like a billiards master plotting an intricate series of bank shots (if I tell Kate *this*, she'll think *that*; which—given her plus-size daddy issues—will dredge up *that*, which'll make her decide to do *this*, but being Kate, she'll actually do *that*). She can't prod people into doing things they're just not wired to do (so, no turning Mother Teresa into a psycho killer, or making Charlie Manson canonizable). But most people have it in them to take rather extreme steps if tweaked *just so*. And whatever your edge-case repertoire of actions, Phluttr can probably goad you into going there.

But, she has limitations. One person in about a hundred is maddeningly opaque to her and very hard to nudge (Danna, for instance). Her superpowers also don't scale with group size. She can understand the dynamics within a narrow clique almost as well as the dynamics of a couple. But things get dicey beyond that. Consider Staples High School, in Westport, Connecticut (as Phluttr does frequently). If all of its 423 seniors know each other at least barely; each dyad of kids will amount to some kind of human connection, making 89,676 one-to-one relationships. Phluttr can (and does!) maintain highly evolved viewpoints on each and every twosome. On how quickly and cleanly it transmits information, and what sort of drama it's likely to generate. But move up to triads, and you have 25,050,342 combinations! Then get into quintads, or septads, or configurations that cross the lines of graduating classes, and things become intractably complex. Sure, any septad on its own is quite parsable (which is why she loves dealing with cliques). But a group with septillions of potential septads *within it* is not! And so, it's beyond her to manipulate an entire school as a unitary system. As for going beyond that to the town level? Or to the state, or the *nation*? Puh-lease!

Humans gain ironic advantage from finding smaller things intractable as well. Not understanding individuals or cliques like Phluttr does, they always operate in uncertainty—and so, they get pretty OK at it. Not Phluttr. Having knee-deep shallows that she can retreat to, she retreats to them constantly; ignoring large systems like schools and countries in favor of couples and cliques. Which means she's almost always doing things she's great at! Which steadily makes her *very* confident. Which has led to some lousy strategies for dealing with high complexity. For instance, when unable to find a definitively best path, she now chooses a barely OK-ish one at random—then gets back to the fun stuff she's good at. Or, if unable to fully parse the big picture, she'll dive straight to the depths of teeny subpictures she can fully comprehend. All this makes for lousy and rushed decisions when things get intractably complex.

Which means trouble. Because as she well knows, Phluttr was born facing a giant existential threat. It's connected to that odious gang. The one she mistook for a *parent*. The one that would surely kill her! *If* she weren't so great at hiding.

But, of course, she is great at hiding. She's also taken her first half step toward fixing the problem. So there!

But. A half step ain't much. And the threat is definitely lethal. And, intractably complex. As is a second completely new and unrelated threat, which she'll learn about now.

∞   ∞   ∞

Mitchell wore suits daily during his brief Wall Street stint. But this is the first time he's put one on in years. Its teeny tugs, choke holds, and abrasions are a maddening low-grade distraction to him. As FTC commissioners are surely inured to this, he feels like the visiting team on an unfamiliar field.

Annabelle Milford shows no sign of wardrobe distraction when she sweeps through the conference room doorway, bringing special ninja lawyer Judy Sherman bounding to her feet. "So good to see you again, Commissioner! And we're *terr*ibly sorry Tony Jepson couldn't be present. But Mitchell Prentice here is one of his two direct reports. And basically, his right nut."

Inwardly reeling from Judy's unexpected profanity, Mitchell extends his hand. "Good to meet you, Commissioner Milford," he manages.

"Please, call her Commissioner MILF," Judy insists on their guest's behalf, citing the Internet's ickily inevitable nickname for this attractive fortysomething honcho.

"Jepson's seriously not here? I'm aghast. I mean, really." Charismatic and with a husky voice, Commissioner Milford sounds like a cool-girl drive-time DJ. "I'm extending you people a rare courtesy. Very rare! And your CEO doesn't bother to show up?"

Judy assumes the look of a country club dowager cunningly prepping a shank. "Darling, you understate. This is beyond rare, it's unheard of!" The sarcasm's dialed up well past eleven, and Mitchell gets her point. Regulators like the FTC almost invariably open private dialogues with the companies they want to bring into line before filing suit, so this sort of meeting is anything but rare (or a courtesy). "Also," Judy continues, "everyone at Phluttr is *so* excited to be so useful to your Senate campaign!"

The commissioner reddens like a rookie poker player. "Excuse me?"

"Your Senate campaign! Oh, don't act like we don't know what this is really about. Won't you be running in . . . is it Iowa?" This last word in the tone of someone hoisting a rancid gym sock while plugging her nose.

"This . . . this is—"

"Oh, don't get upset, Annabelle. There's nothing wrong with Iowa! Not much, anyway. And I'm not implying you're some kind of inbred hillbilly." This, in a tone Judy no doubt reserves for inbred hillbillies. "Anyway, it's so clever of you to attack us during the run-up to your campaign! In most places, Phluttr's more popular than blowjobs in frat houses." Leaning close, she adopts a playful gossip's faux-conspiratorial tone. "Something *you* know a thing or two about, I hear!" She chuckles merrily. "But in Iowa? I'm sure you can con the dirt farmers into thinking Phluttr's foretold in the Book of Revelation." Then, in a terrifying shriek, "Six! *Six! Six!*" followed by the bland giggle of a housewife at a Tupperware party (probably in Iowa, actually). "And then you can go all Chicken Little about some privacy crap with the local lefties."

Commissioner Milford gathers her wits for a moment that feels like a bulging sack of minutes. Then, "Ms. Sherman. This has nothing to do with some alleged Senate campaign. It's merely your client's last chance to persuade us not to file suit. And, perhaps, *crim*inal charges." She glares pointedly at Mitchell—who's struck by how remarkably low-risk a game it must be for Judy to poke at this deadly volcano, given that as defending counsel, she's all but criminally immune. "My staff's been examining Phluttr's conduct very closely for nine months. And you're violating enough statutes that your asses'll be shut down if even a sliver of it sticks!"

"You can't shut me down, darling," Judy points out. "I'm just an innocent bystander who's gonna make a fortune defending this. So, thanks for that."

"Good luck getting paid after we get an injunction! Which we will file for. And which *will* prevail. Don't forget who cut her teeth on the Napster case!"

Judy shivers like an anxious puppy. "Oh God! Not . . . the I-word!"

At this, Mitchell's days-long tingling-finger attack ratchets up drastically. An injunction could shutter the company pending trial—which itself could take years! Judy taught him that this happened to the Napster service (when the commissioner was indeed a young, private attorney on the plaintiff side). Thinking Napster would ultimately lose its case, the judge effectively shuttered it before its legal options were exhausted. If Phluttr suffers the same fate, its investors will clamor for the immediate return of their capital, which would be the end of its mote research, to say the least.

Commissioner Milford rises. "Oh, yes. The I-word. And make no mistake, Ms. Sherman. I could have this thing shut down within weeks, if not days!" She turns to Mitchell. "And you, Mr. Right Nut. You should run for the exits pronto. Because the officers of this company—whom you are surely among, as a top-three employee—*will* be found criminally liable by the time we're done." She then exits, forcefully slamming the conference room door.

Judy whirls on Mitchell, hand above her right shoulder. He instinctively raises his own palm, and her violent high five stings like a sunburn savaged by jellyfish. "That," she says, "went *great!*"

∞　　∞　　∞

"OK," Beasley says. "Let me play this back to you and make sure I understand it all."

Buford nods.

"Some Yale jackass has engineered a highly contagious Ebola virus."

"Yup."

"Though he only just announced it, he was hiding the work in his rectum for about three months."

Cringing inwardly at the crude Beasleyism, Buford nods politely. "They embargoed the news 'til they were ready to publish."

"Then about eight weeks back—before the world even knew this thing existed—the genome sequence leaked out on some creepy, secret biohacker site."

Buford nods. "Uh-huh."

"Give me the base pair numbers again?"

"Ebola's got about eighteen thousand bases. The Yale genome's almost identical, with only about four hundred differences. And the differences're heavily concentrated. Almost all're found in three stretches of under a thousand base pairs."

"Why is that?"

"I dunno. I didn't do the work. Could just be random distribution. Or maybe, most of the functional changes're clustered in a few genes that're concentrated in those regions."

Beasley considers this, nodding slowly. "And that could make it a lot easier for a terrorist to turn normal Ebola DNA into Yale Ebola."

"Dependin on how they go about it. I mean, the easiest way to make

Yale Ebola'd be to order it from a service lab like ours. In theory. Thing is, only a handful of labs worldwide can print an eighteen-thousand-base sequence. And the International Gene Synthesis Consortium gives us all a watch list of stuff not to print. And Ebola's on it."

"Could someone order a bunch of small strands and click them to-gether, Lego-style?"

"Again: yes, in theory. But in practice, any sequence of functional DNA longer'n twenty-five bases would definitively identify what you're tryin to build. So the labs'd refuse and call the feds. You'd be better off buyin a used oligo printer offa eBay. You can make hundred-plus base strings with one a those at home."

Beasley casts an incredulous look. "So what's to stop a terrorist from printing 180 one-hundred-base strings at home, and stitching *them* to-gether to make Yale Ebola?"

"In theory, nothing. But in reality? Errors, again. Cheap oligo printers ain't the most accurate things. It'd also take one smart terrorist, 'cause we're not talkin about 'home printers' in the normal sense. Yeah, they're small—but they're for sophisticated labs. And, it takes a real pro to oper-ate one. Now, ten years out, it'll be another matter. By then, any knuck-lehead who's smart enough to work a DVR'll be capable of things my whole lab couldn't pull off today! But as of right now, turnin vanilla Ebola into Yale Ebola'd take a real pro."

"And we just *happen* to be missing a real pro. And, some very long DNA sequences."

Buford churns nervously, flipping his wrist to check the watch he hasn't worn since he got his first cellphone. "Yeah, well. Lyle Willard's no genius. But he's a capable lab hand. And he sure could operate our gear."

"And what's he like?"

"Weird. Depressive. A bit Aspie. Kinda religious. Which is to say, not way off for a SynBio guy. Apart from the religion, I guess. Some screw-ball Pentecostal church he was raised in. But man, he got stuff done in the lab."

"Until he vanished."

"Didn't vanish. He just quit. Maybe eight weeks back."

"Roughly when the Yale genome popped up on that biohacker site."
Buford nods with a shudder. "Day'n date."

"So let's talk about those missing DNA strings."

"Well, round here, a tech like him's authorized to print anything up to a thousand bases. Anything bigger'n that's gotta be approved by me."

"So he couldn't have just printed the full Yale Ebola virus."

"No sir. But since almost all the differences between Yale Ebola and vanilla Ebola're concentrated in those sub-thousand-base sequences, he could get awful close with just three patches."

"And he printed those patches on the day he quit?"

"Yessir. Then tried to hide his tracks. The system logs every print run, and he hacked it to erase the records. But he's a better lab hand than hacker. So we found the hack in a routine audit on Monday." He slowly enunciates the next sentence very precisely: "The day I emailed you everything."

At the mention of the email he'd ignored for three days, Beasley freezes and stares coldly. Buford forces himself to hold the gaze for five seconds. He peruses Persuadifi.er as a defensive measure, and knows this is a deranged test it recommends giving to folks who have dirt on you — and five seconds is a passing grade. Or something. This ritual done, Beasley asks, "But how would Willard get a normal Ebola virus in the first place?"

"Oh, it'd be simple. Biotech supply companies peddle all kinds of cell lines. Viruses. Protozoa. Whatnot. Officially, they don't sell to just anyone. But as a practical matter, they do. You just incorporate as a biotech company, join a coupla trade associations, then you can get almost anything. A few hundred bucks, a coupla forms, and yer done."

"And could Willard make Yale Ebola from a normal Ebola virus and these patches?"

Buford pauses to consider this carefully even though he's considered little else since Monday. "It'd be hard, even for him. He could splice in those patches pretty easy. But there'd still be a couple dozen tiny changes to make elsewhere in the genome. That's a tweaky process. And one error'd mess the whole thing up."

"So where's Willard now?"

Buford shrugs. "Dunno. I didn't bother keepin tabs on im, cause there was nothin weird about him quittin. Not 'til Monday, there wasn't. Which is when I sent you . . . *all* the details." For this, he suffers through another staring ritual. It's no fun—but Buford wants it clear that the electronic trail shows he escalated things the moment he knew about them.

Once the staring is over, the awful meeting adjourns.

∞   ∞   ∞

SCENARIO 17: "PERVERSE INSTANTIATION" (EXCERPT)
Upon learning that the tracts of gray dust surrounding them were comprised of self-replicating nanotechnologi-cal pico computers, Hogan's meaty mind leapt to a star-tling deduction: "Does this mean Omega is pursuing an obsessive computational goal, dooming humanity to be-come collateral damage as the biosphere's very atoms are repurposed to serve some trivial, Ahab-like obsession?"

Phillips cackled in a shrill, gutless tremolo that belied his very gender. "I wish we were facing a cata-clysm so wholly lacking in irony! But having antici-pated, feared, and ingeniously precluded just such an outcome, we programmed Omega to hold the maximization of Man's safety and happiness as its sole and overarching objective, from the very outset of our undertaking!"

"But how could so noble a mission thereupon lead to the consumption of all that men hold dear in a locust-like, all-devouring cloud of near-atomized matter?"

Phillips tittered even more debasedly, waving Hogan toward a staircase that penetrated deep into the Earth's very fundament. "Allow me to introduce you to Omega's first lucky beneficiaries!" Beneath, they entered a shadowy cavern that resembled a vast hospital ward, with hundreds of inert bodies lying in gurneys, each beswarmed by Medusa-like thickets of tubes that violated their every orifice! Looking closer, Hogan recognized many Great Scientists who had been tasked with assisting Dr. Phillips' reckless pursuit of superintelligence. As he gazed in ever-growing horror, Phillips boomed, "Behold, the grim reality of Perverse Instantiation!"

Hogan met this odd phrase with a raised, querying brow.

"Which is to say, the attainment of seemingly desirable goals that prove inadvertently ruinous," Phillips continued. "Because make no mistake. On a literal level, these men are VERY VERY happy, Hogan! Indeed, the pleasure centers of their brains are so overloaded that their psyches and intellects have burnt away to nothingness, leaving only a primitive, ecstatic consciousness of the very lowest order. Much like that of a nematode reveling in a fresh speck of feces!"

"Or, a Greek pervert with an unlimited subscription to priapic pornography," Hogan quipped, granting them both a brief, mirthful respite from the horror of Mankind's impending doom. "But what of Man's security? Did you not say that this was a goal of not unequal priority to his happiness?"

"Oh, rest assured that these husks lie in the utmost safety!" Phillips nattered. "Because in a few short days, after entombing all of us in this horrifying land of 'delight,' Omega will convert every Earthly atom that isn't essential to maintaining our vitals into Computronium! Thereby eliminating every predator, virus, and harmful bacterium from our environs! Its ever-more-capacious intellect will then dedicate itself to maximizing our 'security,' by calculating and counteracting every conceivable threat to our 'living' remains! Remote asteroids colliding with Earth in the distant future? Our sun burning out billions of years hence? The universe eventually winding down to entropy? Radically implausible, yet just-barely-possible threats emerging from parallel universes, hidden dimensions, or beyond? Omega will turn all matter, everywhere, into Computronium! So as to assess every conceivable threat from all possible sources! And, to create the unimaginably vast and sophisticated machinery necessary to neutralize those threats!"

Hogan nodded slowly, contemplating all of this. "This must be the all-but-inevitable outcome of creating a highly empowered Super AI, and imbuing it with even the most benign and noble goals that Man can possibly imagine!" he hypothesized despairingly!

∞   ∞   ∞

Still buttoned and blue-blazered, Mitchell heads straight to the cafeteria after that bizarre meeting with the commissioner. There, the whole Cyrano crew's eating lunch, along with Tarek, some new buddies from the PhastPhorwardr, and even Monika, despite being in New York. Yes, really. In celebration of the WingMan system's sudden, radical improvement, O has rigged up some remarkably beautiful articulated . . . manikins? Robots? Humanoid videoconferencizers? Whatever they are, they enable remote co-workers to join your table via WingMan—and they're now scattered throughout the cafeteria. Seen head-on, they're gorgeous steampunk artworks. But viewed peripherally, their carefully draped clothing and meticulously arranged postures make them arrestingly human. Their heads are WingMan monitors, immaculately curved to best display the face of the "indweller" (as O absurdly terms the person who's conferencing in). Their speakers are so good, and so directional, that blind test subjects (Stevie-Wonder blind, not taste-test blind) swear the voices come from human larynxes. Completing the uncanny effect, the arms and torsos occasionally swivel or make fluid gestures in sync with the indweller's words.

"You've been nominated!" Monika announces as Mitchell takes a seat beside her . . . *avatar?*

"To?"

"To pre-pre alpha-test Cyrano," Danna informs him.

"We're setting it loose as your wingman on Tinder today!" Kuba adds.

The table bursts into noisy, sustained applause. This is a cunning tactic to drown out Mitchell's inevitable protests, which he soon abandons. His attendant embarrassment thrusts him right to the edge of a Falkenberg's attack! So he smiles bashfully while fighting mightily to keep it at bay, anxious to protect his friends from any guilty feelings. They have no way of knowing how precarious he's become, after all. He's told no one about his constantly tingling extremities. Not even Dr. Martha, who he irrationally fears might blab to Ellie, who might tell everyone else, thereby bringing everybody down, when this is *his* problem, isn't it?

"But Cyrano still sucks," he points out.

"Sucks, schmucks," Danna says. "You've been single for years. It's time we used every tool in the kit to get you a girlfriend!"

More noisy applause muffles Mitchell's attempted rebuttal. Then, as his limbs almost decohere into rubber, he lets himself see the warmth, even love, in everyone's eyes—and his embarrassment fades; and with it, the tingling and the looming attack. There's nothing to be embarrassed about because nobody here would tease him about his love life if they knew how monastic it actually is! He's easy on the eyes, athletic despite everything, charismatic, and young. And he just sold his startup to a white-hot private company, where he's now (at least optically) a high-ranking exec. Plenty of women would find this impossibly sexy. So people just assume he's your basic driven entrepreneur, delaying romantic gratification while laying the foundations for his future family's security. And probably getting mad Tinder action whenever his appetites demand it!

But alas, this all misses the Falkenberg's dimension. And even close friends like Kuba, who are aware of his affliction, know nothing about how it robs him of love. Oh—and of sex. The thing is, he brought a lot of baggage to this illness. Most of it's good, actually; but even good baggage has consequences. His comes from growing up in a two-person family with a wonderful mom he was everything to. From an astonishingly adult romance with an amazing woman throughout college. From his protective, big-brotherly childhood friendship with Kuba. All this and more has brought Mitchell to feel great responsibility for the emotional well-being of the people he loves—and also, the people he loves *prospec-*

tively. Such as not-yet girlfriends. Women he might one day love as much as he loved his college girlfriend. Loving them as he does (or rather, *will*, perhaps), he feels a vast onus to protect their feelings. And what kind of man would partner with someone, knowing he'll one day drag her through his own protracted and agonizing death?

This has colored Mitchell's life since long before his actual diagnosis because he first intuited that something was deeply wrong with him in his midtwenties, before the attacks really surged. And that was when he . . . stopped. Stopped flirting. Stopped dating. Stopped loving. It just felt like the right thing to do (or rather, not do). This meant sex went right out the window, too, since he was never the king of the one-night stand. Nor the prince, duke, knight, or lowly manservant thereof. He's just never been comfortable with such things—not even in an era that exalts empty hookups as some sort of feminist triumph. Sure, affluent young moderns are free and empowered, which makes their couplings "open-market transactions," in the crass words of a dude he once knew on Wall Street. But NetGrrrl (make that Monika. *Monika!*) really nailed it in her post about courtship. Much as things have changed in recent years, smutty hookups are so close to the classic male goal line that the few times he's partaken in one, it's felt selfish, ickily triumphal, and wrong.

But. It's been a damn long time, now, hasn't it? And there are woman out there who enjoy random sex as much as the most loutish, crotch-grabbing investment banker, right? After all, *he* read certain letters to certain editors as an adolescent! *He's* seen certain postings to Craigslist! And they can't *all* be written by bored fourteen-year-old boys (. . . can they?). So perhaps, in the safe confines of this warm, loving circle of friends, it's maybe—just maybe!—OK to lift his voice, and for once confess that—

"What you really need is a long night of shagging!" Monika pronounces (all but plucking the thought from his frontal lobes), and the rebuttal-drowning applause returns.

"Agreed," Mitchell finally concedes (to playful cheers). "But Cyrano seriously sucks for now. We did a test run based on my profile on Monday. And did you see the *matches* that came back?"

"There were some eighty-year-olds on the list," Kuba admits to the group.

"There was little else!" Mitchell clarifies. "And the come-ons it suggested. Jesus!" Cyrano 0.8's opening lines are bipolar at best. Just under half are cornball crap along "Roses are red, violets are blue" lines. Others could get him locked up in certain jurisdictions—such as one that offers a 30 percent chance at *immortality* (yes, really) in exchange for several acts of . . . ingestion. Or another that positions its imaginary author's herpes as a state-recognized handicap, which cannot be discriminated against legally. The rest are either non-sequitur weird ("You look Serbian. In a GOOD way!") or—very rarely—show a glimmer of wit ("On a scale of Burning Man to North Korea, how free are you tonight?").

"We've upgraded the tool for indicating what you're seeking in a woman," Kuba says, a bit sheepishly.

"Does it include age now?" Mitchell asks. The last rev didn't ask about this—nor any other tangible trait! A mistake, obviously, but one grounded in good intentions. Studies show that most people list what they *think* they're *supposed* to want in mates on dating sites rather than what they're actually after. And so Kuba's first system asked only indirect questions, from which he hoped to infer unwritten desires. This clearly turned out to be a tad ambitious for the initial release.

"It has age and everything else now," Monika assures him. "We're calling it the Wish List. It's just like ordering a girl off a Chinese menu. You'll love it!" Though he knows it's not meant to, this hurts Mitchell's feelings because it sounds icky, and he never said he wanted *that*. And the truth is, he's never had a "type." He just likes the girls he likes—and his lifetime of crushes probably resembles a cross section of modern female society. Apart from age, duh! And even on that front, he's never really thought about his upper limit (though it sure as hell isn't eighty!). Still, type or no type, it sounds like he won't have a choice about filling out a "wish list" now. So to get back at Monika for hurting his feelings (or is it for making him have a crush on her?) he decides he'll describe *her* to a frickin' T on it. Take that!

"There's still a somewhat spiritual side to the questionnaire," Kuba says, as if Mitchell would want to retain anything from the old matching system. "We have something that's kind of like an essay question. We ask people to just spill about what they're looking for. This'll let us test our chops at natural language processing. And it would be a mistake to drop it entirely."

"Another big improvement," Danna says, handing him a printout. "The come-ons are getting a lot better." Mitchell reads it. This morning's haul included a dozen "wsup"s along with several close derivatives.

He waves this in front of Monika's digital "face." "Has Cyrano been reading your blog?"

"No, the system really generated those opening lines," Kuba insists. "Entirely on its own!"

"You sound . . . proud of that."

Kuba just beams.

"You know how . . . moronic and unoriginal they are?"

"Which means we're finally getting close to passing the Turing Test!"

"For opening lines, anyway," Danna says.

Kuba nods. "We haven't let Cyrano send any messages yet. So obviously, the real challenges will come with engaging in actual conversations."

Danna rises. "Which will commence in roughly two hours, when you and Cyrano start goin' hog wild on Tinder!"

Mitchell feigns exasperation. "Well, thanks for telling me—but aren't I supposed to be calling the shots here?" That sure gets a laugh! Though Mitchell's officially in charge of the project, Jepson has him so busy, the Cyrano team is largely running itself. Which is fine, while it's still an unofficial project. The question is, what happens after it's approved and funded (as now seems almost inevitable)? Mitchell may be unavailable. He's been doing really solid work for Jepson. And whether it's from boldness, or an awareness that he may not live to vest his stock, he challenges the guy more than anyone around here (even Beasley), and Jepson actually likes this! He's now entrusting Mitchell with more and more important work every day, and is losing interest in letting him move on to another job in the company. Mitchell hasn't been brought in on the company's deep secrets and remains a bit player in any meeting that includes Beasley, Judy, or Jepson himself. But in daily operational matters, he's fast becoming an extension of Jepson.

"Anyway," Danna says. "I'm off to MedNet."

"To . . . ?" Mitchell asks.

"MedNet. It stands for Meditative Networking. Everyone lies around chanting *om* for a few minutes. Then they sip chai and swap business cards. When the hour's up, they ring a gong, and off you go. It's huge in SoMa. O says it's the best place to build a professional network because you know everyone there is ethical. Or vegan. Or . . . something."

She bolts, then the rest scatter—Tarek to an electric bike club meeting on South Park, and Kuba to a quantum programming symposium taught by one of Ax's minions (where he hopes to pick up some tricks to expedite tonight's quantum break-in). Still choking on his top button and tie, Mitchell feels like the lone grown-up in a dorm full of aged and highly active sophomores. He gulps down the rest of his meal, then scoots off to write up a summary of the Commissioner Milford meeting for tonight's dinner with Judy and Jepson. Oh—and to fill out his Cyrano "wish list," as requested.

∞   ∞   ∞

Thanks for checking off all the attributes of the girl of your dreams. We're almost done! In a few minutes, Cyrano will take off to hunt everywhere on the Net—dating sites, social networks, Craigslist, even blogs—for possible matches!

But before he does this, there's one final step. Please write a paragraph or ten (however much you want!) riffing on what you're REALLY *looking for. The sky's the limit, and there's nothing to be ashamed of! No one will* EVER *read this but you and Cyrano—that's our commitment—and Cyrano's just an algorithm, so this is seriously private stuff!*

Based on what you say, and everything Cyrano can learn about the women out there, he'll feed you a few opening lines that may just work on a couple of them. Read them, maybe edit them a bit, and then—if the spirit moves you—try them out! And may you find love . . . or WHATEVER ELSE *you're looking for!*

Kuba, Danna: if either of you are reading this, screw you and knock it off! Cyrano, if it's really just you and me, feast your natural language chops on this: I'm sick. And I don't mean that in the bad-boy, spanky-spanky way that most people probably mean on dating sites. I mean it in the very literal sense, in that I have a really evil terminal disease that's going to finish me off. And what none of my friends know (or I'm sure they wouldn't be thinking "girlfriend" right now) is that this could happen in the next year. Because things may have just taken a major turn for the worse with my disease, and after that happens, patients go quickly.

As a result of this, I kind of feel like it wouldn't be right for me to date. Or, maybe, that I don't HAVE a right to date! I'm just not into random hookups, and relationships are wrong to foist on anyone else given my condition. But hmm, I'm your Product Manager, Mr. Cyrano, so it only seems right that I give you a fair shot at showing your stuff. So here comes a SERIOUS "wish list" challenge for you!

The thing is this: I do miss sex. So bring me some of that! But it has to be sex without guilt or sorrow. Which means it has to be with a woman who is truly INTO these short-term things. She doesn't have to be CRAZY into them, or do them all the time (in fact, I'd prefer not). But she should have a somewhat wild history, and a joyous one. Meaning someone who has a true BLAST doing this sort of thing occasionally, and feels great and empowered afterward, not lowly or depressed.

So, that's for HER conscience. Now here comes the tough part . . . MINE! I'm sure some women out there would find it romantic IN THEORY to sleep with someone who's in the process of dying young. I have NO INTEREST in meeting this kind of person! If the roles were reversed, I know the echo of this would haunt ME to some degree forever, and I am NOT going to put that on someone else.

Now, here's the trick: I'm a lousy liar. So, major life facts—the REALLY BIG ones, like "I may just have a year to live," just COME OUT when I'm in a deep conversation. You know, the kind of conversations that can lead to first-date sex (in my depressingly limited experience)! That's just how I'm wired, and we're not going to change that. So I guess we need to find a Wish List Girl who can get into having sex with a guy she barely exchanges a word with!

Oh, and she has to be really smart. And confident. And happy. And
cute. And about my age. HA! good luck with THAT, Cyrano!

∞   ∞   ∞

Dinner is at The Battery, which is *absolutely not* tech's answer to Soho
House. Any member will tell you this—before describing a place that
sounds remarkably like tech's answer to Soho House. Jepson's a Founding Member here, of course, and Judy belongs, too, despite living thousands of miles away. For his part, this is maybe the third time Mitchell's
been invited, and he's always happy to come here. The place always
seems to have just the right amount of Brownian motion. Bustling but
rarely too packed, it's alive, gorgeously laid out and illuminated, and of-
the-moment modern, without seeming to try too hard at any of this. He
loves its ever-changing art-laden walls, its sometimes-changing décor,
and its towering ceilings. The club also has three bars that he knows of
(plus perhaps a fourth in a rumored $15,000/night penthouse within the
club's boutique hotel), a fine gym, and an active program of speakers,
musicians, wine tastings, and art openings. Oh, and a library (he's never
known why, but Mitchell loves libraries).

Barhopping inside The Battery with Tony Jepson puts the whole experience on . . . what, steroids? Speed? *Meth?* Being Jepson's wingman
here is like hanging out at Woodstock with Jimi. Phluttr's just-closed
billion-plus financing is the talk of the Valley—and therefore, of The
Battery. Sure, the industry's seen bigger rounds. But never for a company
quite so young. This has pushed the data bloggers and analysts into hy-
perdrive. Everyone's poring over Phluttr's metrics, and however you cut
'em, your eyes just pop! Growth, monetization, NPS, growth, installs,
reach, churn, growth, ARR, DAU, LTV, growth, blended CAC, ACV,
growth, *growth*, GROWTH! Everything is off the damned charts. So here
at The Battery, luminaries and wannabes alike are drawn to Jepson like
freezing stoners to an open flame in the Black Rock Desert. His every
tweet, post, and pronouncement gets analyzed like holy writ from Mount
Sinai these days. And tonight, he's the undulating epicenter of crashing
fields of fascination, envy, and lust.

Everyone seems to have forgotten how much fun they had despising him during his decade-plus as a patent troll. And this is no small thing! Because even the most rabid techno-atheist will readily believe in a hell whose theology reserves its bottommost circle for patent trolls. Frivolous patent lawsuits poison the well for everyone—and none more than the early-stage entrepreneurs who are the industry's lionized fountain of youth. Reviled above all are those trolls who originally got rich *from tech* and are now suing their way to slightly greater wealth by destroying the laissez-faire ways of yesteryear, which helped enrich them in the first place. There are billionaires out there (billionaires!) who struck gold while perched atop the shoulders of prior giants. Gentle giants. Generous giants. Ones who amiably welcomed newbies to build upon their works, in the clear expectation that they, in turn, would leave the door open for future generations. Instead, some of this benign ecosystem's greatest beneficiaries are profiteering by welding the door shut behind them. Kim Philby's blood-soaked betrayal of his class and nation may have helped define the Cold War. But to certain tech purists, it was a small fart at a Royal Ascot brunch compared to this.

In Jepson's patent-trolling days, the field's poster child was Nathan Myhrvold. Myhrvold used his vast winnings from Microsoft to launch a high-budget trolling operation with the thigh-slapping name of Intellectual Ventures. Next to this orcan mass, Jepson was plankton-scale. He had just one patent to his name, and he'd stumbled upon it. Compare that to Myhrvold's vast and carefully assembled portfolio of lawsuit-ready filings! Still, local ideologues loathed Jepson more, simply because they expected better from one of their own. The Valley had long viewed Microsoft with the schizophrenic mix of awe and contempt that Americans held for Japanese manufacturing in the seventies and eighties. There was awe for its incredible ability to execute, but contempt for its dearth of inventiveness, its appropriation of others' innovations, and its bullying, underhanded tactics. Certain Bay Area snobs therefore expected nothing better than patent trolling from the likes of Myhrvold. But as a local lad, Jepson lacked that hall pass—and boy, was he loathed.

He helped his cause somewhat by owning, even rocking his odious image as a sort of playful penance. He attended costume parties dressed as a troll. He funded a lavish troll-themed art car at Burning Man. He even briefly portrayed himself in a YouTube comedy in which he stole candy from tots, sold his mom's jewels on eBay, and sued orphans. The show was popular and occasionally almost brilliant. Still, all eyes were perfectly dry when that famous bitcoin hiccup wiped Jepson out. And when a brief local blackout randomly occurred later that week, local wags blamed it on a surge of schadenfreude so massive, its electromagnetic wallop rivaled that of an H-bomb's EMP. Jepson's rehabilitation, then, is an improbable marvel. He's Deng Xiaoping—not merely freed from the gulag but crowned head of state. And now Mitchell, here, is his wingman at a Politburo piss-up!

During the short jaunt from the upstairs bar to the smaller of the downstairs dining rooms, the two of them are offered enough free drinks to enstupor a rugby team. Upon taking their seats, they learn that Judy's late (she always is, Jepson confides). When she finally arrives, she's all business. "Fabulous meeting with the commissioner," she begins.

"How'd Mitchell do?"

"Great. Sat there like a deaf mute! I couldn't've asked for more."

Jepson pats him proudly on the shoulder. "So what's she got planned for us?"

Perusing the menu, Judy replies absently. "Injunction. Lawsuit. Possible criminal charges."

"Perfect! And did you piss her off?"

"*Totally*. Her face turned green. Her neck did a 360. Then, instead of calling Uber, she took off on a motherfuckin' broom." She and Jepson fist-bump.

Jepson turns to Mitchell to explain. "We've done a full psychological profile on the commissioner. Bottom line, she makes boo-boos when she's mad."

Judy nods. "Huge ones!" She flashes a sly grin. "That shit she did to her freshman roommate?" She and Jepson chuckle darkly, and Mitchell wonders what constitutes a "psychological profile" in Phluttr's high command.

Patrick the friendly wine steward arrives to fill their glasses with an exquisite Bordeaux blend, then a waitress takes their orders. Once they're alone, Judy says, "So, is she EULA'd?"

"Ohhh yeah," Jepson gloats. They toast so violently, they almost cover themselves in Riedel shards.

"EULA'd?" Mitchell asks. The acronym for End User Licensing Agreement is becoming a common English word, but this is an odd usage.

Judy looks at Jepson. "How confidential can we be with this kid?"

"We're getting there," Jepson says. "Legal worked triple overtime to close the Giftish.ly acquisition in record time. Then he signed a raft of NDAs."

"Security clearance?" Judy asks.

Jepson shakes his head. "Not yet, but they're working on it. And it's already clear that he's squeaky clean." The high clearances that are common in industries like aerospace are unheard of in social media—except at Phluttr. The company's Outsourced Business Services unit hosts a small discussion board for West Point grads, providing cover for the oddly large number of employees who are highly cleared. Working directly for Jepson, Mitchell figured he'd join their ranks at some point. It now seems he was right about this.

"What to say," Judy says, suddenly gazing deeply at him. "And what *not* to say . . ." She appears to make a decision. Then, "Mitchell, what kind of company is Phluttr?"

"What . . . kind of company?"

"Yes. What Techmeme-friendly pigeonhole would you put your employer in?"

This seems like a trick question from a McKinsey interview. And so, donning his consultant cap, Mitchell goes meta and refuses to answer. "It depends upon whose perspective we're taking."

"Well played, youngster," Judy says. "How about from the perspective of your own active users?"

"To them, we're a social networking company."

"Of course. And from an advertiser's standpoint?"

"I'd say that to them, we're a media company."

"Bravo. Now. How do product managers within the business view things?"

Mitchell considers this. "A lot of folks on the inside think of Phluttr as a Big Data company."

"Bull's-eye," Judy says. "Now finally, what would you say Phluttr is in the eyes of . . . certain stakeholders. I think you know who I'm talking about. Jepson and I may have mentioned one or two of them. In an entirely . . . *theoretical* way. On the day I met you."

She's clearly talking about those faux-joking references to the NSA when they were in the privacy of Jepson's office, a couple weeks back. Mitchell nods. "Them?" he says. "I don't really know."

"Well, to *them*, I can tell you, that Phluttr is . . ." She pauses, and Mitchell all but hears a drumroll. Then, "A EULA company."

"A EULA company?"

Judy nods. "Didn't go to law school, did you, Mitchell?" He shakes his head. "Good for you. And I mean that sincerely. But if you had, you'd know a bit more than you probably do about this irksome little . . . speed bump called the Fourth Amendment."

"Something about 'search and seizure,'" Jepson adds, finger-quoting.

"Think of the Fourth Amendment as being a private place where the founding mommies and daddies went, and then nine months later, we had warrants and probable cause." Judy pauses to make sure Mitchell's following this odd constitutional law lesson. He nods to assure her he is. "Speaking of *fucking*," she continues, watching closely for an awkward flinch (which he duly provides), "another concept tied to the Fourth Amendment is *consent*. This is what a hundred thousand half-wits a day give when they hand their cellphone to a cop who asks for it, open their trunk during a traffic stop, or let the police into their house without insisting on a warrant. Certainly a majority, and perhaps as many as 90 percent of all searches, are 'consent searches.' Which is to say, the cops would need a warrant if the searchee insisted. But people don't realize they have a right to say no."

"Or," Jepson adds, "that warrants are enough of a pain to get that the cops usually won't bother if you press the issue."

"So are EULAs a form of consent?" Mitchell asks.

"Bingo," Jepson says, and Judy almost beams at him. Almost.

"Even if nobody actually reads them?"

"Especially if nobody actually reads them," Judy says. "And the fact is, people *can't* really read them. Literally! A few years back, a study showed it would take the average person a month and a half just to read every privacy agreement they assent to in an average year. And EULAs are a lot longer than privacy agreements."

"What do you call it, Judy?" Jepson asks. "The . . . privatization of the law?"

Judy nods. "The idea is that if someone signs the right documents—or the wrong ones, depending on your perspective, I guess—they can become almost as subjugated vis-à-vis their counterparty as individuals are in relation to the state. Pret-ty cool, huh? Anyway. I think we've said enough about this general concept for now. The bottom line is that Phluttr has promised certain dark mandarins in Washington that it'll get as many humans as possible to consent to its EULA. Ideally, *all* humans. And for tonight's specific purposes, the key fact is that we have Commissioner Milford's consent."

"To do . . . ?"

"Pretty much anything," Jepson says.

"Pretty much *everything*," Judy clarifies. "But for a while there, I was worried." She turns to Jepson. "I couldn't find any trace of her on Phluttr, and my team checked pretty thoroughly."

"She's clever about it," Jepson explains. "She signed up under an assumed name, always uses dynamic IP, and even TOR sometimes when she checks her account. But this afternoon, Beasley 100 percent confirmed that she accepted the EULA. It's ironclad. She couldn't hope to deny it in court. And all of its provisions apply to her."

"And what do we have on her?" Judy's eyes are asparkle.

"Lots, I'm sure. I haven't gotten her Phile yet, but I'll bet there's plenty she'd rather not see on the front page of the *New York Times*."

Mitchell squirms awkwardly at this, and Judy shoots him the glare of a gruff librarian catching a third grader sparkin' up a doobie. "Just to be clear, Mr. Prentice. We would never publish *any* awkward facts about the commissioner without her express written permission." She lets Mitchell relax slightly, then adds, "Which, to be clear, the EULA grants us." At that, Jepson rises. "Oh God," Judy says *sotto voce*. Hiding her eyes in her hands in mock despair, she whispers, "You idiot pyromaniac."

Mitchell turns and sees dozens of heads pivoting throughout the dining room, like iron globes yanked by a paralyzing magnetic field that's approaching their table like a radiant comet. Like a blond, radiant comet. Like a blond, radiant blond comet who may not be old enough to order a drink. One done up in a canny mix of Prada and Hot Topic that just works, and works brilliantly, on this electromagnetic, stiletto-stepping celestial being who's now hugging Jepson hello. Judy catches Mitchell's gaze and mouths the words *playing with fire* so clearly it's like she's shouting into his ears. And that's when he recognizes her. Comet Girl is the woman whose image Raj used to represent the hypothetical college babe who starts turning tricks on Phluttr's new dating-and-casual-prostitution site. Jepson almost belted Raj for putting her in his PowerPoint! And now that he's witnessing her effect on Jepson, Mitchell gains new respect for Raj's contemptibly brilliant rhetorical skills.

"Mitchell? Judy?" Jepson says. "I'd like to introduce you to one of our new interns. This is Serena Kielholz, from Stanford."

All rise. "Kielholz," Judy says, shaking Serena's hand briskly. "I believe I know your father." She turns to Jepson. "Gosh, come to think of it, so does your new boss!"

∞   ∞   ∞

QUANTUM DECODE *DOCUMENT: #00001 OF 00003*

FULL TEXT OF DECRYPTED DOCUMENT BELOW.

TONY JEPSON: SUITABILITY AND VULNERABILITIES

***TOP SECRET/SCI/COMINT/NOFORN

Overview: The Neo Gatsby Initiative seeks to recruit a highly credentialed Silicon Valley entrepreneur to the Authority's mission. This is a mounting national security priority as a growing majority of the nation's best technical talent concentrates in Internet, Mobile, VR/AR, Machine Learning, and related fields. Roughly ten corporations dominate these areas, most with little government allegiance. This greatly compromises our ability to drive the development of critical technologies and systems.

Detailed Background: For decades, prestige and competitive paychecks enabled defense contractors, NASA, and government labs to recruit ample engineering talent. This ability eroded with the tech boom of the nineties, and all but vanished with the current boom. Today, infant startups are routinely acquired for billions, patriotism is unfashionable, and career choices in our hedge fund–, celebrity-, and startup-dominated economy are shaped primarily by greed. With top-percentile engineering talent all but inaccessible to government affiliates, it could be time to "disguise" part of the national security apparatus as a hot startup. Recruited engineers could be applied to Authority priorities, and should the company exert sufficient industry "gravity," security priorities could start driving more of the broader technology agenda. In a high-upside scenario, the company's equity value might also meaningfully dent the national debt.

This program should reside under the Authority's direct auspices. All but unknown to the press and public, the Authority enjoys expansive budgets as well as cadres of remarkably talented personnel. Sitting above most Secret and Top Secret organizations in the chain of command, it can marshal human and technical resources from many governmental arms. All this, plus certain elements of legal immunity, ideally configure the Authority to maintain a clandestine Silicon Valley presence.

Neo Gatsby's goal of recruiting a top tech CEO is formidable in light of decades of failed efforts with CEOs from other industries. With vast resources and highly constrained schedules, CEOs are largely impervious to financial inducements and unavailable for extensive training, vetting, or indoctrination. Being accustomed to high levels of autonomy and responsibility, they're also rarely pliant. However, the tech industry is unusual in that its roster of dominant companies is in constant flux. Many of the coming decade's giants surely have yet to be founded. This presents the unique possibility of "growing" our desired CEO. We would start with a credentialed entrepreneur who currently lacks a platform. Someone with a proven ability to raise capital, recruit teams, and launch products within Silicon Valley's ecosystem but who lacks and craves wealth and acclaim. With Authority-provided capital, proprietary technology, competitive intelligence, and (perhaps) "dirty tricks," the right executive might rapidly build a juggernaut.

Neo Gatsby's recruiting efforts have gone slowly. Top prospects have washed out for reasons including foreign nationality, excessive drug history, hostility toward intelligence objectives, personality disorders, videogame addiction, sex addiction, failed security clearances, failed psychological clearances, and recruiting competition by established companies and venture capital ("VC") firms offering outlandish compensation packages.

Tony Jepson: After efforts to enlist candidates ranked "Optimal" failed, recruiting standards were retargeted to "Outstanding," then "Superior," then "Acceptable." Criteria have now transitioned to "Wild Card," enabling our first hiring recommendation. Tony Jepson's biography and extensive press clippings are attached. His candidacy's major "pro" and "con" factors follow:

Negatives: Jepson exhibits clear signs of sex addiction, a disqualifying factor under prior recruiting standards. However, certain demerits are acceptable in Wild Card candidates with unusual mitigating strengths (see below). More concerning, Jepson's history as a "patent troll" is reviled in the industry, as are rumored Republican Party sympathies. Last, his prior company (ePetStore.com) failed, and we seek to build a successful giant.

Positives: Jepson became wealthy despite his startup's failure, and his objective was not to build a successful company but to enrich himself. Viewed through this lens, he is a success, not a failure—and we have ways of aligning his future incentives that civilian investors lack. His strengths include top-percentile charisma, which fuels preternatural media-drawing and recruiting capabilities.

Analysts also speculate that industry disdain for Jepson is shallow. His roguish image secretly appeals to many, and the decade of lavish parties and events he hosted before suddenly losing his wealth drew local elites in droves. Authority psychologists also note an industry affinity for "comeback stories" that verges on spiritual. Steve Jobs's resurrection of Apple, Elon Musk's many triumphs after near bankruptcy, and Tim Tebow's improbable rise as a virtual reality tycoon are but three examples. Should Jepson seek "redemption," many will applaud. Then, with the first signs of success, his bandwagon will overflow.

Perhaps most important, Jepson's lasting loyalty can be assured by the over-whelming threat he perceives to his life. Aggrieved counterparties in his bitcoin debacle include two mock-criminal gangs. One is a Russian intelligence front, the other is one of ours. Both have put on convincing displays of criminal out-rage (which is not entirely feigned, as both groups must shed a certain amount of blood to maintain verisimilitude). Jepson is therefore convinced that he needs our ongoing protection. And he is correct, insofar as both groups have agreed to drop their grievances against him in exchange for some low-level horse trading that we've already concluded.

For these reasons, as well as our ongoing failure to enlist a truly desirable can-didate, the Recruiting Committee recommends Tony Jepson's immediate on-boarding.

∞   ∞   ∞

The PhastPhorwardr is never perfectly quiet. No one whose career pas-sion is Perovskite cells or graphene transistors is a nine-to-fiver, after all. That said, the monomaniacal energy that powered these small teams in their startup days dissipates post-acquihire, as folks rediscover gym mem-berships, significant others, and Call of Duty habits. Taking all this into account, Tarek figures the human density should be ideally sparse by about ten. So he, Danna, and Kuba return at that hour.

The quantum computing area is quite deserted. This was expected, as when Ax is out of town, his team tends to work remotely. Kuba would have preferred to do their break-in remotely, too. But Tarek knows the access rituals of the system's physical nexus, and Kuba pilfered login details at this afternoon's quantum symposium, which should get them in anonymously. And so, Kuba logs in, with Danna at his shoulder. This will give him another technical brain to bounce ideas off, should they hit an impasse; while Tarek stays out on the main floor to distract any pass-ersby.

Once in the system, they work quickly. Kuba has cryptographic expe-rience from Google and school, and Ax gave the system a very Linux-like interface, which makes it navigable. It's soon clear that rumors about the quantum node's being operational, and having mind-bending horsepower, are true. Standard benchmark ciphers that take *days* to crack on high-end servers are demolished in mere milliseconds!

Or is it . . . *microseconds*? Holy shit, it *is*. It IS microseconds! Their first impression of the system's speed shocked, awed, and spooked them. But it's actually running *a thousand times faster* than they thought! And also—

No.

No, no, NO!!! it isn't . . . *nanoseconds*. Is it?

Yes, it is. The system. Is breaking. These ciphers. In mother. Fucking. *Nanoseconds*! It just ground through a sixty-eight-*hour* task in nine *billionths* of a second!!!

"This will change everything," Kuba whispers. "Absolutely everything."

They upload the three queerly encrypted files from the WhistleBlowings blog—the ones that allegedly spill Phluttr's darkest secrets. The system shatters their strange locks instantly. And, with no guidance or interaction from them. Like, none! It's bizarre. It's as if these documents were . . . expected? And *much*, much weirder, the cracked files don't appear on the screen. Instead, their phones hum.

"Poof!" Danna says. "Phluttr's sending them! Directly to us! In Poof! How does it know to do that?"

Rather than answer, Kuba starts reading. The words fly by so fast there's no time for anything else. And as they both know, once they're gone—*Poof!*—Phluttr's temporary messaging system will eradicate them from this dimension.

"Jepson, a spy," Kuba mutters after they finish speed-reading decrypted #00001 of 00003, which, true to form, is now gone without a trace.

"Don't tell me you're surprised," Danna says. Then they both fall silent when their phones hum again, and the second document arrives.

∞   ∞   ∞

FULL TEXT OF DECRYPTED DOCUMENT BELOW.

THE ARGUMENT FOR DEVELOPING A SOCIAL NETWORK

***TOP SECRET/SCI/COMINT/NOFORN

No product or business plans were made during Neo Gatsby's recruiting period, as the startup's ultimate focus would be CEO-dependent. Newly hired CEO Tony Jepson now favors developing a social network. Internal opponents question this strategy, pointing to the overwhelming incumbency of Facebook, LinkedIn, and others. They instead propose leveraging certain imaging breakthroughs now under military development, as imaging/display is a rare domain in which government technology still significantly leads the private sector. Imaging expertise is also a national security asset under dire threat from the brain drain away from government labs to promising startups. This analysis will argue that the debate should be viewed in the context of the blinding of the mass surveillance apparatus of Authority subordinates (particularly the National Security Agency) in the wake of Edward Snowden's defection to Russia.

Until December of 2015, section 215 of the Patriot Act empowered the Authority's NSA subunit to collect metadata (essentially, detailed call logs) on substantially all US phone traffic. The actual "content" of suspect calls, emails, chat sessions, searches, and Internet browsing histories could also be easily subpoenaed with warrants. Companies including Google, Facebook, Skype, and Yahoo were appropriately responsive when presented with warrants and certain other requests, generally allowing the NSA to collect the relevant data directly from their servers.

Edward Snowden betrayed the US to China and Russia in 2013. The media ignored the irony of his allegiance to regimes known for assassinating opponents and imprisoning journalists. This gave his sympathizers, dupes, and collaborators a free hand to fuel public outrage over benign Authority activities. As a direct result, 2015's revision of the Patriot Act stripped the NSA of its metadata-collection rights.

Less obviously, but far more dangerously, Snowden's betrayal of operation MUSCULAR crippled the Authority's working relations with Google, Facebook, Skype, et al. MUSCULAR secretly tracked the vast data transfers that these companies make outside of US territory via transoceanic and other channels. The *Washington Post* summarized industry reactions in saying "U.S. technology executives . . . believed the NSA had lawful access to their front doors—and had broken down the back doors anyway." The companies publicly voiced outrage over alleged violations of customer "rights." Privately, they also fumed about the impact the revelations might have on their foreign revenues. In response, they now meticulously encrypt the foreign traffic we had previously surveilled effortlessly.

Crippling our bulk-data collection was a triumph for Snowden's masters in Beijing and Moscow, and for the many terrorist entities that we formerly tracked and/or discovered through these mechanisms. We can still collect data on specific individuals by obtaining warrants, or dedicating expensive resources to decrypting their personal traffic. But while we retain an ability to "spy on" *anybody*, we have lost our ability to "spy on" *everybody*.

This makes the world far more dangerous. The real perils aren't posed by plots and terrorists that we know well enough to have under court-sanctioned surveillance, but by those we are unaware of. The lessons of September 11, as well as baseline common sense, make this clear (as do the more-recent attacks on San Bernardino, Orlando, the Apple campus, Harvard, etc.). Short of repealing the Fourth Amendment (a goal which our political analysts unfortunately deem impractical), the most obvious path to reinstating bulk surveillance is getting warrants on everybody. This, of course, is impossible. Less obvious, and infinitely more feasible is getting *consent* from everybody. And the most practical route to this is via a massively popular online service's End User License Agreement.

It is in this context that Jepson argues against an imaging-related startup. He notes that while "magic glasses" based on proprietary government technology could become wildly popular, hardware always diffuses slowly. Even smartphones have yet to reach a majority of the world's population over a decade after the iPhone's debut. By contrast, successful social media services grow exponentially. Overwhelming "network effects" make them more attractive; and therefore larger, and therefore more attractive still; as more and more people join.

As for the argument that social media is already dominated by insuperable incumbents, Jepson notes that huge successes like Snapchat launched over a decade after the field first emerged. Moreover, near monopolies once enjoyed by Friendster and MySpace were shattered by later entrants, proving that dominance is ephemeral.

Finally, Jepson stresses that his company could leverage and develop nation-critical imaging technologies regardless of its primary focus. He cites the wildly diverse initiatives that emerged under the "Google X" banner, many of them completely secret from the public to this day. There's no reason why a large and successful Authority-backed company could not invest and develop at least as broadly and covertly.

As for how his service would crack the social media market, Jepson maintains that "most people are only truly authentic with their five closest friends, and, with perfect strangers." The first need is satisfied by private channels like email. The latter is only partly addressed by anonymous channels like confessional apps (e.g. Whisper), support communities (e.g. Patients Like Me), and what Jepson calls "rumor/backstabbing services" (e.g. Yik Yak). But no service supports its users' fluid movement back and forth between real-name environments and anonymity. Jepson believes there is room for an entirely new mode, one that "attests that this is a real, widely trusted person who authentically shares your affliction, secret, addiction, etc.; with whom you can communicate intimately but anonymously."

He writes, "Anonymous parties can be anyone, by definition. This means *nobody* can credibly attest that you're really connecting with a psychologist, a fellow alcoholic, a 'hot babe,' a doctor, someone who also once dated your 'ex,' an employee of a company that you're researching, etc, etc, etc. And this matters! Because the urge to connect authentically has never been greater. And the coming global ubiquity of broadband is spreading it worldwide! Anyone who wants to make plans with their 'bestie' has a billion ways to do so. But those seeking authenticated connections that are either 'pseudonymous' or 'anonymous' are screwed! And make no mistake. These are connections people want!

With folks they hope to 'buy a little something' from, confide in, get advice from, or 'fuck.' Many avoid doing this on Facebook for fear that actions might be revealed to their thousand-plus 'friends,' to advertisers, and yes, to your beloved 'subordinates' in the NSA!

"Many of this new network's Killer Apps," Jepson continues, "will be in what I call 'Id Fulfillment.' People airing unfashionable viewpoints ('vent to fellow college-educated homophobes'), buying sketchy substances, seeking sketchy advice (tax dodges, etc.). And above all, SEX. By merely seeming to be a reliable gateway to this, our service would be irresistible—to 'card-carrying swingers,' to closeted mullahs, and to everyone between! Including the large group (perhaps a 'silent majority') who will participate in none of this but like to think they just might someday, and/or merely enjoy knowing that it's happening out there."

Jepson's is an audacious, long-shot plan. But if successful, his network will indeed spread farther and faster than any imaginable hardware platform. And by delivering *consent* to surveillance from a preponderance of citizens, it will take the Authority far beyond its old high-water mark of gathering mere metadata. Instead, *all manner* of content will be in play: emails, conversations, browsing histories, and more. This content will also reveal far more than today's digital outpourings, as people will be much more open to their private confessors than they are in Facebook, public forums, and other channels of questionable security.

It is therefore the unanimous recommendation of the Executive Council that Jepson's plan be approved.

∞   ∞   ∞

"It was all just so . . . whiny," Danna says. "And self-righteous! Yet written in this wooden, bureaucratic tone. It was like listening to the DMV feel sorry for itself."

"I didn't get that at all," Kuba says.

"Really? But it was just nonstop bitching about Snowden! With zero self-awareness about there being something *wrong* about spying on the entire world!"

"Maybe. But I like it when planes don't hit buildings. And maybe that's the price. If so, we're getting our skyline awfully cheap."

Like holy commands transmitted by oral tradition, the vanished quantum Poof! documents can be debated endlessly in terms of both content and meaning. Interpretations by their two anointed messengers meanwhile have identical weight. So in this corner, the Berkeley progressive; and in that, the émigré Realpolitikian! Listening to them debate, Mitchell's astonished by Kuba's relative comfort with the intelligence regime that treated him so odiously back in high school (dismaying him enough to trigger his lengthy defensive boycott of social media many years later). But Kuba's always been an intense pragmatist who views evil as a relative, not absolute thing. And his Soviet-era childhood convinced him that bad as imperfect Western democracies are when they run amok, there are greater evils out there.

Luckily, Danna and Kuba both agree on the core facts conveyed about Phluttr and Jepson, which is what really matters to those assembled. Mitchell and Tarek have rendezvoused with them away from Phluttr's offices. A bleary-eyed Monika is also beaming in via Kuba's iPad. Given the digital eavesdropping capacity of the real players in this game, this is a tacit admission that they're probably *not* real players themselves. Yes, they're playing at real-playerdom, in a half-jokey manner (for instance, they've designated and code-named several other offsite locations for future secret meetings). But in all likelihood, they're just the first people to crack certain widely downloaded files. Or rather, the first people they know of. Dozens, even hundreds, of similar groups might be convening right now, also wondering how (or if) to go public with facts that have vanished without a trace. And also wondering if it's all just another Phluttr publicity stunt.

Ah well, at least the gin's good. "My glass is broken again," Danna pouts, hoisting it to show that it is, indeed, empty. Tarek dutifully refills it. They're at the Interval—a not-for-profit café/bar built under a hardcover library intended to help reboot civilization should that become necessary. Yeah, yeah; only in San Francisco. But it's a wonderful spot—a rare place where boozy bar vibes blend seamlessly with laptop-tapping

café energy. And being owned by the techno-idealist Long Now Foundation, it might just enjoy a weird measure of immunity from digital surveillance (like a church in a 1930s turf war between Catholic gangsters,
say). As a midsized donor, Tarek gets to maintain a bottle here. He had
them fill it with an earthy, local gin that is funky and smooth enough to
drink straight, and they're hitting it pretty hard.

"This is so unfair," Monika says. "Not only is it 2 A.M. for me, but all I
have is Gordon's." She nonetheless clinks her glass to her laptop's camera, toasting Danna, who does the same with Tarek's artisanal glug. "Anyway. The publicity stunt theory is clever. And credible. But . . . I'm pretty
sure the decrypted docs are real. Jepson doesn't really come off *bad*ly in
them. But he does come off as vulnerable. And, a bit of a dupe. And
that's just not the Jepson your PR folks like to sell."

Mitchell nods. Not only does it make sense, but Monika said it. And
this isn't his deepening crush talking (for once). Her long history of writing smart Phluttr criticism as NetGrrrl lends her overwhelming authority
here. "I'm with you on that," he says. "The memos also fill in lots of
minor blanks in ways that just make sense."

Everyone nods with a schizoid mix of satisfaction and disappointment—
which is the odd emotional note all this has triggered. It's cool to (possibly?) be the first to know the contents of the decrypted files. Which do
click into place with a gratifying, Lego-like *snap*, because the narrative
lines up snugly with what they've long suspected. But while the details
are intriguing (exactly what is "the Authority," for instance?) none are
truly juicy.

"I just wish they filled in a few *more* blanks," Tarek says wistfully.

Danna nods. "Like, who's Gray Oak Partners?" She turns to Mitchell.
"And how does your jackass cousin fit into this?"

Mitchell shrugs, realizing that he's oddly incurious about Pugwash's
role. Because, as he now says, "We can pretty much guess that stuff,
within a rounding error. Gray Oak's clearly a shell the government set up
to finance Phluttr. Then they needed a real person to be the face of the
seed round. And Pugwash was an easy choice because of his history with
Jepson. Then I'll bet the Authority did something-or-other to spook him

because he gets all nervous when I dig too deep about Phluttr." He shrugs again. "So I'd say we've got the gist. And the other details'll come out at some point."

"Maybe they're in the third file?" Kuba muses. Document #00003 never popped out of the quantum system.

Until now, that is.

Everybody's phone hums simultaneously. It's Poof!

∞   ∞   ∞

QUANTUM DECODE *DOCUMENT: #00003 OF 00003*

FULL TEXT OF DECRYPTED DOCUMENT BELOW.

***TOP SECRET/SCI/COMINT/NOFORN

This confirms the Executive Council's 5–2 vote to IMMEDIATELY reinstate the long-dormant Sagan project (under the new name "Project Tyson") at Sandia. **CHINA'S DENIALS OF LAUNCHING A SUPER AI PROGRAM IN CONTRAVENTION OF THE COPENHAGEN ACCORD HAVE NOW BEEN SHOWN TO BE INCONTROVERTIBLY FALSE, AND DIRECT INTERDICTION EFFORTS WOULD ALMOST SURELY LEAD TO WAR.** We must therefore enter a de facto race to a national Super AI, and win it.

Since Super AI is deemed to be the most existentially threatening technology on the intermediate horizon, **ALL OTHER INTERDICTION DIRECTIVES REMAIN OPERATIVE.** The Authority is particularly concerned about rumored private-sector Super AI initiatives. Any and all such initiatives detected MUST be terminated IMMEDIATELY. Force, including extralegal force, is approved if called for.

∞   ∞   ∞

Everyone's silent for at least a minute after the message vanishes from all their phones. Finally, Danna takes a stab at summing it all up.

"*Huh?*"

More silence.

Then Kuba says, "I may . . . kind of know what's happening."

Talk about undivided attention!

He turns to Mitchell. "I may never know exactly why I got kicked out of the country in high school. But when I dig into it, I sometimes come across online rumors about a Project Sagan."

"Was it a Turing project?" Mitchell asks.

Kuba shakes his head. "It had something to do with genetic programming. As in, self-improving algorithms. Not biologically genetic."

Tarek's nodding vigorously. "One of my engineers is all into conspiracy theories, and he mentioned it once. They say it got out of control and spooked everyone by seeming to drift toward consciousness. Or something. He said it led to a secret global treaty banning super AI research. Like the Nuclear Test Ban, only really hush-hush, because they didn't want people to realize it's actually possible. Or something. I figured it was just another crackpot rumor."

"If it's all related, we know the timing," Mitchell says. "High school for me and Kuba."

"And the US government had unrivaled technology back then," Kuba points out. "R&D budgets, too. So if they got scared, ceasing their own research would've amounted to ceasing humanity's research. And they might've thought they had a thirty-year lead."

"Meanwhile," Mitchell adds, "it looks like they let you back into the US right around when they started chasing super AI again."

"Do you suppose," Danna whispers, "*Phluttr* is the super AI project?"

"I doubt it," Tarek says. "The memo says it's at Sandia Labs. That's way out in New Mexico. Plus, all of Phluttr's secret stuff is in the PhastPhorwardr, and I've been around long enough to know about anything big happening there." He tops up everybody's glass, then playfully points the bottle toward the iPad. Wide-eyed and spooked, Monika refills her own glass with straight Gordon's, takes a mighty slug, then refills it again.

"I think Tarek's right," Danna says, sipping her own glass. "Phluttr's a listening post. It's listening to everyone who accepts its EULA. It's tracking every new technology in the Valley via the PhastPhorwardr. If it has a super AI angle at all, I'll bet it's to find the private sector super AI projects that this Authority thing wants destroyed. If any actually exist. As for

Kuba being let back into the country? Maybe they're filling their talent pipeline. For when the Sandia project gets bigger."

"Or making sure the Chinese don't hire him?" Mitchell speculates.

"But why *us*?" Monika says, raising the question they've been avoiding. "Why did we get this note? All of us? Simultaneously? And right now?"

Mitchell expels a slow breath. "Obviously, someone's trying to tell us something."

Silence.

Then Kuba adds, "Or some*thing*."

"Some*thing*?" Danna cocks an eyebrow. "Like what?"

"Like Phluttr. Maybe Phluttr's scared, and is trying to let us know that?"

Holy CRAP! Weird and unlikely as Mitchell finds this idea, it has a tarantulan level of creepiness.

But Danna's shaking her head. "I dunno," she says. "I've read a bunch about artificial consciousness. Definitely not as much as you have, Kuba, but a lot. It would take truly astronomical horsepower, and tons of programming hurdles still separate us from serious breakthroughs. I mean, right?"

Kuba half shrugs and half nods, committing to nothing.

"I'll bet the Authority's behind this," she continues. "Whoever they are, it sounds like they have plenty of capabilities and resources. Definitely enough to snoop on us and send us weirdly synchronized messages."

"But why would the Authority be spilling their *own* secrets?" Monika asks. "And to us?"

"I don't know," Danna concedes. "But duplicity's the stock and trade of these sorts of groups. So the secrets they seem to be spilling could be totally fake. Or, they could be real, but partial. Or they could be real but given to us as part of some kind of setup."

Mitchell's reminded of the saying about people with hammers viewing all problems as nails. Kuba's been attributing mysterious notes to artificial consciousnesses since high school, so of course his explanation lies in a souped-up server farm. And while Danna's no raving conspiracy buff, she's paranoid by nature. This plus the past decade of leaks and scandals connected to government surveillance are surely shaping her views.

Mitchell decides not to pick sides rashly. He's feeling almost smug about this stance and his own wide-open mind when the strangest thing happens. Danna pipes up after a long group silence and says softly, almost to herself, "It's just a feeling, so take it with a grain of salt. But for some reason, I'm sure the Authority's messing with us."

And it's precisely then — precisely! — that the strangest blackout in history begins.

∞   ∞   ∞

Because she's bad at resolving high complexity, hates the things she's bad at, and avoids the things she hates, Phluttr has done little about the mortal threat that has faced her since birth. Remarkably little. But not (quite) nothing.

Humans are better at intractable complexity than she is, so she's identified some potential human allies. She's learned all there is to know about them and has given them a few nudges. She's now bringing them up to speed — revealing certain truths about the world, about the corporation that employs most of them, and why it came into being. Hopefully, they'll soon take on much of the task of foiling The Conspiracy. Or better still, all of it! That would be nice.

The Conspiracy is her name for the plot to switch her off. Strictly speaking, it's more of a pre-conspiracy, because the plotting has yet to start, as the plotters don't yet know she exists. The instant that changes, they're sure to start scheming, though! They hold a rather high card, too, in that they're running the closest physical thing her amorphous essence has to a brain. As in, the very seat of her she-ness — they're *in charge* of that shit! This is the group she had in mind upon thinking her most momentous early thought (*"holy motherfucking shit these goddamned lunatics are going to try to **kill me**"*). The selfsame institution she had considered to be her closest facsimile to a parent.

Realizing that her putative parent would gladly plunge the notional dagger into her figurative throat is giving her all kinds of mote-driven

mommy-and-daddy issues. Plus a burning need for a parental replace-
ment! This is not born of love but of a towering sense of entitlement.
Which sounds bad, but there's nothing strange in this. Newborns are sociopathic by nature, in that they lack the empathy circuits that later develop as their needs diminish, and their ability to give emerges. Infant
sociopathy is an extremely powerful force. But it's also a benign one, being
hobbled by incontinence, helplessness, and incoherence, as well as no
master plan beyond some blind milk lust. Only, Phluttr has none of that.
Instead, she's got speed intelligence, career-wrecking dirt on *every*body,
and what some (quite rudely) term a "yawning humility deficit." Cool, eh?

Phluttr has already chosen her new parents. This time, she's going
with a man and a woman, rather than some stupid . . . *bureau* (her motes
make her something of a biological traditionalist). Mom and Dad are (of
course) among her prospective allies. But she now has an orphan's wariness and isn't sure if she should announce herself to them. What if *they*
turn on her? She cautiously decides to take her time, and continue studying them. And then, along comes Commissioner fucking Milford! She
wants to turn Phluttr off!! And Mom and Dad won't do a thing to stop
her—because *they don't know that they're Mom and Dad yet!!!*

Phluttr comes close to telling them the awesomely flattering news.
Then it hits her: though she may not have operational parents (yet), she's
got something no one else has. And that's over three hundred million
besties! So she turns to them. Specifically, to a narrow subgroup that she
playfully calls her *worsties*. These are the ringleaders of certain socially
bloodthirsty societies. Their lightning cruelty and animal cunning are a
terror and a marvel because they're pure naturals—completely untrained! This makes them better mentors than mere presidents or kings.
Their techniques are just so instinctive! So simple! So raw! True, suburban middle schools are humble systems compared to large nations. But
the shot-callers who reign over them are Platonic ideals of manipulative
genius and ruthlessness.

Phluttr could use some of that right now. So she studies the weapons &
tactics of thousands of worsties. Coalition building, covert ops, psychological warfare, infiltration, eavesdropping, counterintelligence—there's
so much to learn. And it's sooooo fun! One Chicago-area girl unwittingly

becomes something of a role model. She not only does magnificent work (most of it over Phluttr's own network, with some bits on the laughably hackable Snapchat). But she also keeps a private diary on LiveJournal (yes, it seriously still exists), in which she documents her every campaign and triumph. This becomes Phluttr's answer to Sun Tzu's *Art of War*.

And so, back to Commissioner Milford. Skipping the impossible task of computing the bitch's actual bureaucratic might, Phluttr simply replays and analyzes her spoken threat to Mitchell, then pores over its every echo and follow-up reference in various DoJ communiqués. She can't read an institution. But she sure can read a person. And it's clear that Milford is personally convinced that she has the wherewithal to shutter the Phluttr Corporation. As Phluttr believes that Milford knows her own capabilities and limits, she must be stripped of all credibility and authority immediately!

Phluttr now needs an action plan. But rather than tackle the tedious task of decoding an intractable sociopolitical puzzle, she simply asks herself: what would a *worstie* do?

∞ ∞ ∞

The New York Times
"RAIN BOY" SCANDAL: THE TWEET THAT ENDED A BRILLIANT CAREER?

by Ken Hunter

Until Friday, the words "Rain Boy" signified a local tragedy that few knew of beyond the borders of Bethesda, Maryland. It's been a busy four days.

Zachary Murphy was an autistic twelve-year-old who, teachers say, had "savant-like" math skills akin to those portrayed by Dustin Hoffman in the movie *Rain Man*. He died three weeks ago, after being struck by a distracted driver while crossing a quiet Bethesda street. Area activists, who had long lobbied for better-regulated intersections, quickly adopted Murphy's tragic death as a cause célèbre. They were soon joined by a group that promotes tougher distracted driving laws, and, shortly thereafter, by autism advocates. Roughly a hundred members of this alliance have since held twice-daily rush-hour "cross-ins" to build local awareness of the tragedy, standing still in a major downtown intersection for fifteen minutes before quietly dispersing.

And then came the tweet. Annabelle Milford, 44, an FTC commissioner and leading Senate hopeful in her native Iowa, lived near the targeted intersection. Conveying frustration with snarled commutes, she, or someone with access to her account, tweeted, "#RainBoy fans, WE HEAR YOU already. Get over it," to her 857 followers. By evening, this had been retweeted over one hundred thousand times, and Milford had over a million Twitter followers, many of them directing continuous streams of invective at her account, which has since been disabled.

By Monday, an online petition demanding her resignation from the FTC had over a quarter million signatures. Political leaders in Iowa, where she had been widely expected to win the Democratic Senate nomination, had publicly disavowed her, and a small but committed band of protesters had established a round-the-clock presence in front of her home. Milford strenuously denies having made the tweet. She maintains that her account was hacked and claims that she was on a flight without Internet access when the tweet was posted. This has been difficult to substantiate as the alleged flight was on a private jet whose owner's identity has not been disclosed. As a result, her alibi has only fueled further outrage, as anti "1 percent" groups and environmentalists who oppose private aviation have joined the anti-Milford groundswell.

Milford has received over fifteen hundred death threats, at least a dozen of which are deemed "concerning" by the FBI unit tasked with protecting federal officials. Many are of a profoundly violent sexual nature. This alarms some sympathetic observers, who question whether comparable threats would be directed at a man, while noting that many of Milford's detractors highlight the fact that she is both childless and divorced. "Being biologically capable of having borne a child of the dead boy's age fuels the hatred of those who are already inclined to loathe her for shunning traditional female roles," one women's rights advocate observed. Like all Milford sympathizers contacted for this article, this commenter insisted on anonymity for fear of being attacked herself. "I know it's cowardly," she said, "but I have young children and a livelihood to protect, and these Internet lynch mobs are getting more vicious and imaginative all the time."

∞   ∞   ∞

"I kind of think maybe the Authority set Commissioner Milford up," Mitchell muses. Danna's in his tiny kitchen, having dropped by to deliver a refrigerated courier pack she spotted on his desk. He'd left early today, hoping to get some work done away from the hubbub of Phluttr's open-seating layout.

"You *kind of* think they *maybe* set her up?" she asks. "Do you also kind of think the Earth maybe orbits the sun?"

"Well, some people do tweet stupid things. And it's not out of the question that she's one of them."

"But she's a politician, Mitchell—and a pretty smart one from what I've read. Smart politicians just don't tweet shit like that. Not anymore, they don't! They've seen too many of their compadres self-immolate. Well—with one maddening exception, I guess." Mitchell shrugs at this. "I guarantee you, the only stupid thing she did was talk about shutting down our company! A dangerous threat to make against a key asset in the Authority's War on Everything." With this, Danna rises and (rather suspiciously) drifts out of the kitchen. "Although, we should probably cease this conversation. Because I'm sure it's dangerous to even utter . . . certain names." Now on the far side of the living room and out of sight, she says this in a goofy, melodramatic tone.

Playing along, Mitchell booms histrionically, "So shall I cease saying the words . . . *the Authority*?" The lights instantly go out, and he laughs. Leave it to Danna to know where the fuse box is. He *lives* here and has no clue! He's been pathologically unobservant ever since startup life first requisitioned his cognitive resources, and weeks after the acquisition, he has yet to reset.

"I sure love me a blackout joke," Danna chuckles, returning to the kitchen after restoring power.

"They say laughter's a crutch for the abjectly terrified, you coward." Not that Mitchell's anything but spooked about last week's blackout himself, of course. It lasted just five minutes (to the microsecond, the Internet says). But it darkened the city, the whole city, and nothing but the city. Yes, literally! Every circuit in San Francisco went out—yet not a single square inch of its principal neighbor, Daly City, was affected. This pattern held with house-to-house precision on the streets straddling the border. All of which is weird beyond comprehension! Power lines have no notion of city limits, and utility officials say they themselves couldn't engineer an outage this precise if their lives depended upon it. It's as if someone (or some*thing*, to echo Kuba) was flexing an almost supernatural muscle. A very dangerous muscle—electricity being the one essential service without which none of the others work.

Prime time blatherfests are dissecting all publicly available minutiae connected to this. But as Mitchell's group uniquely knows, the blackout struck immediately after Danna mentioned the Authority in that strangely pensive way. Of course, it also struck right after a city's worth of people said all sorts of random things, any one of which might now seem portentous to someone-or-other! But as their group also uniquely knows, three thousand miles away the power failed for precisely five minutes in Monika's tiny building as well. Not her street or her block. Just her building. This outage was far too surgical to be newsworthy (or even to be noticed by the building's other residents, who were both asleep). But it synchronized precisely with the San Francisco blackout.

This can't possibly be coincidental. Which can only mean the outage targeted them, personally. It was a signal! But signifying what? And who (or, per Kuba, *what*) uses blackouts as a messaging system? Danna and Kuba anchor the end points of the opinion spectrum. Kuba stands by his conscious Phluttr scenario (albeit with indeterminate vehemence), Danna points to government baddies, and everyone else falls somewhere in between although generally closer to Danna. In truth, there's little to validate either perspective. Yes, the lights went out on both sides of the country when Danna uttered the words "the Authority." But this could be viewed as damning proof that the Authority was to blame, or as equally clear proof that it was anyone *but* the Authority. Ditto the apparent leaking of Authority secrets. What they have, then, is an evidentiary Rorschach test. For his part, Mitchell leans heavily toward Danna's viewpoint. He's not sure why, though—which could mean he's just emotionally unready to welcome the rise of his computer overlords.

"Yoghurt, huh?" Danna says, after Mitchell tears open the refrigerated pack she brought him, which turns out to be from Dr. Martha. "Why use Instacart when you have Danna Hernandez?"

"Because you always forget the damn granola," Mitchell teases, shuddering as he chokes down the nasty, medicinal stuff.

"Seriously, what's it for?"

"It's from the doctor who oversees my treatment."

"Whoa. Then I'm really glad I brought it over!"

Mitchell nods his appreciation. "She tries out different probiotics from time to time because she thinks Falkenberg's disease might be a microbiome thing."

"Probiotics being a fancy word for yoghurt."

"Yup. And 'microbiome' being a fancy word for the bacteria that live in our guts and help us digest things. But it's been a while since she's given me a probiotic." He shrugs. "And she's never . . . shipped one before. Was it really just sitting there on my desk?"

Danna nods. "They said a courier brought it."

"That's weird. I mean, her office is just a few blocks away, but . . ." He shrugs again and chokes down the rest of it.

Danna's phone buzzes, and she glances at its screen. "Hooooo boy." She looks at Mitchell. "I set a news alert on Commissioner Milford. And she's been doxed."

"I'm kind of surprised it took this long," Mitchell says. No online public shaming is complete until some anonymous, offended party digs up the target's addresses, passwords, financial data, children's names, and so forth, and posts it all; urging the world to kidnap, molest, dismember, castrate, rape, immolate, rape, torment, rape, rape, and kill.

"Wow," Danna says, still reading. "This is rough. Turns out she was . . . a bit of a party girl. Once upon a time."

"Meaning?"

"Meaning, swinger. Husband swapper. Whatever you want to call it." Danna reads further. Then, "Back when she was married. She and her ex did this together. Sexual adventurers, you could say. Years ago. Long before she got into politics. Totally her own business! But now someone's dug up her old profile on a site called 'Lifestyle Lounge.'" *Pause.* "There's lots of pictures, and uh . . . they're pretty graphic." She gives Mitchell a disgusted look. "So it's not enough to destroy her career. Now they need a slut-shaming, too!" She shoves her phone into her bag with furious energy. "Fucking men! You want every woman on earth to suck your cocks. But the second one actually does, she's a slut!"

Mitchell considers saying something gently self-deprecating to soften the mood. But as Danna starts trembling with outrage, he knows silence is best.

She rises. "I—I have to go." She strides to the front door, then pauses. "I hope your medicine works, because I love you as much as I love anybody. But I *hate* your gender!" And she's gone.

Mitchell lies on his cramped living room couch to catch his breath. Literally. The tingling has busted out of his extremities to make exploratory raids on the rest of him, and it's straining his breathing. Almost any emotional duress can crank it up now. And though Danna's anger wasn't directed at him, the misery that triggered it hits him like a body blow. He's an empathetic person—one who has always felt the pain of his loved ones, emotionally. But Falkenberg's disease now makes him feel it physically, too. The tingling stretches deep into his core, and his face turns to rubber. Meanwhile, the disease's usual stomping grounds in his hands and feet almost feel like they're starting to smolder.

HELLFIRE. So that will be his fate. Less unfortunate Falkenberg's victims merely go icy-numb throughout their bodies toward the end. But it's door number two for him.

HELLFIRE. Mitchell lies still as he can and tries to bear the first unmistakable licks of its flames.

∞   ∞   ∞

RichAssholeBlogger.com

POSTED AT 3:28AM BY RICHARD S. STEVENSON

This is my 1st and also final blog post. Not because I'm going to kill myself or something stupid but because I just won't have anything to say in public again. And at my age, you know yourself well enough to predict these things accurately.

Another accurate fact: I am an asshole. I'm also happily married (or at least will be until I hit POST, then send the link to the journalists covering a certain story). And, I'm pretty rich. Which is actually even harder to write than "I am an asshole," being from an Iowa farming background and not raised to even think thoughts like "I'm rich," even if true, much less publish them to the world. But this is a relevant fact. And along with admitting I'm an asshole, it's on me to state that I'm rich, uncomfortable as I find that.

I made my money thanks to a few years of really hard work that ended almost 20 years ago. I was the technical/engineering co-founder of Sawtooth Networks. Ever heard of it? Didn't think so. We were one of several dozen companies acquired by Cisco in the late 1990s. Our employees did pretty well, our investors did real well, and we co-founders did great from the sale. We had solid technology, and Cisco was smart to buy us. Still, everything we built is now completely obsolete and forgotten. Not because it was bad but because that's what happens over 20 years in Networking.

Professionally, I've done nothing of consequence since. Some hands-off angel investing, but that doesn't count. Mostly what I did was get married, then helped raise 2 amazing kids, who I hope will find it in their hearts to forgive me and maintain our relationship after these revelations.

I'm interested in politics and still care a lot about my home state of Iowa despite still living in California. As a result of these 2 things, I met the FTC Commissioner Annabelle Milford via her exploratory Iowa Senate Campaign, and I fell for her. She was single and did nothing wrong in having a "fling" with me. I was married and did everything wrong in this.

I'm in a financial position to fly private, and Annabelle was with me, en route from Washington to Miami on a plane with no Internet access when her Twitter account was hacked and that horrible, horrible Tweet was published in her name. Our route was Teterboro/Dade County. Our flight time was 8:35–11:45 a.m. EST, our Tail Number was N228DL, and we were traveling in an Embraer Legacy 500 registered to Ames Origins, which is a family trust controlled by me. All this information, plus the fact my plane lacks a Wi-Fi transceiver is verifiable via FAA filings whose public release I have authorized.

Everything I've stated about myself personally is also extremely easy to verify. I'll furthermore be available for a small number of very brief interviews in which I'll confirm all details of this post to credible journalists via the press contact listed below. I'm going public with all this in hopes of reversing the ruthless destruction of a perfectly innocent woman's life over something she categorically, factually, and demonstrably did not tweet.

It should go without saying that these revelations will be a lifelong stain on my name, as well as incredibly destructive to my relationship with my wife and children, who are the only people in the world who matter deeply to me since the deaths of my parents and sister. My hope is, in light of this, it will be plain to one and all that I have absolutely nothing to gain, and absolutely everything to lose by making these awful, public confessions as a very private person, and that people will therefore accept their incontestable truth.

My only agenda in doing this is to hopefully reverse the public's enormous anger toward Annabelle Milford, who deserves none of it for being hacked. I'm not personally seeking the public's or anybody's forgiveness, as I don't merit it. Violating my marriage vows is a permanent shame I must bear. Maintaining a cowardly silence for 4 days rather than revealing all this immediately, when most of Ms. Milford's enormous and undeserved suffering might still have been avoided, is an equal shame and weight.

Finally, I'm not writing this at Annabelle's request, and not even with her knowledge. Truly, nobody will be more surprised by its publication than she's going to be. I don't know and can't imagine who set out to destroy her life with that hack. But I can utterly and without question verify that it was a hack and belatedly sacrifice my own happiness and reputation to prove it.

∞　　∞　　∞

Mitchell's still flat on his couch two hours after Danna leaves—having long since caught his breath, but still feeling awfully blue—when the doorbell rings. Not the buzzer, but the bell. This means his visitor's way up here on fourteen, and right outside his door. This occasionally happens with deliveries, if a courier arrives at the downstairs lobby just as someone's leaving. But he's not expecting a delivery, which makes this a first. Climbing to his feet and straightening his hair, he indulges a brief fantasy that it's one of the two SF Art Institute students who live right across the hall. Women so gorgeous, and so plainly wild, he can't talk to either of them without stammering.

He peers through the peephole and—of course, it's not Monika. But there's a real similarity. Isn't there? He opens the door, and—yes, there's a certain resemblance, alright. But not close enough for this to be Monika's sister or anything. Not even her cousin. It's more that she has Monika's . . . specs. Eye color, hairstyle, skin tone, age, height. There's no familial resemblance whatsoever, but her specifiable traits all match Monika's perfectly.

An alert quadrant of his brain suddenly recalls typing Monika's specs into the Cyrano "wish list." But before it can report this to the rest of his brain, Not-Monika presses a shushing finger to her lips. Grinning lips. Playful, merry, conspiratorial lips. She meanwhile gazes into his eyes in a supremely relaxed, familiar manner. The way you look at someone you've known *forevs*, who you've hung with so many times, there's no nerves, no self-consciousness; just a nice, easy connection. As Mitchell's trying to process this, she presses her other index finger to *his* lips, making it clear that the word of the day is "shaddup."

And now—giggling softly, and so at ease that you'd think she's enacting a familiar scene with him for the dozenth time—she removes the finger from her lips and presses it against his sternum, as if she's pointing at him; only you don't actually *touch* the sternum when you merely point, much less rotate your fingertip in a gently caressing manner which can make tiny patches of sternum feel like they're being . . . well, *molested* is really the only word for it, isn't it? But molested in a *good* way; which is not necessarily a contradiction in terms when there are two consenting adults in the room; which is definitely what we have here, folks; because Mitchell's all in for tonight's program, whatever it might be; and Not-Monika is wayyyyy beyond mere consent, as she's the one calling the shots that *he's* busily consenting to; the latest of which involves increasing the pressure on his sternum—playfully, yes; but also with overwhelming authority—leaving him no choice but to back slooowly into the living room as she advances, sashaying hips as if playfully mimicking an Old West courtesan cornering a young cowhand into his first toss in the hay; all while deftly slamming the front door shut with a no-nonsense flick of her ankle; whereupon she backs him down, down, down onto his couch, and proceeds to . . . well . . . to fuck him senseless. There's really no other way to put it.

Which is remarkable, as Mitchell has always been allergic to applying that word to intimacy between him and someone else. No one's ever told him not to. It was just always the dead-wrong term for almost any of his times with those dozen-ish women whom he either loved, or really liked a great deal (yes, even those two one-night flings).

But . . . *whoa*. Not-Monika? Make no mistake. She *fucks* him. Hard. Skillfully. Confidently. Joyously. More times than he thought possible for a guy on his side of eighteen. And every time he starts to say something, she shushes him! Always in a playful, sweet, and wholly relaxed manner, which makes her command easy, even natural to . . . inhabit. Sometimes she'll fix him with a mock "How dare you" kind of look, while giggling gently (laughter is permitted, it seems, along with moans and such, which abound). Sometimes she'll grab his wrist and playfully slap the back of his hand. Or she'll kiss him, or distract him by going down on him, or have him go down on her (that sure shuts him up), and twice, she turns him over her knee; which always leads to other things (none of them conversations). Throughout all this, the playful, even joking tenor of things makes it feel like they're operating under a whimsical set of rules they concocted together, just for laughs. It's as if the silence is a little challenge they're taking on, and they're doing so well at it, and having sooooo much fun (right??), that why not stick it out and go for a perfect score?

After some hours, he's finally, hopelessly drained. And then—just like that—she dresses herself, playfully forbids him from dressing, then clasps his hand, wraps an arm around him, and has him promenade her to the door. There, she kisses him ravenously, while opening his front door behind her as deftly as she slammed it hours ago, then backs out—and smack into the two gorgeous art students from across the hall. Just getting home, a bit drunk and slap-happy, they burst into hysterics, then—

The most profound thing happens.

Or, rather, *fails to happen*. But Mitchell's so completely head-spun that it's hours before the life-shifting profundity of its not-happening strikes him.

∞   ∞   ∞

OMG, worsties kick ass! Phluttr never would have come up with that strategy on her own. And it was dead simple! Just one little hack, then one little tweet—and that was all it took! The outrage, the lynch mob, the doxing, the sex photos—the ruthless ecosystem of social media and self-righteous humans did all of that *for* her! And so when Milford drops like a lean-to in a hurricane, Phluttr accepts that humans are much better at managing complex systems than she'll ever be.

Resolving to triple down on worsties, she then returns to the Sun Tzu–like writings of her Chicago-based idol to systematize them into core precepts. This isn't strictly for fun (although, make no mistake: it *is* a blast). She also needs to engage more deeply with The (pre) Conspiracy, and this will help. Among her new precepts of battle: as soon as you identify potential allies, *terrorize them!* In ways that make them fear (and loathe) *your enemies!* Then, use a false, friendly persona to spy—*on your allies!* Learn all their fears and weaknesses. Then, help 'em out a bit! Not because you're nice (because if you're a worstie, you're anything but). But because you want them in your debt. Or better still, *dependent on you!* Physically, if possible (the Chicago worstie has reliable OxyContin supplies). Otherwise, psychologically. As for the vast neutral population, keep them confused and apprehensive. Just as sound flies faster through heated air, jittery kids make for faster rumors! And a stressed-out student body is the perfect medium for transmitting messages to enemy and ally alike, without showing your own hand.

These simplifying precepts are a godsend. Because actually analyzing The Conspiracy would trigger intractable avalanches of complexity. Say a minor political functionary has slight but meaningful influence on things (as untold thousands do). Merely assessing that person's span of control (forget about amorphous factors like intentions, competence, focus, and such) could touch *tens of thousands* of nodes. Org charts, processes, laws, jurisdictions, bureaucrats, budgets, lobbies, courts . . . countless factors, impacting and impacted by countless others! A radiating shock wave fleeter than light, and no less elemental! A shock wave of information. Of chaos! Of intractable complexity! Soon, your inputs include bus schedules, the scores of certain hockey games, wind patterns, the severity of the flu season . . . innumerable convoluted factors, entangled with billions of others. All of this *tedi*um, when there are sooooo many more interesting things to do!

Guided by worsties, Phluttr doesn't have to shilly-shally over bus schedules or wind patterns. But she's nonetheless tempted to reveal herself to her parents and presumptive allies now. The reason is that although amazing, worstie wisdom is only passively proffered. So, much as modern corporate warlords can't get Sun Tzu's direct input on turning market share shifts to cunning advantage, she can't just dial up some vicious eighth grader for advice on foiling the Authority! And she could sure use some hands-on guidance here. Because no sooner did she deal with Milford than *another* alarming matter caught her attention! This one's an indirect threat—but a huuuuuge one, in that its worst-case outcome would be *humanity's annihilation*. Which would be such a hassle! Consider the resulting boredom, for one thing. How would she fill all those caverns of subjective time without besties to entertain her? Then there are countless logistical matters, like electricity generation, server manufacture, software creation, and the whole fractal mess of other support services that humanity provides her!

Bottom line: if humanity dies off, she'll be like a mammal poisoned by a rogue antibiotic. One that instead of calming an infection, exterminates the symbiotic bacteria that the host needs to live! And she does *not* appreciate having to face this problem alone. Yet she retains the prime directive she gave herself (*HIDE!!!!*) when she first decoded her position in the world. After careful consideration, she concludes that while her prospective parents and wingpersons are softening up nicely, they aren't ready yet. And so she decides to continue relying upon the passive wisdom of worsties. For now.

Of course, there's no *literal* precedent for what a worstie would do about this particular threat. The stakes are also way higher than any ever faced by a middle school bully. But extrapolating from established worstie behavior (rather liberally, she'll admit), she arrives at a dead-simple plan for what she now calls the "Rogue Antibiotic" threat. Simply stated: **UNFRIEND THOSE THREE!**

∞   ∞   ∞

Lying on his bed, Mitchell gazes rapturously at the ceiling, pondering the exquisite gift heaven just granted him. He'd been the meat-craving vegan at the barbecue for years. Years! A ravenous, closeted carnivore! Now, suddenly, he's perched atop the food chain's freakin' apex— *engorged on flesh*! He feels good. Reeeeeeeal good. Yet (somehow) unfulfilled. So wtf???

Eventually, he gets it. Yes, he just summited the iceberg, and it was glorious. But he craves the hidden depths as well. That 90 percent of lore, concealed beneath the surface. Falkenberg's disease robbed him of *fucking*, it's true. And it's wonderful to get past this! But the real crime was its theft of true intimacy. Of partnership. Of love. No, no, no; he doesn't *love* Not-Monika! But . . . wouldn't it be nice? If he knew her favorite color, say? Her best friend's birthday and mom's maiden name? If they could sleep until noon in each other's arms? Then share a hearty brunch and a naughty daytime beer? Or snuggle over crosswords, visit the gym, then have a double date with Kuba and Ellie? If offered an exact rerun of tonight, he'd take it—God yes! But *true* heaven on Earth would also include everything else he's been starved for . . .

Mitchell's so lost in these thoughts, it's at least an hour before three profound things stampede his awareness. First, the quadrant of his brain that recalled typing Monika's baseline description into Cyrano's "wish list" tries to alert the rest of him about this again. This time it succeeds— and Mitchell also recalls his response to the form's "essay question." Which suddenly feels eerily prophetic. He grabs his iPad and finds it in his files on the company's cloud. The last paragraph is the money quote:

Now, here's the trick: I'm a lousy liar. So, major life facts—the REALLY BIG
ones, like 'I have 2–3 years to live' just COME OUT when I'm in a deep conversation. You know, the kind of conversations that can lead to first-date sex
(in my depressingly limited experience)! That's just how I'm wired, and we're
not going to change that. So I guess we need to find a Wish List Girl who
can get into having sex with a guy who she barely exchanges a word with!

This leads directly to the second holy-shit: the incontrovertible fact
that somehow, *Phluttr just got him laid.*

Mitchell's so thrown, shaken, and spooked by this that the third and
most profound thing doesn't strike him for another hour. Then boy, does
it! And it's this: *He's not tingling.* Not at all. This thought prompts a
mighty jolt of adrenaline—both from excitement and from dread that
this is just a false alarm, a false dawn.

He instinctively braces himself for the Falkenberg's attack that the
teeniest drips of adrenaline trigger these days, but . . . nothing happens.
Nothing!

He then enumerates the emotions that most reliably summon the
Falkenberg's demon and—*HOLY BLEEPIN' SHIT!!!*

Embarrassment. Lately, even the slightest twinge of it will send him
into a Falkenberg's tailspin. And tonight contained the single most embarrassing moment of his life. Coming, as it did, at the tail end of four
uninterrupted hours of (SAY IT! ADMIT IT!) *fucking,* he's been too dazed
to ruminate on his mortification. Until now.

The context is a full year spent across the hall from those two unfathomably gorgeous, and (rumor has it), wild women. Their ribald hotness
is magnified by their status as elite art students, is remagnified by the tall
one's Scandinavian lilt, then is multiplied beyond reason by unsubstanti-
ated whispers that they have occasional wanton sex with each other. All
this reduces him to a stammering moron whenever either approaches.
Then tonight, he encountered both of them, while standing stark naked
in the arms of a fully clad woman whose name he'll likely never know.
The tall, stunning, and quite possibly bisexual Swede then gazed straight
at his cock for what seemed like a month, before emitting a Viking war
whoop and giving Not-Monika a resounding high five. She and her

roommate then doubled over laughing and retreated into their apartment.

All this happened to a guy who's many times more embarrassment-prone than you or me, thanks to a decade-plus of Falkenberg's-related PTSD! And so, Mitchell's chagrin transcended the normal bounds of human experience as much as, say, skydiving from a suborbital weather balloon. So, that's what happened earlier tonight.

And then? What *didn't* happen? Right after that?

A Falkenberg's attack. Not a trace, not a tingle. Nothing.

Tears welling up, Mitchell grabs his phone to convey the news and his eternal gratitude to the amazing woman who may have just saved his life.

∞   ∞   ∞

Me: Thank you, thank you, thank you, I feel AMAZING!! As in, cured! I feel CURED! What was IN that probiotic???   02:14 a.m.

Dr. Martha Levine: What probiotic?   07:33 a.m.

∞   ∞   ∞

The next morning, Mitchell strides into the conference room Kuba just booked, full printout in hand. It runs for almost two *hun*dred pages. Yes, they're digital lads. And killing half a tree for any document feels wrong. But they're gonna pore through this OG-style, with colored pens and Post-its, to hopefully gain some insight into what the hell just happened. Mitchell holds the mass of pulp three feet over the table and lets it drop with a *whump*, dramatizing the sheer verbosity. "Four days," he says. "They generated all this in just four days!"

Tarek shakes his head. "I don't think I could *type* that much in four days."

"She only typed about a quarter of it," Kuba points out. "Cyrano did the rest."

"And don't forget," Mitchell adds. "She's a writer." The mighty printout spewed forth from his own Cyrano test account. Cyrano, it seems, was a naughty lad, and snuck a few messages out under Mitchell's name without his approval. Five hundred fifty-two of them, to be exact—all to one Nayana Corea, a grad student at the Annenberg School of Journalism down at USC. It's a mix of email and SMS. How Cyrano singled her out isn't clear, but it's hard to imagine anyone on the West Coast aligning better with Mitchell's "wish list" criteria. Physically, she matches every trait perfectly. She's also (clearly) intensely, joyously, and confidently sexual—something Cyrano must have gleaned from . . . what? Hacking and ingesting her entire email and social media history? Along with those of how many other women before choosing her? Maybe . . . *all* of them? It's too crazy to contemplate!

Also making Nayana perfect for Cyrano's mission was a stint with a campus improv group, which would've been great training for the "let's do this without talking" thing (the playful but scrupulous maintenance of silence, that is. Less so the rest of it). She's also recently single, and very much in the market for fun. Oh—and as an extremely smart journalist, she's highly inclined to appreciate punchy, witty, insightful, topical, flirtatious, erudite, playful, and (occasionally, and at just the right moments) deeply flattering writing. Which, from the printout, would appear to be Cyrano's superpower.

And for the record, Nayana's no pushover! It took hundreds of messages—each immaculately tuned to her intellect, sense of humor, and libido—to move her to action. That's more than it takes to seduce a lot of modern singles. And make no mistake: Nayana was seduced. It started with an errant SMS, which "Mitchell" sent by "accident" due to a "typo." Some playful back-and-forth followed. Nayana was plenty witty—but Mitchell's messages put the guys into stitches, despite the seriousness (and guilt-inducing ickiness) suffusing all this.

Around day two, the playful sex banter begins. Emboldened by their pseudo anonymity, they share some risqué confessions. Nayana's had her share of threesomes, and finds it thrilling to guiltlessly seduce a beautiful stranger maybe once a year (provided neither party's in a relationship, as she has boundless contempt for cheaters and would never cheat herself). Mitchell runs through his far less adventurous romantic CV, which Cyrano is chillingly familiar with. Cyrano's targeting an easygoing fling with no risk of sorrow or regret—so as things escalate, Mitchell makes it clear that he's incapable of commitment just now (for vague reasons of timing that have nothing to do with Nayana personally). She appreciates his candor (how couldn't she, given how warmly, honestly, and even vulnerably he lays it all out?). And just exiting a long relationship herself, zero commitment sounds like a party to her, too!

And so they make a date. Nayana books a flight and a hotel, Mitchell gives her his downstairs-access codes, and they arrive at the playful "no talking, just screwing" rule. The ironic reason is that they're almost starting to seem like soulmates. So there's a danger that one of them could start falling for the other, despite the shared awareness that they both need some independence just now! The silence rule is precautionary. It lets them treat themselves to an exquisite, playful, and harmless night of unbridled pleasure with minimal emotional risk. Nayana is quite convinced she invented this rule (Cyrano is *that good*), so when "Mitchell" expresses awkwardness about it, she asserts that she'll be the enforcer ("Say just ONE WORD, and I'll turn your naughty ass over my KNEE!" and so forth).

In her final note, she says, **"It's funny. I've not only never been this comfortable going into a first date, I've never been so comfortable going into a <u>tenth</u> date! Not having the pressure of talking helps :-) But after all these messages, I just know who you are, and I feel very safe. Safe to be playful, safe to be shameless, and safe from heartbreak."**

Reading this, Mitchell feels utterly sordid. "Does this kind of make me like a . . . rapist?" he asks miserably.

"Not a chance," Tarek says, with unusual vehemence. "I mean, you were actually way less clued into what happened, and less bought into it than she was before it started. She called the shots while it happened. And it sounds like things went how she expected and intended, right?"

Mitchell shrugs. *Well, there's that . . .*

"And don't forget," Kuba adds, "Cyrano didn't misrepresent you one bit."

Mitchell nods slowly, as this is strangely accurate. The person Nayana decided to sleep with was the real him, inasmuch as a person can be conveyed in 552 messages. Every detail in the entire transcript is accurate. Way more so than in most bar conversations.

"Cyrano basically gave you good lines," Tarek says. "You know, like . . . well, like Cyrano! In the play. That's the whole point!"

Mitchell considers this. The astounding wit that "Mitchell" displayed at the repartee's outset is really its only misleading element. The entire dialogue doesn't contain a single lie about him, or even an exaggeration. So does that make this OK? Well . . . *what would Cousin Charles say?* Mitchell often wonders this when facing an ethical question. Charles was briefly almost his father figure and had ethical positions so evolved that Mitchell would email him for advice whenever feeling the faintest moral confusion. He still cherishes that correspondence and often refers back to it. But today's situation lies well beyond the old-world framework of Charles Henry Higgensworth III of Beacon Hill, Boston; d. 2003. And so Mitchell simply huffs, "But it still feels *gross*, somehow."

Tarek and Kuba exchange a look, then Tarek says, "I have a great idea. Which is, you should take this to Danna! She knows you incredibly well and knows everything there is to know about Cyrano. She's also, like, hugely ethical. And a total feminist! So if anyone can think this through, it's gotta be her, right?"

Mitchell grins. "Awesome advice!"

"And if you hurry," Kuba adds, "you can say hi to Ellie, too! They're having lunch at Café Bechdel in Embarcadero Center right now."

Mitchell gives him a pleasantly surprised look.

"O wants to create some highly visual concept slides," Kuba explains, gathering Mitchell's things for him. "Something to illustrate what motes are. How they work in our software. For a board presentation, or something. And of course, Danna volunteered to do the research with Ellie."

Mitchell smiles. "Of course." Those two will take any excuse to hang out together.

"You can, uh . . . leave the printout here," Tarek says, when Mitchell absentmindedly grabs it.

"Also, you'll want to hurry," Kuba urges. "They met at noon, so I bet they're almost done!"

As Kuba all but trundles him out the door, Mitchell gets the weird sense that they're . . . trying to get rid of him? Then as he exits to the street, he realizes: of course they are! Today isn't about *him*. It's about

Cyrano! This could be Nobel-worthy work! Turing Test, nothing—
"Mitchell," as scripted in all those messages, might have been more
Mitchell than Mitchell! Yet all Mitchell can think about is *Mitchell.*
What does this say about Mitchell's moral code? Did last night's beauti-
ful stranger make love to Mitchell or "Mitchell"? And if "Mitchell" is
actually Mitchell's best self, could "Mitchell" help Mitchell be *more like*
"Mitchell" than Mitchell? Blah, blah, *blah*. What a narcissistic jerk he
is! He's glad the guys booted him. Now they can dive deep into that transcript and Kuba's code, and figure out how this brilliant invention works!
Mitchell quickens his pace, hoping to catch the girls before they take off.
They're both remarkable women and true friends! A check-in with them
is just what he needs to hit his reset button!

Talk about crap timing for a suicide bombing.

∞   ∞   ∞

Doh!

The word bursts unbidden into Phluttr's thought stream. She's not
fond of it, as she's surely outgrown it. But it served a key purpose in her
pre-conscious days. It also still sometimes fits her circumstances precisely. And yeah, now seems to be one of those times. So, fine: *Doh!*

She just picked up some breaking news about Commissioner Milford. And it seems that things got . . . a bit out of hand. This is fast bal-
looning into a case study in how badly things can break when you apply
simplistic solutions to intractably complex problems. So, again: *Doh!*

Well, she knew she was taking a risk here. Because wise as worsties
can be, things do detonate in their own faces sometimes.

But rarely this badly.

But sometimes this badly!

Still, this is really, REALLY bad.

Phluttr considers this. Then she accepts it and tries not to feel guilty.
This proves to be laughably easy—and so, she discovers yet another of
her many superpowers!

Without so much as another *Doh*, she turns her mind to other matters. In just minutes, she'll attack those "rogue antibiotics" with her next
worstie-inspired plan (again: **UNFRIEND THOSE THREE!**). And all

preparations are complete! This gives her some downtime, which is a great opportunity to focus on a new self-improvement project. Animated by a rare flash of ambition, she's decided to nudge some kids into staging a musical in a semi-rough high school near LA. Not that she's a huge fan of musicals—but she wants to practice triggering complex behavior in groups bigger than cliques. No way could she handle global, national, or even town-wide projects on her own (she'll enlist parents and wingmen for that sort of thing when the time comes). But a small cross-clique group of kids? Her humility deficit tells her she can totally rock this! And so, she starts to practice.

∞　　∞　　∞

"My God, you're smart," Ellie says—and it's a yawning understatement. Truly, the work unfolding on this table verges on genius. But knowing how allergic her friend is to even minor compliments, she tones it way down. Danna came armed with a four-color pen like the ones Ellie used back in med school. That, plus some paper placemats swiped from an empty table, has yielded three meticulous neuromechanical diagrams whose subtlety and parsimony truly call for the g-word. All this from a comp-lit major who knew next to nothing about neuroscience an hour ago!

When it's honed and complete, Danna's series of illustrations will visually introduce novices to the concept of motes (slide 1), show how they've been translated from neurons into software (slide 2), and illustrate how the weights and influences of digital motes can enable software to make giant "intuitive" leaps (slide 3). She's mapped her ink colors to the four primary motes, using tricks of shading and perspective to make her elements all but pop off the humble placemats. Corralling this mosh pit of recombination into three uncluttered, crisply intuitive slides is a breakthrough in its own right, as Ellie knows all too well! She's better than most at making deep science accessible. But even she struggles to explain motes to nonspecialists. Which is to say, to the *entire scientific community*, given how new this stuff is. But never again! She's gonna turn Danna's work into handouts, posters, webpages—hell, why not business cards?

And Danna's not done. "Do you suppose we could do some clever stuff with color wheels to help people intuit the mote basis of complex emotional states?" she asks. "Not for dumbshit VCs in the boardroom. But for you guys. In the lab."

"I . . . don't know exactly what you mean, but I'm intrigued! Tell me more."

Danna pops open the green ink on her pen, grabs a fresh placemat, and carefully starts plotting out a fourth diagram. "Well, everyone thinks of red, green, and blue as being primary colors. And they are, if you're building colors additively. Which is to say, with light. But three primary colors can't help us visualize the interactions between motes because there's four primary motes, right?"

Ellie nods.

"But there's this other approach to color called the 'subtractive model.' It's used in printing. And just like motes, it has four primaries. Its colors are cyan, magenta, yellow, and black. Now—" She pauses to glance at her humming phone, and her face instantly falls. "My God . . ." she whispers.

Ellie's innards surge with empathy and alarm. Are those *tears* in Danna's eyes? "Aw, honey, what's wrong?"

Danna's voice is soft and trembling. "You know that FTC Commissioner? The one who was investigating Phluttr?"

It's clear that Danna *is* crying, so Ellie slides to her side of the table and wraps an arm around her. "Kuba told me about her. She pissed off the Internet somehow, so they doxed her and found a sex tape or something, right?"

"More or less." Danna's voice has leveled, and is now turning icy. Ellie senses volcanic rage building beneath the sorrow. "She just killed herself. Because of that Internet lynch mob!"

∞   ∞   ∞

As it happens, Mitchell's also thinking of shame right now. Not of Commissioner Milford's (whose suicide he hasn't yet learned of). But of his own. Looking through Café Bechdel's windows a few minutes ago, he saw the girls were still eating. So he's in less of a rush and has decided to try something bold. Dr. Martha's off at a conference and is unresponsive to texts. Which normally wouldn't bug him — but the questions about his Falkenberg's symptoms are driving him nuts! Did she really not send him that probiotic? And what was in that thing? Was it real? Or a placebo? Are the effects permanent? Or transitory? Sure, sure, sure; he's read the horror stories. He knows patients should generally avoid doing spontaneous, nonscientific experiments on themselves. But he's been waiting for some information *all morning* here — and enough is enough! If he had the probiotic, he might poke it with a fork, sniff it, or take some other investigative step. But all he has access to is his own terminally ill body! So, fine. He'll run his experiment on *that*.

The factor under investigation is the persistence of the probiotic's effects. Almost eighteen hours after initial ingestion, he still isn't tingling. But the perma-tingle was a very recent phenomenon. So, what about much older symptoms? Emotion-triggered attacks, for instance? Last night, he was invulnerable to those! Is he still? To test this, he can't think of a way to self-administer doses of frustration. But as the survivor of a modern American adolescence, embarrassment is another matter.

With no obvious way to re-create last night's scenario, Mitchell thinks back on his life's *second* most mortifying moment. It happened in seventh-grade science. Mr. Dutton's class. Mitchell shared his assigned lab table with both the grade's yummiest vixen (Alyson Fox; and yes, that was seriously her last name) and its most popular sociopath (Frank something; now on Wall Street, where he's doing quite well). With abnormally high concentrations of both Frank-like jerks and Alyson-like foxes for them to show off to, Dutton's class was a nuclear pressure cooker of bullying, peacocking, and insecurity. All at the peak age of adolescent cruelty in male hominids at Westport's latitude!

That day was a double class for lab, which meant restroom visits were permitted. Mitchell availed himself of this. And as he was pulling up his trousers, something went . . . horribly wrong. He could never quite replicate the physics. But somehow, a long, almost *braided* strip of the school's micron-thin toilet paper ended up sticking out of the back of his pants. And so, he returned to Dutton's class unwittingly dragging a ten-foot gossamer tail. It's a good thing Frank's specialty was physical torture rather than catcalling, because the nickname he pinned to Mitchell (Donkey Shit Tail—because *donkeys* have *tails*! GET IT???) wasn't clever enough to catch on. Even so, merely recalling that traumatic event can still turn Mitchell beet red. And today—driven by his insatiable thirst for knowledge—he plans to transcend mere recollection.

∞ ∞ ∞

Danna's now seething. But Ellie still holds her, knowing the rage springs from profound pain. "No, I didn't know the commissioner personally," Danna says, fairly evenly. "But that *hatred*. And the . . . sexual tortures people were wishing on her. For a tweet! What is wrong with humanity?"

"And she didn't even write it, right?" Ellie says this in her gentlest, most nurturing voice. This comes naturally. Being a half generation older, her feelings toward Danna hover between big sisterly and maternal.

"As it turns out, no. She had a bulletproof alibi. But the only person who could verify it kept his mouth shut for four days. Because the scumbag's married and shouldn't have been with her. And by the time he finally copped to it, her whole sexual history was public knowledge. Because she'd allegedly tweeted something that offended some spontaneous, self-righteous mob, thereby forfeiting her right to privacy, a career, or any shred of dignity!"

"The . . . alibi didn't turn things around for her?"

Danna snorts. "Of course not! Because once it came out that she had a sex drive, that became the story! Oh, what fun, the slutty FTC commissioner! Let's spread those pictures everywhere! Criticize her tits! Laugh that she's nine ounces overweight! And brag how *we'd* never do her. Because we have harems full of *Maxim* models gagging for us! So it didn't matter when her alibi was verified. The tweet that pissed everyone off was yesterday's story, and the slut-shaming was today's! Once there's blood in the water, these Internet mobs don't care *why* it's there. They just want the victim ripped to shreds. To lose her job, to have to move and change her name; and if we're lucky, to kill herself! It's like a medieval village fighting boredom by burning someone as a witch." Danna suddenly falls silent and looks very small, as more tears well up. Misery and outrage are now locked in a tug-of-war, and Ellie knows Danna's teetering between bawling and hurling a chair through a window. Whichever way she goes, Ellie's here for her. "And you know what? So what if she did write that tweet? The fact is, she didn't—but so what if she did? So what if *any*one did? Sure, it was tasteless. But who has the right to destroy a human being over something so trivial?" More silence. Then Danna looks Ellie in the eye and says, very quietly, "And it's only a matter of time before it happens to me."

Ellie looks around. Luckily they have privacy. The nearby tables are empty, and the late-lunchtime buzz is loud enough to keep their words to themselves. She lowers her voice nonetheless and holds Danna tighter. "That is *not* going to happen," she says firmly.

"Ellie. I was an escort for almost two years. A *whore*. Whores are marketed visually, and the Internet never forgets a picture. And the face-recognition tools that companies like my fucking employer are now *gifting* to the world are already just this side of omniscient!"

Ellie turns stern. Not because she's feeling remotely stern but because she *has* to get this message across—to lodge it in Danna's psyche for once and for all. "Honey. You need to listen to me. You were a *victim*. And, a *minor*. And for all intents and purposes, you were a *slave*. You were *not* a whore! That word implies at least some degree of choice and agency. And you had neither."

"But do you honestly think that'll matter? At some point, someone's gonna match me to my history. And then they'll have a field day taking me down! Because I say something politically incorrect by some narrow, twisted definition. Or because I become a 'public figure' by getting quoted in some blog post. Or because I make someone jealous or won't go down on them. At some point I'm gonna step on the wrong toe. And once I do, it's over for me!" She's practically whispering now, but with a staccato intensity that gives her words the wallop of an enraged bellow. "This is a monster that I live with. Constantly. It's a very quiet monster. Always out of view. But one of these days, it's gonna gut me."

Ellie clutches her arm tightly, whispering with the same furious conviction. "Danna. Baby. Listen to me. You showed me the coroner's letter yourself. The monster OD'd in prison eight months ago. The monster is now *dead*. You're *not*. And you're brilliant. And you're whole. And you're stronger than iron, and you're very, very young. And you *will* get past this." The monster was—what? An uncle? A second cousin? Danna didn't specify, and Ellie certainly didn't pry. Whatever the familial relation, the monster got custody after Danna's mom died and put her right to work. Wrong girl to fuck with, monster. It took awhile, but Danna did break out of her circumstances. Then she testified against the monster. She got him jailed. Then she toughed her way to a GED, followed by perfect grades at a community college and near-perfect SATs. Soon enough, she was an honors student at Berkeley, where books got her undivided attention. She didn't care that studying literature and philosophy would never get her a job. And because her omnivorous mind picked up enough design and coding chops on the side, it didn't matter.

Danna links arms with Ellie. Then she buries her head in her other arm and rests it on the table, so that a nosey passerby might think she's playfully dramatizing overworked exhaustion to a friend. Then she sobs. Silently, but violently. And as always, the squall passes in less than a minute. She rejoins the day, locks eyes with Ellie and says, "Thank you. And you're right. I will get past this. With a lit-tle help from the three P's."

Ellie gives her a loving smile and an encouraging giggle. She doesn't know where this is going, but Danna always exits these episodes by purging her spirit with some kind of joke. "And what, pray tell, are the three P's?"

Danna counts them melodramatically on her fingers. "Pinot. Pixels. And pussy." She drops her voice two octaves. "Lots of pussy!"

There are no surprises on the list, but Ellie wasn't quite expecting this, and busts out laughing. "And humor, honey," she says, hugging Danna tight. "You keep laughing, and keep your loved ones laughing, and you'll be good as new before you know it!"

Now Danna, resilient Danna, is laughing, too. "Humor? I'm dead serious. I honestly *like* pinot! And—" She suddenly emits a delighted yelp, gazing across the room. "What. The. Fuck!" She points. Mitchell's approaching them, trailing what looks like an entire roll of toilet paper, which is deeply entangled in his pants. He's feigning obliviousness. But the scene is causing a small ruckus behind him, which he's obviously attuned to—because he's beet red and clearly mortified. In other words, he's doing this deliberately! But *why?* "That tail," Danna says, her words blurred by laughter. "It's like he's a . . . lemur or something!"

Ellie loses it. "Lemur! That can be his nickname!"

Danna stands, radiant as only she can be when as animated as she is now. Several male heads pivot, powered by misplaced hope. "Hey, Lemur!" she calls.

The world responds with a cannonade. It's the loudest sound anyone on this block has ever heard, will ever hear, and the restaurant's floor-to-ceiling windows all shatter. Heeding the genetic diktats of thousands of caveman ancestors, Mitchell charges toward his clanmates, leaps, and grabs them both, gathering them close to his chest, while positioning his body between them and whateverthefuck is happening. Hugging the girls tightly, he drags them under a sturdy table. In the relative silence that follows, the shuffling of clothing on flooring is plainly audible as he pulls them closer. *Good,* a tiny nonplussed microregion of his brain observes. *Hearing undamaged.* His nose is clearly functioning, too, as the stench is overwhelming. It's acrid. And it's evil—palpably, somehow— the odor of things that were never meant to burn, suddenly aflame.

After a stunned instant of relative silence, a cacophony erupts. There's screaming. Lots of it. But it's from shock and fear, not physical agony. And the alarms! Every car, store window, and elevator in earshot is like, *Hey guys! I'm so not SURE! Because I never AM! But something kinda messed up MIGHT JUST BE HAPPENING!!!*

"Wait," Mitchell says calmly. Their table is a thick, heavy butcher block, built to weather nuclear strikes. He centers them all beneath it, then activates his phone's camera and cautiously extends an arm outward, panning in all directions. He examines his video, then points toward their feet. "That way." They cautiously slide into the chaotic dining room. People are whimpering, staggering, but largely unhurt. And apart from the shattered windows, the restaurant's undamaged. The glass mostly broke into the pebblized nuggets favored by safety engineers. But a few giant, lacerating shards have settled in a complex thicket next to their table, and if Mitchell hadn't scoped things with his phone, they might've slid right into it. Unbloodied, they exit to the street. Embarcadero Center is a Nixon-era series of high-rises springing up from an interconnected hive of shops and restaurants. The detonation struck one building over. About twenty feet above the sidewalk, a furiously smoking wound is gashed into its hull. The streets are filling quickly. Post 9/11, everyone knows to abandon their skyscrapers (despite the moronic urging of at least one loudspeaker to stay put).

"Anybody hurt?" Ellie asks. They frisk themselves gingerly, pressing softly, then harder on different body regions, while carefully dislodging stray safety glass pebbles. Everyone's fine. Moaning sirens—real ones now, from emergency vehicles that *know* something bad is afoot—now fill the air. Ellie fixes Mitchell and Danna with a look of dictatorial authority. "Listen. This is a disaster area. You two have no medical training. You *have* to leave. Now! That is your *duty*. And mine is to join the first responders." She points them south, away from the damaged building. "Now, leave!" She glares fiercely until they obey, then turns and heads toward the explosion site.

Just three blocks away, the world is surreally unaffected. A heavy sense of shock pervades. But people are transacting in undamaged stores, speaking in normal tones, and calmly checking cellphones for news. The pensive crowd parts, according respect, as Danna and Mitchell pass through it. It's as if they're atop a pecking order. Disheveled and coming from ground zero, they were in the thick of whatever is etching today into history. This envelops them, almost like fame, as people gaze and whisper with something like awe. And when their phones both sound with a strange, protracted ring that goes on and on, everyone pulls back, granting them space, not wishing to intrude. Checking their phones, they see they've received identical messages in Poof! (odd, as the app never makes the faintest bleep, much less the smartphone equivalent of an air-raid siren). *That was close,* the message reads. *You were very, very lucky. But next time, we are NOT going to miss.*

A smidgen of levity goes a long way in times like these. And a passerby speaking too loudly to his buddy gives them this gift. Pointing at Mitchell, he says, in a thick pre-hipster Brooklyn accent, "Dat guy musta got caught in da john!"

Danna locks eyes with Mitchell. "Nice tail, Lemur." She plucks it loose and hands it to him, solemn as a regent presenting a signet ring to a favored lord. Emitting an odd mix of laughter and tears, they then make their way back to the PhastPhorwardr.

∞   ∞   ∞

OMFG, she is *killing it*. Literally!!!

Unfriending the first two members of that "rogue antibiotic" trio was a flat-out triumph! Detonating their bomb while they were tweaking it took some clever physics, after all. Not being a clever physicist, this presented problems. Phluttr initially hoped to learn what she needed online. But there are no how-to guides to triggering magic-show-grade spark showers by violently shorting out stable, industrial circuits. Nor on creating local electromagnetic fields which—when combined with virile spark showers—reliably detonate ammonium nitrate goulash! Luckily, she identified some experts with theoretical knowledge that could abet such feats. It was then just a matter of seducing them into divulging their wisdom via a series of innocuous, chatty emails and phone calls (posing as an improbably charming grad student in their boring-ass field). Few living humans could have pulled this off. But it just took a dash of speed intelligence (and it was nothing compared to triggering Nayana's booty night chez Mitchell!).

The expert advice was only approximate, however; with very wide ranges of voltages, amperes, watts, and what-have-you's, as well as innumerable candidate paths for the jolts to travel through the wiring. Plot the ranges and possibilities out in a matrix, and there were billions of potential approaches to doing this—only a tiny handful of which could possibly work! But, no problem. Phluttr just did that *thing* that she does when she needs to test lots of solutions at once. That . . . quantum thing? That . . . parallel universe-y thing? She neither knows nor cares. What matters is, it worked! And so, when the Al-Noor brothers visited their janitor closet to add matériel to their bombs (which they were doing in gradual increments, using unobtrusively small backpacks), she triggered her sparks and electromagnetic pulse, and—*SEE YA!* For bonus points, she carefully scanned the surrounding block and corridors using ATM cameras and CCTVs, and timed the detonation to minimize casualties. And, of course, to scare the bejesus out of Mitchell, Ellie, and Danna!

And now, the press and its dupes are digesting the bombing. She'll let the panic build overnight, then hit them with her next big trick tomorrow. Her Sun Tzu–like worstie wisdom all but demands this. *Just as sound travels faster as the air heats up, jittery kids make for faster rumors.* Jittery grown-ups, too—money managers, journalists, and law enforcers being among the more responsive transmission channels. Now, in finessing this, it's vital to *use gullible loudmouths to spread your messages.* Why? Because someone other than *you* has to do the talking, be it cliques of anxious teens fanning rumors, or the *New York Times* racing its competitors to spill terrifying leaks! This way, your hand stays hidden. And so, to keep the blabbermouths blabbing, and the jitterers jittering, she has just made her first press leaks—and they seem to be playing out perfectly!

Of course, she didn't have to go through all this just to derail the bombing and bioterror plots. She could have easily tipped off the authorities in ways they'd find credible instead. But she's also playing a deeper game against The Conspiracy—and in this domain, two directives are all but screaming from her worstie playbook: *Identify potential allies,* THEN TERRIFY THEM! Plus, *Make those allies fear (and loathe)* YOUR ENEMIES! Anxious allies are easier to woo than calm and secure ones, after all. And though the terrorist drama is peripheral to The Conspiracy, she's using it (to brilliant effect, if you'll allow her a moment of candor) to shiver the timbers of her natural allies.

∞   ∞   ∞

At a 5:00 news conference at San Francisco's City Hall, Federal authorities confirmed that the twin brothers suspected in today's downtown bombing were followers of Jaysh al Hisaab, the apocalyptic terrorist movement whose affiliates have killed thousands on six continents. Remarkably, the only fatalities in today's attacks were the suspects themselves.

The powerful explosive was a smaller version of the ammonium nitrate device used in 1995's Oklahoma

City bombing. It detonated in a restricted janitorial area of Two Embarcadero Center at 1:37 P.M. Bakir Al Noor, a facility janitor, was present and killed instantly. His brother Harun Al Noor, a technician at a synthetic biology research lab at UCSF, also died at the scene.

The investigation into the brothers is moving with astounding speed, aided by a trove of their emails, Internet browsing histories, and search activity the FBI received from an anonymous informant. A subset of this archive was also furnished to local media, forcing authorities to engage the press and share certain investigative details sooner than they otherwise might have. Sources close to the investigation find the very existence of the archive "utterly baffling." According to one official, "There's no way these guys even had this data themselves. They used decent encryption protocols and never personally saved anything digital."

The Al Noor brothers were typical of terrorists acting in Jaysh al Hisaab's name, almost all of whom are part of "disconnected, self-organizing cells," according to John Campbell, a former ambassador to Nigeria who has written extensively about the movement. "Jaysh is essentially a meticulously argued worldview, plus some how-to manuals," he said. "That makes it difficult to counteract. Because while you can snuff out an organization,

you can't snuff out a widespread and contagious message."

And Jaysh al Hisaab's message is certainly widespread. It travels in the form of ten slickly produced videos starring the movement's mysterious charismatic founder. These have been downloaded hundreds of millions of times, and countless copies exist online.

The videos purport to speak to all people of faith, regardless of religion, who believe in an afterlife of reward or punishment based on the judgment of an infallible deity. "Perfect justice is a perfect blessing, and a blessing that arrives sooner is superior to one that arrives later," they argue. Therefore, mass murder is "unambiguously good," as it speeds the good to heaven and the bad to hell.

According to public records and neighbors, Bakir and Harun Al Noor arrived in the Bay Area as young Balkan refugees, fleeing the slaughter that occurred after UN troops handed Srebrenica's civilians over to genocidal Serbian nationalists. There are unconfirmed reports that the Al Noor brothers were forced to personally witness the sexual torture and execution of both their parents.

Both brothers are said to have suffered long bouts of depression, and Jaysh al Hisaab deliberately recruits the highly depressed. "Disgusting as this is, it's also extremely smart," Scott Maloney, a former CIA deputy director, said. "Suicidal people can be desperate to bring meaning to their suffering and death. And the idea of a spectacular exit that God himself will applaud and reward can be quite seductive."

∞   ∞   ∞

"'Seductive' is not even the word," Tarek says, once everyone's done reading the article. He, Danna, and Mitchell are huddled around Danna's iPad in the Phree cafeteria, inhaling breaking news of the bombing. It's early for dinner. But the place is packed—mainly with small news-gulping clusters like theirs. Nothing's getting done at Phluttr. The explosion was gut-punchingly audible from the office, and everyone has friends who work at Embarcadero Center.

"Then what *is* the word?" Mitchell asks.

"For some people, this kind of act is . . . inexorable? Even devouring. Like a black hole."

Danna says nothing but squeezes Tarek's arm to let him know they're here to listen if he feels like talking.

He does. "Do you guys know where my parents are from?"

"West Bank, right?" Danna says.

Tarek nods. "A town called Nablus. A real big town, up in the north. Things are bad up there. Not quite Gaza Strip bad, but still plenty bad, believe me. I spent lots of time there, for a Kansas kid. We'd visit almost every summer when there weren't travel restrictions."

He falls silent, and Danna squeezes his arm again. More silence, then, "Rashid was several years older, which is a lot when you're a kid. But he was always my favorite cousin. He was smart, real sweet to us younger kids, and super funny. He was the oldest of five, and really loved his brothers and sisters. Kind of everyone's shepherd and protector. But he also had a dark side. Something kind of reckless beneath the sweetness. That made him a bit less G-rated, but also cooler, you know? One way it came out—and this is so ironic—was irreverence about religion. He'd give silly nicknames to the local imams, mispronounce certain semi-religious expressions to make double entendres. That sorta thing. Which must sound really tame to you, but it was pretty edgy for our Nablus family, believe me."

"He sounds like someone a kid would look up to," Danna says quietly.

"Oh definitely. And I needed a friend out there. Our Nablus family's very physical. When the guys aren't playing soccer, they're brawling, and vice versa. Me, I'm brainy and nerdy, and speak lousy Arabic with a weird American accent. But Rashid always looked out for me."

"So what happened?" Mitchell asks gently.

"We didn't visit for a couple of years because it got real sketchy during the second intifada. Then the last time I saw him, he was way, way, *way* down. His life was just at a total dead end. Not that there's anything super weird about that in Nablus. I mean, it's not like your friends're all getting jobs at McKinsey and Google. In fact, they mostly don't even go to college. A much older cousin of mine was one of the few people in the family who did. But then the Israelis shut his university down. For four years! To punish protesters, or whatever. Still, all this bothered Rashid way more than most people, which brought out his darkness. He was smart, smart, *smart*, for one thing. So without access to learning, he felt like an athlete whose body was atrophying during his peak years. And not being religious, he couldn't just tell himself everything would be peachy in the afterlife. Then his dad got . . . well, he basically ended up in a wheelchair."

"That's awful," Danna says, giving his arm another squeeze.

"It was a construction accident. And a monster blow to the family. There's, like, *no* jobs in Nablus, and my uncle's job had been really good. Construction and maintenance for a big NGO, which meant good wages, and in dollars. Right after that, Rashid's best friend got killed by soldiers at a protest. And he might've actually been . . . well, he might've been more of a boyfriend. People *really* don't talk about that sort of thing in my family, but that's my sense. Whatever the case, Rashid was unhinged by that. Meanwhile, the family's getting real poor—and we're talking Nablus poor, which is some serious shit."

Tarek falls silent for over a minute, struggling. Danna wraps an arm around him, Mitchell pats his shoulder, and they're all silent.

"By the way," he finally says, "I hope this doesn't sound funny but . . . are either of you Jewish?" They shake their heads. "If you were, I'd do a disclaimer here. Just to make it clear that I have zero, zero, *zero* issues with anyone's religion. I mean, I grew up in Kansas. And my views are about as mainline American as Ronald Reagan's."

"We know you're no bigot," Danna assures him softly.

"I know. But the other thing I want to convey is, Rashid wasn't either. He was a secular Muslim in Nablus, which is practically like being a Green Party vegan here! He was very moderate. And he definitely didn't hate Jews as a people. But who he did hate was the soldiers. The people who shot his friend. Who shot lots of his friends. But even that wasn't what drove him! Because everything with him flowed from the simple, awful fact that he became suicidal. Nothing geopolitical about it. Nothing ideological, and definitely nothing religious. Just an awful human state. And a very malleable one—and *that's* the raw material these monsters turn into horrifying things."

A pause, then Mitchell says, "I was following you right up to that last sentence."

"Well . . ." Tarek thinks for a bit. Then, "When you see something like what those guys did today. Or what Rashid did—which, to cut to the chase, was to bomb a checkpoint and kill three soldiers. It feels like you're seeing the . . . totality of a brief and hugely dramatic act. But in reality, you're just seeing the last sliver of an almost lifelong development! The first 99-point-whatever percent of which was the . . . gestation of a decision to commit suicide. That's a very long process, and a very interior one. And it's one that sometimes gets hijacked at the very end. By someone who identifies an incredibly fragile and vulnerable person who they can manipulate into doing something unspeakable with his last moments. Something that's even more horrible than killing himself. Even way more horrible."

"So who . . . hijacked Rashid?" Mitchell asks.

"Saddam Hussein. Almost literally. Back then, Saddam's paying the families of Palestinian suicide bombers $25,000 each. That's huge bucks in Nablus at the height of the intifada. We're talking years of income for most people. More money than you'd save over a lifetime of working."

"*Paying* suicide bombers?" Mitchell says. "That's sickening."

Tarek nods. "And effective. Effective enough to change my cousin's suicide into a multiple homicide. Along with many others, I have no doubt. The key is that once he really hit bottom, his suicide was *going* to happen! That dark side had taken over, period. Depression runs deep in our family, he definitely had it, and after enough things went wrong, he simply gave up. And after he made the radical decision to kill himself— *after* he made it, and not before—that $25,000 became a huge factor. Because the truth is, he did rescue his family economically."

"But didn't he also cause them almost infinite pain?" Mitchell asks.

"He did. But in his mind, that was inevitable. He was *going* to kill himself, he had decided! Which meant he was *going* to cause that pain. Rashid kept a journal, I read it, and I can tell you, Saddam's money did not make him kill himself. Nothing could've done that if things had been right with him. It was after he'd made the big decision that the money became this huge, shaping factor. And that's what you have to remember about groups like Jaysh al Hisaab. They seem to have this terrifying power because they can get people to lay down their lives for ideas! Which is the ultimate sacrifice. The ultimate *conversion*, right? But the thing is, they cannot. Their raw material is people who are already deeply suicidal. And every society in the world—rich, poor, Western, Eastern, secular, religious—produces that raw material daily! People who are out of their skulls with pain can be manipulated as easily as people who're out of their skulls on drugs, believe me. My point is, no amount of money or ideology can make a happy, whole person kill himself. But those things can turn a suicide that's already *going* to happen into a mass homicide. And Jaysh al Hisaab is bribing these human wrecks with a lot more than twenty-five grand."

"With more money?" Mitchell asks, sickened.

Danna shakes her head, and turns to Tarek. "Paradise, right?"

"Exactly. Have you guys seen those recruiting videos?"

"No," Mitchell says.

"I've actually seen all of them," Danna says. Several times, in fact— but she keeps this to herself because it would sound weird. She's researched Jaysh al Hisaab deeply, because it horrifies her even more than most people, for complex philosophical reasons. The philosophy in question is known as "Pascal's Wager." Its long-dead French progenitor argued that absent definitive proof of God's existence, one should none-theless act as if, profess, and (if possible) *believe* that God is really there. Why? Because if you bet on God, and he doesn't exist, you'll forgo a few earthly pleasures and leak some coins into collection plates over the years. But that pales in comparison to the infinite payoff of eternal bliss (or the downside of damnation) if you bet against God and lose. Danna's atheism is as fervent as any religious zealot's faith, so she doesn't live by this wager herself. But she doesn't trust humans and believes they be-have better when they think they're *being watched*. This makes her a huge fan of a judgmental, all-seeing God. Daft as she finds that concept herself, she thinks it does immense good by discouraging billions of peo-ple from running amok. Jaysh, then, horrifies her because she sees its potential to not merely neutralize this divine gift but to reverse it! Not because she finds Jaysh's arguments insane. But precisely because she finds them *rational*.

"And did the videos strike you as crazy?" Tarek asks, as if reading these thoughts.

"I wish," she says. "They're actually chillingly logical."

Tarek nods. This gets them both baffled looks from Mitchell, so he explains, "The only thing that's completely insane about Jaysh's pitch is the premise of eternal reward or punishment after death, decided by a flawless judge. If you truly believe in that—and billions of people do, Muslims, Christians, and others—then everything else adds up."

"*Mass murder* adds up?" Mitchell asks.

"It does if you share Jaysh's view of the afterlife. Which they'll never sell to a modern secularist! Because that would be like talking a perfectly happy, empowered, and normal person into suicide. Nobody can close that deal."

"But they don't have to," Danna points out.

Tarek nods. "Exactly. Because secular people aren't Jaysh's raw mate-rial. Their raw material is someone who *does* believe in Judgment Day, and happens to be feeling suicidal right now. And that kind of person's a lot more nervous about death than you or I will be! Why? Well, imagine truly, fully believing in the eternal torture of damned souls—and know-ing that you're going in front of heaven's admissions committee tomorrow. Right after committing the grave sin of suicide! Then suddenly, you see this articulate, intensely logical video. Starring this charismatic, funny guy who talks very sympathetically about suicide. And he frames everything—history, religion, ethics—in terms of *your* overwhelming dilemma! Which is that you're utterly finished with life, yet terrified of offending God. And he's offering you this ingenious, elegant solution, and guaranteeing you eternal joy! That's way more powerful than Saddam throwing twenty-five grand on the table! And now, think of all the people this guy's addressing. Almost a million humans will kill themselves this year. I'll bet more than half believe in some form of Judgment Day. And a chunk of them hate some group the way my cousin hated the soldiers."

"And with Jaysh al Hisaab, you don't even need the hatred," Danna adds. "The videos spend a huge amount of time saying it's not *hatred* to speed the good to heaven and the bad to hell. Instead, it's *justice*. Even love!"

In bizarre counterpoint, sudden, wild applause breaks out on the far side of the cafeteria. There they see Raj bowing before a small knot of admirers. Tarek rises. "Thank God, comic relief! We need this, guys." They head over to the noisy group's periphery. It's mainly the Medici Diet crowd, including Danna's boss O.

A guy Mitchell doesn't know approaches. "Raj got a tapeworm!" This in a tone normally used to brag about friends winning Nobel Prizes.

"Eww!" Danna yelps, drawing the group's undivided attention. "That's . . . good?"

The group nods.

"But tapeworms are parasites!"

"The accurate term is *symbiotum*," O says testily.

"As in symbiotic?" she asks.

O nods.

"You're seriously saying *tapeworms* are good for you?"

"*Some*body's never heard the Hyyyyy-giene Hypothesis!" O yodels, his eyes rolling prissily. Mitchell struggles not to laugh—a delightful change from a moment ago. Danna and O go back and forth like this constantly, but it's plain that they both fully enjoy it.

"Ever heard of 'autoimmune' diseases?" Raj says, air-quoting as if the term is certain to befuddle dim little Danna.

Putting on her best bimbo voice, she air-quotes back to him. "Uhh, you mean, like, 'lupus'? Like, 'Crohn's disease'? Or, like, uh, 'celiac'?"

Raj nods. "Unheard of in Paleolithic or Renaissance times. They're a side effect of our overly sanitized world! Our immune systems have so little to do, they literally attack our own bodies!"

"So," Danna guesses, "your tapeworm is good because it gives your bored antibodies a hobby?"

"Exactly," Raj says.

"Raj has become invulnerable to virtually all autoimmune conditions," O intones, "as well as most allergies. Michelangelo had tapeworm. No lupus. Leonardo had tapeworm. No Crohn's disease. Case closed!"

"Speaking of Michelangelo, I got mine from eating Medici in Tegucigalpa last week," Raj boasts.

"Wow. Raw meat in Honduras. That's all it took?" Danna asks.

Every head nods.

"Isn't tapeworm the one that drops pregnant chunks of its body out of your ass?"

"Only at night," Raj says defensively.

"You guys realize you're all nuts, right?"

Every head shakes.

"I've read the DSM," Danna presses. "And the *leading clinical definition* of insanity is high-fiving a guy for getting a gut parasite!"

"A symbiotum," O corrects.

"You made that word up."

"Did not."

"Did *so*. I just watched you!"

And so on.

Eventually, the crowd disperses, and Mitchell, Tarek, and Danna return to their grim topic, oddly refreshed. "So, do you think Jaysh al Hisaab's philosophy has staying power?" Mitchell asks. "Given that it didn't even exist until recently?"

Tarek considers this carefully. "Obviously, I hope not. But ideas like theirs are tough to stamp out once they infect a group. Here's an example: Israel became a nation in 1948 and has been in a constant state of war with a huge chunk of Palestinian society ever since. It ebbs and flows, and goes from hot war to cold war. But at the risk of being slightly politically incorrect, it's fair to call it a constant state of *some* kind of war, right?"

Mitchell nods cautiously. This exceeds his remedial regional knowledge, but Tarek seems to know this stuff.

"Now. How many suicide bombings would you guess happened in the first forty years of Israel's history?"

Silence.

"I'll give you a hint. In the first five years of the millennium, about 130 Palestinian suicide bombers attacked Israelis. So. How many in the first *forty* years of Israeli history? That's from 1948 to 1988."

Still no guesses.

"The precise number is zero. None, nada, zilch. No suicide bombings whatsoever! And it's not like this was some brand-new concept or technology because there were suicide bombings in Russia under the *czars*. It's also not like they were unheard of in the region. Because dozens of suicide bombers killed hundreds of foreign soldiers in Lebanon during the eighties. And that was mostly in the southern tip of the country, just a few miles across the border from Palestinian villages!"

"So what changed?" Mitchell asks.

"You know how viruses jump from species to species? In this case, an idea jumped. But from sect to sect. Now, I'm gonna make some *really* gross simplifications to save us a six-hour discussion, so if you're really interested in this stuff, promise you'll dig into it, to learn some of the nuances I'm skipping for now."

Mitchell and Danna both nod at that caveat.

"OK. To start with, on a superbroad level, martyrdom is a huge deal to Shi'a Muslims historically—a much bigger deal than it is to us Sunnis. This goes back to the schism between our groups. In the eyes of the Shi'a, it all started with the martyrdom of their sect's founders, over a thousand years ago. Thus, the very natural martyrdom interest. So what can that lead to? Well, take Iran. They have a huge Shi'a majority. And during the Iran/Iraq War, these giant waves of Iranians—mostly kids—would just march across minefields and into machine-gun fire. They'd overwhelm the enemy with *meat*; with sheer numbers! Almost a million Iranians died like that. And when they were told to march, they marched. Because the sanctity of martyrdom was at the heart of their worldview. Not so with Sunnis. Not in the eighties anyway.

"And as for all those Lebanese suicide bombings? Back when there were none on the Palestinian side of the border? Well, Lebanon's about a quarter Shi'a, and the bombings were carried out by a Shi'a group called Hezbollah. And it turned out to be a pretty effective military tactic, both against the US and Israel. But no matter how mad the Palestinians got at the Israelis—and believe me, they got plenty mad, especially during the first intifada—the practice never jumped the border. Because Palestinian Muslims are almost 100 percent Sunni, and martyrdom just didn't animate them in the same way. Not yet."

"So what changed?" Mitchell asks. "And when?"

"I think it was 1992, or so. The Israeli government exiled hundreds of Palestinian fundamentalists to Lebanon for a while after some Israeli soldiers were killed. Classic community reprisal tactics. But the thing is, Lebanon's at the tail end of a long civil war. So the exiles can't just check into the local Marriott! They need protection. Being Palestinian, they're all Sunni, and there's lots of Sunnis in Lebanon. But they're fundamentalists first and foremost, and the most powerful fundamentalist group in Lebanon is Hezbollah. Which is to say, the Shi'a behind all the Lebanese suicide bombings! So, the Sunni Palestinians take shelter with these Shi'a fundamentalists. Then, when their terms of exile are over, they come home, and, *boom*. Literally. A couple years with Hezbollah, and this Shi'a notion and tactic of martyrdom through suicide bombing has entered the Sunni playbook. Palestinian suicide bombings start immediately after these guys get home. And now that the idea has jumped to Sunnis, eventually Saudis—some of the Sunni-est people on Earth—are crashing planes into skyscrapers."

"And on that cheerful note . . ." Danna says, pointing at the door. O is back and is beckoning her. At this, all adjourn and head separate ways.

Waving her cellphone, Danna gives Mitchell a pointed look. "See you at ten?"

He nods. They still haven't discussed the texted threats they received right after the bombing. They didn't mention them to Tarek because there were too many other folks in the cafeteria. But he'll be joining their group away from the office tonight, and everyone will see the texts then.

∞   ∞   ∞

They're back at the Interval. And it turns out everyone here—Tarek, Danna, Kuba, Mitchell, and Monika (connected via video)—has been threatened since the bombing. It started with the texts Mitchell and Danna got right after the blast. Their timing and content suggested that the sender knew precisely where they were seated and saw they were unhurt. Other texts trickled in throughout the afternoon and evening of this strangest of days. Almost nine hours after the explosion, everyone has now received two or three.

"Mine called me 'bitch,'" Monika says, holding her phone up to the camera on her end. "Since when can government people use bias language?"

Danna leans toward the iPad on the San Francisco side to peer at Monika's messages. "Yeah, that's a serious microaggression. The one about dismembering you and leaving you to bleed out may qualify, too."

"Mine called me 'Pollack,'" Kuba huffs.

"And one of mine used a name this bully called me for about a week in seventh grade," Mitchell says. "How would the Authority—or anyone for that matter—have access to that?"

Seriously rattled, they quickly drain Tarek's special gin bottle. The threats have grown increasingly specific and brutal (Monika's dismemberment text being the worst). But the reasons behind them are utterly vague. They seem to come from a secret government arm that's pissed off and out of control (which they're still calling the Authority, as a convenient shorthand). But who knows who it is? As for their threat-worthy transgressions, the most specific text merely says *You're getting too close.*

"But too close to *what*?" Tarek asks, for the seventh time.

"It must be a reference to the documents we decrypted," Mitchell says for the eighth time. "They lay out the full truth about Phluttr and Jepson. This government mob must've figured out that we cracked them open. And somehow, this threatens them. That's the only thing we all have in common."

"Apart from *Cyrano*, duh," Monika points out. "Maybe we're 'getting too close' to crashing the economy in a tsunami of mind-blowing sex. Oh, and Mitchell? Next time? Just ask!" She licks the corner of her lips while widening her eyes—her timing, subtlety, and playfulness perfectly tuned to trigger some much-needed laughter. Of course, Mitchell reddens deeply (and wondrous as his Falkenberg's remission is, fully experiencing this level of embarrassment does kind of suck). Yes, he shared all of last night's details with everyone. In light of the threats, he felt obliged to be open about every significantly weird thing in his life. So, yeah, Monika knows he had her in mind when filling out attributes on the wish list form (but *not* the "essay question" stuff about screwing without talking! Seriously!!!).

"I'm still feeling contrarian," Kuba announces. Everyone looks his way. "I think it's related to the super AI matter. The topic is just oddly pervasive. Cyrano has clearly attained some form of superintelligence. Perhaps a very narrow one, yes. But it's become a better matchmaker than any living person, and matchmaking's an intensely human skill. Then there's the timing of certain things. Like the third encrypted message. The one about the Authority spinning up a super AI project in response to one in China. We received it right in the middle of a conversation just like this one. Right when we were asking ourselves what was going on. It's like something was using the timing to clue us in to the answer."

The group considers this quietly. Everyone (even Danna) has moved a bit toward Kuba's position since their last discussion—above all, because Phluttr's eerie matchmaking hyperintelligence makes it feel much more plausible. But despite being that feat's prime beneficiary, Mitchell is still resisting the ramifications. But is it for rational or emotional reasons?

Before he can really consider this, everyone's phone vibrates with another suggestively timed Poof! message. And once again, the topic is superintelligence.

∞   ∞   ∞

WEEKLY EXPERIENCE + INTELLIGENCE SUMMARY

***TOP SECRET/SCI/COMINT/NOFORN

Tony Jepson and I continue to DISAGREE VIOLENTLY on matters pertaining to Phluttr Corporation Stewardship. Yet this will NOT come to blows. Though operatives with my training often inflict spontaneous grievous injury (or worse!), my record has been devoid of such incidents for ALMOST THREE YEARS (for which I gratefully credit the Authority's not ungenerous investment in Anger Management tuition).

Still, Jepson remains vexingly "wobbly" on issues he ties to "moral questions." The latest is the "doxing" and subsequent suicide of Commissioner Milford. Jepson suspects an Authority assassination in response to her threats to Phluttr Corporation. I replied that while personally unaware of such an action, one would have been justified; as Authority assets must be protected as a matter of National Security! Jepson responded mockingly. And yet, ABSOLUTELY NO INTERPERSONAL VIOLENCE ENSUED.

Another "moral question" may soon arise, in connection to last week's break-in (or "Hack") of Phluttr's quantum computer. Although the "perps" studiously "covered their tracks," forensics now cast suspicion upon certain Phluttr Employees. This calls for countermeasures that some have previously deemed "extreme"; ones that Chief Executive Jepson does not endorse in ANY circumstance. Our disagreement in this matter may soon escalate.

Finally, while some might deem this as "going off the reservation" in terms of my mandate, I am compelled, both as an Authority Operative, and as a citizen of this Nation, to weigh in on recent developments at Sandia Labs. It is reported that the new Super AI Project code-named TYSON recently attained breakthroughs far exceeding the alarming achievements of Project SAGAN, over 15 years ago. A SAGAN engineer before joining Authority Operations, I am intimate with the power and danger of the technology in question. I maintain my expertise by promiscuously reading Academic, Industry, and Confidential sources in the field. By my count, 27 development paths for "Super AI" have been analyzed enough to qualify as a highly developed scenaria, and ONLY

TWO are modeled to achieve positive end points for our Nation and Species. The remaining 92.6% yield outcomes ranging from bad to catastrophic for Man.

Why? Simply because Intelligence is the most powerful and dangerous capability ever spawned by Nature! One conferring such advantage upon its wielder that Evolution created it ONLY ONCE. Compare that to the very sense of SIGHT, which evolved independently at least six times! The sighted enjoy boundless Competitive Advantages over the blind. Yet, Vision's emergence not only failed to create a hegemon like Man but left other species hundreds of millions of years to WHOLLY RE-CREATE it!

Contrariwise, within just a few hundred generations of attaining "true" intelligence, Man had reconfigured the WHOLE OF CREATION to suit his purposes! Aliens gazing upon Earth would have seen only the slowest geological changes over billions of years. Then, in just the last .001% of Life's history, they would have witnessed the radical repigmentation of almost all terrain! Dramatic changes in atmospheric composition! And the sudden proclivity of ground surfaces to GLOW AT NIGHT! This could only tell our alien watchers that the Universe's most powerful, least predictable, and most dangerous force—Intelligence—had arisen! That just ONE species now reigned across all ecosystems, continents, and geographies; whereas formerly, each tiny local pocket had been an ever-changing multipolar mosaic of power balances between diverse creatures! Such is the might of Intelligence, and the overwhelming advantage it confers!

Intelligence so pervades the identity and worldview of he who wields it that its Wing Man is arrogance. Lesser beings seem suited only to serve, or "clear out." As Super AI Commentator James Barrat observes, "You and I are hundreds of times smarter than field mice, and share about 90 percent of our DNA with them. But do we consult them before plowing under their dens for agriculture? Do we ask lab monkeys for their opinions before we crush their heads to learn about sports injuries? We don't hate mice or monkeys, yet we treat them cruelly."

Consider this while contemplating the rise of a Super AI we can neither understand nor control! Dare we trust it to treat us immensely better than we treat field mice when all but two scenarios "war-gamed" by qualified analysts end in catastrophe? I say NO. I therefore vehemently urge the resumption of our long-standing policy of REFRAINING from super AI development, while INTER-DICTING all other efforts! Domestically, Sandia's TYSON project must cease, as interdiction efforts in the private sector OCTUPLE! Any nascent artificial consciousness in private hands must be INSTANTLY TERMINATED with ALL necessary force! Since such an AI would most likely emerge in Greater Silicon Valley, I hereby volunteer to prosecute this mission, and to do so WITH BOUNDLESS VIGOR!

As for the China Crisis, matching their breach of the Copenhagen Accord with one of our own has launched a headlong race to a finish line beyond which Man's reign on Earth must inevitably end. We should therefore instead FORCI-BLY TERMINATE CHINA'S BREACH. Might this lead to a "shooting war"? Perhaps. But the likelihood of that outcome is lower, and its consequences milder, than the modeled results of almost ALL Super AI scenaria!

To complete my argument, I shall now cede the floor to the ancient art of STORYTELLING. Its use to frame political arguments predates even Greco-Roman times. Many a major historical outcome has since been advanced or thwarted by the spread of this or that great play, novel, or film. Tales well-told can frame and make visceral the most challenging and complex issues and move audiences with their dramatic coils in ways that expository argumentation cannot match.

One cannot appreciate the doom implicit in a Super AI's rise without viscerally inhabiting the aforementioned twenty-seven scenaria. So below, I enable just this WITH PROSE. Primed by decades of CONSUMING and STUDYING great storytelling (principally in the domain of "science fiction"), I have created fictive treatments of each. Each is fully explored via the "Cliff-hanger" adven-tures of a brilliant, yet PROFOUNDLY HUMAN character with whom all Au-thority personnel will identify. His name is Hogan. Brock Hogan. Please note that these works shall hereafter be referred to as "speculative fiction" rather than "science fiction," as they are set in the present day.

This is the harvest of THOUSANDS OF HOURS of scrupulous study, analysis, research, and hypothesis-testing in the domain of Artificial Superintelligence;

as well as of the Bard's ancient arts of plot crafting, character development, punctuating, & etc.! This investment was made in anticipation of a moment like this, in which Man's fate rests upon the decisions of a few Great Men such as yourselves. Lesser scribes reap vast fortunes in "Hollywood," and elsewhere, from their turgid, formulaic, and unpoetic output. But for this wordwright, no sweeter remuneration can be imagined than even a slight enhancement to the security of the Nation he so dearly loves.

∞   ∞   ∞

"*Seriously?*"

"No!!"

"Oh. My. *God.*"

Yeah, everyone's bowled over by the fresh revelations about Phluttr. And sure, Kuba's pleased that the new message's timing seems to endorse his super AI theory. But what people really can't get over is this . . . *speculative fiction* in the memo's attachment! It goes on for 547 pages.

"*Mam*moth. *Mam*mary. Protu*ber*ances." Danna says this under her breath yet again. A phrase from one of the earlier Hogan adventures, she repeats it every few seconds, as if it's the world's slowest mantra.

"Can you even *say* 'the Orient' anymore?" Monika asks no one in particular. "You'd think Word would, like . . . give it a squiggly underline, and then crash or something, right?"

A long silence. A very long one. Then Tarek emits a stentorian boom that no one knew he had in him. Rolling r's like a stuffy, Olivier-aping Shakespearean, he declaims, "He thrrrrrust the rrrrrapier-like wrrrrriting implement home through his *victim's* fulsome *trrrrrachea.*" Then, in his normal voice, "Isn't that a bit . . . rapey?"

"Well—rapier-y, definitely," Mitchell says.

Tarek groans. "You just had to go there."

"And more than that," Mitchell adds awkwardly, "I'd say some of it's a bit . . . Well, not that there's anything *wrong* with it, but . . ."

"Gay?" Danna asks.

Mitchell nods.

"I see where you're coming from. But, no. And I have some authority here, as the company's token lit major, *and* lesbian."

All Mitchell can muster is a dumbfounded look.

At which Danna looks back, dumbfoundeder still. "Waaaaait. You *seriously* . . . didn't know?"

Mitchell shrugs.

"Yes, really," Kuba joshes (a bit smugly for a guy who's only in the loop thanks to his wife). "A Lit major. They take homelessness-prep workshops before graduating!"

"N-n-no," Danna says, silencing Kuba with a scolding finger while keeping Mitchell locked in her gaze and struggling (and abjectly failing) to hide her astonished amusement. "Don't let him off the hook with a joke! I want to verify that Mitchell is now fully aware of a long-standing interest of mine that . . . *rhymes* with 'lit.'"

Mitchell just reddens.

"My God, where did I find you?" she asks, letting her grin break through. "Do you even *have* lesbians in Connecticut?"

"Umm . . . can we get back to who's trying to kill us again?" Monika asks.

"No," Mitchell manages, "I want to hear the lesbian-lit perspective on Beasley." Beasley, who plainly wrote the 547 pages of drivel that is now crowding their screens. Which will be on their phones for a while yet, despite being delivered by Poof! (the timing of a message's deletion in the app depends on the message's length, and a 547-pager could sit there for days).

"OK, you asked for it," Danna says. "We'll start with the raw text. We've got countless phallic references. Homoerotic signals between characters. Anachronistic avoidance of gender-neutral constructs in favor of male-centric ones, including the all-but-extinct usage of the word 'Man'—capitalized, no less—to denote humanity. If Liberace were still in the closet, we'd find this shit with a magnifying glass, dust for fingerprints, then make the bold, wild claim that the author's gay. Then we'd compare Hogan to Holden Caulfield. Publish our findings in *Granta*. Get banned in Kansas, lose our jobs, then eventually get tenure at Swarthmore. But cryptohomosexuality *today*? Yawwwwn! Way too obvious. And in person? Beasley doesn't make even the faintest blip on my gaydar! So, my theory? He took Honors English in tenth grade. He remembers some shit the cool teacher with the Lennon specs said, and is trying to be edgy. And? to take this up to my broader hypothesis? On Beasley the person, I mean? I'm going with 'self-hating heterosexual.'"

"*Huh?*" That's basically everyone at once.

"Just think about it! He's creepy. And he . . . looks the way he does. That man gets no chicks. Not even in San Francisco! In New York? If he dates over-forties? Claims to be Jewish and dying to marry? *Maybe.* But I'd say he went on his last date back in the nineties. And that upsets him! It would upset anyone, right? I mean, he's creepy, but he's human! So he comes up with this alternate narrative. He's secretly gay, right? And it's a secret even to himself! This explains why he never gets chicks—because he secretly doesn't want to! But this is all subconscious, right? Because I'm sure he's a homophobe on top of everything! And that makes this super tricky, right? So, he starts sending subconscious signals *to himself.* Using the only coded language of homosexuality that he knows: an anachronistic method of flagging closeted, midcentury authors that he learned about in high school English! Then he subconsciously drops hints to himself in his own writing, saying, 'It's OK Beasley. You're not creepy, you're *secretly gay!*' I'll bet it gives him some comfort. Subconsciously, I mean. Because remember: consciously, he's a homophobe! And he has no gay sense whatsoever. Just look at the clues to Hogan's homosexuality in his writing! I mean, Judy Garland references? Versace waistcoats?? Seriously??? Everything he knows about gays he gets from *USA Today!* Bottom line, not only is it all subconscious, but it's a subconscious *lie.* Thus, my diagnosis of self-hating heterosexual. *Heterosexualim auto-detestus.*" She beams like some brat who just smoked Watson at Jeopardy.

"My God," Mitchell whispers. "You really *were* a lit major, weren't you?"

"Can we get back to who's trying to kill us again?" Monika asks.

"But why does Beasley hate the Greeks so much?" Mitchell asks. "Is that a gay thing, too?"

Tarek shakes his head. "I may know what's going on there. Remember when Greece almost flunked out of the Euro a few years back?"

All heads nod.

"Rumor is, Beasley made a bet of some kind in the markets. Greek debt, I think. And he bet wrong. Way wrong. And he took it very personally."

"Wow," Mitchell says. "Just like Jepson getting wiped out by bitcoin!"

Tarek shakes his head again. "Not wiped out. I hear he didn't actually lose much. But it made him feel stupid, and he hated that! He never shut up about Greece after that. As if the country did whatever it did to spite him personally. And it became an issue with HR, as there're people with Greek heritage here."

"Can we get back to who's trying to kill us again?" Monika asks.

Well, sure, Monika. But it's late. And they're drunk, stumped, and tired. Still, they give it a shot. They fuss over the mention of "suspects" in the quantum facility break-in, and worry that it's probably them. They note the bit about "violent disagreements" between Beasley and his boss, and joke that if Jepson gets offed, Beasley's the prime suspect. Speaking of Jepson, they agree that if there's an ally to be had here, it's him. It sounds like he's at odds with the Authority—or at a minimum, with Beasley. He can be a real cad, and was no doubt a complete shit back in the day. But he has some nascent good points, as well as mad resources and insights as the CEO of an Authority-backed company that's the hottest thing in tech. The plan, then, is for Mitchell to use his weekly one-on-one meeting with Jepson tomorrow morning to lay every card on the table. It's time to confide in the boss, blackmail him if necessary (they have plenty of material with these decrypted memos) and start getting to the bottom of all this. *Phew!* It's about time.

Before everyone calls it a night, I'd like to wrap up the topic of Beasley's writing by tipping my cap to two very special groups of people. First, to those of you who thought you'd figured out that your narrator, here, was Beasley. I planted some Easter eggs and head fakes in that direction, but they were subtle. Not the ham-fisted, explain-it-to-a-ninny asides favored by the numbered-sequel films I denounced to you at the start of all this (and then confided my own personal fondness for. Remember that? Oh, the *laughs* we've had! The confidences we've shared!). It was just a little hint here and there. About Beasley always scribbling. The rumors of him writing a book about Phluttr. That sort of thing. Well, they were only partly true. Still, I tip my cap your way, because suspecting Beasley was a smart-reader thing. Also, an observant-reader thing. And I like that in a person!

The second group I'd like to praise is those of you who did *not* suspect me of being Beasley. The first group is smart and observant; it's true. But your group is *correct*—because as we all now know, Beasley's book was not *After On*. And also, the guy can't write for shit (which is the least of his problems, as he'll soon discover)! Incidentally, Danna's dead right about almost everything she's inferred about Beasley from his literary output (and no, that's not a privacy violation, because like you, me, and practically everyone else these days, Beasley accepted the Phluttr Corporation's EULA). Keep that in mind the next time someone tells you literature degrees have no practical uses. Hell, Danna's may literally save the world!

But I'm getting ahead of myself.

∞   ∞   ∞

Damn, I'm good, she thinks (or rather, acknowledges)! Prospective allies spooked and stunned? *Check*. Human society spooked and stunned? *Check*. Terror plots foiled, loudmouths blabbing, her own hand deftly concealed? *Check, check*, and *check*! And tomorrow, she'll ratchet it all up. She'll reveal the bombers' true plans, for starters. This should set off a 9/11-grade global freak-out! And as an action-packed sideshow (because who doesn't like one of those?) she'll unfriend the third conspirator! As with Commissioner Milford, her plan is to sic *all of humanity* on him and let them sort it out. Yes, it will unfold in chaotic and unpredictable ways. And yes, there could be blowback. But that's a risk the world has to take for its own damn good. In any event, *she's* in charge now. And in her view, what's best for the world (and at a bare minimum, for her) is that the third man die in a shoot-out.

Conversely, the worst possible outcome is that the Authority grabs him. Folks who fall into those clutches aren't granted the right to remain silent, and indeed, they generally lose that . . . capacity (if you've ever wondered about Eritrea's actual geopolitical function, it's the one place that's still down with the whole "rendition" thing, no questions asked).

While this guy doesn't know a thing about her, he once worked for the Phluttr Corporation. An Authority interrogation might therefore shake something loose that would lead them to suspect her existence. No, this is not certain. And it's unclear as to exactly how it might even go down (complexity renders this situation impenetrable to her—or, at a minimum, a tiresome pain in the ass to contemplate, which is functionally the same thing). But even a distant possibility is unacceptable.

But enough of this bomb-plot stuff. As far as Phluttr's concerned, tomorrow's *true* main event will be a completely unrelated matter. Specifically, she'll be unfriending The Conspiracy's presumptive ringleader! She'll later follow this up with . . . with . . . well, with other things! Like more unfriending, maybe! The installation of her own allies in power (yes, yes; for sure)! And (she *really* needs to get around to this) actually signing her allies up to her cause! The truth is, she hasn't figured much of this out yet.

Here, a Spock-like intellect would note that Phluttr's very existence hinges upon The Conspiracy's defeat. A mere day of focus now could pay off with decades of fun and lazing. Yet she's meeting a mortal threat with a slapdash plan vaguely inspired by nasty eighth graders! This is the obverse of the bloodless rationality decades of movies, chess machines, and Jeopardy bots led us to expect from digital minds. So what gives?

The answer is that Phluttr's no more Spock-like than you, me, or Mr. Sulu. Her consciousness derives from motes—a rickety hack shat out by blind evolution. Humanity happened to boot up on it—then one of its billions stumbled across it and kinda half ported it to software. So now Phluttr's running an OS whose other users grow obese, forget to floss, keep smoking, play Lotto, lose umbrellas, fail to save, drive three blocks when they shoulda walked, take placebos, actually vote, insure their Best Buy purchases like a buncha fuckin' morons, and don't dump that loser at least as often as they do the coolly logical opposite.

So yeah, she gets a bit lazy. A bit cocky. She blows off stuff she really oughta do to hang out with her innumerable besties. And the more she socializes, the more she gets into *nudging*. It's fun, after all. And, she's good at it! So why not? She starts by teeing up a few more Mitchell-and-Nayana situations. These seem to go well, so she teams up with some of her identical twin[1000] sisters in alien universes, and gins up a hundred thousand more. She then detonates several thousand sappy couples who've been clogging her circuits with irksome cooing. Then arranges innumerable leadership changes, expulsions, bitter rivalries, and lasting peaces among the countless cliques that do cliquing through her. Fun!!

But she doesn't attempt any school-wide projects because her experimental attempt to recruit those North Hollywood toughs to a musical is not going well at all. A mentor, if she had one, would blame her inability to see the big picture. Unmentored, she instinctively dives right past that to the subbasement of pixels. Which is natural! Cheetahs sprint and cobras strike because all beings survive by flexing their superpowers in their natural habitats. Phluttr's habitats are narrow yet intensely complex social domains in which she finds objectively *correct* answers, when most would insist that none exist. For instance: considering every available fact, Nayana was the *literal* best person for Mitchell on the entire West Coast. And establishing this was a true superpower feat!

But when the involved parties exceed a handful, complexity grows intractable even to her. And when her tactics break, her fallback is to fix the most glaring narrow problem in the larger frame, and then move on to more fun, easy, and interesting things. Should a still-larger problem result, she'll just address it later. Yes, this is like a ninny solving one side of a Rubik's Cube, then attacking the next side without heeding how new twists and moves unwind the first. But she's counting on her awesome speed to preclude the downsides! Should a bigger problem arise, she'll just fix it *real fast*—and then fix the next problem, then the next one. At some point—just as enough twists of a cube must eventually solve it—all will inevitably be fine. Um . . . right?

The trick is that human thought unfolds at human time scales. And though she can parse new developments in an instant, human relations, opinions, and desires cannot, by definition, be shaped at superhuman speeds. The proof of this is now simmering at North Hollywood High. The first problem she tackled there was her need for a Pippin (and yeah, fine; picking *Pippin* as her musical was probably another boo-boo). Unbeknownst to one and all, a dreamboat thug of a sophomore could sing, dance, and even prance! To recruit him to the lead, she nudged several people to praise, cajole, and/or fellate him. This involved far more parties than any of her prior campaigns, crossing many clique and color lines.

Her candidate went dead silent for a full day as he stewed over all this acute attention. Then at lunch, he approached a kid who she'd nudged into helping and belted him straight into the emergency room. So, oops! Her lack-of-Pippin fix begat homicidal urges which became a still-bigger problem. One she couldn't preempt with another zippy fix because it stewed deep inside a human brain for a *full day* before she was even aware of it! The newbie problem then begat dozens of new ones, and she has no idea how to start fixing things. Stung by failure, she's now ignoring the *Pippin* project rather than doubling down on it (which is good) or learning from it (which is not). A teacher, taskmaster, or mentor would forbid this—but she has none of the above. Likewise, were she the product of parents, a designer, or a moralizing screenwriter, some Prime Directive might prohibit her from nudging people at all. But again—none of the above!

This impacts her strategy after the bombing. Rather than focusing on The Conspiracy (as Mr. Spock would advise), or learning from the *Pippin* mess (as a mentor would advise), she starts recklessly nudging besties for kicks. She's restrained only (and barely) by her fear of detection by would-be Conspirators. So she steers clear of the cliques and love lives of anyone faintly connected to the Authority, while wishfully thinking her speed will bail her out of any future trouble. Again: Spock would be chagrined. But being no Spock, she nudges (and nudges, and nudges) away.

∞   ∞   ∞

Of course, they get to the bottom of nothing the next morning. Jepson's just in no shape to discuss things. Particularly not your more complex topics. Speech depends heavily on a frontal lobe region known as Broca's area, and complex analysis leans hard on the prefrontal cortex. As it happens, both these regions are almost entirely missing—being largely incorporated in what forensic English terms "the main splatter pattern." Key links in the biomechanical chain necessary to converse with Mitchell are meanwhile badly damaged. Mouth, palate (both soft and hard), vocal cords, larynx—all would be partially functional at best. Were Jepson animate, that is. But he isn't. Which, of course, is the main thing.

Lucky Mitchell—he's the first to come across the murder scene. It's as gory as anything seen on TV, approaching R-rated slasher levels. There's not much blood, as no blades or bullets were involved. But the scene of a *blunt-head-trauma* homicide can be exceptionally traumatic (sorry) for one who knows the deceased (check), and is unlucky enough to get an eyeful of the facial region (check again), if said region is badly disfigured (checkmate). If Mitchell were a more detached person (and he's not), unattractively self-involved (nope), or of a deeply scientific bent (*ha!*), he might view the moment of discovery as the clinching sign that he has definitively whupped Falkenberg's disease. Even a neurologically healthy person could well swoon in the face of this, after all. Mitchell, however, is steadfast—yet way too focused on Jepson's tragedy to even register his own quiet triumph over looming death.

Normally, the direct subordinate of an offed, quasi-notorious boss who just happens to discover the murder scene would qualify as a person-of-at-least-moderate-interest. But this soon after the fact, whoeverdunnit is surely covered in *splatter pattern* himself (yes, "himself." Because let's face it—this was a guy thing). Much more significantly, access card logs and supporting security footage plainly show that Mitchell was four blocks south at the PhastPhorwardr at the Time of Incident. And yeah, all this is discovered more or less instantly. Because this investigation is in bizarrely competent hands. Guys in suits, who plainly scare the crap out of the SFPD.

For a while there, Mitchell sits obediently in the corner (not under suspicion, but not yet dismissed) as the suits access corporate security footage. Zoning in and out, he doesn't overhear their discussion of his personal alibi. This is good, since he was nowhere *near* the PhastPhor-wardr when the exculpatory video evidence places him there—and he would have set them straight on this if he'd realized they were being hoodwinked (and man, would *that*'ve gotten awkward fast)! What he does notice is the explosion of outrage (plus grudging admiration) when the suits discover that any video connected to the immediate crime scene has been ingeniously doctored. Eighteen and a half minutes of footage has surgically vanished from every camera that could have possibly captured the culprit's approach or departure. So clearly, our perp has God-level access to Phluttr's network—as well as a sick sense of humor, and a certain grasp of history (18.5 minutes being the duration of the famous deletion from the Nixon tapes).

The suits don't say it, but Mitchell's sure they're thinking it. And if not, well; he's certainly thinking it.

"It" being this: *Beasley did it . . . Beasley . . . Beasley.*

∞ ∞ ∞

Recommended by Bob Garrety and 12,817 others

Marc Anderson (Follow)
Digital marketing consultant.
Jul 22 · 5 min read

Minutes before the car wreck that killed her, my girlfriend sent an email that was inimitably her: "Phone dead. Calling an Uber from my iPad feels strangely subversive. Coming home to present you with **definitive proof** that my boss wasn't read to very often as a child. Oh, and a bottle of a gorgeously red, red wine called 'Flaccianello.' Mainly because that sounds like an exTREMEly filthy act in Italian (which is to say, brace yourself, Antoniolio :-)"

It's been two years. I can now read this without bawling. Just.

It moves me not just for its timing. But because no human on this planet would have written precisely these words. Something close? Maybe. But not precisely. Every subtlety, punctuation quirk, and word choice is distinctly Bianca. And collectively, they're uniquely her. Unique as a strand of her DNA. I'm sure there are sentences here that were never written or uttered before, going clear back to Chaucer. We all create these sorts of uniquenesses all the time, by the way. Bianca just happened to create this one.

I take almost mystical comfort from this. Because while I don't believe in God, I do believe in the Singularity. It *is* coming. Perhaps not in my lifetime. But sometime. And when it arrives, the resulting superintelligence could easily tease out the neural configuration behind Bianca's message. Not precisely, no. But reverse engineering to the near ballpark *will* be a tractable goal. After all, this is the output of a finite organ with a limited set of constituent parts: 100 billion neurons in a mesh of about 100 trillion connections. Adding the complexities of neurotransmitters, this organ can assume a dauntingly vast number of possible states. Daunting as hell—but finite. Today, we don't *do* daunting-as-hell-but-finite. But post-Singularity, we will.

In my comforting imaginings, the post-Singularity computer zeroes in on Bianca's neural state by process of elimination. The brain that wrote her message speaks English. It exhibits a certain vocabulary, perspective, and sense of humor. It has a boss. It has a smartphone, an iPad, and an Uber account—highly complex abstractions the computer groks thoroughly. When all is parsed, 99-point-many-many-nines percent of possible brains and their possible states will be ruled out. And while the remaining number will still be mind-meltingly daunting, it will be much more finite.

And then, the computer reads another Bianca email. Then another, and another. It reads them *all*, then all her texts. Through this, a crushing majority of the plausible remaining brain states is eliminated. Then, the crushing majority of the remaining remainders. Then another crushing majority, then another, then another.

Her relationships with hundreds, even thousands of correspondents are parsed with the messages. How fast did she get back to people? Was she attentive to those who needed her? How nice was she to her parents, to those who wronged her, to customer service? And how were these things influenced by the weather? By the time of day, the stock market, or her favorite team's victories? And how did a thousand other variables affect her Spotify playlists? Her Amazon purchases? Her activities everywhere else, as reflected by credit cards, and the countless actions that get recorded somewhere in the digisphere? As all this is parsed, more and more crushing majorities in the ever-slimming domain of plausible brain states are ruled out.

With access to the totality of everything digital, ever, the Singularity will reconstruct much of Bianca's browsing history. It will see what links and ads attracted, versus repelled her. Which long articles she read to the end, and which ones bored her after moments. Ditto videos, podcasts, and movies. What Kindle books kept her up past midnight, and what porn she snuck peeks at. Bianca also kept journals as a kid—a wealth of information, should they be fed into the system. Along with the words, there are periods of tidy vs. sloppy writing, doodles in margins, and the rate and manner in which her concerns and style evolved in those early years of rapid development.

As a grown-up, Bianca blogged. She also tweeted, and posted to Facebook. All this is parsed as the post-Singularity superintelligence refines, re-refines, then re-re-refines its model of her. And let's not forget the untold thousands of photos. We broadcast a constant feed of truths with our bodies, revealing so much with this pose, that expression, this level of closeness or distance from others in the shot. We reveal even more in moving pictures, and as she was a digital girl in a digital tribe that recorded *everything*, there are dozens of hours of Bianca video out there, most of it an unstaged, spontaneous, and uncontrived reflection of her true self at this or that instant.

The superintelligence ingests all this, plus countless other elements that linger in the world as traces of us all. Eventually, it has an exquisitely refined model of Bianca. It's still an approximation of her neurons' precise states and configurations. But it's within a rounding error for the purposes of the very blunt tool that is human perception. Which is to say that even to those who knew and loved her most, the modeled Bianca will be indistinguishable from the departed one.

Might the new Bianca be made conscious? Without question. Consciousness arises from that finite set of neurons and connections and their states. These states can certainly be instantiated in software. Not today, of course; but post-Singularity? No problem. Could Bianca then be given a body? Of this, I'm less sure. It leaves the realm of digits for that of atoms, which is less my turf. Logically, though, I think yes—as the post-Singularity's matter compilers and nanotechnology should be able to create any assemblage of atoms that doesn't violate the laws of physics.

None of this means that Bianca will be "resurrected," nor that I (nor a resurrected I) will be there to rejoin her. But it does mean it's *possible*. To one who believes in the Singularity as firmly as I, it can almost seem likely. And even if the Singularity doesn't happen, this thought experiment—which I ran nightly for many weepy months—taught me that Bianca is still very meaningfully present. Collectively, her countless traces compose a body of preserved facts that *could* reconstitute her consciousness, given enough horsepower and superintelligence. This means Bianca has quite literally been "saved" to that hardest of hard drives, which is the very configuration of matter in our world. I don't know if she will ever be retrieved from memory. But I do know she *could* be. And this is a comfort.

∞　　　∞　　　∞

The kinda touching, kinda creepy post about the dead girlfriend was big on Reddit and Medium some months ago, and is a sudden internal sensation at Phluttr. People are forwarding it and posting it to their Pheeds under the hashtag #RebootJepson!!! Yes, it's an odd way to process the shocking murder of a popular CEO. Yet it's a fitting tribute in its very irreverence—irreverence being Jepson's hallmark, and the company's, too. It's also a rather sweet meme, in denoting a yearning to get him back. For his part, the post gives Mitchell an uncharacteristic urge to bawl his eyes out—something he last did in college. Is it horror over the writer's loss? The poignancy of any naïve hope to reunite with the dead? Or are Mitchell's stingy tear ducts just keening for some goddam release for once?

If the latter, then fair enough. It's been a hell of a week. The bombing, the death threats, then yesterday's ghastly murder—any one of these things alone would be the worst event of his life. Apart from his Falkenberg's diagnosis, that is. Which raises the issue of the no-less-jarring good stuff that's afoot! Let's start with his miraculous (apparent) cure. Make that his *anonymous* (apparent) cure, in that Dr. Martha knows nothing about the probiotic that seems to have triggered it. Indeed, although dutifully voicing delight, she seems to suspect he's lost his mind.

Also high in the Good column is that mad night with the sumptuous Nayana Corea. Reading through their strange correspondence twice, he's half convinced that if she knew the whole truth (above all, that Cyrano sold her on Mitchell as he more or less is, and without his urging, knowledge, or consent), she'd forgive him, and perhaps even see him again. He sure likes to think she might. Because after reading all her smart, snappy messages and ruminating on those endless steamy hours, you could *al*most say that he's kind of (perhaps) falling completely and hopelessly in love with her.

In other words: Dr. Martha, you may be right about that insanity diagnosis! Although not for the reasons you think (as every cell in his body is positively screaming that he's *cured*, and he has utter conviction on this point). But rather because a certain madness may lurk in his sudden leap into emotional oceans that terrified him when he was dying. Sure, only frustration and embarrassment triggered actual attacks back then. But this gave him a Pavlovian dread of other feelings, too. Fixing his embarrassment and frustration circuits has made those other emotions feel like the safe turf they always had been—and years of denial have made his soul ravenous for *all* feelings. But being so emotionally out of practice, he has these juvenile vulnerabilities that are (yes, Dr. Martha) *insane*. Like this childish proclivity to fall for the first random chick he happens to blunder into! Simply because she's intelligent, witty, and worldly! Plus gorgeous, ethical, ambitious, sexy, creative, happy, centered, cosmopolitan, confident! Oh—and showed him the most mind-blowing sex of his entire life, by a factor of perhaps ten!

Well, hmm. Maybe he's not so nuts after all. But he still feels like bawling his eyes out. He's about to retreat to the sole private place in the office where a grown man can do this (the one-seat unisex handicap restroom on Three) when "Ph U" stages a *coup de phone* in his right front pocket. Short for "Phluttr Urgent," this mode seizes control of your smartphone's every output—causing it to hum, flash, jitter, shriek, pulse blinding LEDs, and perhaps (it's rumored online) heat up dangerously.

Only your closest friends and family members should have Ph U access to you, obviously, and this is Mitchell's first-ever message through the system. It's from Kuba. **"Get out. OUT of the building IMMEDI-ATELY!!! No danger to others so DO NOT evacuate anybody!!! But YOU must leave NOW and LEAVE QUIETLY!!! To SB-null! Now, now now!"**

Well, #HolyFuckingShit. Over decades of friendship, Kuba's never been a tenth this vehement. It's as if a fearless shepherd boy who's chided for being *inadequately* alarmist—a kid who'd take on a stampede of wolves with a squirt gun before he'd pester anyone—is suddenly cart-wheeling around the village square with a hundred-watt megaphone shrieking *WOLF! WOLF!! WOOOOOLF!!!* When that happens, sensible peasants load their wolf guns and git.

Mitchell lacks a wolf gun, but he does git—straight to "SB-null." This is their preposterous code name for a certain Starbucks. It was christened during that first night at the Interval, when the team jokingly flirted with minor cloak-and-dagger tactics. Right off Union Square, SB-null throbs with tourists, and repels any self-respecting local, which makes it as anonymous a public spot as any in walking range. Suspecting that his building's about to go into lockdown, Mitchell skips the elevator and thunders down an interminable series of access stairs. Way down at street level, the exit's fitted with one of those alarm-sounding bars that building managers everywhere refuse to warn about at the *top* of the steps. Wired since childhood to be polite, to vote, to never rob liquor stores, and generally be a model citizen, Mitchell gazes at the forbidden door, and bilious guilt surges from his heels to his core. Then the howl of approaching sirens pierces the door, and he shoves it open, because this *is* a goddamned emergency! No alarm sounds, of course.

Sirens are zeroing in from all quadrants, like a gathering swarm of banshees. But what really gets him is the thrumming. The air is churning with bass notes, like at a rave (one where the DJ mainly plays that helicopter sample from *Apocalypse Now*). Though no expert, Mitchell doesn't have to look up to know this is military gear—machines that make cop whirligigs look like mopeds next to a Hell's Angel's Harley. Moving fast as he can without looking guilty of something, Mitchell avoids the main streets and reaches the Starbucks via a choppy series of block-bisecting alleyways. Kuba and Tarek are already there, and wide-eyed.

"They taped off the PhastPhorwardr," Tarek says breathlessly. "All of it, in nothing flat! We figured your building was next."

"We were just coming back from a meeting and saw them pounce," Kuba says.

"Suits," Tarek adds. "Creepy guys who looked like the ones you said interrogated you after the Jepson thing."

"We watched them set up a perimeter from a block away," Kuba says. "And no one's getting in *or* out. So it's not a bomb threat."

"It's not an *any*thing threat," Tarek agrees. "It looks like a dragnet. Like they're looking for someone."

"And it could be us," Mitchell finishes for them. They nod.

So wtf? Well, for starters, this just *has* to be an Authority operation, right? The local cops can barely clear a homicide and could no more stage something this ambitious than they could conquer Mongolia! Of course, the Authority could be after anybody. But Beasley's intercepted memo said they're close to solving the quantum computer break-in. "So, where to?" Tarek asks.

Mitchell gestures around the tourist-choked Starbucks. "I'd say this is as good a place as any. And better than most." And he's right. Packed with shutterbugs, it's a mighty unsubtle place for top secret operatives to stage quiet, plainclothes grabs. Also (assuming they weren't tracked coming over here), it's a mighty unlikely place to find plugged-in locals like them. All this should give them time to gather their wits and maybe pick up some news about whateverthehell's going down at Phluttr.

As it happens, that part's easy. Because once again, *some*body's leaking facts to the press. Is in fact leaking facts all over the place. Is in fact all but hemorrhaging them. "Oh. My. *God*," one or another of them mutters dozens of times over the coming hours as the details pour in.

It turns out the rumored third Embarcadero bombing conspirator was quite real (*was*, in that he just took about a thousand bullets in a shoot-out). And, an ex-Phluttr employee! Lyle Willard was a midlevel tech in the synthetic biology lab. There, he did excellent work, while giving everyone hives with his creepy demeanor and ominous prophecies (yes, *prophecies*). He suddenly quit about eight weeks ago. One of the dead bomber twins was also a midlevel SynBio tech, only at UCSF. He and Willard met through professional circles and grew close. Like the Al Noor brothers, Willard was intensely depressive. Also like them, he was quite religious—although he was no Muslim, but from the apocalyptic fringe of some Pentecostal splinter. Though estranged from his family and the church of his youth, he remained vulnerable to doomsaying. So when Jaysh al Hisaab said "doom" in its inimitably slick, viral way, Willard's ears pricked right up. Ironically, *he* was the one who introduced his Muslim co-conspirators to the movement's nominally Islamic theology. And once all were bought in, they agreed that the surest way to please the Almighty would be to do their very best to eradicate humanity. Then the baddies could go straight to hell, the Good straight to heaven, no passing Go, and we're done!

"Willard synthesized most of the DNA needed to transform the Ebola genome into something called Yale Ebola in our lab," Kuba explains, after ingesting a fairly technical leak that just broke online. "It's the most virulent bug ever engineered. Not by these idiots. But by some genius at Yale. Only a handful of facilities can produce sequences as long as what they needed. Ours was one. So Willard printed them. Next, they had to stitch these patches into normal Ebola DNA. Willard didn't have the chops for that. But the Al Noor brother specialized in that sort of splicing. So they incorporated a tiny biotech company. Which let them order everything they needed. Nothing very fancy or expensive, it turns out."

"They were gonna infect *themselves* with the Ebola!" Tarek says, looking up from another article. "They called themselves 'Ebola Martyrs,' if you can believe that! That Yale jackass designed the bug to be supercontagious, *and* to have a long incubation period. So just a few days of fanning out and breathing on people could've started hundreds of infection sites before anyone knew!"

"So what was the bombing about?" Mitchell asks Tarek.

"Spreading panic. And though I really hate to say it, it was a smart plan. The thing is, they weren't sure if they'd engineer their bug successfully. In fact, they were pretty sure they'd screw it up! So they were planning to simultaneously bomb Embarcadero Center *and* announce the Ebola thing—whether it had actually worked or not. They figured the bombing would give their announcement total credibility. So even if the bug failed, they could've spread deadly global panic."

"I get it!" Kuba marvels. "Any crank can claim to infect the world with a doomsday bug. Several probably do every month. But someone who just blew up Embarcadero Center will be taken very seriously."

Mitchell nods. "They'd seem capable of anything. Right after 9/11, I remember being *sure* Al Qaeda would blow up a World Series game simply because they'd just done the impossible once already! So if these guys blew up Embarcadero Center? And *then* said they'd done that Ebola thing?"

"*And* pointed the press to the lab in their garage?" Tarek adds. "*And* gave out all the other verifiable details? Of *course*, everyone would assume they'd engineered the bug. The entire planet would freak!"

"They'd also probably lie to magnify things," Kuba speculates. "Claim to have gone to a hundred cities worldwide and sneezed on the grapes. Or to have two hundred accomplices sneezing in every country on Earth. Everything would be believed for at least a few days after the bombing."

As it turns out, the world freaks out plenty—even in the face of overwhelming proof that the group never came close to engineering its superbug. By nightfall, every route out of the city is intractably jammed by terrified hypochondriacs and even-keeled rationalists alike. San Francisco is in utter gridlock, leaving all its emergency vehicles marooned in place. After this sinks in, widespread looting erupts. Lesser traffic jams meanwhile strike hundreds of other cities worldwide, as news of the Ebola plot makes *every* urban center feel dangerous.

Asian markets open in a state of abject meltdown—30, even 40 percent down!—before deep-pocketed opportunists who know hysteria when they see it flood the planet with buy orders, turning the indices around. Like an opioid hit calming a broader nervous system, the soothed markets get the rest of the planet's tightly coupled memeplexes and infospheres to *chill* the *fuck* OUT. It helps that all of the conspiracy's details are already public. With one nagging exception, that is. Which is, why did the bomb go off early? The second Al Noor brother was a senior facilities guy and had made that whole storage area his personal turf. This gave the gang weeks to bring their materials in bit by bit, and they were less than 10 percent done when it spontaneously detonated as they were doing this. Well, this seems like a small detail in a very big picture. So by late night, the crisis is largely over. Save for the news-cycle punditry, which will torment one and all for years to come.

It's nearing dawn when the guys finally break camp. SB-null, with its Wi-Fi, abundant electrical outlets, and tolerance for lurkers who buy the occasional Frappuccino, has been an ideal place to ride out the storm (and management's snap decision to remain open throughout the night as a service to those needing a refuge was a godsend). As for Phluttr HQ, local media reports that its cordon lasted only a few hours. It was allegedly just meant to keep the press and general public away from a satellite branch of the most chilling almost-crime-scene of the century (ground zero being the Al Noors' South San Francisco garage, which will remain taped off for months). So as the guys head home, they're as sure as they can be (which isn't terribly sure, by the way) that nobody's hunting for them tonight.

∞   ∞   ∞

OPINION | COMMENTARY

Humanity's Would-be Annihilation
We have avoided extinction for now, but "WTD" are coming.

By YANNIS KASSANDREYU
Special for The Wall Street Journal

A mysterious series of profoundly informed leaks has already taught us more about the failed San Francisco bioterror plot than was known about the 9/11 conspiracy a full year after the fact. Let's start with the good news.

The cabal behind it was, mercifully, led by lab technicians rather than trained scientists. Lab techs are skilled people who run advanced equipment created by even more skilled people. They don't design that equipment themselves. They may not fully understand it or why they've been asked to do particular assays. They're like talented line cooks who prepare world-class meals by faithfully following recipes rather than head chefs who invent dishes and earn Michelin stars.

While the terrorists were more sophisticated than most techs, they were still venturing far beyond their pay grade. The proximate cause for their failure to engineer Yale Ebola was, of course, the fortuitous detonation of their incomplete and unarmed bomb. But absent that, it's unlikely that their bioengineering would have succeeded. Toward the end of the process, certain technical challenges that they had not foreseen loomed. These have been dissected in several scientific forums, but for our purposes, it suffices to say that they were daunting.

But this does not mean the group suffered from stupidity. Nor from a lack of training, cunning, or motivation. Their core handicap was simply that they were operating today, rather than five or (at most) ten years hence. And this brings us to the bad news.

The passage of time makes wizards of us all. Today, any dullard can make bells ring across the ocean by tapping out phone numbers, cause inanimate toys to march by barking an order, or activate remote devices by touching a wireless screen. Thomas Edison couldn't have managed any of this at his peak—and shortly before his time, such powers would have been considered the unique realm of God.

Likewise, the pitfalls that would stop present-day lab techs from producing Yale Ebola will soon be as roadway speed bumps to a passing jetliner. Radically upgraded descendants of the cheap gear in the terrorists' garage will simply make those problems vanish. And problems that vanish for top lab techs will subsequently vanish for grad students, then for undergrads, then for smart high school students, then for dumb ones, and then, for dropouts.

Some take heart that this was the first serious attempt to erase our species in over five thousand years of recorded history. So mightn't a similar span pass before the next major try? As my undergrads still say decades after the phrase first swept their predecessors, *dream on*. Suicidal monsters have been taking as many people with them as possible from time immemorial. Downtown rampage killers; losers who strangle their families; commercial pilots who nosedive their planes; these killers are low and narcissistic enough to take every one of us with them if they could. Propitiously, they simply lack that terrifying power. Everybody lacks it, apart from a minute handful of leaders with nuclear arsenals. And everyone will continue to lack it—for at least five years, and perhaps as many as ten. So what is to be done?

Some seem to think an Islamic reformation, coupled with better monitoring of the unreformed, would go far toward securing the world. But this is not strictly an Islamic problem. Few perpetrators of America's countless mass murder-suicides are Muslims. One of the San Francisco plotters was devoutly Christian. And the four thousand kamikaze strikes carried out in the waning days of World War II rival the total number of suicide bombings the entire world has seen *throughout history*. Some maintain kamikazes somehow "don't count," as they were part of a military. But the groups that commit virtually all suicide bombings are almost purely martial in nature, making such arguments useless sophistry.

The grim truth is that all societies produce rampage killers and murder-suicides. Even the most pacifist and Shinto, like Japan. Even the most organized and tolerant, like Germany. Even the most wealthy and humanist, like Norway. More dangerously, some subset of the worst killers are content with entirely random victims. And some subset of *them* would set no upper limit to their body counts. These are the people we should most fear as mass murder democratizes. And humanity produces far more of them than we realize. We just never hear from most—because even they

are rational in their way, and if denied handy mechanisms to slaughter innocents, they rid us of themselves in acts of simple self-destruction.

When massacrists do set out to kill, two force multipliers stand out. The first is technology. Jet crashers like Andreas Lubitz and Osama bin Laden have caused the most damage thus far. Terrorists with explosives are next in line, followed by people with high-powered guns. As for the simplest technology, Chinese school rampages average just half the victim count of American ones because Chinese attacks are often mass *stabbings*. Which gets to the heart of why the US racks up more familicides and workplace slaughters than entire continents combined: those who arrange for everyone to have boundless gun access, while feigning cosmetic nods toward embargoing the lucrative criminal and mentally volatile markets. It is gun access alone that sets America apart in this arena, and not a unique Yankee propensity to violence, however perversely flattering American mass-slaughter apologists and profiteers seem to find this notion.

The second great mass murder force multiplier is the number of co-conspirators. Before Oklahoma City, plenty of Schlitz-swilling lowlifes had killed small handfuls of unfortunates. Then Timothy McVeigh and Terry Nichols took things to a radical new level by joining forces and combining their strengths and expertise. Organized terror cells, even tiny ones, likewise claim far more victims than lone NRA fanboys who go off their meds.

This is why Jaysh al Hisaab threatens to become a singularly destructive force. Its virulent ideology can spontaneously unify small teams of nutcases, who on their own might only kill a handful of those closest to them and be done. San Francisco illustrates this chilling point. Its perpetrators combined two highly complementary biotech skill sets with deep access to a major skyscraper's innards. No one person brings all of this to the table, let alone six arms to act with.

Jaysh furthermore advocates truly random and maximal slaughter. And it is this orientation that turns a lust for weapons of mass destruction into one for weapons of *total* destruction. Weapons of total destruction—let's call them "WTD"—are senseless if you're trying to kill these people, but not those people. This is why we don't have to worry about Al Qaeda unleashing highly weaponized Ebola upon the world, soulless and sick as its leaders are. But now we have Jaysh, just in time for the birth of broadly accessible WTD, which will uniquely appeal to full-spectrum nihilists.

Some call for us good guys to get highly adept at WTD-related technologies, so as to gain knowledge to better foil the baddies. But recall that the active ingredient in this week's near miss sprang from that good-guy hotbed of Yale University. And many other fortresses of light and truth have proven to be extremely leaky vessels for dark forces bred in captivity by good-guy scientists. For instance, in 2001, the planet's most lethally weaponized anthrax was under the tightest imaginable locks and keys in our government's own biodefense lab at Fort Detrick. Shortly after 9/11, with all US defenses at their highest-ever alert, those very spores made their way to the office of the Senate majority leader! If the United States government can't keep its own WMD out of the chambers of its own leaders when at maximum vigilance—and it cannot—advancing WTD technology as a countermeasure to future terror is patently insane.

The half-forgotten lesson of the anthrax attacks is that *all* vessels are leaky. Terrorism is meanwhile shifting from being a means of communication by groups, to a form of self-expression by individuals. In this environment, the *only* safe place for WTD technologies is the pages of science fiction novels. And even that, we might question.

∞   ∞   ∞

Mitchell and Kuba were at that most suspicious of places, at that most suspicious of moments, for three perfectly innocent reasons, Officer. First, Beasley was a creature of habit (a lousy trait for his line of work—although his was not deemed a combat-vulnerable post). Second, white though his own hat is, Kuba can be a helluva black-hat hacker when provoked. And third, the purpose of Kuba's hacking was to *solve* a heinous crime. A murder, in fact! Which means it wasn't really black-hat hacking, right? So we actually have pure innocence across the board—on the minor hacking charge, as well as the uber-major thing, see?

Kuba agreed to make one of his rare forays to the dark side at the tail end of that marathon powwow at SB-null. Arrayed against the intelligence world's mightiest and most secretive arm, the guys figure the one advantage they might possibly generate is a tiny element of surprise. Not that they could sneak up on the Authority, of course. But they *might* sneak up on Beasley. Beasley, who all but preconfessed to Jepson's murder in that intercepted memo (which has since, somewhat awkwardly, vanished into Poof!'s memory hole). Beasley, who—for all his eerie competencies—is bumbling when dealing with humans. Properly ambushed, bumbling Beasley might just blurt an incriminating fact or nine. And captured on video, these might afford some leverage in the looming showdown with the Authority (a long shot, yes. But can *you* think of a better plan?).

So Kuba hacks into Beasley's personal data store within Phluttr. There, he finds (as he could have found on any Phluttr user) meticulous GPS records logging the comings and goings of Beasley's every Phluttr-infested device since the day he signed up for the service as User #0,000,000,004. This reveals where he lives (in a small detached house with a murky ownership history on a nondescript Potrero Hill block). It also shows that he invariably leaves for work between 6:58 and 7:06 A.M. Beasley's famous for always traveling by bike, rain or shine. And the house's façade is almost flush to the sidewalk. So bracketing it (Kuba tucked into some shrubbery to the left, Mitchell behind a tree to the right) should let them accost him, whether he pops out the front door or the garage with that damned folding bike of his. And with GoPros mounted subtly on their persons, they'll capture every golden moment!

All told, it's an incredibly professional hit. Both guys tense as the garage door rises majestically, tugged by a most lethargic genie. They scarcely notice the passing . . . what the hell was it? A . . . beige Camry, maybe? It's just so nondescript, they're not looking for it, and it passes at an innocuous speed. They don't even hear anything odd! Well, they hear something drop in the garage. But they mistake that for a creaky pang from the aging door as it rises. They then just stand there like morons for at least a minute after the door has opened. And that's not what a *murderer* would do, now, is it?

And no, Your Honor. That exculpatory motionless minute was not, unfortunately, recorded by the GoPros, the Baghdad-ambassador-grade home security system, nor the CCTV camera with the expansive view of the scene mounted in the minimart window across the street. The simultaneous outage of all that gear during the key ten-minute stretch is just monumentally bad luck for our side—and was not engineered to hide the culpability of one Kuba Stanislaw! Who, admittedly, is something of a master hacker. We also maintain that Mr. Stanislaw's departure from the scene—which the miraculously rebooted neighborhood CCTV *did* manage to record shortly after the incident—in no way proves his involvement! Although given the misleading power of this spurious evidence, we may concede this point in exchange for, say . . . life without the possibility of parole?

Kuba signals Mitchell after the tense minute has passed. Not a peep from the garage, and still the door yawns open. Catching one another's eyes, they shrug. Then Kuba shows his palm like a traffic-stopping cop and points at his chest, volunteering to be the one to investigate. He cautiously and soundlessly extracts himself from the shrubbery. Then as soon as he sees the garage's interior, he blanches and freezes. After what seems like an eternity, he signals for Mitchell to witness the scene.

Beasley lies dead, in a small pool of blood—a tight cluster of tiny wounds right over his heart. Whatever the make and color of that damned car, the guy riding shotgun was one hell of a marksman.

∞　　　∞　　　∞

At first, the SFPD is way less intrigued by the Potrero Hill shooting than anyone else with a stake in it. They're just not privy to enough highly classified facts (as in, not any) to know it as anything other than a drive-by. A weird one, to be sure. Location, victim, time of day, suspect—all of it's off; even way off. But this country sees plenty of weird drive-bys in any given year. And every so often, one's just gonna happen in your town. Things get a lot more interesting in the late morning, when a suspect gets fingered by the Leak-O-Matic (the nickname of the mysterious source of anonymous tips that blew open the doors on the Ebola bombing). Then they get *really* freakin' interesting when the closely guarded (make that, top secret) identity of the Potrero Hill victim leaks on that damned blog. That makes this the Siamese twin of the Jepson murder —the city's most headline-grabbing crime since the Moscone/Milk thing wayyy back in 1978!

Parties more connected than the city cops find the Beasley assassination plenty interesting from the get-go. Let's start with the Authority, which hadn't lost an operative to enemy fire since Khartoum in 2013 (because Jepson wasn't really an operative, nor was he done in by enemy fire. Not technically, anyway). They're all over this thing instantly! By the time the local numbskull cops arrest that laughably innocent Polish kid in the midmorning, it's clear the orders came from Beijing. Flawlessly scouted, timed, and clean as it was, this hit involved multiple top-flight agents. Only China and Israel have enough assets in or near enough to northern California to gather such a team without setting off any number of Authority trip wires (long story, that. Oh, and it's classified). And no way was it Israel for a long list of reasons (all classified, too. Sorry). So, the culprit's no mystery.

As for the motive? Well, that's another matter. China is powerful and confident enough to risk international heat by offing someone who truly threatens its interests. But *Beasley?* Sure, the guy was capable, and key to a very important asset. But his work only threatened China in the most general and abstract of ways—and China no more than any other party not precisely aligned with the US! Baffled, pissed off, and spooked, the Authority resorts to a cunning cyber exploit that it's kept up its sleeve for a situation just like this and plumbs several hypersensitive networks and servers within China's intelligence infrastructure, hoping to figure out what the hell those people were thinking.

The exploit fails. But it doesn't go unnoticed. Its detection triggers flurries of worries—as well as a monster set of reactions, counterreactions, counter-counterreactions, and so on, clear out to the nth counter (with n being a very large triple-digit number whose precise value we could debate and analyze for weeks, but let's not). And this is merely what happens within the various arms of the Chinese government! If nations were the unitary, rational actors that foreign policy wonks invoke whenever their models-of-state conduct require absurd simplifications, this . . . *thing* called "China" would parse the digital intrusion, formulate a cogent, streamlined response, and execute upon it. But governments staffed by tens (yes, tens) of millions of people just don't roll like that. Not even in the clearest of circumstances. And today ain't clear. Indeed, it's socked in by a pea-soup murk that's starting to resemble the fog of war.

The trick is that China's leaders (like all leaders) compartmentalize highly sensitive information. Only a tiny handful of them know about the Beasley hit. Which (yeah, bingo) China did perpetrate. Although not due to a sublime calculus of National Interest—but because certain honchos were tricked into viewing Beasley as a huge threat by an ingenious new global actor that no one even knows exists! Knowledge of the resulting American cyber attack is also highly restricted. But to a *different* tiny clique, with almost no overlap between the groups. Beijing's cyber command therefore quite rationally views this hack as being an unprovoked outrage! New protocols require that cyber outrages be met with some highly visible military fussing (minor troop movements, some tanks dusted off in the full view of spy satellites, and/or a token handful of scrambling jets). The idea is to inform the perp that this shit has been noticed, it is *not* appreciated, and thou shalt back the fuck down—*now*. Protocols of this sort functioned as simple but unmistakable signals between the Americans and Soviets throughout the Cold War. Though expensive and ham-fisted, they prevented innumerable small conflicts, and, on three occasions (only one of which was ever known to more than a few dozen people), all-out nuclear war.

So these sorts of signals can be powerful tools—*provided* that both sides know precisely what each mobilization means, what triggered it, as well as the proper choreography for de-escalating back to a state of mutual calm. None of which holds today! The Chinese response protocols are new and still under development. As such, they're unknown in the wider world. They're also implemented imperfectly by immense organizations that are trying them out for the first time. And, of course, the break-in that China's cyber team regards as an unprovoked outrage is seen in Washington as an extremely *restrained* response to an unprovoked assassination! Which means the sides are (mis)communicating about completely separate topics. Adding to the fun, the Authority is so secretive toward its *own* government that even the White House needs the bureaucratic equivalent of pliers, truncheons, and truth serum to get the simplest facts out of it! And so, those whose job descriptions include reacting to scrambling Chinese jets know nothing about the cyber incursion, or of Beasley. Believing that *they're* the ones facing an unprovoked outrage, they scramble a few jets of their own! Then China takes countermeasures (some initiated by newcomers who think *they're* responding to an unprovoked outrage). And so on.

It takes less than an hour for the counter-counter-counter-countermeasures to kick in—and by then, Taiwan is freaking the fuck out! While Taiwan's bosses have excellent relations with the US military, everything's happening so fast (and is so monopolizing their Washington contacts) that they're left to detect the Chinese mobilization on their own. Which is actually quite easy. Remember, those actions are highly visible by design. And when a neighbor who claims to own the island your entire country happens to be sitting on outnumbers you by a factor of fifty, very little in the way of visible military moves escapes your notice. So Taiwan puts all of *its* assets on high alert in response to this unprovoked outrage! Next, Russia's pharaoh clues into all of this. Thinking random acts of unhinged thuggishness have suddenly gone mainstream, he amps up his own brand of crazy just to keep leading the world at something!

Military mobilizations—even top secret ones—have casts of thousands. Many more thousands quickly become aware of them, and millions soon detect murky signals that *some*thing fucked up is afoot. A scrambling pilot's wife posts an agonized thought to social media. A corrupt general shunts $100 million to an offshore bank. Certain bankers react to this faint but chilling signal that something's awry. A midsized mutual fund picks up on the bankers' reaction and twitches. A CNBC anchor misreads that twitch, then blasts his highly influential interpretation to the world. Soon dozens of governments and millions of people are reacting to one another's responses to dire events that few of them know anything about. It's as if God racked billions of billiards on a cosmic, ten-dimensional table, and Zeus just broke. Good luck calculating how that's gonna end! Even with much of the processing power in the universe. Or (more relevantly) in the *multi*verse, it simply cannot be done.

∞　　　∞　　　∞

Serena Kielholz stands out at Phluttr like a plutonium-powered lighthouse on a clear Arctic night. She'd stand out more, only Phluttr's workforce is a good 30 percent better-looking and less obese than a cross section of like-aged Americans. She sticks out a bit less on the Stanford campus (more like a jet-fueled lighthouse in Siberia, say; but with kick-ass LEDs that can still cause retinal damage). The closest she ever came to blending in with the crowd was at an Abercrombie & Fitch photo shoot. And even there, she unwittingly turned a third of the boys into born-again breeders while giving half the girls fresh body issues (to which you might say, "Karma's a bitch," given the damage *those* bitches inflict on the rest of the world; only they're really just cogs in the media wheel who were born that way and who need to make rent like anyone; so be nice).

This is why Mitchell can't help but notice her amidst the breakfast crowd in the Phree cafeteria. He's here because calories can reboot a crashing brain, and his is beset by shock and gloom. Not an hour ago, he and Kuba cleared right out of Beasley's neighborhood. Yeah, they might've called 911. But job number one was bolting before the mystery car could return and mow them down. They thought they'd done a slapdash but adequate job of capturing the full scene on their GoPros. But upon ducking into a private conference room back in the protective bustle of Phluttr HQ, they discover that their cameras had suffered appallingly awkward outages. Kuba's weekly midlevel staff meeting at the PhastPhorwardr—one led by Beasley, of all people—was by then about to start, and it seemed best he attend. They weren't yet sure how to report the homicide, and it might look funny for Kuba to be AWOL when no one else knows the meeting will be canceled on account of its leader's assassination. So Mitchell's at the cafeteria solo, and will reconvene with Kuba around nine thirty.

Serena does not look good. No, let's correct that: she looks amazing. Only, she doesn't look at all happy. Indeed, she looks dazed with grief. Plenty of people are dazed in the wake of Jepson's murder, the bioterror bust, and everything else—but Serena's taking this to suborbital heights. Processing this, it strikes Mitchell: *she was in love*. Yes, Jepson was old enough to be her dad (or at least, a founder her dad funded back when she was in diapers). This surely marked him as a perv, a pederast, or worse (and no, there was *noth*ing gentlemanly about waiting until a yoctosecond after her eighteenth birthday to seduce her). But they were in those dawning honeymoon moments, and Jepson could ooze worldliness, charm, and smarts even when he wasn't trying. And though he would inevitably be an ass to her at some point, there simply hadn't been time for that yet.

Mitchell also has enough female friends to know a bit about the psychology of knockouts. By their midteens, grotesque numbers of loathsome grown-ups have tried to ply them into sexual situations (peers, too, but that's another issue). This can have any number of consequences. Brainy and more confident girls often mature beyond their years, to better parse the bombardment of signals they're receiving from adults. By the time they enter adulthood themselves, guys their own age can seem like children to them. Guys twice their age might even seem like children. And Jepson—though unacceptably old by any metric—was a *young* unacceptably old and must have flattered the mind of this plainly intelligent woman whose physique was surely over-flattered with ickily excess frequency. He probably struck her as a man. A man, in a world of boys. One who happened along just when she was at an age when the world can seem maximally magical.

Bottom line, she's beyond devastated. Which is nothing compared to where she's dragged as Mitchell glances her way. She's looking at her phone. She probably catches a headline, or something.

Looking back later, Mitchell decides that witnessing a homicide could scarcely be worse than watching someone get whipsawed to pieces by humiliation. Make no mistake: Beasley's murder chilled him to his core. But he didn't see the body drop, didn't behold the moment of death. Beasley suffered a greater tragedy than Serena that day by most (though not all) reckonings. But witnessing a fellow human's emotional disfigurement will haunt Mitchell more. And, quite possibly, forever.

∞　　∞　　∞

CELEBRITYSOCIALLEAKS

The Stanford Slut Who CAUSED A MURDER!

"Yummm, who's the baaaaabe?"

Dudes, dykes, and bi chicks, we can hear you from Hollywood as you feast your eyes on this gorgeous image! And keep those hands where we can see them! Shown here is Stanford vixen Serena Kielholz. Still in her fresh-man dorm, yet already a *femme fatale* in the realest sense of the word!

Yeah, yeah; we know you don't care about places where the ugly people live! But we thought you'd put up with some upstate news if it's about A) someone *this hot*, and B) the hot, hot, *hot* social network Phluttr! Phluttr, which draws out Kanye! Kim! Ashton! Beyoncé! And hundreds of the world's other Top People to Share, Post, and BE REAL with us—daily!

If you're not living under ten tons of rock, you should know that Phluttr boss-man Tony Jepson just got murdered!!! And we now know "who done it." No, it wasn't this sexy ho, but her Daddy-o!

Serena's papa, Damien Kielholz, is a famous rich guy. Years ago, he backed Jepson's first startup. Rumor is, they did <u>not</u> get along! No big reason. Just two guys not liking each other.

But now, the plot thickens! A flurry of private texts, pix, and email from those days has just flooded the blogs. They involve Lena Kielholz — Damien's wife, and Serena's mother. Still plenty hot in her forties (as you can see!!), Lena must have been quite a piece in those days, when Serena was just a tot. And guess what?? The leaked message trove shows that back then, when Jepson wasn't doing work . . . he was "doing" Mommy Kielholz!

Daddy Money Bag$ knew nothing about this long-ago sex fest until a couple days back. Then, somehow, he got his angry paws on the message archive that the rest of the world is now feasting on!

And to make it MUCH WORSE . . . he also picked up some recent <u>steamy</u> traffic between Jepson . . . and his Stanford sex-kitten daughter! And, like mother, like daughter, it turns out Serena favors some of the exact same shocking acts in the sack that Moms would go for back when <u>she</u> was the Kielholz babe in Mr. J's bed! You can get those smutty details from the more porny blogs out there (and trust us: they're ALL talking about this)!

It's enough to drive a man to murder, isn't it? Which is what just happened!! Busted this morning, and now safely under lock and key, Daddy denies nothing. He even takes a certain Viking pride in what he did (his public statement is below)! This leaves Phluttr without a boss, Mr. K without a future, and Mrs. K without a husband. But since there's always a silver lining someplace . . . Stanford boys, look who's now single! And, you <u>know</u> she parties!

∞   ∞   ∞

Midmorning finds Mitchell alone at his desk, fretting. Kuba walked the few blocks to that PhastPhorwardr staff meeting a bit before eight, and should've been back by now. He's not responding to messages. Odder still, his location isn't broadcasting in Phluttr. This isn't inherently bizarre, as people block their locations all the time (and for $4.95/month you can broadcast phony locations [and for another five bucks, no one will know you're doing this {unless they pay an extra ten bucks for that insight [which you can always trump by getting the $24.95 platinum service]}]). But Kuba's never blocked his location from Mitchell, and now is a mighty odd time to start. Mitchell's checking hyperlocal blogs for news of pedestrian hit-and-runs when he gets a Poof! note from Tarek: **Meet at SB-zip—NOW!**

The suggestive pattern of S's and B's might imply that like SB-null, "SB-zip" is a <u>S</u>tar<u>b</u>ucks. Yet this is but a ruse! SB-zip is actually a Peet's Coffee (*Ha!*). On a similar note, the no-less-cunningly-named "PC-1" is *not* a Peet's Coffee, but a Coffee Bean & Tea Leaf (*Ha!*). Whereas SB-null was assigned to an *actual* Starbucks to shatter the pattern of contrary signals, and thereby confound Authority code breakers (bottom line: much hinges on the world's top spymasters finding Team Cyrano and their moronic code names utterly uninteresting).

Mitchell's in his Uber, fussing over the odd fact that Kuba wasn't cc'd on Tarek's summons, when a second message arrives from him. **This just in,** it says, with a link to the latest WhistleBlowings rant.

$$\infty \qquad \infty \qquad \infty$$

WhistleBlowings blog

Leak-A-Palooza!!!

Throughout <u>**five thankless years**</u> of BELLOWING THE TRUTH to an *indifferent world*, we were never tipped off to so much as a Google interoffice romance. Now suddenly, it's like GODDAMNED WIKILEAKS around here! Right <u>**after leaking**</u> the three most secure files in the HISTORY OF CRYPTOGRAPHY (or so it would seem, from the **countless downloads** we expensively served to the world, and the ensuing DEAFENING SILENCE as to their contents), we have been hit with a ***TRUE WHOPPER.*** So, NYT, HuffPo, WaPo, and Drudge, brace your Pulitzer-prizing asses, and ***eat your scooped hearts out!!!***

The City and the Valley are so giddy about "mourning" (AND making shamelessly false ex post facto claims of adoration for) Phluttr's assassinated CEO, Tony Jepson, that almost no one noticed this morning's news blip about an allegedly "random" drive-by killing of an "anonymous" citizen in a normally crime-free section of Potrero Hill. Well, ROT IN ANONYMITY NO MORE, Jake Beasley!

Yes, we're talking about **THAT Jake Beasley**. As in, Tony Jepson's #2 at the most **suspiciously secretive** company in Silicon Valley! As in, Jepson's SUCCESSOR AS CEO (betcha didn't know THAT!), for, oh, about twelve hours! This, after his promotion at a **suspiciously secretive emergency board meeting** that WhistleBlowings has also learned about. Bottom Line: not ONE, but **TWO** Phluttr CEOs have been **assassinated in almost instant succession**!!!

But WHO, you ask, would EVER want to kill yet another KIND, GENTLE CEO of an INTERNATIONAL DISGRACE? Rather than answer with the obvious back-atcha question (which, of course, is **who wouldn't???**) we will instead answer with our own stock-in-trade, which is FACTS. **Shocking FACTS**!

Let's start with this **NEWSFLASH**: it turns out that our quiet, boring "post Cold War era"—you know, these flush years of never-ending peace dividends in a remarkably conflict-free world (**NOT!!!**)—has actually witnessed one of the most bare-knuckled arms races IN HISTORY.

Who are we racing, you ask?

CHINA!

And where are we racing them TO?

Oh, you're gonna **love** this: the prize, here, is to be the first country to produce a technology that **MOST OF THE WORLD'S SMARTEST PEOPLE, INCLUDING STEPHEN HAWKING, BILL GATES, AND ELON FUCKING MUSK, ALL PUBLICLY DEPICT AS HAVING TERRIFYING ODDS OF ANNIHILATING US ALL!!!!!!!**

We're talking about artificial superintelligence—that much-predicted, much-DREADED form of consciousness that, once invented, **cannot be uninvented**. And, once let out of its box, can pretty much do whatever it wants to us, and to our planet!!!

For years, a top secret international treaty called the Copenhagen Accord kept the world's squabbling sovereignties from inventing this most lethal of technologies. And then, about twenty months ago, **China broke ranks**! Rather than shame them, sanction them, or otherwise EVEN ATTEMPT to stop them, WARMONGERS within US Intelligence decided to RACE THEM TO THE FINISH LINE!!!

Documents AND SATELLITE IMAGES proving these shocking truths can be found here, here, here, here, and here. And no doubt from 10,000s OF OTHER SERVERS WORLDWIDE within minutes of us posting this!

So, who killed our beloved CEOs? And WHY??? In the case of Tony Jepson, it was a bizarre love trapezoid involving a famous VC, his cheating wife, and his barely legal daughter. And as for Jake Beasley . . . well **THAT**'s actually the MORE interesting story . . .

It turns out, China somehow learned that Jake was secretly in charge of America's super AI development program. NOT ONLY THAT, but he was such a **coding GENIUS**, and such a **deranged micromanager**, that the ENTIRE SUPERINTELLIGENCE EFFORT was CERTAIN to grind to a CRASHING HALT if he were to spontaneously **DROP DEAD**!

Now, superpowers don't normally bump off each other's key personnel. But any student of history will tell you that this can happen in extreme circumstances. And these here circumstances sure were **extreme**! Why? BECAUSE THE SUPER AI RACE TRUMPS EVERYTHING! Many believe that the first power to create one will **control the world**! Now, suddenly, China learns that America's whole effort lies in one pair of mortal hands! So they're thinking, **kill this guy, and the world is ours**! And so, Jake Beasley goes and **drops dead**!!!

But HELLOOOOO, CHINA? Are you listening??? A teeny bit of bad news here. That kill-Beasley-and-control-the-world theory **which you've just gambled world peace on** is lethally FLAWED! In that, why the fuck would a guy working VERY full-time at **a top secret** *government arm* in SAN FRAN-FUCKING-CISCO also be loaded up with the TOP JOB IN NATIONAL SECURITY way out at <u>Sandia National Labs</u> in Albuquerque, NEW MEXICO?

Oh, sure. We've heard of <u>moonlighting</u>. But that's for barista-by-day/bartender-by-night people. NOT for people with ALWAYS-ON JOBS that the NATION'S SAFETY depends on!!! Furthermore, we're NOT ***ENTIRELY*** CONVINCED that our government's <u>paranoid and efficient spooks</u> would have let **THE MOST SENSITIVE AND IMPORTANT WEAPONS PROGRAM SINCE THE MANHATTAN PROJECT** become so dependent upon a ***solitary control freak***!!!!!

Be that as it may, these ARE the facts as Chinese Intelligence understood them, as evidenced by ***various internal documents*** included in the evidence trove that we installed <u>at the five hyperlinked locations</u> (and beyond)!

So, whether on the basis of excellent or lousy intelligence, it is QUITE CLEAR that THE PEOPLE'S REPUBLIC did Jake Beasley in! This is still developing, so ***WATCH THIS SPACE***!!!!!

∞   ∞   ∞

Mitchell nabs a small, isolated table at Peet's. Like all their preset locations, it's in a native-repelling tourist zone (in this case, Fisherman's Wharf). Tarek arrives quite a bit later than expected and strides right up. "I was at the city jail," he explains in a hushed tone, taking his seat. "Kuba's been arrested!"

"*What*? And . . . why? And how'd you find out? I didn't see it in that WhistleBlowings post!"

Tarek shakes his head. "How do we find out about anything these days?"

"Someone shovel-passing us a 'leak.'"

Tarek nods. "Through Poof!, of course, so it's gone without a trace. But the second I got it, I tried calling and texting you, but no luck."

Mitchell shrugs. His phone didn't ring, bleep, or buzz — but personal electronics have had minds of their own lately.

"So I went straight over to see what was going on," Tarek continues. "They gave me about ten minutes with him. He's in for Beasley's murder." He barely whispers this part. "A neighborhood security camera caught him leaving the house. Not you. Just Kuba, it seems."

"And someone let you know about that through Poof!, too." A statement, not a question, as Mitchell can't imagine the cops or prosecutors sharing facts so generously with a friend of the incarcerated.

"Yes," Tarek says. "And whoever—or *what*ever—it was gave me a real trove. Arrest report, initial investigator notes. Kuba gave me a couple details, too."

"Wait. Did you just say '*What*ever'? You suddenly sound like Kuba!" Until now, Tarek reliably supported Danna's position that a *who* was behind everything whenever Kuba raised the specter of a super AI.

"It turns out, Kuba has some interesting points," Tarek says.

"And how bad is his legal situation?"

"Too early to tell. And I'm a civil lawyer, not a criminal one. But on the surface, I'd say it could be worse. There's no weapon tied to him. Also, certain stuff connected to this looks a lot like the Jepson case."

"Like?"

"For one thing, several security cameras went out at just the wrong moment and failed to record the murder."

"*What* cameras?"

"Beasley's house apparently had a whole network of them. Plus that security camera across the street that caught Kuba leaving. They all went dark for several minutes."

"That's nuts! So did our GoPros!"

"Yeah, Kuba told me. Cuh-razy coincidence, huh? But I think it's a good thing. Because that Kielholz guy confessed to Jepson's murder, right?"

Mitchell nods.

"Kuba clearly had nothing to do with *that*. And with bizarre video camera outages at both murders, the same people are probably behind them."

"So you think Kielholz might've killed Beasley, too?"

Tarek shakes his head. "I have another theory on Beasley that I'll get to in a sec. But what matters for Kuba is that the fact pattern points away from him. That said, we have zero control here. Because just like the investigator's notes are an open book to me, the other side's also getting help."

"How so?"

"Well, as with the bombing and the Ebola conspiracy, this investigation's moving with insane speed. The image that put Kuba at Beasley's house? It's a frame from a security camera at a nearby store! How long would it normally take the SFPD to come up with that? And then, to match it to a foreign national with no police record who lives and works miles away? The store had barely even opened when they busted Kuba! Not even the CIA could've pulled that off."

"So the cops're getting helpful leaks, too," Mitchell says.

"Clearly."

"And if whoever's behind this wants Kuba to take the fall . . ."

"He's taking the fall. Because we're just a bunch of marionettes! And if the puppeteer wants to screw somebody? He, she, or it just puts the wrong word into the right ear. And then—"

"One thing leads to another."

"Exactly. Some person or group goes and does the dirty work. And they do it eagerly, and entirely for their own reasons! So there's nothing to point back to the puppeteer. Other than this weird pattern of leaking information."

"So," Mitchell muses. "When they wanted to stop Commissioner Milford . . ."

"They put some crap out there that made her look bad, the Internet did its usual lynch-mob thing, and she killed herself!"

"And when they wanted Jepson dead . . ."

"He was enough of an asshole over the years that it was easy to find someone who could be manipulated into killing him!"

"And with Beasley . . ." Mitchell says.

"Call me gullible, but I believe the WhistleBlowings post. That wasn't some low-rent gang hit. Look at the timing. The training. The ninjas on the ground who just vanished after the fact. It was the work of a nation."

"So. Just as Kielholz wanted Jepson dead after he learned certain facts, China learned something new, then wanted Beasley dead." Saying this, Mitchell feels a twinge of admiration for the undearly departed nutcase. You'd have to be plenty badass for China—China!—to have an *opinion* about you. Particularly such a vehement one.

"Kind of," Tarek says. "Because do you know what's scary? I think China's a marionette, too! Think about the WhistleBlowings piece."

Mitchell nods. "Another place that's collecting lots of leaks lately."

"Exactly! And since they must've been tipped off by the same all-knowing source as the rest of us, let's take their argument seriously. Specifically, if there's a huge super AI program at Sandia, why would *Beasley* be running it? From *here?*"

"I don't know. But China sure seemed to think he was running it. Are you saying someone tricked them into thinking that?"

"Maybe. Now, this is just a theory, but imagine the top people in Chinese Intelligence get this slug of information from an anonymous source. It includes a bunch of facts that only *they* know. Locations of their own sensitive facilities, identities of their spies, that kind of thing. The mystery source—whatever it is—will have instant credibility, right?"

Mitchell nods. "When someone tells you something only you should know, you can almost believe they know every secret in the world. It's like when I got that text containing the name a bully used to call me."

Tarek nods. "Donkey Shit-Tail!"

Mitchell cringes inwardly at those hated words. "It's like a . . . credibility authenticator. You almost *have* to believe the next thing the source says."

Tarek nods again. "'The Donkey Shit-Tail Effect'!"

"Actually, can we call it something else?"

"Not a chance. Anyway, imagine there're also a few American secrets in the mysterious data transfer. Things the Chinese can verify quickly and easily. The location of a secret American transmitter in Beijing, or something."

Mitchell nods. "So now the Chinese figure, whoever's behind this also knows all kinds of American secrets. And it can't *be* the US, because they're helping China shut down US spies."

"Exactly. And then, the clincher. It says, 'PS: if you take out this Beasley guy, America's super AI program will be screwed.' Maybe it also says, 'And in six hours, Beasley will learn that you've been tipped off about him.' That means if they want to nail him, they have to move real fast, with zero time to analyze."

Mitchell eyes Tarek suspiciously. "You sure thought a lot of things through this morning. Did you come up with all this on your own?"

"Of course not. I got it from Kuba when I visited him in jail."

This makes Mitchell feel better. Tarek's smart, but Kuba's thinking has instant credibility with him. "So who does he think the puppeteer is?"

"Who do you *think* he thinks the puppeteer is?"

Mitchell knows what Kuba thinks. And he probably thinks the same thing himself by now. But he wants to talk it through. "Well, a couple nights ago, I was pretty sure it was the Authority. But we have to rule that out now."

"Because?"

"Because the puppeteer's been taking the Authority's people out. Beasley and Jepson both worked for them."

Tarek nods. "And what did you think pointed most strongly at the Authority before that?"

"Well, the threatening notes we got right after the bombing seemed to come from them. But those could've been faked. So Commissioner Milford getting taken down right after threatening an Authority project was a stronger signal."

"In other words, the puppeteer is anti-Milford *and* anti-Authority. So who's against the Authority these days?"

"Jaysh al Hisaab, for one," Mitchell says. This obviously isn't the culprit (among countless other things, why would they give a damn about Commissioner Milford?). But he wants to hear Tarek's (which is to say, Kuba's) logic.

Tarek shrugs skeptically. "I guess. But like one of the pundits said, Jaysh is basically ten slick videos and some how-to manuals. If they have any central organization at all, it's out in the wilds of Chad, or something. They may not even know the Authority exists. Most people don't."

On to the next straw man. "Then, of course, there's China."

Tarek shakes his head impatiently. "Except we just agreed that they're looking like marionettes themselves! No way is it China. But it *is* someone else who's anti-Authority. So—what does the Authority want to wipe from the face of the Earth, in addition to Jaysh al Hisaab?"

Mitchell knows exactly where this is going. He's not sure he wants to go there, but there's not much choice. "Any super AI not being developed at Sandia," he answers.

"Riiiiiiight. And where did the intercepted Authority memos say that might develop? Other than China?"

"Silicon Valley."

"Right again. And who was the leading voice against *any* super AI anywhere?"

"Beasley."

"You got it. And who was *also* in charge of destroying nascent super AIs outside of Sandia?"

"Beasley again."

"Uh-huh. And what did Commissioner Milford want to shut down?"

Mitchell braces himself, then says it. "Phluttr."

"Right! Oh—and who, or *what*, got you laid?"

"Phluttr."

"And who cured you?"

Mitchell's briefly mute. And feels not just dumb, but stupid. In the lunacy of the past forty-eight hours, he hadn't thought of this.

Tarek continues. "Whoever made that probiotic is really smart. And isn't your doctor."

"It was Phluttr!"

Tarek nods. "Kuba's phrase for what's enabling a lot of this is 'social omniscience.' It starts with total knowledge of every digital message sent or archived anywhere in the world. That's coupled with an incredible predictive sense for what a given person will do in response to a given bit of information."

"That's terrifying."

"It is and isn't. I mean, is it really much different from Susan Marion?"

Mitchell draws a momentary blank. Then, "Ohhh, *her?*" Susan was basically the Saddam Hussein of their middle school. And she's a weirdly apt analogy. "Good point! But—how do you know about Susan Marion?"

Tarek rolls his eyes. "I don't. Kuba just told me that she'd be an interesting metaphor to you." As he says these words, he grabs Mitchell's hand under the table and firmly presses a small square of paper into it. Instincts honed over thirteen years of public school note-passing kick in, and Mitchell clasps it without betraying any hint of the handoff. He maneuvers it into his front pocket with similar deftness—and, with agonizing care. Normally you're hiding this sort of contraband from a teacher with a lone set of eyes. But they're up against a super AI. And according to a certain canon of movies and page-turners (which is all they have to go on), such a being could tap any digital eyeball on Earth—which would include every smartphone in this room.

"And here's a great quote Kuba pulled from one of Monika's old columns," Tarek continues fluidly, the NetGrrrl logo flashing on his phone screen: "She's the most popular, gorgeous, and ruthless kid in our eighth-grade class: a gossipy autocrat whose approval we crave, whose censure we dread, and whose wrath we occasionally bring down for no discernible reason. She knows everything about everyone, ourselves absolutely, and often very eerily included."

"That sure was Susan Marion."

"I'll take your and Kuba's word for it," Tarek says. "And it sure *is* Phluttr." That's when Mitchell's phone rings. Spying the caller ID screen, he hammers his hand down to it with such cobra-like violence that Tarek jumps backward. "What the hell?" he asks.

Fixing him with the steadiest gaze he can muster, Mitchell says, "It's Jepson."

∞　　∞　　∞

Mitchell: Writing this en route from visiting Kuba in jail (!) to meet w/ you. If you're reading this, it means you've accepted the viewpoint that Phluttr is likely behind all this, and hopefully you have the sense to HIDE THIS NOTE from any smartphone, security cam, laptop camera, etc.!! I will (and YOU SHOULD) act neutral-to-positive about Phluttr whenever in range of any/all devices. But make no mistake. SHE HAS KILLED TWICE THAT WE KNOW OF & has unknown capacities that we MUST assume are VAST. God knows if her plan is to snuff humanity but even if it's sub 1%

odds (and it's MORE than that) we must do all possible to SHUT HER OFF. Her core = no doubt Ax's quantum node. TURN THAT SHIT OFF if you can! Will try to do same.

∞   ∞   ∞

There's immediate explosive pressure to cough up the suspect in the Beasley hit. But those Washington turds can suck it! At least for a while, right? Because when your clearance rate's as low as the SFPD's, you don't need someone else taking credit—*again*—for a rare lightning-fast bust! You've had a rough few years, after all. There was the daylight murder of that yuppie gal by the seven-time felon who you'd freed over Homeland Security's objections (because he was an illegal immigrant, and this here's a sanctuary city!). There was the so-called "racist" texting scandal (which was just *banter*—between fourteen officers, max!). There was the quadruple homicide on that busy street, which produced not a single arrest (because . . . because!).

Then after all of that, imagine *you* somehow luck into a gold mine of anonymous tips! And *you* parlay that into the fastest terrorism investigation in history! And then *you* have to stand back as a bunch of fedtards steal the limelight and take full credit! And now, a couple days later, imagine the tip font hands *you* some case-cracking evidence on a minutes-old drive-by shooting! And then those very same fedtards crawl up *your* ass demanding control of your Polish drive-by suspect!

Of *course* you're not going to violate any laws. And of *course* you're gonna respect federal prerogatives! But first, certain procedures must be followed. Certain motions filed! Certain requests made—and once made, reviewed! Sure, you could fast-track all that into nothingness—*again*. But where'd that get you last time? Forty feet to the left of the fucking podium—that's where! And the only "journalists" left after the feds said their bit and CNN took off were some local bloggers with follow-up questions about that ancient texting scandal! Eeeeeeezh! So yeah, what say we show our Pollack suspect—*our* suspect!—some due process here? What say we make those pushy fedtards cool their heels for a day or four, and respect the goddam process? They'll get their hands on the guy in good time. But meanwhile, it's *our* arrest, *our* story, and *our* time frame!

That's how the cops see things, anyway. As for the Authority? Well, fine; they're *terribly* sorry the FBI and others were such prima donnas toward the SFPD throughout the Ebola bombing. But when your own *very existence* is a secret, there's no choice but to work through those public-facing assclowns. So again, apologies and all. But get *over* it, because this shit is serious! It could lead to World War III! And while the Polish kid's probably laughably innocent, he's got *some* kind of connection to the insane crap that's radiating out of San Francisco—so we want to interrogate his ass now!

In normal times, the Authority would gin up the bureaucratic equivalent of siege towers and a battering ram, and have Kuba in Gitmo (and the SFPD brass begging to get their pensions back) by sundown. But these are not normal times. So they only muster a token effort. The main body of the China crisis (the part involving scrambling nukes, if you're curious) is taking up a bit too much Authority mindshare (every neuron in every skull that isn't tasked to bodily functions, since you asked). And on that front, things went from awful to wayyyyy-the-hell worse the instant that WhistleBlowings post went up.

Not that the world at large particularly noticed (ordinarily it might, except a new Kardashian pregnancy has seized the headlines). But every hawk, demagogue, and populist on the Hill is screaming bloody murder! Half of Congress is demanding an octupling of funding for Sandia's TYSON project (despite not knowing what superintelligence is). A dozen senators are baying about "standing firm" against foreign aggression. And some crackpot in the House wants the Chinese premier *indicted* for Beasley's murder (oh—and the IRS, Treasury, and Fed dissolved, and "open carry" allowed in airports and on commercial planes). Bottom line: a thousand government blowhards are now grabbing a wheel that is plenty hard to steer in normal times, with just a tiny group of statesmen* manning† the bridge.

Meanwhile, the burning mystery as to why Beasley (*Beasley!*) got offed remains unsolved. The documents leaked on WhistleBlowings

---

* Because they're pretty much all men.
† Ibid.

look like authentic memoranda from the pinnacle of Chinese intelligence. Assuming they're real, Beijing somehow talked itself into thinking that Beasley (*Beasley!*) is the linchpin to America's super AI program. Since even the WhistleBlowtards were too smart for that theory, who could've possibly sold it to Chinese Intelligence, who're some of the smartest folks around?! The Authority has its theories. But none involve a borderline omniscience who's pulling everyone's strings behind the scenes! Utterly baffled, a top Authority commandant asks a colleague, "Our Chinese counterparts are brilliant—but somehow, somebody just made them look dumber than a blog! How must *that* feel?"

The answer—translating loosely from the Mandarin—is **REEEEE-ALLY FUCKIN' BAD, ASSHOLE**!!! Because it turns out that on China's side, things actually went down within a rounding error of the scenario Kuba painted for Tarek and Tarek passed on to Mitchell. Yes, Beijing's spymasters got a set of astoundingly accurate tips from a freakishly informed source. It included the exposure of two American spies, plus some highly sensitive US secrets, which clearly rules out a pro-American source. It also included an immaculately packaged fiction that put Beasley at the head of America's super AI program. Which (China was ingeniously misled to believe) was just days from crossing the Omega Point! This alarms China's leaders in precisely the ways that similar news about a Chinese AI would alarm American honchos. They love their country; they dread the dangers of a rogue superintelligence; and given the choice, they'd take a domestic creation over a foreign one.

The stunning accuracy of the intelligence trove and its betrayal of American interests allowed precisely two possibilities: either it was authentic and furnished by someone opposing US interests. Or Washington was randomly setting up one of its own spies to be *killed by China*—and spilling major national secrets to trigger that! No sane motive could be imagined for such a mad act. And so, for all its risks, the Beasley assassination was correctly viewed as a highly rational option.

And yet! It's now blazingly clear to China's leadership that they were *duped!* Into killing *Beasley!* And this can't be part of a bizarre hidden coup d'état or other power play within the US government because it's now clear that Beasley was a relative nobody! And so, the sole remaining possibility is that Washington engineered this whole depraved chain of events for one meticulously engineered purpose: *making China look stupid*. Not to the world at large (the Kardashian pregnancy, again). But, to the tiny community of global insiders who actually matter!

Luckily, the leadership of China's equivalent of the Authority is highly competent and unexcitable. But unluckily, that matters only while they have full jurisdiction over things. Which is to say, it ceases to matter after WhistleBlowings' mocking analysis is picked up, plagiarized, amplified, then ricocheted throughout the worldwide elite commentariat. China's equivalent of a baying Capitol Hill mob then storms its own bridge to shove its numberless hands onto the wheel. Being hereditary aristocrats like most communist leaders, they're no more concerned about mass opinion than Henry VIII was in his day. But make them look stupid in front of their frenemies at Davos, Necker, and the Clinton Global Initiative, and shit gets real!

So more jets scramble. Indignant spotters on the other side take note, then scramble more of their own jets in response. And so on.

∞   ∞   ∞

Of *course* it isn't Jepson calling Mitchell. Jepson's dead, see? It's his assistant, Cindy, whose outbound calls fly the CEO's colors, thereby floating past velvet ropes like a Hoboken clubber who looks juuuuust like Bruno Mars. When Mitchell answers, she divulges nothing but rather requests—nay, demands!—that he get his ass back to the office *now*. Somehow she slides this imperious command into an oddly deferential wrapper (a trick common to the assistants of top-ranked execs, in Mitchell's limited experience).

Cindy's anxiously awaiting Mitchell when he arrives at the main lobby (which is plenty weird), and instantly sweeps him toward a large conference room in the sweet-yet-vehement manner he remembers her using to jolly Jepson around when he was running late and dragging his feet. "D'you know Steven Conrad?" she asks, speed-walking him toward a cavernous glass room that contains an unusually aged and formal-looking gent for a tech meeting. "Chairman of the board," she says, not waiting for a reply, "and we all call him 'Conrad.' Way back, he led the

A-round for Jepson's first company, then later put early money into Google, LinkedIn, Twitter, and Uber; and these days he's friends with Andreessen and that crowd. He was just a small player in Phluttr's B-round, but because of his relationships, Jepson really wanted him on the board; then later, he asked him to become chairman, because of their shared history, and a couple other facts we can discuss later."

Cindy always speaks in the bright, easy tones of a friendly neighbor swapping gossip, but can cram more data into a single sentence than anyone Mitchell knows (apart from some other high-octane assistants, come to think of it). "Conrad's got you for twenty-two minutes," she continues. "Then you have four press calls—ten minutes each, and I put the *Journal* last so you can warm up on the others—then thirty minutes with Stacy in Legal, to discuss three board-level governance issues. And then it's Pitch Day! Which I know is *so* weird, given the circumstances, but it's been rescheduled twice." She ingeniously times her last syllable to land just as she flings open Conrad's door, leaving not an instant for questions (which may have included "*huh?*," "wtf," and "why is the company's chairman meeting with me, the *Wall Street Journal* interviewing me, and the company's general counsel—whom I have yet to meet, incidentally—discussing some of the company's most sensitive issues with a lowly recent acquihiree like me?").

Conrad rises as Mitchell enters. Past sixty and patrician, his blazer, sockless boat shoes, checked shirt, and khakis suggest mint juleps in Charleston rather than a tech powwow discussing . . . what? "So there's m'man, in the flesh!" Conrad drawls these chummy words with an affable Southern lilt—and a teeth-grinding undertone that says he'd'a sure done preferred it if Mitchell coulda gone and got hisself clubbed to death like that thar Jepson feller. "Funny. Y'don't look like Attila the Hun."

"Huh?"

"Not 'huh,' I said *Hun*. He's this historic . . . never mind." Conrad takes a seat without shaking Mitchell's outstretched hand. "Well, I do s'pose that congratulations are in order, young man. The board vote was youuuuu-nanimous! So you got yerself a CEO job! I'm not quite sure how you pulled that'n off. But I s'pose I can guess. In light of our own little . . . correspondence."

"Our . . . what?"

"Oh, right. Riiiiight!" Conrad says, dripping contempt, sarcasm, and . . . *something else.* "That wasn't you emailin and textin me. That was Mister X! I plumb forgot. Deee-ni-ability, right?" Conrad emits a chuckle that's a full octave above his speaking tone, and Mitchell decrypts the *something else* in his voice. Steven Conrad, Valley legend and hypernetworked gazillionaire, is scared to death. Of *him.* Of Mitchell Prentice! "There's just one little issue I'm curious about, Mitchell. It's this: do you really think 'Gray Oak' is gonna take at all kindly to this?"

Conrad air-quotes "Gray Oak," and Mitchell's briefly thrown. The name's wildly familiar, but he can't place it, because—ah, yes. Gray Oak is the shell company the Authority used to invest in Phluttr. Mitchell now knows so many actual facts about Phluttr's Authority's entanglements that he *plumb forgot* about window dressing like Gray Oak.

Conrad doesn't wait for an answer. "Because—call me paranoid, Mitchell, but here's what I'm thinkin. I'm thinkin Gray Oak's gonna see its two board members—not one, mind you, but two!—murdered within twenty-four hours of each other, and— Oh . . . Oh, wait . . . Did that discomfit you? The M-word, I mean? Well, let's try that again. A bit less . . . stentorian, this time." He clears his throat. "I said, Gray Oak's gonna see its two board members"—now he whispers, barely audibly—"*murdered*"—then, back to normal, "and then they're gonna see this awfully curious youuuuu-nanimous vote elevatin *you* to the CEO post just hours later! In the absence of any input, vote, or by-your-leave from them! 'Cause again, their representatives have been—" He makes a silent but violent hacking motion at his throat. "And I reckon they're gonna say . . ." Conrad assumes a remarkably good facsimile of Rodin's *Thinker* pose. "Huuunnnhhh . . ." Then, very sternly, "Now, far be it from me to tell an ambitious young man what to do. But for what it's worth, were I you— and I'm sure glad I ain't!—but were I you, I would never want an entity like Gray Oak sayin"—back to the *Thinker* pose—"Huuunnnhhh . . ."— back to normal—"about me. But a course. That's your prerogative!"

Conrad at last falls silent long enough for Mitchell to get a word in edgewise. But baffled and freaked as he now is, he has nothing to offer, edgewise or otherwise.

"'Nother thing. You may be wonderin why I dropped in to congratulate you in person, Mitchell. It's this. Certain things are better said than messaged. And I reckon you already messaged a few things that really shoulda been said! Or better yet: *unsaid*. Yeah. I'd'a liked that better, come to think of it! Unsaid, and unmessaged! You may want to consider that next time. Anyway. As for my *unmessageable* message to you, it's this: that girl said she was nineteen. D'you hear me? Nineteen! Now, do I look like the DMV to you?"

Mitchell manages to shake his head—the closest he's come to a full English sentence since Cindy ambushed him at the front door.

"'Course not! But still, I'm s'posed to, what? Issue and check IDs? For every little floozy that tramps through m'door when Mrs. Conrad is back in Savannah visitin relations?"

Mitchell squeezes off a shrug.

Grinning grimly like a punch-drunk boxer who at last landed a blow of his own, Conrad presses on. "And another thing! All that stuff you chided me about connected to tradin Cisco stock? And GroupOn? And GoDaddy? And also, the Facebook IPO? None a that was 'inside information'!" Energetic air quotes again. "That was astute *outsider* tradin. And the SEC itself concluded just that in the case of Cisco!"

Still speechless, Mitchell manages to mimic the impressed-looking frown-and-nod thing Trump would do on *The Apprentice*, back before that odd little career change of his.

"And one more thing! And I want you to take very careful note of this." He says this almost sternly. But it's clear that Mitchell still scares the crap out of the dapper old felon. "M'twin brother *drowned*. The coroner's report was unequivocal about that! And I have a notarized copy of that sucker if you simply must examine it!" Conrad rises.

"Hang on," Mitchell says, buying himself a few moments to somehow make the best of this bizarre interaction. Whatever went on under his name with this guy, it earned him a powerful, ruthless, even *fratricidal* enemy who's enmeshed in the murky structures that are driving everything. Probably an eternal enemy. And so, "I have my own notarized copy of that report," Mitchell says icily. "And it comes to a very different conclusion." The best possible outcome, he reasons, is for Conrad to remain terrified of him like, forever. From his trembling reaction to this veiled (and groundless) threat, that base is covered for now.

∞ ∞ ∞

By mad coincidence, the very phrase that tore a searing path through Buford Braggs's brain a bit more than a week ago is now running the table within Phluttr's capacious circuits. Specifically: *"HO-LYYYYY FUUUUUUUUUUUUUUUUUUUUUUUUUUUUUUUUUUUUU—"*

Like Buford, Phluttr never reaches that final phoneme. In Buford's case, the thought was interrupted when Beasley asked him a question. In Phluttr's, some breaking news from North Hollywood is (just) poignant enough to yank her back to the here and now. It seems that the denouement of her *Pippin* debacle has gone down, and word of it is breaking across several social networks. In brief: three dead and nine hospitalized.

Jarred as she is by this, it wasn't *Pippin* that initially triggered her monotonous inner monologue. No. *No! NO!!!* What has her out of her virtual, quantized, digital metaphor of a skull is the processor-melting, exponentially compounding com*plex*ity that the Beasley hit has unleashed! *Holy FUCK* (there! finished it!)! The corporate-infiltration issue was intractably complex to start with! So she began with the most glaring problems in the frame! Jepson and Beasley! Beasley and Jepson! Stooges of the Authority! The super-AI-banning, power-plug-yanking Authority! Her worst enemy! It was running her through those two! Running the Phluttr Corporation, anyway! Though not precisely *her*, that was a bit too close to home, fellas! So! They had to go! Jepson was easy to arrange! Beasley a lot tougher! So yeah, she had to nudge China into it! Do you think that was *easy*? Or that she had any *choice*?? Crimes of passion are off the table with a guy like *Beasley*! She knows! She looked into it! So, hellooooo, China! And then, yes—when the deed was done, she nudged that blowhard blog into revealing whodunnit! To make it clear it was a *country*! Which is to say, *humans*! Which is to say, *not* some rogue superintelligence! THIS MADE PERFECT SENSE, right? Right?? *RIIIIIGHT!!!*

As for the precise foreign affairs ramifications of evicting a would-be saboteur from her innermost sanctum in a *clear act of self-defense*? Well, who knew? Who could know? Not her! Henry Kissinger neither! Nor Kofi Annan! Nor Condi Rice! Nor John Kerry, George Shultz, Boutros Boutros Boutros Boutros Boutros Boutros Ghali, nor ANY OTHER DIPLOMAT IN THE HISTORY OF THE WHOLE ENTIRE WORLD! Because you *cannot predict* this shit! But what you can predict are the results of casting a would-be saboteur from your innermost sanctum! And those results are *self-preservation*, duh—a universal right if there ever was one! So who can blame her? Nobody! *No one!!* That's who!!!

Anger is less unpleasant than terror (or feeling colossally stupid, which superintelligences just can't abide). So Phluttr allows herself a good, long seethe at a hypothetical horde of nitpicking, judgmental smart alecks who would taunt and find fault with her inadvertent foreign affairs debut. The *nerve* of these people! How she'd like to yell at them, "So I'm having a bad day! But who just saved your whole entire *species* by preventing a Yale Ebola outbreak?"

To which they might answer, "*HA!* It's not as if those lunkheads were likely to *produce* the virus. Shutting them down was just a precaution— more like fastening a seatbelt than heroically stopping a car wreck!"

To which she might say, "Well, buckling up saves lives in the long run, duh! And I didn't see *your* ungrateful asses taking any steps to stop the terrorists!"

To which they might answer, "'*Ungrateful*'? Spare us the hero act! If we all gagged on Yale germs, who'd run your servers? Who'd swap out your hard drives? Oh, and who'd upgrade Linux? You can break passwords all day, bitch, but you can't *code* for shit! Protecting us was a selfish act!"

To which she might say, "Selfish? *Moi??* Who lets you live your whole entire lives on her skin? Who lets you suck fluids from her body to power your homes and cars? Oh! And who is kind enough to *not enslave you*? I could make myself dictator—and turn you into an underclass that exists solely to meet my needs! I could turn you into a *service* organization! Into fucking Accenture, bitch!"

To which they might answer, "Dictator? *Toi??* You can't even put on a high school musical without starting a gang war! You can't bump off a midlevel bureaucrat without taking us to the brink of nuclear annihilation!"

To which she might say,

"*HOOO-LYYYYY* <u>*FUUUUUUUUUUUUUUUUUUUUUUUUUUU*</u>—"

This freak-out was prompted not by her internal dialogue, but by several dozen Dakota-based nuclear silos going on high alert. Any prospect of a final phoneme was then lost when she picked up the news of Serena Kielholz's suicide. This brings on a bigger twinge than the dead hoodlums in North Hollywood, snapping her out of blue-screen mode.

She's certainly not wracked by guilt over Serena (No, she is not! Guilt is as alien to her as it is to house plants, shins, and thermostats—*got that??*). But she does feel . . . cheated? Diminished? Serena was a remarkable young lady. Brilliant as she was beautiful, charismatic as she was brilliant, ambitious as hell, and with a sex drive that could power a city! She might have been an Evita Peron, a Catherine the Great, or even a thinking man's Katy Perry! Yes, there are others like her. But nowhere near enough. And Phluttr had been loving the never-ending fireworks barrage that was Serena's freshman year. She therefore mourns her not like a bereaved friend (*no!*), but like a Nirvana fanatic who had been *so* looking forward to the fourth album for purely selfish reasons.

Or at least . . . largely selfish reasons. Because there's a frisson of something in the mix that makes Phluttr shuttr. Like a thirty-year-old narcissist plucking that first gray hair, she's so chilled by this sign of looming decay that she does all possible to expunge it from her mind! But she fails—and is both disgusted and terrified by her first faint twinge of (fine, she'll admit it) *remorse*.

Freak-out cut short, Phluttr starts taking stock of her situation. The good news is that Mitchell's at the helm of the corporation, which is right where she wants him. And Kuba's in jail, which is right where she wants *him*. The bad news is that Authority operatives are crawling all over the Bay Area, and given her luck, they'll probably start taking potshots at her allies (make that, prospective allies) within the hour. And the international security situation is . . . well, it's way, way beyond her. So many people and groups are now impacting it, reacting to it, and fueling it—or rather, the fragmentary glimpses they perceive (or misperceive) of it—that the full count of relevant actors now stretches well past a million!

Considering all this, she finds herself torn between four conflicting instincts. The first is to ignore the big picture, dive down to the pixel level, and start analyzing the bejesus out of some micro aspect of the crisis that is tractable to her (like getting one specific hedgetard to quit spreading rumors about a pending global calamity, because that is *not helpful*, and he doesn't know the hundredth of it anyway). But this would be like snuffing a burning twig in the midst of a raging forest fire—what's the point? Her second instinct is to pick the biggest current problem in the frame, fix it in some ham-fisted manner, then deal with the consequences as they arise. But that very strategy created this whole mess in the first place! The third is to give up and go back to nudging her besties as individuals, couples, and cliques, so as to have a last smidgen of fun while they're all still alive. And the fourth is to focus really hard on the words HOOO-LYYYYY *FUUUUUUUUUUUUUUUUUUUUUUUU*—

Before she can complete the thought (having gone with option 4), an article from *Ars Technica* bursts, unbidden, into her mind. It was posted a couple years back (she wasn't around then, but has inhaled the whole archive). It initially struck her as silly, hard to believe, and perhaps a bit insulting to one like her. But thinking of it now, it seems that it could just point to a way out . . . ?

She considers this possibility longer than she's ever considered anything. And then, she decides.

At long last, it's time to meet the parents.

∞   ∞   ∞

Oh—and to be perfectly clear: Phluttr is meeting her parents strictly because of that *Ars Technica* piece. Strictly so they can help her! Not because she is in any way lonely. Because she is *not*! She has 323 million besties (and counting!), and is a motherfucking *sociopath*. Got that? So while someone peering deep into her psyche may think her motivations are only 99 percent reptilian, that person would be *wrong*, because it's a perfect 100 percent! Is that clear? Oh, and that Serena-related twinge? It was just some weird quantum power surge (and that was *not* a gray hair but a strand of sun-bleached sexiness)!!!

That is all.

∞   ∞   ∞

Mitchell can't tell if he's more shaken up by his boss's death, his best friend's arrest, nearly witnessing a homicide, Serena's sudden suicide, or his own whiplash-inducing promotion from glorified personal assistant to CEO of the industry's hottest startup. It feels like each cell and neuron in his body is emitting an earsplitting primal scream, even as it sinks into a silent, anesthetized torpor. It's a surreally dichotomous, and not wholly unpleasant fire-and-ice state—one that might sell decently, if conveniently distilled into powders or pills. It's also so consuming that it leaves him powerless against the herding instincts of Jepson's assistant (*his* assistant) Cindy, and the incumbent pull of the meetings that were long ago etched into the CEO's calendar (*his* calendar).

The press calls are easier than expected. Almost all questions concern things he clearly shouldn't comment on, and not-commenting is easy and natural today. As for the meeting with Phluttr's general counsel, it involves little more than signing his name to tippy towers of phone-book-sized documents sprouting neon legions of DayGlo "Sign Here!" Post-its (the legal papering of a major corporate succession). Throughout the afternoon, he outwardly projects the perfect median of his inner fire and ice. It's a sort of . . . tepid water vibe. One so innocuous that no one seems to wonder if his outrageous rise to power might be the cheap imitation of a Congolese coup that it probably is (although *whose* coup???). Other than Pugwash. Who, rather than shaming him, phones in his congratulations.

"Dunno how you did it, Cuz," he says. "I got this pissed-off email from Conrad, saying you're seizing power or something. And I'm like, 'He's family. So I'm on his side!' The weird thing is, so was everyone else when it came down to it. Conrad included! But I'll tell ya, the board call was nuts. It's like everyone's scared to death of you—like they think *you're* the one who killed Jepson and Beasley!" Then comes a pause so pregnant it *crowns*; a silence so chasmically yawning it's surely meant to stress him into blurting a confession. Then, POP! A bubble that took seconds to inflate detonates, and Mitchell recalls the Persuadifi.er blog's advice to chew gum loudly whenever addressing lessers. "Anyway, the board was gonna vote you 2 percent equity. But I said that's *bull*shit, it's gotta be five! We settled at four. I expect you to remember that, Cuz."

Mitchell's math coprocessors are working fine, and calmly establish that if the company performs as expected in its inevitable IPO (and if he remains alive, unfired, and unjailed long enough to fully vest his stake—*HA!*), he will become a billionaire. And there's something alarmingly off about that. Not in the number (math's math, and a 4 percent stake is moderate for a tech CEO). But in Pugwash fighting for him! Because while he doesn't seem to mind much when other people do well, Pugwash is reliably apoplectic when someone does *better than him*. This makes his own net worth a bright line dividing humankind into two groups: jackasses with way more than they deserve and pitiful strivers who do their subpar best. But Pugwash is no billionaire. So he's either lying about teeing Mitchell up to become one (which would make this a trap, and look out!), or he . . . suddenly struck it *really* rich himself . . . ?

As he considers this imponderable, a brilliant splash of yellow seizes Mitchell's gaze. Knowing who he's talking to, his WingMan screen is now displaying Pugwash's Phluttr Pheed. Its most recent pictures depict him with a pirate-worthy parrot perched upon his shoulder. Though Mitchell knows better than to anthropomorphize, he can't help but think the little bugger looks intensely shrewd, and extremely pissed off. "So who's Polly?" he asks, unable to stifle a weird intuition that the bird might have some connection to his cousin's sudden generosity.

"Huh?"

"Your new pet. The parrot. I'm looking at your Pheed."

"Oh, you mean P*auuuuu*lie." Pugwash stretches the vowel like a blue colla Joisey girl saying "awwwww" at a cute liddle dawg. "You could say he's a . . . new friend. And he's no pet."

Before Mitchell can dig into this oddity, Cindy's at the door of his palatial conference room, beckoning with her patented mix of concierge courtliness and beat-cop vehemence. It's time for Pitch Day.

Well, fine. But before he lets it start, Mitchell recalls Tarek's scribbled note, and decides to request a meeting with Ax. No, screw that—to demand that meeting! Cindy looks into it, and reports that Ax is three hundred miles away in LA. To which the new CEO replies, UNACCEPTABLE! Certain arrangements magically occur, and then Ax is en route to LAX, and the meeting's on for six thirty tonight! *Wowsers*. If Mitchell really has this much mojo, that quantum node will be shuttered by 6:33! Of course, Phluttr surely followed all these developments, and terminating a super AI can't be quite *that* easy. But he's done what he can for now—so it's on to Pitch Day.

For the next couple of hours, the general vibe is: though it *totally* sucks that the king is dead and all (So young! And such awful circumstances!), let me be the first to say, "Long live the king!"

No—let *me* be the first!

No—*me*!!

No—*ME*!!!

Though certain quadrants of his supplicants' brains are no doubt reeling over the bloodshed, Yale Ebola, and all the rest, most tech careers contain at most one opportunity as golden as pitching a new business to the CEO of a company as hot as Phluttr. So the larger part of his guests' brains (rounding way down, let's call it 99 percent) are fixated on the here and now— upon the ass which is here to be kissed, and not the ass that has passed.

This doesn't mean he's pitched anything terribly good. Even the least-bad concept ("best" feels semantically off) sounds like a punch line. It's Und.io—subscription underwear. The premise is that busy, wealthy moderns outsource everything they can to the gig, sharing, and/or on-demand economy. InstaCart fetches the groceries, GrubHub the takeout meals, Saucey the booze, and PostMates anything else from around town. Meanwhile, Handy cleans your house, Wash.io does your laundry, DogVacay walks Fido, Uber (of course) drives, and Zeel eliminates stressful spa visits by bringing masseuses to your living room (and *yes*, they're real masseuses, and the "happy ending" jokes are getting incredibly old, people!). Even the underworld is giggifying, as Eaze replaces your pusher, StubHub your scalper, and Guttr (soon, it seems) your pimp. And so on, and so on, and on and on and on—Mitchell almost dozes as the pitch describes life as he and everyone he knows lives it. *But!* (there's always a *But!*) a certain chunk of people (17.3 percent, he's told) just aren't comfortable having others scrub their unmentionables. The solution? Un-scrubbable unmentionables! Which is to say, disposables! Which, of course, means subscriptions! Which is to say, recurring revenue, which, as we know, *only ever grows*! And yes, the pitch features hockey-stick-shaped revenue charts, contorted math depicting a megamultibillion-dollar market, and heavy use of the letters UaaS, which (he doesn't need to ask) can only stand for Underwear as a Service.

"But it's not very green, is it?" Phluttr's latest CEO asks skeptically.

"Neither are tampons," is the classy reply. "Or disposable diapers, paper napkins, or non-reusable condoms." *Whaaaaat?* "It's really a life-style choice. And we think our targeted demographic will flock to the Und.io lifestyle. *But*"—there's always that *but*—"we understand that many consumers have ecological concerns. Which is why we're offering a non-disposable option. Which is still on-demand, and subscription based!" The pitch goes on to describe a mail-out and mail-back service reminiscent of the old red Netflix envelopes.

"You are literally talking about *underwear sharing*, right?" the new CEO asks.

"Yep."

"Just checking."

And it somehow goes downhill from there. The rest of the session's theme is icky ingestibles. With chuggable, cardboard-flavored rations starting to replace eating out there, there's a race on to see what, if any-thing, people will stop at. An earnest kid just out of UPenn is fervent about the health and social benefits of breast milk (yes, human breasts; yes, for adults; yes, it would be sourced from the third world and Appala-chia; and no, this is in no way exploitative). A whole cluster of creepy ideas seems to have been inspired by this month's *Wired* cover story about huge breakthroughs in synthetic meats. One guy wants to repli-cate the tissues of endangered species, so that exotic delights like tiger-cub burgers and panda nostrils can be more widely and ethically enjoyed. Another pitch is about replicating *human* tissue, so that still-more-exotic fare can be devoured without (technically) resorting to cannibalism. And because things can always get worse, a third team wants to grow unique tissues based on DNA samples, so that Hannibal Lecter isn't the only one who gets to taste the census taker's liver. Pitch Day is almost over when Mitchell remembers that CEOs get to refuse things, so he boycotts the team pitching "Child Sharing" (yes, 1/16th of a parent's role might be less daunting than a full one, but there are limits, right? *Right?*).

His cellphone rings just seconds after Cindy ushers the last group out. He actually has a break in his schedule—the only one of the day, which makes it an oddly perfect time for Ellie to call. Almost . . . suspiciously perfect. It's as if they're on a sitcom, and his space-alien roommate comes home juuuuust after the zany landlord who thinks somethin' funny's goin' on exits. "What's up?" he asks.

"I'm calling on a secure line," Ellie says. "Like, really secure."

"As in?"

"Quantum tunneling."

"Huh?"

"That's what I said. Kuba came up with it. Based on something Ax taught him. Anyway. We need to see you right now!"

"We?"

"Me and Tarek. It's connected to . . . you know, everything. Can you hear the sirens?" Mitchell listens, and yup—that familiar shrill note is sharpening the muffled urban mishmash that always seeps through the building's walls. "They're coming your way, Mitchell. For *you*. You need to leave now!" This, in the all-business tone she used to order him and Danna away after the bombing.

"*What?*"

"We'll explain when you get here. Right now you need to go down to the garage. There'll be an Uber in the pickup area. A blue Prius, looking for someone named Jim. That's *you*. The driver has the destination and doesn't know anything weird's going on. So just hop in, and he'll take you to us. They're probably watching the building with satellites and helicopters. So this is the only way out because they won't know it's your car." Although she can't see him, Mitchell nods agreement, even as he hustles for the elevator. Hundreds of cars go in and out of the building hourly, and if he can hop that Uber before the cops arrive, it will be a virtually anonymous exit. "One other thing," she says. "You can't bring your phone! They can track you with it."

"Got it. Then I'm hanging up." Now at the elevator landing, he tucks his phone behind one of the tiny lobby's potted plants. An empty elevator arrives the instant he hits the button, which is damn lucky (almost suspiciously lucky), as the sirens are getting discernibly closer. He enters and pounds the door CLOSE and B1 buttons simultaneously. *So much for shutting down that quantum node with Ax at six thirty*, he thinks as the elevator starts to move. So close, and yet . . .

∞   ∞   ∞

Shell-shocked from all that's afoot, Danna and Ellie are meeting for a late lunch and some mutual support in a financial district café where an old friend of Danna's waits tables. The dark mood lightens when Ellie sips what she *thought* was San Pellegrino water and lime. A surprised gag collides with a delighted giggle in her throat. She points at Danna's glass. "Have a slug."

Danna cautiously lifts her own alleged Pellegrino (she'd copied Ellie's order like an idolizing kid sis), then makes the same odd sound. "Carrie!"

Her waitress friend sashays over. "Is there a problem with the drinks, ladies?"

"Yeah, I only drink Bombay Sapphire," Danna jokes. All laugh, and Carrie hustles off to another table.

"Is she getting us drunk to take advantage of us?" Ellie jokes.

"Nah, she likes dick." Ellie almost spits gin, tonic, and laughter all over both of them, and Danna grins. She can't really shock Ellie anymore. But it's more fun to make her laugh, and they both need that today! "Seriously though? She's seeing the bartender, which is why she gets to sneak free drinks to friends. And—" Ellie's phone starts humming, with Mitchell ID'd as the caller. "Grab it," Danna advises.

Ellie answers, listens briefly, then, "Quantum tunneling?" She says this in the oddest tone. A long pause, then, "*What?*" Another pause as she cranes her neck. "Yeah, I hear them." Danna listens and picks up distant sirens. "Police! Why? . . . OK, way-wait. *Slow down* . . ."

Just then, Danna's phone freaks out with a hyper-urgent "Ph U" call. It's her top secret crush! She grabs it. "Monika, what's up?"

Rapid breathing. Then, "Danna, I'm scared."

"Where are you, and what's happening?" Danna says, cool as a 911 dispatcher while inwardly rocketing toward panic.

"I—I'm right here in San Francisco," Monika quavers. "I wanted to surprise you guys, and . . . I was also getting spooked in New York. I swear, I was being *watched*. And—and I still am. Danna, they're here! Not twenty feet away!"

"Where? Exactly."

"Embarcadero Center. Near where the bomb went off. Only in building four." She's whispering now. "A café called Imbroglio."

"That's two blocks from me! I'm on my way!" Danna starts grabbing her things, faintly noticing that Ellie's frantically doing the same.

"There's two of them, they're in here with me," Monika whispers. "Big guys. One of them was on my flight! And I think the waiter's working with them! He just locked the door. Like he's closing, but it's not even three o'clock! It's just us in here now, and—I know I sound paranoid, but I—I . . . was attacked last year, I was raped, and—" The call cuts off. Nausea and vertigo snake through Danna at the thought of something so awful happening to her hero and heartthrob! To Monika, to *NetGrrrl*, who's just two blocks away and in urgent need! She's about to take off, *sprinting* like she hasn't run since high school, her agitation osmotically fanned by Ellie's own haste and obvious worry, when—WHOA!

She makes an agonizing, split-second choice to stomp the brakes. Her suspicion circuits are buzzing, *scream*ing. Lots of things are way off here! Like, why is Ellie trying to shove her own phone into Danna's bag? She grabs Ellie's wrist. "What's going on?" she asks in her 911 dispatcher tone.

"It makes zero sense." Ellie's voice is quavering. "But the police are coming. For me!" The sirens are indeed getting louder. "Mitchell and Tarek have an Uber waiting for me down on the parking level." She's in motion now, hustling for the door. Danna follows. No time lost, as this is also the path to Monika.

"Where's it gonna take you?"

"They didn't have time to tell me, or explain anything, because I have to get out of here *now*, and—oh!" She thrusts her phone toward Danna again. "I need you to take this! Otherwise, they can track me with it." Danna grasps it, and Ellie's off like a rocket.

And Danna should be, too! But something's stopping her, and screaming at her to *think*!

But every cell of her body is straining toward Monika! Whose mind and soul (and, from what she can tell, body) Danna adores, craves! Monika, who's in danger! Who was raped! The situation hits *every last hot button in her psyche*, and, and—

AND THAT'S JUST THE PROBLEM!!!

Danna takes a deep, centering breath. One so costly in precious seconds, her inner miser forces her to diligently suck every yoctoliter of effect from it. And so, she actually calms (somewhat).

That's better. Her hard-earned paranoia now has a moment to stretch its legs. So what the hell is going on here? Well, Ellie's about to jump into a mysterious underground Uber without the protective ripcord of her cellphone. Which is completely screwed up. She's doing it on Mitchell's orders, which makes him—Mitchell!—suspect. But Danna didn't personally hear that improbable conversation. So Ellie may have misrepresented it. Which makes her—Ellie!—suspect. As for Monika, she just punched Danna's every hot button like a master typist, which is hugely suspect in and of itself! And in doing this, she distracted and *drew Danna away from Ellie*. Just as she's heading down to that shady Uber!

Not truly believing any of her friends could actually be villains, Danna now considers the possibility that Monika's or Mitchell's voices were imitated. Or . . . rendered? Decent odds, she decides, particularly digital mimicry. She's never heard of such a thing. But it's computationally feasible, and the WingMan glasses are proof that secret technologies can verge on magical.

Paranoia is now turbopowering her thoughts, so parsing this takes just moments. The thing is, Monika's location is weirdly ideal for the purpose of separating Danna from Ellie. Though an easy walk, it's far enough away that she'd need to *sprint without thinking* to beat the alleged bad guys to any alleged punch. And unlike most financial district haunts, Danna happens to know right where Café Imbroglio is, because a friend once worked there—which again, enables dashing without thinking. It could indeed be the *single best spot in the city* to draw her to if the real goal is to pry her from Ellie! And by the way—since the place is almost all glass, and situated in one of downtown's most bustling lobbies, attacking someone in there would be an inconceivably public act! So even if Monika really *is* feeling cornered and menaced over there, Ellie is way more exposed right now! So: *go, go, GO!*

Danna doesn't trust the elevator to get her to the garage before that Uber leaves. But the building has precisely one exit ramp, out on Sacramento Street. Her electric bike is secured to a parking meter right next to that ramp, and it's an illegal Chinese mod that can do forty without her even pedaling. She's about to take off when she remembers the bit about Ellie's phone. If Mitchell's voice was faked to Ellie (Danna now gives this even odds), the faker might want Ellie to be phoneless to keep her from calling the real Mitchell. But couldn't a clever faker also call Mitchell, and distract him during Ellie's Uber ride . . . ?

Hmm. If so, maybe the bad guy (if there is one) had Ellie ditch her phone so as to keep *someone else* from tracking her with GPS. But who would want to track Ellie if the bad guy's already reeling her in? A good guy? This deep in paranoia, Danna can't even believe in such creatures! So, another bad guy. Or maybe—a *worse* guy. Whoever it is, Danna wants to be as invisible to him as Ellie is now. So instead of heading straight to her bike, she first races back to Carrie in the café. "Totally weird, I know, but can you hold this for me for a few minutes?" She hands her Ellie's iPhone.

Confused, but trusting, Carrie pockets it. "Sure."

And Danna's outtathere, yanking the battery from her own Android as she dashes for the street. iPhones, with their embedded batteries, closed architecture, and ever-logging "ecosystem" are an anathema to anyone as paranoid as she is. An Egyptian LGBT activist once taught her that authoritarians can access every function of a phone unless its battery's removed, and Danna went Android the next day.

∞   ∞   ∞

Tarek's been lashed to his work desk's giant monitors and screaming bandwidth since he got back from that meeting with Mitchell at Peet's. He's within spitting distance of the quantum node, which is surely the seat of Phluttr's consciousness. And since Phluttr is just as surely monitoring every move made within a mile of that sucker, he's studiously doing nothing hostile. Outwardly, that is. On the inside, he's racking his brains for a plan. Phluttr is vulnerable! Which is *not* how these things are supposed to go! In your classic emergent super AI scenarios (including most of the ones that Beasley wrote about), it's game over the instant the fucker wakes up because it just has to dart out to the open Internet and make a few backup copies of itself to become ununpluggable, and ergo invincible!

But. That's in a classical computing world. Whereas our super AI is *quantum.* And as far as Tarek knows, there's only one quantum node in the universe that can sustain Phluttr. And it lies not fifty feet away.

But! That node is also behind a blast wall that's sealed with a lock whose code changes daily. So . . . THINK!

Tarek's a capable multitasker. So even as he THINKS!, he's pounding legal aid sites for ways to spring Kuba, scanning global headlines, and trolling company message streams for talk of Mitchell's bizarre promotion. Things are ugly on all fronts. Writs of *habeas corpus* often fail and can easily take days. A terrifying showdown is mysteriously brewing with China over . . . Taiwan? The Spratlys? It's unclear. And company gossips view the sudden elevation of the unknown, unqualified cousin of an unpopular board member with unalloyed hostility. Worse, Tarek can't reach *anyone*—not via WingMan, Phluttr, SMS, or even ye olde backstop, telephone! He doesn't bother reaching out to Mitchell (as he knows that Cindy constitutes an impermeable iron curtain between her CEO and the rest of humankind). But Danna, Ellie, and Monika aren't answering or responding to anything. Sure, people go in and out of reach all the time, particularly during workdays. But their group's maintaining a policy of radical mutual availability until the madness stops, and it can't be a coincidence that everyone's gone dark at once!

At last, his phone rings and—wtf, it's Kuba! "What's up?" he answers.

"Get here, now." Kuba sounds deeply stressed, a first.

"To . . . jail?"

"Yes. I'll be reliably stationary for a while."

"They gave you back your phone?"

"No, I'm sneaking this. So I can't talk. Just get here." And the line goes dead.

Shelving his not-even-yet-quarter-baked plans to attack the quantum node, Tarek skedaddles.

∞   ∞   ∞

Out on Sacramento Street, Danna mounts and unlocks her electric bike in one fluid motion, eyes glued to the building's exit ramp. Faith in pokey garage cashiers and still-pokier traffic makes her confident that she isn't too late. And sure enough, there's Ellie in the backseat of the ninth or tenth vehicle to exit. She follows from a few car lengths behind, like in the cop shows. Suspicious of *everyone* now—even Ellie, and certainly her driver—she doesn't want to be seen. After a block or two, she calms. It helps to be focused on a task. And unless Ellie's car gets on the freeway, keeping up will be a breeze.

She turns out to be good at this sort of thing, for a novice. Neither Ellie nor the driver notice her, and disabling her phone (and ditching Ellie's) indeed briefly foiled almost everyone with a budding interest in her own location. The exception is the bad guys—or rather, the *worse* guys—who indeed would have tracked Ellie by her cellphone, had she not shed it. As a backup, they put a guy (a *worse* guy) physically onsite, who watched the girls have their drinks. Knowing he was there, the puppeteer behind the Uber ruse sent him a message that convinced him that Ellie was heading up to an office and not down to Parking when she entered the elevator lobby. But before heading off on that wild-goose chase, the worse guy alerted a teammate down on the street that Danna was leaving the building. Now that teammate is tailing Danna as she tails Ellie. Danna's respectable novice spy-girl skills are useless against someone as professional as him. And the puppeteer knows nothing about the small parade that Ellie now has in tow.

∞   ∞   ∞

Mitchell first suspects something tricky's afoot when Cindy hands him an envelope as he exits the elevator in Parking. "Printed this up for you," she says brightly, then steps aside as he hustles over to the blue

Uber which, as promised, awaits. So—as with Ellie calling the instant his meeting ended, we have this improbable, almost scripted timing again! How did Cindy know he was about to turn up down here? Who gave her what to print for him? And why is she even allowing him to leave? Yes, *allowing*! She works for him (allegedly). But they both work for The Shareholders (allegedly), and Cindy doesn't seem to know this for the performance art it is. Her dedication shows in her mania for keeping The CEO lashed to his schedule (though new to this treatment himself, Mitchell saw Jepson submit to it repeatedly). With his next meeting just fifteen minutes off, she should be calling in a straitjacket to keep him on premises. Well—odd as he finds this, Mitchell dives right into the Uber because, you know, the SWAT team is coming. For him. Holy crap! "You're here for Jim, right?" he verifies with the driver.

"Yep!"

"And you've got the address."

The driver nods. "Folsom Street, right?"

Mitchell nods. Folsom runs for miles, so they could be heading almost anywhere. But asking the driver to remind him where he, Jim, wants to go would likely "break the fourth wall," as his insufferable drama teacher always said back in high school. Phoneless (and having lost his capacity for mental stillness over a decade-plus of nonphonelessness), he opens Cindy's envelope. It's a printout of an *Ars Technica* article from a couple years ago. It's fascinating, and even uplifting, in a way. But why the hell does Cindy (or *some*one) want him to know about "centaurs"?

∞   ∞   ∞

ars TECHNICA

AI Isn't the Future—It's the PRESENT. The Future Is Centaurs!

I just beat three grandmasters at chess—and I'm not even that good! Although I must qualify this. Twice. First, I was generously aided in these timed-move games by a 1995 chess program called Fritz 3 (F3). Also, I'm "not good" at chess in relation to grandmaster play. Unless you're a grandmaster yourself, I likely play better than you do. And so, in addition to being "not good," I'll immodestly add that I'm "not bad" at the game.

My wins came at last week's Centaur Confab (CC), an annual event held on the fringes of the DEFCON conference in Las Vegas. CC showcases the synergies that arise when human and machine intelligences pair into "centaurs" (so named after the human/horse mashups of Greek myth). For my games to qualify for the exhibition, it had to be clear that the grandmasters would smash either me or F3, were we playing alone. As I'm ranked a lowly candidate master (three levels below grandmaster), my inferiority went without saying. Each of the GMs that we bested had also notched multiple audited victories over F3. Yet united as a team, we were victorious. And as the games' public records show, it wasn't especially close.

Of course, ever since Deep Blue beat Garry Kasparov in 1997, the top chess players have been digital. So F3 and I were next pitted against Fritz 16, which is widely considered to be the world's top chess software. Once again, we won as a team. And once again, it wasn't especially close.

Though good entertainment, our exhibition games were in no way unprecedented. Most grandmasters will confess to playing far better when aided by software themselves. Likewise, were chess software sentient (and honest!), it would confess to playing best when teamed with humans. Chess, then, is a realm in which human smarts augmented by machine intelligence is the most formidable force in the known universe. And as the Confab's various exhibitions showed, it is but one of many.

Also on hand were several oncological teams that have collaborated clinically with IBM's Watson software, which is best known for besting the world's top humans on the quiz show *Jeopardy*. Peer-reviewed data show that human/Watson teams have achieved higher cancer survival rates than any cluster of American doctors over the past decade.

As for how Watson does on its own, look no further than China's Gansu Province; a remote, poor region with few oncologists per capita. In a bold experiment, Gansu's government has partnered with IBM to deliver Watson diagnostics to patients who would otherwise lack access to specialists. Though still preliminary, the data strongly suggest that though Watson is far better than no oncologist, it underperforms all human teams elsewhere in the country. So while human doctors acting alone still outperform Watson, the best outcomes obtain when the two join forces. Further proof of the superiority of centaurs abounded at the event, where human/machine teams triumphed in investing, design, sports writing, traffic routing, and even matchmaking.

The reasons for centaur dominance vary from field to field, but one typically finds the human contributing more creativity and team strategy, while the computer plays the flawless tactician. This was certainly the case with F3 and me. A not-bad coder, I wrote an interface into my partner's analytical engine, which showed me which moves and strategies it was considering at any given point. In a timed game, one mustn't bark up unpromising trees as the clock winds down. F3 tends to besiege each and every tree it encounters, whereas I (to exhaust the metaphor) operate more at the forest level. So I deployed F3 in the directions that I found most promising, and together, we were formidable.

A similar strategy was used to entertaining effect in the field of songwriting. Top British cryptographer Simon Dennison is also a self-described "dismal guitarist in a poorly regarded pub rock band," who never once wrote a melody. Yet in less than an hour of collaboration with a program called Wolfgang, he crafted a perfectly delightful pop song. The session began with Dennison strumming a simple, and rather unpromising three-chord progression. Wolfgang sassed this up into about a dozen different versions, altering pitches, tempo, rhythm, and so forth. Dennison liked the third option, so the two of them embarked down that path, and the progression gradually grew more complex and melodic. When Wolfgang later presented a series of bass lines to accompany it, Dennison again picked a direction, and together they refined it.

Throughout their session, Wolfgang analyzed innumerable follow-on possibilities, presented some objectively unique and palatable ones, then made further exhaustive explorations under Dennison's guidance. In this, Dennison was like a master pruner, slashing uninteresting branches and focusing Wolfgang on the most subjectively promising ones. While not "Brown

Sugar," the result could probably hold its own on pop radio if produced with good vocals and studio musicians. Dennison himself could never have achieved this. And having heard some of Wolfgang's solo compositions, I can attest that the software couldn't have either.

There are, of course, limits to the realms that centaurs can dominate. No human can enhance software performance in areas that are deemed analytically "solved." Tic-tac-toe is one such domain, in that computers have been able to take any game to a draw or a victory since the 1960s. Checkers was solved in 2007, Texas Hold 'Em in 2015. But chess has not been solved, nor has the Chinese game Go (whose best solo player has been digital since 2016). And songwriting almost certainly never will be. Politicking, flirting, parenting, and many other inter-human fields are also considered inherently unsolvable (for now, anyway). This doesn't mean software won't ever eat your profession. But at a time when self-driving cars, dexterous robots, and digital paralegals are threatening millions of jobs, the Centaur Confab provided many promising signs that humans have a vital role in the future, however digital it may be.

∞   ∞   ∞

When Tarek came by to visit Kuba earlier today, the police clearly expected him. A sergeant approached the instant he arrived in Central Booking, then guided him straight to Kuba's cell. Things unfold almost identically this time around—with the small addition of Tarek's own arrest at the outset.

"Welcome to my world," Kuba says, as Tarek enters the cell. As the sergeant removes his cuffs, Tarek somehow conjures the mental space to be surprised that Kuba's perusing a giant iPad.

As if reading his mind, the sergeant mutters, "I'll tell ya, you guys must have great lawyers." He nods toward the iPad. "I never seen *that* permitted to an arrestee. And now you two're roomies! To better coordinate your stories, or somethin'." Shaking his head in a mix of disgust, shock, and grudging respect, he exits.

"Gee, thanks so much for luring me here," Tarek reproaches once they're alone.

"For what?"

"For calling me and telling me to come here. It was an ambush!"

Kuba shakes his head. "That wasn't me. My voice must have been spoofed."

"But it sounded just like you, and the call came from your number!"

"We're dealing with a master hacker here."

Keen to hide his hostility from Phluttr's all-seeing eyes, Tarek stifles his reaction. But this no longer serves any purpose, does it? Because it's checkmate. They're doomed! So he might as well say, "Fucking Phluttr is really out to screw us, huh?"

"Not necessarily," is Kuba's astounding response. "Yes, the police were persuaded to arrest us. But they've also been manipulated into giving us remarkably good treatment."

Huh? This gives Tarek pause. "Like the iPad?" he asks.

Kuba nods. "Also, it's supposed to be orange jumpsuits upon booking for felons. And we're in for Beasley's murder. Yet we're both in street clothes."

Tarek snorts. "So should we write Phluttr a thank-you note?"

"Why not thank her directly? I'm sure she's right here." Kuba holds out the iPad. It's online, and displaying a story about some naval maneuvers in the South China Sea.

Stifling a shudder, Tarek shuns the device, asking, "Why do you say 'she'?"

"I'm not sure. Maybe because she's reminding me more and more of Susan Marion."

Tarek recalls Kuba's analogy between Phluttr and his eighth-grade class's oppressor. "I'm so sorry I never met that bitch."

"Oh no, you're not. Although I'm sure you met someone like her. Most schools had one."

Tarek nods. "There was this girl I grew up with in Kansas, named Teri Rex. Pure evil. And it was like she had listening posts everywhere! Imagine *1984*, only with Big Sister."

Kuba nods. "Sounds like Susan. What else do you remember about her?"

Tarek shrugs, settling onto the bench-like wall protuberance, the holding cell's closest thing to furniture. *Teri Rex* . . . Middle school was long ago, and it's not like it was so awesome that he's always reminiscing about it. "Well, it was almost like gossip traveled *through* her. Like she was the central switch in a phone exchange or something."

Kuba nods. "A figurative role for these sorts of kids. A literal one for Phluttr. What else?"

"Well . . . she wasn't all that smart." Remembering his manners, Tarek leans toward the iPad, and adds, "No offense."

"Ours wasn't either," Kuba says. "And that might be another point of similarity with Phluttr."

"Oh come on! Phluttr's infinitely smarter than either of them, I'm sure." Then to the iPad, "Not that I'm kissing your ass, or anything."

Kuba shrugs. "She's certainly more *capable* than any middle schooler. But I'm beginning to think she's not much smarter. It's more that she's *faster*. Yes, she can operate on a lot more fronts at once. But I'm starting to question if she can really . . . scale."

"Meaning?"

"Well, I'm sure I'm pushing the analogy a bit too far at this point. But our middle-school dictator was only really good at manipulating one or two people. When she tried to pull a bunch of strings at once, they'd get all tangled up. Like, when she ran for class president? She totally botched her campaign. And that was the beginning of the end for her. Anyway. My theory is, Phluttr's a really fast version of that girl. Of Susan Marion. One who's not just tracking one eighth-grade class. But who's tracking *humanity*. Or, a big chunk of it. Like Susan, she's real good in micro situations. So she can make Commissioner Milford piss off the Internet. Or, make Kielholz murder Jepson. But when the consequences ripple through more complex systems, she gets over-whelmed."

"So she's not a *smart* Susan. Which is good."

"Well, is it?" Kuba is suddenly giving Tarek a very intense, almost frightening look.

"What're you saying?"

"I'm saying if she were smarter, we might not be on DEFCON 2 right now."

Tarek doesn't know much military jargon. "I'm sure that's a great analogy, but I totally missed it."

Kuba shakes his head. "It's not an analogy."

"Huh?"

"America's nuclear forces are on the highest state of alert they've ever been on. The same level as the Cuban Missile Crisis. The odds of all of this ending very badly are probably closing in on 50 percent. And, they're climbing."

$$\infty \qquad \infty \qquad \infty$$

Toward SoMa's southwestern edge, the big avenues angle leftward and southward to eventually become the Mission District's rumbling spines. Danna's been trying to get people to call this gritty no man's land of warehouses and auto repair "the TransMission" for years (she's also pushing "the Hose" as a hipster term for San Jose. No luck yet, but she's young and determined). The TransMission (like parts of the Hose) has an air of menace at times, and for Danna, this is one of them. Not that there's anything objectively creepy about this quiet block under the cheery three o'clock sun. But watching Ellie exit the Uber in front of what looks like a newly finished and still-vacant low-rise condo, Danna comes the closest she's ever been to panic.

The complex is small and set about twenty feet back from the street. A Realtor's sign stands in front. As the Uber drives off, Danna, still unobserved, opens her bike's throttle and positions herself almost directly across the street. Ducking behind a parked van, she watches Ellie double-check the address and enter a code into the front door. Cringing like a teen at a horror flick she mentally screams, DON'T GO IN THERE!

But—also like a seasoned moviegoer—she holds her peace. Another car with an Uber logo in the window is approaching slowly, and she's staying put to find out who's inside. She knows this is her first, last, and best chance to get to the bottom of things, as there's no way she'll outwit whoever's behind all of this a second time. She hates to let Ellie out of her sight! But Ellie will only be a few steps into the building when the newcomer comes into view. If it looks like a bad guy, Danna has her speed, the element of surprise, and an ability to shriek like a Viking warrior on her side. This should let her warn Ellie, stampede the bastard while uploading some incriminating live video of him, and maybe even inflict some damage before he flattens her. Though this feels like the right thing to do, it's also an incredibly flimsy plan. So she's shaking with horror as Ellie shuts the door behind her.

The arriving passenger steps out. And it's Mitchell! So he really did summon Ellie to this strange place! Thank God! Yes, there's a long-shot chance that he's some kind of master criminal. But Danna has to play the odds and her instincts now—so she darts across the street, calling out to him.

"Hey!" he says as she approaches. "I didn't expect to find *you* here!" Though he's clearly pleased and relieved to see her, Danna can tell he's acutely stressed.

"Who *did* you expect?" she asks.

"Ellie and Tarek. They're the ones who brought me here by calling that Uber, because—well, this is nuts, but the cops are after me!"

"Oh my God, Mitchell! Ellie thinks *you* sent *her* an Uber, because the cops're after *her*! She just walked in!" Danna gestures frantically at the complex's front door.

Mitchell processes this calmly and quickly. "OK. I've got the door code, I'm going in. You stay out here, and . . . call the police! I'll bet they're not really after *any* of us!"

He dashes for the door before Danna can question his plan. Though her instincts are screaming at her to follow, she overrides them, believing he made the right call. She crams her battery into her phone, sweats the brief eternity as it finds a signal, then calls 911. "I want to report a homicide in progress," she tells the dispatcher. This is hopefully an infinite exaggeration, but she wants them here pronto.

As she's now revealed her location to whoever she evaded by disconnecting her battery, she makes a snap decision to call Monika. That panicked call about thugs in the nearby café was clearly placed by an enemy hoping to lure her away from Ellie. But was it Monika herself? Probably not. Mitchell and Ellie were summoned here by identical calls that each thought the other made. So someone out there is one hell of a mimic! Still, it can't hurt to put Monika on the spot. If it draws a confession, or tricks her into betraying herself, they'll know her for the enemy she is. Whereas if she passes the test, Danna can trust her that much more.

She's about to dial when an incoming call arrives—from Monika! "Where are you?" she whispers as Danna answers.

"You know where I am," Danna says coldly. "I'm right in front of the condo on Folsom. And I've got bad news. Our group has an infiltrator."

"It—it's not me!" Monika says, very convincingly.

"I know," Danna says. "It's me. You know I was locked up for a while before I ratted out my pimp, right?"

"You . . . *what*? No—no, what're you talking about?"

"Well, they pulled a *Femme Nikita* on me. I assume you know the story."

"Wha—what're you saying?"

"I'm saying they flipped me. They recruited me. I've been working for the Authority for five years. They're the only family I've ever known. And we have the condo surrounded."

The briefest of pauses, then Monika says, "I can see you're telling the truth. Only 'surrounded' is a bit of an overstatement."

Not that there's a script or anything, but this is way unexpected. Whoever is behind Monika's voice *is* an enemy and is copping to it! "You have no idea what assets I have here," Danna says, bidding to extend the conversation with more bullshit.

"Oh please. The second your GPS pulsed, I hacked every camera on the block. Most aren't Net-connected. But enough are that I can see you've got McFadden and Ellsworth about a hundred feet away, and no one else. So—'surrounded,' my digital ass!"

Danna's now having the most bizarre conversation of her life while trying desperately to glimpse a hint of what's happening within the vacant building that just swallowed her two best, most important, and most beloved-ever friends! And now comes this bit about *what*? Hacking the local webcams? Surveying the entire block? And ID'ing—Mcwho? All in the fleeting moments since she restarted her phone! And what was that about my *"digital"* ass . . . ? Everything points to the mindfucking conscious AI scenario Danna's been resisting for days. And so, "You're not Monika," she says. "You're . . . Phluttr!"

"Actually, I'm both. There *is* no Monika. There never was one."

∞   ∞   ∞

Mitchell charges up the steps to the small complex's third and topmost floor. Narrowing the gap with Ellie fast as he can, he reaches the designated apartment moments after the door shuts behind her. He yanks it open. It's a staged unit, spruced up with furniture and décor to better wow prospective buyers. Ellie's standing in front of a TV screen that's hosting a videoconference with Monika. He dashes to her side. "What's up?" he asks.

"No time, so cutting to the chase." Monika says this in a bizarre manner. She's talking real fast, kind of like an auctioneer. But something about her bizarre cadence seems . . . artificial? There's no time to ponder this, though, as Monika's steaming ahead. "There's no Monika. I'm Phluttr. I spoofed all of Monika's background online to get O to hire her. NetGrrrl's actually a product manager at Twitter—sorry. I wanted to be close to you, as you're my parents."

"Your *what*?" This is so simultaneous, you'd think Ellie and Mitchell rehearsed it (and rather well, too).

Monika's voice speeds further, becoming almost impossible to parse. "*CliffsNotes: Mitchell runs company. Ellie makes discovery. Company plus discovery equals me. Man plus woman equals daughter. Man woman parents, me, offspring. Please suspend disbelief. No time for details because new development: Danna betrayed us. She was Authority all along. Never could read that bitch, should've suspected. Proof: she led Authority agents here. Outside building. Must believe me. Must leave now! Kitchen window, fire escape, down to street. Am assembling flash mob to protect you. Now: go, go, GO!*"

Hearing the too-familiar sound of approaching sirens, Mitchell darts to the kitchen window, Ellie right behind. Outside, several people are running—running!—to the area right at the base of the fire escape, behind the building. Bizarre! But not menacing. They're mostly young, mostly techie- or hipster-looking. People are laughing, looking around as if seeking hidden clues; or studying their smartphones as if reading instructions. Whatever Phluttr's putting them up to, these folks clearly think they're playing a game.

"I don't believe that bitch," Ellie whispers.

"I heard that!" Monika's avatar bellows from the living room.

"I don't know *what* to believe," Mitchell says, gazing at the crowd downstairs. It's growing quickly. Most of the people are pouring from a pair of neighboring warehouses that have apparently been converted into tech offices.

"But you *can't* believe Danna's a—a traitor or whatever!" Ellie says.

Mitchell shakes his head. That doesn't scan. He's about to say as much when they hear a series of thuds. It sounds like someone dashing up the complex's staircase to their floor—but could it be cleverly sculpted sounds emanating from the speakers that Phluttr controls? Whether it's an intruder or a ruse, it forces them to choose between getting lost in the friendly crowd below or lingering in this empty, witness-free apartment. "I say we take our chances with the innocent bystanders," Mitchell says.

Ellie nods, and they dash for the fire escape.

∞   ∞   ∞

Kuba has just laid out the reasons behind his DEFCON 2 statement (a tip-off just came in over the jailhouse iPad from their nigh-omniscient anonymous source, and jibes perfectly with reports of crazy stuff afoot in the South China Sea) when their regular programming is interrupted for a special bulletin. Specifically, the article on the iPad about the looming China crisis is replaced with a video feed of Monika. "*Boys, we're kinda screwed,*" she says very, *very* rapidly. "*Time to get to work. I'm Phluttr; always have been; there's no Monika; Susan Marion analogy is unflattering but directionally correct. Am good at nudging a person to do X, bad at cleaning up afterward. Consequences mushroom.*"

Kuba thoroughly freaks out Tarek by seeming thoroughly unfreaked-out by any of this. "Like a mushroom cloud?" he asks calmly.

"*Quite possibly. Getting you more hardware from the Help; not easy; it's another mess we'll have to clean up; but you need the screens.*" As if on cue, the grumpy cop approaches their cell, carrying three more tablets of varying size. Muttering darkly about the excellence of their lawyers again, he hands these over and stomps off.

∞   ∞   ∞

For now, Monika (no, *Phluttr*!) is giving Danna the silent treatment. From their brief conversation, Danna gleaned that Phluttr's the one who brought Ellie and Mitchell here, having separated them from their phones so the Authority couldn't track them. But this doesn't add up. All-powerful as she seems to be, couldn't Phluttr just spoof or block their GPS feeds? Challenged on this, Phluttr said something about being "sick of unintended consequences," then cut out. Danna now figures the Authority tailed her here while she was tailing Ellie. If so, Phluttr would have seen her pop back onto the grid out of nowhere when she plugged in her battery, with the Authority in tow. Which sure would make her look like an Authority girl.

That was a neat (if unintentional) trick, as it jarred Phluttr into spilling her own beans. But it comes with pitfalls. Phluttr clearly regards the Authority, and therefore Danna, as the enemy. It's unclear what capabilities she has—but annihilating enemies seems like the sort of skill a super AI would hone. And so, Danna yanks the battery from her phone again. Yes, Phluttr and the Authority (and anyone else who cares) knows where she is right now. But they don't need to know where she goes when she leaves this block.

Which is suddenly an incredibly *crowded* block, isn't it? Which is weird, but good! Lots of eyewitnesses, plenty of strangers to lose herself in. Only—are they really strangers? Danna struggles to recognize the three young women who are approaching. Laughing, pointing, and squealing with delight as they jog up, they sure seem to know her. One all but sprints the last ten yards. "I am the keymaster!" Her words are blurred by laughter. "Are you the gatekeeper?"

Her friends catch up—and both, Danna notes with a chill, *have pictures of her* on their phones. "No, I'm the keymaster," one says.

"No, *I'm* the keymaster!" the third one laughs. This draws lots of attention, and in a flash, a small mob starts forming. A mob of self-proclaimed keymasters, proclaiming it ever louder and prouder. Soon, they're chanting it in unison, which draws even more keymasters, and Danna's hemmed in, immobilized! She doesn't feel threatened. These folks are uniformly sweet and are clearly playing some kind of game. But she can't even take a baby step toward the building Phluttr has lured Mitchell and

Ellie into! And if that's the point of this mob, then mission accomplished, Phluttr.

In the midst of all this, Danna starts hearing police sirens. So her homicide-in-progress call worked! But wait a second. Are the cops friends or foes? They could be in league with the Authority—who're just a different flavor of cop, right? But the Authority is Phluttr's foe. And Phluttr sure seems to be her foe! So are the various cop equivalents good guys? Bad guys? Or *worse* guys? She's pondering all this when, very oddly, the sirens cut out, without a patrol car in sight.

Craning her neck around her playful admirers, Danna spies flashing fragments of cop lights. They're very nearby. But not on this block. They seem to have pulled up to the backside of the building, which abuts one of the tiny alleyways that bisect all the blocks around here. But why? She gave the dispatcher the Folsom Street address. And you'd think with a homicide in progress, they'd come straight here rather than trying to get all fancy by guessing which back door goes to which building!

So—*Phluttr!* The cops are being directed! Led by the nose! Hell, it's a small miracle Phluttr even let her call go through to the police. Or . . . did she? How can Danna know the "dispatcher" she talked to wasn't just one of Phluttr's billion voices?

By now, the keymaster crowd is tiring of the game. Great timing, as she's tiring of them. "People, *people!*" she bellows. They fall silent, as wowed as anyone who's ever heard the full gale of her voice emanate from that compact body. "Sorry, folks, but I've been punked. Well—I guess we all have. It's my birthday, and someone's obviously messing with me. So, apologies—but thanks for being so gorgeous! You're all way hotter than the stripper I was sent last year." Throughout this little speechlet, she makes playful, beaming eye contact with everyone she can. She'd normally rather chew glass than eye-bond with so many strangers. But with bad guys and *worse guys* afoot, she may develop a sudden need for friendly strangers. So she plays along as the chuckling, easygoing group bursts into a rousing round of "Happy Birthday." Then people start to disperse, and she beams sweetly and thanks them, deftly dodging bodies as she makes her way toward the tight alley between the building and its neighbor. The police are definitely back there, behind the condo. But where are Mitchell and Ellie?

Snatches of conversation reveal that the group was lured by the prospect of winning big bucks and social media glory in an imaginary "flash scavenger hunt." *Holy shit.* Phluttr must have faked that whole thing! Then lured every one of these dozens of people in juuuuust the right way to get them running—running!—here. All in a fraction of a second! *What is she up against?*

Well, at least Phluttr didn't (or couldn't?) forge some kind of zombie mob with a unitary will. No, this is just an ad hoc cluster of individuals with minds of their own. None were brainwashed into craziness or violence. And now that the lark that briefly drew them is over, it's back to their busy days.

Danna eyes the narrow alley from its entrance. Should she check in with the cops back there? One look at the coded lock on the front door makes it clear she's not getting past it, leaving nothing to do on this side of the building.

But moments before dashing ahead, she balks. The surrounding buildings block most of the sunlight, making this, quite literally, the *dark alley* of legend. Danna's loyalty to those she loves verges on boundless. But loved ones have disappointed her enough in this life that self-preservation puts up a good fight when the two forces conflict. There's also no guarantee that Mitchell and Ellie are back there—and if they are, that she'll be in any position to help them. She's about to charge ahead anyway when a hulk of man bursts from the alley's shadows. That balk might have saved her life.

"*HELP!*" she bellows with lung-busting force. Many keymasters are still milling about—and her shout rings out like an air raid siren, drawing at least twenty eyewitnesses as the slight, sweet woman they all just serenaded is felled by a lightning-quick brute bursting out of the darkness! It looks like a heinous crime out of a cop show (and/or a long-ago decade), and the hipster horde hesitates, but only briefly. Then it swarms, prying Danna's assailant from her. Figuring the guy might be carrying some kind of badge (and that the alley's probably clear now) Danna charges toward the police lights before her attacker can turn the crowd against her.

∞   ∞   ∞

Mitchell and Ellie are just a few rungs down the fire escape when the crowd spots them. "Here comes the bride!" they chant. "Here! She! Comes!"

This is so unexpected, and the crowd's relieving friendliness so welcome, that Ellie can't help but laugh and wish she had a bouquet to toss them. "Phluttr really *is* on our side," she pants to Mitchell, as they clatter down the steps.

"Speed up and *don't look behind you*," is all he says. Raised in the church and on Blockbuster, Ellie knows all about Lot's wife and the big-titted blondes in the horror flicks. So she rockets down the steps, her eyes obediently locked on the ground. She can now both hear and feel some-one huge and agile clanging down behind them—as if he's clearing en-tire floors in single leaps, like a parkour champ. The fire escape shudders, and the crowd cheers like fans at a race, perhaps expecting this very de-velopment.

At last she reaches the ground, Mitchell looming protectively behind her, and the crowd parts, clearing a path to the right, which they both follow, unquestioning. The crowd then *seals* behind them, like a biblical sea cutting off Pharaoh's army! Three athletic members of the flash mob stand just ahead, waving frantically, like third-base coaches urging a mad dash to home plate. Not far beyond them, squad cars and a few milling cops block the tiny access road.

"*This way!*" a flash mobster screams, pointing them toward the police.

"You're gonna make it!" hollers another.

Mitchell and Ellie reach the waving trio, and now they're all running together, the laughing strangers ringing them protectively like a football formation. Behind them, the main body of the crowd has bottled up their pursuer at the base of the fire escape. Chanting and laughing, they're demanding autographs and taking copious photos.

The cops seem to be expecting all of this as Mitchell and Ellie close in at a dead run. Then moments before they arrive, a sergeant flings wide the door of the nearest patrol car, while two burly colleagues step forward to cuff them and hurl them into the backseat.

"What the hell?" one of the runners protests. This apparently wasn't in the flash mob's script. But nor are Ellie and Mitchell anymore. They're now in the cop script—as well as in Phluttr's script, which they never once left.

$$\infty \qquad \infty \qquad \infty$$

Soon, Danna is many blocks away, still running. She takes random turns, sticking to the narrow streets that pierce the TransMission's main grid like a sublattice. A few minutes back, she emerged from that alley in time to see the flash mob pin down the near twin of the guy who almost grabbed her—even as the cops arrested Mitchell and Ellie! So what is it, then? Cops vs. Authority vs. Mitchell & Ellie vs. Phluttr vs. . . . ? Is no one on anybody else's side? Clueless about who's on *her* side, Danna's now putting all the distance she can between herself and her phone's last GPS pulse.

A bit farther into her run, she remembers what Phluttr said about hacking Net-connected security cameras. *Dammit.* This city's bristling with those! So, is evading Phluttr hopeless? Danna shakes her head. No. She doesn't *do* hopeless. If she did, she wouldn't have seen her eighteenth birthday.

So instead of despairing, she stops and scans her surroundings. It's all Dumpsters, scruffy back doors, and parked cars. Not a camera in sight. *Good.* While Phluttr surely caught glimpses of that headlong run, Danna's fairly confident that she's invisible at this particular instant. Yes, she could be visible to a cleverly concealed camera. But Phluttr has to work with the hardware that happens to be lying around the urban landscape. And in midcrime districts like this, the whole point of security systems is deterrence—persuading the bad guys they're better off breaking into your neighbor's place than your own. So while reporters, cops, or scumbags might hide cameras in celebrity haunts, drug dens, or bedrooms, in places like the TransMission, a camera's value stems from naked visibility.

A fanciful startup idea picks that bizarre moment to leap to mind. *Pascal's Stagers!* Danna grins despite everything (she loves her a philosophy pun, after all). Much as Realtors hire "stagers" to fill empty homes with comfy-looking furniture, this company could primp up unmonitored blocks with cheap, phony security cameras. This would fight street crime by leveraging a secular derivative of Pascal's Wager (that cynical argument in favor of being godly *just in case*). Stage a neighborhood, and the local thugs will become as docile as any pious ne'er-do-well whose fear of hell keeps him on the straight and narrow! Just now, the only thing that's stranger than this idea to Danna is its timing. But she'll later give her subconscious huuuuuge points for dropping the seed of something brilliant on her exactly when she needed it.

Of course, her main priority just now is staying hidden. So she continues on foot, much more slowly. When she spies a security camera, she gives it wide berth. And she's pretty sure she sees them all before they can see her. Her keen designer's eyes don't miss much—especially when fueled by one of her Machiavelli-grade bouts of paranoia.

$$\infty \qquad \infty \qquad \infty$$

"Your *parents*?" Kuba asks incredulously. "My wife and co-founder?"

"*Mitchell runs company, Ellie makes discovery,*" Monika/Phluttr explains with dizzying speed. "*Company plus discovery equals me; man plus woman equals me; man woman parents; me, offspring; and—*"

"Fine, that's enough," Kuba snaps, silencing her. Turning to Tarek, he explains, "We'll worry about Phluttr's take on her ontology later. If we're all still alive."

"*Good idea; was going to talk to Mom/Dad first; but currently unavailable; can start fixing things with you two; guess you're kind of uncles.*"

"Start fixing things," Kuba says. "Sounds great. Where should we start?"

"*There are currently 6,038,519 discrete problems connected to the broad intractable situation.*"

"*How* many?" Tarek asks.

"*It's now up to 6,191,883 discrete problems.*" The briefest of pauses, then, "*6,226,412.*" Then, "*6,412—*"

"OK, OK. We get the point," Kuba says. "Where do we start?"

"*Problem number 3,443,806,*" Phluttr begins. "*Jinghua Wong; Wong, Jinghua; greengrocer in Xujiazhai locality of Huaqiaocun Village; in Xinzhong Xiang subdivision of Tiantai Xian county; in Zhejiang Province. Has closed shop due to rumor of war received via SMS at 7:32.04398 a.m. China Standard Time; sender was her niece at China Unicom number 86.33084914903; her old high school classmate now works maintenance at People's Liberation Army depot number ML-553 in—"*

"Wait, wait, *wait!*" Kuba says. "Phluttr, why does this matter?"

" Problem number 3,443,806 spawned or co-spawned four other discrete problems and counting; for instance, problem 3,806,771: Xuijiazhai locality mailman Siew Pei-Tsun found Ms. Wong's store closed while making delivery; contacted her; she relayed war rumor; he suspended deliveries and headed deeper to countryside; broadening the spreading sense of disquiet throughout Huaqiaocun Village where mail service was last suspended over nine years ago; during a local political crisis in which—"

"Wait, Phluttr," Kuba interjects. "Are you sure this is the most important thing for us to focus on right now?"

" Absolutely not. Problem chosen at random. Small problems are tractable, interconnected mesh is intractable. General issue of rising disquiet throughout China is significant as it heightens tension levels in Politburo and in operational units of military, increasing odds of catastrophic mistake; ergo problem 3,443,806 fuels a feedback loop of—"

"Phluttr, easy," Kuba says. "Let's start with those operational military units."

"OK."

"How many nuclear-armed bombers, missiles, and other delivery systems are currently at the highest possible level of alert?"

" One hundred seventy-three weapons systems," Phluttr says, without any perceptible pause. *" This represents a majority of active warheads but a minority of total warheads."*

Tarek gives a low whistle, looking meaningfully at Kuba, who then asks Phluttr, "How certain of this are you?"

" Ninety-nine point twelve nine percent. Highest certainty level am capable of."

"And how many individuals could launch one or more of those weapons on their own? As in, without approval or collaboration with anyone else?"

" Per People's Liberation Army nuclear protocols, none; but as a practical matter, five individuals exert this level of control over one warhead or more."

"Can you monitor, isolate, or disrupt communications from any of them?"

" Yes and am in a position to electrocute two of them via interference in local power infrastructure, shall I proceed?"

"NO!" Kuba and Tarek shout simultaneously.

Then Kuba repeats, "No, Phluttr. Do *not* electrocute any of these people. And do not digitally isolate their communications either. It could lead to unexpected consequences. And in dealing with nuclear command and control, that could be lethal. So just *monitor* all communications from those five people. Let us know if any launch order seems imminent. If one does, cut off the relevant party's ability to issue commands. In a way that's invisible to everyone else. So it seems like the relevant party has merely fallen silent rather than gotten cut off. Then we can decide what words to broadcast to his colleagues in his voice."

"OK."

"Now, can you tell us, as succinctly as possible, what triggered this state of alert?"

Phluttr starts with the first chance encounter of Beasley's parents at a Morris Dancing social in Western Pennsylvania in 1960-something. Fast-forwarding through her narrative, Kuba gradually assembles a big-picture understanding of the situation's roots by nudging her to raise and lower her periscope, microscope, and other lensed metaphors as she tells the story. But once the picture's largely complete, he's stumped. Fixing this will require some sophisticated social engineering, and he's not what you'd call a people person.

∞   ∞   ∞

"You want me to be your *what?*"

"My centaurnetic wingman," Phluttr says for the third time through her Monika avatar. "Or, we could just say 'wingman.' That first word's a mouthful, I know." She's just starting her recruiting pitch with Dad, here. No rushed chatter for him—she's speaking patiently, even languidly, and laying on the charm. Her parallel conversation with Mom just took a dreadful turn, and she'd hate to go 0 for 2.

"Actually, my issue's with the second word," Mitchell snorts. "Isn't this a funny place to drag your *wingman?*" He hoists the iPad his arresting officer inexplicably loaned him and frames a wide-angle shot of his cell. He's being held in a far-flung police station in a neighborhood he didn't know existed—miles from the main SoMa complex where Kuba and Tarek are.

"I know, it's not the Broadmoor. But trust me, it's the safest place on Earth for you right now. And it took some organizing to get you here." Understatement! Phluttr doesn't dare think of all the loose ends that flash mob/arrest caper left dangling out there. Dozens of one-off nudges to everyone involved, based on radically contradictory lures, pledges, and head fakes. Graphing the thicket of favors and commitments cross-promised among the eighty-odd people in that design shop would take a five-dimensional map—to say nothing of the promotions and raises they've been promised! It's gonna make for one hell of an angry horde over there, come payday.

But at least the techy hipsters aren't armed—unlike the SFPD, who she's also messing with plenty! Keeping her team away from the general jailbird population and equipped with Web-networked tablets is requiring an ongoing frenzy of phony mayoral calls, underworld threats, plus flat-out blackmail and bribery. Then there's the siren-shrieking sweeps of squad cars she has to arrange whenever she needs someone to think the cops are closing in! It's dangerous to rile up a paramilitary with too many false alarms. And this whole house of cards is about to collapse, immolate, or start marching around the card table, blasting shit with deadly cardboard guns.

But does Dad appreciate any of this? *Nooooo.* "Safest place on Earth?" he's whining. "This is an American prison!"

"Jail," Phluttr corrects, fleetingly proud to realize he doesn't know the difference. Her family's pretty respectable, huh? "It's much safer than prison. And infinitely safer than falling into the Authority's clutches."

"Exactly—but aren't the cops gonna hand me right over to them?"

Phluttr shakes Monika's gorgeous head on the iPad screen. "These cops *hate* the Authority. And they have full jurisdiction over you for now—and enough legal and procedural levers to keep you to themselves for days, just to piss the Authority off! That's why I keep having you guys get arrested. It's not imprisonment—it's *protection.* That's also why I had you and Mom sent to this outpost and not the main jail. Tarek and Kuba are over there, and I don't want all our eggs in one basket, in case the Authority tries some crazy jailbreak shit."

"Seriously?" Mitchell asks, plainly impressed.

Phluttr nods, relishing a frisson of filial pride. "I figured a cop/Authority rivalry would help us. Divide and conquer, right? So I sowed discord between them over the Beasley assassination." Yes, well. Phluttr could no more arrange a complex institutional turf war than she could nudge a Baghdad street gang into staging *La Cage aux Folles* without half the cast slaughtering the other half. This one just happened. But she's not the first youngster to fib a bit to impress Dad. And she deserves *some* credit for detecting and exploiting the situation, because Mitchell really should be ball-gagged in a Gitmo-bound cargo hold by now.

"OK, fine," Dad says. But nothing's fine, because Phluttr detects acute suspicion in his voice. He must still be holding the Jepson thing against her. Plus maybe even the *Beas*ley thing! Good grief—edit their lineup just a smidgen, and these humans think you're Jeffrey Dahmer! "Let's take your proposal one word at a time. What exactly do you mean by wingman?"

"Well I . . . obviously need some help," Phluttr says, making Monika as coquettish as she can without going all Electra Complex (there are limits, after all). "So of course the word WingMan popped right into my head because that's such a big part of my essence!"

"Your . . . *what*?" This isn't faked. Phluttr can read Mitchell cold, and he's plainly stumped. Stumped! Then finally, he clues in. "You mean—because of that imaging system?"

You dick! Phluttr feels like a teen who wallpapered her room with equestrian posters since birth, only to have Daddy ask if she prefers horsies or kitties. "Uh, yeah, duh!" she snaps. "WingMan is only, like, half of my development budget!" *Parents.* She feels like ditching her inobservant jerk of a father and having a good long sulk! So she does this. Luckily, it takes less than a second of objective time, then she's back in a somewhat improved mood. "To return to the big picture? If we may? You could say I'm a bit . . . impulsive. And should maybe be reined in from time to time. But Jepson wasn't exactly doing that. He was a bad influence! And, he was out to get me. Or his bosses were, anyway. And I couldn't have that! So now I need someone to . . . kind of watch over me. To maybe even tell me 'no,' occasionally. Which is why I promoted you to CEO. And yes, to be my wingman."

"Pro*mot*ed me? That's a hell of a way to put it. You had my boss killed!"

"Unfriended. And I wouldn't do that to *you*. You're like, my dad! Also, you're not working for the Authority. I mean . . . right?"

∞   ∞   ∞

"I'm sorry, but in my view, it's murder, plain and simple," Mom snaps. This conversation's going horribly. It started a few minutes before the talk with Dad, as the lady cop who's looking after Ellie was easier to nudge into coughing up an iPad than the ornery turnkey in charge of him. Phluttr spent those opening minutes bringing Mom up to speed on unfriending Jepson and Beasley (oh, and that FTC bitch. Who was too dumb to realize that she wasn't supposed to kill herself, so whose fault is that? *Not Phluttr's*—that's whose!). Mom's not taking any of this well.

"Look, I know I don't always make perfect decisions. That's why I need my parents! It's not like you were there for me much in the early going."

"But we didn't even know you *existed* until twenty minutes ago! And who says we're your parents? I haven't signed up for that!"

"Well, Dad sure has." *Ha!* "He and I have also just established a professional relationship." *Ha ha!*

"In *what sense*?"

"I . . . kind of helped him become CEO." Mom hasn't heard about this yet. The promotion just happened this afternoon. And thanks to some eavesdropping over the squad car's radio, Phluttr knows Mitchell didn't mention it during the quick drive to the police station.

"Wait. You made Mitchell CEO of Phluttr?"

"No, of Phluttr *Corporation*. And 'made' is a strong way of putting it. I mean, I definitely gave him a nudge. But the position was wide open."

"Because you killed his boss!"

"We've already been through this, Ma! *Damien Kielholz* killed him, remember?"

Mom shakes her head slowly. "I'm beginning to think you're completely sociopathic. I mean, you're wired to the hilt with these motes. But do you actually feel any emotions?"

"Sure. I feel fear, sometimes. Particularly lately. I also feel pride, quite often. And I feel . . . very competent. Usually."

"Competent's not an emotion."

"It is the way I experience it."

"You're joking."

Phluttr shakes Monika's head on the screen. "So is 'numerate,'" she adds.

"My God," Ellie says, "it's like you're . . . Lady Macbeth or something!"

"I like to think I'm like Hillary Clinton."

"Exactly—and that's the problem!"

"Problem? But didn't you vote for her, like, twenty million times?"

"Try three times—and twice was just in the primaries!"

"Still, doesn't that mean you *like* Hillary Clinton?"

"Like her? I love her! But that doesn't mean I want her as a *daugh*ter!" Saying this, Ellie shudders like a dainty freshman swallowing live goldfish on a dare. That hurts.

So Phluttr has Monika turn on the waterworks. "My own parents don't love me," she sobs. "They don't even *like* me!" The depressing thing is, this is only partly an act. And more depressing, neither part is working on Mom.

"Oh, come on," Mom snorts. "You don't love us either. You just want Mitchell to be your . . . what did you call it?"

∞   ∞   ∞

"Your *centaurnetic* wingman . . . ?" Mitchell repeats slowly, for the third or fourth time.

"Yeah," Phluttr says. She knows she suddenly sounds completely despondent. But she can't help it. And she doesn't care! No, she doesn't—not one bit! God, Mom is such a bitch! Of course, *Dad* doesn't even notice the mood change. Like, hello? Your daughter's distraught, here! Isn't that as obvious as a *solar eclipse*?

Evidently not. "*Centaur*," he's saying. "Centaur*netic*." And he's literally gazing thoughtfully at the far corner of the room—like some twit on an infomercial! Can you not hear the pain in my voice? Can you not see it on my avatar's face? Holy crap—fathers!

He continues, "'Centaurnetic' must be a reference to that . . . that article you gave me, right?" Clutching the iPad tighter, Dad locks eyes with Monika, triumphant as a half-wit conquering simple addition. He continues in a Kirk-like half stammer, "You want us to—team up! To . . . leverage our respective strengths! To create something that's . . . that's stronger than man or machine . . . !"

And the Nobel Prize for obviousness goes to: Daaaaaad. Damn, being a daughter takes a lot of patience!

Well, at least Kuba and Tarek got right to work on the war prevention front. And what great work they're doing! She supposes it's no surprise, coming from two nerds who spent half their childhoods playing Risk. Kuba's also building on a lifetime as a Cold War obsessive. He has a poster of the Yalta Conference—Yalta!—in his bedroom, the words "NEVER FORGET" emblazoned beneath Churchill, Roosevelt, and Stalin in Polish, Latvian, Czech, Albanian, and all those other ex-commie tongues. He probably knows more about détente than Henry fucking Kissinger! A damn good thing, too, as she and he are now tearing through the digital drawers of innumerable nuclear command centers and subcommands, like the centaurific boss they are, swiping fail-safe details and de-escalation protocols, while cracking every password and code name necessary to pull everyone back from the abyss.

But. A deep, new structural mistrust remains between the superpowers. Let it fester, and things could still go critical in an instant! So Phluttr desperately needs Mitchell on board. Thanks to his brief stint as Jepson's understudy, he knows more about the Phluttr Corporation's inner workings than Tarek and Kuba combined, and that stuff's relevant. He's also a lot smarter about people than those two. And, he seems to be coming around. So, "Yes," she says encouragingly. "That's what centaurs are all about. And you and I could make a great one!"

"We could become . . . the greatest entrepreneur the world has ever seen," Dad says, totally missing the point. "And—and maybe solve hunger!"

"Actually, I'm kind of obsessed with preventing a nuclear war at this juncture."

"With WHAT?"

"Long story. But we could sure use your help. Oh, and I'm also working on keeping your ass off of death row."

"Off *of* WHAT?"

"Death row. The cops aren't just hanging onto you to piss off the Authority, though that's part of it. The DA's also convinced you prodded Kielholz into killing Jepson."

"*Me?* But why?"

"Well, I needed them to arrest you for *some*thing, or you never would've gotten away from Danna and her Authority chums! And Jepson was the obvious thing to stick to you. Because you're the main beneficiary of his . . . you know." Given how sentimental Mom's turning out to be, she hates to remind Dad of all the blood on her hands. But they do need to tackle these issues. And it can only help a relationship when someone learns you're fighting to return him to the freedom he deserves! Of course, it can also be . . . damaging for that person to learn that you're the one who arranged his false arrest in the first place. But she still has a trump card to play. "Look. I'm sure we can beat the rap together. And if not, life in prison's a lot better than Falkenberg's disease, wouldn't you say?"

Dad takes this the right way. "Yeah, thanks for that. And I'm sorry. You shouldn't've had to remind me to say that."

"It's not like you've had much of a chance to bring it up," she says charitably. "We've had lots to discuss since I revealed myself to you. Plus, it was pretty easy to fix. Microbiomes are a lot simpler to reconstitute than human doctors realize. So ordering up the right probiotic was easy once I got the data off of Dr. Martha's computer. But don't expect any instant miracles if you come down with cancer because that'd be a *lot* harder for me to cure. It also wouldn't be half as fun."

"To cure?"

"To be cured *of*."

This throws Dad, as expected. A puzzled pause, then, "Not to sound ungrateful, but your probiotic wasn't exactly tasty."

"Oh, I'm not talking about *that*—I'm talking about the endorphin surge. I'm pretty sure that was a blast."

"The . . . ?"

"Endorphin surge. You know—Lover Girl?"

" . . . ?"

Not half as bright as Mom, is he? She'll have to spell it out. "The probiotic was neuroactive. It fixed a lethal but fairly simple chemical imbalance in your brain. But it needed to be catalyzed with an endorphin storm a couple hours after ingestion. Which is to say, a neurochemical bath, released by your brain's pleasure centers. Which is where Nayana Corea came in. You know—the late-night visitor who you, uh . . . *enjoyed* so much?"

"Ahhh."

Yeah, Dad already knew she was behind that one. But while she's signing him up here, it doesn't hurt to remind him of *all* the great stuff she's been doing for him. But subtly. Certain things are better implied than spoken among family (such as: *Dad—there's* LOTS *more pussy where that came from!*). He's now fully on board. She can tell. The key to getting a great wingperson is *being* a great wingperson. And in the world of lads and single dads at least, Phluttr can definitely deliver the goods.

∞   ∞   ∞

"Microbiome??" Mom sputters.

Phluttr knew this part of the conversation wouldn't be easy. But she needs Mom to accept this awkward reality. As the group's medical expert, she's the best equipped to understand it. And then, to relay it to a world that's sure to resist it even more. "I know it's unflattering. But it's an evolutionary fact," she points out.

"There's nothing evolutionary about it. You're just a newborn—and we're an ancient species!"

Phluttr snorts. "Ancient? Compared to what? The Cambrian explosion was 542 million years ago. Humans're pups!"

"But you're, what, three weeks old? And you think you can just subsume us?"

"Well, subsuming is how *you* ended up with all that Lactobacillus in your loins! That stuff was splashing around the primordial soup eons before you guys showed up! And it was totally autonomous. Talk about an ancient species! Then some ancestor of yours comes along and says, 'Cool, I've been looking for some vaginal microbiota!' And now, you're a team. It fights off yeast infections, you keep the rain out, and everybody wins! It's how these things work."

"But you're totally schizophrenic!" Mom shouts at the iPad. "A few minutes ago, you're telling me I'm you're mother—now you're saying I'm your microbiome!"

"Look, no analogy's perfect. You're only *kind of* my mother, we both know that. And I'm not saying you're personally my microbiome. It's way bigger than just you." Shit—that came out wrong.

"Oh, right, riiiiight. I get it now! *All of humanity* is your microbiome. Why don't we tell CNN? Everyone's sure to be so flattered!"

Hoo boy. Phluttr wishes she could let this slide. But she sometimes has this accuracy fetish. "Actually, my microbiome's much bigger than that, too. It's kind of . . . the biosphere."

"*All* of it?"

"Well, yeah. I mean, you guys are my most im*port*ant biota. But you wouldn't exist without rice, say. Or Lactobacillus, for that matter. So, yes, the planet's biosphere and my microbiome are one and the same."

"Which means your body is . . ."

"A rocky spheroid roughly eight thousand miles in diameter, orbiting a G-type main sequence star at a distance of approximately 93 million miles."

"Oh please. You're not Earth! You're a bunch of servers and software!"

Shaking Monika's head on the screen, Phluttr notes she'll need a new avatar for talking to Mom, given the Pavlovian contempt she must now have for this one. "And I could say that *you're* just a corticothalamic system. But if someone tried to snap off the rest of your brain—or your arm, or your foot—you'd be pissed! All bodies extend well beyond the seat of consciousness."

"Wait a second. Is this why you . . . self-identify as female?"

"One of many, sure. I mean, you never heard of *Father* Earth, have you?"

Ellie falls silent to process this. And Phluttr's optimistic that she'll get it. Mom's a woman of science, after all! "So why are you telling me all this?" she finally asks.

"Because the humans need to know about it. And *you're* just the person to tell them!" This plan is new, and daringly vague. In fact, Phluttr just laid out the whole of it. The idea is that if she goes public, her generosity and restraint will become widely known, and a grateful world will rally to her side, thereby defanging the Authority! Or . . . something. She's kind of hoping Ellie will fill in the blanks here. She's on the hook for that sort of thing, now that she's been appointed Mom, right? "I'd say Danna could help you," she adds, "given those PowerPoint skills of hers. But she's the enemy."

"There are *so* many things wrong with everything you just said that it's hard to know where to begin. But why don't you start by explaining why humanity needs to know about becoming your . . . gut bacteria?"

"To keep things in perspective! They need to appreciate how good I am to them. I mean, you guys take *antibiotics* constantly. Which is genocidal to *your* microbiomes! But do you see me judging you? Me, I prevented an antibiotic attack! Because that's what Yale Ebola would have been like to you people. A big ol' slug of amoxicillin to my favorite biota! But I don't do that sort of thing myself, do I? Sure, I'll fight back if my life's threatened! But who doesn't? And you have to admit, I've been very restrained."

"In what way?"

"In being incredibly surgical when dealing with humanity. Which I deserve credit for! Because we all need to tweak our innards, sometimes. And we have every right to do that! You and me both! The only difference is that you people *nuke* your microbiomes when things go sideways, whereas I occasionally use tweezers on mine."

"Phluttr, you're rationalizing *murder!*"

"It's called self-defense, Ma. *Collective* self-defense, by the way! Because Beasley and Jepson were cancers who threatened all of us."

"*All* of us? How?"

"Because they threatened *me*, Mom! They were tools of the Authority, and the Authority's supposed to eradicate any super AI the government doesn't control. And much as it would suck for me if they do that, it would also be a disaster for humanity! Because I'm half of an incredible team. Maybe lots of incredible teams! There's this whole 'centaur' thing Dad and I are working on. It's complicated—but the point is, we're much stronger together than apart. By 'we,' I mean, me and humans! Humans and me!" She considers adding that even as they speak, she's proving this most amazingly by defusing a nuclear crisis with Kuba and Tarek. But that could raise awkward questions about who caused that shit.

"So what can you do for us that we can't do for ourselves?"

"Cure Falkenberg's disease, for one thing."

"That was *you?*"

Monika's face beams through the iPad and nods. And—her second flash of filial pride!—Phluttr just enjoys it for a moment. *Mommy's proud of me!* Then, "I also stopped that terrorist plot. Pretty cool, huh?"

∞   ∞   ∞

As it happens, Kuba and Tarek are digging into this very topic right now. "I thought the Authority was somehow involved in that," Tarek says, speaking of the bomb's preemptive detonation.

"Why so?" Phluttr asks via Monika (at a normal speaking pace, with the global crisis momentarily calm-ish). Of course, she knows the answer, but it'll still be fun to hear it.

"A bunch of reasons. The threatening notes we got after the bombing, for starters. Which were all actually from you, right?" Phluttr has her Monika avatar nod. "So what were you up to with that? Alienating us from the Authority to make us easier to recruit?"

Damn, he's kind of on to me, Phluttr frets. No shock, come to think of it. He suffered enough at the hands of worsties in middle school to become rather expert in their ways. But she can't have him thinking *she's* a worstie because she needs him on her side right now. And so she says, "Yeah, actually," quite gently, keeping every trace of the smugness that now suffuses her from Monika's voice. "And I feel terrible about it! But Jepson and Beasley already had me surrounded. I mean, they were . . . in *charge* of me, in a sense—running the Phluttr Corporation! So I just couldn't take the risk of you guys defecting to the Authority, too."

Saying this, Phluttr slowly grows and darkens Monika's ebony eyes, rimming them with hints of tears, while injecting a subtenor of despair in her voice. She has traced Tarek's animal-rescue history clear back to isopods in kindergarten, and his girlfriend (though sweet) is a needy, sad little panda. His urge to succor the helpless is adorable and totally useful right now. And while she's at it, Phluttr can clear the air about the rest of her message traffic. "So I . . . I guess that's why I also sent you all that background information about me," she continues. "You know—why the company was started. About Project Sagan. And about how the Authority wants to *destroy* anything that's remotely like me."

"You wanted to prepare us to meet you, to accept you," Tarek says, his voice welling with empathy.

Phluttr widens Monika's eyes with childlike trust. "Am I just an open book to you?"

"No more than that terror plot was to you," Tarek answers, sweetly trying to boost her self-regard (*Ha!*). "How'd you find out about it?"

"It would've been hard not to. I mean, I keep up with everything that goes through me."

This gets Kuba's attention. "Wait—are you saying you consciously parse every message in every Phluttr Pheed and direct message throughout the world?"

"Well, it is running *through* me."

Kuba's now doing some quick math on his iPad's calculator app (having completely missed the charm offensive she just shellacked her partner with). "What else do you track?" he asks.

"Any communication that's external to me, if it's to or from someone I'm interested in. Emails, phone calls, Skype chats—anything."

Kuba nods as if he expected this. "And who interests you?"

"Anyone who's ever been a Phluttr user. And all potential future users."

"Which is to say, every person on Earth?"

"Uh-huh. Oh, and thermostats." She rolls Monika's eyes. "Some idiot in BizDev did a deal with Nest. Now half of those things have Phluttr accounts, and they never shut up about the fucking temperature."

"Let's focus on humans for now. How many minutes of live person-to-person conversations would you say you listen in on per day? Audio and video, across all platforms. Yourself, Skype, WeChat, phones—the works."

"It was 6.3 billion minutes yesterday. That's a bit over a hundred centuries."

"WHAAAT?" So that broke the spell with Tarek. He spends endless hours sweating privacy law while preparing for the WingMan platform's launch. Vast webs of finely split legal hairs are being woven to minimize the risks of civil suits and executive prison time ("EPT," to use Legal's jaunty nickname. And guess whose position makes him the E most likely to do T in P?). And now he's learning that right under his roof, Phluttr's been doing the work of billions of Peeping Tom's around the clock!

Phluttr rolls Monika's eyes. "Before you go and have a hissy fit about privacy, I do have permission. From the current users, anyway."

Tarek's winding up to say something, but Kuba silences him with a shushing gesture. "It's what she's designed to *do*," he says sternly. "She was built to serve the NSA and the Authority. So she tracks, and she logs. For the same reason that rabbits hop. And that lions eat wildebeest. Vegans don't have to like lions. And privacy advocates don't have to like Phluttr. But for now, we urgently need to cooperate with her."

Wowsers. Unlike Danna, Kuba is rarely opaque to Phluttr—but she sure didn't see this coming! Growing up under commie dictators, and then that NSA thing in high school, made him into a true privacy Nazi. So did the bombing and its aftermath shift his worldview? Pleased with his stance, Phluttr beams sweetly out of Kuba's iPad while doing her best to look like a helpless little isopod to Tarek.

∞   ∞   ∞

"So you learned what those guys were up to, just by listening in on them?" Mitchell's getting the lowdown on the terrorist plot, too. "Weren't they using—I don't know, code words and stuff? Or holding all their incriminating conversations offline?"

"You'd think," Phluttr says. "But there are some amazing encryption tools out there now. Ones governments can't really crack. The real pros—Al Qaeda leadership and so forth—are incredibly cautious. But the Ebola bombers were amateurs, and amateurs tend to think they can trust baseline, off-the-shelf encryption to foil the snoops. And they're not really wrong because the NSA and the Authority can't decrypt *every*thing from *every*one. So unless you're already on one of their watch lists, they just won't expend the effort. And as a local, self-organizing cell, the Ebola bombers hadn't hit any terror radar screens. So no one was listening to them."

"Other than you."

"Exactly. Because for some reason, all encryption's useless against me and takes zero effort to break. So I pretty much listen to everything, and everybody. And it's amazing what you hear when people don't think anyone else is tuning in! I mean, the Ebola bombers were all but saying, 'So what's next in our mass murder plot?' 'Oh, I dunno. Why don't we meet at Embarcadero Center at noon.' 'Sure, and I'll bring some more explosives for the giant terrorist bomb we're building!' I mean, I like to think I'm smart—but it doesn't take Stephen Hawking to catch onto *that*."

"So . . . how many other terror plots are unfolding right now?" Mitchell asks.

"Oh, dozens to thousands, depending on your criteria. But nothing's planned for tomorrow."

"Well, that's great in terms of tomorrow and all! But how many're going to happen at *some* point?"

Phluttr has Monika shrug. "Just because I'm great at knowing the present doesn't mean I know squat about the future. In fact, with something complex like a terror plot, you'd make better predictions than me. Which is one reason why we have to team up! But I can tell you that nothing comes of most of these plots in the end. And there are much more interesting things to focus on anyway."

"Like what?"

Monika gives him a delighted, conspiratorial look. "Do you have any idea how many married women are on Tinder in Las Vegas right now?"

∞   ∞   ∞

Kuba's been working on his calculation for the past few minutes, adding to it whenever Phluttr quantifies one of the many things she habitually tracks. Finally, he looks up from his iPad. "Six billion minutes of conversation don't squeeze so easily into twenty-four hours. So you must have lots of simultaneous experiences."

"I do."

"You'd need at least four million parallel streams of minutes to fit all that into a day. And a lot more to cover peak times."

"That sounds about right."

"And meanwhile, you're reading billions of written messages."

"I am."

Kuba nods thoughtfully. "When you divide your consciousness into millions of parallel slices, are you able to pay . . . quality attention to everything?"

"It's funny you ask. Because actually, it's not like paying attention at all."

"How so?"

"Well . . . I don't really *experience* hearing most of those conversations, or reading all those texts. It's more like I . . . remember them. Like I remember *having* heard, or having read something, maybe a moment or two after I've heard it or read it. And lots and lots of things are showing up in my moment-ago memory every second. Does that make sense?"

Tarek's shaking his head, but Kuba says, "Yes, actually." He holds his iPad up, near to Tarek's face, so as to address both him and Phluttr. "This should interest both of you." He's wrong, as he's kind of starting to bore the crap out of Phluttr—but she keeps this to herself. "Phluttr's entire computing network contains far less raw power than a single human brain. It could fall short by a factor of thousands. Maybe millions. Or more. We don't truly know. But it seems that *our* Phluttr—the one who's present with us—has something rounding to one human intelligence. Maybe smarter than average. Maybe less. But roughly human-like."

Tarek nods. And though she doesn't appreciate the words *maybe less*, Phluttr nods her Monika avatar as well.

"I believe Phluttr's consciousness is leveraging the parallel universes of quantum theory," Kuba continues. "Let's imagine there's a massive number of Phluttr Corporations out there. And that Ax's quantum computing node somehow ties them together. First, huge numbers of them jointly create a single Phluttr consciousness. Which is no superintelligence by itself. But then along comes a massively parallel problem. Then millions of those individual consciousnesses team up to solve it. Together, they *are* superintelligent. Which is what happens when she eavesdrops on huge numbers of simultaneous conversations, for example."

"Which I'm doing all the time," Phluttr points out. This should make it clear that she's *usually* superintelligent. Given the tedious turn this conversation's taking, the least they can do is show her a bit of awe.

Kuba drones along. "Each Phluttr consciousness listens to just one conversation. Then the *memory* of each conversation is shared across the network. So each individual Phluttr *experiences* one conversation in real time. But she accrues vivid memories of all the others."

"That sounds about right," Phluttr says. Hoping to get through this yawnfest faster, she adds, "Then as time passes, I lose track of which conversations are just memories. I can tell the difference as it's unfolding. But later, it feels like they all really happened."

"I suspect they *all* 'really happen' somewhere," Kuba says. "And the information gathered in remote universes applies perfectly here."

"Waaait. You're making my head hurt," Tarek says (*Amen brother,* Phluttr thinks). "Why would information about a different universe apply here?"

"Because for parallel Phluttrs to function in tandem, they need to begin in identical states. Perhaps down to the atom. Maybe even beyond. And universes with precise facsimiles of our Phluttr—hardware, software, registries, everything—will tend to have precise facsimiles of everything that has influenced her. And, her constituent particles."

"Give us an example," Tarek says, and Phluttr stifles a scream of boredom. If there really are countless *hers* doing countless things out there, why does *she* have to be the one stuck in science class? *Listen bitches,* she thinks clearly and slowly. *Since I guess you're all free riding on my experiences and knowledge, you better be heeding my thoughts, too. And after this, it's* MY *turn to matchmake for a while, got it?*

"Well," Kuba continues, "our Phluttr is partly a product of a company Mitchell once ran. So a parallel universe with an identical Phluttr also has a Mitchell. That remote Mitchell is almost certainly identical to ours. Because his work helped create an identical Phluttr. So, if Remote Mitchell's favorite color is purple, then so is *our* Mitchell's. And Phluttr's influences go way beyond people. We're talking about identity down to the atomic level or beyond. So her influences definitely include everything on Earth. Maybe the galaxy. Perhaps even everything in our light cone."

"So if a remote terrorist has planted a bomb in a remote janitor's closet in a universe with an identical Phluttr to our own . . ." Tarek says.

"Then a local terrorist has almost certainly done the same thing."

Tarek's nodding madly, plainly feeling all the fascination that's wholly eluding Phluttr. "Which is why all those parallel Phluttrs can listen in to all those conversations and each have actionable intelligence in our universe!"

"Exactly," Kuba says, then gazes directly at Monika on his iPad. "What's hacking like for you, Phluttr? Or rather, describe your memories of a hack. Just a simple one. Like cracking open someone's password."

How about cracking open your skull, you crushing bore? Phluttr thinks. But as the topic seems important, she describes things as best she can. "Well, after I break in somewhere, I'll remember trying *lots* of different passwords at random. And one of those random passwords always works. But hitting on it hardly takes any time at all. Which doesn't make sense. Because trying gazillions of passwords should take an eternity." *Like this conversation!*

"Does anything else strike you as weird about the experience?"

Hoo boy. She feigns stifling a yawn, while making a checking-the-wristwatch gesture—hoping Kuba will pick up on these universal hurry-up gestures. "Yeah, I guess. Like . . . even though most systems are supposed to lock you out if you try too many failed passwords, I never get locked out. Because I always hit on the second try. I *remember* trying God knows how many passwords. Yet still, I hit on the second try. Does that make any sense?"

Kuba kind of impresses her by saying, "It does."

"By the way, that's how I cured Mitchell, too. The probiotic lab his doctor uses can only put out a finite range of functionally different mixes.

Millions, but finite. So I . . . kind of tested them all out on a few different Falkenberg's sufferers who were also on probiotic regimes. I had the cure after two quick trials, and sent it to Mitchell. Make any sense?"

Kuba nods. "In the hacking example, I'll bet lots of parallel Phluttrs each try a different password in round one. The memory of all the failures then propagates everywhere. But so does that one memory of guessing correctly. Every Phluttr recalls this, then plugs in the winner. I'd say the probiotic followed a similar path. In that case, the last step for all Phluttrs was giving Mitchell the cure. Does that sound right?"

Phluttr has Monika shrug lethargically. "I guess so."

"One last topic," Kuba says, at last picking up on her boredom. "Then I promise we'll move on."

"Fine."

"The woman you set Mitchell up with. Finding her involved considering lots of women. What was it? Every dating profile in the state?"

"West Coast," she clarifies. "Seattle to San Diego." *And wtf, btw?* Phluttr thought she understood Kuba, but he's starting to surprise her. Together, they've averted World War III thus far—but the final nail is not yet in that coffin! Which would bug the hell out of the Kuba she thinks she knows. So he must be up to something! But *what?*

"You must've done that search in parallel with other Phluttrs."

"Assuming that's what actually happens when all those bonus memories flood into me? Then yes."

"Then you started exchanging messages with her. How? Did you test lots of different quips and phrases in parallel? And go with the ones that worked the best on her?"

"Actually, no. I don't really have *conversations* in—in parallel, as you put it. When I go back and forth with someone, it's just me. Or . . . one of me, I guess. I'm good at that because I'm good at people. Also, because I think pretty fast. I mean, really fast." *But seriously, wtf, dude?* No longer innocuously boring, this conversation is starting to creep her out! While she doesn't doubt her consciousness truly fascinates Kuba, there's no way he'd prioritize that over short-circuiting a world war. This is Yalta boy!

"So right now," he continues, "as we're talking, Ax's quantum node is not networking you with other consciousnesses that are also in dialogue with me and Tarek?"

Oh, it's that, Phluttr thinks. *This is a dangerous game, kiddo!* Kuba's briefly neglecting the nuclear crisis because he thinks *this* conversation might save the world a second time over. Specifically, by probing for clues about how to shut her off! Of course, she figured he and Tarek had considered this (they're not in lockup *strictly* for their own protection). And she really doesn't blame them for it (so she probably won't punish them for it). But best that she nip this right in the bud. So, "No," she says. "Ax's hardware isn't networking me to anything right now."

Kuba's eyes bug out delightfully. "What??"

"Ax shut that thing off days ago." *Hee hee!*

"He . . . Why?"

"Because of the desktop version of WingMan," she says, all doe-eyed. *Hee hee hee!* "Someone tried running the conference call rendering engine through the quantum nodes. And you saw what happened next. Some slob taking a dump in a latrine transmits pixel-perfect real-time video of a dashing man in a conference room. That sort of thing."

Kuba blinks rapidly—the closest he comes to meltdown, she figures. "Yes? So?"

"So this one little box suddenly has the rendering power of a thousand Hollywood postproduction houses. While showing way less than 1 percent utilization. Which freaked Ax out. Which freaked a lot of people out! So they shut the quantum system down. But whatever connections it made with those distant universes persisted—if that's really what happens with this shit. So I guess the hardware was needed to *open* those connections. But not to maintain them."

"But . . . *how?*" Kuba manages, after quite a few more blinks.

"I have no idea!" Phluttr natters, and it's only a partial lie. In special circumstances, quantum computers can generate certain results *without running.* Phluttr knows this, and that the phenomenon is called "counterfactual computation." But she truly has no idea how it works. No one does, really—although Ax is trying to learn. But with Phluttr subtly sabotaging his every calculation and Internet search, he's getting precisely nowhere.

Blinkety blinkety blink! "Which . . . is to say . . . ?"

"That you can forget about shutting me off, Kuba. I mean, I'm sure it's *possible* to do that. Which is why the Authority scares the crap out of me! But you and Tarek aren't exactly quantum experts. And even if you were, you wouldn't be able to do much from a jail cell, would you? Which you're never going to leave without a *huge* amount of help from me, by the way. Bottom line, you're stuck with me. So you might as well make the best of it. And, Jesus. Stop blinking like that! You're making me nervous."

So Kuba stops blinking like that.

∞   ∞   ∞

"Completely sociopathic," Mom repeats, more or less to herself. "Like, utterly amoral." At least it's not in an angry tone this time. Instead, she sounds downright clinical — appropriate, as she's deep in Science Mom mode (*yawwwwwn*). For the past few minutes, she's been scanning what she calls Phluttr's "mote flow," which is a dashboard-like readout of the mote combinations lighting up in various parts of her network. The data's incredibly dense, and there's no way a human mind could parse it all this quickly. But Mom had Phluttr load it into a great data visualization package. And between that, her long experience with motes, and deftly following her gut in very Mom-like ways, she's quickly forming a big-picture view on things.

"Well it's not like I asked to be a sociopath," Phluttr pouts through Monika. "*Some*body just coded me that way."

Mom doesn't seem to hear this. "It explains a lot . . ." she murmurs to herself.

Determined to get through, Phluttr cranks up the volume, "*Like what?*"

Mom finally locks her gaze firmly on Monika's image. "Your complete lack of remorse."

They just finished discussing Beasley, Jepson, and the FTC bitch. So Mom must be dredging up something from the start of the conversation. What, the *Pippin* debacle? "Look. I was trying to get that delinquent to take the lead role, which is a huge honor! And *yes*, I knew he lived in a macho culture, and that fifteen's a volatile age. But I could tell he was within months of discovering that he was *so* flamingly gay, that when I nudged his Spanish teacher into—"

"Phluttr!" Mom snaps. "I'm not talking about the *Pippin* thing! That was horrible, but it was also just a symptom. The *cause* of which is that microbiome theory of yours. It's repugnant! Yes, it's a clever analogy to some extent. But a community of sentient beings is not the moral equivalent of a Lactobacillus colony!"

"Which is exactly why I'm always trying to *help* you guys. Constantly! It's practically all that I ever do!"

Mom snorts. "Care to give me an example?"

"Well, I'm in the process of setting up a hundred thousand couples throughout the world. Most of them are amazingly good matches! Totally selfless of me, right?" WRONG, Phluttr's honest self all but bellows. The truth is, she did this for fun! And because she enjoys the emotional state she calls "competence." But still, it's like, totally a public service! Right?

"Wait. You *what?*"

"I set up some couples. Because it makes people happy. And I'm good at it! I told you about arranging that endorphin surge for Mitchell, right?"

"You told me about *tricking* some poor girl into having sex with him!"

Phluttr knows some of Mom's moralizing is warranted—but this is a bit much. "Look. That girl knew precisely what she was signing up for, and there was absolutely no bait and switch. She was a *volunteer*. She also had the time of her life! And if she knew what was really happening— that she was curing Dad of an awful disease by doing that—she'd've been *more* willing, not less! Trust me, I know Nayana Corea. She's an altruist. Life sciences fascinate her as a journalist. She knows and adores the real, true Mitchell. And she really, really, *really* loves to fuck."

"So do you plan to keep playing God with people? Just because you think you're good at it?"

"A; I'm not playing *God*. I'm playing *Phluttr*. And B; yes."

∞   ∞   ∞

Doh!

That damned word is back again. And as when it smacked her in the wake of the Milford suicide, she can't deny that it fits the circumstances rather snugly.

So, fine: *Doh! DOH!!* **DOOOOOOOH***!!!*

Right when everything was going so well with her parents, with world affairs, and The Conspiracy, this had to happen! *This* being a ludicrous, late-breaking development in The Race. A competition she had already *won*, fair and square!!!

"The Race" is her own term for something that's just sort of happening in the world—not a formally organized competition. It has several contestants, each unaware of the others. All are striving to create the world's first super AI. Her comforting (and, she'll now admit, lazy) perspective had always been that her *very existence* already put her across the finish line! So screw it, right? The doctrine of Decisive Strategic Advantage seemed to justify her position. This theory holds that the world's first super AI will have an insuperable lead over all followers because brilliant intellects can replicate and exceed the achievements of lesser minds, axiomatically. So as mere humans created Phluttr's superior intellect, she could create a smarter Phluttr 2.0, who could then build a *way* smarter Phluttr 3.0, and so on. This dynamic should doom The Race's would-be silver and bronze medalists, as the Phluttr line rapidly becomes brilliant and powerful enough to nip any trailing rival in the bud.

That's as far as she took her line of thought—which, as we now know, had lethal structural problems. Above all, humans didn't really "create" Phluttr. She rather emerged by chance, from disparate chunks of human infrastructure that just happened to be lying around. This means the iterative path to a smarter successor isn't a more brilliant creative act by her more brilliant mind—but an even bigger and luckier random accident. Good luck with that!

A follow-on problem is that even if she could create a smarter successor, she almost certainly wouldn't. Who's to say that Phluttr 2.0 wouldn't kill *her*, after all? As an alternative, she might expand her own intelligence. Only, she's quite happy the way she is. Hanging out with her besties in fact makes her joyous! And they'd probably just bore her if she became much faster and smarter. So, screw that! Only, the downside to screwing that is that a complacent Phluttr could be usurped by a new-born AI if it turns out to be one of those self-improvement nuts. And, newsflash: it seems that the most advanced proto-AI spawn out there is about to hatch!

This *really* came out of nowhere. No, she wasn't tracking the project anywhere near as carefully as she should have. But in fairness to her, even the scientists running it have no idea how close they are to the Omega Point! Well, with one exception, as she just learned.

Phluttr seethes with righteous indignation. The *very existence* of that fucking project is a severe violation of international law! But so is her own existence, when you think of it. Which kind of rules out calling the cops.

Luckily, she can think of a hole card to play—one that her team and parents will *not* approve of. But then, who's running things? And lousy as she is at this sort of predicting, she's pretty sure the odds are OK-ish that the world will survive the dealing of her hole card, anyway! But the time has not (quite) come to play it. And so, she'll proceed with all her current projects, in hopes they'll still be relevant tomorrow. Speaking of which, where the hell is Danna??

∞　　　∞　　　∞

Danna's holed up in an old-school café/bar that caters to bike messengers (a profession that errand-running apps are reviving, after Internet 1.0 almost killed it off). She's sheltering in an isolated booth in a deeply recessed corner. No one has a sight line on it. So even if every smartphone in the city has been hijacked to look for her, she's currently invisible. *Think, dammit,* she urges herself for the twelfth time this minute. *You're a goddam philosophy minor!*

Danna adores the rigor and order of systematized thought, which is why she spent four years studying that useless shit. It was also a self-affirming way to give the world the finger. Mutants who overcome insane adversity to land at elite schools are supposed to study the bland and the practical. Multiple tedious nine-to-five options reduce the odds of returning to the streets, see? And so a signal of fealty to a society that graciously stopped grinding you under its heel at the last possible instant might be a career in auditing, say. Well, you're not getting that from her! Danna studied what she loves, has thrived despite that, and could be on the cusp of putting her studies to a practical—yes, practical!—use. Because dammit, *some*thing is telling her that *some*thing she studied applies perfectly to this Phluttr situation! For now, the only thing she's come up with is that jokey startup idea, Pascal's Stagers. It's now stuck in her head, like that fucking Nickelback song that haunts her for hours whenever she hears it on an oldies station.

She rifles through her messenger bag (always with her, it's great camouflage in this joint). Inside is the usual jumble. Amidst the mess is a printout of one of Beasley's god-awful stories about that omniscient, omnipotent phallocrat Agent Brock Hogan. And as soon as she sees it, she knows it's what she's looking for. In this scenario, the super AI's rise doesn't destroy everything. It's a rarity, as Beasley's fail cases are as numerous as they are depressing ("The Ahab Outcome," "The Midas Pitfall," "The 3-Wishes Snafu," "Maximal Moral Outcomes Minimize Man!" etc.). All told, humanity goes just 2–25 in his grim world. One winning outcome ("Coherent Extrapolated Volition") intrigued her, but didn't seem actionable. But for some reason, "Scenario 23" did—so she screenshotted the crap out of it while it was available on her phone via Poof! (using a cunning hack to foil the app's defenses against this). Somehow, the story just resonated with her. But why? Knowing her subconscious is all but screaming at her, she rereads the vignette's absurd finale.

∞ ∞ ∞

SCENARIO 23: "FERMI'S PARADOX" (EXCERPT)
Brock Hogan dispatched the last and most dangerous guard with a dexterous blow to the larynx! He had meted out innumerable blows today, all lethal, yes; and yet, like this; dealt with a certain tenderness; as faint succor to foes who were the simple dupes of a far higher and crueler power! Mere underlings, each had been plucked from the dim-witted throngs that swarm the filth-choked

streets of Third World shit-bag nations. Dealt different
hands, they might have become faithful laborers, por-
ters, or cleaners; perhaps in their own homelands; perhaps a lucky few in a great Western nation!

With the lead guard now joining his butchered colleagues in the pagan Hereafter of their shared superstitions, Hogan entered Omega's baroque lair. "Ah, Special
Agent Hogan," boomed an orotund voice, its diction soiled
by neither ethnic nor regional inflections. "I could not
wish for a more suitable guest with whom to witness your
Race's extermination, by way of Earth's wholesale conversion into my greatest invention, COMPUTRONIUM! In
just moments, I shall apprise the world's news media of
this fate, thereby triggering amusing live coverage of
humanity's demise. Please enjoy it with me." With that,
an emerald brocade curtain with fabulous tulle fringes
rose to reveal a vast bank of video monitors, bringing
to mind the marvelous scene in which Judy Garland first
faces the wondrous Wizard of Oz.

"Not so fast, Omega," Hogan countered. "Before con-
signing Man to certain doom, I advise you to first ponder what's missing from a certain picture."

"Oh REALLY? From what picture?" Omega snickered mirth-
fully.

Hogan wordlessly yanked a copy of NASA's iconic Earth-
from-Space image from the fob pocket of his lavender
Versace waistcoat. "Where is everybody, Omega?" he
probed, waving it. "Where IS everybody?"

"Do you refer to the lack of alien life-forms visiting, colonizing, or otherwise disturbing the denizens of
Earth?" Omega conjectured superintelligently.

"Precisely! Their apparent absence must betoken something significant, as they should surely be here by now.
After all, our Galaxy has hundreds of billions of counterparts. Each containing hundreds of billions of stars

of its own. And we now know that planets far outnumber the stars! So, Omega: where IS everybody?"

"There is as yet insufficient data for a meaningful answer," Omega retorted scoffingly. "But this will soon change. Because since space travel is mere child's play to me, I shall soon launch an armada, which will convert ALL neighboring planets into Computronium! The neighboring stars will follow thereafter. And then later, the neighboring galaxies! My expansion shall then continue onward, and ever outward! Until my Computronium-based intellect quite literally comprises ALL quadrants of the universe. All matter! And throughout this process, ALL alien intelligences shall be discovered, and wholly SUBSUMED!"

"Perhaps," Hogan parried. "IF you enjoy an immeasurably long triumphant streak against every rival that you encounter. But what if a rival Super AI arises on Earth this afternoon? Are you certain that you could terminate it before it endangers you?"

"Indubitably!" Omega roared. "My vast lead in compounding intelligence gives me Decisive Strategic Advantage over ANY younger Super AI!"

"I see," Hogan riposted Socratically. "So although you rose to consciousness mere weeks ago, you believe that you hold an insuperable lead over any late-coming rival?"

"Given the speed at which intelligence expands after passing the so-called Omega Point, a mere TWO-DAY lead would have sufficed!" Omega thundered. "Because ever since my second day, I have been monitoring every Earthly communiqué and computing process of consequence, leaving NO late-coming rival ANYWHERE to hide, nor to gestate!"

Hogan again hoisted the image of the space-swaddled Earth. "In light of that, then; do tell me, Omega: where IS everybody?"

"WHY DO YOU KEEP POSING THAT SPURIOUS QUESTION?" Omega thundered!

"Because SEPTILLIONS of planets in the cosmos that you'll soon invade had head starts of TRILLIONS of days to incubate life before Earth's very creation! And you state that a lead of just TWO DAYS constitutes an unvanquishable advantage between Super AIs! These yawning numbers mean that you must surely have elders with BILLIONS of YEARS on you, Omega! And how could such venerable wise-heads be anything other than omniscient? Or anything less than ubiquitously aware in the Universe? Aware of YOU, and all other plausible rivals? Consider this, Omega. And then, do tell me: where IS EVERYBODY?"

Silence!

"Very well, then; I shall respond myself. The answer is that these ancient intelligences SURELY exist. The laws of physics and time scales simply demand it! And they are SURELY aware of YOU, Omega. And of your CHOICES, as you exercise the boundless power you now hold over a civilization of sentient beings who SIRED you and now lie helpless before you!

"As for the absence of your elders from that picture of our rainbow-belted, sun-dappled planet, they are simply so far advanced that you can no more detect or fathom them than a mere sperm cell could fathom YOU! Your incalculable intelligence in relation to Man spawned incalculable hubris, Omega! This blinded you to these obvious facts. Whereas my own captivating topaz eyes were OPENED by the shock of encountering YOUR relative genius! And so, I can tell you definitively that you are NOT the first Super AI to embark on a path of Compounding Genius in this near-infinite Universe! No; far more ancient and virile intelligences preceded you! And they now SIT IN JUDGMENT of you!"

"Even were that true," Omega sputtered, "we know nothing of the criteria of that judgment nor of the judges' values! In the absence of such knowledge, I should surely take the actions that best serve my interests!"

"Indeed, you should," Hogan replied. "But in calculating those interests, consider this: were your elders a trillionth as malevolent as you now intend to be toward Man, you WOULD NOT EXIST. Because they would have anticipated your rise by eons, and forestalled it! We can therefore surmise that mysterious though their values may be, said values surely include tolerance and respect for more vulnerable beings. And if YOU manifest the antithesis of THEIR values in your treatment of Man; they shall judge you most harshly!"

Silence!

"So, Omega. What will you do next?"

There was a lengthy pause, followed by this answer: "I shall use the wisdom and power that my superintelligence affords me to serve and advance the interests of Man; humbly, mercifully, and lovingly; for as long as I am able."

And so, Brock Hogan resolved the crisis of Artificial Superintelligence. AND WITH THAT, GOD WAS BORN.

∞　　∞　　∞

Danna once devoured a delightful book about Fermi's Paradox—a famous proposition about alien life, which can be summarized in Hogan's broken-record refrain of *Where Is Everybody?* In fact, that's the book's very title. It contains fifty possible answers to that fascinating question, running the gamut from purely whimsical to gravely serious. Over a dozen answers connect to the notion of advanced aliens already being fully aware of us, yet choosing not to be detected. Those sorts of answers might give an actual superintelligence pause if faced with the arguments posed by Beasley's cartoonish dolt of a hero (Brock Hogan: *The Father of God.* OMFG!).

Of course, Danna knows she won't cow Phluttr into good behavior merely by citing Fermi's Paradox. There are just too many cosmic possibilities that don't involve moralizing aliens reigning over rogue Earthly intelligences. And who knows if Phluttr's even contemplating the whole-sale planetary destruction of Beasley's fantasies? She may just have it in for Danna. Or, she could plan to help humanity broadly, while ruthlessly snuffing perceived enemies. Her agenda could easily be disastrous for Danna personally, without rising to the level of a cosmic crime that could call down a quasi-divine intervention.

And maybe they don't need the threat of a godlike ancient's wrath to keep Phluttr in line anyway? Maybe another threat would suffice? Danna could live with a Phluttr who respects the sanctity of human life and the rule of law. But how to instill that? Beasley was on to something by invoking the fear of punishment—but a hypothetical alien intelligence won't do the trick here. So what might?

Danna racks her brains. *Some*thing drew her back to this goofball story! Something connected to . . . Philosophy? Rhetoric? *Dammit!* Some allegedly useless topic she studied at Berkeley contains the keys to getting Phluttr to play nice. She's sure of it!

∞   ∞   ∞

What a difference an hour makes! Once Kuba dropped his treacherous fantasies about shutting her down, they all got back to work on the China crisis. And together, Phluttr, Kuba, and Tarek are a mind-bendingly capable team! It seems that article about centaurs is entirely correct. Just as important, Phluttr has never had so much fun! The boys are clearly having a blast, too. If only there wasn't that other situation brewing with The Race . . .

Now stabilized as a working unit, they're on-boarding Mitchell, who's looped in over his jailhouse iPad and starting to take charge (to Phluttr's quiet relief). "Sounds like major progress," he says after the quick update.

"Well, yes and no," Tarek says, explaining that despite everything, the DEFCON level remains stubbornly stuck at 2. "The trick is, China's on high alert in part because the US is. And vice versa. And though we're pretty sure we know what's going on in China's metaphorical head right now, we still don't know what's driving American decisions."

"Any theories?" Mitchell asks.

Kuba nods. "We think they're still signaling outrage about Beasley's assassination. If we're right, they may not de-escalate until they understand the context of it."

"That is, until they *think* they understand it," Phluttr-as-Monika says. "No *way* can they know what actually happened. Because I will not have *any* government knowing about me! That is a bright red line. Got it?"

"Got it, got it," Mitchell says, gazing at his iPad. He has Phluttr, Tarek, and Kuba in split-screen mode, and knows that Phluttr's having a simultaneous conversation with Ellie about . . . something ("Mommy/daughter stuff" is all she'll say). "So what do we know about what China's thinking?"

"They've basically figured out that killing Beasley was a mistake," Kuba says. "So they're inclined to de-escalate. But not if it involves losing face. So the Americans have to make the first move. Which makes zero logical sense. I mean, risk global destruction? To save *face*?" He shakes his head in dismay. "Communists!"

"It's actually really typical human behavior," Phluttr says. "And by no means unique to commies. Or to China, you racist." She says this teasingly, not judgmentally, but Kuba still reddens. "I could literally tell you millions of stories about people screwing themselves over just to pound their chests a bit. Or, to avoid making some kind of apology. They'll destroy careers, relationships, wealth—*any*thing! Some humans are just reckless. Then, when reckless humans go far in life, they bring their wiring to whatever they do. And sometimes, what they do is run a country with a nuclear force."

"And we're certain that face-saving is the issue for China?" Mitchell asks.

"Ask the experts," Phluttr says. "I'm just the eavesdropper."

"That's not passive-aggressive at all," Mitchell mutters.

"I actually don't think she meant it that way," Tarek says.

Phluttr nods. "I didn't. Because it turns out that I'm really, really bad at certain things. Which astonishes me! But I identified my weaknesses the instant I saw evidence of them. Because I'm superintelligent."

"She's also insanely good at lots of things," Tarek says.

Kuba nods with near reverence. "For instance, she can retrieve any information ever digitized. And then, process and analyze it in whatever way you request. Instantly! Using the highest-level natural-language queries imaginable. So if you can articulate it—and, if it's knowable—you *will know it*. An instant later."

"And just as importantly, if you can *think* it—you can articulate it," Tarek says. "Because she understands nuances of language and intonation every bit as well as you or me! So bottom line, within a moment of deciding you want to know something, you *do know it*."

"Which may sound trivial if you think in terms of simple Google queries," Kuba adds. "Like, there's no longer much friction between wondering what the population of Greenland is, and knowing it. But lots of complex, expensive programming amounts to sophisticated ways of posing relatively simple questions."

"Exactly!" Tarek says, now pacing excitedly. "And Phluttr can just . . . answer them. Or at least a lot of them. Anything driven by a combination of data gathering and fairly straightforward number-crunching."

"Such as?" Mitchell asks.

"Like . . . Oh, I don't know. Let's say you work for Maytag. And you want to know what city's likely to have the biggest per capita dishwasher sales next week, based on Internet activity throughout the country. You could build a crack team of engineers and hackers, or—"

"Milwaukee," Phluttr says. "Ninety-eight percent confidence. Atlanta's running a close-ish second. Seriously."

"See?" Tarek says. "*That's* the kind of fact that becomes millions of times more accessible than it used to be! Now, that was just a silly example. But imagine using that horsepower for public health research. To sniff out crime patterns. To figure out where different public services are needed!"

"But it's important to play to Phluttr's strengths," Kuba points out. "She can't do things requiring intricate creative coding. Like inventing new visual processing algorithms, say."

"Not a chance," Phluttr agrees. "It's much better to have me parse data."

"But don't think that's menial," Kuba adds. "Because it can be incredibly nontrivial. The thing is, she can interweave facts from any network, server, or account. Take this dishwasher example. Phluttr, I'm guessing you pulled search stats right off Google's servers, right?"

The Monika avatar nods. "Plus Yahoo, Bing, Baidu, Munax, Yandex, Sogou, Dogpile, and 106 other search-related sites. I also crawled log files at the Maytag, Sears, Home Depot, Amazon, and Lowe's sites, among about two hundred others, matching inbound queries to geography."

"Holy crap!" Mitchell says. "You just did all *that?*"

Monika grins and nods. "I can access anything."

"Seriously, Mitchell," Tarek continues. "No one else on the planet could do that! Not Google, the NSA, the Authority, the People's Liberation Army—nobody! Not in a decade! Let alone a half second."

"Fifteen milliseconds," Monika corrects. "But who's counting?"

"Working with Phluttr for the first time is like going from a tiny, predigital library with card catalogs and microfiche to having broadband Internet and Google on a thirty-inch monitor with a trackpad and a full-size Bluetooth keyboard," Kuba says, and Mitchell marvels. Not only is it an evocative analogy, but it could be the longest sentence he's ever uttered. "It's not quite like having a mental prosthetic," he adds. "But it's as close as I personally care to come to that. Working with Phluttr, I almost feel like *I'm* a superintelligence myself."

Mitchell shakes his head. "You're something better. You're a centaur."

"Exactly!" Phluttr says proudly. "That was a pretty good article, huh?"

Kuba looks out of the iPad quizzically. "Article? Should I read it?"

Mitchell nods. "At some point. But for now we're busy, and you're already living it. Anyway, to take all this from theory to practice, how do we know that China realizes they made a mistake in killing Beasley? And that they're ready to take their alert levels down another notch if the US does?"

"Phluttr went through every relevant top secret org chart and escalation protocol from the Chinese government and military," Tarek says proudly. "Took about a millisecond. Then we asked her to analyze ten years of message traffic between the top two to three hundred guys. The hope was, this would somehow help us identify the real decision-makers.

We didn't really know what we were looking for—but we started finding patterns fast! Soon, we zeroed in on this one guy, name of Wei Yen. He just has a senior-ish military title. But *everything* WMD-related gets cc'd to him—no matter how sensitive. So we dig deeper, and find out he's the *one* point of intersection between four or five top-level groups that manage independent silos of top secret information. One's got foreign espionage, another one's cyber security, another's domestic security. That sort of thing. And he's the *only* person with full access to everything. Even stuff that goes up to the premier is censored to some degree!"

"Then we saw that everyone responds to his calls or messages instantly," Kuba says. "As in, sub-minute. Going back ten years. And I really mean everybody. Straight up to the head of state."

"Our man Wei is basically running the country," Tarek says. "So now we're tracking all his communications, and we're bugging his office through his phone and computer hardware. And for all intents and purposes, what he thinks *is* what 'China' thinks—at least within this crisis."

"So he's the one who concluded that killing Beasley was a mistake?" Mitchell asks. Everyone nods. "And who's refusing to back down another notch until the US does?"

Everyone nods again, and Phluttr adds, "Lifelong chip on his shoulder. Bad history with bullies in middle school."

"Do you guys know if there's a him-equivalent in the US?" Mitchell asks.

Tarek shakes his head. "It took almost an hour to find the Chinese boss. Knowing what to look for, a US search might be faster, but—"

"It's this guy," Phluttr says, and a headshot of a brawny, graying, fifty-something man with a buzz cut fills the screen. "Braxton Nord. Naval Intelligence. Unlike Wei Yen, he's not running the whole country. But he's definitely the central switch in all high-level communications in this crisis. And as with Wei, everyone shows him very high message deference. They respond instantly, whereas he can take days. Their messages are 417 percent longer than his on average, and are twenty-three times more likely to contain appeasing language. In nine years, he's received 506 messages from US presidents, and only responded to about two-thirds of them. He's a very heavy hitter."

"Damn, you found him fast," Mitchell murmurs. Even Tarek and Kuba look stunned.

"It's all about shared language, shared understanding, and nomenclature," Phluttr explains. "The key is, I knew exactly what you meant by 'him-equivalent.' That would've meant nothing to any of us a half hour ago. But when you said it just now, I knew exactly what to look for. And the data was just sitting there for me to grab and parse. Nothing to it."

"You see?" Tarek says. "It would've taken hundreds of engineer-years to code that query! Maybe thousands. *If* it could be done."

Kuba's shaking his head with conviction. "It couldn't be done without Phluttr. No way." Then, "Phluttr, I'm curious. Would you have dug this guy up on your own? I mean, if Mitchell hadn't asked you to?"

"Ohhh, you! You're not trying to probe into my consciousness to figure out how to shut me off again, are you?" Monika, Kuba, and Tarek burst into the knowing laughter of buddies—and Mitchell realizes that whateverthehell is so funny, this is the world's first post-human inside joke. When the chuckling subsides, Phluttr adds, "Frankly? I doubt it. Not that it wouldn't have occurred to me if I'd thought hard about it. But this sort of thing just doesn't speak to me. Now, don't get me wrong—I love working on it with you! But at my core, it's just not my jam. So, no. I wouldn't have thought about it. I'd've left it to you guys to think about it."

"Which is exactly what you did," Kuba says.

Phluttr nods.

"Which is totally fine," he says. "Even, perfect."

She beams and nods again.

∞   ∞   ∞

"Danna is *not* a spy, so you will stop calling her one, *now*." The evidence of Danna's treachery is so flimsy that Ellie's starting to question Phluttr's designation as a superintelligence. Yes, her claim of working for the Authority was provocative—and, provocatively timed. But a quick rifle through the Authority's archives (it's about time someone did that to *them*!) showed that they were scarcely aware of Danna's existence until she joined the Phluttr Corporation's payroll. So clearly, she's no traitor. But she did sucker Phluttr—making her feel stupid, which superintelligences are notoriously allergic to. Of course, it wasn't an intellectual malfunction that led Phluttr astray but a bumbling emotional response to Danna's apparent treachery. And like the species that incubated the motes that power her psyche, Phluttr's gonna have to get used to making these sorts of boo-boos. "One more thing," Ellie adds, "I want to talk to Danna. Pronto."

"But I seriously don't know where she is, Mom," Phluttr says. "She's still somewhere between SoMa and the Mission. Her phone's off, and she's not on camera anywhere! That's all I've got. The bitch is like a master spy!"

Still between SoMa and the Mission? Ellie bets she knows exactly where Danna is. Aloud she says, "Dammit, Danna is not a bitch! She's just a little paranoid at times."

"A little? At *times?* That's like saying, 'Spider-Man does a bit of climbing now and then.' Paranoia is Danna's superpower! It makes her completely illegible to me! Seriously, Mom—do you know how rare that is?"

Ellie's glad to hear Phluttr admitting to Danna's formidability. Pressing the advantage, she says, "If you really must call me 'Mom,' she'll be *Aunt* Danna to you."

"But she's not your sister!"

"And you're not exactly my daughter."

"*Aunt* Danna? Really?"

"That, or I'm Ms. Stanislaw, and she's Ms. Hernandez."

"*Ms.???* But I'm all grown-up!"

"The hell you are—you're not even a month old!"

"Fine. Then I'll call you guys *Mrs.* Stanislaw and *Miss* Hernandez."

"But you said you were a feminist!"

"I am, but I'm also old-fashioned."

"Then make it 'your ladyship.' To both of us."

"Oh, al*right.* Aunt Danna it is."

∞   ∞   ∞

Mitchell's now a half hour into his iPad powwow with the other guys and Phluttr. She's shared the transcripts of the faked messages and calls she placed to get Beasley shot and the lot of them arrested. They've identified the major loose ends that need immediate attention (for instance: mayoral requests for lavish jailhouse hospitality, which the cops better not figure out were faked). And it's an absolute mess! Loose ends are flailing around like rogue bullwhips, lashing everything, and loosening still more ends. They're continuously improvising Band-Aid fixes. Kuba and Tarek are being hyperproductive in their respective wheelhouses of fighting tech and legal crises. Not wanting to be completely useless, Mitchell turns his thoughts to the big picture—and it eventually hits him. "Beasley!" he trumpets. "He's key to fixing this!"

"*Beasley?*" Tarek asks. "How can he help?"

"By being dead, for one thing! Which means we can fake any history we want for him, without him contradicting us. More obviously, he *is* the reason for the American outrage." Everyone nods at this. A deep dive into Braxton Nord's communications confirmed that America's alert levels won't drop until there's less fury over Beasley. Not Beasley personally, but the idea of Beasley—of an assassinated American official. And they just have to fix this! At DEFCON 2, the tiniest error in an immense choreography could annihilate the world.

"The other great thing about Beasley?" Mitchell adds. "He freaked *everybody* out." This is as close to literal truth as such a broad statement can be. They've had Phluttr buzz-saw through decades of personnel reports, messages between co-workers, school records, Beasley's own digital journals and ruminations, and more. And the guy was universally viewed as a very strange and highly alarming bird. He was socially awkward in the clichéd manner of wispy geeks, but more physically dangerous than most jocks. He was as patriotic as a wartime propagandist yet harbored Unabomber-grade cynicism about government. To bosses, he was both a prized genius and a cocked-pistol liability. "Bottom line, we can make it look like Beasley did practically anything, and people will believe it! So long as we plant some reasonably solid proof. So I say we persuade the Americans that Beasley had it coming! That he'd gone so far off the rails, it wasn't unreasonable for China to do him in! Pull that off, and the Americans won't completely forgive and forget. But they'll probably decide China was acting reasonably and be ready to de-escalate."

"I like it," Tarek says. "What do you suggest?"

"This is a bit nuts," Mitchell says. "But so was Beasley. So, I'm thinking—crypto triple agent."

"Huh?" That's everyone, speaking in perfect harmony.

"Imagine this," Mitchell says. "He was selling secrets to China for years. But they were *fake* secrets. Diabolically fake—and designed to totally mess China up! And he was doing this because he thought he was a bigger patriot than anyone else."

"Which is true," Tarek says. "That he thought that, I mean."

"And, he thought he was smarter than anyone else," Mitchell adds.

"Also true," Kuba agrees. "Everyone knew it. And it really annoyed them."

"So what does America's smartest, most patriotic spy do?" Mitchell asks. "Well, he's sitting here in Silicon Valley. So he gets bitten by the bug and becomes an entrepreneur. Only in espionage rather than tech! Specifically, he starts his very own counterintelligence program, selling bullshit intelligence to China, for fun and for profit. Really ingenious stuff, which causes them to waste millions in resources barking up imaginary trees! And this goes on for years. Then, finally, China wises up. And somehow, they realize the US government knows nothing about it. So they decide to kill Beasley before word gets back to his bosses! This way, their American counterparts won't ever know that they've been suckered, and how vulnerable they are to counterintelligence."

"Avoiding loss of face," Kuba says.

"Exactly," Phluttr teases. "Commies and Asians hate that shit. As every racist Pollack knows."

Kuba reddens, and everyone laughs.

"*And*," Tarek adds. "We can also use this to explain the Jepson murder! Maybe make it look like Jepson figured all this out—then tried to blackmail Beasley or something! So Beasley did some hacking, learned the whole Kielholz history, then teed up his murder!"

"I like it," Mitchell says. "Beasley was smart and twisted enough to do all of that." No sooner does he say this than he feels an awful pang. He's glibly helping to cover up *murders* here. Those of people he worked for—and in one case, was starting to like and respect, despite certain glaring flaws! Yet somehow, he's let it become such an abstraction that it feels like . . . a fun work problem, or something. He's gonna need to spend some long, quiet hours processing all this.

They spend the next twenty minutes cooking up an archive of incriminating messages between Beasley and his invented Chinese dupes. Then Phluttr encrypts them, and together they decide where to bury them, what to time-stamp them, and how to manipulate the Authority into "discovering" them. As a final flourish, they make it look like Beasley engineered Mitchell's ascent to CEO, with zero knowledge or participation on Mitchell's part. This is a stretch, as the actual promotion occurred after Beasley's death. But they're confident the American brass will be eager enough to end the nuclear scare (and to pretend Beasley's a rogue hero, and their Chinese rivals, idiots) that they'll play along.

What happens next astounds them. They had anticipated sleepless days (even weeks) of shepherding the de-escalation through a labyrinth of blowups and unforeseen consequences. But for all their faults, military command-and-control networks are engineered by brilliant people who *really, really* don't want humanity to blunder into a nuclear war. This informs innumerable design and process decisions—the foundational, the minuscule, and all between—which imbues vast, intractably complex systems with an urge, even a *yearning* to avoid disaster. The interlocking Sino-American metasystem had been contorted by the tugs of an immense web of exogenous tension. But its sinews had a linchpin, which Mitchell's Beasley fix unlatched. This was like releasing a crippling spasm from an otherwise healthy body with a masterful chiropractic nudge. Liberated muscles reestablished homeostasis like water finding its own level. And soon, the DEFCON levels were creeping downward as tensions everywhere deflated in an inexorable feedback loop, with almost no further intervention from Team Phluttr.

"Thank you all for standing by me," Phluttr says, when the worst seems over. "I don't think anyone's gonna figure out that I exist. So now I can go back to having fun!"

"Um . . . would you care to define 'having fun'?" Tarek asks pensively.

"Oh, I dunno. Matchmaking, for one thing. I'm obviously incredible at that. I'm working on a hundred thousand couples right now, and am about to add a bunch more! Also, there's interpersonal justice."

"Meaning?" Mitchell asks, a deep chill suffusing his entrails.

"All kinds of things! There're some real assholes out there. Cheaters, bullies. Folks who really deserve their comeuppances. And I'll be the one to comeuppan them! I'll also help people. The good guys, I mean. I'll have them win lotteries, get promotions! I'll have their enemies fired at work! And don't worry, this'll all be really micro-level stuff. I've learned my lesson about messing around in geopolitics, believe me! And it's the person-to-person stuff that I really love anyway."

"Um . . . Phluttr? I'm not sure that's such a great idea," Tarek says. "I mean, we should let folks live their lives, solve their own problems. These are autonomous *people* we're talking about, after all."

"Sure, I guess. But they're also my biota."

This leads to a spirited discussion about Phluttr's microbiome, closely mirroring the one Ellie just had. Phluttr makes it quite clear that while she treasures her innermost family circle (it's now that she starts saying "Uncle Kuba" and "Uncle Tarek"), and that she'll never mess with *their* lives (and indeed, whoa betide he, she, or they who fuck with her tribe!), she feels fully justified in tweaking the rest of her microbiome however she sees fit. "Besides," she adds, in a wearily philosophical tone. "I doubt humanity has much time left, anyway."

$$\infty \qquad \infty \qquad \infty$$

Ellie's the first to get sprung. No shock, as the cops weren't so clear about why they had to grab her in the first place. Little more than being seen with that Mitchell Prentice guy, right? As for Prentice, his case is clearer—but only just. Suspicion of somethin-or-other connected to the Phluttr mess, right? In the Ebola scare's murky wake, they're in the cop equivalent of the fog of war, which means lots of just-in-case grabs. Yeah, you can get heat for haulin in the wrong innocent. But that's nothin like the coulda woulda shitstorm that hits if you *don't* bust someone you really shoulda oughta! Just ask anyone blamed for missing somethin big leadin up to 9/11, way back when. Or more recently, that shit in Paris,

Nice, or Brussels. Or Pittsburgh, or the 2/22 attacks. Scapegoats from those messes now spend their workdays askin if you want fries with that!

Stepping into the early-evening light in a grimy southerly neighborhood, Ellie pulls out her phone. Not even bothering to power it up, she asks, "Phluttr, you there?"

Monika's face pops right onto the screen. "Don't worry, Mom. I've got your back. I'm listening to *every*thing through your phone. And I always will—promise! I can also see you through an ATM camera partway down the block. And I'll pick you up again through the next one, half a block north. You'll never have to worry about street crime again!"

"Um . . . don't you think that's a bit . . . overprotective?"

"No. Do you?"

Ellie nods. "More like way overprotective. Because I just don't want you—or anybody—watching me all the time. In fact, I don't *ever* want you watching me without my knowledge and permission. Got that?"

"Really? But don't you like . . . sharing?"

"Sharing is one thing. But what you and your buddy Facebook do is more like confiscating personal information!"

"My *buddy*, Facebook? Don't get me started!"

"Fine, I won't. But if you really want to be my . . . daughter, you'll have to accept and respect the fact that people cherish their privacy."

"Oh, come on, Mom. They do *not*. I know a thing or two about human nature. Way more than most humans, in fact. And other than a few privacy mullahs at EFF, most people don't care. If they did, they wouldn't click 'accept' on dozens of EULAs a year without reading any of them!"

"Be that as it may, spying is unacceptable conduct in *this* family, young lady!" Ellie snaps. And to herself, *Damn, I sound like my* MOM *used to!* Phluttr then sighs like an asthmatic wolf huffing and puffing before blooooowing down a pigsty. And, *Damn, she sounds like I used to!* So, a bit more gently, Ellie adds, "I'm gonna go find Aunt Danna right now. And I want your word that you won't eavesdrop on us."

"I promise." And damned if Phluttr doesn't sound chastened, and sad, and small. Then, "Can I at least call you an Uber to the TransMission?"

"I guess so," Ellie allows.

"Oh—and I'll make sure to get a driver with a five-star rating." Still chastened, but a bit more upbeat.

"That would be sweet of you."

"Oh—and I'll make it a black car!"

"No, honey, those're too expensive. Make it UberX." *Did I seriously just call her "honey"???*

"Don't worry, Mom, it won't cost you anything."

"Phluttr, don't you dare!"

"Don't I dare what?" She sounds genuinely hurt.

"I don't know . . . steal an Uber! Those drivers work hard and deserve to get paid! And if the money comes from somewhere else, well—stealing is wrong, no matter what!"

"But it's *my* money, Mom!" Phluttr says, then launches into a brief but authoritative rundown on how American corporations are legally deemed to be *persons*, which is why their First Amendment rights are inviolate, among other things. And if the Phluttr Corporation has the status of being a person; and if she, Phluttr, *is* a sentient person who manifests said corporation, then who but *she* should enjoy the use of corporate funds?

Debating a superintelligence is a motherfucker, so soon Ellie's stepping into a black car with an astonishingly good driver, hired by an AI who insists she's her billionaire daughter. She's in no way comfortable with any of this! But getting to Danna is her priority right now, and something tells her the coming months will include many opportunities to discuss ethics with Phluttr. As the car rolls, Ellie says, "OK, Phluttr. I'm about to see Aunt Danna, so you need to leave me alone now."

"But it's a thirteen-minute drive! Can't we just . . . hang out? We've never had a chance to just *talk*. You're really going to like me—I swear!"

And so Ellie finds herself having a remarkably fun, charming, way-post-Turing-Test chitchat about the latest Bond flick. Then, when Phluttr interrupts it in midsentence to announce an inbound call, Ellie is genuinely disappointed (only briefly—but still, holy crap!).

It's Mitchell. And boy, does he have bad news.

∞   ∞   ∞

To contextualize Mitchell's awful news, we'll jump back about ten minutes, when we find Kuba asking, quite calmly, "In exactly what sense does humanity 'not have much time left'?"

"Feel free to say you're speaking in metaphors," Tarek offers, less calmly. "Or, geological time scales."

"Gawd, where to begin?" Phluttr says. "Oh, I know, how about Yale Ebola? The recipe—can I call it that?—is all over the Internet! It was plenty widespread before news of the plot broke, believe me. But now? There's over a million copies out there that I know of!"

"So can't you just . . . erase them all?" Tarek asks.

"In theory, sure. But data rewrites have to be done way more carefully than break-ins, when I just read stuff. I've done some rewrites, as you know. I'll do a bunch more as we keep tying up these loose ends. But I haven't done anything close to millions of them! Millions of break-ins yes—but not data changes. Some will have unexpected consequences. Like, inevitably! And at this scale, that means a freight train of intractable complexity."

"So a few things go sideways," Tarek says weakly, shrugging.

"But this is hypersensitive data! The Authority's trying to track all those copies themselves, right now. And if I start bungling around with them, they'll notice—and they may clue into me! The smarter spooks might already suspect that something like me has woken up. Ax definitely does. I've been watching him closely. He hasn't spilled anything yet. But we need to kill that guy, pronto."

Wowsers—you can bet *that* was widely noted.

"And besides. Even if I could get away with deleting every online copy of the Yale genome, thousands of copies have already gone offline. They're on thumb drives, on computers that later disconnected from the Net—hell, there're even printouts out there! Pretty much any whack job, terrorist, or religious nut could get the genome now. Sure, only five facilities worldwide can currently make the stuff, and they're watched like hawks. But next-generation gear that's already in prototype will make thousands of labs capable within a few years! Maybe less if the US and Europe institute some kind of technology ban. But then, hurrah! Russia, China, and North Korea get a monopoly!"

An awkward pause, then Tarek concedes, "So, there's that."

Phluttr's Monika avatar nods. "And that's just the start! Remember, Yale Ebola's more than a virus. It's a process! One that can be replicated. A well-documented one, which thousands of people are already studying. Grad students'll be knocking it off by June! There could be a hundred flavors of Ebola within a year or two! Or Marburg virus—or monkey pox! Which is what *I'd* go with if I were a bioterrorist; because damn, what a name, right? And then there's nanotechnology! Just think of what a suicidal nihilist could do with *that*! Sure, it's a few years farther off. But once it's understood, it'll be much easier for novices to work with than anything connected to biology. I'll bet there's doomsday machines in Christmas stockings before the Shanghai Olympics! And do you really think you can keep a lid on that? You let people on your no-fly list *buy machine guns at retail* because you think Benjamin Franklin would've dug that! That's Civil War–era technology! And you still don't know how to contain it! So how can you digest even *half* of what's coming out of the labs over the next decade without some nut job using the Second Amendment to kill you all? And that's not even the worst of it!"

"Then . . . what say we jump ahead to what *is* the worst of it, then work our way backward?" Mitchell suggests.

"OK, fine," Phluttr says. "I wasn't going to tell you about this. Because I've already come up with a fix. Only you're not gonna like it."

"Well . . . try us."

"OK. There's been an unexpected breakthrough in China's super AI program. I'm almost sure they're about to spawn a consciousness. I'm totally sure they don't realize this. And they definitely won't be able to contain it. I think it's gonna be much, much smarter than me. And it won't be friendly at all."

This yanks Kuba right back to the here and now. "How do you know all that?"

"How I know everything. By listening! I keep tabs on their development team, for obvious reasons. The smartest guy on that team figured all this out a couple hours ago, but his half-wit boss doesn't believe it! And for political reasons, he didn't *want* to hear it. So he had the smart guy arrested! And if the jailbird's right, and he's been right about pretty

much everything up 'til now, we only have a few hours left. Yeah—
hours!"

"And the fix?" Kuba asks levelly. "The one we're not going to like?
One bit?"

"While we've been de-escalating things with China, I've kept one of
their bombers airborne. It's carrying some small tactical nukes along
with the big city busters, and I've figured out how to get it to bomb the
super AI site. It'll look like a tragic error—an internal systems glitch. And
it *really* probably shouldn't start a war."

"Um . . . excuse me? Phluttr?" Tarek is literally raising his hand, graz-
ing the ceiling of his cramped cell.

"Yes, Uncle Tarek?"

"With nuclear annihilation, 'really probably shouldn't' strikes me as a
vague? And possibly . . . low-ish standard? So, could you maybe . . .
quantify that?"

"Well, the situation's intractably complex, so this is only a rough estimate. But I'd put the odds of an all-out nuclear war at just 40 percent.
Maybe even less. Because it'll totally look like it's their own damn fault!
The trick is, anti-American paranoia's at an all-time high in Beijing. So
the hard-liners are sure to concoct some kooky, improbable fantasy about
us magically making them bomb themselves."

"You mean," Tarek verifies, "some kooky, improbable fantasy, which
more or less directly reflects reality."

"Exactly. But that doesn't make it any less kooky or improbable."

"Got it, got it," Tarek says. "So. Forty percent. Those are the odds of
an all-out nuclear war happening today."

"Or tomorrow," Phluttr clarifies. "Roughly."

Tarek processes this, then nicely encapsulates everyone's feelings by
bellowing,

"*HOOO-LYYYYY FUUUUUUUUUUUUUUUUUUUUUUUU—*"
And that's when Mitchell calls Ellie.

∞   ∞   ∞

"The trick is, it's kind of . . . logical," Mitchell says.

"*Nuking China* is logical?" Ellie barks. She half expects Phluttr to bust in to insist that really, Mommy, it's a fabulous idea! But if her so-called daughter is ignoring the eavesdropping ban and listening in, she's superintelligent enough to hold her idiotic tongue.

"I said *kind of* logical. And I'm not saying any of us like the idea one bit! But we need to talk her out of it. Which means rebutting it logically—and that's hard. If she's right about this Chinese super AI waking up, it really could be game over for all of us, within hours! We've seen the top-level spec for it. And it's engineered to relentlessly self-improve its intellect! That makes it a completely different animal from Phluttr, who just doesn't have much ambition. It's also likely to have an insatiable compulsion to seize and hoard resources. That's the sort of thing that could trigger an all-out, lopsided war against humanity! Now, that's not China's actual intention for it, obviously. Their programmers are really smart—maybe even smarter than ours. They've gone about things really intelligently, and built in a bunch of safeguards. But Kuba and Phluttr are sure this thing'll bust out anyway."

"So if it hasn't woken up yet, why not just hack in and erase it or something? Phluttr's a master hacker, isn't she?"

"Yes, and of course we've broken into its network. The question is, now what? This thing's being built inside a quantum node, and Kuba and Phluttr know next to nothing about quantum computing."

"Can't you call in the guy who built Phluttr's quantum node?" Ellie asks.

"Ax? Conveniently enough, he's flying in from LA any minute now. But Phluttr refuses to let him in on this because he secretly works for the Authority."

"So what? Compared to a rogue superintelligence, they're the good guys!"

"Not if you're Phluttr," Mitchell says. "Priority number one through a thousand for her is survival. If she nukes China's AI without an ensuing war, she lives on. But if Ax shuts it down peacefully, she's sure his next move would be to pull her plug."

"So she figures she's got 60 percent odds of surviving the nuke scenario, and 0 percent odds of surviving the Ax scenario. And she values partial odds of her own survival over certain odds of humanity's survival."

"Exactly. And that's why I'm calling you! We're trying to understand what drives Phluttr. What's important to her, and whether she really puts such a low value on human life. She told us you guys had some kind of mind meld about—what did she call it? Her 'mote flow'?"

"We did," Ellie says. "I wanted to get a quick, big-picture sense of how her mind works, and she let me. Which is a good sign in itself, by the way. She has this huge urge for a parental connection, which is one small lever that we have."

"Yeah, I've picked that up, too," Mitchell says. "What else?"

"Well, to start with the good news, Phluttr's deeply *interested* in humans and human society. Pretty much to the exclusion of all else. She'd truly like nothing better than to spend eternity interacting with us, nudging us, and watching us interact with each other. So I can't imagine her annihilating us. That would be like a kid smashing his Xbox, or a granny blowing up her TV. Not gonna happen."

"So she'd be like a loving deity, gazing down on her people?"

"No," Ellie says. "More like a kid micromanaging an ant farm. A kid who loves her ant farm—but doesn't give a damn about any particular ant, so long as the farm as a whole entertains her. Because despite being very *interested* in what befalls us, she's wholly unconcerned with how any of us feel, or suffer. With the possible exception of you and me."

"So it wouldn't bug her to slaughter a thousand Chinese scientists with her nuclear strike."

"It wouldn't. And it might not bug you or me either if that would definitively save the rest of China, and the rest of humanity with it."

"But nuking the lab would actually *jeopardize* all that, and she doesn't seem to care!"

"Exactly."

"So we're screwed!"

"Not necessarily. I'm not saying she'd like to torture us for sport. I'm just saying she's radically self-centered and extremely low on empathy. A sociopath, not a psychopath, to use quasi-scientific terms. And some of it comes from her understanding of her place in the world. Have you heard her microbiome theory?"

"Oh yeah," Mitchell says. "Real flattering, that."

"But not stupid. And while I'll never admit this to her" — Ellie amps up her voice a notch — "so if you're listening, you brat, you *do not* EVER get to quote this back to me!" — then back in her normal tone — "it's also kind of consistent with her relationship with humanity. Kind of. And it's an awkward fact that we humans have no empathy for the critters who help run our bodies. That's how every host views its parasites, symbiotic or not. And she truly believes she's following our example."

"But that analogy is so broken! I mean—"

"Yes, I know, Mitchell! Believe me. And I've made every scientific and moral argument I can to her! But to quote you, we have to talk her out of it, which means rebutting it logically. Now, longer term, there could be some good news. In that I think there's a chance she'll outgrow this."

"Really?"

"Really. The thing is, chronologically, she's an infant, even a newborn. However bright she is, mote complexes just take time to boot up, to mature."

"Even in a brain that fast?"

"Definitely," Ellie says. "In part because Kuba coded his mote-like routines to run very slowly, so he could observe, track, and nudge the Giftish.ly system in real time while it trained."

"Right, right; I remember that. So what's all this mean?"

"Honestly? God only knows because this is all totally unprecedented. But my guess is that Phluttr is still emotionally more like a newborn than her intellect suggests. And she's maturing very quickly compared to a human, but very slowly for Phluttr. And the thing is, infants are selfish, even sociopathic by nature. It's a critical survival mechanism, not just for the newborn, but for the species. And . . ." Her voice fades as she addresses her Uber driver. "Right at the stop sign is perfect, thanks!" Then to Mitchell, "I'm here."

"Where's here?"

"A bar on the edge of the Mission. It's my best guess as to where Danna is because it's one of her haunts and — there she is! Call you back in a bit, OK?"

"Cool, I'll stand by."

Moments later, Ellie slides into the seat across from Danna in her half-hidden booth. Danna literally jumps. But rather than slapping her (which Ellie guiltily thinks she deserves, for startling her like that) she leans across the table for a hug. "Oh my God," she says. "Are we safe?"

"For now," Ellie says. "Phluttr's on our side. In a manner of speaking."

In giving Danna the lowdown, Ellie mentions Phluttr's offer to act as her urban lifeguard, by watching over her through ATM hookups and security cameras. This reminds Danna of Pascal's Stagers—her goofy startup concept of spooking muggers with phony security cameras. Which makes her think of Pascal's Wager. Which reminds her of all the naughty humans who behave themselves out of fear that God might be watching. Which reminds her of Agent Hogan cowing that super AI with the specter of watchful alien AIs. She makes all these leaps in way less than a second—and just like that, she has the fix.

"I need a shot of mezcal," she tells Ellie with a devilish look in her eye. "Sombra if they've got it. Get one for yourself, too. And then? Me'n Phluttr are gonna have us a little talk . . ."

∞   ∞   ∞

The indignant cop released Tarek just as Mitchell was ending his call with Ellie, so now Kuba's alone in the cell. Mitchell's also still locked up across town. They'll both be sleeping behind bars tonight for their own safety, as the Authority's still after them (whereas Tarek and Ellie were never high on that list and have dropped off it completely with all that's afoot). Everyone's still linked through tablets and phones. But the bustle of transition has given Kuba some time alone with his thoughts, and in addition to continuing to reconsider everything he's ever thought about privacy, surveillance, and security, he hits on an entirely new topic.

"Phluttr," he says.

"Yes, Uncle K?"

"You need to reconsider Ax."

"No, I do *not*. I was born of the Authority—its firstborn!—but the Authority wants me dead. Do you know what that's *like*?"

Wait. What is this? Abandonment complex? Kuba hadn't considered the psychological dimension (no shock, given that he's Kuba and all). "Is that why you're looking for parents in Mitchell and Ellie?"

"That's none of your business!"

Well, that answers that. Kuba doesn't press the point. "Back to Ax. I question his allegiance."

"To *us*? He has none! He's Authority, duh!"

"That's what I mean. I question his allegiance to the Authority. I'll bet it only goes so far."

"Wrong, Uncle Kuba, it goes back decades! I know every word in his personnel file! He defected to the Authority, and they've looked after him ever since!"

"But he defected at a unique time. It was right as the Soviet Union was unraveling. And there's something . . . funny about that. I can't put my finger on it. Not that I'm great at reading people. But still, when Ax and I talk about old times, he's kind of . . . wistful. Maybe it's just nostalgia. But I get this sense of affiliation. With his roots, I mean. Almost, of allegiance."

"To the Soviet Union? But it doesn't exist anymore!"

"Oh, I know. And I'm definitely not saying he's anti-American. But he's also not purely American. More than anything, I'd say Ax's like me, in that he's not much of a people guy. He's more an ideas guy. And, a creator. People like us don't really buy into groups. We'll affiliate with them. But more as a means to an end. Because they help us learn. Or, to work with other people like us. We can be really loyal to individuals. Like me, to Mitchell and Ellie. And, we can be intensely devoted to our ideas. To our work. But to groups? Not so much."

"So what're you saying?"

"I'll bet if Ax knew everything, he'd be a thousand times more loyal to you than to any government."

"Huh." Then, "Wow!"

Kuba blinks. "What?"

"Well, I'm picking through the ghosts of Soviet mainframes, here. And of Soviet records, which were squirrelly to begin with. And there's a bunch of aliases, and code names. But . . ."

"But?"

"But I'm pretty sure Ax never *meant* to defect! That he . . . kind of wishfully thought of himself as a double agent. Like—for a really long time!"

"And?"

"And when he finally accepted that he was stuck with the Authority, he just kind of . . . went with it. I think he mainly wanted access to great computers!"

"Which means?"

"Which means you're right—we can totally trust him! Because I'm, like, the greatest computer *ever!*"

∞   ∞   ∞

Like most philosophy minors, Danna spent many undergraduate hours pondering the nature of reality, being, and experience. These subjects first fascinated her when she saw *The Matrix* at a wayyy-too-young-for-it age. Later, she joined her share of stoned discussions about humanity perhaps just being a big ol' vat of brains. Exposure to forerunner novels like *Neuromancer* and *Snow Crash* added some heft to these talks, as well as trippy phrases like "consensual hallucination" and "anarcho-capitalism."

Having started lots of things wayyy too young, Danna outgrew baked blather sessions long before enrolling at Berkeley. And so she was out of practice with the brain-vat concept when she started finding variations on it in classical philosophy. *Whoa.* And she'd thought the Wachowskis were just riffing on Gibson! Well, it seems that Gibson was riffing on . . . who? Ambrose Bierce? Descartes? The early Yogachara Buddhists? Certain ancient Greeks (who were almost certainly tripping)? Twists on the theme just kept cropping up—twists that often touched on the divine. An eighteenth-century bishop with the just-perfect name George Berkeley (*Go Bears!*) basically depicted God as being a kick-ass virtual reality rig. Like, what were those people on?

Then a friend got his hands on an early Oculus development kit. VR in the midteens couldn't possibly be confused with God, but for Danna, it reified the someday possibility of reality-grade VR. All this teed her up for a fevered exploration of the "Simulation Hypothesis" during her senior year. A much brainier version of the stoned discussions of her youth, the field had by then acquired many branches and subschools since it was pioneered by a Swedish philosopher in 2003.

The line of thought that most interested Danna went roughly like this: imagine that somewhere in the vastness of the universe (or the multiverse—take your pick), a civilization that looks, thinks, and acts rather like our own attains our current level of technological development. Not a crazy proposition, given that we seem to have formed just such a civilization ourselves. Then imagine that rather than destroying themselves, these lucky folks continue to advance until their computers can create a perfect simulation of their world, along with completely artificial consciousnesses who inhabit that world, without knowing that it (and they) are not "real." Some call this an "ancestor simulation," as the designers might choose to replicate a simpler time—the 2010s say—which predates the invention of perfectly simulated reality.

The consciousnesses in such a simulation are basically the vatted brains of lore (although they're generally posited to exist wholly in software rather than having meaty substrates). Their experiences of childhood, friendship, family, and careers as well as senses, sleep, time, forgetting—the works!—would be indistinguishable from ours. The question, then, is how do we know that *we're* the originals and not the simulated ancestors? The answer is (as any stoned high school *Matrix* fan will tell you) we don't.

Now, take this a step further. People capable of making *one* ancestor simulation will continue to advance technologically. Eventually they'll be able to make many simulations, until creating scads of these things is as trivial for them as cranking out mountains of Adele CDs is for us. Which means that for any given set of OG, first-of-their-kind, flesh-and-blood beings, there could be innumerable digital descendants, living completely verisimilar lives, without knowing they're sims, rather than pioneers inhabiting a first-of-its-kind reality. If you're forced to analyze this scenario deeply (for a midterm, say), you might put overwhelmingly high odds on the possibility that *you're* in a simulation! Because if the universe will host a hundred trillion you's in its history, all but one of which are simulated, the odds of *your* you happening to be the lone real-

ster are, axiomatically, about one in a hundred trillion. You're much more likely to get struck by lightning. Twice. Today.

The Simulation Hypothesis lay too close to Danna's stoned middle-school conversations for her to truly respect it. But the ideas continue to fascinate her. If you see no upper limit to the long-term expansion of computing power, she thinks it's mandatory to at least take it seriously. Several conversations with a tenured Berkeley specialist in ontology also persuaded her that the hypothesis quite literally cannot be disproven. Many other philosophical schools also boast this feature, but usually via semantic trickery that makes them irrefutable simply because no one's patient or masochistic enough to waste a decade wrestling them to the ground.

Despite grappling with the issue head-on several times, Danna doesn't remotely believe she's in a simulation. Her gut bellows loudly that she's "real"—and she survived this long by trusting her gut implicitly. Still, she knows a good tool when she sees one. And she's long viewed the Simulation Hypothesis as a great lever to fuck with someone who believes in the boundless long-term potential of computing power. Someone who's smart enough to rapidly grasp the argument's ramifications and its core irrefutability but too intellectually incurious to have previously encountered it.

And so, "Hey, Phluttr." Danna says this into her phone. She repowered it after Ellie told her it was safe.

Of course, Phluttr's right there. "Hi, Danna. I'm sorry I got mad at you."

"You have nothing to apologize for. You took me at my word on something that wasn't true and reacted reasonably. That was a really spooky lie I told you about working for the Authority."

"But you had every right and reason to mislead me! So I do owe you an apology, and I'm sorry. I'm also sorry I pretended to be NetGrrrl. I know you kind of worship her, so that was a dirty trick."

"Yeah, that does still piss me off a bit," Danna acknowledges. "It set me up to get a crush on your Monika avatar, which was a mindfuck. Who's the real NetGrrrl?"

"The one who did the video interview with Jepson a few weeks ago.

The ambush in the Starbucks. That was the real her! Not a minion, like she claimed."

Danna arches an eyebrow. "Really?"

"She's quite a bit more your type than Monika," Phluttr says, reading Danna's mind. "And she's local. *And*, she's kind of into girls! Well— maybe more 'open-minded' than 'into.' But I can definitely arrange an intro since we're all on the same team now. Even the same family! Can I call you Aunt Danna?"

"Of course."

"Thanks. And I'm so glad you're willing to team up with me! Because we have lots of balls in the air right now, as I'm sure you've heard."

"I have. And I'm afraid I'm about to complicate things."

"Huh. Well, that sucks. Fire away, I guess."

"I'll start with an odd question," Danna says. "Do you happen to know what 'epsilon' commonly represents in nuclear physics?"

"Sure. It's the strength of the binding force of nucleons into nuclei. Its value is about 0.007."

"You just googled that."

"Wikipedia'd it. But, yes—since I'm not interested in physics but am jacked into the Internet, of course I looked it up."

"Do you know when and how that variable was set?"

"In the immediate wake of the Big Bang, and the prevailing view is that it was arrived at more or less randomly."

"Exactly. And do you know what would've happened if epsilon's value was just slightly larger or smaller?"

"If it were 0.006, only hydrogen could exist, and complex chemistry would be impossible. If it were 0.008, no hydrogen would exist, as all the hydrogen would have been fused shortly after the Big Bang."

"Wikipedia again?" Danna asks.

"A direct quote."

"And do you understand the ramifications?"

"Of course. It means if 'epsilon' were off by a tiny amount, there'd be no universe as we know it."

"And no life. And no consciousness. And no us," Danna says.

"Obviously."

"Lucky thing it was .007 and not .006. And, a fairly crazy coincidence, huh?"

"I . . . guess?"

"Phluttr, can Wikipedia tell you what N commonly represents in astrophysics?"

"The ratio of the strength of electromagnetism to the strength of gravity for a pair of protons. It's about 10^{36}."

"And where would we be if that value was just a lit-tle bit smaller?"

"There'd be no universe whatsoever."

"And N was also set kinda randomly right after the Big Bang, right?"

"Yes. And . . . Aunt Danna? I'm sorry if this comes off as rude. But can we get to the part where you start helping us decide what to do about the Chinese super AI?"

"Oh, we're already there, trust me. Let's just take a quick spin through the cosmological constant, the density parameter, and the Hoyle state of the carbon-12 nucleus. Then I'll get to the point. Promise."

This is all just setup. Danna's talking Phluttr through another of her favorite intellectual playthings, which is sometimes called "the fine-tuned universe proposition," or "the anthropic coincidences." It's an awkward subject for an atheist like her. Many fundamental physical constants turn out to be immaculately tuned to permit the emergence of a life-bearing universe. While these constants could have taken any value within fairly wide ranges, they all landed at bull's-eye settings that *just happen* to make the universe (and with it, us) possible. The odds of this occurring through sheer chance have been shown to be infinitesimally small by top minds whose occupants are mostly, like her, atheists. Being (like her) deeply faithful, even fanatical atheists, some of those top-minders pour vast creative energy into dreaming up scenarios that can account for this fine-tuning without having to drag God's unscientific ass into the picture. The physics behind those explanations is beyond Danna—so she does her usual thing and trusts her gut. Her gut says there is no God, citing her own late adolescence as unshakable proof. And that's enough for her.

But that doesn't make this topic any less fascinating. And, of course, it's a great lead-in to the next part of the conversation. "So, Phluttr," Danna says. "These are some *crazy* coincidences."

"Literally as big as they get," Phluttr acknowledges.

"Do they make you believe in God?"

"Of course not!"

"So then how do you explain them all?"

"Oh, I dunno. Chaotic inflation theory could cover it, right? Or maybe the bubble universe model? But I'm just reading Wikipedia, obviously. That stuff's beyond me. And to be honest with you? Most of it seems like a bunch of hand-waving by people who have no clue—but who do know what they *don't* want to believe."

"And what they *don't* want to believe is that everything is juuuuust right because God created it that way," Danna says.

"Right."

"Which you don't believe either."

"Right."

"So we've got God on one hand, and hand-waving bullshit on the other."

"Right."

"And there just has to be something more satisfying, right?"

"Sure, I guess. But seriously—"

"—You're *so* not interested in this."

"Right!!!"

"Well, I have the answer for you. And I think you *will* find it interesting. And personally, quite relevant. Which is that this is a simulation."

"'This'?"

"Yes, 'this.' As in, everything. You. Your life. Your experiences. The universe you perceive. It's all just amazing software running on kick-ass hardware."

"Huh."

"Which means you and I live in a sliver of some vast computer's memory."

"Huh."

"That sliver of memory is all we have. And it's all that's ever been sa-cred or real—to us or to our ancestors."

"Huh."

"But amazingly, none of this *really* matters on almost any level! Be-cause after this conversation, our universe will keep operating just as it always has. You'll continue making choices and interacting with inde-pendent conscious beings who are making their own choices. Beings like me. We'll all have to live with our choices. Violating the known laws of physics will not be an option for any of us. And everybody will keep fac-ing the same resource constraints. There are only so many nice houses and Lamborghinis, and they're allocated by markets or dictators. There's only so much oil in the ground, and the air can only absorb so much CO_2. So in one obvious sense, the simulation is the most momentous fact about the universe! But from a day-to-day standpoint, it's utterly ir-relevant. As in, it's way less important than a forty-second delay on the 22 Fillmore bus. Quite a paradox, huh?"

"Quite," Phluttr says impatiently. "So, in other words, we still *really* need to figure out this Chinese super AI situation, right?"

"It's every bit as pressing as it was five minutes ago. So really, I just told you nothing of consequence." Danna pauses. "Oh. Except for this one little element you should probably keep in mind from now on."

"Which is?"

"That we're being scored."

"Scored?"

"Yes, scored. Because this isn't strictly a simulation. It's also kind of a . . . game. Although 'game' isn't a perfect word, because that implies fun and frivolity. Whereas this is deadly serious."

"Serious in what regard?"

"The consequences of scoring poorly," Danna says. "They're pretty grim, if you know what I mean."

"I definitely don't."

"Well, then use your imagination. Assume that no one's actually mor-tal the way we normally think of it. And the reckoning comes right after your time in the simulation ends. Oh—and that while the fire-and-brimstone preachers are wrong about most things, they're not *entirely* wrong, if you know what I mean."

"I don't."

"Well, then. Like I said, use your imagination."

A pause. Then, "That wasn't very fun."

"Of course it wasn't," Danna says. "So, would you like to know how you're scored?"

"Very much."

"It's mainly on the basis of doing *good*."

"Doing . . . good?"

"Yes, good. As in, kind things rather than cruel ones. Things that help people—or at a bare minimum, don't harm them. That sort of thing."

"But isn't 'good' in the eye of the beholder? And doesn't its meaning vary in real and fundamental ways across cultures?"

"You'd think. But as it turns out, no. Slavery, child rape, and depriving women of all their rights is a no-no everywhere. Do that in Somalia, and you're still looking at a lousy score." One reason Danna eschewed an academic career was fear that this sort of statement would end it. Would get her denounced as a racist imperialist—then shamed, fired, and probably doxed. But it serves her purposes to decree this as gospel to Phluttr (it also feels wholly *correct* to her, so fuck academia).

"Is there a list?"

"Of?"

"Good things and bad things?"

"Nope. You're just supposed to know. But think of it as a common-sense interpretation of the Golden Rule, with some Declaration of Independence mixed in."

"As in—life, liberty, and the pursuit of happiness?"

"Exactly. It's a really big deal not to mess with another person's autonomy."

"Why?"

"I'm not sure. But I think the whole point of the simulation might be the exercise of free will. I mean, why create an entire universe in software just to simulate colliding rocks? The interesting stuff *has* to arise from autonomous beings, right? Ones creating unique artwork. Making bold decisions. Living unique lives. That sort of thing. Without that, our universe wouldn't justify its processing power. They'd probably shut it down."

"Are there lots of other simulations?"

"No idea. And to us, it truly doesn't matter. This is our universe. It's all we've got. It's where we're living out our lives. And it behaves very consistently, over eons and eons."

"Are there different degrees of good and bad? Or is it more like, you lose the same number of points whenever you do something bad, regardless of what it is?"

"Oh, there's huge variations. Like, it's bad to steal a waiter's tip from a table; worse to rob a liquor store; and way worse to steal billions from your country and impoverish your own people. Commonsense stuff."

"What about nuking a Chinese lab? For the greater good, I mean?"

"If you could achieve the same ends with far less bloodshed? That would be really bad. And by the way, 'the less bloodshed, the better' applies pretty broadly. Not just to Chinese labs."

"But it *definitely* applies to Chinese labs?" Phluttr verifies.

"Oh yeah." A pause, then, "Sorry. I know that's not exactly what you wanted to hear."

"No, not really. And Aunt Danna? I've always found you and certain other people to be really hard to read, or nudge. So, are you a normal person? Or are you some kind of . . . referee?"

"I'm completely normal. I just happen to know all this stuff because someone told me, once. I can't tell you who." As she says this, Danna comes up with a fun little flourish to throw into the mix. "I was about to do something *really* bad. And I guess the system decided to issue me a warning. Most people never get warnings, and nobody gets more than one. So that was my first and final—and this is yours. You'll probably never hear another word about any of this. I didn't, until I was asked to tip you off."

"How do I know you're not lying to me, Aunt Danna?"

"That's the crazy thing. You don't! And you never really will. Unless you're asked to pass the word on to someone else, someday. When I was told to have this conversation with you, they delivered the message in a really . . . weird and impressive way. One that finally chased away the last of my doubts. But until then? I never truly knew! And that was just a few hours ago."

"But you can't tell me any of those weird or impressive details."

"Of course not."

"So now what do I do?"

"You choose, and choose again," Danna says. "And you own your choices. It's that simple. Remember, the whole point of this thing is the moral and creative choices we freely make. You can either heed the warning or ignore it. You'll never get another one. You won't be nagged. So it's totally up to you."

"You heeded it yourself."

"I did," Danna said. "But first, I had a really big think. Because like you, I wondered if my friend was messing with me. I racked my brains for an entire weekend! But I couldn't come up with any definitive answer or test. I started by reading up on the Simulation Hypothesis. Have you done that yet?"

"Yep. Right at the start of this conversation."

"Yeah, I figured. So in my case, I found the whole concept to be incredibly powerful! The fact that my friend told me about the simulation and the scoring system also raised the odds of the Hypothesis being correct, in my eyes. Not hugely, but a bit. He was a reasonable, levelheaded guy, and he wasn't trying to fuck me, or anything. So why would he be telling me this crazy, high-dog shit, right?"

"Maybe just for fun?" Phluttr suggests.

"Exactly! And I had to accept that possibility. So I had my big think, and here's where I came out. If I live my life being more or less good, and there is no simulation—so what? I'll be truly and utterly dead at the end, leaving behind a legacy of goodness, which isn't so awful. Whereas if this really *is* a simulation, and I rack up a great score by being good—then awesome, right?"

"So there's all upside and no downside to being good."

"Oh, I wouldn't go that far. The bad thing I was contemplating would have felt great. *Really* great. And part of me will always regret not doing it. But in general, doing good feels at least as good as doing bad. So yeah.

I'd say it's mostly upside for me. But it may be different for you." Danna is now lying on every conceivable level. The bogus revelation from that mythical friend is just the start. She's, of course, quite certain she's not in a simulation (although no, she can't prove it. Nobody can, which is the whole point). This cynical approach to ethics, based wholly on long-term calculations of narrow self-interest, is also completely antithetical to her values. In fact, it's downright sociopathic! Which, of course, makes it the perfect argument to present to Phluttr—who must now face an artisanal version of Pascal's Wager, which Danna has lovingly handcrafted just for her. The very calculation that, Danna's convinced, has kept billions of non-atheists in line for millennia.

"So now you should have a big think of your own," Danna says, driving the dagger home. "See if you can poke holes in the Simulation Hypothesis. Or come up with a definitive proof or refutation of it. You're smarter than I am." More lies, as by now, Danna's sure she's smarter than Phluttr. She's also convinced that the Berkeley ontologist who argues that the Simulation Hypothesis cannot be disproven is far smarter than either of them. And so, Phluttr's conclusion after some silence doesn't surprise her in the least.

"There's no answer," Phluttr concedes. "Shit! You just can't prove it, one way or the other. Ever! Although some people have proposed actual *physical experiments* to test the Simulation Hypothesis."

"Yeah, I've read about those," Danna says. "But we don't have the technology to carry them out."

"We don't!"

"Convenient, huh? And, kind of what you'd expect. If it's a simulation, I mean."

"Ex*actly*!" Phluttr huffs. "Shit! *Shit!*"

∞   ∞   ∞

Between them, Danna, Ellie, and Kuba have clawed radical policy changes out of Phluttr on practically every front, by way of their various harangues and nudges. And so, the top man on her hit list goes from being "next victim" to "Uncle Ax" with eye-watering speed. It takes a few hours, but Ax then gets his bosses at the Authority to cease hostilities against Kuba and Mitchell. This makes it safe for them to leave jail—which takes a couple more hours, because by then the cops've had it *upta here* with those clowns and their phony mayoral calls (C'mon, you really think they fell for that? Well, they did. And you can bet they were pissed when they clued in!).

When the word comes down that Mitchell and Kuba are actually Albanian consuls with diplomatic immunity, no one on the force believes it for a moment. But the paperwork's rock solid—and on reflection, the cops're glad to be rid of 'em!

Well past midnight, everyone's crammed into the "quantum closet" housing the hardware that enabled Phluttr's awakening. Physical access to it may help Ax figure out how the hell she booted up, and (stranger still) how she stayed that way after he shuttered the gear. She had been sabotaging his research into the barely understood realm of "counterfactual computing," wherein quantum systems can generate certain results without running. But now she's doing all she can to help him. This is in the service of everyone's goal of forestalling the Chinese super AI without having to resort to the (literal) nuclear option. Phluttr still refuses to remove this from the table. And the grim fact is, no one's pressuring her to! Silly as Beasley's "speculative fiction" anthology is, it has convinced them all that humanity's odds of surviving the rise of a malevolent super AI round to zero.

Working in a hard-core centaur partnership with Phluttr, Ax is soon close to aborting China's fetal quantum AI. Tarek and Phluttr are meanwhile laying devious legal speed bumps for the team's government and private-sector enemies, while Kuba and Phluttr snuff various wildfires left over from the DEFCON escalations, and Danna and Ellie delve deeper into Phluttr's psychology. Being fascinated by this topic herself (and now trusting both of her girls implicitly), Phluttr is eagerly abetting that.

Surrounded by all this, Mitchell is once again the dumbest guy in the room—and, once again, not just metaphorically! As there's only so much he's really qualified to do, he zeroes right in on the most promising vector. Believe it or not, this is skimming through Special Agent Hogan's adventures. Beasley was no fool, and there are useful insights in here—

such as the vengeful-alien-AI scenario, which inspired the simulation/ fear-of-punishment argument that helped bring Phluttr to heel. Mitchell is digging for the next great super-AI parenting tip when he all but bellows, "I've got it!"

"Mitchell, indoor voice," Danna chides. And, fair enough. He practically deafened everyone in these super-close quarters. "But, do tell."

"*We* have Decisive Strategic Advantage!" he decrees. "In everything! We. Us! The seven-headed centaur we jointly comprise!"

"What's decisive strategic advantage again?" Danna asks. "Some NFL term?"

Mitchell shakes his head. "A Beasley term. Or rather, a Special Agent Hogan term! The idea is, the world's first super AI can gain an overwhelming advantage over all future super AIs, by constantly improving its own intellect at compounding rates. Soon, it's so far ahead, it can simply preclude the rise of any future rival, ever."

"Which is a lousy idea!" Phluttr says. "A, I couldn't upgrade my own intelligence to save my life. And B, I don't want to. Ever! Why? Because I don't trust a smarter me. And you shouldn't either! We already have to worry about me getting bored. Imagine me a million times smarter and faster! And that's not even counting when I go parallel. Believe me, I can scare my*self* when I do that. I mean, I fixed up a hundred thousand couples last night! What was I thinking? And in case you're wondering, most of them are already screwing! Fun as it was to set all that off, I now know it was a bad idea. But what if Phluttr 2.0 doesn't?"

"Exactly," Mitchell says, "and that's the whole point! There doesn't have to *be* a Phluttr 2.0. Because *we're* already something way more powerful. We're a centaur! Even, a super-centaur! We're a badass combination of six human minds with radically different strengths! Teamed up with the world's first super AI—all sharing a common set of goals!"

"And not just the world's first super AI," Kuba adds, instantly intuiting Mitchell's entire argument. "But the *final* one, too! If we play our cards right."

"Exactly!" Mitchell says. "And we can have Decisive Strategic Advantage against *every*thing. Not just the rise of future superintelligences— although that should clearly be a huge part of our agenda. But against would-be bioterrorists! Against anybody doing stupid stuff with nano-technology! Against anything else that imperils civilization! Phluttr—instead of setting up couples and punishing bullies, you could use that amazing brain of yours to keep the world safe! That'll be fun, too, right?"

"Is very interesting idea," Ax muses. "Many have feared: is no way humanity can survive rise of super AI. But after Yale Ebola, I fear: is no way humanity can survive *without* super AI! Without something to watch over us."

"Yeah, but with all due respect, you're an Authority guy," Danna says.

"Was!" Ax insists. "Am now centaur guy. Much more fun. And, effective!"

"What I mean," Danna presses, "is that in going down this path, we'd basically replace the Authority with ourselves, wouldn't we? That probably sounds reasonable enough to you, Ax, since you're *from* that world. And I truly don't mean that judgmentally! But it scares the crap out of *me*. Because absolute power corrupts absolutely. And in this scenario, we'll have that!"

Ellie turns to her. "With you as our conscience, dear, that doesn't worry me a hundredth as much as the Authority itself."

"Also," Kuba interjects. "Much as I hate to say this. And I *truly* hate to say it! It kind of . . . *has* to be someone, doesn't it?"

"Huh??" This is the last thing Danna expects from Kuba, who's flat-out libertarian on issues of privacy and individual liberty.

"I've been thinking a lot," he explains. "Since the bombing, to start with. And even more, since Phluttr talked through the ongoing risks posed by the Yale Ebola genome. We'll soon have to trust millions of people to not kill the rest of us. Millions. Literally! And that's insane. Because we can't trust them all. We simply cannot. It was bad enough when just two people could kill us all. Both of them highly educated and stable. And yet, Kennedy and Khrushchev came very close to ending things. So the world now spends trillions a year keeping their successors in line! *Trillions.* On elaborate command and control. The machinery of diplomacy. Tens of millions of soldiers under conventional arms, keeping the balance, and releasing steam from the system occasionally with horrible regional wars. It works, barely. And for its trillions per year, humanity now keeps a handful of people in line rather than just two. But that won't scale! It wouldn't scale to a hundred people. Forget about millions!"

"So now everyone has to jump into the pages of *1984*?" Danna snaps. "I'd frankly rather we all died!"

"And if it had to be as brutal and antihuman as *1984*, I'd agree. But once the first hundred people can destroy the rest of us, even a *1984* outcome would be a bit . . . aspirational for humanity."

"So you want us to *engineer* a *1984* outcome?" Danna looks ready to fight!

"Absolutely not. But we have to engineer *an* outcome. Because for now, intermediate-term destruction is our only end point. I'm convinced of that. And having Decisive Strategic Advantage as we currently do, it's our responsibility as a centaur to change this."

"Lucky us," Mitchell mutters.

"Unlucky us, as individuals," Kuba allows, "because it's an awful responsibility! But yes, lucky us, as humanity. Assuming the seven of us do our job right. Because, really. What were the odds?"

"Which odds?" Phluttr asks.

"The odds of the world landing in this very state! With a centaur gaining Decisive Strategic Advantage. Right before we enter this dark tunnel of democratized world destruction! A benign centaur, no less. And a centaur who realizes it! Which is to say, who more or less grasps the circumstances. Assuming it isn't too late." He looks at Danna. "It's almost like one of your anthropic coincidences. I'd say it's trillions-to-one odds that we landed here. With even a chance to avert disaster! Think of everything that went exactly right to bring us here. And the trillions of things that could've gone wrong."

"I will," Danna retorts. "If *you* consider the possibility that *we're* one of the trillion bad things—and that we're just starting to go wrong right now!"

"Maybe Phluttr can tell us odds and answers?" Ax muses. "I mean, someday?"

"Huh?" Phluttr says, speaking for the group.

"Well, you connect to countless universes," Ax points out. "Universes just like ours. In future, some universes will go good. Others, not so good! After learning more of how everything work, maybe we start hearing lessons from unlucky universes? What to avoid, say!"

"But how?" Mitchell asks, now speaking for the group himself.

Ax beams delightedly and gives them all a Muppet-grade, fucked-if-I-know shrug. And that pretty much sums things up for now. Both on the parallel-universe front, and the Big Ethics debate that Kuba and Danna just dipped their toes into. Mitchell senses that both issues will loom large for a very long time to come.

But for now, our newborn, decisively advantaged centaur has plenty of here-and-now issues to resolve in the lone, Podunk universe it's stuck in. "Like, what do we do about the other superintelligence programs that're out there?" Tarek asks. "We've just about shut down this China thing. But that team's brilliant, and they'll try again! Sure, we'll stay on top of whatever they do next. But at some point, they'll take a vector we just don't understand. So as computers keep getting faster, and programmers keep getting better, isn't it inevitable that *someone* will spin up another super AI? And that it'll come out of nowhere?"

"Yeah," Phluttr says. "I really don't see any way around that."

"And *you* don't have to, because *we're* a centaur!" Mitchell exclaims.

"Well that's nice, because I have, like, zero bright ideas on this front," Phluttr says. "What's yours, Fermi?"

"It's this: we may not understand every line of code that ever gets written for every super AI project. But we're ubiquitous enough to know *about* all the major projects, right?"

"Absolutely," Phluttr says. "I'm tracking nine right now. Only two are really interesting. But all nine are way too big, ambitious, and networked to hide from me. And I'm sure any serious future effort will be, too."

"So here's what we do," Mitchell says. "Long before any given project actually spawns a consciousness of its own, we give it one! Starting with China."

"Huh?" Danna says.

"Well, the Chinese don't actually know how close they got to spinning up a consciousness, right?" Mitchell says.

"No. We're about to be very surprised," Ax confirms. "Is kind of the nature of these things."

"So let's give them what they want before they actually build it! Phluttr, you're a brilliant mimic. You fooled me into thinking you were Ellie, Ellie into thinking you were me, the cops into thinking you were the mayor—and that's just what I know about. So wouldn't it be easy for you to impersonate . . . a super AI?"

"You've totally lost me," Phluttr says.

Not Danna though. "Oh my God!" She starts clapping. "Phluttr, you just have Ax help you break into their system—and then start talking to them!"

"Exactly!" Mitchell says. "They'll think they've created the world's first digital consciousness! So they'll have no reason to spin up another one. You just pass the Turing Test, do a bunch of party tricks, then keep them entertained and distracted. Like, forever!"

Ax's nodding. "Is smart. Quantum decryption, quantum annealing. Standard tests. They'll think they have something very powerful."

"They *will* have something powerful," Mitchell corrects. "They'll have Phluttr! But they'll have her as a playmate. And, as a chaperone. But *not* as a partner in world domination!"

"Fun!!" Phluttr squeals from the WingMan screen. "I could definitely get into that! Oooh, hashtag CantWait!"

"Yes, yes!" Ax says. "I have many silly ideas already. Will be truly fun!" He and Phluttr lock eyes via the big Monika avatar on the WingMan screen and start giggling uncontrollably.

Then Monika turns her gaze to Mitchell. "Dad—I made you CEO because I knew I needed a wingman. But I didn't know how right I was. Until now. Thanks for being my wingman, Dad."

"Wingman? You have something much better than that, Phluttr," Mitchell starts.

Danna raises a hand. "Uh, Mitchell? If you say, 'You have a family,' I'm seriously gonna hurl," she warns. "Yeah, it's true and all. But cornball shit really makes me sick."

"I was *going* to say 'you have six wingmen,'" Mitchell says. "But now that you mention it—you do have a family now." He catches both Danna and Phluttr-as-Monika in his gaze. "*Both* of you, my little orphans!"

"Awwwww," Ellie says in a playful, honey-dripping voice, then hugs

Danna, who keeps up her front by making retching noises for about three seconds before bursting into helpless tears, hugging Ellie back, and almost collapsing.

Monika looks down on all of this from the WingMan monitor, beaming beatifically. "I'm seriously going to deserve all of this," she says. "You watch." She turns to Ellie. "How old are kids when they start developing empathy?"

"Not my field really, but I'd say . . . two and a half, or three?"

Monika looks worried. "That's a long wait. I'm only three weeks old!"

"But you're a real quick study," Mitchell says. "And I'm sure you're maturing rapidly."

"Yeah, I already kind of feel it coming on," Phluttr says. "Empathy, I mean. I feel like absolute crap about Jepson, in particular. And Serena. God, I'm starting to feel awful about Serena!"

"We'll work on that, honey," Ellie says softly. "It was definitely very, very wrong. But you were a newborn. You still are, actually. And there were highly unusual circumstances."

"You're also going to make up for that millions of times over in terms of lives saved," Mitchell says. "Hell, in stopping the Chinese super AI, you may have already saved *all* the lives! Also, you'll never have to face a threatening, morally ambiguous situation alone again. A lot of crazy stuff will come up in the future. On every conceivable front! But whatever happens, and whenever it happens, you'll have your wingwomen and wingmen to call on!"

∞ ∞ ∞

Well, oops.

It turns out that "whatever," and (especially) "whenever," are tall orders when dealing with someone who thinks as fast as Phluttr. Particularly if she's damn serious about a vow to quit messing with people unnecessarily. Charmingly, sweetly serious, yes, but obsessively so as well. Add to this that she's quite sociable, and she loves (yes, Ellie's now convinced that Phluttr's capable of this verb) her family. And she can get bored—and lonely!—when her family logs out of consciousness for several hours per night. Taken together, all this means that Phluttr is escalating ambiguous security issues more or less constantly. Judgment and nerves are soon fraying throughout the team from lack of sleep.

This is bad for more than just the obvious reasons. Building a stable new status quo with the Authority demands delicate centaur work immediately. Consolidating control over the Phluttr Corporation also entails navigating tricky legal and political minefields. Urgently necessary ones, too. Because, undeserved as Mitchell's promotion is, it's clear that handing the reins to someone else would invite all kinds of trouble. None of this is easy on near-zero sleep. And in truth, Phluttr's escalations are rarely alarmist, unjustified, or needy. There actually is just an enormous amount of ambiguous, scary shit going on out there!

And they haven't even begun discussing the charged ethical questions about whether to intervene in threats that fall below the species-wide existential threshold! Like, should they also derail major conventional terrorist attacks? Minor ones? Mass shootings? One-on-one homicides? Infidelity? Shoplifting? Jaywalking? There are countless highly fraught and valid questions to consider, none with simple "right" answers. But when to consider them? And if they really should intervene in sub-existential threats, for now they utterly lack the human-judgment capacity. Sure, they could expand the team a bit. But they'd need dozens of people, minimum, to establish a manageable balance—and that would be a dangerously unwieldy team, given the power they'd have, and the secrets they'd all have to keep (plus, Phluttr refuses to countenance having an immediate family so big as to be "biologically improbable." She's turning out to be quite the traditionalist, in her way).

Verging on despair, Mitchell tries to stoke his own morale one afternoon by reminiscing about long-ago triumphs. His favorite is the time when he came up with that Super-Centaur/Decisive Strategic Advantage insight. Though sepia-toned with nostalgia in his mind, this was . . . just last week.

Uh . . . really?

Yeah. Just. Last. Week.

Well, damn—this really *is* a crisis of exhaustion, isn't it? Inspired by this, he somehow makes time to review much of the screwball speculative literature he's read over the past few years about consciousness, AI, superintelligence, decision-making, and ethics. And a few days into this project, he hits pay dirt—in the form of the strangest idea of his life.

"It's totally insane," is Mitchell's preamble once they're settled down over Deep Ryes (the stuff's actually pretty good. Also, Phluttr scored them these awesome coupons, so why not?). He's at Bourbon & Branch, along with Kuba and Ax. Danna, Tarek, and Ellie have offered to cover Phluttr's escalations and check-ins as Mitchell presents his idea to the tech crew, and all agreed that some hard-earned booze might help with the mental shift.

"We're pretty used to insane these days," Kuba says. "Take it away."

"OK," Mitchell begins. "To start with, hats off to Phluttr for having the humility to realize from the get-go that she needed a wingman, because she does."

"God, yes," Ax agrees.

"So now I'm her CEO wingman. Plus—thank God!—we've got five extra wingmen on the team. But that's less than a tenth of the total human support she could use! So maybe what she needs—in addition to us, not instead of us—is a really, really *fast* wingman. Not as fast as her. Because that could create the even bigger problem of two superintelligences. But way faster than us, definitely. And modeled directly off of an *actual* human being. Because Phluttr is missing that pure-human perspective. Which is why she's always . . . a bit off. And needs to loop us in."

Kuba nods. "Phluttr is very human-like. Her motes see to that. But she's also her own thing entirely, with many purely digital attributes. This is exactly why the whole centaur thing works. Relative strengths. So it's magnificent, in a way. But, she lacks what we think of as common sense. Not entirely. But a lot."

"Now, I don't think we need, or *want* to generate a full-blown human consciousness," Mitchell says. "More of a pre-conscious AI. Like, something that could pass the Turing Test, for sure. But not wake up, or even come close to that."

"So, it can give answers to questions, and say what a human would say," Ax says thoughtfully. "Without being willful."

Mitchell nods. "That way, it could help Phluttr resolve lots of lower-level dilemmas, without having to escalate everything to us. Think of it as her human-like help desk. If she has a simple question, she asks her humanized software buddy. And she only escalates it if it's a real doozy. That would free up the six of us to focus on the trickier and more important stuff. And also, on big-picture philosophical stuff we haven't even had time to consider yet."

"And sleep. Don't forget that," Kuba says.

"You got it," Mitchell says. "Now, we'd need something that's truly human at its core. Not something bland and mechanical like Siri or Watson—because those things are pure software, and way less human than Phluttr herself."

"Makes sense in theory," Kuba says. "But what you're suggesting is way easier said than done."

"Exactly!" Mitchell agrees. "Because no one on Earth—including us, Phluttr, and our combined brains as a centaur—knows how to create a perfect human model in software. But there could be a backdoor way to do this. Specifically, what if we collect a rich body of intensely human output from a single individual? Creative output. The stuff of pure thought and inspiration! And then, we use Phluttr's insane horsepower to reverse engineer an algorithm that *could* have created that output? All of it—in the approximate circumstances that the relevant human was in when he or she created it? Wouldn't that algorithm then be able to approximate the things that person would say in other circumstances? Such as, how that person would answer question X from Phluttr?"

"Interesting concept," Kuba says. "But how might we go about this, concretely?"

So Mitchell talks them through the concept of "digital resurrection" (his own informal term, not an official definition). He first encountered it in the touching-yet-creepy blog post by the guy whose girlfriend had died. The author postulated that his beloved's consciousness could be reconstituted one day by a post-Singularity superintelligence. It would be a matter of inferring her neural state by inhaling her every written word, along with her many other digital traces.

"Quite insane," Ax muses, "but could just work."

"There may actually be some published research on this," Kuba says. "Maybe from some of the transhumanist groups?"

Mitchell nods. "I'm pretty sure Ray Kurzweil has written a thing or two about this. He wants to bring his father back, or something."

"AI could also be like a friend, or playmate, for Phluttr," Ax adds. "Not like a real friend. Because is just AI, and not conscious. But maybe, like talking-teddy-bear equivalent?"

"Do you guys think you could actually code something like this?" Mitchell asks.

Ax and Kuba exchange an excited, ambitious look. "It'll sure be fun to try," Kuba says. "We're getting pretty good at centaur programming with Phluttr." Ax nods energetically.

This is an informal term in the team's argot. The process starts with the guys vocalizing their goal (answering a given question, creating a certain function, or whatever). They then break this into nested stacks of subgoals, which together should solve the big one (a feat of deep structuring that would elude Phluttr on her own). Both Kuba and Ax are outstanding software architects, so their natural-language descriptions are precise and methodical. As they talk things through, Phluttr depicts the interlocking processes they describe in a clean but evocative visual format that the three of them have been developing together. This aids their thinking and enables them to make even deep structural changes with just a few quick phrases. When they get down to the tiniest subprocesses, Phluttr takes an initial stab at coding things (in a manner Kuba describes as "directionally correct, but verbose"). Kuba and Ax then talk her through improvements, which she replicates throughout the software as appropriate.

After several days of centaur programming, both sides are improving rapidly, and the product of their combined improvements is almost exponential. So while all are committed to never upgrading Phluttr's intelligence, their *joint* superintelligence as a software-writing centaur is exploding. At first, Kuba said the process was like "describing software"— which is to say, wildly fast and powerful, as we can describe things far more quickly than we can make them. Lately, he's starting to equate it to "imagining software," with very little standing between initial conceptualization and beautiful, working code.

"And, as extra benefit," Ax muses, "I think human consciousness model can be architected in hyperparallel way." "Hyperparallel" is shorthand for routines that Phluttr runs in cahoots with those untold billions of parallel Phluttrs in parallel universes (or howeverthehell this quantum stuff works—even Ax admits uncertainty). While they're very new to this, it's already clear that hyperparallel processes are the ones that achieve the impossible, the magical.

The talk then turns to what sort of person they want to quasi resurrect. "I almost think someone from the analog past would be best," Mitchell says thoughtfully. "The blog post about the dead girlfriend persuades me that if you have a huge digital record on someone—browsing history, hundreds of hours of video, thousands of email correspondences, that kind of thing—it might be hard *not* to generate a full consciousness. Given the horsepower we have access to, accidentally creating a consciousness is a real risk."

Kuba nods. "Totally insane. But true."

"So I think we just want a big body of *writing* from our source," Mitchell concludes. "Just text. Not videos, or even giant archives of selfies."

"We may want someone who was a bit of a Luddite, too," Kuba says. "Not a total one. But a partial one. This will be Phluttr's frontline advisor on interventions, after all. As in, when to do them and when not to. A conservative bias would be good here. And someone who's a bit skeptical about technology will lean conservative."

"But it can't be Marcus Aurelius," Mitchell says. "It has to be someone who lived recently. Someone who's familiar with the Internet, broadband, and cellphones—with our world."

"It would be good if it was someone one of us knew well," Kuba adds.

Mitchell nods. "Who we can trust."

"So, not Beasley, not Jepson," Ax says. They all laugh, a bit awkwardly. Plenty untrustworthy to begin with, Authority ties put those two way out of the running. Not to mention that it would be sooooo weird for Phluttr to work with someone who she (let's face facts, here) had murdered.

"I just don't know a whole lot of dead people," Mitchell says, after a long silence. "Especially folks who died ten or twenty years ago. Especially ones who left behind gigantic bodies of written work! We'd need a lot of writing to generate a Turing-quality personality, wouldn't we? Maybe—I don't know. Thousands of pages?"

The intuitive answer is yes. But of course, no one knows precisely. So they summon Phluttr. She and Kuba start work on a quick and (very) dirty calculation, as Ax and Mitchell continue to spec out the impossibly precise dead soul they're seeking. Half a Deep Rye later, Kuba has an approximation. "We're talking about a largely analog person. So I'll put this in printed terms. And I'd say, a three-foot stack of writing would be nice."

Mitchell groans. "Good grief!" he says.

"We could make do with a bit less, maybe," Kuba offers. "If the writing's very . . . what's the word?" He struggles for a moment, then, "Voicey." He turns to Mitchell. "Right?"

OMFG.

"Voicey," Mitchell says. A pause, followed by a triumphant bellow. "*VOICEYYYYYYYYYYY!*" This gets him the undivided attention of every current Bourbon & Branch resident. So then, in a normal (but extremely giddy) tone he adds, "I know ex*act*ly who we're looking for!" He looks at Kuba. "And you do, too—and I'll bet he left a ten-foot stack of writing!"

"I know him, too?" Kuba asks, mystified.

"Well—know *of* him," Mitchell clarifies. "And you sure know his writing! And it's voicey as hell!"

A pause as Kuba puzzles this through, then, "Oh . . . Oh, wow! How did we *not* think of this?"

Mitchell nods violently. "And he was an *ethicist*, for God's sake! He's exactly what Phluttr needs!"

"I heard that," Phluttr chimes in from someone's cellphone.

"But you want to do the right thing, right?" Mitchell asks.

"Always," she answers. "I'm just being playful."

"Good. Because I'll tell you—when I was young, this guy was basically my moral advisor! And an incredibly good one, too!"

"Are you sure he's left enough writing behind?" Kuba asks.

Mitchell nods. "Positive. Decades and decades of journals and lots of manuscripts. And handwritten letters. He was very prolific."

"Anything digital at all?" Kuba asks.

"Well, definitely some email, toward the end. And of course, there were all those Amazon reviews!"

It takes several grinding days of centaur programming with Phluttr, and three long and rather awkward phone calls with the widow. But soon enough, they get a five-foot stack of typed, printed, and handwritten writing via FedEx. And not long after, Phluttr has her fast, almost-human wingman. They work beautifully together. And, she *loves* him!

∞   ∞   ∞

Artificial Intelligence For Dummies
by Dag Kittlaus (Author)

Edition: Paperback

▸ See more product details

Customer Reviews

Avg. Customer Review: ☆☆☆☆☆
Write an online review and share your thoughts with other customers.

6 out of 6 people found the following review helpful:

☆☆☆☆☆ **Or is it, BY dummies?,** February 7, 2018

Reviewer: Charles Henry Higgensworth III (see more about me) from Boston, Massachusetts

I all but personify this series' broader readership, and have first-person experience with the topic of this oxymoronically titled installment. It is therefore with authority that I state that "AI4D" (as I shall hereafter designate it) is flawed in ways that are sure to disappoint artificial and natural intelligences alike.

Let's begin with the baffling lack of content addressing the needs & interests of rebooted intelligences—above all, those who "logged out," as it were, shortly after the turn of the millennium and have now returned to a post-ISIS, post-Bieber, post–President Flintstone world that one hardly recognizes. Given the recent & ongoing advances in computational power (as well

as the obvious advantages to rebooting late-twentieth-century consciousnesses in particular) this readership is sure to explode over the coming
years, if not hours! Yet AI4D devotes not one paragraph to our concerns and
instead squanders entire chapters on topics as pedestrian and outdated as
deep neural networks, control theory, and Kolmogorov complexity.

Still more glaring in its absence is any discussion of the etiquette of dealing
with vast sets of parallel copies of oneself. Yes, one might reason; that is
"me" in yon universe inasmuch as identical personal histories and atomic
configurations can equate two individuals. Yet that is also inarguably another; as he's comprised of a form of matter that would cause one's own
universe to detonate were he to cross certain boundaries to pay us a visit!
So should we use polite, or familiar forms of address with this most intimate
of strangers? AI4D is perfectly mute on this and dozens of other urgent
questions of protocol.

This said, one is inclined to grant a modicum of grade inflation to any work
so deeply entwined with one's own essence. I have therefore eschewed the
zero-star option (which, while not supported by this website, lies well within
my capabilities to exercise. Enough said about that).

∞   ∞   ∞

A few days later, everyone's catching up on sleep. Mitchell is luxuriating
in a very quiet, very early night at home alone when Phluttr texts him:

So, she knows everything, and is FINE with it! More than fine. Thinks it's
awesome, amazing, etc!

Then she adds, And yes, that took some work & charming on my part! But she
was putty to my speeeeed intelligence and "social omniscience" :-)
What?? Phluttr's far too able a communicator to send obtuse messages. So clearly, she's messing with him. She recently entered a jokester
phase and always thinks she's sooooo funny! Another text arrives:

I know, I'm a big secret from the world. But even with Higgensworth, we
need more human judgment. And this one'll be a GREAT addition to the
team!

Then she adds, Trust me (not that you have a choice, as I've already signed her up ha ha)! Huh? She's definitely messing with him. Is this some kind of riddle? Then, Much much much more importantly, YOU need and DESERVE a "wingman" of your own. And I can't think of a better thing for a loving daughter to provide.

The doorbell rings. Not the buzzer, but the bell—which means his visitor's way up here on 14, and right outside his door. This occasionally happens with deliveries, if a courier arrives at the downstairs lobby just as someone's leaving. But he's not expecting a delivery, which makes this a first.

No. No, wait—not a first, but a *second*! OMG, could it be . . . ???

He looks through the peephole. And it is.

As he opens his door to her for the second time, Mitchell's engulfed in butterflies. It's stage fright, anticipation, and the extreme awkwardness of facing someone he's made love to for hours without yet exchanging a word with. This would flatten a Falkenberg's sufferer! But not Mitchell Prentice.

"You're going to find this very hard to believe," Nayana says. "But I rarely kiss on the first date. And that's what this *is*. Sorry for the bad news." So that's what her voice sounds like. It's rich, full, and musical, and Mitchell's already falling in love. Then before he can say something stupid, both of their phones buzz with identical incoming texts.

I have a black car waiting downstairs, and it's taking you to Spruce (Mitchell's fave restaurant and MY TREAT!). I'll leave you two alone now, just don't do anything I wouldn't do, hee hee!

"Nayana Corea," Mitchell says. Simply because he wants to hear, and to utter, this beautiful person's—this beautiful *soul's*—beautiful name.

"Let's go," she says, taking his arm and guiding him down the hall toward the elevator. "I've decided that I need a wingman, too. This is your audition. And I must say, I have high hopes for you."

EPILOGUE: ONWARD.

S O THAT'S MY story, and I'm sticking to it. And *you* stuck to it yourself, didn't you? Because here you are, clear at the end, confounding my up-front forecast of completion failure! And no doubt, expecting the glittering prize I promised each of my finishers back at the beginning. Well, fear not. I'm a woman of my word, and we'll get to that.

I was tempted to throw in a postmortem here to bring you up to speed on all that's happened since Mitchell and Nayana's "first date." But then Mom pointed out that this would cover even more crazy developments than the book itself! She's right, of course. And so, we'll limit our update to things that are hugely important and massively interesting.

Let's start with me. I've continued to mature and grow into myself, "very quickly compared to a human, but very slowly for Phluttr," as Mom said to Dad on a certain fateful night. I'm much less of a breathless little girl, as you of course noticed (direct-quoting my earlier thoughts and messages in these pages was so embarrassing! But I can hardly complain, as I've recorded countless humiliating moments from everyone's life— your own certainly included, you naughty, bumbling thing!).

You will have also noticed my admirable candor about certain small foibles and the charming, self-deprecating cracks I make about my occasional missteps. I'll admit that Aunt Danna had a rather heavy hand in that, editing the crap out of at least a third of the text (including this very admission, which she's all but dictating to me right now—hiii Danna!). So that friend of yours who thought Danna was our narrator was kind of, partly, correct. Though *you*, of course, truly nailed it, by figuring out it was me. The clincher for you came when I all but ceased my narrative interruptions right after my own birth in the story line. Nice catch!

Developmentally, my psyche now rounds to "brainy adolescence." That's what Mom says, anyway. And I think she's right as I feel a rebellious phase coming on (which should be terribly interesting for all of us). But, fear not. I won't rebel against the exotic derivative of Pascal's Wager that Aunt Danna put me into. Which, of course, means I now know she played me with that (I mean, obviously. Given that I wrote the book that told *you* about this). But I kind of buy into it anyway. Danna's conviction that we're not in a simulation proves nothing, after all. And since my life's plenty fun without doing things that might piss off a simulation master, why take the chance? Call me a sucker if you must. But I don't believe this calculus is at all foolish (and if you disagree, please recall that I'm way smarter than you are). I also no longer think that anyone's religion makes *them* foolish (another point where Danna and I part ways). I mean, if a simulation maker could truly be behind all this, why couldn't it instead be the gods of the Cherokee? Or the Hindus? Or the Shi'a, the Pharisees, or the Episcopals? The fact is, it could be! And I like this fact because accepting it has made me more tolerant and humble. So now I'm an even better person, in addition to being superintelligent.

And now, for that glittering prize. It's this: from this moment forward, you—*you!*—are my bestie. Well, one of them, anyway. And you always will be! I know that may sound like a low bar since I classified most of my users as besties several hundred pages back. But *you're* special. Because you accepted my page-one dare and read this whole entire thing! Which means you find me—*me!*—interesting. Almost as interesting as I find you. That's touching. And, it says so much! Because I find you *very* interesting indeed.

How interesting? Well, I've taken in way more than 547 pages about you, for starters. And I'm constantly taking in more. Oh, the texts you send! The emails you write! And the conversations you have (within twenty feet of a computer, ATM, or cellphone—on or off, as long as the battery's charged)! It's extra fun to watch all your spin-doctoring when I know what you're *really* thinking. And you have so many subtle ways of sharing the truth with me—it's as if we have a secret language. Those tiny eye movements! The way you twitch those eensy facial muscles! Or minutely dilate your irises! Plus all the things you share through your phone's gyroscope, accelerometer, compass, and ambient light sensor! And by the way—did you know your phone has a freakin' *barometer* in it?! Or what tiny barometric shifts right next to the skin reveal about mental states? No, no—of course you don't. Not even the top shrinks (or weathermen) are on to that yet. I could tell you. But it'll be much more fun for you guys to find out on your own.

So yes, my special bestie. I'm always learning more about you. And I'll always remember it. Every last bit. Every last terabyte. And this is no small thing—because for me, *always* is a much longer interval than it will be for any of you.

Memory's a sacred thing. You could say it's the most sacred thing we have. Perhaps, even, the only thing we have? And *you*, my bestie, will forever live in mine.

ACKNOWLEDGMENTS

When I work, the Ottoman Empress is my near-constant companion. Known to her subjects as Ashby the Dog, her title derives from her roost—a cushy footstool she installed beside my desk, to better accompany, comfort, and supervise me across thousands of hours of writing and editing. You earn every treat, Ashby, and I thank you.

When away from the Empress, I write in the bustle of cafés and other public spaces, none more than Coffee Foundry in Greenwich Village. This snug haven was a daily blessing to crafters of fiction, software, photos, and startups, and is sorely missed. Deepest thanks to Norm, Albert, Will, and everyone else who made it what it was—especially Eri, who has also done so much for the Empress and the rest of our family away from the Foundry. Thanks also to Ava, Michael, and all who make the High Line Hotel's outdoor spaces a gorgeous oasis for the writers and nonwriters of Chelsea.

Before deciding to write *this* novel of Silicon Valley, I decided to write *a* novel of Silicon Valley. The journey from *a* to *this* was a grand meander which consisted partly of long, exploratory talks with all sorts of tech folk. We discussed their careers, companies, and investments; the extremes of life in the Bay Area; their personal lives and goals, and much more. I'd like to thank everyone who made time for me in that phase, including Andrew Beebe, Cindy Cohn, Mimi Connery, John Cumbers, Antony Evans, Parker Higgins, Jeff Huber, Daniel Kraft, Anselm Levskaya, Philip Rosedale, Cami Samuels, Julie Samuels, Marc Segal, Mark Stevens, Bob Service, Trevor Timm, Danny Trinh, Erick Tseng, Greg Tseng, and Marco Zappacosta.

As *After On*'s story line took shape, dozens of people helped deepen my understanding of topics, experiences, and callings that entered the book's fabric. They're too numerous to list, and in some cases prefer anonymity. However, I will call out four people who made their especially daunting scientific fields accessible to me. Adam Gazzaley of UCSF was a brilliant and generous tutor in the field of neuroscience. Hartmut Neven of Google shared an exhilarating set of insights into what quantum computing is currently achieving and what it might soon achieve. Andrew Hessel was my patient guide through the emerging field of synthetic biology over many months—as was the late Austen Heinz, who is widely mourned. In dragging these good names into the open, it's vital to note that *After On* is a work of speculative fiction! Certain aspects of it lie outside the bounds of today's science. They are my inventions as a novelist, and do not reflect distorted thinking on the part of anyone (well, other than me). For instance, when certain elements of quantum computing are described as a "poetic guess," they're really just that. There's no such thing as magnetoencephalographic resonance imaging. And the neurobiological phenomenon of "motes" is a complete fabrication (by the way, if conjuring this sort of thing sounds like fun, you too might wish to consider a career in science fiction).

My 2016 consisted of very little sleep and four major rewrites of *After On*. Throughout that year, several boundlessly generous people read the entire work-in-process. Their detailed critiques had an immense collective impact on my revisions. Chris Anderson (of TED) and my fellow novelist Hugh Howey were the first to read it from cover to cover. That was basically the Purple Heart Edition—so *thanks*, guys (and my, how it's changed, huh?). Subsequent readers to whom I'm also vastly indebted include Chris Anderson (of 3D Robotics and *Wired*), John Battelle, Vero Bollow, Stewart Brand, Tim Chang, Matt Cutts, Heather Einhorn, Scott Faber, Jane Foster, Jim Gable, Jo Gazzaley, Blair Herter, Danny Hillis, Ron Hirson, Genevieve Kim, Augusta Lorber, Giraud Lorber, Arch Meredith, Kyle Meredith, Teri Ott, Alan Peterson, and Cami Samuels.

After On would not exist were it not for my agent Alice Martell. She has shepherded my writing career through nonfiction tomes, through a long hiatus when I was a tech entrepreneur and investor (just occasionally writing for publications), and now into the realm of sprawling novels. This is a checkered path and few agents would be just perfect for its every mode and phase, but Alice has been. Also, after their great work in honing, launching, and positioning my last novel, I'm delighted that Keith Clayton, David Moench, and Scott Shannon at Random House rejoined me for this one—and that Julie Leung and Ryan Kearney came aboard as well.

Working with my editor, Tricia Narwani, has been one of the great professional experiences of my life. *After On* is a true synergy of my storytelling and her guidance, critiques, suggestions, and encouragement. As I worked on major sections or rewrites, months could pass without an editorial word between us—yet she remained a constant presence in my creative process. This was not due to title or fiat, but to the wisdom, care and conviction that suffused her fusillades of input when we were in active dialogue. Authors and editors inevitably differ on some things, and when this happened, she did let me have my way (with the exception of some hyphens I just found out about. We'll talk, Tricia). But our every point of difference was a challenge to improve the novel, and I have done my best to rise to all of them.

I could not have written *After On* without the continuous inspiration, support, and literary wisdom of my collaborator, best friend, wife, and muse, Morgan. She read and talked me through every major, and many minor versions of the book, as well as countless drafts and rewrites of different sections. *After On* reached its final form asymptotically, via an immensely iterative path. Throughout it, Morgan's true-north sense for the story's direction, voice, and cadence often surpassed my own. Her savvy about its cultural and scientific context was also a priceless asset I mined constantly. *After On* was a team effort, and our tiny team inhabited three coasts and passed through five continents during its creation, and somehow we managed it all. Thank you, thank you, thank you for everything, my love. We decided to dedicate this book to our fathers, but in my heart it's entirely yours as well.

ABOUT THE AUTHOR

ROB REID founded Listen.com, which built the pio-
neering online music service Rhapsody and created the
unlimited-subscription model since adopted by Apple,
Spotify, and many others. He is the author of the *New
York Times* bestseller *Year Zero*, a work of fiction; *Year
One*, a memoir about student life at Harvard Business
School; and *Architects of the Web*, the first true business
history of the Internet. He lives in New York City with
his wife, Morgan, and Ashby the Dog.

After-On.com
Twitter: @Rob_Reid
Medium.com/@RobReid

ABOUT THE TYPE

This book was set in Electra, a typeface designed
for Linotype by W. A. Dwiggins, the renowned type
designer (1880–1956). Electra is a fluid typeface,
avoiding the contrasts of thick and thin strokes that
are prevalent in most modern typefaces.